Woodcraft;

or, Hawks about the Dovecote

Woodcraft;
or, Hawks about the Dovecote

A Story of the South at the Close of the Revolution

William Gilmore Simms

Critical Introduction by James Everett Kibler
With a Biographical Overview by David Moltke-Hansen
and Explanatory Notes by George F. Hayhoe

The University of South Carolina Press

New material © 2012 University of South Carolina
Explanatory notes © 1979 University of South Carolina Institute
for Southern Studies, reprinted with permission

Cloth original published by Redfield, 1854
Paperback published by the University of South Carolina Press
Columbia, South Carolina 29208

www.sc.edu/uscpress

Manufactured in the United States of America

21 20 19 18 17 16 15 14 13 12
10 9 8 7 6 5 4 3 2 1

ISBN 978-1-61117-023-8 (pbk)

Published in cooperation with the Simms Initiatives, a project of the
University of South Carolina Libraries with the generous support of
the Watson-Brown Foundation.

William Gilmore Simms: A Biographical Overview

David Moltke-Hansen

Introduction

Harper's Weekly put it succinctly in its July 2, 1870, issue: "In the death of Mr. Simms, on the 11th of June, at Charleston, the country has lost one more of its time-honored band of authors, and the South the most consistent and devoted of her literary sons" (qtd. In Butterworth and Kibler 125–26). Indeed no mid-nineteenth-century writer and editor did more than William Gilmore Simms to frame white southern self-identity and nationalism, shape southern historical consciousness, or foster the South's participation and recognition in the broader American literary culture. No southern writer enjoyed more contemporary esteem and attention, at least after Edgar Allan Poe moved north. Among American romancers (or writers of prose epics), only New Yorker James Fenimore Cooper was as successful by the 1840s. In those same years, Simms was the South's most influential editor of cultural journals. He also was the region's most prolific cultural journalist and poet, publishing an average of one book review and one poem per week for forty-five years.

Before his death Simms saw his national reputation fall along with the Confederacy he had vigorously supported and with the slave regime that many in the North had come to despise. Nevertheless reprints of most of the twenty titles in the selected edition of his works, first published between 1853 and 1860, appeared up until World War I. Thereafter only *The Yemassee*, an early romance about an Indian war in South Carolina, continued in print. The tide began to turn in the 1950s, when five volumes of Simms's letters appeared and a growing number of his works were issued in new editions. Publication in 1992 of the first literary biography, by John C. Guilds, and establishment of the William Gilmore Simms Society and the *Simms Review* the next year at once reflected and fostered this revived interest. Yet not until the 2011 launch of the digital Simms edition of the South Caroliniana Library of the University of South Carolina did scholars of southern, American, and nineteenth-century culture have the prospect of ready access to all of Simms's separately published works. With the University of South Carolina Press's cooperation, readers also will have access to sixty works in paperback editions by the end of 2014. Simms himself never saw nearly so many of his works in print at one time.

Clearly the decline in the critical standing of, and historical attention to, Simms and his oeuvre in the century after his death has reversed in the years since. The last three decades of the twentieth century saw more published on Simms than the previous hundred years (Butterworth and Kibler 126–200; MLA International). The last decade of the twentieth and first decade of the twenty-first centuries saw more dissertations and theses on him (forty-one) than had appeared in all the years before. This is not to say that Simms is yet given the attention directed to some of his contemporaries. For the first decade of the twenty-first century, the Modern Language Association International Bibliography lists roughly four times as many scholarly publications on James Fenimore Cooper, more than ten times as many on Nathaniel Hawthorne, and sixteen times as many on Edgar Allan Poe. Not surprisingly, therefore, Simms is not yet included in most anthologies of American literature, although he is a subject or a source in an expanding and ever more diverse body of scholarship.

To prepare to read Simms, it is important to see his writings in multiple contexts. He rarely wrote about himself outside of his more personal poems and his letters (some fifteen hundred of the many thousands of which survive). Yet he systematically drew on his background, personal experience, and relationships in his work. He also shaped that work through a progressively developed poetics and philosophy of life, history, and art. He did so in the context of his very broad reading of both contemporary and earlier Western literature and in the midst of multiple professional engagements and responsibilities. The richness and variety of these writings and involvements make Simms a key figure for future understanding of the literary culture, issues, and networks in mid-nineteenth-century America.

Background

Simms's family history reflected the dynamics that fueled the spread southward and westward of the populations, plantation economy, and society of the South Atlantic states. Simms's ancestry also reflected the Scots-Irish and English roots of what became identified as southern culture by the 1830s, a generation after the end of most immigration to the region. Two of Simms's grandparents, William and Elisabeth Sims, were Scots-Irish and migrated to South Carolina from Ulster. One, John Singleton, was an American-born son of putatively English immigrants, who had come to South Carolina from Virginia. The fourth, Jane Miller, was daughter of two Scots-Irish and Irish descended people—John Miller, of North and then South Carolina, and Jane Ross. Ross's family also migrated to South Carolina from western Virginia, where members lived cheek by jowl with other Scots-Irish families, who migrated to the Carolinas (White, *Ross*). Simms's father and Uncle James migrated in 1808 from Charleston to Tennessee, then to Mississippi. This was after the bankruptcy of the elder William's business and the deaths of his wife and their other two sons. Following the last of these losses, the elder Simms's hair turned white in a week. To his anguished eyes, Charleston appeared "a place of tombs" (qtd. in Guilds 6, 12).

For the son, however, Charleston was home—so much so that he refused to leave his maternal grandmother and move to Mississippi when his uncle came to get him in 1816. Then the fifth largest and by far the wealthiest city, as well as one of the greatest ports, in America, Charleston was at the peak of its influence (Moltke-Hansen, "Expansion" 25–31; Rogers). Cotton culture on the sea islands to the south, begun in 1790, and rice culture in impounded lowcountry tidal marshes meant that the port was filled not only with sailors of many lands and languages, but also with enslaved people of many African and Creole cultures and speech ways (slaves continued to be imported legally in large numbers until 1808). This street life made vivid the transnational nature of plantation agriculture and the fact that the developing region's dramatically expanding borders "were not just geographic; they also were human, historical, and intellectual" (Moltke-Hansen, "Southern" 19).

Even more important for the future author, the expanding region's borders and nature were taking imaginative shape. The West of the senior William Gilmore Simms and the first Creek War in which he fought, the Revolutionary War of the young Simms's maternal grandfather, the backcountry of many related Scots-Irish settlers, all these became grist for a lonely, energetic boy, who spent as much time with books as he could (Simms, *Letters* 1:161). The possibilities of such settings, incidents, and characters were not confined to history alone. Simms reported that he "used to glow and shiver in turn over 'The Pilgrim's Progress,'" while "Moses' adventures in 'The Vicar of Wakefield' threw [him] into paroxysms of laughter" (Hayne 261–62). Sir Walter Scott's Border and medieval romances and James Fenimore Cooper's Leatherstocking tales also deeply colored his imagination (Simms, *Views* 1:248, and Moltke-Hansen, "Southern" 6–15). As affecting were the ghost stories and Revolutionary War tales of his grandmother and the verses sent, and tales told, by his father.

These diverse tales became reasons to explore—in books, but also on the ground. As a boy, Simms ranged through the city and along the banks of the Ashley River, which fed into Charleston Harbor. He did so in search of scenes of colonial and Revolutionary battles and incidents (*Letters* 1:lxii). He first heard his uncle's and father's many Irish and frontier stories when they visited in Charleston in 1816 and 1818, respectively. He heard more on his trips to Mississippi during the winter of 1824 through the spring of 1825 and again in 1826. The first trip took him through Georgia and Alabama, where he saw elements of the Creek and Cherokee nations. At the time, Simms later reported, he was a boy "cumbered with fragmentary materials of thought, . . . choked by the tangled vines of erroneous speculation, and haunted by passions, which, like so many wolves, lurked, in ready waiting, for their unsuspecting prey" (*Social* 6). When he first got to Mississippi, traveling partly by stage, partly by riverboat, and partly by horse, Simms learned that his father had just come back from "a trip of three hundred miles into the heart of the Indian country" (Trent 15). Later father and son "rode together on horseback to various settlements on the frontier of Alabama and Mississippi" (Guilds 10–11, 17–18). Simms recalled as well "having traveled 150 miles beyond the Mississippi" (Shillingsburg, "Literary Grist" 120). The next year he returned to the Southwest by ship. "During this [second] trip he carried a 'note book.'" There he jotted episodes, encounters, stories heard, characters seen, and descriptions of the landscapes unfolding around him. He also wrote "at least sixteen poems" (Kibler, "First"; Shillingsburg, "Literary Grist" 123).

Simms took a third western trip five years later, writing letters back to the newspaper that by then he was editing (*Letters* 1:10–38). Together these three trips provided materials for his writings over more than forty years. "The first . . . produced mainly short fiction; the second inspired much poetry; . . . the first and third . . . yielded three novels written in the 1830s" (Shillingsburg, "Literary Grist" 119). This was, in part, because of the trips' timing. Sixteen years after the first trip, Simms told students at the University of Alabama that in the interval their world had changed from a howling wilderness into a place of growing civilization (Simms, *Social* 5–6). Had he not gone when he did, he would have been too late to see the frontier. Later travels took him many other places and also provided much grist for his writing. Never again, however, did he experience the frontier firsthand. Furthermore, on these later trips Simms was a practiced professional writer, no longer that boy haunted by passions.

Personal Life

After the ten-year-old boy's momentous refusal to leave Charleston, his grandmother sent Simms for two years to the grammar school taught on the campus and by the faculty of the nearly moribund College of Charleston. By then he already was "versifying the events of the war [of 1812]," just concluded, publishing "doggerel" in the local papers, and learning to read in several languages (*Letters* 1:285). His trip west a decade later helped him decide to pursue both literature and a career in law, but back in Charleston—this despite his father's urging that he stay in Mississippi. Upon his return home, he began to read law and also launched a literary weekly, the *Album*, which ran for a year. He became engaged as well to Anna Malcolm Giles, daughter of a grocer and former state coroner.

A year later the young couple married. This was six months before Simms was admitted to the South Carolina bar, on his twenty-first birthday, not long before he was appointed as a city magistrate. Although living up the Ashley River in the more healthful, less expensive village of Summerville, Simms kept a law office in the city. Shortly after using his maternal inheritance to buy the *City Gazette* at the end of 1829 and moving down to Charleston Neck, just north of the city limits where he had lived as a boy, Simms lost both his father and his maternal grandmother. He also found himself attacked because of his Unionist stance in the Nullification crisis resulting from South Carolina's rejection of a federal tariff. Then, in early 1832, Simms's wife died. Soon after, he took his four-year-old daughter back to Summerville to live and determined to sell his newspaper and leave the state for a literary life in the North.

Fueling his ambition was the correspondence Simms had begun several years earlier with an accountant whom he had published in his *City Gazette* but not yet met—Scots immigrant James Lawson. At the time Lawson, seven years Simms's senior, edited a New York City newspaper and, in addition to writing plays and poetry, was a friend (and, later, informal literary agent) to a wide circle (McHaney, "An Early"). Simms's trip north in the summer of 1832 saw the two begin a lifelong friendship, cemented as they squired ladies about and interacted with Lawson's literary circle. In subsequent years Simms multiplied the number of his friendships, in both the North and the South, making them in some measure a replacement for the family that he had lost. Lawson remained the closest of his northern friends, while James Henry Hammond, a future governor and U.S. senator, became his closest friend in South Carolina.

Late in 1833, after his Summerville house burned, Simms wrote Lawson to say that he was enamored of "a certain fair one" (*Letters* 1:73). Seventeen-year-old Chevillette Eliza Roach was the daughter of "a literary-minded aristocrat of English descent" with two plantations on the banks of the Edisto River in Barnwell District (later County) (Guilds 70). The courtship was protracted, as Simms felt it necessary first to clear debts that friends had bought up on his behalf. He also was determined "to marry no woman" before he was "perfectly independent of her resources, and her friends" (*Letters* 1:78). Therefore he did not propose until the spring of 1836. The nuptials took place seven months later, and as a result, Simms came to call the four thousand acres of Woodlands Plantation, with its seventy slaves, home. It was twenty years, however, before he took over management of the plantation and, then, only in the wake of his father-in-law's final sickness and death. Five years after that, he lost his wife, the mother of fourteen of his fifteen children. Nine of the children Chevillette bore him had already died, devastating Simms repeatedly. Five were still living (three sons and two daughters), as was Simms's daughter by his first marriage, who helped raise the youngest of her siblings. Those remaining children—even Gilly, who fought in the Confederate army—all outlived their father. Gilly and a brother-in-law ran Woodlands after the war, when Simms, though dying of cancer, was earning what he could by writing again for publications in the North and editing one or another South Carolina newspaper.

Career

The trip north in 1832 did not result in Simms moving there. Except during the Civil War, however, he returned almost every year. This was because the contacts he made, and the exposure to literary culture that he enjoyed, helped him define his future as an author. Earlier he had written fiction and criticism as well as journalism, filling the pages of several short-lived cultural journals and his newspaper, but between the ages of nine and twenty-six Simms had focused his literary efforts primarily on poetry. Beginning with his first book of verse in 1825, he had published five small volumes in Charleston. A couple had received positive notice in New York, and in the fall of 1832, J. & J. Harper issued the sixth anonymously from there, *Atalantis: A Story of the Sea*. Coming back the following summer, Simms had in hand for the Harpers a gothic novella, *Martin Faber*, and after his return south, he also would send the manuscript of his first two-volume border romance, *Guy Rivers: A Tale of Georgia*.

The reception of these and the romances and short stories that followed quickly made Simms one of the nation's most successful fictionists. He continued to issue poetry as well—roughly a collection every three years over the thirty-seven years that he worked as a professional author. But this output was dwarfed by the fiction—on average a title every year (counting several serialized works but not counting the many revised editions). Then there were the two dozen separately published orations, histories, and biographies as well as edited collections of documents and dramas and a geography of South Carolina. Add to these the revised editions and the further printings and issues of his own works and it appears that Simms saw a title coming off the presses at the rate of one every three months or so. Making that figure all the more astounding is the fact that, during more than a dozen of those years (the early-to-mid 1840s, the late 1840s-to-early 1850s, and the mid-to-late 1860s), he also was editing a cultural journal or newspaper. Furthermore he contributed reams of reviews and poems, hundreds of op-ed pieces and columns, and dozens of short stories and public addresses, which were never collected and published in volume form.

His career mapped an arc. It ascended meteorically in the 1830s and peaked in the early-to-mid 1840s, before beginning to descend. One reason was the popularity of the historical fiction that Simms began to write. When he left behind the law, his first newspaper, and the Nullification controversy, as well as his sadness, historical fiction was all the rage. Sir Walter Scott had fueled the craze, beginning with the publication of his first Border romance in 1814. He died in September 1832. Seventeen years Simms's senior, James Fenimore Cooper, the closest America had to a Scott at the time, was at the peak of his reputation and success, having started publishing his romances in 1820. Thus the way had been prepared for a writer of Simms's historical imagination and preoccupations. Within five years of his first trip north, moreover, Lawson's (and now his) circle became loosely affiliated with a nationalistic and Democratic group, self-styled Young America, this after Young Italy and similar ethnic, nationalist, European, cultural and political movements (Moltke-Hansen, "Southern"). Edgar Allan Poe and other members gave Simms's first fictions positive, if not uncritical, attention.

By the end of the 1830s, paradoxically, Simms, like Cooper, found his success attracting unauthorized editions of his works because Britain and America did not have an international copyright agreement. Further, in the wake of the panic of 1837, Americans bought fewer books. Simms's response was to diversify his portfolio. He turned to biography and history, including his hugely successful *Life of Francis Marion* (1844). He also returned to the editor's chair, overseeing one and then another cultural journal. These were unlike the ones he had edited in the 1820s: they included contributions by numerous authors, not just those from Charleston, but from the region and also the North. The ambition motivating the journals was to connect and promote Charleston intellectually. Consequently the journals more closely resembled metropolitan quarterly reviews in their offerings.

The mid-1840s saw Simms involved in politics, even serving a term in the South Carolina legislature. By the middle of the Mexican-American War in 1847, he had concluded that the South needed to become an independent nation. Thereafter, although he maintained ties with many in the Young America circle, he no longer promoted his writings as fostering Americanism in literature (*Views*). Instead he increasingly emphasized the ways in which his three romance series—the colonial, the Revolutionary, and the border—were making tangible and meaningful the origins and development of the future southern nation and the sad but inevitable consequences for Native Americans (Watson, *From Nationalism*; compare Nakamura).

Sectional politics colored more and more of Simms's perceptions, speeches, and private communications. The rising tide of abolitionism had him aghast. It also fed his growing sense that his position in American letters was slipping. He returned to editing, and his poetry, which was more often explicitly about the South, became increasingly patriotic in tone. Although his first biographer, William Peterfield Trent, insisted that Simms's declining standing reflected the change in literary fashion from historical romances to realistic novels, Simms in fact wrote more and more as a social realist in the 1850s (Wimsatt, "Realism").

The Civil War consumed Simms. As he wrote Lawson, "Literature, especially poetry, is effectually overwhelmed by the drums, & the cavalry, and the shouting" (*Letters* 4:369–70). He did manage to editorialize often and to rework and finish things long on his desk, including poems, a novel, and a dramatic treatment of Benedict Arnold, the northern traitor in the Revolutionary War. Then, in the wake of the Confederacy's loss and the failure of his vision for the South, he found himself recording the loss in a new newspaper, dealing with the trauma in his poetry, and becoming more existential and psychological in his fictional treatments. Simms's old New York friends tried to help. He did edit and see through publication a volume of Confederate war poetry. Yet it is a measure of his reduced stature that the several new romances he published appeared only in serial form. In part this may have been because he was in a sense competing with himself. Publishers were beginning to reprint volumes out of the selected edition of his writings. Many of Simms's works were available in book form, just not new works.

Associations

As the *Letters* testify, Simms had complex, overlapping networks of friends and colleagues. As a boy and young man, he received the friendship, patronage, and commendation of a variety of well-placed people in Charleston, including Charles Rivers Carroll. It was Carroll with whom he read law, to whom he dedicated his first romance, and after whom he named a son. Both men were Unionists during the Nullification controversy. So were Hugh Swinton Legare (later U.S. attorney general) and the considerably older William Drayton, as well as lawyer and editor Richard Yeadon and Greenville, South Carolina, newspaper editor Benjamin Franklin Perry. Also considerably older was James Wright Simmons, who had joined with Simms to launch the *Southern Literary Gazette* in 1828, when Simms was twenty-two. Through him Simms had direct contact with such British literary figures as Leigh Hunt and Byron (Kibler, *Poetry* 15).

The next group of influential friends and collaborators that Simms acquired were members of the Lawson circle and included such figures as Edwin

Forrest, the Shakespearean actor, and Evert Duyckinck, who published several of Simms's volumes in Wiley and Putnam's series Library of American Books, which he edited. Among the many others were poets and editors William Cullen Bryant and Fitz-Greene Halleck. Simms also made nonliterary friends in New York and Philadelphia, such as John Jacob Bockee and William Hawkins Ferris, the cashier at the U.S. Treasury office in New York who, after the war, helped Simms, Henry Timrod (poet laureate of the Confederacy), and others.

As a Barnwell planter, Simms met a widening circle of South Carolina's leaders and literati. For instance his acquaintance with James Henry Hammond began in the late 1830s and deepened into a friendship in the early 1840s. It was in the early 1840s, too, when he again was editing cultural journals, that Simms became friends with many southern writers. He regarded several of them, including Virginians George Frederick Holmes, Edmund Ruffin, and Nathaniel Beverley Tucker as members, together with Hammond and himself, in a "sacred circle." Uniting the circle were members' devotion to the South and a shared sense of the marginal status and critical importance of the life of the mind in a largely rural and unintellectual region (Faust, *Sacred*). Others of Simms's wide connections in the region did not interact as much with each other, but Simms long corresponded with Maryland novelist and lawyer John Pendleton Kennedy, Irish-born Georgia poet Richard Henry Wilde, Alabama lawyer and writer Alexander Beaufort Meek, and Louisiana historian and assistant attorney general Charles Gayarré, among others. By the 1850s, when Simms once more returned to editing a cultural journal, many of the writers whom he recruited were members of a younger generation. Poets Paul Hamilton Hayne and Henry Timrod were two. Often they and a half dozen others of Simms's and their generations met in John Russell's Charleston Book Shop and adjourned to dinner at Simms's Smith Street home, "dubbed 'The Wigwam'" (*Letters* 1:cxxxvi). Shortly before his death fifteen or so years later, Simms wrote Hayne, "I am rapidly passing from the stage, where you young men are to succeed me" (*Letters* 5:287).

Thought

The welter of Simms's works disguises unities and dynamics of the thought underlying them. From early on Simms was convinced that art ennobles or transforms, as well as gives voice to individuals and societies; therefore it must be cultivated assiduously. Without the potential for high artistic attainment, he insisted, societies are not ready for the independence and regard of free peoples. This is where Simms the historian joined Simms the poet. Societies develop, he argued (using the stadialism of the Scottish historical school), from imitation through self-assertion to achievement and also from savagery through strife to settled agricultural communities and, ultimately, to a hierarchical civilization supporting a rich artistic life. It was the job of the artist to help envision the goal, inspire the pursuit, and inform the process. That process was at once progressive and dialectical. Order, without dynamism, stifled development, as did the obverse—the dominance by ungoverned impulses or uncontrolled license. This was true in the individual, but also in societies as a whole. War was necessary for civilization, but its success was measured in the securities of the home, the center of cultural production and reproduction.

Whether in the public or in the domestic arena, "the true governor, as [Thomas] Carlyle call[ed] him—the king man—" guided rather than impeded the forces of change and progress (Simms, "Guizot's" 122). There were few such men with the capacity to lead. The same was true of nations. Neither all people nor all peoples were equal in either capacity or attainment. That was why Native Americans were overrun and Africans had been enslaved by European peoples in the New World. Indeed, Simms argued, "slavery in all ages has been found the greatest and most admirable agent of Civilization," giving education and examples to less evolved peoples (*Letters* 3:174). The degree to which a people had evolved mattered. That was why, he held, Americans had won independence from the most powerful empire in the world. They had done so through their Revolution, led by an elite that felt correctly its time had come (Simms, "Ellet's" 328). By mid-1847 that also was Simms's judgment for the South: the region had evolved enough to become independent (*Letters* 2:332). The hope inspired and then failed him and the people he sought to lead.

While not all men could rise to the highest rank, they all had the same responsibility at home. There the father was patriarch, protector, and head, while the mother was nurturer, moral instructor, and heart. There, too, children's characters and minds were formed by age twelve ("Ellet's"). Children's upbringing was critical to citizenship, and it was through her sons and the support of her husband, father, and brothers that a woman shaped the public sphere. The culture and character instilled in the child expressed and informed not just the household, but the larger society—the people.

"The history of peoples and their embodiments in institutions, states, and artistic productions—these were the great subjects" in Simms's view (Moltke-Hansen, "Southern" 120). Yet "poets were the only class of philosophers who had recognized" this until his own day, when at last "we now read human histories. We now ask after the affections as well as the ceremonies of society" ("Ellet's" 319–20). Peoples or races—that is, ethnic groups—were not unchanging any more than were their politics and their cultures. They either advanced or were overrun by history. Further, new peoples emerged, and old identities were submerged. The Spanish conquistadors were the creation of centuries of conflict with the Moors: their motivation was the glory of conquest, not the routine of trade or the plow. On the other hand, the English settlements in North America reflected the impulse to transform the wilderness into verdant farms and build society (*Views* 64, 178–85; *Social* 8). The same impulse drove Americans westward in Simms's own day and gave Americans their Manifest Destiny.

To explore these facts of the South's settlement and its place in international conflicts, Simms wrote all together, between 1833 and 1863, two romances set in eighth-century Spain, two set during the Spanish exploration and conquest of the Americas and two during the later English colonization of South Carolina, seven set during the American Revolution, and—depending on how one counts—perhaps eight set on the borders of the nineteenth-century South. After the war he published one more Revolutionary romance and two more that, like it, were set beyond the boundaries of civilization. He also left two unfinished romances, also set beyond society's normal reach. These late works, however, no longer had as their framing justification the cultivation of the South's future and civilization.

White southerners had their independence foreclosed by the war. In his last works, therefore, Simms found himself exploring the psychological, philosophical, and historical impulses that led to the Confederacy's demise and what, in the aftermath, it meant to be a good man and to build for the future, however impoverished. On the first score, he argued that the impulse to idealism behind abolitionism ignored historical realities, becoming inhuman in its consequences. On the latter score, he affirmed responsibility for one's dependents and the virtues of stoicism, as well as a continued commitment to the beauty and truth of art and the impulses to the cultivated life and fields. Therefore, in the face of the burning of his Woodlands home and library in February 1865—during Sherman's march and in the midst of desperate circumstances—he insisted that home, or the ideals and past characterizing its potential, still was at the center of true civilization, but only if elevated by art (*Sense* 8, 17). It was wrong to measure civilization by the getting, spending, and mad dashing, or material progress and utilitarianism, characteristic of both a capitalistic North and also many southerners. These traits he often had attacked even before the war, insisting that "the work of the Imagination, which is the Genius of a race, is only begun when its material progress is supposed to be complete" (*Poetry* 12).

Writings

Simms expressed many of his ideas most personally in letters and most cogently in essays, speeches, and occasional introductions to his books. But he illustrated them most fully in his fiction and poetry. By the time he arrived in New

York in 1832, he had formed many of the core ideals and beliefs that would shape his work. His application of them, however, modified his understanding over time. Growing as a writer and growing in knowledge and experience, he also grew as a thinker.

In his hierarchy of values, poetry came first. It was a prophetic calling as well as evocative of the deeply felt (or, sometimes, the fleeting) and thus testimony to the perdurance and transcendence of the beautiful and the human spirit. Yet, as Simms often ruefully reflected, prose spoke to many more people. That was a principal reason why he turned to writing prose epics or romances. He gave his most concerted consideration of poetry's value and roles in three lectures in Charleston in 1854. Over the prior three years he had given portions of them in Augusta, Georgia, Washington, D.C., and Richmond and Petersburg, Virginia. Entitled *Poetry and the Practical*, they did not see print until 1996, as Simms never found the time to expand them as he wanted. On the other hand, his last address on the same themes, *The Sense of the Beautiful*, was issued soon after he delivered it, also in Charleston.

Many of his important reviews have not yet been gathered, but Simms collected some in 1845–46, and *Views and Reviews in American Literature, History and Fiction* came out in 1846 and 1847 in two "series." Beginning with a consideration of "Americanism" in literature, the first series explored the themes and periods of American history for treatment by the novelist. Simms argued there, and in forewords to several of his romances, that fiction rendered the past more truthfully, interestingly, and tellingly than histories and biographies could because fiction—like poetry—required imagination to look beyond what is not known or expressed. The second series examined additional American writers and what distinguished them, for instance, in their humor.

Despite their early success, Simms's romances, novellas, and stories provoked mixed reviews. Poe eventually concluded that Simms had become "the best novelist which this country has, on the whole, produced" but also insisted that "he should never have written 'The Partisan,' nor 'The Yemassee.'" This was in a review of *Confession*. That novel, like the gothic *Martin Faber*, demonstrated, Poe contended, that Simms's "genius [did] not lie in the outward so much as in the inner world." Yet he nevertheless wrote of Simms's short-story collection *The Wigwam and the Cabin* that "in invention, in vigor, in movement, in the power of exciting interest, and in the artistical management of his themes, he has surpassed, we think, any of his countrymen." Other critics, especially in the genteel and Whiggish Knickerbocker circle, joined Poe in condemning what they considered to be the excessively graphic and vulgar qualities of many characters and scenes, and Simms's prolixity and sententiousness, in his romances (Butterworth and Kibler 64, 50).

The violent realism and earthiness of the romances did not result in realistic novels. Although Simms received early praise for his characterizations (particularly of women), he used the romance formula, with its stereotypic heroes and heroines, predictable themes, and conventional polarities. People were on quests or had lost their way or were fighting long odds or were carrying forward the banner of (and modeling) civilization or were mired in the slough of despond or were resisting all the claims of civilized society and behavior or were pursuing love interests. Deceitfulness, selfishness, and greed opposed honor, high-mindedness, and honesty against the backdrop of the South's development from the earliest days of Spanish exploration to the westward movement in Simms's own youth.

It was only gradually that Simms married the psychological acuity of some of his portraits of the interior struggles of his gothic characters and fiction to the historical romance. Helping him think through how to do so were the biographies he wrote in the mid-1840s, but also the incidents on which he focused particular fictions, such as the murder in *Beauchampe; or, The Kentucky Tragedy* (1842). However incomplete the blending of realism and romanticism or of stereotypical and socially individuated renderings through the 1840s, by the 1850s Simms fundamentally had made the transition to social realism in such works as *Woodcraft* and *The Cassique of Kiawah*. Indeed some scholars have considered *Woodcraft* the first realistic novel in America (Bakker; Wimsatt, "Realism").

In some sense disguising the transition is the fact that Simms also increasingly wrote as a humorist and, in so doing, often rendered his late narratives fabulistically, when not writing social comedy or stories of manners. This dimension of Simms's work was largely hidden, however, until the 1974 publication of *Stories and Tales*, volume 5 in the Centennial Simms edition. There, for the first time, readers had access in print to "Bald-Head Bill Bauldy." There, too, for the first time one could read together that story, "Legend of the Hunter's Camp," and "How Sharp Snaffles Got His Capital and Wife," which was published posthumously in *Harper's Magazine* in October 1870. These and other stories and tales made it clear that Simms was a fecund contributor to southern and American humor.

Humor let Simms take up issues that he could not otherwise address in print and still expect to be well received. He did so both during and after the war. The war also pushed Simms past the emerging fashion of social realism. Having destroyed the familiar, the preoccupation of much realistic fiction, the war made the liminal central (Shillingsburg, "Cub"). While his romances and tales had often explored life on the edge or in extreme circumstances, whether in war or on the frontier or on the verge of madness or in fanciful realms, it had done so against a backdrop of, and with the goal of affirming, social norms and development. In the war's wake that goal seemed absurd. Mythologized memories of a healthy past might nurture a sense of the beautiful but could not help one deal with the present. Thus Simms's conclusion, in a March 1869 letter to Paul Hamilton Hayne: "Let us bury the Past lest it buries us!" (*Letters* 5:214). Fifteen months later he lay dead in the 13 Society Street, Charleston, home of his oldest daughter, with the shell holes in the walls of the bedroom he had shared with several children.

Posthumous Reputation

The twenty years after Simms's death saw him often respectfully treated, first in obituaries, later in memoirs and columns, and also in literary dictionaries and encyclopedias. Yet Charles Richardson's 1887 *American Literature: 1607–1885* proved a harbinger of a shift: Simms, Richardson observed, was "more respected than read," having "won considerable note because he was so sectional" and then having "lost it because he was not sectional enough," although he showed "silly contempt for his Northern betters" (qtd. in Butterworth and Kibler 130). Five years later Trent's biography of Simms appeared. It was the first full-length, scholarly treatment. Its central thesis was that Simms's environment frustrated his abilities: the South was inimical to art and the life of the mind, and Charleston high society's hauteur marginalized Simms despite his talent and character. Trent's second thesis was that Simms's commitment to the romance and his romanticism meant that his works had become largely unreadable in an age of literary realism. Although Vernon Parrington and later scholars recognized Simms's impulses to realism, the two theses long shaped Simms criticism and, indeed, also helped frame study of antebellum southern literature and intellectual life (Parrington 119–30).

A Virginian born in 1862, Trent was a progressive who wanted a New South radically different from the old. He saw his pioneering study of Simms as an opportunity to criticize what the Civil War had made untenable. From his perspective the Old South was not the expanding and rapidly developing environment, with a deep history, that Simms portrayed, but a place where slavery stultified and stunted the growth and progress displayed by the North. Southern—especially South Carolinian—writers occasionally challenged Trent's agenda and conclusions, but those critiques had little impact. Not until after publication of the Simms letters in the 1950s did scholars begin to consider the author in the historical and contemporary contexts that he had rendered in his poetry and fiction. And not until after the centennial of his death did a growing number of scholars, having concluded that southern intellectual history was

not an oxymoron, begin to study in detail the culture in which Simms partici-
pated and to which he contributed so voluminously and variously.

Some of these scholars also have had agendas: they have wanted to see
Simms included in the American literary canon, for instance, or they have
wanted to defend the heritage that in their view Trent, and so many others,
inappropriately belittled or ignorantly dismissed. More fruitfully, other scholars have begun to reframe the understanding of nineteenth-century American
intellectual life by stripping away preconceptions that characterized earlier
evaluations of Simms and his contemporaries. They are closely examining the
historical record and transatlantic and other contemporary contexts and developments in the process. Although the pursuit of canonical status in a post-
canonical age seems quixotic at this point, the explosion of the canon is leading
to more varied fare being offered and may, therefore, mean that Simms, once
his work is widely available, will be more often anthologized as well as studied. Defensiveness about Simms and the antebellum South may warm the
hearts of like-minded people, just as critics of the Old South have been encouraged by shared presuppositions and disdain. Yet dueling cultural ideologies do
not advance comity and may only reinforce mutual incomprehensions. Continued, deep research in original sources and the theoretical reframing that
Atlantic history, the history of the book, and other perspectives offer — these
approaches promise most for further study of Simms, his works, and his world.

Works Cited

For amplified readings by and on Simms and on his world, go to http://simms.library
.sc.edu/bibliography.php.

Bakker, Jan. "Simms on the Literary Frontier; or, So Long Miss Ravenel and Hello Cap-
    tain Porgy: *Woodcraft* Is the First 'Realistic' Novel in America." In *William Gilmore
    Simms and the American Frontier*, edited by John Caldwell Guilds and Caroline Collins,
    64–78. Athens: University of Georgia Press, 1997.
Butterworth, Keen, and James E. Kibler Jr. *William Gilmore Simms: A Definitive Guide.*
    Boston: G. K. Hall, 1980.
Faust, Drew Gilpin. *A Sacred Circle: The Dilemma of the Intellectual in the Old South, 1840–
    1860.* Baltimore: Johns Hopkins University Press, 1977.
Guilds, John C. *Simms: A Literary Life.* Fayetteville: University of Arkansas Press, 1992.
Hayne, Paul Hamilton. "Ante-Bellum Charleston." *Southern Bivouac* 1 (October 1885):
    257–68.
Kibler, James E. "The First Simms Letters: 'Letters from the West' (1826)." *Southern Liter-
    ary Journal* 19 (Spring 1987): 81–91.
———. *The Poetry of William Gilmore Simms: An Introduction and Bibliography.* Columbia:
    Southern Studies Program, University of South Carolina, 1979.

McHaney, Thomas L. "An Early 19th-Century Literary Agent: James Lawson of New York." *Publications of the Bibliographical Society of America* 64 (Spring 1970): 177–92.

Moltke-Hansen, David. "The Expansion of Intellectual Life: A Prospectus." In *Intellectual Life in Antebellum Charleston,* edited by Michael O'Brien and David Moltke-Hansen, 3–44. Knoxville: University of Tennessee Press, 1986.

———. "Southern Literary Horizons in Young America: Imaginative Development of a Regional Geography." *Studies in the Literary Imagination* 42, no. 1 (2009): 1–31.

Nakamura, Masahiro. *Visions of Order in William Gilmore Simms: Southern Conservatism and the Other American Romance.* Columbia: University of South Carolina Press, 2009.

Parrington, Vernon L. *The Romantic Revolution in America, 1800–1860.* Vol. 2 of *Main Currents in American Thought.* New York: Harcourt, Brace and Company, 1927.

Rogers, George C., Jr. *Charleston in the Age of the Pinckneys.* Columbia: University South Carolina Press, 1980.

Shillingsburg, Miriam J. "The Cub of the Panther: A New Frontier." In *William Gilmore Simms and the American Frontier,* edited by John Caldwell Guilds and Caroline Collins, 221–36. Athens: University of Georgia Press, 1997.

———. "Literary Grist: Simms's Trips to Mississippi." *Southern Quarterly* 41, no. 2 (2003): 119–34.

Simms, William Gilmore. *Atalantis: A Story of the Sea: In Three Parts.* New York: J. & J. Harper, 1832.

———. *Beauchampe; or, The Kentucky Tragedy.* 2 vols. Philadelphia: Lea and Blanchard, 1842.

———. *The Cassique of Kiawah: A Colonial Romance.* New York: Redfield, 1859.

———. *Confession; or, The Blind Heart. A Domestic Story.* 2 vols. Philadelphia: Lea and Blanchard, 1841.

———. "Ellet's 'Women of the Revolution.'" *Southern Quarterly Review,* n.s. 1 (July 1850): 314–54.

———. "Guizot's Democracy in France." *Southern Quarterly Review* 15, no.29 (1849): 114–65.

———. *Guy Rivers: A Tale of Georgia.* 2 vols. New York: Harper & Brothers, 1834.

———. *The Letters of William Gilmore Simms.* Edited by Mary C. Simms Oliphant, Alfred Taylor Odell, and T. C. Duncan. 6 vols. Columbia: University of South Carolina Press, 1952–82.

———. *The Life of Francis Marion.* New York: Henry G. Langley, 1844.

———. *Martin Faber, the Story of a Criminal; and Other Tales.* 2 vols. New York: Harper & Brothers, 1837.

———. *Poetry and the Practical.* Edited by James E. Kibler. Fayetteville: University of Arkansas Press, 1996.

———. *The Sense of the Beautiful: An Address . . . before the Charleston County Agricultural and Horticultural Association, May 3, 1870.* Charleston: Charleston County Agricultural and Horticultural Association, 1870.

———. *The Social Principle: The Source of National Permanence. An Oration, Delivered before the Erosophic Society of the University of Alabama . . . December 13, 1842.* Tuscaloosa: Erosophic Society, University of Alabama, 1843.

———. *Stories and Tales.* Vol. 5 of *The Writings of William Gilmore Simms.* Centennial edition; introductions, explanatory notes, and texts established by John Caldwell Guilds. Columbia: University of South Carolina Press, 1974.

———. *Views and Reviews in American Literature, History and Fiction.* 2 vols. New York: Wiley and Putnam, 1845 (1846).

———. *The Wigwam and the Cabin.* 2 vols. New York: Wiley and Putnam, 1845–46.

———. *Woodcraft, or Hawks about the Dovecote: A Story of the South, at the Close of the Revolution.* New York: Redfield, 1854.

Trent, William Peterfield. *William Gilmore Simms.* Boston: Houghton, Mifflin, 1892.

Wakelyn, Jon L. *The Politics of a Literary Man: William Gilmore Simms.* Westport, Conn.: Greenwood Press, 1973.

Watson, Charles S. *From Nationalism to Secessionism: The Changing Fiction of William Gilmore Simms.* Westport, Conn.: Greenwood Press, 1993.

White, William B., Jr. *The Ross-Chesnut-Sutton Family of South Carolina.* Franklin, N.C.: Privately printed, 2002.

Wimsatt, Mary Ann. "Realism and Romance in Simms's Midcentury Fiction." *Southern Literary Journal* 12, no. 2 (1980): 29–48.

Critical Introduction

WOODCRAFT

James Everett Kibler

Woodcraft is the fifth novel composed in Simms's saga of the American Revolution. Set during the chaotic close and aftermath of the war, it is the last (eighth) Revolutionary Romance in terms of chronological action. As the work opens, the British are evacuating Charleston in December 1782. Then the novel shifts to a ruined rice plantation, Glen-Eberley, on the Ashepoo River south of Charleston, where the plantation community is striving to establish relative civil order and comity. To resist being stolen by the British, some of the plantation's slaves have hidden in the swamp, and as their master, Porgy, returns, they come forward to seek normalcy and put in a crop to feed the near starving. In achieving order, some of the "woodcraft" maneuverings of both war and survival in wild nature must be utilized. Hence the title. As Porgy will state, life, even in peace, is eternal civil war. Proper woodcraft is necessary at every turn and juncture if man is to survive intact as whole human beings.

The general critical consensus for the last hundred years has been that *Woodcraft* is among Simms's best novels. Many, in fact, deem it his masterpiece. Donald Davidson, perhaps still the most perceptive critic to have written on Simms, for example, wrote in 1952: "It is not too much to say that *Woodcraft* is Simms' highest achievement. Certainly it stands…without a rival in its day and time, and hardly excelled or even paralleled later in its peculiar vein" (*Letters* 1:xlv). It is a many-faceted, exceedingly rich and complex work. Critics have rightly discussed it from a multitude of vantage points, but the full measure of the novel has yet to be taken.

Like its themes, the composition history of the novel is among the more complex of Simms's works. It first appeared serially in the Charleston *Southern Literary Gazette* a year after the serialization there of *The Golden Christmas*, to which it bears some thematic affinities and related imagery (Kibler "Pairing," 13–16). Its title in the *Southern Literary Gazette* was *The Sword and the Distaff; or, "Fair, Fat and Forty," A Story of the South, At the Close of the Revolution."* The novel ran from February to November 1852. In a letter to James Henry Hammond on 18 August 1852, Simms reported the novel finished (*Letters* 3:193). Before the last section of the serialized version appeared, the complete novel appeared as a separately published work in Charleston from Walker and Richards (publisher of the *SLG*) in September 1852. It was still entitled *The Sword and the Distaff,* and bore on its title page "Second Edition," which is actually the first book edition, created from the typesettings for the *SLG*. It was reissued by Lippincott, Grambo of Philadelphia from the same plates and with the same title in 1853.

This early title effectively represents the complicated mesh of contrasts and opposites that fill the novel. The sword here is emblematic of war and the male world. The distaff (a part of a spinning wheel, or in heraldry, the distaff or female side of the family) stands for the peaceful domestic sphere, the home and hearth, and the female world. In other words, the novel is Simms's *War and Peace,* seventeen years before Tolstoi. The subtitle "Fair, Fat and Forty" refers most specifically to the Widow Eveleigh, Porgy's love interest and plantation neighbor, who stands in contrast to him. As a British officer says of her, she is more of a man than some men, while Porgy is inactive, passive, and of less than heroic nature. Like Falstaff, who is partly a model, he is a likeable comic, mock heroic figure. His unusual name likely derives from a scrappy fish common off the Carolina coast. Its shape, like Porgy's, is round and fat-bodied. The fish was usually only eaten by the poor, owing to its boniness. Just as the worlds of male and female get blurred by Porgy and Eveleigh, the world of domestic peace gets mated with the maneuverings of war.

Simms asked his friend Hammond to comment upon the work, and in a letter of 8 July 1853, he called it "fully equal to any of your novels." He went on to advise Simms to "strike out" the subtitle "Fair, Fat and Forty," because it was "decidedly vulgar." He also noted several inconsistencies and a "fault in your geography" (*Letters* 3:243). Simms revised the novel, subsequent to its Lippincott, Grambo appearance in 1853, along the lines Hammond suggested. The new, revised edition appeared from Redfield in late September 1854 as *Woodcraft or Hawks About the Dovecote. A Story of the South at the Close of the Revolution.*

William P. Trent, Joseph V. Ridgely, and later critics could see no apparent reason for the change and felt the new title had no bearing on the text. Yet it is equally effective, perhaps even moreso than the first. It broadens the focus. Woodcraft is the figurative image of maneuvering through life, full as it is of pitfalls and dead ends. In this way, with his new title, Simms highlights the *Bildungsroman* novel of character development (especially for the main character Porgy) and in general broadens the psychological implications outside the smaller (albeit still epic) panorama of war and peace, of the "soldier's pay" of coming back to normalcy in a ruined, war-ravaged land. In twentieth century fashion, the outer world of the landscape mirrors the scarred inner world of the characters, especially the returning veteran Porgy, who in the early stages of the book, is fatalistic, self-indulgent, and self-pitying, and says that he might best slit his own throat. Simms's belief in the flawed nature of man and his insistence on human frailties and limitations has always been a hallmark of Southern literature.

Likewise, Porgy's overseer, Sergeant Millhouse, is only a partial man, as reflected by his loss of an arm. As in Flannery O'Connor, physical deformity is an outward sign of an inner lack, a spiritual deficiency. Although he may seem more "practical" than Porgy in his thorough-going materialistic attitude toward the world, he is close to being a grotesque. It is no wonder that slave Tom can assess his shortcomings. He concludes that Millhouse lacks the proper balance for dancing, which he forswears as frivolous.

In addition to the new title, Simms made a few substantive changes and cleared up inconsistencies. For example, Corporal and Sergeant Millhouse become consistently Sergeant Millhouse, as suggested by Hammond. Unfortunately, the Redfield Edition also bears Redfield house-styling and what appears to be some substantive editorial tampering. The Redfield Edition has two unsigned illustrations by F. O. C. Darley, engraved by Whitney, Jocelyn, and Annin in South Carolina. The title page verso indicates that the text was stereotyped by C. C. Savage of New York.

Both editions of the novel are dedicated to Joseph Johnson, MD. Johnson (1776–1862) was a Charleston friend and author of *Traditions and Reminiscences Chiefly of the American Revolution in the South* (1851). To Duyckinck in 1854, Simms declared Johnson to be "one of the best living reminiscents" of the war (*Letters* 3:343). In the dedication, Simms suggested that the novel is a *roman à clef*, peopled with fictional portrayals whose real-life antecedents Johnson would surely have no trouble recognizing: "The humorists of 'Glen-Eberley' [Porgy and his comrades at his plantation] were well-known personages of preceding generations, here thinly disguised under false names and fanciful localities, which, I am inclined to think will prove no disguise to you. I shall keep my secret, however, as a matter of course" (*Woodcraft* 3). Simms went on to state that Johnson was under no similar obligation to remain silent about the true identities of the characters, and in fact, was encouraged to name them.

George Hayhoe writes that Johnson's *Traditions* (p. 408) describes "a widow lady of great respectability,—'fair, fat, and forty,'—who entertained the soldiers, and one young officer who flattered himself that he might acquire her wealth by marrying her" (Hayhoe 524). Hayhoe feels that this "description is quite probably the germ of the novel," considering the fact that Johnson's "fair, fat, and forty" became the subtitle of *The Sword and the Distaff*. The phrase in Johnson, incidentally, likely derives from Sir Walter Scott's *St. Ronan's Well*

(1823) and/or *Redgauntlet* (1824). Hayhoe might also have used the fact that *Traditions* had just appeared the year before Simms wrote his novel to explain it as the impetus for Simms's composition.

As for the Eveleigh surname, the Eveleighs were well-known in early Lowcountry and Charleston Revolutionary War history. Legend has it that it was from the window of the George Eveleigh house on Church Street in Charleston that Francis Marion leapt to avoid capture by the British. A Nicholas Eveleigh of Charleston had an illustrious revolutionary history.

Of Porgy, Hayhoe writes, while he bears resemblance to Falstaff, "it is likely that much of the inspiration for Simms's portrait...is derived from a sketch of Dr. Alexander Skinner of Lee's legion in Alexander Garden's *Anecdotes of the Revolutionary War in America* (1822). Garden describes Skinner as 'an honest fellow, just as ready to fight as eat' (136) and points out his 'strong resemblance to Falstaff' as well as Sancho Panza" (Hayhoe 527). Hayhoe continues: Garden also notes that Skinner was unsuccessfully trying to court the widow Mrs. Charles Elliott of "Sandy Hill" plantation, but even though she refused him, the fact that he had "a kind invitation to feel himself at home" in her house, "the most hospitable mansion in the State, made Skinner the proudest and happiest of men" (Garden 138; Hayhoe 527). These details fit Porgy perfectly.

Simms's character colonel Moncrieff is based upon James Moncrieff (1744–1793), a Scot who served as a military engineer for England during the siege of Charleston in 1780. He supervised slaves stolen from outlying plantations for resale, and in March 1782, Colonel Balfour suggested he lead a brigade of blacks against the Patriots. Moncrieff is known to have shipped eight hundred slaves to the West Indies, where he sold them as his own property. According to Hayhoe, "such exportation of slaves was illegal but was such a common offense that Cornwallis had issued orders forbidding it without his express permission on 2 August 1780" (Hayhoe 524). M'Kewn is likely based on James McKloun, a Scot and loyalist, whom the Patriots did not banish after the war.

Porgy's body servant and cook, Tom, as well as slaves Jenny, John, Jupe, Maum Sappho, Charlotte, Betty, Sally, and Bob, "may be based on or named after Simms family slaves" (*Letters* 1:clii, 2:590–1). The novel is peppered with allusions to historical figures such as Harden (Colonel William Harden) and Withers (William Withers), Captain Henry Barry, General Francis Marion, General Henry Lee, Horatio Gates, Nathanael Greene, General Charles Cotesworth Pinckney, General Alexander Leslie, Colonel Nesbit Balfour, Major John Andre, and others. Porgy's consistent praise of the Patriot militiamen of South Carolina reflects Simms's attitudes toward the South's role in the Revolutionary War.

There is no known counterpart for Samuel Bostwick, Dory Bostwick, or Lance Frampton, though their family names are common in the time and place. There is a Frampton plantation ("The Hermitage") near Pocotaligo, whose master, John Edward Frampton (1810–1896), was a state senator from 1842–1846, while Simms was in the legislature. He was one of the largest planters in Prince William's Parish of Beaufort District and had ties to Simms's Barnwell District. He married there in 1842. Long active in the Nullification Movement, Frampton attended the Southern Rights Convention of 1852, and signed the Ordinance of Secession. Lance Frampton, an admirable, sober, common-sensical farmer-soldier, may have been either an ancestor, or a tribute to the senator from one who obviously shared his political beliefs. In courting, Frampton is Porgy's superior. The Widow Griffin, Millhouse, Absalom Crooks, Dr. Oakenburg, and Geordie (George) Dennison may be purely fictional creations, though as Hayhoe suggests, "it is possible that, although Simms used published anecdotes and traditions such as Johnson's [and Garden's] as the basis for some of his characters, he modeled others on figures he had heard Johnson and others talk about" (Hayhoe 521).

Woodcraft appeared during a period incredibly fruitful and rich for both Simms and American literature. The decade of the 1850s has been named the American Literary Renaissance by historian and literary critic F. O. Matthiessen (1902–1950) in his landmark volume *American Renaissance: Art and Experience in the Age of Emerson and Whitman* (1941). Although Matthiessen makes no mention of Simms, *Woodcraft* would be legitimate there squarely in the middle of the brief period that produced *The Scarlet Letter*, *Moby Dick*, *Walden*, and *Leaves of Grass*. Interestingly and significantly, if placed there, Simms's work would be the only humorous novel of the decade, and well before *Huckleberry Finn*. A persuasive case has been made by recent critics, most particularly Jan Bakker, that it is as well the first realistic novel in America.

The novel incorporates a complex system of character contrasts, pairings, and comparisons in Faulknerian manner. As in Faulkner, plot and action are driven in this way; and character provides order, structure, and themes. Themes grow out of character rather than the other way around. The centrality of character is likely what lifts the work from the rhetorical to the dialectic and accounts for its literary stature. In general, abstractionist theme-driven, rhetorically conceived fiction is not as effective, and *Woodcraft* escapes these limitations by a Shakespearian, Dickensian focus on the complexities of human personalities in conflict with themselves and each other.

This is not to say that ideas and views and philosophies are not present, but they grow out of character that is alive (not flat cardboard), believable, engaging, and memorable. Captain Porgy had first appeared in *The Partisan* (1835) as a rather simple supporting figure and, frankly, at times something of a bore. He makes a cameo appearance in *Mellichampe* (1836), is resurrected fully and effectively in *Katharine Walton* (1850), and later appears briefly in *The Forayers* (1855) and *Eutaw* (1856). But here he takes central stage as chief protagonist. He is the most beloved character in Simms's work but nevertheless elicits debate as to just how sympathetically we should see him. Wimsatt has made a good case for Porgy as very sympathetically human despite his exasperating self-indulgence and self-pity early in the novel (168–72). William Taylor has him the perfect embodiment of the Cavalier plantation South, with all its strengths and defects (288).

Wimsatt treats the novel's "dominant mode" as a "comedy of plantation manners" (167). One question *Woodcraft* poses is whether plantation civilization and its traditions will survive. Involved in this focus is a definition of community and how such communities are kept whole and vital. For the community to persist, there must be hospitality, neighborliness, tolerance, good naturedness, and nurturing through food, fellowship, and friendship—as opposed to self-centeredness and extreme individualism outside society (Kibler, "Pairing" 13).

Beyond these considerations, *Woodcraft* bursts with life in all its infinite possibilities. Its world is full of miracles and mystery. The spiritual suffuses the empirically real. As Porgy says, the "devil is at our elbow" (410), ready to delude, defraud, degrade, and destroy. He continues, and "with foes among those who surround us, and the vices and vanities at our own hearts to second their labors, unless Heaven help us in season, and with all its angels, hope and humanity stand but a poor choice for happiness" (410). In this struggle to survive and maintain community, life is war, civil war, very much like the military conflict that has just ended. It is chaotic, confusing, contradictory, paradoxical, violent, and absurd enough in its particulars. It requires the maneuverings of woodcraft to get through it, often in a dark wood, and along winding, circuitous, and dangerous paths. The novel's sometimes tedious first hundred pages, set in the woods, are necessary to frame the figurative comparison. There are all sorts of snares and false paths throughout the novel, false "ologies" and "isms" that lead to dead ends and sometimes to death. Two such are atheism (as expressed by the squatter Samuel Bostwick) and utilitarianism (as demonstrated by Millhouse), but there are numerous others as well. Many times the novel's paths (in and out of the woods) go in circles, leading nowhere. What Simms provides here, beyond "ology" and "ism" or specific concerns (like, for instance, answering *Uncle Tom's Cabin*), is a way of seeing the world, a *Weltanschauung*, that encompasses and transcends topical issues. This way of seeing opens doors to possibilities rather than closing them with easy explanations that oversimplify and thus distort truths. Simms felt, and had his omniscient narrator suggest, that transcendentalism, abolitionism, utilitarianism, hedonism, realism, naturalism, empiricism, determinism, Marxism, spiritualism, and other passing ideological approaches all, in the final analysis, are flawed by shortsightedness and single-mindedness. Any angle of truth, held too tightly, becomes a falsehood. "My writings are not to be estimated by things of a clique or of a day," he wrote. He was aware of literary trends, but was equally the possessor of a strong historical consciousness and was cognizant of the broader context and the constants of literature, which a grounding in the Classics gave him. In the final analysis, in this instance, if not always in his fiction, the shifting fashions, while they made an imprint on his work, seem only superficially secondary when placed against these constants.

The novel's doors indeed open to mysteries, unexplainable riddles, and miracles that are at the heart of life. This world has miracles at every turn of the path. The characters learn practical woodcraft in going down the novel's paths, but real wisdom comes from the particular way of seeing man as finite, flawed, and imperfectible, but yet still capable of transcendence of his animal nature. It is a book that centers around transcendence and transfiguration, both sought and rejected, both accomplished and not achieved.

Man's animal nature, determined by animal desires in an animal world that ends in death, is a part of this novel's realistic universe; but equally realistic is man's capacity for salvation through faith. The character Dory Bostwick is essential in this respect. A faith in miracles is essential to the anti-empiricist way of seeing. Empiricism clearly leads to a diminished world that is joyless and hollow. The characters in the novel stand in stark contrast as those who realize potential, and the possibilities for growth and transfiguration confront those who reject salvation and end their lives in the failed horror of spiritual emptiness.

Woodcraft is thus a book about possibilities, especially the possibilities for redemption and transcendence. Actions matter and character is fate, but the results of these actions are not always pat. Wisdom is a matter of learning that life, with its deep, sad, and grand mysteries, can never be fully fathomed—that it is both inscrutable and unconquerable. Evil exists. It comes from within and is not imposed from without. The novel is thus a grappling to discern the very nature of life as a constant struggle with the devil "at out elbow." Thus, *Woodcraft* is anti-determinist. Men are not fated, not determined by environment and heredity. Simms even left the resolution of his main plots open to conjecture, but the conjecture alone is enough to undercut rigid determinism (Kibler, "Dory" 211). What is clear is that at the novel's end a character's treasure of faith is proved true and life affirming, while his foil's reliance on the material proves false and leads to emptiness and a death that is at once physical and spiritual. One of the novel's primary miracles, Dory Bostwick, daughter of a cruel and malignant squatter, "blossoms" in her squalid shack. Man's animal world is still ordered in its larger design by a Providence which allows miracles even for the humblest.

Clearly *Woodcraft* (1852–1854) is close in spirit and philosophy to Simms's *Poetry and the Practical* (1854), in which poetry, or the way of seeing that it requires, is the only truly practical. The novel's main character, Porgy, accepts the mysteries of life, sees the true value of music, poetry, and dance, values the eccentricities of human personality that would prevent easy case-book explanations of human nature, and refuses (like Simms) to allow life to be explained only by uninspired science and the cash nexus or by the pragmatic, empirical, and practical alone. Porgy tells us "The true man does not live by money…. There is still better food than that for which I hunger" (*Woodcraft* 235).

On the other hand, Porgy's foil, his utilitarian overseer Millhouse (shades of John Stuart Mill and the mill house of industry) can see no good in allowing slaves to coon hunt or dance or Porgy to entertain poets and guests who cannot pay their way. He would turn out immediately foppish, eccentric Dr. Oakenburg, that "puzzle in a bottle" as Porgy calls him, and poet Geordie Dennison, who is chronicling the late war and its heroes in his verse. Dennison rides with Marion, and who will be there to pass down his exploits and their meaning if not sung by the poet? To summarize the novel in terms of "finance vs. romance," however true the phrase rings, is not the whole story. Although Simms himself famously said that the novel was "probably as good an answer to Mrs. Stowe as has been published" (*Letters* 3:223), his answer was more philosophical than direct. To treat it simply as a reply to *Uncle Tom's Cabin* is to miss many even more important dimensions and to greatly impoverish the novel.

Porgy's "woodcraft" in the novel has not led to perfection, but he is a tolerant and much wiser man by novel's end. Furthermore, the circumstances of the novel and the plot prove Porgy to be correct in his major assumptions and surmises. His woodcraft has led him a long way; and learning to be less self-indulgent has opened up the larger possibilities of life. He has not gone in circles in the dark like the embittered, demonic Bostwick.

Porgy, the cook for his band of soldiers, now becomes the food provider in peace for those on the plantation who look to him for protection and sustenance. The novel's complex patterns of food imagery thus provide depth of meaning and thematic unity. That Porgy's name derives from a fish — perhaps a sacrificial one suggesting the abiding early Christian symbol IXθΫΣ, the Ichthus, the Greek word for fish that became the acrostic for Christ, with connotations here of the Christ-fish that fed the multitudes — becomes all the more relevant. Porgy *is* his plantation. His imposing round body is imaged as both host and rice barrel from which his rice plantation community draws its life. The feeding, feasting, and food imagery takes on great importance in delineating both Porgy's character and the novel's themes. So does the imagery of dressing, clothing, and *sans culottism* (324).

As in the ancient Celtic Arthurian legend and Fisher King myth, Porgy's kingdom can be only as healthy as he is. That is another reason that it is crucial that he lift himself out of hedonism, self-pity, and despair--and act manfully. Many are depending upon him. The very existence of the complex little plantation kingdom is at stake. Porgy finally accepts responsibility, imagines himself as the head of a body, with many hands to direct, and understands that this head must be kept soundly functioning. His body servant Tom is a key in that soundness. In a sense, he is the cook who feeds the cook (mentally, spiritually, physically), who feeds the plantation. Both *Woodcraft* and *The Cassique of Kiawah* (1859) show that it is through the noble sacrifice of the rare individual that civilization is able to survive at all—even if only by the skin of its teeth.

At the novel's end, the reader is left wondering what will happen to Porgy's plantation community. It seems to be enduring the fortunes of war. Dory may marry Arthur and the plantation world return to harmony. Or maybe Porgy's bachelor world will doom the plantation to a dead end. We should not forget, however, that *The Sword and the Distaff* was preceded in the *Southern Literary Gazette* by *The Golden Christmas* the year before—another comedy of manners set in a Lowcountry plantation community. The setting is 1850, and the fact that the agrarian society is still intact and functioning strongly suggests that *Woodcraft*'s chaotic world will finally be survived one way or another through accommodation. In 1850, the plantation community has its own new struggle, with the outcome once again determining whether that community will continue into the future. This time it is the prejudice and pig-headedness of family that might be the end of the plantation. *The Sword and the Distaff*, following on its heals as flash-back to an even more crucial time, might tip the scales into an over-riding optimism premised by the wisdom that the community has been there before and survived. And, after all, survival is triumph enough— indeed is a southern specialty. It is one of Simms's key themes throughout his works. The home and hearth abide. As David Moltke-Hansen makes clear, Simms's 1850 review of Mrs. Ellet's *Women of the Revolution*, declares that it "is from the home that 'spring all the virtues and securities of the nation,' even in the midst of wars and political turmoil" (12).

But for *Woodcraft*, Porgy's way into the light of responsible action has been the path through the dark tangled wood of the returning veteran, physically and psychologically burned out. At first depressed and at brief moments even suicidal, repairing his ruined plantation lands had seemed too much. Such a treatment thus fully qualifies *Woodcraft* as a "soldier's pay" novel ahead of Stephen Crane, Faulkner, and Hemingway. Porgy's complex psychology is only one of several superb, complex characterizations in the work. The others are Bostwick, the Widow Eveleigh, Dory, and Arthur Eveleigh, all very complex and memorable figures.

Porgy stands opposite to Millhouse, Tom to Porgy, Porgy to Bostwick, Millhouse to Dennison and Oakenburg, M'Kewn to Bostwick, Tom to Millhouse, Lance Frampton to Millhouse, Frampton to Porgy, the Widow Griffin to the Widow Eveleigh, but the most important central contrast is of Porgy, surrogate father to Dory, and the Widow Eveleigh and her son Arthur. This double pairing may achieve its resolution at novel's end in classic romance fashion, with the strong likelihood that Dory will marry Arthur and the couple will eventually take possession of both Porgy's and the neighboring Eveleigh lands. All this is left to conjecture however. *Woodcraft* is too sophisticated a book for a pat conclusion. The world it portrays is not assuring a happy ending. What is clear, however, is that, in the end, Dory's and Porgy's treasure of trust and faith are proved true and life-affirming, while M'Kewn's and Bostwick's lust for gold proves false and death-dealing, miring them in their own personal hells in a culture of death. Appropriately, the novel's image patterns associate Dory with the light and Bostwick and M'Kewn with the dark. Dory herself is the gold of genuine treasure. Perhaps her name is a play on the Spanish *D'Or*. The title of Chapter 34, in fact, gets specific by calling her Bostwick's real "Treasure."

It is clear that bachelor Porgy has become Bostwick's replacement in his fatherly protection of Dory. He sees her worth and the "miracle" she is—this flower blossoming in a mud puddle. Although separated by class, she shares much in common with Porgy. They appreciate the non-utilitarian but, more importantly, are both striving for redemption. That search thus becomes a central theme of the novel, one that has universal implications. To treat *Woodcraft* as a social thesis, a probing of history, a critique of the antebellum planter, a close depiction of landscape, a definition of community, a defense of slavery, or a weighing in on various topical issues, while helpful in understanding the great expansive world of the novel, is only to see one or another facet of this work, whose depths are still to be properly plumbed. What elevates the work to greatness is its verisimilitude of complex, engaging character, its believable settings, effective poetic use of imagery and image patterns, and above all its universal themes of redemption and transcendence.

Woodcraft, as Wimsatt shows, is congenial social comedy of manners. Its comic surface has its charms, but the surface belies the true nature beneath, which is anything but humorous and placid. In fact, it is this contrast that often provides the dramatic tension—say, for example, in Simms's attitude toward nature, which can be both a peaceful sanctuary (as for Marion's men), or a place where danger lurks in the form of "varmints," both animal and human—hence, Simms's very complex view of life as a thing of illusions, masks, violent contradictions, and strongest paradoxes. Life can bear its rose among the thorns, but it is more often the twisting path through the dark woods, demanding "woodcraft" at every turn. A man's woodcraft in this light most often involves coming to terms with the world by regarding even its harsher aspects as having ends (a Providential design) that one does not and can never fully comprehend.

Simms uses his tangible, carefully limned, accurate local physical settings to explore the nature of mankind and his world in general and through the ages. From his broad reading and well-developed historical consciousness, Simms learned early that despite shifting social forms and fashions, man's nature is always constant in revealing the same vices, in all times and places. He found these in the society he knew, but just as certainly fully recognized that they were not original with or limited to that society. Simms saw the hypocrisies and weaknesses in his local scene were the same that all flesh is heir to. He was capable of diving below the surface and thus reaches the great universal depths and profundities. He was always fond of saying that in poetry, as in fiction, a writer should find out the depths of feeling within oneself, and then he would know and be able to portray the same in human nature.

In portraying these depths of universal human nature, he presents us with the man God intended, and his opposite, the retort-made, self-made, monomaniacal modern man. The latter loses the whole man as a result of his selfish will to greed, hedonism, and the narrowly utilitarian, thus robbing life of meaning, beauty, and interest, and reducing living to the mechanical routine of going through the dull motions. Man preempts God's place; and the accompanying loss of values reduces him to "the creature he was not made." In this way, man is diminished to the animal, and reality is shrunk to scientific empiricism in a greatly impoverished universe. Such is the trap of determinism and empiricism. In its modernist image patterns of retort-made, obsessive, narcissistic men going in circles in the dark and getting nowhere, placed in the healthy context of whole self-sacrificing men held within a Providential design, the novel is a bridge from Old America to the New.

Yet another of the novel's strengths is that, despite its length and unlike so many works of its day, the novel has little that is superfluous or extraneous. A case in point is a minor character, Geordie Dennison, who is, after proper consideration, not minor at all. Dennison is the resident poet, and Millhouse rants and raves that he is not providing food or wealth to keep the plantation going.

Porgy understands his value, however, and counters that the world must have its "singing birds" as well as poultry. Furthermore, James Cantrell accurately reinforces Davidson's view of Simms as saga-man by discussing his creation of Dennison as the Irish-descended bard with the mission of that central figure's keeping and furthering of the people's story and cultural identity. Davidson writes: "The real strength of Simms is his unselfconscious nearness to what might be called...folk tradition, which is pre-literary or pre-bookish....The best fiction of Simms is not a long step away from saga and folk tale" (*Letters* 1:lii). Cantrell writes: "Throughout the Revolutionary War series, Dennison is shown to be the folk poet, the natural bard of both the war and South Carolina and its culture" (90). Simms understood well the mission of the bard, and *Woodcraft*, his humorous mock epic in prose, shows clearly that he deserves Davidson's appellation and accolade. There is a further dimension to consider as well. *Woodcraft* draws heavily on legend, reminiscence, and folk culture. Simms was committed to capturing in print the oral lore that Cleanth Brooks claimed characterized the traditional South as primarily an oral folk culture (332–8). By the mid-nineteenth century, many Europeans were similarly exploring their traditions, myths, and memories with great literary consciousness. The Southern writer, as Brooks shows with his comparison of Faulkner to Yeats, was not alone in this. Davidson again hits the mark even more precisely: "As a writer of fiction, Simms belongs to another age—a heroic age....He became what might be called the 'saga-man' of that age."

The other member of the minor pair of impractical ones for whom Porgy serves as patron is the eccentric Dr. Oakenburg. He cannot be figured out or classified, and that keeps Porgy constantly aware that people cannot be reduced or oversimplified to figure, statistic, or idea. Empirical science is good at recording and quantifying, but not explaining. The thorough-going materialist could never understand Porgy's honoring the riddle and celebrating the mystery. Oakenburg, minor character that he is, is thus, like Dennison, not so minor after all. The abundance of small side-bar touches like these coalesce to contribute to the novel's major strengths to make *Woodcraft* the masterpiece critics have found it.

The novel's reception was favorable from the start. It was not widely reviewed however. Only ten reviews and notices appeared from 1852 to 1854 (Butterworth and Kibler 84–98). Simms blamed his publisher for not disseminating the volume. Many notices were short and non-specific, placing into question whether the reviewer read the volume. The more specific reviews rightly praised Simms's verisimilitude, humor, authentic use of locale, and "actual scenes and circumstances" (*Courier* 21 October 1852; Butterworth and Kibler 86). Attesting to the work's continued popularity, however, *Woodcraft* was reprinted many times by a number of northern publishers in the late nine-teenth century. Several paperback editions have been available for the last half century. The 1854 Redfield Edition is still the standard text, but imperfect owing to copious house-styling.

Woodcraft has continued to elicit favorable response along a spectrum of critical interests, illustrated by the bibliography which follows. As for its influ-ence on later writers, perhaps the most significant early one is from pages 222–223. The passage concerns Dory's reading to her father. George Hayhoe finds a close similarity to Chapter 5 of *Adventures of Huckleberry Finn* (1885), where Huck reads to his father. He notes that "Huck's father and Bostwick are essen-tially the same type of character—poor whites who drink too much, abandon their families and are criminally involved" (Hayhoe 539–40). Charles Frazier's reference to Simms in *Cold Mountain* is the latest. Odds are that *Woodcraft* will continue to find an appreciative audience, as well it should. As Kibler declared in 1990, "It is destined for proper appreciation because it effectively addresses universals" ("Major Fiction" 94–5).

Works Cited

Bakker, Jan. "Simms on the Literary Frontier; or, So Long Miss Ravenel and Hello Cap-tain Porgy: Woodcraft Is the First 'Realistic' Novel in America." *William Gilmore Simms and the American Frontier*. Ed. John C. Guilds and Caroline Collins. Athens: U of Geor-gia P, 1997: 64–78.

——. "Simms and the American Apocalypse: Woodcraft and The Cassique of Kiawah." *Studies in the Novel* 35 (Summer 2003): 149–56.

Beatty, Richmond Croom. Introduction. *Woodcraft*. By William Gilmore Simms. New York: Norton, 1961. vii–xvi.

Brooks, Cleanth. William Faulkner: *Toward Yoknapatawpha and Beyond*. New Haven: Yale UP, 1978.

Butterworth, Keen, and James E. Kibler, Jr. *William Gilmore Simms: A Reference Guide*. Boston: G. K. Hall, 1980.

Cantrell, James P. *How Celtic Culture Invented Southern Literature*. Gretna, LA: Pelican, 2006.

Cecil, L. Moffitt. "Simms's Porgy as National Hero." *American Literature* 364 (Jan. 1965): 475–84.

Cook, George Allan. "The Beginnings of Porgy." *The South Central Bulletin* 27.4 (Winter 1967): 51–57.

Dale, Corinne. "William Gilmore Simms's Porgy as Domestic Hero." *Southern Literary Journal* 13 (Winter 1980): 55–71.

Davidson, Donald. Introduction. *The Letters of William Gilmore Simms*. Ed. Mary C. Simms Oliphant, Alfred Taylor Odell, and T. C. Duncan Eaves. 6 vols. Columbia: U of South Carolina P, 1952–1982.

Dean, Paula. "Revisions in the Revolutionary War Novels of William Gilmore Simms." Ph. D. Dissertation. Auburn Univ, 1971.

Dye, Renee. "Narrating Social Theory: William Gilmore Simms's Woodcraft" *Simms Review* 4.1 (1996): 23-43.

Frazier, Charles. *Cold Mountain*. New York: Grove, 1997.

Guilds, John Caldwell. *"Long Years of Neglect": The Works and Reputation of William Gilmore Simms*. Fayetteville & London: U of Arkansas P, 1988.

——. *Simms: A Literary Life*. Fayetteville: U of Arkansas P, 1992.

Hogue, L. Lynn. "The Presentation of Post-Revolutionary Law in Woodcraft: Another Perspective on the 'Truth' of Simms." *Mississippi Quarterly* 31 (1978): 201–210.

Hayhoe, George F. Explanatory Notes. *Revolutionary War Novels. 8. Woodcraft*. By William Gilmore Simms. Spartanburg, SC: Reprint Co., 1976.

Holman, C. Hugh. "William Gilmore Simms' Picture of the Revolution as a Civil Conflict." *Journal of Southern History* 15 (Nov. 1949): 441–62.

Kibler, James Everett. "On the Pairing of The Golden Christmas and Woodcraft." *Simms Review* 2 (Spring 1994): 13–6.

——. "The Major Fiction of William Gilmore Simms." *Mississippi Quarterly* 43 (Winter/Spring 1989-90): 85–95.

——. "Simms as Naturalist: Lowcountry Landscape in His Revolutionary Novels." *Mississippi Quarterly* 31 (1978): 499–518.

——. "William Gilmore Simms." *Encyclopedia of American Literature,* Ed. Steven R. Serafin New York: Continuum, 1999. 1039–43.

Kolodny, Annette. "The Unchanging Landscape: The Pastoral Impulse in Simms's Revolutionary War Romances." *Southern Literary Journal* 5:1 (1972), 47–67.

Moltke-Hansen, David. "Southern Literary Horizons in Young America." *Studies in the Literary Imagination* 42:1 (Spring 2009): 1–32.

Okker, Patricia. "Serial Politics in William Gilmore Simms's Woodcraft." *Periodical Literature in Nineteenth-Century America*. Ed. Kenneth M. Price. Charlottesville: UP of Virginia, 1995, 150–65.

Ridgely, Joseph V. "Woodcraft: Simms's First Answer to Uncle Tom's Cabin." *American Literature* 31.4 (Jan. 1960): 421–33.

Simms, William Gilmore. *The Letters of William Gilmore Simms*. Ed. Mary C. Simms Oliphant, Alfred Taylor Odell, and T. C. Duncan Eaves. 6 vols. Columbia: U of South Carolina P, 1952-1982.

——. *Poetry and the Practical*. Ed. James Everett Kibler. Fayetteville: U of Arkansas P, 1996.

Taylor, William. *Cavalier and Yankee: The Old South and American National Character*. New York: George Braziller, 1961.

Watson, Charles S. "Simms's Answer to Uncle Tom's Cabin: Criticism of the South in Woodcraft." *Southern Literary Journal* 9.1 (Fall 1976): 78+. Academic OneFile. Web. 18 May 2011.

——. Introduction. *Woodcraft*. By William Gilmore Simms. New Haven: New College and UP, 1983. 9-27.

Wimsatt, Mary Ann. *The Major Fiction of William Gilmore Simms: Cultural Traditions and Literary Form*. Baton Rouge: Louisiana State UP, 1989.

Woodcraft

WOODCRAFT

OR

HAWKS ABOUT THE DOVECOTE

A Story of the South at the Close of the Revolution

BY W. GILMORE SIMMS, Esq.

AUTHOR OF "THE PARTISAN," "MELLICHAMPE," "KATHARINE WALTON,"
"THE SCOUT," "THE YEMASSEE," "GUY RIVERS," ETC.

NEW AND REVISED EDITION

REDFIELD
110 AND 112 NASSAU STREET, NEW YORK.
1854.

STEREOTYPED BY C. C. SAVAGE,
13 Chambers Street, N. Y.

MY DEAR DR.—

I THINK it very likely that you have encountered, in your early days some of the persons of this domestic novel. They are all drawn from the life, and are sufficiently salient, I trust, to be remembered. The humorists of " Glen Eberley" were well-known personages of preceding generations, here thinly disguised under false names and fanciful localities, which, I am inclined to think will prove no disguise to you, I shall keep my secret, however, as a matter of course; but you are under no obligations to do so, and will please remember what you can and relate what you please. You have so long wandered in the interesting periods of the Revolution, and among the generations which immediately followed that event, that I am persuaded to believe that you will find pleasure even in the perusal of a record so imperfect as my own. I owe so much to your kind communications, and to your own researches in this direction, that I derive great satisfaction from the hope that you will find pleasure in perusing my story, and that it may stimulate your memory into recalling many things which it may be agreeable to you to resuscitate.

With great respect and regard, I am, dear sir, faithfully, your friend,

THE AUTHOR.

WOODCRAFT.

CHAPTER I.

A BRAVE WIDOW.

THE provisional articles of peace, between the King of Great Britain, and the revolted colonies of America, were signed at Paris, on the 13th November, 1782. The British forces in Charleston, South Carolina, prepared to abandon that city early in the following December. The event took place on the 14th of that month. Prior to this period, the enemy had been confined to the immediate precincts of the garrison. The gradually contracting arms of the Americans had established a cordon about them, which they had found it impossible to break; and the rival armies, the one unable to take the field, and the other too feeble to force the garrison, lay watching each other, like a couple of grim tigers, who have learned, by frequent combats, to regard their opponents with respect, if not affection. Both were exhausted. Exhaustion, not wisdom, or a better state of feeling, was the secret of the peace which was finally concluded between the two nations, and of which, South Carolina, and Charleston in particular, was eagerly expecting the benefits. For more than two years this region was in full, or in partial keeping, of the enemy. The days had been counted by skirmishes and battles, by fears, hates, anxieties, persecution, and blood. The time for repose was at hand. Peace was agreed upon; the British army was about to evacuate the city; the Americans were crowding about their outposts, eager to come in. Meanwhile commissioners from both were in the city, preparing for a peaceable restoration of prisoners, chattels, and soil. There was much to be re-delivered, which irked the stomach of the British captor, and his allies among the loyalists. The latter had many fears of meeting with their ancient brethren.—Both the British and themselves had much plunder which it was becoming difficult to make away with. The American commissioners were particularly solicitous in respect to this matter. South Carolina had already lost twenty-five thousand slaves, which British philanthropy had transferred from the rice-fields of Carolina, to the sugar estates of the West India Islands; and there were yet other thousands waiting to be similarly transported. But how to conceal them from the lynx eyes of the commissioners, who were studiously attentive to the mode of fitting up the transport-ships, and their accommodations provided for passengers; and especially heedful that they were not too much crowded with the black, for the comfort of the white inhabitants. Such vigilance was the subject of much soreness on the part of those who exercised their charities for the African race, without desiring to give their labors any unnecessary publicity. The anxieties of the one party, and the vigilance of the other, were duly increased as the moment drew nigh for the exodus of the British.

It was but three days from this event, when Colonel Moncrieff, of the latter—whose philanthropy on behalf of the blacks had been exercised on a most extensive scale—was surprised by an unexpected visitor. We may add, an unwelcome one. He was sitting in his office, books and paper around him, swords upon the wall, pistols among papers upon the table, and with but one companion. This was a person of rusty complexion, sharp visage, small bulbous-shaped nose, a low, broad forehead, and sinister expression of mouth and eyes. The latter were of a light grey, keen rather than bright, and significant of cunning rather than character.

These two persons appeared to be busy in long details, figured out on several sheets of paper, and a confused array of arithmetical propositions. But there seemed no difficulty between them; the business, which equally interested both, seemed mutually satisfactory. Over some of the details they chuckled pleasantly. They were thus employed, when the door was suddenly thrown open, and a white servant, partly in military habit, appeared at the entrance.

"Well, Waldron," said Moncrieff, scarcely looking up, "what now?"

"A lady, sir."

"A lady? Who, pray? What's her name?

"Didn't tell me, sir—is here—the lady says she must see you."

"Well, if a lady says she *must* see me, the necessity is hardly to be escaped, I suppose. Show her in."

The servant stepped back, and the lady entered—a fair and comely dame, scarcely forty, with a fresh, healthy expression, a bright, cherry blue eye, a sweet, intelligent mouth, as indicative of character as of beauty, and a frank, buoyant expression of countenance. Her figure was tall, yet somewhat inclined to *embonpoint*, though her carriage was equally dignified and graceful.—The gentlemen rose promptly at her entrance. Moncrieff advanced politely and handed her a chair, which she took with a quiet ease and promptness that showed her to be accustomed to society.

Moncrieff was evidently and immediately impressed by her presence. It was quite apparent, however, that she was entirely unknown to him. Not so with his companion, whose visage put on a look of blank dissatisfaction at the moment of her entrance, which at once dispersed the smiles that had mantled it only a moment before. But neither of the other persons in the room seemed to notice *his* disquiet. He drew apart, and went toward one of the windows, but kept his eye upon the two, with an oblique glance eminently his own; and his ears were keenly alive to what was spoken.

"May I have the honor, madam, of serving you?" was the question of Moncrieff, with all the courtesy proper to an officer in his Britannic majesty's service. The answer was prompt. In a clear, frank, musical voice, the lady said—

"I bring you, sir, a billet from his excellency, General Leslie, which will fully explain my business. My name is Eveleigh, the widow of the late Major Eveleigh, who once held the office in your army that you now hold."

"I remember, madam; I had not the pleasure of knowing

Major Eveleigh personally, but his rank and character are fully known to me."

"Here, sir, is General Leslie's letter."

She took it from her bag, and handed it as she spoke. The brow of Colonel Moncrieff clouded as he read.

"You will perceive sir," said the lady, "that his excellency, General Leslie, requests you to see that certain negroes be restored to me, my property, which are now within the garrison— their names are in this paper, and a description of them individually, by which they may each be identified."

Moncrieff read the second paper with increasing gravity of aspect. His male companion crossed the floor to him, and looked over the paper as he read. The widow Eveleigh observed the movement—and the man—with some interest. After a few moments, Moncrieff, with something of annoyance in his tone, remarked—

"Why, madam, it is very doubtful if there be any such slaves within the garrison. You are aware that we have been delivering them up, as fast as they can be found, to the American commissioners. They may be concealed—"

"They *are* concealed," answered the lady.

"If that be the case, Mrs. Eveleigh," answered the other, with a soothing smile, "we must try and find them for you. We shall institute a thorough search, and should they be found, they shall be delivered to the commissioners."

"I thank you, sir; but something of this trouble may be spared you; and I should prefer—as the ownership of the property is unquestionably in me, as I have satisfied General Leslie —that they be delivered to myself."

"That, too, my dear madam, I cheerfully promise, should we find them."

"It is the trouble of this search, sir, that I would spare you. I have already found them."

"The devil you have, madam?" cried Moncrieff, starting to his feet, and evidently disquieted—"and where, pray?"

"In the old hulk, sir, at Market dock, in company with some two hundred others, upon whom I have no claim, but who, I have no doubt, will find claimants fast enough if they be once exposed on the wharf to the examination of the American commissioners."

"'Pon my soul, madam, for a whig-American, you calculate largely upon the generosity of his majesty's government."

"Very far from it, Colonel Moncrieff. I calculate nothing at all upon the generosity of his majesty's government. My calculations are all based upon what seems the necessity of the case, and the policy, which his majesty's officers seem generally to recognise, of performing the condition of the treaty in good faith. You speak of me, sir, as an American and a whig.—I am not ashamed to say that I am both; but remembering that my late husband was a good loyalist, and a faithful and trusted officer in his majesty's service, I have forborne, with a due regard to his memory, from taking any active part in this contest. On this subject, however, General Leslie has been long quite satisfied. I feel proud that I may number him among my friends. You have read his letter—it appears to me that nothing more is necessary to be said."

"Well, madam, allowing all this, it appears to me that what is expected of us, is the delivery, to the rebel commissioners, of all the negroes claimed as fugitives—"

"Let me interrupt you, Colonel Moncrieff. The commissioners are employed only to represent the *absent*. I am here *present*. I can identify my negroes—I have done so—and now I demand of you their redelivery."

"But, why of me, madam?"

"For the best of reasons, sir. They are entered in the hulk-book in your name."

"The devil they are, madam!"

"I forgive your irreverence, Colonel Moncrieff, to myself; but regret that your tone should be so disrespectful to his Satanic majesty."

Moncrieff could not forbear a laugh.

"Begad, madam, you have me! By what names do you distinguish these negro subjects of yours?"

"Here is the list;—they have been identified by my overseer as well as myself."

"But, madam, I am somewhat curious—pray how did you—yet, no matter! You say, Mrs. Eveleigh, that you have, yourself, seen these negroes at the hulk?"

"I have, sir, and spoken with them."

"Then there can be no doubt! But—" Here he paused, looked hurriedly over a pile of memoranda before him, bit the tip of his goose quill, and seemed, for a few moments, to meditate; then turning to his former companion, he said—

"M'Kewn, I must confer with you. Will Mrs. Eveleigh excuse me for a few moments?"

The lady bowed her head, and the two gentlemen left the apartment. The brave widow was left alone.

CHAPTER II.

THE WIDOW MAKES SOME DISCOVERIES.

"M'Kewn!" said the lady in an under tone. She appeared to muse for awhile. Then, looking up, her eyes seemed to become interested in the furniture of the apartment, which, as it was that of a military bachelor, was somewhat curious and contradictory in its character. The floor of the room was cumbered with chests, trunks and boxes. The walls were hung with pistols and sabres. Interspersed among these, were sundry articles of unmentionable clothing, to say nothing of military, parade, service and undress coats;—Moncrieff was something of a carpet-knight.—Great boots lay sprawling beneath the table. An elegant *chapeau bras* rested upon it; and, in near neighborhood, protruding from beneath a pile of papers, was a pair of pistols of extraordinary beauty and finish.

The widow possessed some rather curious tastes for a lady. She rose, took up the pistols, and examined them without any of that shuddering feeling which most ladies would exhibit at the contemplation of such implements. They might well attract the attention of a person not an amateur. The weapons of that day were of much more curious and costly workmanship than ours. There was an antique richness in the ornaments of the pistols which was calculated to gratify the eye. The stocks were quaintly inlaid with *fleurs de lis* and vines, done in filagree of variegated gold. The butts were capped with gold, in the centre of which was an elaborately-wrought eye, with a small amethyst forming the pupil. The barrels were plain, but exquisitely polished. They were of rifle-bore—the duelling pistol in fact—a weapon more in use then than now, and in the workmanship of which much more care and ornament were expended.

The inspection of these beautiful tools of murder seemed to afford considerable interest to our widow. She finally laid them down in their places. As she did so, her eye was arrested by a paper which lay open beside the weapons. Her own name caught her glance. She uttered a slight ejaculation of surprise, and caught up the paper, which was one of those enormous sheets of dingy foolscap which were in common use at that period. Her interest increased as she examined the writing, and she felt justified in reading it. It afforded her some curious intelligence in regard to the very business in which she was engaged; containing, in fact, a long catalogue of names, evidently those of slaves—Sam, Tom, Peter, Dick, Pomp, Cudjoe, Dembo, Cush, Binah, Bess, Bathsheba, and a hundred more—and all parcelled off in sections, embraced in brackets, opposite to each of which were the names, also, of their respective owners. To some, the names of places, or estates, were appended. There she beheld her own name in connection with the slaves she claimed. There was something further. A memorandum, against each column, contained a reference to the source from which they had been obtained. She read the name of " M'Kewn" as that of the person who had put her negroes in possession of Moncrieff. There was Moncrieff's acknowledgment and signature. There were M'Kewn's memoranda with his own handwriting, as she supposed, and rightly; and other matters, all in detail, which she saw, in a moment, comprised a large body of conclusive testimony that might be very useful.

This, then, was the document which the British colonel and his companion had been studying when she came in. She laid the paper down in its place. But her lips became rigid with resolution. She hastily seized the paper and folded it.

"I am dealing," she said to herself, "with enemies. This document may become necessary yet to secure my property.

The villains! Shall I scruple when I am in such hands? Shall I suffer them to defraud my son of his rights, when it is in my power to prevent them? Away with such childish scruples. It is war between us, perhaps, and I owe them no courtesies, no forbearance."

She put the paper into her pocket.

"M'Kewn! M'Kewn!" she muttered. "Where have I heard that name before?

She heard footsteps approaching from without, and hastily resumed her seat and her composure. Her face on the instant became one of singular calm and simplicity. She was a woman evidently of equal good sense and nerve, and seemed totally unconcerned and unemployed, as the outer door was thrown open. The orderly, Waldron, again made his appearance, followed by another person. He looked about the room for his superior.

"He is not here—the colonel?" he remarked inquiringly.

"He is within," answered the widow, pointing to the chamber to which Moncrief and M'Kewn had retired. As she spoke, she observed that the person who followed Waldron, started, and seemed disposed to retire. Her eye quickened with intelligence, but she ceased to look at the new party. A single glance had sufficed. Waldron advanced, calling to his companion to follow.

"Come this way," said the orderly. The person addressed, hesitated for a moment, then, rapidly moving to the side of Waldron, put him between himself and the widow. They crossed the room together, and, without reserve, entered the inner apartment, the door of which they closed behind them. Mrs. Eveleigh followed them with a careless but intelligent glance. When they had passed from sight, she muttered—

"I see it now! Bostwick has been the creature of M'Kewn in this business, as M'Kewn is the creature of Moncrieff. The ungrateful wretch; and I have fed his family for years; his wife and child—when they were sick and starving. Oh! what a frightful, fiendish thing is poverty, when it is linked with ingratitude!"

The widow had discovered, in the new-comer, the squatter on a plantation which adjoined her own. The single glance which she had given him, had sufficed to identify him ; and she was too circumspect to allow him to perceive that she had made the discovery. She was satisfied to look no further. His slight form, sidelong gait, low, swarthy features, and long black hair, which hung down heavily upon his cheeks and shoulders, were not to be mistaken. She smiled sadly as she mused upon the ingratitude, which had been fed at her hands without thanks, and which had robbed her of her property without remorse. Let us leave her for a while, and become parties in the conference between Moncrieff and M'Kewn.

CHAPTER III.

ROGUES IN CONFERENCE.

" This is a d——d awkward business, M'Kewn !"

" What's to be done ?" said the person addressed, in rather sullen accents.

" Ay, what ? That's the question," answered Moncrieff; " I see no way to escape it, my good fellow. It robs us of some of our profits."

" But will you give up the negroes ?"

" Eh ! to be sure ! What else ? Show me how it may be managed, saving me scot-free with old Leslie, who, though three parts old woman, is yet a Tartar when you cross him—and I'm for any remedy. But it seems to me impossible."

" Can't *we* get off the negroes while you keep her in play ?"

" Scarcely ! She has identified them, and found them entered in my name. How the devil she has done this, I can't see. What could that Hessian, Dort, have been about."

" He was drunk, I reckon ! He was the last man to have been trusted with them. I feared it. But, it strikes me that we might run the negroes without committing you."

" How so ? Remember, my honor as a British officer—"

" May be kept safely, if we can prove that they broke out of keeping and took boat up the river."

"Indeed! Half a dozen negroes break away from a score of Hessian guards—"

"All being drunk."

"Unchain themselves—secure a boat, and make their way up the river through a fleet of three hundred vessels of all sizes! No! no! M'Kewn! That won't do! Old Leslie is too shrewd a soldier to listen to such a story. My answer would be an arrest and a court of inquiry. You must think of something better."

M'Kewn remained sulkily silent.

"You are gravelled!" said the other. "So am I! I do not see but that we shall have to make a merit of necessity, and the sooner we do so, the better. If we delay about it, we shall have a host of other claimants; and the danger will be, not only that they will prove three hundred slaves in our keeping, but that something will come out showing how they came into our keeping. You, for example, might be required to explain some queer histories. My notion is, that we must yield handsomely to the handsome widow—a devilish fine looking woman, by the way, with a head of her own!—and, by promptness in her case, avoid the danger of other visiters. We must discharge her chattels, and transfer the rest to the 'Tartar' before day, to-morrow. By the way, does this woman know you?"

"I think not. Her husband did. I have seen her repeatedly, and have been on her plantation. In fact, I am somewhat interested in an estate in her neighborhood. But this need not concern us now. It is a matter of some concern with me, as I am to remain in the country, that she should not know me in connection with this affair. I shall avoid showing myself when you return to her."

"You see no means, then, of evading the surrender?"

"None, but that already hinted."

"That is out of the question," said Moncrieff, rising. "I will take the physic without wry faces. But, as soon as she goes, do you see to the transfer to the 'Tartar.'"

"It will be well, too," added M'Kewn, "if you put them under some better keeper than that drunken Hessian."

"It shall be done. Well! How now, Waldron?"

At this moment, Waldron entered the room, followed by Bostwick, the squatter. At his entrance, M‘Kewn looked disquieted, Waldron was immediately dismissed.

" You here ?" said M‘Kewn to Bostwick. " Did you see the lady ?"

" The widow — Eveleigh ? — Yes !"

" Did she see you ?"

" Don't think ! Jest as I caught the shine of her eyes, I dodged ahind the sargeant. Don't think she made me out at all. Didn't look as ef she did."

" Do you know what she comes about ?" demanded Moncrieff.

" Reckon I does, colonel. She's been to the ‘hulk’ and seed the niggers herself."

" Remain here, both of you, till she is gone. Take care that she sees no more of either of you. If she has made you out, Master Bostwick, your best course will be to get into his majesty's transport, as soon as you can, or she will hang you when the rebels take possession here."

" She hain't seen me yit, I reckon," answered the squatter, though a dubious expression darkened his swarthy visage as he spoke. Moncrieff, meanwhile, proceeded, rather reluctantly, though hurriedly, to give his answer to the widow's requisition. M‘Kewn resumed the subject with Bostwick.

" That woman has eyes to see through a stone wall. Do you think she got a glimpse of you at all ?"

" I seed her first, I reckon."

" You are not sure ?"

" No ! nobody's sure of nothing, no-how, it seems to me, in this world," responded the squatter.

" Well ! Even if she did see you here, it would only prove to the rebels that you were in bad company as well as myself. I have my excuse — my reasons, for being here — which, indeed, would silence suspicion ; and you being seen with Moncrieff and myself would only provoke suspicion, not confirm it. We must be cautious, that's all."

" Well, now, look you, squire, there's no caution without money, and I'm mightily needing the article. I must have some, right away."

" Why, you had five guineas last week, Bostwick."

" I've lived a week since, and fed and drank—"

"Ay, and got drunk upon food and drink. Five guineas ought to last you a month, if you were a sober, prudent person."

"Look you, squire, I'm too bad a fellow to be sober or prudent. I ain't in love with myself, at all, when I'm sober; and, as for being what you call prudent, why, the thing's unreasonable. Ef I'd been a prudent person, would you have seen me here? Would I be doing for you all them dirty little transactions?"

"Pshaw! you're well enough as you are."

"I reckon'd you'd say so. You'll let me have the five guineas, squire?"

"I suppose so—for this time; but the business is nearly done up now, Bostwick. I do not see that we can be of much further use to one another: and all that's to be done, is to close up the old accounts. Don't you suppose that you're pretty well paid up for the past?"

"I don't know what you mean by being paid up. I ain't any better off for all I've done for you and him. You're pretty rich, I reckon. I'm as poor as a wood-rat."

"And whose fault? You've had money. Why didn't you keep it?"

"I've had precious little, anyhow; and I had to live—me and my wife and children. What I've got, always came by driblets, and went as fast as it came."

"You talk of your wife and children, Bostwick, but I'm thinking they got but a small share of your money. You've drunk it up and gambled it away, and to keep you in money, when it goes as fast as it comes, is clearly impossible."

"I must have it, that's sartain, squire," answered the other, doggedly. "I've been working mighty hard, and not at good work neither, for a mighty long time. You've got rich by my labors. You and he" (meaning Moncrieff) "got all the niggers —more than two hundred, I reckon. If I had got for them niggers—all of my bringing—what they *focht*, or will fetch, to you—I'd ha' been as rich as any."

"Yes! perhaps! But without him and me, you could have got nothing for them. He had the ships to carry them off, and the king's stores to pay for them, and but for him you wouldn't have had the price of the hair of a negro for your pains. You must not suppose that what you've done could have been of any use but for us. Still, you have been paid, according to agreement. You've had a good deal of money—"

" In driblets, I say."

" And stores—clothes—"

" Yes, the king's stores; and ef I was to blow *him* to General Leslie, for it, where would he be? And if I was to blow you to the rebels, where would you be?"

" Pshaw! you might blow to all eternity, Bostwick, and would only hang yourself the faster. You sold me negroes, and gave me your titles for them. I have your hand and seal on it, my good fellow—all fair business transactions. Don't be a fool, Bostwick, as well as a knave. Keep your senses as long as you can. You shall have the five guineas as soon as Moncrieff comes back; but the question then will be, how much more you are to have? I suppose we can present you with a good chance of stores which you can sell to the rebels at your own price. They are monstrously in need of clothes."

" I hain't made much by what I've sold yit, and I'm jest as poor a man as ever. That ain't reasonable. Arter all I've done to make a little money, losing my character, and my own right feeling, I ought to have something to show for it."

" Well, as the British are going, there will be pretty leavings, and Moncrieff won't stand upon trifles, in helping a fellow that has been faithful to him. If he leaves you stores, which will bring a hundred guineas, you ought to be satisfied. Don't you think so?"

" Ef I kin do no better," was the somewhat sulky answer.

" Well, I suppose that something of the kind will be done, and that will settle off for the past. I may give you good business hereafter. Moncrieff's coming now, and we'll fix your affairs for you at once."

The approaching footsteps of Moncrieff arrested the conference between the two. He soon after appeared, looking excessively disquieted. Let us leave the three for a few moments, while we return to the Widow Eveleigh.

CHAPTER IV.

THE WIDOW BECOMES TROUBLESOME.

WE left the brave widow in an apparent calm of mind, which she did not altogether feel. She was a person of that temperament which does not affect repose—to which it is rather restraint than rest—and which, having grateful performances before it, regards delay with disgust, and feels the necessity to wait as an evil rather than a virtue. But the good had schooled her moods with considerable success, and, if she felt the feverish impatience which prompts one to be up and doing, she was yet able to subdue its exhibitions when these might come in conflict with duties equally requiring forbearance. She amused herself, as we have seen, in examining the more curious portions of the furniture of the apartment in which she was required to wait. We have noticed her examination of the beautiful duelling pistols of Moncrieff, and the discovery to which this examination led. Her eyes were soon caught by the swords and sabres hung upon the wall. Among these was a Turkish scimitar, with a handle of mother-of-pearl, at the sight of which she slightly started. In a moment she had arisen and taken the weapon from the wall. She drew it fairly from the scabbard, and surveyed the polished and beautiful blade, unstained and unspotted, with a degree of interest which seemed to arise from other causes than its simple beauty. She waved the bright steel upward, with a somewhat gladiatorial air, then held it before her eyes, and it was while she was thus employed, and in this attitude, that Moncrieff suddenly re-entered the apartment. He absolutely recoiled at the spectacle, with an expression of wonder on his countenance, which he did not seek to conceal.

"By Mars, madam, you terrify me! Positively, I must arm myself, and get me a shield. I shall believe in the Amazons after this."

The lady smiled sadly, and restored the weapon slowly and

carefully to its sheath. A tear was in her eye, but it escaped that of Moncrieff She said in low tones, as if apologetically—

"I know this scimitar, Colonel Moncrieff: I have seen it often, with its former owner, at my dwelling. It was Major André's."

"You are right, madam; and I do not wonder at your curiosity. Poor André! What a cruel fate!—and he, with such tastes, such sensibilities, and such ambition!"

"Too much lacking pride, however."

"How, madam, pride?"

"Yes; or he had never suffered himself to be put to such base uses."

"I do not see, Mrs. Eveleigh, that fidelity to one's king, can properly be so stigmatized."

"There is a higher fidelity to one's self, one's honor and individual character. But he paid the terrible penalty, and we must not dwell upon his weaknesses. He had tastes, and sensibilities, as you say;—he loved music and poetry, and could make the song and find for it the fitting harmonies. He has frequently joined me on the harpsichord, and would forget, at our evening fireside, all the habits of the soldier. He was not fitted for such a life, and he felt it. I have listened to his own self-reproaches, for having chosen the profession. He did so in an hour of disappointment—of weakness—and was only not courageous enough to abandon it when he felt his unsuitableness for it."

"But, André was a brave man, Mrs, Eveleigh."

"Yes; in one sense of the word. He had conventional courage, but not intrepidity. He would have shown himself fearless in the sight of armies—he would have fought his man without flinching in the sight of friends; but he had none of that gladiator spirit—that Hunnish blindness—which belongs to the soldier from choice. Had he possessed this quality, he would have disdained the petty employments which finally cost him his life."

"Well, madam, you have given me something to think upon, though I knew André well. We exchanged swords in proof of friendship—though, by the way, mine was the most costly weapon of the two. It was a genuine Damascus, while this, though a very beautiful imitation, is not!"

The widow looked at the speaker with an unalloyed expression of disgust. Her glance did not escape him, and his face was slightly flushed, as he added—

"Though, of course, the difference of value between the weapons was not a subject of consideration. Indeed, if I remember rightly, the first proposal to exchange came from me. It was just when he was about to embark for New York, with Sir Henry."

He paused, and the lady was also silent. She appeared willing to drop the subject. Moncrieff then promptly recurred to the business upon which she came.

"I have made you out the order, Mrs. Eveleigh, for your negroes, if they are, as you say, in the custody of Captain Dort."

"Captain Dort, sir! I know nothing of him, and have named no such person. The negroes are in the 'hulk' at Market Dock, and their keeper I have not seen."

"He is Captain Dort, madam, a Hessian, and the keeper of the 'hulk.' Had he not been drunk, madam, you would possibly have seen him—and possibly not your negroes."

This was spoken with unsuppressed chagrin. He added :—

"Here is the order, madam."

"I thank you, Colonel Moncrieff. And now that my *own* affair is settled, suffer me to draw your attention to that of one of my neighbors, and an old acquaintance. I discovered in the 'hulk,' while looking for my own slaves, seven others, who belong to Captain Porgy, a planter on the Ashepoo. They knew me, and I them, in an instant. They implored me to obtain their restoration to their owner, and I shall be obliged to you for an order to this effect also."

"By the powers, madam, but this is quite too much! One would think that you might be content with having secured your own property."

"Not so, Major Moncrieff! We are taught to love our neighbor as ourself, and such love can be shown in no better way, perhaps, than in giving heed to his interest at the moment when we attend to our own. Indeed, sir, I do not know but that, as a good Christian, I should have thought *first* of his concerns."

"Oh! you are scrupulous, ma'am! But, in truth, this Porgy, is a fierce and pestilent fellow—one of the gang of Marion—who has made himself particularly conspicuous as a malignant. He has certainly no reason to expect favor at our hands."

"Oh! surely not favor! The question is one of right, simply. Either these negroes are Captain Porgy's or not. I can *prove* them to be so."

"But not that he has not sold them?"

"His bill of sale would show that."

"Madam, you should have been a lawyer."

"But a little while ago, your opinion was that I should have been a soldier."

"Egad! madam, it is difficult to say what profession you might not have chosen successfully."

"Thank you sir for the compliment, however equivocal. But you will give me the order, will you not?"

"Oh! to be sure, if there really be such negroes in our possession."

"They are entered in the 'hulk-book' in your name."

"The devil they are! It is strange that people should take my name in vain so eternally. I must see to it. These cursed Hessians, Mrs. Eveleigh, are the greatest rogues and drunkards in the world. I will see to the matter. If the negroes are there, when I make the inquiry, I will send you an order for them. Let me have your address, if you please."

"I am with my friend, Mrs. Merchant, in Church street."

"Mrs. Merchant," writing. "The Merchants are all our friends. And now, Mrs. Eveleigh, as I have already said, if the negroes of Captain Porgy are really in the 'hulk'—"

"You forget, Colonel Moncrieff, that I have just told you that I myself have seen them there."

"Pardon me, madam; I do not forget. But you do not know these Hessians. If they have had the audacity to enter these negroes in my name, they will not scruple at doing worse. They will be very apt to hide them elsewhere, the moment they suspect that they are in danger of detection."

"So much the more important, Colonel Moncrieff, that I should have the order for them promptly, and before they get wind of their danger. But, in fact, there is no chance of their doing as you suppose; for, before I came here apprehending this very danger, I procured the assistance of three vigilant friends, who are now watching every movement at the 'hulk,' and will follow the negroes wherever they go."

"Then, madam," answered the British colonel, with evident chagrin, "I may as well give you the order out of hand."

"I shall thank you, sir."

"I trust, madam, that your requisitions stop here; for, though very happy to oblige the ladies, and to do justice, my interference will make me many enemies among these rascally Hessians."

"Oh! sir, you will survive that danger. But this is the extent of my demands. I have no doubt that there are many other slaves, about to be fraudulently taken from their owners, but I can advance no proof to this effect."

"The names, if you please, madam, of the negroes, whom you claim for this rebel, Porpoise!"

"Porgy, sir," was the correction, with a quiet smile, as the lady beheld the evident chagrin of her companion.

"Well, madam — Porgy — though both names are sufficiently fish, and of the two, the Porpoise is decidedly the most dignified."

"But less fit for the table, sir," answered the widow, as she proceeded to give the names of the negroes. Moncrieff wrote as she spoke. A few moments were thus consumed; then he threw down his pen, looked at the lady, then among his papers, rose at length with a dissatisfied air, and hurried again to the inner room where he had left M'Kewn and Bostwick. In a few seconds he again returned, still with a manner of some disquiet. Again he stirred up, and glanced over the papers upon his table, but without seeming to satisfy his search. Resuming his seat and pen, at length, he finished ths order for the delivery of Porgy's negroes, and rising, handed it with great politeness to the widow, expressing at the same time, in very stately language, the profound delight which he felt in being able to comply with the wishes of a lady whom General Leslie was so well pleased to honor. The widow was not to be outdone in conventional graces. She answered him in terms equally polite and profound; and, with smiles and courtesies, took her departure. He waited upon her to the entrance. When the door had fairly closed behind her, he gave full expression to his chagrin in a burst of wrath and denunciation.

"The d——d cool and confident creature? Hark you, within there, M'Kewn come out!—and you, too, Master Bostwick!—that I may have somebody to curse till I am comfortable. We are handsomely bedevilled, i' faith, and by a woman. But such a woman! In truth, she *is* a woman, and worth half the men I know."

CHAPTER V.

THE OVERSEER, FORDHAM.

THE excellent lady of whom these words were spoken, had, meanwhile quietly taken her place in the carriage which had been awaiting her in the street. The driver was a black, in the livery of Mrs. Merchant, to whom the establishment belonged. Mrs. Eveleigh was not its only occupant. On the back seat, beside her, sat a white man, who had held possession while she remained within the quarters of Moncrieff. Here, he had studiously kept himself from being seen, but had not been the less disposed to maintain a vigilant watch upon all without. He received the widow, on her return, with a manner which was equally attentive and respectful. The appearance of this person was that of one who had not been accustomed to a place so distinguished. He was not abashed, but awkward. He was evidently a backwoodsman, in humble life, wearing the costume of the woodsman of that period, a rather snug-fitting suit of blue homespun, with a sort of hunting-shirt of the same color and material, though without the customary fringes which made it the military garb of the forest rangers, or militia. His face and hands were well embrowned by the sun. The latter were large and rough, and had been well exercised in splitting their two hundred rails per day. The features of his face were large and rough also, but mild, and full of honesty. His great blue eye was expressive of much benevolence, but mixed with a decisive and earnest manliness. The widow addressed him as Mr. Fordham—nay, she called him "Fordham," familiarly, without the prefix, and it did not at all lessen his deference, this freedom. He was, in fact, the overseer of her plantation, and had been the *employée* of her husband. A long experience had perfectly assured them both of his fidelity and worth. That the widow had chosen him as her companion, on the present occasion, was due to the objects she had in view, and to the necessity of the case. He had been the agent who had successfully discovered the place in which her negroes were confined. By his scheming, the Hessian guards at the "hulk" had been drenched with Jamaica, and access had been procured to that prison, and to the books which identified the slaves with their several British appropriators. In this business he was much more efficient than any of the more eminent friends of Mrs. Eveleigh could have been; and the work being an unpleasant one, she had preferred to employ a person whose services she could compensate, rather than those who, however well pleased to serve her, would yet have found the particular duty somewhat disagreeable. But the good lady, though an aristocrat, was not disposed to underrate Mr. Fordham, as a friend, while employing him as her overseer. She really respected the man, and, as he never trespassed upon her indulgence, she felt that she might safely honor him with her friendship, as well as her interests.

"Well, Fordham," she said, as soon as she had taken her seat beside him, "if you have kept your eyes about you, you have, probably, made a discovery."

"Indeed I have, ma'am! You mean the squatter, Bostwick."

"I was not mistaken in the fellow, then! You saw him?"

"Oh, yes, ma'am; there's no mistaking such a fellow! He came up soon after you went in—pushed in without knocking, jest as ef he was at his own home. But, did he see *you*, ma'am?"

"Yes; but I rather think he believes that I did not see him. Are you sure that he did not see *you*?"

"Quite sure, ma'am. He never once looked this way, and seemed a little beflustered and in a mighty great hurry. I reckon he's found out what we've been after. He's at the bottom of this business."

"I have no doubt of it now. Yet, who could have believed it?—that the wretch could be so ungrateful—and his wife and children living, as it were, out of my hands!"

" He's jest one of that very breed, ma'am, that does this sort of things. No good ever comes out of sich a cre'tur' no more than out of a snake. Warm 'em as you please by your own fireside, and feed 'em kindly out of your own hands, and it makes no difference. Once warm, they're sure to bite you. All their vartue, they seems to think, lies only in their venom. What will you do with him, ma'am ?"

" I don't see that anything can be done with him. The proofs against him are, at present, only in our suspicions. Besides, for the sake of the poor, broken-hearted woman, his wife, and his wretched children, I prefer that he should go free."

" Why, yes, ma'am, if one could be sure that he would do no more mischief. But you're not sure of sich a cre'tur' a minute. He's always at something wrong. 'Twould be a monstrous sight better for his wife and children ef he'd clear out with the British. He's as good as one of 'em."

" Perhaps he may."

" A good riddance then for all. But lynching might be of help to him before he goes."

" Nay, I'm not sure of that."

" 'Twould *hurt* him then, and that's, anyhow, as much as we ought to care about. But, one thing, I'll tell you, ma'am. Ef he don't clear out when the British go, he'll be of trouble to us yit. We'll have to keep all eyes open, ef he's to stay in the country."

" I must use your eyes then, Fordham, for this purpose, as I have done for so long a time already. I have every confidence in your vigilance and ability, Fordham.'

" You may rest on me, ma'am."

" Thank you, Fordham. I feel sure of that. I need not tell you, Fordham, that I have the order for the negroes."

" Captain Porgy's too, ma'am ?"

" Yes, both."

" Good! It must have been like physic to the British colonel to have to give 'em up."

" Yes, indeed! But here are the orders, both for Captain Porgy's and mine. You must take the negroes into your own keeping—take them to Moore's house, ' up the path,' and Moore and his two sons will take turns with you, for a few days, in watching them. We will keep within the garrison till the British troops leave, and our own people march in, and shall then escape any danger from detachments about the country. In a week or ten days we may safely depart. I will leave town with you. Here we are, at Mrs. Merchant's. You will take the carriage, and go at once to the 'hulk.' My friends there, Miles, Johnson, and Sturgis, will help you to procure the negroes, and here is General Leslie's order for keeping them in your possession undisturbed. I will get the protection of our commissioners also, who will be in town to-morrow. Now, Fordham, I leave all in your hands. Good-morning."

CHAPTER VI.

THE OLD ROGUES MAKE NEW PLOTS.

"MAY the foul fiend deliver us from such a woman!" was the exclamation of Moncrieff, as his two confederates entered the apartment; and he swore terribly as "our army did in Flanders."

"Why, what's the matter? anything more—anything worse?" demanded M'Kewn.

"Ay, indeed!" answered Moncrieff, busily looking among his papers—and he told of the further requisition which the widow had made for the negroes of Porgy.

"But you did not give them up?"

"How the devil, could I help it?" was the fierce response of the British colonel. M'Kewn was almost as furious.

"I'd have seen her d——d first!" cried the other.

"Oh! you would, would you? but she would have had the negroes, though you d——d her into the deepest part of your own future dominions."

And he then told of the precaution taken by the wily widow —how she had placed her friends in watch upon the "hulk," leaving them no opportunity for evasion. For the time, they were in her power.

"I would have baffled her if the thing could have been done;

but I saw no way of escape. She has the order, and it will not be long before the negroes are in her keeping."

Moncrieff and M'Kewn were equally savage. Bostwick, who had nothing to lose, and could not be made to disgorge, was comparatively cool and indifferent. The anger of the two former having subsided a little, they began to congratulate themselves that the matter was no worse—that they had got off, in fact, so easily. The requisition might as readily have relieved them of two hundred as of twenty negroes. The question with them was, in what way to save the residue. The widow had only to report what she knew, to the commissioners of the American army, to wrest from them all of their ill-gotten fugitives. Fortunately for them, the commissioners were not then in the city. They were in the American camp, procuring all possible forms of proof for the reclamation of the goods of citizens. They might, and probably would, return to the city, in the space of another day, and the first object with our Arcadians, was how, meanwhile, to secure the rest of the stolen negroes. But the parties interested had their mode of operation, and were not without experience. It will suffice here, if we mention the fact that, but very few of the two hundred remaining in the "hulk," after Mrs. Eveleigh had secured hers, were ever restored to their owners. The next morning, at dawn, found the "hulk" empty, while one of the transports had hauled out into the stream, ready to depart at a given signal. To arrange these matters, our companions needed little discussion.

"And now," said Moncrieff, "now that we have resolved what is to be done, I will give you the order without delay. That drunken rascal, Dort, must be relieved of all such trusts in future. This woman, through some of her friends, has practised upon his love of Hollands. She had never got a peep at those books otherwise. We must give their charge to Witsell. Do you keep here, M'Kewn, and see that Bostwick does not expose the beauties of his face until I send Waldron to you. He will tell you if the coast be clear. For his own sake, it will not do to identify him in my quarters. Indeed, I don't know but that my own character needs the same precaution. You are not, Master Bostwick, the handsomest piece of humanity that the world has witnessed."

"I am jist as God made me, Colonel Moncrieff," responded the squatter, sulkily.

"Pooh! pooh! Bostwick, that's all a mistake. Do you suppose that God made *you* at all? If he did, do you presume to say that you are in just as good condition as when you came out of his hands?"

"Ef I'm changed for the worse, colonel, I know who has helped to change me," and the fellow's eyes looked alternately to his two companions.

"What! you would give us the credit of your bad improvements; but you know better, Bostwick. We found you as you are, a ready made rascal, my lad; and employed you in a business for which your education was complete. But you want money, M'Kewn says? Well, we must give you a little. Five guineas you say? There it is. And now, Master Bostwick, you are pretty well paid. In fact, considering our losses this morning — the seven of the widow Eveleigh, and the seven more of the rebel, Captain Porpoise — seven, is it, or six? — where the d—l can those memorandums be? — I say, considering these losses, you are something overpaid. But we won't be tight with you, my good fellow; and, as M'Kewn hints, I will leave you, at parting, a tolerable supply of stores with which you can do a clever little business, hereafter, with your rebel friends. How does this plan suit you?"

"I reckon it must do, colonel."

"Do! By ——, my good fellow, you are about the most ungrateful, and not easily satisfied scoundrel of my acquaintance!"

"And it's a mighty large one too, I reckon." was the answer of Bostwick, with a grin that seemed to show that he was fully conscious of the sarcasm contained in his reply.

"You are right, my handsome fellow—many rascals in it, no doubt, but no one, by ——, who seems so little grateful for little favors as yourself. But, where, the d—l, are these memorandums? Have you seen them, M'Kewn?"

"You mean those of the negroes?"

"Yes; to be sure! I had them here but a while ago;" and as he spoke, Moncrieff looked suspiciously at Bostwick. He tumbled over the papers on his table, but without effect. He failed to find what he sought. M‘Kewn interested himself also in the search.

"Could the widow have laid hands upon them?" he suddenly asked, with some anxiety.

"No! Impossible!" said Moncrieff, and his eyes again glanced at Bostwick, who sat sullenly beside the fireplace, looking down upon the hearth. M‘Kewn also glanced in the same direction; but his mind reverted again to his former suspicion.

"If the widow has laid hands on them, it will be a bad business," said he, apprehensively.

"Pshaw! she wouldn't have touched them for the world. A lady, M‘Kewn—a lady."

"If she *did* take them, there's no way of getting them from her."

"I should certainly be the last man to think of demanding them. But, continue the search, M‘Kewn. Look among the papers in the other room. I must hurry off to Dort, and see to this business."

When he was gone, M‘Kewn exclaimed—

"Lady or no lady, I'll lay my life, that woman has pocketed the papers!"

"What papers?" asked Bostwick, indifferently.

"The papers that will hang you like a dog, fool! The memorandums of all the negroes brought in during the last month, and who brought them, and whence they were taken. My name and yours are both upon the paper."

"Who put 'em there? I can't write. You must ha' done it."

"So I did. I had to keep your accounts as well as my own, with Moncrieff. Look you, Bostwick, we must find out if she's got them, and if she has, we must get them from her, or the country will be too hot to hold us."

"I don't see. There's a paper, you say, with your name and my name; but anybody can write *my* name, and I'm not answerable if I don't write it myself. I reckon, if there's anybody in danger, you are the man."

"You reckon so, do you?—as if my evidence won't convict *you*, should the paper convict *me*;—for I must show how the negroes came into my hands. Don't be a fool, Bostwick. We must get those papers!"

"Well—how? I'm agreeable to anything."

"I'm glad to hear you say so, and to make the necessity seem more reasonable to you, let me hint that we must not only get the papers back, but the negroes. They're as good to you as ready money."

"How can it be done?" asked the squatter.

"I must find out when the widow and the slaves leave town. You can easily pick up half-a-dozen of the fellows of Huck's gang, can't you?"

"For good pay, and guineas in hand, I reckon."

"You shall have them. If we can find out when she leaves town, you can intercept her and recover the papers and the negroes. We shall have a transport sloop at the mouth of the Edisto, off and on, for the next two weeks. In that time the negroes must be off for the plantation, as they will be wanted pretty soon for breaking up the rice land. If you can recover them, you can push down the Edisto in boats, where Barton and Drummond will be on the lookout for you. Do you see?"

"Yes—cl'ar enough. But there's no gitting the boys, without the guineas *in hand*. I'm rather owing them something now, and they won't b'lieve me unless I kin show them the gould."

"You shall be provided. Leave it to me to procure the necessary information, while you go and pick up the refugees. Half-a-dozen stout fellows, in all, will probably answer, and you, yourself, can make the sixth man. The fewer the better. They are more manageable, and the pay will be larger to each. When you have engaged your men, promise *the cash*, and come to me for the money."

Waldron at the moment entered.

"The Colonel says all's clear, Mr. M'Kewn."

"Then I'm off;" said Bostwick. "I know where Dick Norris and Rafe Burke keep, and they can show me the other men. I'll come to you at your own place to-night, Mr. M'Kewn."

"Very good, only be sure and keep sober. You will need all your senses."

"I'll walk a crack with you any day," answered the other, as he hurried out of the room with Waldron. For a moment after his departure, M'Kewn sat musing. Then, appearing to recover his thoughts, he proceeded anew to search for the missing papers among the piles which lay upon the table.

"I'll look," he muttered, "but something tells me that woman has got them. The may do mischief with them, and, unluckily, it's just in her neighborhood now that must of my interest lies. There's that estate of Porgy: my mortgage covers his land.—There's Gillon's, which I've bought out and out—all, as I may say, alongside of her. If she has the papers, though they may absolutely prove nothing certain, they prove too much. She will hardly make use of them *now*. The British going out, and the Americans coming in, will cause a stir for sometime, and she'll be quiet 'till all the hubbub's over. Then!—But that will give us time, and time is half the capital of a wise man. She's a monstrous fine woman. What an eye she carries in her head! What a head! I must see her again! She has fine estate, almost joining those I got of Gillon."

We need not follow him in his musings. Enough to say that his search was fruitlessly continued, for sometime longer, after the missing papers.

CHAPTER VII.

NEW ISSUES BETWEEN OLD ALLIES.

Saturday, the 14th of December, 1782, was the day, memorable in the annals of Charleston, for the evacuation of that city by its British conquerors. They had held possession of it for two years, seven months and two days. Painful to them was the necessity of departing from a region in which they had been so successful in combining profit with pleasure. They had spoiled the Egyptians with a vengeance—had luxuriated in their flesh-pots for a long season, and naturally tore themselves away with reluctance. Nobody suffered more grievously from the necessity than our thirsty colonel of engineers, Moncrieff. Yet, no one, probably, had so successfully engaged in the business of "appropriation." His portion of the spoils, in negroes alone, is estimated at eight hundred. These had been shipped, at various periods, for the West India islands, as soon as it became obvious to all that the war was about to close, and the evacuation was inevitable. Fully two hundred slaves, as we have seen, were about to accompany his departure, all to his credit; the profits of which, in some degree, served to alleviate the disquiet that he felt at the discontinuance of a career, the fruits of which had been so abundant. In respect to these, there was a final conference between himself and M'Kewn, at the dawning of the day assigned for the exodus of the British. M'Kewn sought the British colonel in his chamber, and while the latter was yet yawning dismally, not thoroughly awake, at once over his own broken slumbers, and the cheerlessness of the prospect, the former opened the last business interview that was destined to take place between the parties, by a somewhat abrupt reference to the one matter which particularly concerned himself."

"You have not found the memorandum, colonel?"

"No, d—n it, it is gone, certainly. I have searched everywhere but in vain. Your rascal, Bostwick, has it, in all probability. I can hardly persuade myself that the woman took it. She is too much of a lady."

"That may be, yet I doubt; and, indeed, I'm not so sure that, even as a lady, she need have any scruples at putting in her pocket a document which so much concerned her own interest."

"Ah! and that's your opinion?" said Moncrieff, yawning, with an insolent contempt in his manner. "But, permit me to say, M'Kewn, that your habits in life, and business, are not, perhaps, the best calculated to make you a judge in such matters. The rules which govern the conduct of ladies and gentlemen do not necessarily occur to persons in trade. They are, perhaps, almost exclusively understood by those only whose life from the beginning has been in society, and among that class which finds its chief occupation in this very study. Now, you are a shrewd man of business, M'Kewn—devilish shrewd as a man of business—one may say wise, indeed—certainly, monstrous knowing—but you will admit that you have paid but small attention to the affairs of polite society. You can not well understand them, my good fellow.—Permit me to repeat that

Mrs. Eveleigh, who was born in the purple chamber of aristocracy, never could have taken this paper:—never! never!"

M'Kewn's brow became contracted as he listened to this offensive speech. It betrayed the contempt, without any desire for the concealment, with which the insolent official regarded him. All motives for concealing this contempt were at an end. The intercourse was over between them. The orange had been fully sucked, and M'Kewn could no longer be of use to the avarice of his employer. He felt all this, in an instant, but it was not his policy to express the indignation which it provoked. A sharp sarcasm, indeed, almost forced its way between his teeth; but he crushed them together, at the peril of his lips, and held his peace until the impulse was over. Then he said, quietly—

"Bostwick, I know, could not have taken the paper, for the scoundrel can't read a syllable, and knew not that such a paper was in existence. The temptation to the widow, Eveleigh, was great, and if she has it in her possession, the affair becomes a very serious one to me."

"Why, yes," rejoined the other, with an air of the greatest sang froid, "it might hang you, M'Kewn."

"Hardly that; but it would ruin me."

"You have managed badly. Why did you invest in real estate? How could you expect to make away with it? How could you expect to remain after our departure? Whether this paper arises or not, you are surely committed irrevocably with the rebels. Here you have been a contractor for the British army—you were one of the addressors of Sir Henry—an unforgivable offence. That you are a creditor of some of the rebels, and hold mortgages upon their estates, are only additional reasons for the confiscation of your property, and the endangering of your personal safety. It has always seemed to me the greatest folly that you should think to remain. It is not too late to determine more wisely. Abandon these villanous acres, these liens, which will be wholly worthless to you, and get yourself aboard the fleet before the army moves."

M'Kewn seemed to brood upon the suggestion for a few moments, then looking up suddenly, replied—

"No! it is now impossible. I should be a beggar elsewhere. My whole capital consists in these lands, and these liens are my whole stock in trade. I must take my chance. I do not think that my debtors, though rebels, will take advantage of my situation; and but for this accursed paper——"

"Oh! d—n the paper! Let's hear no more about it. You see my desk there. It contains the only papers in my possession which I have not destroyed. These will go with me, and can never rise against you. I can say no more on the subject. I repeat, you are an idiot if you stay. You can not hope for safety. Take to the fleet, and be aboard as soon as you can. This is my last and best counsel."

M'Kewn longed to utter the savage answer which he could have spoken—longed to snap his fingers in the face of the insolent Briton, and tell him that while he fancied that he used him, he was himself used—that he had guarantees of safety of which the other did not dream, and which, had he known, would have have probably insured him a British, quite as soon as an American gallows;—but the moment for such daring had not come by several hours. He reserved himself for this relation to the moment when the American army was fairly within the city. A slight smile, therefore, was employed to shadow his future purpose. Moncrieff did not perceive the sinister meaning of this smile—he added—rather contemptuously than kindly—

"If you reject my counsel you will deserve your fate. Yet, I assure you, M'Kewn, it will distress me to hear that so shrewd a business man has been suddenly made to ride a wooden horse, and unprovided with stirrups."

"I see that you have nothing further for me, colonel," was the only answer of M'Kewn.

"No, my good fellow, nothing. Take yourself off, now, while I make my toilet. There is the morning gun. You can see me on the march if you desire it; but i' faith, the ceremony of parting is usually so dismal and distressing, that I do not know but we may well dispense with it. At all events, for the present, M'Kewn, good morning—good morning."

"The selfish and narrow-minded scoundrel!" muttered M'Kewn, as he slowly wound his way down the staircase.

"What a bore!" exclaimed Moncrieff, as the other disappeared. "With his d——d memoranda! What do I care if they do hang him! That he should presume to know the laws of honor for gentleman or lady. He deserves to be hanged for that, if nothing else. Ho! there, Waldron."

And ringing his bell furiously, our excellent colonel entered upon the duties of his toilet.

Meanwhile, the business of the day was fairly begun in the American camp, and within the lines of the garrison. By a plan previously agreed upon between General Leslie of the one, and General Greene of the other army, the British column was to be in motion at the firing of the morning gun, withdrawing from the lines, near Shubrick's farm, and moving through the city to the wharves. At the same moment, the advance of the Americans, under General Wayne—who had been approaching from Ashley Ferry, where Greene's army lay—was to follow slowly upon their footsteps, until the city, abandoned by the one, should be fully occupied by the forces of the other. The fleet of the British, more than three hundred sail, lay at anchor in the roads, stretching, in a beautiful crescent, from Fort Johnson to Five Fathom Hole. "It was a grand and pleasing sight," says old Moultrie, who accompanied Greene in his triumphal entry. Not less pleasing to the war-worn and returning patriots, and the brave glorious dames, who cheered them in their weary struggle, was the progress of the troops of the conqueror, sullenly retiring from their places of pleasure and pasturage. The windows, balconies, housetops, in all the principal streets, were crowded with happy smiling faces, beholding with equal joy the departure of the one dynasty, and the reappearance of the other. At an early hour of the day the embarkation of the British began, but it was not till near eleven, A. M., when the rear-guard began to file, with measured steps, through the centre of the city. Wayne's detachment, consisting of three hundred light infantry, twenty artillery with two six-pounders, and eighty of Lee's cavalry, following them at an interval of two hundred yards only, constituted the advance of the American army. It was a novel situation for both parties to approach to such propinquity yet keep from blows; and the British evinced no small feeling of disquiet, as, in the impatience of the former, to obtain possession of that city for which they had so long been striving, they pressed forward at a pace which promised to unite the two armies in one indistinguishable mass.

"This must not be," cried a British officer, riding up to the head of the Americans; "you are too fast upon us, gentlemen —you press upon us too closely."

The American general was compelled to call a halt—and then the shouts rose from the housetops and the balconies, while trumpets blared, and a thousand palmetto banners were flung out in air as the cry went up—

"Welcome, welcome home, brave hearts! God bless you, gallant gentlemen!"

"How the brutes howl!" muttered Moncrieff to one who at that moment jogged his elbow. "Ah! is it you, M'Kewn? You are just in time to say farewell."

"But I shall not say it, sir," was the reply, in a tone, and with a manner which at once drew upon the speaker the astonished attention of the British officer.

"Eh! what's the matter now?"

"Read that at your leisure, Colonel Moncrieff," said M'Kewn, handing him a billet where he stood, curbing his chafing steed, beneath a low balcony near Chalmers, in Meeting street. Moncrieff took the paper, and proceeded to open it on the spot.

"It will teach you, sir," continued M'Kewn, "that you were never more *my tool* than when you thought me yours!"

With these words he disappeared within the dwelling before which the scene took place. Moncrieff, astonished, looked about him, but not seeing the speaker, he turned to the billet. In a moment his eyes glittered with sudden rage, and in the next instant the voice of M'Kewn from the balcony above gave new impulse to his fury.

"Rather a new feature in the history, Colonel Moncrieff!"

"Ha! villain, but you shall not escape me!" and, thus speaking, he dashed up to the balcony, which, on horseback as he was, his drawn weapon might have reached. But the side walks were covered with spectators, who were not disposed to give way, and one of these, an old man with a great white beard, but sturdy and fearless, grasped the bridle of the horse and forced him back. At the same moment, Major Barry hurried forward, threw himself between, and drew Moncrieff away. The procession was again in motion.

"What are you at, Moncrieff?—this will never do. A single

rashness will bring their whole force upon us, and three fourths of our army are already embarked?"

"D—n the scoundrel!" was the exclamation of Moncrieff as he suffered himself to be led away. "I would give fifty guineas for a chance at his ears!" and, glaring as he spoke, like a hyena, at the balcony where M'Kewn stood, the centre of a crowd of men and women, he was answered by a grin from his former ally which added a hundred-fold to his vexation. The concourse beheld this singular scene, and many of them heard the language which the British colonel had employed. The circumstance raised M'Kewn inconceivably in their estimation. The man who had provoked the ire of Moncrieff, was necessarily, in that period and place, a patriot. But the procession moved on, and the parties were soon separated.

The clamors increased. The trumpets rang forth more merry peals. As the rich scarlet uniforms of the British disappeared into Broat street, great festoons were swung across Meeting, which they had left, and the crowds increased in the balconies. Then, as Wayne pressed forward with his blue coats, in double quick time, the shouts went up in redoubled peals. Rolled onward the solemn artillery — galloped forward the gay horsemen of Lee's squadron — while the rattle of drums in the distance announced the gradual approach of the main army of the Americans. At 3 P. M., the rear-guard announced the approach of General Greene; the governor of the state, Mathews; with the council of state; closely followed by General Gist and the brave old Moultrie, and accompanied by a noble civic procession. This *cortege* halted in Broad street, opposite the spot now occupied by the Bank of South Carolina, and the shouts of welcome which hailed the appearance of the defenders of the country, announced the final embarkation of the foe. Trumpets sounded merrily — drums rolled from a hundred conspicuous points, and the cannon belched forth their mighty thunders, in echo to the general voice of public thanksgiving.

CHAPTER VIII.

PLOTS ALL ROUND THE TABLE.

THE day passed off in pleasurable excitements which did not end with the night. An illumination followed, and every house was thrown wide for the reception of friends and visiters. The military bands were in full requisition; and the merry violin, sounding from this or that great house, in almost every street of the city denoted the extempore dancing-party, and the joyful reunion of long separated friends and dear ones. Formality interposed to mar none of the conviviality. There were no tedious ceremonials. The strangers were known friends, and successful valor, and unquestioned patriotism, were to be honored and rewarded. There had been little time, and less means, for any stately ceremonials. Invitations had not been given out, but were commonly understood; and every gentleman knew that he was welcome at every whig mansion. Doors everywhere were thrown wide, and the gay cavalier passed from one to another dwelling, sure to find in all an attraction and a welcome.

It was at one of these dwellings, in Broad street, that Mrs. Eveleigh was, for the evening, an honored guest. A considerable party had assembled, when General Greene made his appearance with his suite. Moultrie came soon after, with good-natured visage, looking the very personification of peace and good-will to men. There were stately cavaliers in train from Virginia, Maryland, and Delaware—the old North state was honorably represented in more than one tall and portly soldier, while Georgia had two or three handsome blue-eyed and round-faced youths, following the wake of the fiery Wayne. The assemblage, hastily conceived and promiscuously brought together, was nevertheless, comparatively, a brilliant one. We do not propose to describe it more particularly.

It was while the rooms were most crowded, that Mrs. Eveleigh was suddenly surprised by the entrance of M'Kewn, whom she had known only as the associate of Moncrieff, and by the memoranda which she still held in her possession. He approached the hostess, Mrs. W———, with the easy assurance of one who has no doubt of his reception. Mrs Eveleigh watched curiously to see what that reception would be. To her increased surprise, she found it affable in the extreme. M'Kewn was next seen among the gentlemen. With these, also, he seemed to enjoy an excellent understanding. Her surprise underwent still further increase, as she discovered in the persons with whom he seemed most at home, none but unquestionable patriots. By one of these she saw him led up to General Greene, and introduced; a few words were whispered in the general's ear by the gentleman who did the courtesy on this occasion, and Greene was then seen to shake M'Kewn's hand with a hearty and nervous grasp. Good Mrs. Eveleigh knew not what to think. She turned to a gentleman who sat beside her, whom she well knew, and asked:

"Who is that person just introduced to General Greene—he to whom General Moultrie is now speaking?"

"His name is M'Kewn—he is, or was, a Scotch merchant here, but I believe he has declined business recently. He is a man of substance."

"The general seems to view him with favor."

"Well they may, if all's true that is said of him. He is one of the few Scotchmen who have been with us during the war. He was one of the addressors of Sir Henry Clinton, but his ostentatious loyalty was only employed as a cover for his revolutionary principles. He has been one of the spies, in part, upon the garrison, and has frequently served Marion with information of the state of affairs."

"His being a Scotchman, yet a spy for us, does not speak much for principle of any kind. I suppose he feathered his nest by it."

"Ah!" with a shrug, "we must not be too scrupulous about the quality of the tool we use if we pick the lock with it."

"Perhaps not: the necessity of the case is to be considered, surely. But is it certain that Marion got any really valuable information out of him?"

"That is a problem. But you seem curious in respect to this person. Have you any reason for it?"

"I have; and I must consult you in regard to it and him. But not now. I see that he approaches."

The companion of Mrs. Eveleigh was, in that day, a very celebrated Carolina lawyer, and, subsequently, the widow unfolded to him the discoveries which she had made.

"I am not at all surprised at it," was the reply. "It is certain that M'Kewn has grown wealthy. He is proprietor of several large estates, or rather has liens upon them, for advances made at enormous interest. A foreclosure of these mortgages, at this moment, when there is no money in the country, would give him these estates at his own prices. These papers which you possess would be fatal to him. But, unless he proceeds to extremities with his debtors, it may be well not to use them."

"Should he not be made to disgorge?"

"Yes, if there be any good whig who suffers by him. But in all probability most of his debtors are tories, and they will scarcely oppose his action."

The good widow shook her head.

"He has other victims. I know of one at least, a true patriot —a strange creature—of many eccentricities, but of many noble qualities and of much real talent. He has been the loser already by this M'Kewn. I recovered half-a-dozen slaves for him, when I got my own out of the hulk."

"You mean Porgy?"

"Yes!"

"Oh, we must save Porgy—and we will! But, for the present, keep perfectly quiet. We are yet in the storm. Government is only nominally established—we know not what may follow; keep an eye on the fellow—that is enough for the present—and, with these papers, we can bring him up with a short cord at any moment."

Enough of this conversation—which took place the day after the party at Mrs. W————'s. To that let us now return. The approach of M'Kewn to the place where Mrs. Eveleigh sat, followed very soon after the moment when she discovered his presence in the assembly. He appeared to see her suddenly; but, we may state, from our own knowledge, that his motive for appearing in that particular assembly, that night, was the result of his previous knowledge that he should be sure to meet her there. He had taken sufficient pains to satisfy himself on this point. His object in desiring to see her should be obvious to the reader. He was deeply interested in knowing whether she had possessed herself of the missing paper which so greatly compromised him. His notion was that, as a woman, she would in some way betray her knowledge — by look, word, manner — and thus enable him to determine upon the necessity before him, and the game which he would need to play. But the Widow Eveleigh was no ordinary woman. She was a good whist-player, and when you find a good whist-player among women, be sure that she knows how to keep a secret. Her trumpet never announces the number or the value of her trump cards.

A smile and bow — a look and manner of the profoundest courtesy — mingled with that sort of triumphant pleasure which might be supposed to appear in the faces of all good citizens at such a moment — distinguished the address of Mr. M‘Kewn, as he stood before Mrs. Eveleigh. The lady acknowledged his address with a courtesy sufficiently decided to make no revelations. M‘Kewn took the seat beside her, which her late companion had just vacated, and, in the current phrase of the hour, congratulated her on the grateful change which the country had undergone. She answered him in a manner of perfect good faith, avoiding with care every look or word which the most jealous nature might construe into suspicion or sarcasm.

“It is certainly an event at which every good citizen should rejoice, Mr. M‘Kewn. Our people have gone through a terrible trial. They have shown themselves worthy of the liberties they have won. It is to be hoped that they will now prove themselves worthy to retain them.”

“A more difficult matter. But we must hope, my dear madam. It is something in proof of their capacity to keep, that they have shown the capacity to win. I found you lately engaged in a somewhat unpleasant business. I trust you were successful in getting back your negroes.”

“I was, sir.”

“You were then much more fortunate than some of your neighbors. I have much trouble with Col. Moncrieff in removing some of my own, and was only in part successful.”

“Indeed.”

"Yes; I have lost a number, and was quite satisfied not to have lost all. The British have had their emissaries all over the country, and some of those creatures, madam, were such as we should little suspect. When you found me with Colonel Moncrieff, I was endeavoring to procure some clews to their detection, for it is impossible but that some of these wretches will still remain in the country."

"Were you successful in your inquiries, sir ?"

"Not altogether; but I fancy I have some clews in regard to one or more of our neighbors. You are aware, madam, that I have become the proprietor of an estate near yours on the Ashepoo ?"

"No, sir, I was not, whose, pray ?"

"Gillon's.—I took it for a debt; shall send up negroes to work it, and hope to find myself one of your neighbors in the spring, if not before."

The lady bowed rather stiffly, but said nothing. The wily M'Kewn construed her manner into a confirmation of his suspicions. If it had been her object to baffle his scrutiny in regard to the missing paper, she had lost a point in the game. There was a brief pause in the conversation, which M'Kewn, at length, resumed by returning to the subject of his interview with Moncrieff. He told a very pretty little story of the ingenious processes by which he had succeeded in recovering his negroes, and concluded by stating that Moncrieff and himself had quarrelled finally.

"But I had the last word, Mrs. Eveleigh, and one that he will remember. I was compelled to bear his insolence while the British garrison was yet in possession, but, in the moment of his departure, and when he could no longer exercise his power, I gave him my opinion of his character."

He then told of the final passage already detailed between himself and Moncrieff. The note which he had put into the hands of the latter, he described as full of the most stinging insult. The lady could not forbear the sarcasm, which she yet uttered very quietly, and with a seeming unconsciousness of its latent meaning.

"Certainly, a very daring proceeding, Mr. M'Kewn. But, if I recollect rightly, Wayne's advance was within a hundred yards of you at the moment. Of that, however, you were unaware."

A slight flush tinged the dark cheeks of M'Kewn; but he answered calmly.

"No, indeed, Mrs. Eveleigh—I knew it well enough; and knew that, were it otherwise, I should have perilled my neck to have done what I did. There would have been no sense or even courage in speaking freely, what I thought of the scoundrel, at a time when I should have no power to contend with him. I did all that I properly could in expressing my sense of his rascality."

The lady appeared to hear him indifferently. He discovered this, and soon after withdrew from her side.

"Fool!" thought Mrs. Eveleigh, as he moved away. "Does he think to delude me with his inventions?"

"She *has* the paper!" muttered M'Kewn, at the same moment; "and now to ascertain when she leaves town."

His spies were set accordingly; and instructed to watch every movement of the widow. They did their duty faithfully. The very next day. the squatter, Bostwick, was in attendance upon his employer.

"Well, Bostwick, have you got the fellows?"

"Five of the best bloodhounds in the country. But I must have money for 'em. I'm at great expense in keeping 'em. Jest simple meat and drink won't answer to keep 'em quiet. You must soak 'em and stuff 'em;—ef you leave an empty place in 'em, they begins to be good and religious-like, and to talk about sins and sich like matters."

"Pshaw!"

"It's mother-truth, I'm telling you. There's no keeping 'em properly sinful for your wants, onless I'm a drenching and stuffing 'em. It is something's a-wanting from morning to night. They wants everything they sees or thinks about, and they say they've a right to all I can git."

"But you forget—you agreed with them for a certain price."

"Yes! that was the pay when the work was done. But I was to keep them in the meantime, you know, and it's mighty hard work. They're all asleep now at Broddus's, up the path. They was most eternally drunk last night, broke all the windows, and killed Broddus's dog—so them's to be paid for. Broddus says the windows is two dollars, and the dog cost him two guineas."

"The devil! And you expect me to pay me this fellow?"

"In course—it's only reason—seeing as how these boys is in your keeping."

"But I'll do no such thing."

"You'll hav' to, M'Kewn, so it's no use to kick agin it. They will git drunk, and when they're drunk, they will splurge and shine. There's no hendering 'em."

"And you?"

"Oh! I must drink with them, you know——"

"And splurge and shine too, I suppose; break windows, kill dogs, and expect me to square the bill."

"In course. It's the life we lead, and belongs to the business, and one part jest as much as the other. The man what sells himself to the devil, must in nater hev' a sort of devil's edication, and must play devil's tricks. It keeps the hand in for devil's business."

"Well, it's some consolation that we shall not have the keeping of such rascals very long. This woman leaves town next week."

"Which day?"

"Friday, I think—but we shall find out."

"Friday, a bad day for a start. Hangman's day."

"Yes; a bad day for her, as she will start then. You will set out the day before, and choose your place of ambush. Remember, Bostwick, you are not to fail. Your pay depends upon it;—the negroes you will recapture, depend upon it—and your neck depends upon it; for she certainly has got the paper."

"I reckon it's *your* neck jest as much as mine, M'Kewn, so you'll jest please to stop with that sort of talking. Nobody likes to have the rope and gallows constantly flung in his face, jest when he's thinking of other things. As for my name on the paper, it oughtn't to consarn me so much, seeing as how I didn't put in thar. But you did, and you put your own too, and I reckon when they're h'isting me on the cross-trees, they'll be swinging you off to make room. Ef you wants me to be reasonable and do your business, you'll jest stop with a sort of talk which makes my blood bile agin you."

"Well! well! since you're so nice about this hanging, I'll say rope to you no more."

"Better not—t'ain't *advisable, no how. It's better to talk of the business atween us. I must have money for the keeping of the boys."

"Here is three guineas——"

"Why, there's six on us."

"If there were sixty, I have no more money about me."

"It takes pretty nigh a guinea a day to keep 'em, as they expects to be kept."

"Damn their expectations! Do they suppose me to be made of money? You must make them more reasonable, Bostwick, for you yourself will lose by it in the end."

"I don't see."

"But I do!—make these three guineas answer for the week and come to me at the end of it."

"I'll be sure to do that, whether the week's at an eend or not. Tiger-cats must be fed."

"Ay, but as tiger-cats only, and not as lions. Remember the difference, if you please. You have taken care that none of them know me in the business?"

"To be sure? make yourself easy thar'."

"Make yourself ready, and see that they are quite sober when the work is done; and when you have got the negroes and paper, push down the Edisto, where I will contrive to meet you, and get the negroes off to the transport sloop. But we'll talk over these particulars before you start."

Here the conference ended. We have been content to give a sample of it only. There was much more said, unavoidably, between the parties, which it is not necessary that we should chronicle. The week passed, and M'Kewn was called upon to disgorge other guineas, and meet other bills for damages done by his dogs in keeping. Meanwhile, Mrs. Eveleigh was making her preparations. On Wednesday, not on Friday, she set out for her plantation, accompanied by her negroes, and those of Porgy—her overseer, and her son—the latter a youth of fifteen. But we shall introduce this lad more formally hereafter.

CHAPTER IX.

THE SOLDIER SURVIVES HIS OCCUPATION.

WE must now change the scene of operations, and introduce new parties to our drama. Let us present ourselves at the camp of Marion, at the head of Cooper river. The reader will, perhaps, have observed that, in speaking of the departure of the British forces from the city of Charleston, and the grand entry of the American troops at their heels, we said nothing of the militia, the rangers, the famous Partisans, cavalry and foot, of Marion, Sumter, Maham, and the many other brilliant cavaliers, whose sleepless activity, great audacity, and frequent successes, had, perhaps more than any other influence, kept alive the hopes and maintained the cause of liberty in Carolina, at a period when Fate seemed to have decreed the utter subjugation of the country by the enemy.

The fact is, none of these gallant spirits were permitted to be present at the reoccupation of the metropolis by the patriot army! They had shared the usual fortune of modest merit; had served their purpose, and had survived their uses. The work done, the game won, they had been thrown aside, as the orange sucked of its contents, with no more scruple or concern. It will scarcely be believed, but such is the fact, that the militia of the country were especially denied the privilege of being spectators of the departure of that enemy against whom none had battled more ceaselessly, more fearlessly, or with better success, than themselves. It might have been that they were too *nude* to be seen on such a brilliant occasion. They were, verily, very nigh to utter nakedness. They were mostly in rags. Their rents of garment were closed by bandages of green moss. Their shoulders and hips were thus, in like manner, padded, as a protection against abrasion by the belts which they had to wear, bearing their arms and ammunition. They were commonly shoeless and hatless. Raw hides made the shoes of many, wrought roughly, moccasin fashion, into mere troughs for the feet, the seams running down, and gathering up the edges of the leather, from the instep to the toes. A fragment of coarse cotton, or a ragged handkerchief, wound about like a turban, was the substitute with many for a hat; while, with a still greater number, the skins of "coon or possum," untanned, untrimmed, and with the tail jauntily stuck out on the side, made caps of every pattern, and of fashions the most extraordinary. Their weapons were of similar diversity; from the long ducking gun of the planter, to the short fusee of the German yager; the heavy tower musket of George the Third, to the long rifle of the mountain rangers from that section of the Apalachian slopes, which divides, or rather unites, the states of North and South Carolina and Georgia. Sabres, wrought from mill-saws, with handles of common wood, graced the thighs of half the dragoons.

Such equipment would scarcely have made a brilliant showing in a scene so brilliant as that witnessed at the recovery of Charleston. Whether it would not have been most noble and impressive, as illustrating the true worth and honest patriotism of the partisans, is a matter which the reader will take into consideration. It, certainly, was not considered by the ruling powers at that period, or considered only as calculated to subtract from the splendors of the triumphal pageant. But the reasoning by which the militia were excluded from the scene was really of a more offensive and objectionable character. An unworthy fear — a dread of the power of a body of troops who were supposed to be less easily brought under the control of authority — who were known to be dissatisfied, and who, it was felt, had just cause for discontent and dissatisfaction — was the true secret of their exclusion from the scene. Badly armed and worse clad, fighting for years amid a thousand other privations, without pay, and almost without thanks or acknowledgment, their achievements slurred over and disparaged, as they have been too frequently since — while the deeds of others were exaggerated and clothed with a false lustre;—it was apprehended that, with the withdrawal of the enemy, they might be disposed to assert their rights, and do justice to themselves. It is possible they might have done so; since humanity is not to be supposed capable, always, of forbearing the exhibition of a just indignation, under continued wrong and provocation. But the possibility was still a very faint one. They had given no reason for the suspicion. Nay, they had been called in, and kept ready, more than once, under Marion, to suppress the apprehended outbreaks and insurrections of some of those very continental troops who had been deemed worthy to be present at the event which they were denied to behold.

A deep feeling of indignation, naturally enough, was awakened among our partisans at this ungenerous exclusion. But it did not declare itself, and could not, while under the leaders who had so nobly conducted them throughout the war; and now they were about to be disbanded—to separate from their leaders—to pay the last honors of salute to the colors they had so often watched in the heady storms and vicissitudes of battle, and to retire to their homes—such homes as a war of seven years had left them—homes in ruins;—and to sink unhonored into an obscurity which held forth little promise of distinction in the future, and still less of improving fortunes.

It was in that tract of country, so often distinguished by his active enterprise, lying near the head waters of Cooper river, that Marion assembled his brigade for the purpose of dissolving his connection with them, and their existence as a military society. Their number did not much exceed four hundred men, infantry and horse. At an early hour of the morning, the stir of preparation was begun, and, by nine o'clock, the rolling drums and sharp clamors of the bugle, summoned them to the area of a noble wood of ancient cedars in which they were to take leave of their well-beloved chieftain. At ten, the general appeared among them, attended by all his staff. He was received in deep silence—a silence expressive of emotions too solemn for shouts or words. His face, usually grave, wore a still graver expression than was its wont. His words, always few, were scarcely more copious now, when so much was to be said, even if much was to be left unspoken. There was more than his usual hesitation, in his manner, as he addressed them. His tones slighty trembled, and thus spoke directly to their own feelings. He spoke of their long services, their fidelity to himself and country; the honorable termination of their labors in the field, and the necessity of now sinking back to the no less honorable duties of the citizen. He assured them that, in him, his old soldiers should always find a personal friend, who, whatever might be the changes of the future, could never forget his sympathy and connection with the past. At the close, they gathered about him, each eager to seize his hand in friendly gripe. Nor was he the man to insist upon the dignities and formalities of his position at such a moment. The commander was forgotten in the friend, and the leave-taking was such as might be expected, at the breaking up and dispersion of the members of an ancient and loving household. It was midday before he left them, riding slowly away, attended by his suite, and escorted by a small detachment of cavalry. Night found the scene of the encampment silent—no drums rolled—no trumpets sounded—no fires were lighted. The cedars at Watboo, were as lonely, as if they sheltered the graves only of the brave fellows to whose living heads they had so long afforded the most grateful protection.

We can not follow the fortunes of our scattered partisans, pursuing, as they did, a score of different routes, each with his thought and heart turned upon some special home and object. Bands of fifty might be seen, on horse or a-foot, taking the route for Orangeburg ; other groups went northward, bound for Waccamaw and Peedee; others again moved down the river, taking one or other of the two routes conducting to Charleston, while sundry squads sped directly southward, aiming for the Ashley, the Edisto, the Ashepoo and the Savannah rivers; from all of which regions they had severally been drawn.

We will accompany one of these parties, a group consisting of four persons, all well mounted, and, comparatively speaking, all well armed and caparisoned. Two of them in fact are officers. One of these is a stout, and somewhat plethoric gentleman ; full, and smooth, and florid of face, with indubitable signs of a passion for the good things of this life. His features are marked and decisive, with a large capacious nose, a mouth rather feminine and soft, and a chin well defined and masculine. But for the excessive development of the abdominal region, his figure would have been quite worthy of his face. He rode a noble gray, of great size and strength, good blood and bottom, and with his fires but little subdued by hard service.

Beside this person, whose epaulettes showed him to have held
a captain's commission, rode a youth, who could not have been
more than nineteen years of age. He was slender and tall, but
wiry and agile; with features rather pleasing and soft, than expressive; and which might have seemed somewhat lacking in
manliness but for the dark bronzing which they had taken from
the sun. He was well mounted also, tolerably well dressed, and
wore the equipment of a cavalry ensign.

The third person of this party was a man of altogether inferior appearance, tall, rawboned, and awkward, with features
harsh and irregular, redeemed only by a certain frankness and
honesty of expression, which was derived from a large and gentle
eye of hazel, and a broad good-natured mouth. He carried an
enormous beard almost of lemon color, and his hair streamed
down his shoulders in waving masses, that faintly reminded you
of a falling mountain torrent. A stout chunk of a horse, of frame
not unsuited to his own, bore his weight. He wore no other
uniform than the common blue frock, or hunting shirt of the rangers, a cap of coon skin, and, for weapons, a broadsword, of immense dimensions as from the primitive forges of a son of Anak,
and a pair of common pistols. These weapons, we may add, he
could use with the left hand only—the right being wanting.
He was one of the few who, in the miserable deficiency of the
militia service, had survived a hurt which had completely shattered the limb. His safety was due to his own stout heart, and
the unflinching promptness of the friend and superior whom he
followed. His right arm, torn into strips by a brace of bullets
from a musket held within a few paces, was stricken off at his
entreaty, by his captain, and the bleeding stump was thrust instantly into hot, seething tar. The wounds healed, Heaven
knows how, and he recovered. But for this proceeding he must
have perished. At that time, there was not a surgeon in Marion's brigade, and every hurt which affected the limbs of the
victim was certain to end in death. Sergeant Millhouse, the
man in question, became the devoted adherent of a superior,
who had the firmness to comply with the stern requisition of the
patient, and himself perform the cruel operation, which the sufferer bore without a groan.

The fourth party in this group is a negro—a native African

—the slave of the captain; a fellow of flat head and tried fidelity; of enormous mouth. but famous as a cook; of a nose that scarcely pretended to elevate itself on the otherwise plain surface of an acre of face; but of a genius for stews that commended him quite as much as any other of his virtues to the confidence and regards of his master. Tom had a reputation in camp, for his terrapin soups, which made him the admiration of the whole brigade. He well knew his own merits, and was always careful to be in condition to establish them. The sumpter horse which he rode was covered, accordingly, with a variety of kitchen equipage. Pots and kettles were curiously pendant from the saddle, strapped over the negro's thighs, or hanging from his skirts. A sack, which exhibited numerous angles, carried other utensils, to say nothing of pewter plates, iron spoons, knives and forks, and sundry odds and ends of bread and bacon. Tom was really buried in his kitchen baggage. But this seemed to offer no impediment, nor to be felt as an incumbrance. He kept close to the heels of his master, and had as ready an ear for all that was spoken, as any of his superiors. He was not wanting, also, in the occasional comment — the camp-life having done much toward perfecting the republicanism of all the parties.

Our company had ridden a couple of hours from the time of their withdrawal from the " Cedars," and the separation from their ancient comrades; and had compassed, perhaps, eight or ten miles in this interval. Yet, but little conversation had taken place among them, and, though they rode together, they maintained comparative silence. Our captain, who bore the name of Porgy, was almost the only speaker. He was one, in fact, who possessed a liberal endowment of the gift of language, and greatly delighted, on ordinary occasions, in his own eloquence. But he, too, was influenced, in some degree, by the scene through which they had so recently gone; — by thoughts which were now, perforce, required to meditate the future; and by the sterile country through which they were passing — reaped by the greedy sickles of the enemy, and sending up no cheerful smokes from the homesteads of welcoming friends.

The day itself, from being bright at sunrise, had become overcast with clouds. Chilly, without being cold, it added to the feeling of chill which the circumstances of the day had naturally occasioned in their hearts. Nor did the solemn, stately, and ever-murmuring and monotonous pine-forests through which they rode—by no means enlivened by occasional tracts of scanty oak, stripped wholly of its foliage, or by the ruins of ancient farms and decaying fences—contribute to lessen the feeling of melancholy which sensibly possessed our little group of travellers.

At length, however, Captain Porgy broke the silence, as he alone had hitherto done, by something that sounded monstrously like an oath, but which we may render into more innocent language.

"By St. Bacchus, Lance, I must drink—I must eat—I must be guilty of some fleshly indulgence! Let us get down here. There is a branch before us, the water of which I have tried before. We have still a bottle of Jamaica. Tom must knock us up a fry, and we must eat and drink, that we may not grow stupid from excessive thinking. If one must think, its most agreeable exercise, to my experience, is over toast and tankard. Tom, 'light, old fellow, and get out your cookables. Lance, you carry that Jamaica; I would see if it loses any of its color in these dark and drowsy times."

The command was instantly obeyed: though, to descend out of his piles, to fling off straps to which hung pot and kettle, bread and bacon, &c., was, to Tom, a sort of performance which needed equal discretion and deliberation. He was extricated, at last, though only with the assistance of Sergeant Millhouse; and, having relieved his horse of its luggage, he adjusted himself to his tasks. Very soon, his box of tinder, flint and steel, were in requisition, and he had kindled a pleasant blaze within twenty steps of the running water. To this Captain Porgy, accompanied by Lance, his lieutenant—Lance Frampton being the full name—had at once proceeded; and already had he brightened the clear, but rather unmeaning complexion of the water, with the rich, red liquid of Jamaica. A pewter mug, of moderate dimensions, sufficed for the embraces of the separate fluids; and having first, with his nostrils, inhaled the fragrance of the rum, our captain held it to his eye for a moment, surveying it with a glance of decided complacency, before he carried it to his lips. He drank, smacked his lips with a sense of cordial satisfaction, and offered the cup and bottle to Frampton. But the latter declined the liquor respectfully, and, stooping to the brooklet, drank directly from the running stream. Millhouse, the sergeant, was more easily persuaded, and Captain Porgy, as he beheld him pour with liberal hand into the cup, might have entertained some reasonable doubts of the propriety and wisdom of suffering a man with but one hand to adjust his own measures, particularly where the source of supply was so distressingly small. But he suffered the soldier to help himself, and, retiring a few paces, let himself down—no easy matter— at the foot of a pine, where the straw of previous seasons afforded a couch of tolerable softness. Hither, when the horses were fastened, came the ensign, Frampton, while the sergeant, Millhouse, bestowed himself more particularly upon Tom, the cook. A hoarse sigh, that, issuing from a plethoric chest, might have been held a groan, betrayed, in Captain Porgy, a more than usually serious sense of his situation. The ensign, who had thrown himself down on the opposite side of the tree, modestly remarked—

"I think, Captain Porgy, you are more sorrowful than I ever saw you before. Indeed, I can't say that I ever saw you sorrowful till now."

"Well: quite likely, Lance;—I have reason for it. Othello's occupation's gone."

"Othello, captain? Was the gentleman a soldier?"

"Ay, indeed, a Moorish soldier!—a blackamoor—a sort of negro—of whom, it is quite likely, you have never heard—of whom you will, probably, hear no more than I shall tell you. He was a famous fighter in his day; but there came a day when his wars were ended—like ours—and then!—"

"And then?"

"He swallowed his sword through an artificial mouth!"

"What? How? Swallowed his sword?"

"In other words, cut his throat!"

"What! because he could no longer cut the throats of other people?"

"Partly that—and reason enough, too! Throat-cutting was his business. Nobody ought to survive his business. Now, if I were quite sure that my wars were wholly ended—that I should

never be permitted to cut throats again, according to law—
I should certainly request of you the favor, Lance, as an
act of friendship, to pass the edge of your sabre across my
jugular."

"I should do no such thing, Captain Porgy."

"Oh, yes! you would—that is, if I particularly requested it;
and I don't know but I shall have to do so yet. You will certainly oblige me, Lance, when the necessity shall arrive, and
when I make the entreaty."

"I don't think, captain. No! I could never do it."

"Oh, yes, you will; but the necessity is not apparent *yet*,
since my nose tells me that Tom has still some material left, by
which my throat shall find agreeable employment. I suppose,
so long as one may tickle his throat with fish, flesh, and fowl,
and soothe it with Jamaica, he may still endure a life relieved
of its usual occupations. But, this is the doubt, Lance. How
long shall there be fish, and flesh, and fowl, and Jamaica? I
am a ruined man! I go back to the ancient homestead of my
fathers, to find it desolate. Negroes gone, lands under mortgage, and not a rooster remaining in the poultry-yard, to crow
me a welcome to dinner. Such a prospect does not terrify *you*.
You have not been reared and trained to position, and artificial
wants. You are young, just at the entrance of life, my dear
boy, and can turn your hand to a thousand occupations, each of
which shall supply your wants. Such is not the case with me.
At forty-five, neither heart nor head, nor hand, possesses any
such flexibility. A seven years' apprenticeship to war has left
no resources in peace. Othello's occupation's gone!—gone!
There is little or nothing now that I should live for;—family,
wife, friends, fortune—I have none;—loneliness, poverty, desolation—these are the only prospects before me!"

This was spoken with so much real mournfulness, that it compelled the warmest sympathies of the youthful hearer, who, in
spite of many eccentricities on the part of the speaker, which he
failed to understand, and a strong and active selfishness, which
he comprehended well enough, had yet a real affection for his
superior. He crept near to Porgy, and said—

"Oh! it can't be as bad as all that, captain. You have many
friends. There's General Marion, and there's our colonel, and

many besides; and you've got a fine plantation, and I reckon some of your negroes are left——"

"Tom only!   The last accounts reported that every hair of a negro was gone—all carried off by the tories, I suppose, or the British.   As for the plantation, it's under mortgage to a d——d shark of a Scotchman; and, even if it were not, it would be worth nothing without the slaves.   I tell you, boy, I see no remedy but to get my throat cut like a gentleman, and die in my epaulettes and boots."

"Oh! something will be sure to turn up, captain.   Remember what old Ben Brewer used to say when anything misfortunate had happened—'Look up, I say,—God's over all!' God's your friend, captain."

"Well, in truth, Lance, I've so seldom called upon him, among my other friends, that, perhaps, he might do something for me now."

The irreverence was rebuked by his young companion in the following terms—

"Oh, captain! don't talk so!   He's been doing for you all along!   Who has taken care of you till now, when you're forty-five years old?   Who saved you so often in fight?—and that's another reason, captain, why you should have faith in his mercies.   I reckon God always puts in, at the right time, to save people, if so be they only let him!   It's we that *won't* be saved, and that's continually fighting against his mercies."

"You talk like an oracle, Lance!   One thing's certain, that at times, when a fellow discovers that he can do nothing to save himself, the best philosophy is to confide in powers superior to his own.   Of one thing, rest assured, my lad—I shall never hurry my own case to judgment.   I should fear the judge's charge would be against me, let me plead as I might, and be his mercies as great as I could hope for.   It will be always time enough to end one's own history; and since I've escaped the British bullet and bayonet, during a seven years' service, I shall certainly not use either to my own disquiet. The smell of Tom's fry, makes my philosophy more cheerful.   It is, indeed, surprising how a man's griefs dwindle away toward dinner time.   Ho! Tom! are you ready?"

"Jes' ready, maussa," was the prompt reply of the cook.

"Let us eat, Lance. I see that Millhouse has his cleaver out already. Help me with an arm, my boy, while I rise to a sitting posture. I am no small person to heave up into perpendicularity."

Leaving our little group of partisans, for a while, let us return to the widow Eveleigh, on her route homeward.

CHAPTER X.

AMBUSCADE.

MRS. EVELEIGH, as we have already stated, left the city for her plantation on Wednesday, instead of Friday. The change in her arrangements, called for a corresponding change in those of M'Kewn, and the squatter, Bostwick. The latter, with his five confederates, or *employeés*, took their departure on Tuesday; and, well knowing the route to be pursued by the widow, sped rapidly for the Edisto, in the neighborhood of which river, they proposed to plant their ambush. Their departure was quite a relief to M'Kewn, as it greatly lessened the expense to which he was necessarily subject, so long as they remained in idleness, and in a vicinity so full of temptations.

We need not note their progress. Conducted by Bostwick, they were not long in reaching their hiding-places, and in taking such a position, west of the Edisto, as would enable them to fasten upon their prey at a bound. The excellent lady, unsuspicious of danger, set forth after breakfast on Wednesday morning, in her great family carriage drawn by four stout horses. The lumbering vehicle of that period need not be particularly described. It is very well known that the carriages of that day were huge, unsightly and heavy machines, very solid structures of wood and iron, which, even when entirely empty, were a sufficient burden for their teams. When occupied by our widow, her son, a youth of sixteen, a maid-servant of no small dimensions, sundry trunks, bags and boxes, filling up every foot of space—and condemned to a lonely progress over rough and heavy roads, it was inevitable that its movements must be slow. Accordingly, it made no more rapid progress than the plantation wagon which accompanied it, and in which several of the negroes found a place. One or two of these were mounted on mules, while others, the more vigorous, walked, easily keeping up with the carriage.—Among these were the half-dozen negroes, belonging to Captain Porgy, whom, as we have seen, the widow was so fortunate, and so firm, as to recover, with her own, from the clutches of Moncrieff. The overseer of Mrs. Eveleigh, Fordham, led the *cortege*, mounted on a clumsy, but powerful, sumpter horse, and armed with the well-used long rifle of the country. He carried, besides, in holsters, a pair of large but common pistols. Young Eveleigh was similarly armed. He rode, sometimes with his mother in the carriage, but occasionally left the vehicle for a little 'marshtacky,' or poney, of Spanish breed, such as is to be found very commonly about the parishes of South Carolina to this day—a light, hardy, lively creature, very small, but of great endurance. Young Eveleigh was a tall, handsome and vigorous youth, full of spirit, of a strong will and resolute character.

Properly armed, the party, including the negroes, might have laughed at any demonstration which could be made by the force under Bostwick; but, unsuspicious of danger, they had taken no precautions against it, and travelled as carelessly along as if their course lay through the pathways of the peaceful city. Sometimes, Fordham and young Eveleigh rode together ahead; and other moments they were to be seen about the wagon and negroes, in the rear; and, not unfrequently, when riding ahead, they were out of sight both of wagon and carriage. Bostwick had made all his calculations with due regard to what he knew of the travelling habits of the people on such occasions. The party had been suffered to cross the Edisto at Parker's, and had made some progress upward and toward the Ashepoo, when the hour for "nooning" approached. Of course, carriage and wagon were both well provided with the necessary supplies of provisions; as the lodging houses along the route, few at any time, and with long intervals, had been very generally broken up during the war, upon any but the great thoroughfares.

Fordham and young Eveleigh had ridden forward to find a

branch—a stream of water—or a spring, at which the party might stop. A turn of the road had taken them out of sight of the carriage. The region was well wooded; and the vehicles were passing through a defile of the forest, more than commonly dense. They had just passed an ancient Clubhouse, such as may be found, to this day, throughout the parish country of South Carolina; where, after the day's hunt, the gentry of the surrounding district rëassembled for dinner. The house had been disused for this purpose, during the war, and was now in ruins. The planks had been torn off from the frame, which stood up an almost naked skeleton. The floor was gone—the roof could afford no shelter. Weeds and grass, still in rankest luxuriance, environed the decaying fabric, in which, no doubt, during the heats of summer, the serpent and the wild-cat found frequent harborage.. Just beyond this spot, a heavy timbered forest spread away to the south, over a low, mucky tract, which the deer and the bear could alone inhabit. The road wound along the edges of this low region, pursuing the higher grounds. It was while the carriage was passing through the dark shadows of this defile, that it was suddenly arrested. The horses were made rudely to recoil, and wheeled about; the vehicle was thrust directly across the road so as fairly to close it up. The shock awakened Mrs. Eveleigh from a drowsy mood, while the cry of the servant-maid who accompanied her, warned her of some event which required her attention. At first, she fancied that the horses were unruly; but she was soon undeceived. The words of the negro-girl—

"Oh! missis, look a' dem black looking man! He da ketch de horse by de head."

At that moment the driver cried out—

"Hello! da'—wha' you gwine do wid my hosses?"

He was silenced with a blow from a bludgeon delivered by a hand which he had not seen, and which tumbled him fairly from his seat. Two or three men, covered with masks, and dressed with long, shaggy black hair, through which their wild dark eyes only were visible, now appeared at the side of the carriage, the door of which was torn open in an instant.

"Who are you? What do you mean by this violence?" demanded the widow, looking very pale, but speaking very firmly.

One of them replied harshly, seizing her by the wrist as he spoke —

"Come out, my good woman!—that we may have a good look at your han'some visage!"

"I will come out! Release me. I need no help."

"All right, ma'am; I'm all ciwility!" said the fellow, as he made way for her to descend. The negro-girl sat trembling in the carriage, after her mistress had got out.

"Out with you, Jenny!" cried the spokesman, taking the servant by her ears, and with so much effect that she screamed violently.

"Shut up your fish-trap, you ——," he cried, with a terrible voice and oath, "or I'll tear out your tongue, and eat it without bread or gravy."

The threat, and the action by which it was accompanied, caused her to redouble her screams, and to cling the closer to the vehicle; upon which, the other jumped in, and tumbled her out headlong, as if she had been a bale of cotton. He then proceeded, with singular industry, to search the carriage: possessing himself, among other things, of a richly inlaid mahogany case, which he drew from beneath the seat. By this time, his confederates had cut the traces, and freed the horses. The servant-girl continued her screams, until flung down, and her mouth bandaged—an operation which was performed by one of the assailants, with the celerity of an old practitioner. The widow Eveleigh, meanwhile, stood silent, anxious, breathless, with expectation and apprehension, but maintaining a noble and fearless demeanor. At this moment, a pistol-shot was heard ahead —then another, and another. At the sound the lady could not suppress the murmur—

"My son—my son! My God! protect my son!"

She clasped her hands with increasing apprehensions, while the new terrors in her face were too strong for concealment; her knees trembled beneath her, and she sank back for support against a tree. Two of the assailants had remained with the carriage. These started into activity as the sound of the fire-arms reached them. They came from the road in front, along which young Eveleigh and Fordham had ridden. A moment only did the outlaws pause; then, simultaneously, darting forward, they hurried in the direction of the scene of action. The widow watched them with eager terrors, as they sped along, chiefly under cover of the trees, pursuing the roadside, but avoiding, as much as much as possible, the exposure of their persons. Suddenly she saw them crouch beneath opposite trees, and, in a second or two after, the tramp of a horse, at a run, smote their ears. At the sound, one of them raised a light carbine which he carried, and which he cocked in readiness. He had scarcely done so, when young Eveleigh came in sight, pushing the pony to the utmost. Then was heard the cry of the mother—at the top of her voice—but very faintly, at that distance;—reaching the ears of the banditti only:—

"Back, Arthur, back, my son. Beware! beware! There are enemies in ambush!"

The youth seemed to hear, and appeared disposed to gather up his horse: but he was anticipated by the ambush. A shot was fired, and the little steed went down, forward on his face, pitching the youth over his head. The two assailants then darted out of their place of hiding, and threw themselves upon him as he was feebly endeavoring to rise. He struggled as well as he could, being evidently somewhat stunned by his fall; but what could his unhardened sinews avail in a struggle with two ruffians, practised in all sorts of encounter, with frames well set, and in the full vigor of manhood! While they held him down, preparing to bind his arms, the mother rushed toward them, crying aloud—

"Spare him, spare my son, and you shall have all—all! Any thing! only spare him! Let him rise!"

She did not wait to see the effect of her entreaty, but pushed in between the assailants. It was a noble exhibition of maternal courage, reckless for herself, moved only by the one impulse of love and devotion to her young. One of the ruffians seized her and bore her back, while the other kept his knee upon the breast of the youth.

"My son! my son! Spare him! spare him!" she continued to cry, "and I will give you everything."

"Shut up, good woman, shut up! There's no danger, ef the young cub will only keep quiet. There's no harm done him yit; and none will happen to him ef so be he has sense enough not to provocate us. I reckon he's done some mischief a'ready. See, Fire Dick"—to his companion—"both pistols is empty."

As he spoke, two fellows, masked and bearded like himself, with false hair, and great handkerchiefs muffling their heads and faces, ran toward them from above. To these, the bandit who had just spoken addressed himself—

"Well! How goes it?"

"Bad enough! Bill Sykes is on his back, and hasn't a word for a dog. This young bull-pup has laid him out with a bullet through the head."

A fierce glance from all parties was addressed to the young man; and, having secured the prisoners from whom they had most to fear, they drew aside for a moment to consult.

"What hev' you done with the overseer, Fordham?" demanded one who seemed to be the leader, and who was, in fact, the squatter, Bostwick.

"He's fast."

"You hevn't killed him?"

"No; only stunted him with a backstroke over the head and neck, and then tied him down to a sapling."

"Is he safe?"

"I reckon! He don't move, and kaint!"

"How was it?"

"Why, he got down to drink at the branch, and when he was drinking, Bill Sykes jumped out of the bush, and knocked him into the water with the butt-eend of his rifle. As the young fellow seed that, setting on his horse, he let fly at Bill, first one shot, then another, though I reckon 'twas the first bullet that did the thing. Then he wheeled about, and went off at full speed. I pulled on him, but 'twas only a snap; and we had to turn about, Sam and me, to manage Fordham, who had raised himself up out of the water, and was aiming to get at his horse and holsters, where we saw he had two pistols. But I gin him a settler, side of his head, which sprawled him, and Sam took up his horse."

"Well, we must see to business. Bill Sykes, you say, wants no help?"

"He's ate his last bacon!"

"Let him lie then, till we see to our work. We must pick up the niggers, and be off. There's not much time."

"Did you gut the carriage, Bost?" demanded one of the fellows.

"No! there's nothing much, I reckon."

"No money?"

"Not that I see — but I hevn't looked in yet."

"I'll see to that," said Fire Dick, otherwise Dick Norris.

Each of the parties darted off in the direction of the carriage and wagon, except Bostwick; who, having already quietly possessed himself of the mahogany box of Mrs. Eveleigh, which he had somehow contrived to conceal from all parties in the bushes, seemed to take the further adventure quite coolly. To him, as he stood, apparently meditating, the widow now advanced. Her son lay bound and writhing beside the road.

"Is your purpose plunder?" she demanded of the squatter. "Take, then, all that is in the carriage and wagon — money, goods — but release my son, and let us go."

"You've got money in the carriage?" asked the squatter.

"Fifty guineas only, which you will find in a small mahogany box beneath the seat."

"Hem! Well! What else in the box?"

"Nothing but a few papers of value to nobody but myself."

"We must see to that! Do you come with me. The young fellow has killed one of our people. That must be paid for — for, as the Bible says — 'life for life!'"

"Take all!" she exclaimed, "all — as I said before, and let us go."

"'Twon't do! We've got all that's *here*, a'ready. There must be *more*, ef you would save the young un from a dog's death."

"What, more! How shall I pay you? What sum? When?"

"We'll think about that! But, jest now, look you, I must put a little hitch about your arms."

He pulled a bundle of cord from his pocket as he spoke.

"You will not dare!" exclaimed the lady, drawing herself up with loathing and indignation in her face. Her indignation was felt by her son. The youth shrieked in fury, and writhed desperately in his bonds. But the ruffian was unmoved, and laid his hand upon the arm of the widow. At first she recoiled — her eyes were filled with such gleams of anger, as promised desperate struggle. But she subdued herself; feeling that any effort at resistance must only expose her to worse indignities. With this reflection she held out her wrists.

"Well! I call that sensible and civil," cried the ruffian; "but the other way, ma'am—behind your back, ef you please. You see, ef I was to tie your hands in front, you might gnaw through."

The calculating rascal! Again the lady recoiled with a natural feeling of loathing and indignation; again, however, the reflection of a moment caused her to subdue it.

"Now, ma'am, ef you please," continued the ruffian, "you'll jest set down with your back to this sapling. You kin lean agin it, you see. 'Twill be a help to you."

She sat down passively, and suffered herself to be fastened to the tree.

"Now, I'll jest warn you to keep quiet. 'Twill be no use to bellow, for there's nobody to hear you but our own people; and they'll not be overquick to help you, onless it's out of the world; for they don't like a woman's hollering when there's no help for it; and it won't take them much to make 'em knock you and the young fellow over the head."

With no more words, having made both the parties as secure as possible, the bandit turned off to join his comrades, leaving the widow with a soul swelling to bursting with fruitless indignation, with fear and ill-suppressed rage, for which she could find no relief even in feminine tears. But, when she looked upon her son, terror, in respect to his danger, suspended every other feeling.

"Oh! Arthur—my son! my son! What is to become of us? They will kill you, my son; they will kill us both!"

The son groaned in answer, and once more writhed desperately, but vainly, in his bonds. Exhausted with his ineffectual struggles and humbled by the sense of shame and impotence, tears, big and scalding, gushed from his eyes, which he closed, in very mortification, as if to conceal the weakness which he could not control.

CHAPTER XI.

A CHANGE IN THE ASPECT OF AFFAIRS.—THE MOUSE GNAWS THROUGH THE LION'S MESHES.

HALF an hour might have elapsed, or even a longer period, and the outlaws had all disappeared from the sight of the two fettered parties—having now addressed themselves to the duty of capturing the negroes, and overhauling the wagon, which slowly followed in the rear. But few words had passed between the mother and her son. They had nothing consoling in their thoughts, and no motive, accordingly, for speech. They crouched, gloomy, wretched, and full of apprehensions, on the spot, and against the trees to which they had been separately fastened; when the ear of the widow caught a rustling sound among the bushes behind her, and a moment after heard a voice, which she readily recognised as that of her maid-servant, Jenny. It was at this moment that she remembered that the ruffian who ordered the girl from the coach, and finally hurled her out of it, had called her by her true name—a fact to be remembered.

The girl had been much more fortunate than her mistress. It is true, the outlaws, provoked by her clamors, had bandaged her jaws; but they had neglected, in their anxiety to secure the widow and search the carriage, to bandage her arms also. The sly negro, in the general confusion, and not being a conspicuous personage, was allowed to crawl away unperceived into the bushes; and, in the variety of interests which the outlaws had to consult, remained, for a time, altogether unremembered. While the two, having charge of the widow, ran forward to plant an ambush for the son, the girl had found close shelter in the thickets—had succeeded in stripping the bandage from her jaws, and had so far recovered her wits, or her instincts, as to feel the desire of being useful. Keeping still the cover of the thicket, she had wound her way along the road, though at a safe distance from it, toward the spot subsequently marked by the struggle with young Eveleigh, and the pinioning of himself and mother; and now she stood, but a few paces distant in the woods, seemingly afraid to venture out upon the public road, on the margin of which the captives had been bound. Her object was to feel if the coast was clear. She could see her mistress and the youth, from her place of harborage, but the highway, up and down, was beyond her survey.

"Hi, missis, hi! Da me! Da Jinney! I jis' want for know ef dem black people gone."

"Oh! Jenny, yes; I don't see them!"

"Look up de road, missis, ef you kin. Le' me yer [hear] wha' you kin see up de road, fus, 'fore I come."

"I see nothing but the carriage, Jenny. I see no person about it. They are gone, but I hear a noise."

"I yer dat noise too, but he's fur away on de road. I kin come out den?"

"Yes you may—but look sharp, Jenny."

"Yer's me!" cried the girl, emerging from the wood. "Lor' a mussy!—an' he tie you, and mass Art'ur! De black debbils—he tie you, missis? You got knife?"

"Put your hand in my pocket—you will find one."

"I hab 'im—le' me cut you loose."

"Arthur first, Jenny," said the mother, earnestly. But the girl was already slashing away at the ploughlines which had been used to secure the mistress. In a moment her arms were free. The mother then seized the knife herself to perform the grateful office of giving freedom to her son. A few more seconds sufficed for this, and the youth sprang up with a new sense of manhood, and full of a fierce desire for the conflict.

"Now, Arthur, my son, fly to the woods—hide yourself—see if you can find a horse, and speed for help."

"No indeed, mother," cried the youth, resuming his empty rifle and pistols, which had been suffered to lie where they had fallen in the scuffle; "do you and Jenny take to the woods. Push down for the swamp, which is only a few hundred yards below, and there hide yourself."

"What do you propose to do, Arthur?" she asked in some trepidation, seeing him proceed to reload his rifle; the outlaws

having thought it quite unnecessary to deprive him of his pow-
der-horn and pouch.

"I must see after Fordham, mother. They may have killed
him, or bound him, as they bound us. If he lives, there are
two of us, both armed—"

"But two, Arthur, against six."

"Five only, mother, *now!* One you recollect—"

"Yes, yes!"

"Well, two against five, both armed, is no bad ambush: and
we shall surprise the rascals. You will see."

"But if poor Fordham should have been killed, my son?"

"I will revenge him!" cried the noble boy, driving home the
bullet, and, immediately after, bounding off along the road in the
direction of the spot where Fordham had been knocked down.
His mother wrung her hands passionately. She dared not call
out after him, lest she should alarm other ears; and it was only
with a great effort of will that she controlled her feelings, and
adopted the youth's counsel, by burying herself in the woods
beyond. Yet she only put herself in partial cover. Her anxiety led her still to pursue a course parallel with the road, keeping the same direction with her son.

It did not require many minutes to enable Arthur Eveleigh to
cover the space between, and to reach the borders of the creek
where the outlaws had attacked the overseer and himself.
There were all the signs of the struggle between Fordham and
the ruffian who assailed him; but Fordham was not to be seen.
While the youth looked about in wonder, he heard his name
called by some one in the wood, and reasonably conjectured the
person to be the one he sought. He pushed through the bushes
to the spot, and found him, bruised and beaten, hardly well recovered from the stunning blow by which he had been felled to
the ground—but otherwise not injured. He was tied down to
a sapling, as the widow and the youth had been; and beside
him, within a couple of feet, lay the corpse of the outlaw, stark
and stiff, whom Arthur himself had slain—a spectacle which
made the boy shudder, and grow suddenly sick; but which poor
Fordham had been compelled to endure for a goodly hour!

But time was pressing. The exigency of the case did not
allow Arthur Eveleigh to give way to any nervous emotions,

however natural. Their assailants, as the two reasonably apprehended, might be soon again upon them, and the youth, strongly exerting his moral nature, overcame his sickness, and cut the cords which fettered the overseer. Fordham, on his feet, rapidly recovered himself. His own rifle, and that of the dead man, lay together, with an old pistol belonging to the outlaws. Of these, Arthur and himself took quick possession.

"And now," said Fordham, "I want to see if I can make out this carrion."

And he stooped to examine the body of the slain man. But Arthur turned away—though a strange fascination seemed, a moment after, to compel him to gaze upon the face of the victim, from whose head Fordham had removed a wilderness of false, black, and matted hair. The whiskers came off with like readiness.

"He's a stranger to me," said Fordham. "He's a mighty bad face, and here's a cut over his cheek, a great slash, that looks as if 'twas done with a broadsword, and it hasn't been so very long. I reckon he was some tory. Your shot was well p'inted, Mr. Arthur—it's gone, I reckon, straight through his heart. It's worked a most amazin' big hole in his bosom. See to that."

The youth looked as directed, but turned away quickly.

"Enough, Fordham! We have precious little time. We had better be loading, and putting ourselves in readiness."

"What's to be done? Where's your mother?"

"In the woods with Jenny. I told her to push into the swamp where she could hide so close that a hundred men couldn't find her in a three days' search—"

"Onless it so happened! But you are right. And what now are we to do?"

"There are two of us—there are four or five of these outlaws. They have gone down the road, but will probably return. We can ambush them, as they ambushed us; we have three rifles, and as many pistols."

"Good, Mr. Arthur! But to ambush *them*, we must hide t'other side of the spot where they tied you and your mother. If they git to that spot and find you gone, they'll take the woods on us."

"True! Let's push for it, Fordham."

"I'm consenting," answered the other, who had just finished loading the two rifles. These he took on his shoulder. The pistols were loaded also, and the whole stock of arms pretty equally divided between the two. In a few moments they struck into the woods, Fordham taking the lead, and following the edge of the road, with a bold stride, yet a vigilant eye to every bush that stirred. He had recovered all his energies, and now showed himself, as he was, a thorough master of woodcraft. We leave the two in their progress; having almost reached the spot where the carriage had been halted and turned across the road. At this moment, and when Arthur, seeing nothing, was about to push forward, Fordham caught his wrist, suddenly, and drew him back into the shelter of the thicket. Let us leave them, and look after our outlaws for a while.

CHAPTER XII.

HOW BLACKBIRDS ARE TAKEN, AND HOW BLACKBIRDS FLY.

HAVING, as they fancied, secured the only persons who were likely to give them any trouble — having ransacked the carriage, and taken into their own keeping any small valuables which had previously eluded their search — our banditti, under the conduct of the squatter, Bostwick, now prepared to turn their attention upon the negroes and the approaching wagon. This vehicle might have been three quarters of a mile in the rear of the carriage when the latter was arrested, the inmates taken captive, and the assault made upon Fordham and young Arthur. Of these events, the negroes, by whom the wagon was accompanied and driven, had no sort of conjecture, at the moment when they happened. The road was one of those admirably circuitous ones, so common in our forest country, which seldom afford you a direct survey of the route for three hundred yards together; and, trudging on, with tongues incessantly employed, singing or talking, the negroes had ears for no sounds but those which they themselves produced. The wagon was mostly filled with stores, sugar, coffee, flour, bacon, blankets, and negro clothes. These loaded it rather heavily for the six mules by which it was drawn. To this load you may add, at intervals, two or three of the negroes, who, from temporary lameness, or a less degree of strength than the rest, were permitted, occasionally, to relieve their fatigue by a lift in the wagon.

One of these negroes, belonging to Captain Porgy, was, by the way, an expert violinist. His only possession was a cracked and ancient fiddle, the seams of which had been carefully, but roughly, closed with resin from the pine trees, gathered as he passed. With this instrument he contrived to increase the noise and the merriment which still accompanied their progress, and to lessen the consciousness of fatigue on the part of his companions. Pomp, or Pompey—that was his name—as might be expected, was a great favorite; and his plea of lameness, we may add, was not examined too closely by the driver of the wagon, when it was remembered that his violin could be made to work while he *played*. The negroes were fourteen in number, seven of them being the property of Mrs. Eveleigh, the rest of Captain Porgy—all of whom, with one exception, had been recovered from the clutches of the insatiate Colonel Moncrieff and his colleagues. These were all walking, with the exception of the wagoner, Tobias, Pomp, the violinist, and Dembo, a young fellow of sixteen—the two latter being within the wagon—Dembo looking out from the opening of the cover, in the rear, while Pomp occupied a similar position in front; the post of honor being naturally claimed for the violin. Tobias bestrode the wheel-horse immediately in front of him, and when Pomp was not actually playing, he and Tobias kept up a running commentary upon the ways before them, the events through which they had passed, their recent captivity in the British hulk, and their fortunate escape at the very last moment. Thus travelling and employed, the party at length wound its way slowly into the plain, at the farthest opening of which—perhaps a quarter of a mile distant—the carriage of the widow could now be seen, awkwardly enough, turned directly across the road.

The situation of this vehicle was first beheld by the pioneer of the party, an able-bodied, fine-looking fellow, named John, or John Sylvester, as he preferred to be called, after a former owner by whom he had been reared. John was a calm, and rather thoughtful fellow, of quick comprehension, keen sight, and good judgment. He stopped immediately, looked earnestly about him, and, after surveying, for a few moments, the situation of the carriage, he turned quietly back to the wagon and his companions.

"Look yer, Toby"—speaking to Tobias, the wagoner—"dem hoss of missis nebber tu'n dat carriage 'cross de road, as you see 'em. He hab somebody for tu'n 'em so, for sure."

"Ki!" quoth Tobias, looking out and drawing up his team, as he gazed. "wha' dat? He choke up de road for sure. Sartin, John, de hoss nebber tu'n 'em so hese'f [heself]!"

"Nebber!" continued John; "and you see nudder t'ing, Toby—de hoss tek' out and gone! He nebber tek' out hese'f."

"Da's true! Wha' dis!"

"Now, Toby, you hab eye! Look to de little wood ob scrubby oak; you see? You see hoss hitch, and der's a coal black hoss hitch wid udder hoss in dat scrubby oak?"

"I see! Coal black hoss dey, for true, John."

"Missis ain't got no coal black hoss, Toby."

"Nebber."

"Toby, I'm jubous, der's somet'ing wrong in dis bis'ness. Boy, you 'member dat d——n poor buckrah, Bossick? He hab big, rawbone, coal black hoss, same time he catch we, and carry we to town."

"You sure he been Bossick was catch we, John?"

"Enty I know! He big beard like goat, and head o' hair like wolf, nebber been blin' me so I can't tell the d——n blear eye son ob a skunk. I smell 'em out, same as pole-cat in my nose. I tell you, Toby, Bossick was the same poor buckrah been nab we. He de same one was ride de rawbone black. He can't fool dis nigger. I'm jubous dat is Bossick hoss you see dey in de scrubby oak. I'm jubous Bossick is yer in dese parts. I t'ink I feel de smell of de pole-cat in my nose jes' now. Dat carriage aint cross de road for nuttin' [nothing]."

"Well—wha' for do?" demanded Toby, in considerable excitement.

"Da's de t'ing;—but I tell you Toby, John Sylvester nebber guine le' Joe Bossick put he dirty, poor buckrah paw 'pon him shoulder agen! I nebber guine back to dat d——n salt-water hole in de wharf, ef I kin help it. You mus' do wha' you kin! You can't lef' de hosses—dat you know. But, dis nig-ger will hide hese'f in de wood, and be ready for a run; and you better gi' all dese niggers a chance. Better we bury wese'f up to de neck in de swamp, where we knows de varmints, dan le' 'em carry we off to de British hulk, I'm a t'inking."

"You right! But wha' *me* for do?"

"You stick to de wagon. You will hab for dribe, you know. But Pomp kin skip out wid me; and Dembo dere; and any ob de fellows wha' chooses, kin mek' track [run] same as you see me mek' 'em."

"But you aint guine run 'fore you see wha's a-coming?"

"No! But I guine to stan' ready for wha's a-coming, boy. You see dat close t'ick [thick or thicket] 'pon de lef' ob de road? I'm jubous der's some d——d varmint, like a poor buckrah, da's a-lyin' close 'pon de lookout in dat same t'ick. You dribe slow; I watch 'em. Da's all. You yer [hear], boys? Jes' wha' you see me do, ef you hab sense, you guine do de same as me. De lame nigger wha' can't run, le' 'em lie close and kick! Ef Bos-sick nebber see nigger legs 'fore to-day, I 'spec he will hab sight dis time! Yer!"

Thus warned and counselled, the negroes were all on the lookout. John Sylvester, for his own part, took care to suffer the wagon to keep between himself and the suspicious wood he had pointed out. Pomp, the violinist, slipped out of the wagon, still keeping his fiddle in hand, and followed in the steps of John. The other negroes, with one or two exceptions, seemed rather stupefied and undetermined, at the notion that they were in some peril of a return to captivity. They crowded together at the tail of the wagon, as a flock of sheep threatened an all sides. Tobias drove slowly, keeping up a soliloquy, in under-tones; which betrayed his fear to his mules if to no other audi-tors. In this way, the party had advanced about a couple of hundred yards, when a shrill whistle was heard from the thicket to which John had pointed. Tobias drew up at the same in-stant.

"You ye'r [hear] John Sylbester?" quoth Tobias.

"I ye'r, Toby! You dribe on! Don't you stop! Ef you see anyt'ing like trouble, gee de mule de whip, and push. We only seben mile from home, I t'ink."

"Wha' dat?" cried Tobias. "I see buckrah, for true."

"In de t'ick?"

"He da peep!"

"Ha! de d——d snake in de grass!" was the brief commentary of John, as, squatting, he peered beneath the wheels of the wagon. The mules were again in motion. Hardly had they advanced ten paces, when there was a rush from the thicket. A couple of fierce looking brigands, black with hair, and beard, and smut appeared a little in front of the mules, each carrying a rifle in his grasp. At that moment, John Sylvester disappeared in the opposite woods; Pomp, still carrying his fiddle, close in his wake. They had barely gained the cover, when three other bandits made their demonstration close beside the wagon.

"Stop, there, you d——d black Belzebub!" was the cry of one of them to the wagoner, who now began to whip up his weary and sluggish mules. The negroes, recovering their consciousness and energies, proceeded to scatter in various directions; but in a state of confusion, which left them doubtful which way to go. The mules were forcibly arrested, and taken out of the wagon. Tobias was tumbled from his perch, still grasping the lines.

"Hello! mussa! wha' dis?" demanded the poor fellow.

A rude blow of the fist, dexterously planted in his jaws, muzzled him completely; and while one of the party roped him, the others scattered in pursuit of the flying negroes. A terrible summons, followed by a pistol-shot, fired over their heads, brought three or four of them to a dead halt. In fear and trembling they suffered themselves to be caught and corded by a single pursuer. With these, Tobias, and a lame fellow in the wagon, the brigands found themselves in possession of six of the the fugitives. There were still eight to be taken, and, leaving one of their number in charge of the captives, two of the four dashed into the opposite woods whither most of the negroes had been seen to fly; while the remaining two hurried back to their horses, in order the better to resume the chase.

CHAPTER XIII.

"TOO QUICK ON TRIGGER."

It will be remembered, at the close of the scene that witnessed the extrication of young Arthur from his bonds, and the recovery of Fordham, the overseer, that these two had advanced to the place where the assault had been made upon the carriage; and that, when the former was about to emerge eagerly from cover, he was arrested suddenly by his companion, in consequence of some discovery which had been made by the latter. The discovery was that of the horses of the party, which, as we have seen, were all fastened to swinging limbs of trees, in the cover of a little clump of scrubby oaks. The quick, sagacious experience of Fordham, at once showed him the advantages which were promised by this discovery.

"Stop, Mr. Arthur;—we must think a little."

"What do you see, Mr. Fordham?"

"The horses! Our horses, and those of the inimy."

"Where?"

"Yonder;—in them scrubby oaks."

"We have them!" cried the youth eagerly, seeing the uses of the discovery at a glance.

"Perhaps!" replied the other. "The first thing is to know if any one watches the horses. We must see to that. We must fetch a compass through the woods, and come in on the back of them. I must give you a lesson in woodcraft. We are to see without being seen. If they see *us*, we lose all that we have gained. A rifle shot from behind a log may tumble both of us, and these rascals won't stop at a shot, if they see us making at them with we'pons in our hands. Let us round this thick, and git across the road above."

The caution necessary, rendered the operation a tedious one; but it was managed with perfect success by the practised woodsman; Arthur Eveleigh following promptly in his track, and emulating his circumspection. They wound their way under cover to the horses, and found them without any guard—the bandit needed all their forces for the pursuit of the negroes. In silence, and with great deliberation, Fordham proceeded to strip the horses of their saddles, which he concealed in the thicket. To remove the bridles was the next operation.

" What's the use of this, Fordham ?" was the whispered query of his young companion.

" To gain time—to make the horses as useless to the inimy as possible. But we will leave two of the nags saddled, and if you will lead these quietly, through the wood ahead, and get them across the creek, where we can find them at a moment, they will help you and your mother to git on. These rogues are all below us, I reckon, and looking out for the wagon. It's cl'ar they're aiming at a great plunder. They'll gut the wagon if we let 'em."

" But, couldn't we mount, and ride the rascals down ?" demanded the youth.

" And draw a rifle-shot from every bush as we pass ? No! no! Mr. Arthur, that would be to *spile* the whole business. We've got a *leetle* the advantage now, and I'm for keeping it. I'd much rether cut the throats of all the horses than mount them, *now*, when these scamps are scattered through the wood. But let us stir ourselves. Will you take the two horses down to the creek, while I keep watch ?"

" Yes; but what will you do with the rest ?"

" Turn 'em loose, and let 'em pick about the woods. They'll be so much harder to be caught."

" But why not take them all over the creek ?"

" I'm afraid; lest we should be caught, and be attacket *ona*wares. It's better so, as I tell you. Ef you don't like the job, Mr. Arthur, say so, and I'll do it while you keep watch here; though I'm rather the better hand, I'm a-thinking, to do the watching part of the business."

" No, Fordham; I'll do it."

" Hurry then, Master Arthur, and be back as soon as possible. With our three rifles, we can make these rascals feel very sore, taking them *ona*xpectedly out of these bushes. I'll not turn the other horses loose till you git back."

The youth had but three hundred yards or so to go, and he executed his duty with sufficient celerity, and with success. He crept back, and into cover, alongside of Fordham, with all the stealth of an experienced woodman. He was on his best performance, and taking his first lesson in war; and proud and solicitous accordingly.

"And now that we are ready for the rascals, I'll jest slip the bridles and let the horses free. Do you lie close, keep behind that log, and see that you havn't spilt your priming."

A few moments sufficed to let the horses loose, and then Fordham crept to a thick clump of bushes, some ten yards from the spot occupied by Arthur, and laid himself at length behind it. The horses, for a while, as if unconscious of their enlargement, stood with heads down in the same place. Soon, however, they began to turn, now to one side and now to the other;— anon they thrust their noses to the earth, and nibbled at the meagre grasses; gradually, they began to wander, and, after a short interval, to scatter themselves about the wood. Meanwhile, the wagon appeared in sight, and our party, lying *perdu*, beheld the rush upon it from the wood, and saw the result, as we have thus far described it.

Their turn was about to come.

"I count the whole five, Mr. Fordham," murmured Arthur crawling nigh to his companion.

"Yes; and they've work to do before they catch Jack Sylvester. He's off. It's him, I know, that walked this side of the wagon; and Captain Porgy's Pomp was jest behind him with his fiddle. With two horses only, the rascals will never catch them all in this world."

"They've gone after them."

"Three of them, I think. No; only the two mounted men. I still see three, near the niggers they've caught. They're tying them. Well—that's strange! I wonder what they can mean? They surely don't intend to steal 'em ag'in, now the British have gone."

And Fordham raised himself uneasily, as if disposed to take the field.

"Lie close, Mr. Fordham—they're coming this way.

"Sure enough: two of them! They're coming after the

horses, I reckon.   Well, with two off, in chase of the runaways, one minding the wagon, and only two to manage at a time, I think, Mr. Arthur, we ought to manage 'em. If we can pick off these two skunks, it 'll take more courage than I give the other chaps credit for, to bring 'em down to attack us in *our* ambush. Now, don't be too eager, Mr. Arthur—keep down your heart. Shet your lips close, and spread out quiet on your left side. Don't you cock your we'pon 'till you're ready to let drive. There's always time enough for that. Perhaps you'd better wait 'till I give tongue with *my* rifle, and then yours can follow at the chap that you see still standing."

"Let *me* shoot first, Mr. Fordham, if you please ?" murmured the youth eagerly.

"Well!   But I'm afraid you'll be too *on*steady ;—you talk like it."

"No! no !" answered the other, "you'll see."

"Well! well!" replied the overseer, good naturedly—"young fellows must begin sometime or other!   Only, Mr. Arthur, don't waste the bullet when you show where you take your rest. Don't let your heart thump so as to knock your eye out of the range.   See to that."

"I will !" in a subdued, yet agitated voice.

No more was said between the parties ; the approach of the two brigands requiring their utmost silence and attention.   On a sudden they were seen to halt.   They had discovered that the horses had escaped from their place of fastening.   One of them pointed to a couple of the animals which had wandered some fifty yards from the cover, and were now feeding up through an open pine ridge.   They both turned aside in this direction.   At this moment they were within long rifle range of the ambush.   The course they now pursued was calculated to take them entirely beyond it.   Arthur Eveleigh saw this, and, in his eagerness, his unwillingness that they should escape him, and perhaps from a miscalculation of the distance, he pulled trigger upon them.

"Too far--too far !" muttered Fordham—"I was afear'd he'd be too quick on trigger."

"He's got it," cried the youth, almost too loudly for prudence.

"Only a taste—a flesh-wound, Mr. Arthur," said Fordham, who could better appreciate the effects produced by the shot.

The man aimed at was certainly hit. He was seen to spin round for a moment like a top, while his right hand caught convulsively the left arm just below the shoulders.

"A little more to the left, Mr. Arthur, and the bullet would have bored him through the heart. Now it's only grazed the arm. He's got a taste, however, that'll operate mightily like a scare. They'll fight shy of us now, and we must watch that they don't fetch a compass round us. Lie close and reload."

Meanwhile the companion of the wounded man hurried to his assistance, and they both retired in the direction of the wagon. Here they were seen to tear off the coat of the sufferer, to examine and to bandage up the wound. The fellow laid himself down, leaning with his head against a tree. The dressing was soon performed, and Arthur Eveleigh was mortified immensely to discover, what was sufficiently apparent, that the hurt, as Fordham had said, was to the flesh only. Not a bone was broken and the blood was quickly stanched. The wounded man was seen to lift his arm without assistance, and, after a few moments of repose, he got up and joined his comrades who had now retired to the woods, as if for consultation.

CHAPTER IV.

LESSONS IN WOODCRAFT.

The whole aspect of the affair had now undergone a serious change in the eyes of the outlaws. We must enter into their councils for a moment. Close by the side of the road, but concealed amid the shrubbery which skirted it, three of the party had assembled, including the person who had been left in charge of the captured negroes. These, as they had all by this time been well secured with ropes, and were now grouped together at the side of the wagon, needed perhaps no close *surveillance.* Still, the party at the roadside, but a few paces distant, were ready, should there be any movement among the slaves. But they lay quiet, crouching close to the earth, and entirely subdued by their terrors. The two absent outlaws were still in pursuit of the fugitive negroes in the woods opposite. The three whom we now find in council consisted of Bostwick, the squatter, Ralph Burke, and Dick Norris—distinct persons all, certainly, but with such a family likeness among them, the result of great beards, mammoth wigs and whiskers, all of glossy black, and similar habits, that they could really only distinguish each other by their voices. Bostwick, as was proper, was the person to open the conference upon the state of their affairs.

"Well, boys, here's a trouble. These chaps have got loose, and how, is the puzzle."

"No puzzle, I reckon," answered Burke. "They've been ontied by that wench that you let slip out of the carriage. That's the how."

"I reckon it must be so," answered Bostwick.

"And how you come to let her slip, is a matter I can't see. You *would* take the carriage to yourself, and shet your eyes to hafe [half] the business."

"Yes; whar' was your eyes, Bostwick?" quoth Norris.

"In the widow's pockets, I reckon," muttered Burke, with a shrewd approach to the truth.

"I miss'd it sartain, somehow," replied Bostwick, composedly; "but that's not the matter now. It's *now* to see how we hev to mend the slip. It's sartin sure that Fordham and the young man are loose, and it don't matter by whose hands. I suppose the widow's loose too?"

"There was only one shot, Bostwick," quoth Norris.

"Well, what of that?"

"Well, that would show there was only one man. Now, it's not so cl'ar to me that Fordham's loose. He had quite too hard a hit o' the head to git the use of his eyes and fingers so mighty quick, ay, or his senses either. Now, if it should be only the young un."

"Hardly. He's not got the sense for it yet, though he's spunky, I know—I know him of old. I've seen and talked with him years ago, when he wasn't knee-high. Ef 'twas only him, we could soon sarcumvent him. But it's not so easy work with Fordham, who is a sort of man-fox, I tell you; as cunning as a sarpent, and with a mighty hard head and fist in a fight."

"There was but *one* shot!" quoth Norris, pertinaciously.

"Yes, and Fordham wasn't the man to shoot *that*, I'm thinking," said Burke. Ef he's the man you say, he'd ha' held back, *on*til he could ha' made a better mark with the bullet. It's the boy, I tell you."

"But suppose the man's along with him?"

"Would Fordham ha' let the chap shoot a minnit before the time?"

"I reckon he couldn't help it. The boy was always mighty hard-headed. But whether there's one or two, boys, there's only one way before *us*, and that's to find out, and take the back track upon 'em. So, up with you, Rafe Burke; we're the men for this business! We'll leave you, Norris, to keep an eye on the road and the negroes — seeing as how you're a wounded man; you're an *on*combatant, as they say, and kin only do hospital sarvice."

"Psho! I kin do as much as ever. This here is only a scratch, and a mighty leetle one at that."

"It come mighty nigh to making your cross, old fellow. The same bullet, only a *lectle* to the left, would have worked out a buttonhole in your ribs that no plaster could have shet up again. But, whether you kin do much or leetle, aint a matter now. You kin use your rifle at a push, and that's enough. Keep your eye on the niggers, and if Jeff Brydges and Tony Hines come in afore we git back, keep 'em in till you hear the whistle three times — three short whistles and a long one. You know what that means? Then bring all hands to bear. We'll want you."

"What's your first aim now, Bostwick?"

"To git on the back of these fellows, and see after the widow. Ef we kin git hold of *her* agin, supposing they've cut her loose and hid her, we sh'll be mighty nigh to making what tarms we please with her son and Fordham."

Such was the ruffianly policy of the parties. Bostwick and Ralph Burke now disappeared, pushing deeply into the woods, and carefully giving a wide berth to the precinct still occupied by the carriage, where they now knew the two honest men to

be in ambush. Meanwhile, what of these companions, the overseer and young Arthur?

We must not suppose that Fordham was so inexperienced a
woodman as to continue in occupation of the spot which they
had distinguished by the discharge of firearms. He knew better the necessity, so admirably practised among all the partisans
of this region, of changing the ground the moment they had
struck a blow, or in any way given reason to an enemy to think
that they occupied it. Scarcely had Norris and Bostwick retreated from before young Arthur's fire, than the overseer said
to his inexperienced companion—

"Now, Mister Arthur, this is jest no place for us! We must
creep out and off, and shift quarters. Don't you *rise*, for you
don't know what spies may be looking out in this direction now.
Take your rifle in your right hand, and crawl, as well as you
kin, sideways, tell you git to the end of that log, then twist
round, and crawl fora'd, in a straight track for the crossing at
the creek."

"What's to be done now, Mr. Fordham?"

"Jest now, nothing, but what I tell you! To creep out of
quarters in front of which you've cried aloud from the mouth of
a rifle, 'here your inimies camp.' You ain't to think that five
rapscallions like these, aiming at plunder, will give up the s'arch
when they know there's only two ag'inst 'em. They'll be upon
us ag'in, and it's my notion now to take up a position jest where
they mightn't look to find us."

"Shall we not push down to the swamp where mother's
gone?"

"No, no, Mr. Arthur!—there's some birds about your own
fields that could teach you better than that. They takes care,
when you're birding, to fly jest the farthest from where they
hides their family; and they take pretty good care, by crying,
and chirruping, and screaming, and dipping about all the time,
to make you believe jest the contrary. Leave your mother to
herself. I reckon they'll never do her any mischief, more than
robbing her of all she has about her. But *we* hain't got the
protection of a petticoat, and we mustn't risk anything by having a petticoat in our way. Do you jest follow now, as I show
you, never rising up once higher than you do now, tell I give

the word. One never knows when he's quite safe in sich an expedition as this; and the only chance is in jest playing the scout, as ef you had a wolf on one quarter, and a yellow painter [panther] on t'other. Pull up now—it's slow and tiresome walking, this, on all fours, or belly to the ground like a snake; but it's more sure than any other, and won't last very long."

Fordham led the way with a will, crawling forward with a degree of ease and rapidity which was quite surprising to young Arthur, whose practice had never been in this sort of woodcraft. He was for ever arrested by boughs of trees, fragments of the storm; by holes and hillocks; by vines and roots, that, bulging out upon the surface, and concealed by dried leaves, caught foot or hand, or rifle, alternately, and to his perpetual annoyance. He was, a dozen times, on the point of springing to his feet, and braving every danger, but that he was partly subdued by the reflection that his recent precipitation had already brought about mischievous results. Besides, he was watched by Fordham, who ever and anon put in his exhortation judiciously, to "take it coolly," "don't be in a hurry, Master Arthur," "only a *leetle* bit longer," and "it will soon be over." When the patience of the youth was almost exhausted, Fordham uttered the grateful words of relief.

"Now, Master Arthur, we can lift ourselves. We're in a pretty close thick, you see of gall and 'hurrah-bushes,' where it would puzzle the prophet Daniel to look us out. Here, do you lie quiet for a bit, tell I take a view of the field of battle. I'll not be long; and you shall hear me hoot, like an owl, when I'm coming back."

He disappeared almost with the words, affording young Arthur, who was buried on every side in the thicket, no opportunity for a single word. The place in which the latter found himself was a sort of wolf-castle, as, in the southern country, such places are apt to be called. The wild, matted, tangled, tough, and altogether indescribable shrub, which the woodman described as the "hurrah-bush," and for which we have no better name, constitutes, in poor soil, and on the edges of swamps and drowned lands, one of the most formidable and impenetrable of forest-walls; while the gall-bushes, which are apt to associate with it, mass themselves together with a luxuriance of top which effectually closes every aperture of sight. Beneath them the bear and wolf, of the wilder regions, or the hog and wild-cat in the more civilized, find their way, making the only avenues of egress and entrance; and these of a sort to require the hunter of them to crouch almost to their four-footed levels, with his feet half the time buried from sight in mud-puddles, while his hands labor incessantly in pushing the thick masses of shrubbery from his eyes.

Poor Arthur grew monstorus impatient in this gloomy abode. Fortunately, the season had been dry, and he had no inconveniences to endure beyond those of restraint. But, to a youth of his eager and restless temperament, this restraint was the worst of evils. His horizon was within reach of his grasp. The great trees above shut out the heavens. The wall of shrubbery about him left him no other objects of survey but the one monotonous wilderness of dull, green waste; and it was only by squatting and crouching almost to the earth, that he could pierce to the distance of a few yards along the dark and sinuous beast-paths that ran below—the highways of deer, and bear, of fox, and 'coon, and 'possum.

But Fordham was not long absent. Soon the faint hooting of the owl was heard, and suddenly the youth discovered the overseer within a few paces of him, winding along beneath the bushes like a black snake, seemingly without motion, and certainly without noise. The stealthiness of his approach caused the young man to start. His enemies, approaching with such facility, would have fatally surprised him. He learned a new lesson of woodcraft, and his humility increased with his caution, in the growing conviction that he had a great deal yet to learn —a fact which fast young persons are very unwilling to believe, and rarely discover for themselves, unless with the penalty of frequent bruises.

"They're travelling, I'm sure," quoth Fordham, with evident anxiety. "They're not idle, I could take my Bible oath;—but whar'? That's the question! They make no signs. They're fox-bred, all of them, and are now winding about in the woods, without turning up a leaf. We shall have to git closer into the swamp, Master Arthur, and put some good-sized pond on the back of us, so that, if they find us, they'll have to take us in front. Then we kin manage; only, you must let *me* tell you when to shoot. Ef we throw away another shot, it's next to throwing a scalp along with it, and I'd rather not part with mine; and I'll die hard, Arthur, before I see them finger your'n."

The youth caught the hand of the overseer, and pressed it warmly, but without speaking.

"We must back out of these 'hurrah-bushes,' and git upon the tussocky places, among the pines. Jest now, do you follow me close; I reckon we kin go ahead boldly in this quarter, sence it's *on*possible that these rascallions kin have got quite to these parts. Here, away, and don't be *on*easy."

"But my mother, Fordham!"

"Well, we shall push for one side of the same swamp that you told her to make for. As I told you, I'd a'most rether that she shouldn't be with us; for, though she's a mighty strong-hearted lady, your mother, yet there is no answering for any woman in a sudden bloody skrimmage, with, maybe, sharp shooting, and a wild Ingin-shouting at the same time going on. There's no telling what sort of supper these fellows mean to get ready for us. Stoop a bit, now, Mister Arthur, and keep close to the bushes; we've got to cross a leetle rising ground jest here, before we reach the swamp."

They were moving pretty quickly over this track, when, seeing Arthur a little too erect, the woodman caught his wrist and pulled him down.

"Squat—close—quite now—*es* [as] you are!" said Fordham, in a whisper. "Hist now, don't you hear?"

"Nothing! What is it?"

"There was a whistle, jest there to the right—hist! Again! Don't you hear it?"

Arthur fancied he did hear something like a whistle, but added—

"It's a bird's, Fordham."

"Ay—but a sort of bird that's born without feathers, Arthur! Creep, now—hands and knees—and take care not to jostle a bush—a leetle more this way. We must make for them cypresses, jest ahead; there is, likely, a pond behind them, and we'll put it to the back of us."

All this was said in a whisper. The two moved forward;
Arthur exerting all his will in subduing the eager anxieties that
diffused a feverish glow over his whole system. He was almost
breathless when Fordham paused, on the edge of a small tract
of soft ooze, which indicated the terminus of the little rising
ground over which they had been crossing.

"Now," said the latter, still in a whisper, "we'll work round
this little ooze, and git upon the tussock among them big cypresses. There are, you see, some *bay* bushes jest in front of
them, which will do to cover us. We must still crawl, for that
whistle is a little nigher than you reckon, and we must use all
our caution."

He led the way in the manner he described. Never did fellow, carrying two rifles, exhibit such agility. Arthur could
scarce conceive, though he beheld it, how the thing was done.
He found his one rifle, though a short one, and his pistols, a sufficient burden, pursuing such a progress, and, half the time, in a
crouching, or crawling attitude. But one of the rifles carried by
Fordham, was the German yager, short, and with a strap attached, which the overseer contrived to bind pretty close to his
body, and beneath it, when he crawled; the stock being just
under his left shoulder. His right hand grasped the long rifle,
which he held above the ground. The two soon reached the
designated tussock, and crouched quietly behind the bay or
laurel bushes.

"Now," said Fordham, "let us reprime. I reckon we've spilt
the powder from our pans."

He himself lifted the cover of his rifle pan with great deliberation; But the incautious Arthur threw his open without heed,
suffering the click to be sufficiently heard.

"Ah! Mister Arthur," whispered the woodman, reproachfully,
"that will never do. You've got a mighty deal to l'arn. That
click kin be heard jest as far as the whistle of that ere bird.
One talks to the other so as he kin *on*derstand. In these
swamp woods, so still as they are now, I kin hear the click of a
rifle fifty yards, and ef I'm not mightily mistaken, these scamps
can hear it too. We'll try 'em! Now—are you primed?"

"I am."

"Jest then give me your cap. Lie close now, and keep ready.

We'll just draw their shot, ef so be they're in rifle distance. You'll see what eyes these fellows have for an inimy, ef so be they've got round, as I'm thinking they hev', to the edges of the swamp."

He elevated the cap upon the rod of his gun, just beside one of the cypresses, showing the cap only, above a bunch of laurel. Scarcely had he done so, when the report of a rifle was heard. The rod was lowered instantly; the cap was untouched—the aim had been six inches below it—and the ripping of the bullet through the bark of the cypress, showed how narrow would have been the escape of a man occupying the same position.

"You see!   The cussed skunks!"

"Can't we get a crack at them, Fordham ?"

"Ef we could, I'd say take it; but lie close, and keep your fire.   I'll *riconn'itre.*"

And the shrewd woodman crept away down the bank-side and disappeared. Arthur soon lost sight of his person among the bushes on the right, and everything remained as still as if the region had never been inhabited.

CHAPTER XV.

THE FAT TURKEY WALKS INTO THE TRAP.

WHILE the youth remained, thus, *perdue,* confused and impatient, but, by this time, fully tutored in the necessity of keeping quiet and watchful where he had been placed, ten minutes might have passed; to him seemingly a good half hour. He was suddenly awakened to increased agitation and anxiety, by hearing a second rifle-shot about twenty paces on his right. He conceived, rightly, that this shot was from the overseer, and eagerly began to anticipate the necessity, himself, of taking part of the action. But a deep silence again followed, and ten minutes more may have elapsed, when he was suddenly conscious of a sound among the bushes as of a stick broken. He turned his eyes in this quarter, gauged it with his rifle, and, though expecting Fordham, stood prepared to meet an enemy. He was reassured by a chirp, not louder than that of the cricket from a split-log, and the next moment the overseer glided up the bank.

"You shot! What have you done?"

"Nothing much, I reckon! I didn't expect to do much, but mostly to give the skunks an idee that we were in different camps, and that they couldn't git at one fairly, without putting themselves in the way of eating the bullets of the other. I was tempted, as I seed a little motion in a heap of tallow-bushes; and, as I reckoned that was pretty much about the spot where their shot come from, I kept my eye upon it, and when I saw the top of the bush move again, I aimed pretty low down and blazed a way.'

"Well?"

"Nothing come of it, so far as I seed! I reckon I was a *leetle* too quick on the trigger, jest like a younger person, Arthur. But let us slip down this bank, and get farther along up the swamp."

"But when you drew their fire, by the cap, Fordham, why didn't you offer for a rush at them?"

"How was I to know how many rifles they had, with mouths full of bullets still? No! no! Master Arthur;—we are but two, and they are five, may be—certainly four—and ef thar's to be a rush made, why they are the proper persons to take the resk. We must resk nothing. We're on the defensive, *all* the time. What we must aim at is to sarcumvent them. We must fetch another compass, and change ground constantly."

Having, by this time, reloaded his discharged rifle, Fordham led the way for his young companion. Creeping along the hedge of laurel, but not so near it as to disturb a sprig, the two glided down the tussock, and soon made their way into the deeper shelter of the swamp. They now moved steadily upward, aiming, though by a circuitous progress, in the direction of the creek where Fordham was surprised in the opening of the affair. While thus moving, let us look into the camp of the enemy, and pierce their policy, if possible.

We need not detail the several fetches by which the two bandits, Bostwick and Ralph Burke, approached the point where we find them. Their route, like that of the party we have hitherto accompanied, has been a circuitous one—in recognition of the vital necessity, which existed, that they should not unadvisedly happen upon their foes. A proper knowledge of woodcraft, led Bostwick and Burke readily to conjecture what would be the game practised by Fordham. They aimed, accordingly, to accomplish a circuit so sufficiently wide, as to bring them, finally, in the rear of the overseer, no matter how much the compass he, too, might have allowed himself in the desire to attain a similar object. In this progress, they measurably accomplished their aims; and, but for the retreat to the "Hurrah" and "gall berry bushes," and the short pause of the overseer and Arthur in that place of refuge, they would, probably, have arrived at better opportunies than those which they enjoyed.

It was while fully conscious, from certain discoveries which they had made, that the fugitives were nearly within striking distance, that the two outlaws hid themselves for awhile; keeping a sharp watch, rifle in hand, within twenty paces of each other. Their instincts led them to divine that Fordham would seek the cover of the swamp;—and, upon this region they kept their eyes, from the centre of that elevated ground over which the overseer had so cautiously crept, leading his inexperienced associate. While lurking and watching thus, the eyes of Burke were the first to catch a glimpse of the youth's cap elevated above a clump of laurel. The bait took and he fired; to the great annoyace of Bostwick, who had seen it also, and had suspected the *ruse*. The parties rejoined, a moment after this shot, and, with a brief wrangle in respect to it, separated as before, and once more shrouded themselves among the myrtle and tallow bushes. It was, while recovering this position, that Bostwick drew the fire of Fordham;—suffering a narrow escape, the bullet actually cutting the cape of his coat, and razing the skin of his shoulder as if a cowhide had been laid on with a will. The fellow writhed under the smart, but made no other movement, and, after a brief pause of watch, in the hope that the secret enemy, whose bullet he had escaped, presuming on a more fatal result, would show himself, he readily conjectured, from his forbearance to do so, that he had changed his ground. But he waited still awhile longer; then, as all continued silent, he whistled to Burke, who answered him from his place of shelter, and both drew backward, crawling away in snake-fashion, and scarcely stirring the foliage which had given them shelter.

"We can't play these cards too nicely," said Bostwick to Burke, as they went some yards in the rear of their late position, and with the "hurra bushes" effectually concealing them from sight. "This chap, Fordham, is a whole team of foxes, and no mistake! We must git *across* the road, and push down quick for the swamp on that side—cross the creek and road at the same time, and come in on 'em from that quarter."

The plan was agreed on, and at once put in execution. Once in the forest, on the opposite side of the road, the two bandits made rapid progress upward; reaching the margin of the swamp in which, as we have seen, the widow Eveleigh had previously taken shelter, very nearly as soon as Fordham and young Arthur. But a considerable space now lay between the latter and their hunters, destined, however, to be rapidly overcome, as the overseer and his companion were also bending their steps toward the same creek which the bandits are now crossing. Once on the opposite side, the two latter struck into the swamp, proposing to pursue the course of the creek which wound through it, and place themselves in ambush among the willows and laurels by which it was skirted. But they had not gone far, preserving the caution which had hitherto marked their movements, when they discovered such proof of the near neighborhood of other parties, as made them momently forgetful of Fordham. The anxieties of the widow Eveleigh, in respect to her son, had made her unwilling to leave him, while there was any prospect of his suffering from an encounter with his foes. Though she had crossed the creek, and had consented to go forward on her route —keeping still the cover of the wood, under the guidance of Jenny, the servant-maid—yet with a fearful fascination, which she could not withstand, did she again return upon her own footsteps. Her track, going, had been detected in the soft ooze along the margin of the creek. It was followed instantly by the outlaws.

"Let us but git our hand on *her* ag'in," quoth Bostwick, "and we'll git a purchase on her son and Fordham."

Such was the cold-blooded calculation.

"Right!" responded Burke. "Son or mother, the one kin always be made to sell out for the other."

"That's jest as they have vartue and nateral affection. These will do it—but, let me tell you, 'tain't the case with many hundred others. 'Gad! there's some people that'd rether sell mother and grandmother, and son and grandson, then give up the hair of a nigger, or the shine of a dollar. I've known many of that sort—but it's no use to talk. There's man-beasts, Burke—wolf and tiger, fox and shunk, 'coon and 'possum, snake and spider—who don't know no law but jest to strike and swallow—and makes snares and steal, when they can't strike; and run, rether than fight, for their thievings! I don't know, old fellow, but we b'longs to some one of these breeds, ourselves; and we'd be bad enough, ef we wa'n't willing to resk our lives as well as our honesty. There's one I know, but——"

"Who?"

"Never mind—he's one who would cut his inimy's throat with *your* knife or mine, and take his neighbor's money with *our* hands; he's—but no matter. Now, this widow and her son are of the true grit—people of raal blood; and *raal blood*, Burke, is a vartue by itself, and by natur'. They'd die for one another!"

" We won't hurt 'em, Bostwick?"

" That's as it happens. We don't know what we may hev' to do. One must help himself, no matters who he hurts! We must use one of 'em to bring the other to reason. So—stop! —hist!"

The two crouched instinctively into cover.

" The turkey's walking straight into trap!" quoth Bostwick.

A whisper between the parties, and they stole off, still under cover, in different directions. A few moments only had elapsed, when Bostwick laid his hand on the unconscious shoulder of the widow Eveleigh, taking her by surprise, while the fingers of Burke griped Jenny, the servant-maid, rather tenderly than otherwise, about the nape on her neck.

"Jest taking a leetle liberty, my lady," said Bostwick, in a gruff and disguised voice.

She started and shuddered, but submitted with dignity; vexed to the soul, and humbled, that. once free from his clutches, she had not followed the instructions of her son and the overseer, and pushed rapidly from the scene of danger. She felt, in an instant, all the advantage that her second captivity would afford to the enemy. Jenny, the servant-maid, was overwhelmed with her terrors, and screamed, and continued to scream, until the enraged Burke, throwing her to the ground, crammed her distended jaws with moss enough to make an infant's mattress.

"I must take the liberty, ma'am, of giving your arms a hitch as I did before, but, this time, you must walk with me. I sha'n't leave you a second time out of sight."

"What is your design upon me, sir? Speak out! If it is money—you are already in possession of all I have about me. —If you require more for my ransom, and that of my friend, say so, and if it can be procured, I will consent to any sum, sooner than submit to this treatment!"

"Directly, ma'am;—that's for afterward. But, jest now, you must foot it along with me. Quick, ma'am, I've got no time to waste."

"But whither must we go?"

"Back to your carriage! I reckon we'll put you in it, right away, and send you home safe enough, after a leetle while.— That's ef you ain't obstropolus."

"Who are you?"

"A wolf, ma'am, or a tiger, ef you axes after my family and name. Come, ma'am, walk, or by —— I'll lace you with a hickory. I will, by thunder!"

This was plain language enough. The widow bestowed but a single glance of her large blue eye upon the ruffian, calm and strong, under the threat and indignity; then quietly moved forward in the direction which she was bidden to take. What was only a threat in the case of the widow, became an experience in that of the servant-maid. Gagged and on the ground, she resolutely refused to rise, till the enraged Burke, cutting a rod from a neighboring bush, laid it thrice over her shoulders. The argument proved sufficient, and she set forward with a speed that was studiously calculated to leave a space of five feet or more between herself and assailant; who still continued to threaten with the rod which he found no longer necessary to use in any other way. Again the party sped across the creek, and into the opposite forest, making rapid progress, and keeping vigilant eye upon the road which separated them from those woods, in the unknown retreats of which Fordham and young Arthur continued to find shelter, and where it was very well known they lurked and watched. Let us now return to them.

CHAPTER XVI.

SKIRMISHING.

THE overseer and his young companion, having struck somewhat deeper into the swamp, were necessarily compelled to make a considerable circuit in approaching the point where the outlaws had succeeded in recapturing Mrs. Eveleigh. The swamp, of irregular figure, thrust out a huge horn between the parties, the extent of which Fordham had not calculated. This was always pretty full of water, and not passable, except with great difficulty and inconvenience. The two were on one side of this horn, or arm of the swamp, itself a lake—while the outlaws skirted the other—the creek being between the parties also— when the screams of the servant-maid of the widow smote sharply on the ears of our wanderers. The first instincts of Arthur led him naturally to suppose that the cries were from his mother.

"My poor mother!" he exclaimed, passionately. "They have found her, Fordham. Hear! It is she! These are her screams. They are ill-treating her."

"I don't think!" returned the other, with interest, but still calmly. "Don't be scared, Arthur. I reckon they've found your mother, and have made her a prisoner agin, though she ought, by this time, to have been a mile farther on the road. But 'tain't *her* that you hear a-screaming. It's Jenny, the gal, I reckon. Mrs. Eveleigh ain't the lady to scream, I'm thinking. It ain't *like* her."

"But are we to stand here, Fordham, when there's no knowing what these villains are after ?"

"That we must try and see, Arthur. We must push on, that's sartain; but we mus'n't push on any faster than we've been doing. The only way to save her, and to save ourselves, is jest to play scout tell we kin git some advantage. Jest you leave the thing to me, and ef so be we're to work out of this trouble with whole bones, it's only by showing not a white of the eye to these skunks, until we kin speak to 'em safely by the mouth of the rifle. Let's push on, along the edge of this lagoon, as we're a-doing. It'll bring us out upon the road after awhile, and we'll see. Now that these rascals have got your mother, as I reckon, they'll not be able to work their way through the woods so easy as afore."

The youth felt that everything must be left to Fordham, in whose ingenuity and courage, as well as fidelity, he had full confidence, and the two pushed forward, still with great caution, worming their way along the edge of the swamp, Fordham taking the lead with equal energy and circumspection. They reached, in this way, the road, just where the creek crossed it, and there Fordham halted.

"Now," said he, "Arthur, do you keep close here in this cover while I take an observation of the country. I'll be gone only a leetle while."

He was gone somewhat longer than he himself had anticipated, and young Eveleigh was getting quite impatient, when the overseer suddenly reappeared. His countenance was grave and anxious.

"Well, Mr. Fordham! my mother?" demanded Arthur.

"Them's mighty sharp rascals, Mister Arthur," replied the overseer. "They've got back to the carriage, and they've put your mother and the gal into it. But there's no scaring the scamps. They've put your mother on the seat of the driver, and they've tied her to it, and the gal's tied inside. Besides, they've carried off the two horses."

The youth gnashed his teeth.

"You've seen her then—my mother?"

"Yes! she's put so that we *could* see her,—the d——d varmints! By that I know'd they're on the watch for us. They think that when we've seed her, and not them, we'll be such

blind buzzards as to show ourselves. But I see the trap as well
as the cheese. We'll not take the bait, Arthur."

"How do you know she's tied?"

"I reckon so from the way she sits, though I didn't go nigh
enough to see. I calculate that these scamps are lying on both
sides of the carriage, close in the bush, with their eyes running
close along their rifle-barrels. They know we're between them
and the creek. Now, as that's the case, our first business is
to work round on t'other side. We must take another fetch
through the woods."

"Let's be moving, then," said the youth, impatiently.

And the overseer struck out at right angles, as if wholly leaving the road. He pursued this course for a while, with a comparatively swift motion, and, after compassing a couple of hundred yards which brought them once more upon the swamp, he
turned suddenly to the left, and took a route parallel with the
road, which he followed with little variation for about thrice the
distance. Then, making another turn to the left, he made his
way forward, seeking a point near the highway, but at some
distance in the rear of the carriage. When he caught sight of
these objects, which taught him to believe he had gone sufficiently far, he restrained his youthful companion. They both
crouched, and went forward, steadily keeping under cover of the
shrubs, bushes, and long grass which covered this region. After
a brief space consumed in this way, during which they had
drawn nigher to the carriage, Fordham paused and whispered
to Arthur.

"Now you lie down snug. Ef I calculate rightly, these skunks
are now within reach of along-tongued rifle. I reckon that one
lies on t'other side of the road among them oak-bushes, and in
that tall dry grass. The other is, I'm thinking, on this side of
the road, somewhere among them water-myrtle and willow
bushes. Do you see your mother in the front seat of the
carriage?"

"Yes!"

"Well, I reckon ef she could speak, she could tell us jest
where these critters harbor. They're on a sharp lookout for
us now from above. But we're *here*, Arthur, and its always
half the battle when your inimy don't know where to look for

you, and when you can reasonably p'int your finger and say, 'Thar *he* is!' Look back, Arthur, and see ef there's anybody in the shape of a white man nigh the wagon."

"I see the negroes only, and only half of them, I reckon."

"Well, ef I could only tell how many of these chaps was here in front of us; but whether one or a dozen, there's no help for it now but patience. Keep you quiet now, while I do a little *snaking*."

And, so speaking, the woodman crept forward, close to the ground, frequently pausing to listen, and sometimes raising himself, whenever a sufficiently dense cover enabled him to do so with safety. In this way he continued to advance, until a space of thirty or forty yards alone remained between himself and the carriage. He was still pursuing this serpent-like progress, when Arthur suddenly heard his mother's voice, the tones eager, and full of anxiety and agitation.

"Beware Arthur—beware Fordham! You are seen! Your enemies watch you!"

Fordham was down in an instant, but Arthur, excited by his mother's voice, on the same instant, raised himself to his knees, rifle in hand, and eyes that seemed to have acquired all the far-penetrating and piercing power of the eagle. Almost in the same instant a shot rang through the woods, which whistled through the bush beneath which Fordham crouched, rending the leaves and twigs immediately above his head.

"Blast you!" cried Ralph Burke, who had fired, addressing himself, in the same moment, to the widow, "ef I hear another word out of your head, I'll cut your tongue out!"

He had scarcely spoken from his bush—for he also was buried among the leaves—when the bush was seen to be hurriedly agitated, and the widow heard another shot, but from what quarter she could not conjecture. It was her son that fired.

At her words, which had called him up from his crouching attitude, he had caught a glimpse of the flash which had preceded the shot of Burke, and obeying his impulse, he had drawn trigger at the same moment upon the spot from whence it issued. He knew not if any effect had ensued from his fire, for a deep silence overspread the scene; and he began bitterly to reproach himself with the precipitance with which he had again emptied his rifle without first making sure of his object. But, had he then known the truth, he might have congratulated himself in the language of Hamlet—"praised be rashness for it"—that he had obeyed his impulse without regard to the seeming impolicy of the proceeding.

> " Our indiscretion sometimes serves us well,
>   'When our deep plots do pall ;"

and so it was in the present instance. The almost random bullet of the youth had buried itself in the brain of the ruffian, and, with a single fearful spasm, he lay dead beneath the cover which had lately formed his ambush.

CHAPTER XVII.

THE CONFEDERATES CHANGE THEIR GAME AND WOULD CLAW OFF.

FROM the deep silence which covered the region, one might suppose that all the parties had suddenly disappeared. Mrs. Eveleigh had been warned to silence by the brutal threat of the ruffian, Burke ; and having, as she thought, sufficiently informed her son and his companion of the proximity of enemies, she was not unwilling to respect the warning. She knew not of the effect produced by her son's shot. The fact that it was fatal, was unknown, indeed, to any of the parties. Fordham had been suddenly made more than ever cautious by his narrow escape from Burke's bullet, and lay in supreme quiet in the bushes which sheltered him. Young Arthur had also sunk back into cover, quite ashamed of his own (assumed) rashness and indiscretion, and congratulating himself that he had not drawn the enemy's fire also.

Bostwick, in the meanwhile, conscious of the fact which Fordham had no reason to suspect, that the parties were now equally matched, and that all his hope lay in the excellence of his own stratagem, crouched more closely than ever in his place of ambuscade, with every sense quickened by the feeling that he had an enemy before him who, thus far, had shown himself a match for him in Indian artifice. In the practice of woodcraft he was now willing to acknowledge that Fordham was quite as good a man as himself. Of that which had been exercised by the opponents respectively, we have been able to report but imperfectly. It would need more space than we can afford to chronicle minutely those details, of which we have given an outline only. The fox-like doublings, the snake-like crawlings, the subtlety, stealth, keen sight, and foresight, equally, which had been shown by both sides, in their several approaches to, and recedings from each other, had been of the best school of stratagem, as practised by the red-men of America. The little practice of our *dramatis personæ* will, on a small scale, exhibit the characteristic features of Indian warfare, which, first of all, recognises the necessity of risking nothing, and of making a clear gain, without equivalent loss of all its advantages. Where the number is so small on both sides, the first necessity is to economize it. Art is to supersede brute valor. No perils are to be incurred except in cases of extreme necessity, and when the issue of main force is absolutely inevitable.

In the present instance, Bostwick and Fordham were equally impressed with the necessity of avoiding loss. Neither dared show himself, with the view to an assault, or any bold demonstration, as long as an enemy lay concealed and on the watch, with a rifle-barrel still unemptied. Thus, accordingly, after the space of ten or fifteen minutes after the several shots of Burke and Arthur had been delivered, neither of the parties had moved or spoken.

The first sounds which struck the ears of Fordham and Arthur were the faint whistles of a partridge. The latter, in his inexperience, really supposed them to proceed from the bird; but Fordham knew better. He now held his breath, if possible to distinguish from what precise quarter the sound had issued. He knew it to be a signal. It was repeated at slight intervals, and he found that it came from the opposite woods—the carriage being, in fact, directly between himself and the sound. He supposed it to be forty or fifty yards distant. Thrice did he hear it, and always from the same precinct. He could perceive no answer to it. Either, therefore, his late assailant was nigher to him than he had imagined, and therefore dared not answer, or he had succeeded in drawing himself off from the scene of action. He never once fancied anything so agreeable, but so little probable, as that the hasty shot of Arthur had done his business. But the conjecture of Bostwick led him more nearly to the truth. The failure of Burke to answer his signal—for it was his—filled him with doubt and apprehensions. He repeated it thrice, as had been agreed upon between them, and listened vainly for the reply. He at once reviewed all his ground, and, for the first time, began to lose his confidence in the enterprise.

"I'm jubous," he muttered to himself, "that Burke has got his fodder! There's but one way for it, and that's to back out. It's high time. Better half a loaf than no bread. Six niggers sure, is better than a dozen, with a ragged bullet to chaw into the bargain. I must shift the ground—git back to the wagon, bring the boys together, and take what we've got."

These results were slowly arrived at. Once resolved upon, the execution was immediate. Bostwick, with habitual cunning and caution, withdrew from his place of hiding, drawing back into the deeper woods, and without provoking any suspicion of his movement. The widow, from her seat in the front of the carriage, and who without actually seeing the squatter in his place of ambush, was yet aware of the spot in which he harbored, was totally ignorant of his departure. Once in the deep thicket behind, Bostwick rose to his feet, and sped down the road with all possible haste, in the direction of the wagon. There, also in concealment, he found his colleague, Norris, who, having heard the firing, had become exceedingly uneasy.

"Well—how goes it, Bost?" he inquired, as the other drew to his side. "Where's Burke?"

"Not in heaven, I reckon! Maybe in a worse place, if the preachers know anything about it."

"What? You don't mean—?"

"I reckon he's chawed his bullet. He don't answer the call. That d——d eternal Fordham! They've had a shot apiece, and the widow cried out, and Burke, like a bloody fool, must git out of the bush, and curse her, and shake his fist at her, and so draw'd the inimy's fire. Sence then, he's laid quiet, and don't answer to the call."

"But you ain't sure? You hain't seed for sartain?"

"No! He may be only barked a leetle; but there's no telling. I durs'nt ventur', as Fordham still keeps close!"

"And what's to be done?"

"Claw off—that's the how! Take what we've got sure, and be off. The boys not in?"

"Yes; they're after the horses. They caught another of the niggers, and we've tied him with the rest."

"Makes seven?"

"Yes."

"We must be satisfied with that, and be off. It's been a mighty hard business, and I'm getting tired, and scary too. We'll be having somebody upon us, ef we stay much longer. Better mount, and drive the niggers we've got, and make for Dooley's Cove. We ought to be there before moonrise."

"But don't you think we kin git something out of the wagon? A jug or two of rum, I'm thinking, and *pre*haps some other little fixings that we kin carry on the saddle?"

"Well, I suppose we might make a s'arch; but you mustn't be long about it. I reckon the boys hev' got the horses by this time. There's been nobody to hender, this time. Where did they go to?"

"Yonder, in the open piney wood, where there's grass, I'm thinking.. It's thar' the boys went. Hesh—thar' they come, bringing all the critters. What shall we do about Burke?"

"Do! What should we do? Mind what the Scripter tells us—'Let the dead bury the dead.'"

"But we don't know that he's dead."

"And we mus'n't resk the life of a live man to find out. Ef he's living, I reckon he knows what to do. We'll make a divarsion in his favor, and he kin then snake away to the swamp. Ef he's dead, there's an eend to his troubles, and we kin take care of his horse among us, and spend his share of the money! Ain't that sense, I ax you?"

"Right! But about the divarsion?"

"Well, look you—these chaps—this overseer Fordham—d—n his quarters, I say!—he and the young chap lie about the carriage now, a'most within pistol-shot. I'll put myself in the thicket thar'"—(pointing to a spot some fifty yards farther on the road, one third of the distance, perhaps, between the wagon and the carriage)—"and jest cover the track with my rifle, while you s'arch the wagon. Let Brydges and Tony Hines lead off the niggers. Have our horses ready to follow. Tell 'em to take the woods down for a mile or so, then strike into the old road for the burnt church; we can push a'ter them at a smart gallop, and overtake 'em any time. Anything more?"

"No! go ahead, and put yourself on the watch, and I'll make the s'arch. We must pick up some litte vallyables, if we kin."

"How's your arm?"

"Feels a little numbish, but don't hurt. It's only a skin transaction!"

"Now, don't be long about the wagon s'arch; and don't stop to try the liquor. That's your danger, Dick, you know."

"Psho! u taste kin do no man any mischief."

"But your taste is never less than a swallow, and a swallow, like what you takes, damages mightily the sight-seeing for a rifle. Be quick, now, in what you do, for the sun's lowering fast, and we've been too long a'ready about the business."

"Be off, Bost, and keep a sharp look out. I'll take care of what I'm after."

Thus the parties separated. A few moments sufficed to put Bostwick in his new place of ambush, covering all approaches from the direction of the carriage; and to set Norris at work in exploring the contents of the wagon. The two confederates, meanwhile, came up with the horses, which now, with one exception, had all been safely recovered. The negroes were then roped together as they were, set in motion, and slowly disappeared from the road; driven before the two outlaws on horseback. The movement did not escape the keen eyes of Fordham; and he groaned, in the bitterness of his spirit, as he beheld, first a box, then a sack, then a keg, pitched out from the wagon, as from invisible hands within the vehicle.

"Thar's the sugar," he muttered; "thar's the coffee; thar's the kag of rum! The varmints! Lord, ef I could only git a sight of the chap that's so active—it's not quite two hundred yards I reckon—I'd try what vartue's in a good rifle at longer shot than I like to use it in common shooting. But, Lord! what can be done?"

The soliloquy reached no ears but his own. He did not yet dare to speak aloud, or to show any sign of life. The very silence that prevailed around him, led him still to apprehend that his enemies were near him, and still on the watch; while Mrs. Eveleigh, still bound, and still in sight, preserved the quiet of one who was conscious that she had hostile listeners.

The overseer readily conjectured the game which the ruffians were prepared to play. He saw the negroes marched off by *two* of the outlaws. There were yet three as he conjectured, with whom he had to contend. Two of them were still, he supposed, in the precincts of the carriage; and the fifth man was in the wagon. To move against *him*, or to attempt to pursue the *two*, with the negroes, would be to expose himself and companion to the fire of the two whom he assumed to be on the watch for him. He was thus completely masked, and felt himself bewildered. To draw off from this dangerous neighborhood was his best policy, yet he dreaded the attempt under the *surveillance* (as he supposed) of his two enemies. We must add, in justice to our overseer, that his chief anxieties were on account of young Arthur. The devoted fellow never once forgot how precious in the mother's eyes was the safety of her only son. To remain quiet still longer, and wait the further development of the schemes of the highwaymen, was the conclusion to which the meditation of Fordham conducted him. To lie close, keep dark, and wait events, is, perhaps, the best policy, always, in any such contest, where we do not see clearly the prospect or propriety of action. He did not adopt this policy in vain. Hardly had he come to this resolution, when the scene was changed by the introduction of other parties. For these, however, we must open another chapter.

CHAPTER XVIII.

THE LAST DROP OF JAMAICA IN THE VETERAN'S BOTTLE.

THE reader will, perhaps, find it advisable to go back with us
to a certain small group of Marion's partisans, whom we left, *en
route*, from the camp of that chieftain, for the ancient settlements
upon the Ashepoo, which they had abandoned at the opening of
the Revolutionary struggle, to undergo the capricious events of
war. Captain Porgy, and his little suite of three persons, having
been making easy progress since we left them—have advanced
considerably on their way homeward, and are now almost within
striking distance of the Ashepoo. A few miles beyond it, and
the captain will once more be able to contemplate his ancient
homestead—the paternal house and hearth, the well-known fields
and woods—a once valuable property which had been transmit-
ted to him through three or more careful generations—he, alas!
being the only careless one of the race—in whose hands their
continued accumulations had constantly undergone diminution,
until now, when, what with his own profligacy and the misfortunes naturally following the sort of war through which the colony had just gone, his homestead was almost wholly desolate,
stripped of negroes, and covered with debt as with a winter garment.

Porgy had been a *fast youth*. He had never been taught the
pains of acquisition. Left to himself—his own dangerous keeping—when a mere boy, he had too soon and fatally learned the
pleasures of dissipation. The war found him pursued by debt
and embarrassments, as unrelaxing as the furies that hunted the
steps of Orestes.— He had found temporary relief from the hands
of usury, and may thus be described as falling from the grasp
of the Furies, into the worse keeping of the Fates. He held
himself very nearly a ruined man, when the war began; and
the loss of numerous negroes, carried off by the enemy, gave
him no reason to doubt upon the subject. His lands were mort-

gaged, the negroes gone, his debts cried aloud against him for judgment, and he had reason to know that his chief creditor was on the watch for his return. The cessation of war, which stripped him of his occupation, was an event which necessarily restored the common law to its fearful activity. The camp was now doomed to pale in the shadow of the court; arms must give way to the gown; and the laurels of war soon wither, in sight and from remembrance, when the tongue only is allowed to carry on the contests of human antagonism. The *pillars* in war, are notoriously the *caterpillars* in peace, and there was no blessed exemption, in the lot of Captain Porgy, from this distressing prospect. Of that he was well assured. He did not once deceive himself. He could, with sheer force of will, expel from his presence the gloomy prospect, but he had no imagination such as would enable him to look on it, till he made it grateful and encouraging.

To the strongest—nay, to the most reckless nature—there will be always something humbling and oppressive in the survey of such a situation. The questions "what is to be done?"—"whither am I to turn?"—"of what am I capable?"—"where is my resource?"—to be asked of himself, for the first time, and by the man who has already passed middle age, are well calculated to fling a pall over the prospect, and make the heart to shrink at the entrance upon the unknown void of life which yet spreads before it. Porgy was the man to feel, thoroughly, the discouraging and sad, in this survey; for he was a man really of good sense and many sensibilities;—but he had moral resources which kept him from basely cowering and whining beneath the cloud. He was only not so blind as not to see it with oppressive distinctness—to feel its pressure, to acknowledge the doubts and embarrassments which crowd upon his path;—not to shudder at them basely, or to yield to any weaknesses of mood, in consequence. Besides, he had a taste for pleasure, was not a little of an epicure—there may have been, indeed, some affectation in this characteristic—and he prided himself upon the fact that he could extract his morals always from his appetites. He took philosophy with him to his table, and grew wise over his wine. So, at least, he claimed to do.

We have seen him, in a previous chapter, resorting to this sort of remedy against the cares which he was yet compelled to contemplate—appealing to his appetites against his griefs, and seeking consolations against thought, in his last bottle of Jamaica. It so happens that in resuming our acquaintance with his party, we find him again similarly engaged. It is noonday and past. Our partisans feel the necessity of stopping for refreshment, on the route.

They have reached a pleasant spot upon the roadside, a rill of sweet water trickling across the sandy highway from a green copse that shelters it—and there are still a few bright drops in the corpulent bottle of Jamaica—one of a shape and size that we do not often see in use in these degenerate days. It was, in shape, an oblong square, with portly capacities, holding, perhaps, a trifle under a gallon. A netting of wire-grass envelops it, affording it comparative safety against the vicissitudes of travel.—The party have tasted of the beverage ere we come upon them. The bottle leans against a tree just above the streamlet. Tom, the cook, has been again made to descend to unstrap his wares, and prepare his hoe-cake and bacon. The feast has, already, in a great measure, been enjoyed. The only persons who still show an unrelaxing appetite, are the sergeant, Millhouse, the one-armed veteran, and Tom, the African. You may see that each of these carries in his hand certain fragments of bread, and broiled ham of corresponding dimensions, the latter *done to a turn*. The sergeant eats as if duly conscious of Tom's excellence as a cook, and—for no other reason. He is not silent when the expression of his gratitude is becoming.

"Tom," says he, " I shall never be able to eat br'iled ham of any other cook but you! You knows what a br'ile ought to be, Tom, and what hog-meat naturally desarves."

" I ought for know, Mass Millhouse! Maussa show me how for cook 'em hese'f. Mass Porgy fus'-rate cook! He 'tan' [stand] ober me when I fus' begin for l'arn. May-be he no cuss when I sp'ile 'em! Sometime I do 'em too much, sometime I do 'em too little; he cuss bote times, and sway [swear] he'll make me see h—l ef I do 'em so nex' time. Wha' den? I no want for see h—l, and I min' [mind]. I l'arn! Once I l'arn, I nebber forgit. Maussa hole me to 'em. He quick for cuss—

like the debbil!—Sometimes he lick! But, wha' den? I always hab good share of wha' I cook. Ef Maussa only hab skin ob de pig, he sure for gib me de yays [ears] and tail."

"He's a d——d good fellow, Tom—Cappin Porgy. I'd 'a been a dead dog ef 'twa'n't for him. But he seems mighty dull, these times, Tom;—droopy, I may say; like a young turkey in wet weather."

Tom looked with interest toward his master, who was sitting some steps off—reclining, rather than sitting—beneath a tree, with young Lance Frampton, the ensign, in attendance. In the low tones of voice employed by the sergeant and the negro, in this conference, they were quite unheard by the subject of their dialogue.

"I sh' um [see 'em]," responded the negro. "De trute is, Mass Millh'us—de bakin is most gone; de buttle, I 'spec' [expect] hab room 'nough for fill agen;—I most 'fear'd der's no quite 'nough lef' in 'em, to gib you and me anoder dram; and de army's broke up, de British and torys, day say, all gone; and nobody lef' for we ravage 'pon, and git new supplies. Da's it! Wha' we for do now, is de t'ing. It's dat wha', make Mass Porgy look like young tukkey in rainy wedder."

"Tom, old boy, we'll have to work for the cappin."

"You work, Mass Millh'us?—wha' you kin do when you only got one han'?"

"But I'm got a h—l of a big heart for my friend, Tom, by thunder; and when there's heart enough in a man's buzzum, Tom, he kin always find arms enough to sarve his friend, even if so be both hands are chopped off."

"Der's trute in dat, Mass Millh'us," answered the negro gravely with an assured shake of the head.

"Truth! By thunder, Tom, it's all truth! It's the body and soul of truth, and I'm the man to prove it! I'll work! The cappin shan't want! He can't do much, Tom, for himself, seeing that there's to be no more fighting, which is the only work that a gentleman kin do, without s'iling his fingers."

"Mass Porgy is gempleman for true."

"Let anybody stand up and say he ain't, and I'll gallop through him, by thunder!"

"I trot t'rough arter you, Mass Millh'us."

"But he don't need that. He's the man to do all his own fighting, and mighty glad of the chance."

"Fight like de debbil, Mass Millh'us! You take some more of dis br'ile?"

"No, Tome, no more;—and yet, you do br'ile it so bloody fine that—yes! You may fork over that bit. The small bit, Tom, keep t'other piece for yourself."

"I done! Ef der' was only de smalles' drop o' dat Jimaica in de bottle!"

The fellow looked wistfully toward his master. The eye of Sergeant Millhouse took the same direction; but neither of them would have dreamed of doing, or saying, anything, which might declare their wants to their superior. But it was in proof of Captain Porgy's claim to the character they had both been pleased to assign him, that of the gentleman, that he always duly considered the claims of the inferior, and anticipated their reasonable desire. As if divining their wishes, he seemed to waken up at this moment, and cried out from his tree, to Millhouse :—

"Sergeant, there's still a drop of the Jamaica for you in the bottle. Give what you leave to Tom. There's, perhaps, a tolerable sup for you both; but it's the last. I suppose, whenever we deserve it, the good Fortune will send us more."

Millhouse did not wait for a second invitation. Tom smacked his lips as the sergeant approached him with the bottle.

"Wha' I bin say, Mass Millh'us? Ef Mass Cappin had only de skin ob de pig, he will gib we de tail and yays."

"He's a born gentleman, by thunder; and we'll work for him, Tom, more hard than any nigger he ever had."

"I 'tan [stand] up wid you for dat, Mass Millh'us. I cook myse'f 'fore I guine le' Maussa want for dinner. So long as dere's 'coon and 'possum, squerril and rabbit in de wood, pat-tridge and dub [dove]—duck in de ribber, and fish in de pond —so long, I tell you, Tom will always hab 'nough somet'ing to cook! As for de corn, we kin make dat too. Ef you no got two han' for hoe, Mass Sergeant, you kin drop de seed."

"But I kin hoe like h—l, with one hand jest as well as two! Why not? By thunder, Tom, you must think me a sort of child, old fellow, ef you think I kaain't!"

"Well, Mass Sergeant, I know you hab de strengt', but it don't come so easy to de one-hand man. You hab de strengt'. You will help me pack up de pots and kettles, when we ready for start, Mass Sergeant?"

"Why not, nigger? To be sure! It's for your maussa, Tom, and I love him, boy, and I'll be his nigger, too, when it ain't *on*decend—that's to say, when there's no company. Ef a great colonel or ginneral should come to visit the cappin—Colonel Singleton, maybe, or the 'Old Fox' himself, maybe, or Ginneral Greene, or any other big person—why then, Tom, don't say work to me them times! I must be in my rigimentals when they comes, and stand jist behind the cappin."

"Da's right? I comperhend, Mass Millh'us! Every nigger to he own sawt o' bizzness. But, hello! Wha' dis I see. Der's strange pusson, Mass Millh'us, coming out de bush! Wha' for dat? Man da run! Nigger da run! He holla! Ha! look da' Mass Millh'us. Two nigger da' run. Enty I know 'em? Stop! Le' me see. Sure as a gun, Mass Millh'us, one ob dem boys is our Pomp. I lef' 'em a boy! He's grow a man! Wha' Pomp! Da' you? Ha! ha! ha!--ho! ho! ho! Lord ha' mussy [mercy] 'pon my eyes! Dey blin' wid water!"

We must account for these broken apostrophes hereafter. We owe it to Captain Porgy and *his* companion, to bestow our attentions upon them also, and see what have been their meditations while at dinner.

CHAPTER XIX.

PHILOSOPHY IN THE BEGGAR'S WALLET.

THE moment we choose for rëintroducing Captain Porgy, and his late lieutenant to our readers, is one which is usually found to fulfil all the conditions of happiness to the ordinary mortal. They have dined. Crouched at ease, under the shadows of an enormous oak, they have feasted upon the simple fare provided by the hands of their excellent cook, and have done the amplest justice to the thin slices of broiled ham, "done to a turn," and the brown hoe-cake, in the proper composition of which, Tom had established in camp the most enviable reputation. These constituted the sum total of their commissariat. The sufficient potations of oily old Jamaica had followed ; and with a sense of physical satisfaction which greatly brightened the prospect, Captain Porgy leaned back against the shaft of the tree, and closed his eyes in order justly to enjoy it.

That complacent sort of revery which usually occupies every mind, after the noon-day appetite has been subdued and satis-fied, had already seized upon our corpulent captain. Under its present influences, the state of his affair began to look less gloomy. The circumstances which more particularly pressed upon his thoughts at this juncture—the loss of his late employ-ment, the involvement of his estates, the supposed abduction of all his negroes, the danger which threatened at the hands of certain creditors—sharks, in shoals, lying in wait, like tigers of the land, seeking what they may devour—these crowding and dismal figures upon his landscape which, before he dined, had rendered his thoughts a very jungle, worse than Indian, of lions, tigers, and snakes of mammoth dimensions—with the consumma-tion of the noon-day meal, retreated from before his path, dis-armed of most of their errors, and, though still lurking and still hostile, looking so little capable of doing mischief, that our cap-tain began to wonder at his own feebleness of soul which had, but a little while before, so greatly alarmed him on their account.

A mild and soothing languor of mood, as if by magic, changed and modified all the figures in his landscape: and Nature, having gained time—which is the best capital, after all, as well in morals as in war—it was surprising how grateful and agreeable became the philosophy which she had taught our captain. He actually—to the amusement of Lance Frampton, who had tried in vain to soothe his melancholy mood as they rode together before dinner—began to chuckle aloud, yet unconsciously, during his revery, and finally afforded to his young lieutenant an opportunity to twit him, good humoredly, upon his sudden change of humor, by snapping his fingers in the air, as if at the flight of some enemy, whom he had successfully combated.

"Well, I say, captain, you don't seem quite so sick of life as you said you were before dinner. I reckon you won't be shooting yourself, as you threatened, only a little while ago."

"Well, boy, what then? Is life less loathsome because one learns to laugh at it as well as hate it?"

"But you don't hate it, captain—not now."

"No, and for a good reason—because I no longer fear it. I see the worst of it. I see all that it can do, and all that it can deny, and I feel, let it do its worst, that I'm the man for it."

"And what's made you so much stronger now to bear, captain, than you were only an hour agone?" asked the youth, with an insinuating chuckle.

"Dinner, you dog, I suppose—dinner and drink. Is that what you mean? Well—I grant you. We are creatures of two lives, two principles, neither of which have perfect play at any time in the case of a man not absolutely a fanatic or a brute. The animal restrains the moral man, the moral man checks the animal. There are moments when one obtains the ascendency over the other, and our moods acknowledge this ascendency. Before dinner, my animal man was vexed and wolfish. It rendered me savage and sour. I could not think justly. I could not properly weigh and determine upon the value of the facts in my own condition. I exaggerated all the ills of fortune, all the evils before me, my poverty, my incapacity, and the ferocious greed of my creditors. My soul was at the mercy of my stomach. But, the wolf pacified, my mind acquired freedom. The wild beast sank back into his jungle,

and the man once more walked erect, having no fear. Philosophy, my boy, appears once more to comfort me, and the landscape grows bright and beautiful before my evening sun."

"Well, all's right then, captain, until you get hungry again."

"Poh, poh! boy — sufficient for the day is the evil thereof.
God will provide. Vex me not with what to-morrow may
bring forth, or refuse to bring forth. To-day is secure. That
is enough; and the philosophy which to-day has brought, will,
no doubt, reconcile me to-morrow. Hear you, Lance? It is the
first policy in a time of difficulty or danger, always to know the
worst — never to hide the truth from yourself — never to persuade yourself that the evil is unreal, and that things are better
than they really are. When you know the worst, you know
exactly what is to be done, and what is to be endured. In time
of war, with the enemy before you and around you, you are
required to see his whole strength, give him full credit for what
he can do, and ought to do, and determine, accordingly, whether
it be your policy to fight, or fly, or submit — whether you can
fly — what will be your treatment if you yield, and what is the
reasonable chance of safety or victory, if you resolve to fight.
In time of peace the necessity is the same. Peace is only a
name for civil war. Life itself is civil war; and our enemies
are more or less strong and numerous, according to circumstances.
One of the greatest misfortunes of men, and it has been mine
until this hour, consists in the great reluctance of the mind to
contemplate and review, calmly, the difficulties which surround
us — to look our dangers in the face, see how they lie, where
they threaten, and how we may contend against them. We are
all quite too apt to refuse to look at our troubles, and prefer that
they should leap on us at a bound, rather than disquiet ourselves, in advance of the conflict, by contemplating the dangers
with which we think it impossible to contend. I have just succeeded in overcoming this reluctance. I have arrayed before
my mind's eye all my annoyances, and the consequence is that
I snap my fingers at them. As old Jerry Sanford used to cry
out when he was in a fight, 'Hurra for nothing!' Jerry was a
true philosopher. His motto shall be mine. Hurra for nothing
seems to me to embody the full amount of most men's matter
for rejoicing."

"Well now, captain, it's a fine philosophy, I reckon, that'll bring a man to such a sort of feeling. But, if I may take the liberty, I'd just like to know, how such a philosophy can put a stop to the trouble, make the enemy quit the field, drive the creditors off the plantation, and fill the corn-crib when it's empty? I ask these questions with your permission, captain, seeing as how you've been good enough to talk to me upon your affairs, and your debts, and the troubles from the sheriff that you're so much afraid of."

"Afraid of the sheriff, boy! Who dares to say that of me? Never was I afraid of a sheriff in my life. D—n him! Let him come. I have the heart, or I'm no white man, to take the whole *posse comitatus* by the snout."

"*Posse comitatus!* Oh, I reckon you mean the deputies?"

"Ay, ay — the host of deputies — a legion of deputies if you will, from the Pedee to the Savannah. But you haven't caught my ideas, Lance. I must try and be more intelligible."

"I thank you, captain."

"You know, Lance, as well as anybody else, that I've been a d——d fool in my time."

"Yes, captain, to be sure."

Porgy's self-esteem was not pleased with so ready a concession.

"Well, boy, I don't mean exactly that. How the devil do you know anything of my folly?"

"Oh, I can guess, sir."

"Can you, indeed?" with a sardonic grin. "You are too knowing by half, sir—presuming to know, for one so young as yourself. I mean, boy, that I've done a d——d sight too many foolish things. This don't make a man utterly a fool."

"No, captain."

"Unless he continues to do foolish things, mark you."

"Yes, captain, I see."

"Most men, the wisest, do foolish things. I don't know, indeed, but that wisdom itself requires to go through a certain probation of folly, in order to acquire the degree of knowledge, which shall teach what folly is —what shape it takes, and how it will affect us. I suppose that it was in obedience to this law of nature, that my follies were performed. But my error was that

I continued my probation quite too long. I was ambitious, you
see, of the highest sort of wisdom. I made too many experiments in folly, and found them too pleasant to abandon them in
season. The consequence was, that I began to grow wise only
as I forfeited the means for further experiment. My wisdom
had its birth in my poverty, and as it was through my follies
that I became poor, I suppose, logically, I am bound to say
that I was wise because I had been so great a fool. Do you
comprehend me ?"

"A little, captain; I think I see."

"You will understand me better as I go on. I wasted
money—a great deal—ran into debt—sold negroes—mortgaged others—and when I joined the brigade, my plantation
was mortgaged also—I can't tell you for how much. But,
even if the British and tories had not stolen all the rest of my
negroes, the sale of the whole of them would scarcely have paid
the debt then, and there's some six years' interest since. A
very interesting condition of affairs, you will admit, for my contemplation now."

"Very, sir."

"Now, to look fully these affairs in the face requires no
small degree of courage. I confess, until I had finished dinner
to-day, I was scarcely the man for it. But that last draught of
that blessed and blessing old Jamaica—did Millhouse and Tom
get a good sup of it ?"

"Pretty good, captain."

"They require good measure, both ! Well Lance, boy, that
last sup of the Jamaica seemed to warm up my courage, and I
resolutely called up the whole case, didn't suppress any of the
facts, looked at all the debts, difficulties, duns, and dangers, and
said to myself, 'A fig for 'em all.' Let the lands go, and the
negroes go, and still—I'm a man !—a man !"

"That's the way, captain," responded the youth, with enthusiasm, seizing the extended hand of his superior, and pressing it
with a real affection.

"It was just when I had come to this conclusion, Lance, that
I snapt my fingers. I couldn't help it. It was the spontaneous
sign of my exultation; and as I did so, I thought I saw the
d——d mealy face, blear eyes, hook nose, and utterly rascally

whole, of my creditor M'Kewn, back out from before me, and take to the woods at a full run. Along with him went the sheriff and the whole swarm of deputies, all of whom have been dodging about me the whole morning, shaking their d——d writs, ca. sa's, fi. fa's, and a thousand other offensive sheets of penal parchment in my face. I discomfited the wretches by that same snap of the fingers; and the adoption of old Jerry Sanford's cry of battle—'Hurrah for nothing!' has made me able to back poverty and the sheriff into the woods!"

"I'm so glad, captain!"—after a pause, was the response of Lance Frampton; but, with some hesitation, and perhaps not well knowing how to shape the question which he only desired to intimate—"but, captain, is that all?   Will it end so?"

"End how?"

"Won't the sheriff come again?"

"What then!   Give him another snap of the fingers, and the war-cry."

"But won't he take—"

"The property?   Yes!   I suppose after a while I shall have to surrender; but we'll make a d——d long fight of it, Lance; and we'll get terms, good conditions, when we give in—go off with our sidearms, flag flying, and music playing the grand march 'Hurrah for nothing!'"

"But, captain," continued the youth, "I don't altogether know. You're a man of learning, and can tell much better than me; but I'm rather dubious. When I was a boy, old Humphries of Dorchester, father of our Bill, you know, he sent the sheriff after my father, and took him, and took all the property besides, even to the very beds and bedding. Now, won't they take you, captain, if you can't pay?"

"Take me, boy!   Do I look like a man in danger from the claws of a sheriff?   No, no!   There will be blows in that business. They know better, Lance. In fact they are content, dealing with a gentleman and a soldier, to take his baggage-wagons, his *impedimenta*, and that purely out of kindness, as they desire to free him from all incumbrances. They will hardly attempt more. That d——d harpy, M'Kewn, will be quite content, I suspect, to take the plantation. There are no negroes left, I fear."

"But Tom ?"

"Tom! oh, ay! And you think Tom liable ?"

"Ain't he, then ?"

"Well, I suppose so. Tom is certainly a negro. Tom is certainly mine. As mine, Tom is liable for my debts, and it *may* be that some d——d fool of a creditor or sheriff may fancy that he can take Tom. But he shall have a hint in season of the danger of any such experiments upon my philosophy. I love Tom. Tom is virtually a free man. It's true, being a debtor, I can not confer freedom upon him. But let a sheriff touch him, and I'll put a bullet through his diaphragm. I will, by Jupiter ! If I don't do that, Lance—if there's no escape for Tom—for they may seize him when I'm napping—after dinner, perhaps—then, I shall kill Tom, Lance; I'll shoot *him* —him, Tom—in order to save him. The poor fellow has faithfully served a gentleman. He shall never fall into the hands of a scamp. I'll sacrifice him as a burnt-offering for my sins and his own. Tom, I'm thinking, would rather die my slave, than live a thousand years under another owner."

"He *does* love you, captain.

"And I love him. The old rascal, I do love him. He makes the finest stew of any cook in Carolina. He shall cook for me as long as I'm able to eat; and when I'm not, we shall both be willing to die together."

"Well, but captain, you was saying—"

"Ah! yes. We are supposing that all's gone, lands, negroes, baggage—all the *impedimenta*. Everything but Tom— and what then ? That is the point which I have reached, and to which my philosophy reconciles me. It is still possible for me to live."

"Oh, yes, sir !"

"How the devil should you know ? To be sure, I could live precisely as you and a thousand others would live; but you see, Lance, life is a very different thing to different persons. One man lives like a dog, a hog, a skunk, a 'coon, or even a cabbage. With such a person, you can despoil him of nothing by any process. You can not rob him. Thieves can not break into his premises and steal. Take all he has, and he loses nothing. He can still find grubbage—water lies conveniently before him in every puddle—and he may swallow air without even vexing the fears of a chameleon. He acknowledges only the principle of distension, not of taste or even appetite, and there is no stint of grass and weeds for a starving heifer. 'Root pig or die,' is with him the whole body of law; and his snout has long since been practised in finding its way into the potato-hills after the crop has been withdrawn. But to reconcile a man, with my training, to such a life, requires a rare philosophy indeed. How, with such tastes as mine, am I to live?—how dig?—where find potatoes, and with what substitutes for tea, and coffee, and Jamaica, refresh the inner man? That I should be able to cry 'Hurrah for nothing!' with perfect good-humor, after such a survey of my case, is the glorious triumph that I have this day achieved. Would you believe it, Lance, that I go out of the war with a paltry eleven guineas in my pocket? And this is all I really own in the world; but—"

"Captain!"

"Well!"

"I've got a *lettle* more than that. Here's twenty guineas that Colonel Singleton gave me more than a month ago. If you're willing, we'll put yours and mine in the same bag, and you shall have the keeping of it."

"You're a good boy, Lance, and I love you; but d——n your guineas. What should make you think that I want 'em? What should make you think so meanly of me as to suppose that I would rob you of your little stock in trade?"

"But it's no robbery, captain—I'm glad to—"

"Pooh, pooh! Put up your guineas, Lance. You'll want 'em all. Don't I know you? Are you not going to marry that pretty little witch, Ellen Griffin?"

"Well, sir—I reckon. Yes, sir, Ellen and me—"

"Give her the bag to keep! Don't trust yourself with it, or, in some fit of folly, you'll be for giving it to some other person, who will take you at your word. You will want all that, and even more, to begin your career in this world. As for me, I see exactly what I am to do, and will tell you."

"I'll thank you, sir."

"There was, many years ago, an old Frenchman, that came into our neighborhood. He was the most dwarfish and dried-up little fellow in the world. He was as poor as Job's turkey—"

"Why was Job's turkey so poor, captain?"

"I suppose that, being a favorite with Job himself, his wife never fed it. But don't interrupt me by asking such a d——d unnecessary question, Lance! As I was saying of this Frenchman, he was wretchedly poor, in purse as in body, owned no goods that I could see except the clothes on his back, and a miserable little single-barrel bird-gun, small in bore, but something taller than its owner. The only luxury that the old fellow indulged in was snuff; and with this, his upper lip, his shirt-bosom, coat-sleeve, and vest pocket, were all dyed deeply with a never-fading saffron brown. His snuff, gun, a supply of powder and shot, and an old box with some mean cooking apparatus, were his only possessions. I doubt if he had an extra pair of breeches. He alighted suddenly in the neighborhood, and presented himself before me, with a polite bow, and a most persuasive grin.

"'Monsieur Porgy, I yer of you! You s'all let me live on your plantation! Dere is one house ob log by de *leetle* swamp! Dere s'all be nobody live in him! 'Spose you s'all soffre me, I s'all live in him! I have no money to pay! I live by my leetle gon! I s'all shoot your little—de dove, de—what you call him, patridge, de squirrel, de rabit, all de leetle beast. I no trobble de deer, and de big bird—de torkey! Yuo s'all soffre me dat leetle house, and to hill, for my leetle dener, dese leetle bird, and de leetle beasts, I s'all be votre tres homble sarvant two t'ousand times, and s'all t'ank, t'ree, seven, eight, fiv' times ovair!'

"I consented to the very moderate entreaty; but offered that he should live with me—offered him money—but he refused everything but the simple privileges which he applied for, 'to liv' in de leetle pole house, by de leetle swamp, and kill de leetle birds and beasts.' There, accordingly, this poor fellow lived, for seven years, literally on nothing. He would accept no gifts, and even strove to put me under obligations. If, for example, he shot a pair of fine English ducks, which was sometimes the case, he would bring them to me with a grateful grin—

"'Monsieur Porgy, you s'll do me de ver' great honneur.'

"At first I accepted, but when he steadily refused my help, I refused his game, except as a purchase. His wants were few and easily provided. His powder and shot, his snuff and coffee, salt and sugar, oil and vinegar,—these he procured from a pedlar who went the rounds of the parish at stated periods. To procure these articles, he sold at the cross-roads, or to neighboring families, his surplus game. He planted a couple of acres of corn and peas, just about his habitation, which, under his cultivation, yielded twice or thrice as much as any two of my best acres. His food, besides, was wholly procured by his gun, yet he was not a surprising shot. But he was indiscrimate in his slaughter of 'de *leetle* birds.' He showed few preferences. If the dove and partridge did not come immediately in his way, he shot down woodpecker and blue-jay. The hawk was not rejected from his cook-pot. He luxuriated in 'coon and 'possum when he could get them, and with this object, he frequently went on the night-hunts with the negroes. His taste required that his birds and beasts should be utterly stale before he ate them. His larder was hung with birds, of all sorts, almost dropping to pieces, before he thought them well flavored enough for his palate. Then, with a little salt, oil, and red pepper, he made his meal with the relish of one who has eaten of a princely feast. He was always cheerful as a lark. He sang and even danced alone beneath his trees. He had been on the place for about a year, when he went off suddenly, on foot, to Charleston. When he returned, he brought back with him an old violin, the vilest looking thing in the world, but stuffed to the core with the sweetest music, which the old fellow brought out with singular skill. The instrument was a genuine Cremona—a famous fine one—which, as I found out afterward, he had left in pawn in the city. His happiness was quite complete when he had redeemed it. I often strolled out to hear him play. He had no apparent griefs. He never complained—never even fretted—was always ready with a grin of good humor—smile he could not, on account of the peculiarly ill-formed mouth which he owned;—and so, for seven years, he lived, entirely companionless. Yet he had visiters, and of his own countrymen. At Christmas, he sometimes had no less than three or four guests, who came again at the close of spring. Without bedding or covering, except the scantiest for himself, they remained with him more than a week on each occasion. I was curious to see how he would entertain them, and always paid him a visit when I heard of their arrival. He received them with open arms. They were welcome to all he had. True, he had nothing; but what then? He made room for them, gave place by the fire-side, spread a third of his room with pine straw, ground an extra quantity of corn and coffee; then, as they had finished their morning meal, he would say—'*Allons!* my friends—we s'all go shoot de leetle birds!' Each had brought his gun, and they knew that each was expected to find his own dinner; and he did so. I have encountered them on their return from a morning's excursion, and their bags were full—and such an assortment! They killed everything that crossed their paths, taking care, however, to spare the 'big birds and beasts.' *My* Frenchman, Louis Du Bourg, scrupulously respected his pledges. But, in fact, they all lacked the enterprise which required long and remote wanderings. Their largest visiters, of the bird kind, were the duck; the squirrel and the rabbit were the 'small deer' which satisfied their ambition in respect to large four-footed game.

"Now, Lance, what I have told you is a history. Poor old Louis Du Bourg is dead: but he has left me his example! I see exactly how I may live, as happily and as independently as he —that is, when all's over, and I have seen the worst. I shall then turn to killing 'de leetle bird and de leetle beast,' squatting on some great man's property. I can surely get this privilege from some of my old associates; and, with two acres of tolerable land, I shall hoe and hill my own corn; sow and dig my own potatoes; cook my own hominy; sell my ducks and birds when I want powder and shot, and be able, possibly, as I was once something of a hunter, to carry enough venison to market to procure me an occasional demijohn of good Jamaica. Perhaps, in process of time—but I need look no farther. Enough, Lance, my boy, that, like my old Frenchman, I shall be able, once or twice a year, to entertain my old friends. You shall come and see me, Lance, you and our friend here, Sargeant Millhouse; he shall help me set my snares, and you will help me kill my leetle birds and beasts,' and with a 'coon and 'possum hunt, by night, we shall lay in sufficient store of venison for a week's entertainment of any friends. There, boy, is a prospect for you; and, after surveying it, I can sing out heartily, and with a philosophy that is quite consoling— Hurrah for nothing! Let the world slide!—Sessa.'"

"Oh! captain," cried the youth, seizing affectionately the hand of his superior, "you sha'n't work—you sha'n't hill and hoe corn and potatoes, while I've the hands to do it for you! I'll come and live with you, and work for you—"

"You forget, Lance, you are soon to have a wife."

"True—to be sure," answered the other, staggered for a moment; but quickly recovering, he cried—"Then, captain, you must come and live with me. Ellen will be glad, and—"

"You're a good fellow, Lance, my lad, and I love you, though I don't think that I shall ever be able to become *your* guest. 'Twouldn't suit, Lance. It would be all right that you should live with me, and I must insist upon that, boy, until you are fairly married. For me, at the worst, old Louis Du Bourg's plan is the only one. It will have a look of independence, at least, and that is always a matter of great value to a person of my temper. But, hey! what's the outcry from Tom, and who are these? Help heave me up, Lance, and see to your weapons. It looks like a surprise!"

By dint of great exertions on his own part, and with the strenuous help of his lieutenant, the huge bulk of Captain Porgy was lifted into the perpendicular, and, in a moment, Lance and himself were prepared to make battle as if an enemy were upon them. The cause of the alarm was soon explained; and Tom, the cook, accompanied by Sergeant Millhouse, rapidly approached at the command of Porgy, bringing with them two of the escaping fugitives from the wagon of Mrs. Eveleigh; namely, John, otherwise Sylvester, the slave of the widow, and Pompey, junior, belonging to Captain Porgy himself.

CHAPTER XX.

TO HORSE! THE CAMP IN MOTION.

"Here's a smash-and-tear-it sarcumstance, Captain Porgy, as ever you did see," quoth Sergeant Millhouse, advancing before the fugitives.

"Der's John Sylvester, Mass Porgy, b'long to widow Ebleigh, and dis"—thrusting his hand familiarly into the wool of Pompey, and pulling him forward—"dis da' our own little Pomp, you know."

"Little! The fellow's as tall as you are. Why, Pomp! is that you, boy? Where have you been? What are you doing here? They told me you were carried off by the British."

"I git 'way, maussa! Dey tief me, but I git 'way! How you bin, Mass Cappin? God A'mighty! I so glad for see you;" and the fellow ran forward and shook his master's hand with the eagerness with which one welcomes the best friend in the world.—"Oh! maussa, it's de blessed t'ing you is come. You hab sword and gun. You mus' mek' haste now. De tory got we—got Ben and Bill and Josey, Little Peter, and all of we, and Toby, and Jupe, and Sam, an' all of dem b'long to Miss Ebleigh: and he hab catch Miss Ebleigh, shese'f, and his son, Mass Art'ur, and de obe'shar, Mr. Fordham, and de wagon, and little Peter, and all—only Mr. John Sylbester, yer, and me, Pomp, show 'em legs, and git 'way."

"What the d——l does the fellow jabber about? What's the rigmarole?"

"It's a surprise, cappin, and no mistake," put in Sergeant Millhouse, "a smash-and-tear-it business! as I said before. You see, the tories, so they call 'em, half a dozen or more, in mighty strange clothes and looks—"

"He face and head all bury in hair and whisper, maussa, da's true," interposed John Sylvester.

"Yes—you see?"

" Well !"

" Have laid an ambuscade for this lady, her son, overseer, wagon, and negroes, and these two chaps have slipped out of the scrape."

" Eh! What's this ?" demanded Porgy, at once beginning to perceive that the affair possessed some essentials of importance. " Do you mean to say that this ambush has been set to-day — that these things have only now taken place ? How long — fellow — you — what's your name ?"

This was said to John Sylvester.

" What! Mass Porgy, you no 'member me, John Sylbester, wha' b'long to widow Ebleigh ? I sure I 'member you fas' 'nough."

" No matter ! To be sure I remember you, John, and your great grandmother, too, if you desire it, but we need say nothing of either now. Where is your mistress, John ?"

" In de wood, Mass Cappin — on the road guine home to de plantation, jes' down by de leetle creek wha' run out of Turkey swamp. Dere we meet dem man in de hair and whisker. He shoot — I fear'd he kill Mass Art'ur and de obe'shar [overseer] — he catch misses — den he jump out 'pon we people wid de wagon, and I reckon he catch we all, only we two, me and Pomp, get off in de woods. Dey push arter us, but we lef' 'em in little green bay, and run, I 'spose must be most four miles, 'fore we see smoke. We creep up, and Pomp say — 'Da's maussa Tom, me fellow sarbant! I know 'em, like me own fadder !' "

" Yes: da me !" quoth Tom, interposing to confirm the report.

" And this *but now*, and only four miles off! and here, you d——d pair of long collards, you've taken a good hour to tell it. Boot and saddle, Lance ! Millhouse, to horse ! Tom, gather up and follow as fast as you can. John Sylvester — up behind Lieutenant Frampton. You, Pomp, jump up behind Sergeant Millhouse, and show the way between you. Ride apart, Lance, you and Millhouse, and see to your priming. Let these fellows tell when we are within three hundred yards from the spot where the affair took place. Give the whistle then, and haul up and move with caution. Don't dismount — we may have to dash in upon the rascals headlong.   I'll take the woods between you—let there be some twenty yards between us each.   And now, at a smart gallop, as soon as you can !"

It required but a few minutes to prepare the party in order for the march, as required.   John jumped up behind Frampton, Pomp took his place in the rear of Millhouse, and Captain Porgy, setting these two horsemen in the proper direction, dashed forward through the piney woods with a spirit and celerity that seemed scarcely consistent with his great bulk, and the languor which he had exhibited but a little while before.

CHAPTER XXI.

SCAMPER AND SCUFFLE; FLIGHT AND FIGHT.

THE negro guides did their duty with the exactness and promptitude of persons who knew exactly what was required of them, and what was the object of the arrangement.   They stopped the rapid motion of the horsemen when within three or four hundred yards of the spot where they conjectured the wagon had been left, and with that happy instinct which marks the faculty of the southern woodsman, they uttered their several warnings nearly at the same moment.   The horsemen drew up carefully, the negroes, John and Pomp, leaped down, and kept along on foot with the horses, which were now held at a walk; and, in this way, they approached the opening of the road, within eighty yards of the place where the wagon stood.

Here, Porgy was enabled to get a practical glance of the state of affairs.   They arrived at a fortunate moment.   The negroes, who had been captured, roped together in pairs, were marching off under the charge of two of the ruffians, who were both mounted, and were still to be seen moving slowly away into the pine forests in the distance.   Four other horses were discovered fastened to the swinging branches of a tree some ten or fifteen steps from the wagon.   The wagon-horses were hidden in the woods. The vehicle, itself, however, presented a singular appearance o!

vitality. The cover had been thrown off, and lay upon the ground on one side of it. On the other were to be seen bales, bags, boxes, and barrels; and, every now and then, something was seen to upheave itself within the wagon, to revolve slowly over the sides, and come down upon the ground with a heavy squelch.

Were the robbers all in the wagon, the two excepted who were to be seen going off with the negroes? That was Porgy's first question, which he soon answered, as he saw that the contents of the wagon were thrown out slowly, and separately, giving evidence of the presence of a single worker only. Where were the other three? In ambush somewhere—but where? A moment's reflection led our troopers, in a brief conference, to the conclusion that they were somewhere in front, between the wagon and carriage; and not in the rear, or on the route which they were pursuing.—The carriage was to be seen, and Lance Frampton fancied that he could distinguish the garments of a woman in it. Porgy surveyed the field with a military eye. A dead silence prevailed, broken only by the dull, heavy sound of the falling packages from the wagon.

"There is some bush-whacking going on still," said he— "some hiding and seeking, but it's not hereabouts. The fellow in the wagon works coolly and composedly, as if he had no apprehensions. If there had been any suspicion of danger from our side of the woods, the ambush would have been so placed as to have kept us from working so far forward. Our first duty is clear: we must pursue these fellows who are marching away, cut them off, and rescue the negroes. This will compel the ambush to show itself. We may draw their bullets, as we appear; but if we are sudden, with a shout, and go forward at full speed, we are very apt to escape the taste of lead. We can ride those rascals down! They are but two. Lance, you will keep back, and, with John and Pomp, contrive to capture the fellow in the wagon. Don't kill him if you can help it. We must get his despatches, and cut the secret of this expedition from under his tongue. Do you hear?"

"Every word, captain."

"Very good; now, if you will dismount, fasten your nag in the bushes, and creep forward with John and Pomp toward the wagon, you will probably have a good chance, the moment after we make our rush. The rascal will then jump and make for the bushes, or for the horses. In either case, you ought to be able to grapple him. See to it, and let the boys understand you."

The negroes were soon instructed, and betrayed a patriotic eagerness to be up and doing. Seeing that Frampton had fastened his horse, and was already advanced upon his way, with his sable allies, in the direction of the wagon, Porgy gave the signal, and, with a terrible shout from the throat of Millhouse, the two dashed headlong out of the wood in pursuit of the robbers who had charge of the fugitive negroes.

At this sound, as Porgy had anticipated, the outlaw, Norris, who had been at the work of unlading the wagon, naturally popped up his head to see what was the matter. The vigilant eye of Frampton saw it. He could have shot the fellow even in the single instant of opportunity which was thus afforded him; but he remembered his instructions, and forbore; wisely, it seemed, for Norris, seeing the charge of two well-mounted horsemen upon his companions, and recognising them as new-comers, whose reinforcement to the two customers whom they had already found so troublesome, might well lead to doubts of his own safety, concluded to see to this matter, without any regard to the spoils contained in the wagon. Seizing his rifle, accordingly, he leaped out of the vehicle, but with singular ill-fortune. His feet alighted upon a hamper of Irish potatoes, part of the contents of the wagon, which rolled away beneath him, and laid him at length with his face to the ground.

Before he could recover himself, Lance Frampton was upon him. The rifle of the outlaw was wrested from his grasp; and, with the vigorous young lieutenant grasping him firmly by the throat, John Sylvester by the legs, and Pompey, junior, literally sitting astraddle upon his back, Dick Norris resigned himself to his fate, after a few spasmodic but ineffectual struggles! The whole affair consumed but a few minutes, and was concluded by Lance Frampton securing his prisoner within the wagon by the strongest cordage, scientifically knotted; while John Sylvester, pistol in hand, was seated at his head, instructed to quiet him with a bullet, should he prove troublesome. Frampton, meanwhile, with Pomp, stole away to the bushes opposite, prepared to afford succor to his friends whenever there should be need and opportunity.

Meanwhile, Bostwick, the squatter, lying snug in his place of watch, contemplating his enemy only in the direction of the carriage, was confounded by the sudden appearance of the horsemen in his rear. With their shout and charge, he became almost instantly aware of the assault upon, and the capivity of Norris; for though the struggle had taken place on the opposite side of the vehicle, of which he had but a very imperfect view from the spot where he crouched, he could yet see enough to assure him of such an inequality of force between the parties as must be fatal to his colleagues. He was too heedful of himself to incur any unnecessary perils in the effort to succor his companion; and, indeed, could not well have done so, at least at that distance and with his rifle, as it was impossible so to distinguish any of the writhing figures upon the ground, as to be sure that he should not draw his bead upon his friend, rather than his foe. Besides, he well knew, that to show himself, in any demonstration upon the new enemies in the rear, he must only become exposed to the shot of those whom he felt to be somewhere harboring, and on the watch, in front.

To crawl backward — to increase the distance between himself and *all* these parties, his own as well as the rest — became now the selfish policy of the squatter. He could do nothing to help his comrades — the negroes would be recovered — two of his associates were slain already — he himself was in danger, unless he moved promptly away; and besides, he was already in possession of the most valuable of the *portable* spoils — the strong-box of the widow, having the important papers, as virtually important to the rich M‘Kewn as to the squatter, Bostwick — to say nothing of the fifty guineas in money, which, he had the widow's word for it, was in the strong-box also; and of which he had already determined to betray nothing to his comrades. It required no great argument to persuade him to be content with his acquisitions, and to draw off in season, no matter what fate should befall his companions. He crawled back, accordingly, slowly and with admirable circumspection; and so changed his ground as to place himself out of immediate reach of either of the several groups into which his assailants were divided.

But one anxiety alone prevented him from utterly taking his departure. He would, unhesitatingly, have gone, were he sure that his comrades were *all* slain, or certain to be slain, *without speaking*. But the doubt occurred to him.

"Norris is taken! Should he confess? Should others be taken and confess? Thar's the trouble. Thar's the danger and the resk."

This reflection disquieted him. He lingered in sight of the field of action, fully assured that he ought to fly, yet with that incertitude of mood which left him incapable of determination.

"If they confess," said he to himself, "there's nothing for me but to cut and run. The country would be too hot for me!"

Why should he not leave it? is the question that might occur to anybody else. But the wretch was not without his ties, his affections, his sensibilities, such as they were—and when he thought of the necessity of leaving the country, a picture of three young children—one tall, sad-eyed girl among them— grew vividly up before his eyes. He had a wife, too, but he saw nothing of her. It was the three children alone that formed the spell, so potent, about the heart of the bad and seemingly heartless man. Strange that such a creature should so feel and think at such a moment! Yet not strange either.

Let us follow our partisans. The wild halloo of their onset soon made their presence and purpose apparent to the persons they pursued. Looking about them quickly, one cried to the other :—

"Jimini! They're Marion's men, as I'm a sinner! Here's a fix! Cast the niggers loose, Jeff, and use a bloody spur ef you knows how. We must scatter."

"How many do you see, Tony ?" cried the other.

"Only two as yit; but they rush as ef there was a dozen. They've got the heels of us too, I reckon! There's no racing with such a nag as this. I'm for the swamp, Jeff! I can't trust the run, I must try the dodge! And you better do the same, but make your push for the hammock lower down. We must scatter !"

Wheeling to the right, as he spoke these words, one of the

outlaws made off for the denser woods which conducted to the heart of the swamp, and was soon lost to the sight of his companion in the thick undergrowth of that region. The other, whether less apprehensive of danger, or more confident of his horse, which was young and of tolerable swiftness, seemed to hesitate. He bade the negroes run ahead, and hide themselves; then, once more looking over his shoulder, he felt the necessity of going off at all speed, and did so with the best impulse of whip and rowel. Porgy and Sergeant Millhouse were soon up with the negroes, who cheered them with hearty shouts as they drew nigh.

"Da maussa!" was the cry of his own people, almost with one voice. "Hurrah, maussa! Gorrah Mighty bress you! How you do?"

"Young, boys, young and lively! God bless you! How many of these tory rascals are there?"

"Only two ob them, maussa; one push right ahead t'rough de woods—t'udder one gone keen for de swamp. Push hard, maussa, you sure for catch 'em. He hoss no better dan cow for run."

"Don't mind the fellow in the swamp, sergeant! We can look for him as we return. Go back, boys, to the wagon, and help Lieutenant Frampton to put the things into it again, or you will lose all your chance for coffee and molasses. Now, sergeant, as you are left-handed, take the right of this robber, while I take the left. His nag will be a good one, if we do not overhaul him between us in the next three hundred yards."

No more words! They were off, separated by an interval of fifty yards, perhaps, and coursing through the pine woods at a tearing gallop. A few minutes hard riding gave them a fresh glimpse of the fugitive. He was making up for lost time, and going through the undergrowth, and among the thick-set trees, which began to approach each other more and more closely, at a rate, which, to those who have never beheld a fox chase in the south, would seem sheer desperation. The fellow was a good rider, however, and an experienced hunter, born in the bush, and of kindred to the fox himself!"

"He goes well, but it can't last!" muttered Porgy, as he applied his *persuaders* anew to the flanks of his own high-spirited courser. It was wonderful to see how well the animal sped with such a bulk upon his back! But the steed was a powerful one, chosen heedfully with reference to the severe duty which he was required to perform. The fugitive looked about him as he fled.—The partisan captain could already count his gains. The space was reduced between them. The outlaw soon made this discovery. He extricated one of his pistols from the holster, and knit his teeth firmly together, with the air of a man who already anticipates the worst. Porgy was too good a soldier not to calculate on a certain degree of danger, in such an enterprise as that which he had in hand;—but, as he was apt to phrase it himself—

"Danger is a part of the contract! It is to be counted on, but not considered! He who stops to consider the danger never goes into battle! No wise man, embarking in such an amusement as war, ever considers its mischances as likely to occur in his own case. He knows the fatal sisters have singled out certain favorites for Valhalla, but he always takes for granted that they have overlooked *himself!* He relies, always, on his peculiar personal star, and goes into battle—not to be killed, but to kill!"

With such reflections, our Captain Porgy, corpulent as he is, was very apt to behave in battle, as we are told the Berserkirs, or wild warriors of the Scandinavians, were wont to behave. To dash, with a sort of frenzy, into the worst of dangers, totally heedless of them all, as if bearing a charmed life—and only seeking to destroy! And such a practice, by the way, is very apt to carry with it its own securities. A rage that blinds the champion to all dangers, and makes him totally unconscious of all fears, is very apt to inspire fear in the enemy who beholds his approach. The onset of Porgy was well calculated to prompt such feelings. A mountain in a passion, and in progress —a human avalanche descending upon the plain—crashing, rending, overwhelming, as it goes—such, in some small degree, was the image presented to the mind of the trembling enemy, seeing the headlong rush of our plethoric captain!

Our outlaw was soon enabled to distinguish his chief pursuer. He knew his man as he approached—knew his character—his fierce, headlong valor, the power of his arm, the fleetness of his steed. His mind became oppressed heavily, with the sense of whelming danger, as he saw the space lessening momently between them. He now saw his other assailant, Sergeant Millhouse, who, less rapidly, but quite as certainly, was making toward him on the right. He felt very sure that the game was up with him unless some interposition of good fortune—call it, if you will, his gallows destiny—should baffle the pistols, or the swords, of his pursuers. The outlaw had no remarkable properties of mind or courage;—he was only one of the myriad of ordinary men, who, as we are told by the dramatic poet, issue from one common mould; nature, after their being cast, ashamed of her own handy-work, and sending them forth into the world without putting any mark upon them! But he was a drilled and practised ruffian; had served for years as a soldier; as a robber; as a pirate;—and, from habit, and induration, was a man with whom the exigency only brought out the coolness, the determination and resource. He did not show his pistol, but he cocked it! He saw the course which Porgy rode, and he slightly inclined his horse to the right, in order that he should use his pistol-hand more freely. Porgy suspected his object and made a corresponding change in his own course. He was now sufficiently nigh to the robber to make himself heard. He accordingly cried out:—

"Halt, you d——d outlaw, and surrender, or I'll cut you down in your tracks!"

The fellow, slightly glancing over his left shoulder, "grinned horribly a ghastly smile," but made no answer. The captain was near enough, by this time, to fancy that he heard the click of the pistol lock; but it was fancy only. The outlaw had cocked it several seconds before. The latter glanced uneasily at Sergeant Millhouse, who was now approaching him on the right; and felt the necessity of crippling one of his enemies at once. By this time, Porgy was preparing himself also; but his slightest motion seemed to become apparent to the fugitive. Sharply applying both rowels to his horse's flanks, the great sabre of the partisan captain was drawn in an instant, and the flash of it, as it suddenly waved in air, gleamed unpleasantly in the eyes of the man it threatened. He kept his coolness, however, and his course; and, as Porgy came on with a speed suddenly accelerated, and while he was measuring the distance which he should first overcome before rising in his stirrups to execute the fatal stroke, the outlaw pulled trigger under his left arm.

The steed of Porgy swayed round at the flash, threw out his fore-feet wildly, then settled heavily down upon the earth, in the immediate agonies of death! Porgy, however, had sufficient warning that the animal was hit, and, releasing his feet from the stirrups as the beast was falling, he escaped from being crushed beneath his weight. He recovered his legs with some effort, but without injury. The horse of the outlaw kept on: but there had been a pause in his progress, which, however brief, had enabled Sergeant Millhouse to get almost within striking distance. But he was on the *right* of the outlaw, who, ignorant of the left-handed, and single-handed, condition of the remaining pursuer, fancied that some change in their relations was necessary to enable the other to use his sword. But he really saw no sword, and his object was simply to escape the pistol. But, against this, Millhouse was desperately resolved. He had hitherto kept his steed rather in hand. He now plied him with the terrible Spanish rowels which he wore, and which he never used but in extreme cases. To the surprise of the outlaw, who had judged of the horse by his previous performances, the animal made but a single bound or two, to bring his rider within striking distance; then, as the outlaw fumbled to extricate his remaining pistol from the left holster, he beheld, to his increased surprise, a gleaming sabre suddenly plucked from an invisible scabbard, and wielded, with a wonderful ease, in the left hand of his enemy! He bowed his body to the opposite side of the saddle, drove the spurs into his beast, bore down upon the curb to the left—almost swinging the horse about as he rode—and all this in a single moment—but all too late! A swift, sharp flash, as of lightning, seemed to darken his sight, and the next moment the keen, heavy steel might have been heard to gride through the solid skull of the victim. Down he sunk, hanging to one stirrup, while the frightened horse, dragging him forward, darted blindly into a clump of scrubby oaks, and became tangled and held, until caught by Millhouse. Captain Porgy came up a few seconds after; almost as soon, indeed, as Millhouse, who had just alighted to extricate and examine the body. They both bent over the fellow in this scrutiny, but to neither was the victim known.

"The face of the rascal is strange to me," said Porgy, "and that's a strange fact in my experience; for, in this seven years' war, I fancy I've made the acquaintance, in some way or other, of all the rascals in the country. Do you know anything about him sergeant?"

"Only that he *is* a rascal, captain, or was so a while ago; and that he's dead now as Job's turkey, with a loss of all the profits of his trade. I never *seed* him afore."

"The scoundrel! Had he been Christian enough to have suffered himself to have been cut down five minutes ago, and before that last pistol-shot, I could have been sorry for him! But he has done for my noble gray, the best of friends; a horse that has borne his own flesh and mine so long to the satisfaction of both! I feel, sergeant, as if I could blubber like a boy over his first colt!"

Our two partisans did not waste any unnecessary time, you may be sure, in a fruitless examination of the outlaw's body; nor did they consume much thought in speculating upon an event that had too frequently occurred in their experience not to leave them comparatively callous.

"See what the rascal has about him, sergeant," said Porgy; and, like a good trooper, perfectly aware of what such cases usually required, Millhouse searched the clothes, and turned out the "silver lining" of the pockets of the dead man, with all the dexterity of a Parisian chiffonier. He stripped him of everything of value; and, seeing that he wore a tolerable pair of English boots, he had them off in the twinkling of an eye;— though how the thing was done—*our* chiffonier with one hand only—it is as difficult to describe as to conceive. His search into the pockets of the outlaw was productive of no very astonishing results. They yielded up only a few English shillings and sixpences, an empty flask—the odor of which still pungently declared for its former contents—a clasp, and a dirk-knife, extra flints and steel, a small finger-ring, and the fragment of a bracelet or necklace. The ring had been worn about the neck, suspended by a faded and soiled riband, which had once been blue. Of what was this the miserable token? Was it love, or gratitude, or a filial feeling, which had hung this ornament about the neck of the ruffian? There is no record! The memorial was of a nameless virtue!

Captain Porgy surveyed these things, as they were severally produced by the search of the sergeant, and, after the scrutiny was over, he yielded them, with the grace of a feudal baron, to the possession of the latter.

"Keep 'em, Millhouse, until you find the proper heirs for them."

The sergeant grinned, as he replied—

"I reckon they'll be rether slow, cappin, to ask after 'em."

"Send them to me, should they ever be so bold, and these shall furnish my answer," quoth Porgy, at the same time taking possession of the holsters and pistols—a very useful pair of the bull species—which the outlaw had carried.

"These and the horse shall be mine, Millhouse; and then I lose by the exchange. My brave old gray! He was worth a score of such nags as this!"

And here he walked round the still trembling animal, taken from the outlaw.

"Yet he must do! He has bone and strength enough, perhaps, for a season in camp—peace and no active service! He will do to ride about the plantation, and for a Saturday hunt. He *must* do. The devil take the unchristian dog who should kill a man's horse in sheer wantonness, and when it couldn't profit him at all!"

"He worn't to know that, cappin," was the suggestion of Millhouse.

"He's wiser by this time! He *should* have known it. Did he expect to escape us both? Did he think I'd leave such an animal as mine unrevenged? If you hadn't cut him down, sergeant, and I had laid hands on him, I'd have scalped him! As it is, considering his condition, I forgive him. God forbid that I should harbor malice against the dead. But, were he living!— were he living!"

CHAPTER XXII.

DELIVERANCE.

OUR captain of partisans, after this ebullition of pagan feeling and Christian philosophy, having mounted the horse of the ruffian, taken, perforce, in exchange for his own, proceeded, in considerable sulliness, in the direction of the scene of former action, and where Lance Frampton remained in possession of the wagon. He was followed, more slowly, by Millhouse; that excellent trooper, following a practice that had been too much taught by the cruel war through which he had gone, leaving the carcass of the slain outlaw upon the spot where he had fallen— having no sort of notion, apparently, that humanity required him to give it better sepulture than that afforded by a wintry forest. We shall see, however, that the sergeant's omissions were repaired, at a more becoming moment, by his superior.

The negroes, meanwhile, still roped in pairs, had returned in safety to the wagon, and had been set free from their villein bonds by the ready *couteau de chasse* of Lieutenant Frampton. Our captain, on his return, found the latter in quiet possession of the field of action, with the ruffian Norris well hampered with ploughlines under the tail of the wagon, and yoked to one of the wheels. He deigned but a single glance at the captive, who lay coiled up like a snake, looking quite as full of venom, and just as ready for the spring at his enemy's breast. But the ability no longer seconded the will. Captain Porgy could spare as little of his regard to the grouped negroes, who were all busy in repacking the wagon with its contents, which had been so unceremoniously tumbled out by the captive outlaw. He had recognised the voice of his own slaves, even in the hurry of his pursuit of the fugitives; but he had not then scanned their faces. Their familiar features, and affectionate assurances of love, touched the soul of the sensual and the selfish soldier, who was not wholly made of clay.

"Thank you, boys—thank you, my good fellows. God bless you! I'm really glad to see you again, all of you; and to see that the tories havn't quite eaten you all; but, as for shaking hands just now, that's impossible. We must do our work first. Keep at yours, like good fellows; shovel in the kegs; and you shall all be rewarded. But now to business; and first, Lance, about the carriage, the widow and her party, and the rest of these robbers. What is your report? What have you seen? What heard? Speak—we have no time to lose!"

"Well, captain, there's nothing to report but what you see for yourself. *There's* the lady, I reckon—it's a woman, you see, sitting bolt upright in the front seat of the carriage. At least, it looks like a woman, by the dress; but I hain't seen it move once since I've been watching it. I've seen nobody, and nothing else, though I've kept a bright look out over all the track between, and the boys have been scouting jest about here, and within reach of my rifle. I didn't want them to risk themselves by going too nigh to the carriage."

"You were right, particularly as you could see nothing stirring in that quarter. *That's* something singular. Our demonstration should have caused Fordham and young Eveleigh to show themselves, unless, indeed, they were hurt, or felt themselves to be watched by enemies. Have you kept your eyes, Lance, on that long grass around the carriage?"

"Yes, sir, pretty much, but couldn't see so much as a sparrow stirring anywhere. It's a dead calm, as far as I could see."

"Strange! We've chased two of these rascals. Here's a third. Are there more of them? John and Pomp reported half a dozen or more. They were probably mistaken. How now, Pomp—John?"

The two negroes disagreed; but they were positive as to five or six assailants on the ground.

"S'pose you ask *him*, captain," said Lance, pointing to the captive outlaw.

"To be sure—right! Hark ye, fellow, who are you. What's your name? And how many had you in your company?"

The fellow glared up fiercely at the inquirer, but made no answer.

"Sullen, eh? Well, we will find a way to make you speak!

There's no use to waste words upon this scoundrel. We must put him to the hempen question! A rope, with a swinging limb at one end and a rogue at the other, will probably find an answer quick enough, and sometimes even rises into eloquence. The short way, now, is the best. Mount you, Lance, and we'll all three make a rush for the carriage. We can't be mousing all day with fruitless conjectures. Here comes Tom, too, just in season. We can trust him to keep watch over this rascal. Here, Tom, 'light, and take these pistols—keep them within six inches of this fellow's head; and give him his physic, a full dose from both bottles, if he offers to give you trouble, or if anybody comes to help him. 'Light, I say, you lazy rascal, and be quick!"

"Ki! Mass Porgy!—you talk as ef I hadn't a hundred poun' of pot and kettle on dis nigger t'ighs [thighs]! Gib 'em time, I tell you! Here, you boys! You Pomp, and John, and Dick, and Bob—enty I know you all, you han'some pot-black rascals! You no see wha' I want? Help tak' off some of dese pretic'lars wha' I hab yer—'nough to bury any man, eben ef he bin name Samson!"

The negroes eagerly went to Tom's assistance.

"Why, brudder Tom you *is* load mos' like a mule," quoth John almost pulling away the thigh of the cook in the endeavor to withdraw a gridiron, without first remarking that it was well strapped to the member.

"An' you pulls to *on*load dis mule, berry much as ef you was an ass, brudder John! Dere—you hab 'em now: you see the 'pen' (depend) 'pon dat little strap and buckle!"

Tom was relieved after a while, and, now alight, was provided with the pistols taken from the outlaw whom Millhouse had cut down. He placed himself at the head of the captive, Norris.

"Now, buckrah," said he to the ruffian, "jes you be easy and cibil, whey you is, or I'll g'e [give] you the benefit of dese yer two barking puppies!"—showing the two pistols in ugly proximity to the outlaw's jaws as he spoke. Tom was an old soldier; cool and confident; who stood ready at all times, to execute his master's orders without the smallest scruple. He always rose too, on an occasion like the present, in his sense of what was due to his elevation.

"Niggers!" said he to the clustering slaves, "you kin stan' back dere, and not crowd too close 'pon de buckrah wha' I got to shoot, may-be!"

Captain Porgy, mounted, as we have seen, upon the horse of the outlaw by whom his own had been shot, having seen that his two comrades were quite ready, now gave the signal, which was responded to by a tremendous shout from the throat of Sergeant Millhouse. The worthy captain took the lead, and, allowing a little interval between them, the three partisans darted forward at a smart gallop, riding, as they had every reason to apprehend, into something like a wolf-trap. The trap had, indeed, been set, as we have sufficiently shown; but we have also seen in what manner its teeth were drawn. Our gallant partisans were unassailed by any foe, and encountered no strange presence, until they were thirty yards of the carriage; when the overseer, Fordham, sprang up from the bushes in which he had so long been crouching, and cried out his welcome to the strangers.

"Friends! friends!" he shouted, dropping his rifle to the ground, and clapping his hands. "We're none but friends here, now, I reckon, captain. God be praised for sending you jest at the right moment!"

The troopers drew up suddenly.

"Who is that?" demanded Porgy.

"Why, don't you remember me, Captain? Fordham, you know, that you used to see at Major Eveleigh's, and——"

"Ah! Fordham;—yes! How are you, my good fellow, and all? Are you all well?"

"Yes, thank God, and mighty glad to see you, as you bring us safety! Glad to see you at any time, captain; but pretici-larly jest now, when we didn't know whether we should ever have to sup upon anything better than lead and cold steel agin! We've had a mighty sharp scrimmaging here for more than three hours, and been in such a stew as I don't want to be in ag'in."

"Not like the stews of Tom's making then," quoth our captain, *sotto voce;* "they are such as a man might swim in without feeling too hot with the exercise, or getting beyond his depth at any time! Stew! do you say, Mr. Fordham! I trust I can say 'well done' to you!"

"Well, it's pretty well, then, I tell you!   I'm thinking, considering all things, we made a pretty good *out* of it—Master Arthur Eveleigh and me!   But God be praised for bringing you when he did; for I don't know·how it would ha' turned out in the *eend*.   Even *ef* we could ha' stood it out *tell* dark night, then, their greater number would have brought them down upon us; and on which side, there would be no telling.   You've saved us, captain, I tell you; and thank you for it—and bless God for it, and all other marcies."

By this time, they were joined by young Arthur Eveleigh, who showed himself, rising out of the bushy fastnesses, as soon as he heard Fordham cry aloud in tones of confidence and cheer. He promptly came forward and joined the party, and was hurriedly introduced by Fordham, to the captain of partisans, but not before the worthy fellow had embraced the youth with such a sense of joyous relief, as was natural to a heart so loyal under the circumstances.   He then brought the youth forward, saying :—

"This, Captain Porgy, is Master Arthur Eveleigh, son of the widow Eveleigh, whom you remember.   He's done mighty good sarvice in this scrimmaging business.   He'll be a man, I tell you, ef ever there was one."

"Good!" answered Porgy, alighting and grasping the hand of the blushing youth, with an encouraging frankness, "You've begun early, and well, Master Arthur; and a good beginning is always half the battle!   I'm glad of it for your sake, and that of your parents!   But, talking of your parents, reminds me of your excellent and amiable mother, whom I claim as an old friend.   Let us go to her assistance.   I trust that she's not hurt."

And the captain of partisans turned and proceeded toward the carriage, accompanied by the others.

"I think not; I hope not," answered the youth anxiously, while hurrying forward ahead of the rest, his stride increasing to a bound and run, as he advanced.   The eyes of Porgy followed him.

"A fine, vigorous lad; well made; looks like his father in form, his mother in face; bating the eyes, which are not blue, and which look far less amiable.   I should say the lad was a bold, rash. high-spirited fellow.

"He's all that, captain! He'll fight, too, like the devil. Twa'n't so easy to keep him back and quiet; to keep him from putting his head up as a mark; but he'll soon l'arn, with proper edication!—It's surprising how well he could take the track and keep it. The work was to keep him *down*; but he had sense enough to see how 'twas needful! We've been watching here—jest covering the ground with our beads, for a good hour, not daring to stir—not knowing how soon we should hear the crack of an inimy's rifle."

"How many of these rascals were there?" demanded Porgy. "We have one of them, a prisoner; one was cut down by Sergeant Millhouse; and another made his escape into the swamp, half a mile or so below. That accounts for *three* of them."

"There were six in all, at first, I reckon; but its not so certain but there might have been more. Of these *we* killed *one*."

"There are then, at least, two yet to account for. They must be about—are probably not far off. But they will keep snug and quiet for awhile. It's hardly likely that they will attempt anything farther at present. But keep your rifles primed, and your horses at hand. We must not let ourselves be surprised!"

These orders were given more in detail to Lance Frampton He and Sergeant Millhouse made themselves busy, and took the necessary precautions. Meanwhile, Capt. Porgy proceeded toward the carriage, having considerately delayed his own and the movements of Fordham, in that direction, by saying:—

"A moment or two, Mr. Fordham! Let the young man release his mother himself!"

The youth, meanwhile, had sprung with proper alacrity to this grateful duty. The mother and son embraced with mutual tears and thankfulness. The glad widow held the happy boy apart from her, gazed fondly in his face, and then, even where she stood, in the box of the coachman, sank down upon her knees in silent prayers to Heaven. The boy instinctively sank down beside her, and both yielded themselves, in the sight of Heaven, to frank and fervent but silent prayer.

CHAPTER XXIII.

THE SOLDIER AND THE LADY.

THE good sense, and good taste, of Captain Porgy, sufficed to prevent him from interrupting such a scene. He stood apart, conferring with Fordham, seeming to see nothing at the carriage; but his eye took in all the sweet picture of maternal love; of all the forms of love, perhaps, the most pure, the least selfish, the longest lived! At length, the voice of the widow was heard calling our partisan.

"Captain Porgy—will you not suffer me to thank you?"

Our captain, as we know, was not one of the most sprightly of living cavaliers. Agility, as he himself freely admitted, formed no part of his physical virtues; but he certainly made the most astonishing efforts, at this summons, to appear agile; and did succeed, we allow, in reaching the carriage in a tolerably short space of time, and without appearing too greatly breathed from the exertion. As he drew nigh, the widow, supported by her son, alighted from the box, and extended her hand to the grasp of her deliverer. Conspicuous on each of her wrists was a dark ring, the mark of the cords with which she had been tied by the ruffians.

"How much ought I to thank you, Captain Porgy—how much do I owe you, sir! See from what indignities you have rescued me?"

"Would I had been with you some hours sooner, my dear madam," cried the captain, seizing her hand and carrying it, in courtly fashion, to his lips. Those were days, be it remembered, of more lavish ceremonial than ours; and the act was held one of mere grace, rather than of gallantry. At all events, it seemed to occasion no emotion in the bosom of Mrs. Eveleigh, and lessened, in no degree the warmth of her acknowledgments.

"That you have come in season for our safety—to relieve

my dear son, and this brave man to whom I owe so much, is quite enough to make me thankful to God, and for ever grateful to you! Ah! sir, I have passed a terrible hour and more! How I bore up against my own terrors, thus fettered, and unable to act, or even to speak, without going mad, I know not! But all is over now, I trust! There is no more danger?"

"I hope not—I believe not, my dear Mrs. Eveleigh; and, now that it is over, perhaps I ought to congratulate you on what has taken place. It has had its good along with its evil. It has brought out the manhood in your brave son, and shown the admirable stuff which he has in him for future work. Mr. Fordham has given me a glowing account of his conduct. I am really sorry, for his sake, that our wars are ended. I should like to take him into my keep as my ensign."

The tears again gathered into the mother's eyes, while the boys cheeks became crimson. Some further conversation ensued between the widow and the partisan on this subject, so grateful to the mother, until the lad himself interposed, and in a whisper, taking her hand, said—

"No more, mother, if you please! If Captain Porgy knew *all* that I had done, he wouldn't be so ready to praise me, I assure you."

The partisan half heard the words, and guessed the meaning of the rest; and rejoined good naturedly and sensibly—

"Ah! my dear fellow, you are conscious of some mistakes, perhaps; but that is only another proof in your favor. A fool is never aware that he has made any blunders—never! To be conscious that you have done so, is the first proof of wisdom— the necessary process by which to avoid them in future. You were too quick and rash; too hasty; and fancied you understood the whole game, when you were only taking the first lessons in it. An error, doubtless; but one, my dear boy, that seems natural to our climate; where one usually dates his manhood from the moment when he instructs his father in what way properly to break his eggs. You will soon get over all your mortifications of this description—too soon, perhaps."

But we do not propose to report the whole of the dialogue, as it took place between the parties;—a dialogue, such as can readily be conjectured under the circumstances, and at the meeting of old friends, after such a long interval of time, occupied by war and its worst vicissitudes. Captain Porgy, himself, not regardless of duty, soon brought the merely amiable in their conversation to a close; though it was, evidently, very grateful to him. It seemed to restore him at once to the social sphere from which he had so long been an exile. He thus changed the topic—

"But we must reserve these matters, Mrs. Eveleigh, for a moment of greater leisure. We must not forget our duties now. The sun wanes, and you have yet to find your way home. We have accounted for all these outlaws, but two; and to do our work thoroughly, we should give an account of *them*. Two have been slain outright, one by your party, and another by mine; one is even now our prisoner; and the fourth man we have seen making his escape into the swamp, below, where we can not now hope to hunt him up. There are still two others, somewhere, lurking in the neighborhood, of whom we must ascertain all that we can within the next two hours, or before dark."

"I am somewhat bewildered," said the lady, "and have suffered so much from the sun in my eyes, and the cords about my arms, that I may have allowed things to pass under my very sight without being altogether conscious of the fact; but, just before the last skirmish of Mr. Fordham and my son, there were two of them harbored very near the carriage; one on that side," pointing to the right, "whom I could not see after he first proceeded in that quarter; while the other was hidden among these myrtles just in front. Now, I've never seen *that last one* leave his position."

With a few bounds, as he heard these words, Lance Frampton was at the indicated spot. He stooped—then cried out—

"He's here, sure enough; stone-dead, with a bullet through his head!"

He drew the body out of the bushes as he spoke.

"That was *your* bullet, Master Arthur," said Fordham.

"And a *chance* bullet too," replied the ingenuous youth. "I felt so *much* ashamed at having fired, thinking that I had thrown the shot away!—for I felt that I had taken no aim at all!"

"Ah!" said Porgy, "you know not how wonderfully the hand

seconds the eye, and both the will, when there is no time left for preparation. The best shots are frequently those which are taken when we are so conscious of a *purpose*, that we are wholly unconscious of an *aim*. If the will is right, the hand and eye obey, as implicitly as the slave of an Eastern despot!"

"I remember the moment that you shot, my son!" said the widow, with a shudder of horror, as the body was drawn out of the bushes. "He rose out of that very clump of grass and myrtle; swore, and shook his fist at me, and made some horrible threats. It was because I had called out to warn Mr. Fordham, whom I had seen approaching, where they were in concealment. I only *saw* Fordham; but I concluded you were somewhere with him, and I trembled at the cunning ambush which they had set. It was all over in a moment. It seemed as if I heard the outlaw and the shot all in the very instant when I was speaking."

"No doubt," answered Porgy. "There's now only one for whom we can not account, and of him we may be sure of this— that he will not remain long in a neighborhood the climate of which has been so unfriendly to the health of his people. At all events, Mrs. Eveleigh, it would be only looking through the haystack for the cambric needle, to attempt to hunt him up, at this late hour, and on the edges of this swamp! And yet"— looking round upon the dense thickets which indicated the swamp fortresses—"poor as I am, I would give the last hundred guineas for a couple of good Scotch blood-hounds, or Spanish, for a single hour! But the wish is idle. There are, nevertheless, some things within our power, Mrs. Eveleigh, and the first is to get you homeward with all despatch. We must use promptly all the daylight that is left us; and, with all our efforts, it will be a little in the night before you can possibly get home. Still, there can be no danger now! Neither of the two rogues whom we shall leave running, will be so hardy as to attempt anything new in this quarter; and you will have quite a sufficient escort in your son and Mr. Fordham. They have already managed successfully a force of *six* assailants; they will have no difficulty in managing a *couple*. But even these two, it is likely, do not hunt together. The one we drove into the swamp, took its shelter some two miles below. The other scoundrel, as last reported, had his perch rather above than below. Be it as it may, you must push on for home, before night, under your escort. You need not fear these ruffians, who, even if they had nothing to apprehend from *our* superior force, bringing up the wagon and the rear as we propose to do, would never attempt your carriage now, guarded by your son and Fordham. Leave me to secure your property, and guard your negroes home. The more grateful duty would be to guard yourself, but the more arduous is here. Fordham will now be on *his* guard against surprise; and, to render you quite safe and sure, I will confide a few pistols to some of your most courageous negroes—your fellow Sylvester, for one. These will suffice. With my party I will remain, and see to the repair and reloading of your wagon, the horses of which, I perceive, my people have already recaptured. It shall follow you as soon as ready. But, the sooner you start the better. You have hardly an hour of sunlight left, and the rogue sees better in the night than the honest man, as the owl sees better than the chicken."

The widow was quite sensible of this good advice, and prepared for its adoption. Her servants rapidly got her carriage ready, the traces, where they had been cut, being supplied with plough-lines. The appearance of his own negroes assisting in this duty, reminded our captain of the active agency of the widow, in recovering them for him from the British hulks—a circumstance of which she had entirely foreborne to speak.

"I, too, have my thanks, my dear Mrs. Eveleigh, since, as I learn, but for your keen eye, and fearless spirit, my negroes would now be on their way to the British West Indies. But I must take a less hurried moment for making my acknowledgments."

"Don't speak of it, my dear captain; I did only as a neighbor should have done. But, of course, you will accompany my people to my house. Your own will scarcely give you a proper shelter just now."

"No, thank you a thousand times, but I have some of my old and young soldiers with me——"

"I have room for all," said the hospitable widow.

"I thank you again; but I must see to these negroes; and—"

The captain paused. The widow fancied there was some lit-

tle embarrassment in his manner. She fancied there was a slight
flushing through all the bronze on his cheeks. Mrs. Eveleigh
was a woman of good sense and good feeling. Such a person
always receives an apology—for what is it worth; at least she
never disputes it, driving the apologist to the wall, and exposing
to himself the poverty of his excuses. She behaved, accordingly, in the right manner. She forebore annoying him, the moment she discovered him resolved to excuse himself. She took
for granted that he had his reasons, proper enough for himself,
which it might not be proper for him to unfold. This was
enough.

"As you please, captain. Remember, from this moment, I
take for granted that you will feel yourself always welcome, and
at home, at *my* house. Your old and young soldiers will share
this welcome—all whom you command. Pray believe, in addition, that I shall desire to see you at an early moment. I have
much to hear from you, and something to communicate. Why
not ride over and dine with me to-morrow, or the day after, and
bring your friends with you?"

"And very much delighted, indeed, to do so, Mrs. Eveleigh,
if it be possible. At all events, I shall let you know in due season, if I shall not be able to come to-morrow. Believe me, I
have not been living so long in camp as to have quite lost my
relish for a good dinner."

"Visit her now," quoth Porgy, turning away to see after the
coach and wagon, "with such a beard—mixed grey and brown,
salt and pepper—and in this travelling gear—a break under
the arm, a rent in——"

And he paused as if at some unmentionable difficulty—then
proceeded—

"No! no! One puts on his best favors and front, when he
goes to court, even in a republic. This grizly beard!"—

Here he stroked his chin reproachfully—literally took himself
by the beard—and added—

"Who the devil could have anticipated such an adventure!—
That I should have put away my best things in my valise!"

He was brought to think of other matters by the approach of
his lieutenant. Meanwhile, all were busy. To gather the negroes and horses together, repair the harness, and set the coach-

man once more upon his box, was a task of no great labor with so many hands. Fortunately, the outlaws had left behind them an abundance of plough-line, and there was a bolt of rope in the wagon. The harness was quickly put in strong travelling order, and all ready for a start in a much shorter period of time than had been anticipated. The widow, accompanied by her son, Fordham and the servant girl, bade Porgy and his followers a friendly farewell; repeating her thanks to all, and giving separate and warm invitations to each to visit her; which all parties promised. When they were fairly out of sight of the troopers, she called the overseer to the side of the coach.

"Mr. Fordham, have you been lately to Captain Porgy's place ?"

"Not later than a month ago, ma'am, or thereabouts. I pass it constantly, you know."

"It is all destitute, I think; almost in ruins ?"

"The house is good, ma'am, wants a little repairing; but there's not a stick of fence, and——"

"Ah! that's not what I mean! Do you suppose he has any provisions there ?"

"Not the feather of a chicken, ma'am—not the hair of a hog! How should he ? The niggers eat him out before the tories took 'em off. They left nothing. There may be a few cattle in the swamps, and perhaps hogs; but it's worth more than they'd bring to look 'em up."

"How then is he to feed all these people ?"

"God knows, ma'am; it's a wonder to me."

"Mr. Fordham, we must take care of him and them for the present. Men who have so long served, and helped to save, the country, and who have so lately served and saved us, must not be suffered to want. I'll tell you what you must do."

"To be sure, ma'am."

"When we reach his place, we shall be so nigh our own that there can scarce be any further danger from these outlaws. You will, accordingly, stop at Captain Porgy's, and stop the wagon there also, when it arrives. Knock open the sugar barrel, and leave him a fourth of it; give him a like proportion out of the coffee sack. There are, I think, four boxes of candles, leave him one. Put out for him, also, a dozen of the blankets, and if you can think of any other matters, that may be useful from among our stores, leave him a like supply. When I get home, I will send him some meal and bacon. Oh! don't forget to leave him one of the jugs of Jamaica. These soldiers are all fond of spirits, you know."

Porgy would have retorted—How else should they have spirit?

The plethoric old soldier little dreamed, at that moment, what the charities of the amiable widow had decreed for his creature comfort. As little did she conjecture the sort of business which, at the same time, occupied his hands. Let us return to him and note the progress of events.

CHAPTER XXIV.

JUDICIAL DIGNITY IN THE FOREST.

OUR captain of partisans would have gladly undertaken the escort of the widow, had circumstances—in which the condition of his travelling costume must be included—allowed. But he felt, as leader of the party, so suddenly engaged in such an adventure as that which followed his encounter with the outlaws, that a serious further duty had devolved upon him; and, however selfish or luxurious his character might be, it was seldom that he permitted his tastes, or his love of ease and enjoyment, to thwart the performances to which he was professionally bound. He was a soldier, not less than a *bon vivant* and gentleman. True, he had been regularly dismissed from duty. He was no longer an officer in command. There was no longer an army. But he had character. He was sure of his own honesty. He felt, and understood, the lawlessness which prevailed throughout the country; and, in the deficiency of courts and sheriffs, he resolved that he was still a captain of militia, and that each militia officer was, *ad interim*, in the commission of the peace.

The old idea of *regulation* was as much the fashion through-out the country as ever. It was now as much the *necessity* of the region, as it had been in the early stages of society when the practice originated. The woods were filled with outlaws and offenders? and, to await the slow processes of the courts of law, at such a period, and in a country so sparsely settled, was to sacrifice all the securities of the better sort of people. Society, in such cases, always resorts to the necessary means for sustaining law; and the morals of law always will, and should, sustain what are the obvious necessities of society. In this you have the full justification of the code of regulation; a code which is, no doubt, sometimes subject to abuse, as is the case with law itself, but which is rarely allowed to exist in practice — among people of Anglo-Norman origin — a day longer than is absolutely essential to the common weal. Captain Porgy simply fulfilled the conditions of this code, when he resolved on subjecting the captive outlaw to the tender mercies of an extempore court of justice, all the members of which had been trained in a severe military school, the rules of which recognised no limits to its own powers, and usually threw upon the accused the burden of proof, in establishing his own innocence.

The wagon of Mrs. Eveleigh, reloaded, and despatched upon its way, under an escort composed wholly of the slaves of the widow — several of whom, including John Sylvester, had been armed with the view to its defence, should either of the two outlaws in the woods be prepared and in the humor to attempt further mischief, which was held to be scarcely possible — our captain established himself under a goodly oak, planted himself comfortably upon a heap of dry leaves at its roots, and instructed Sergeant Millhouse to bring the offending outlaw before him.

This order was promptly obeyed. His coat off, his arms bound behind him, the outlaw, Norris, was pushed forward by Millhouse, his *one* hand diligently applying the point of his sword to the fellow's haunches, whenever he halted or seemed unnecessarily reluctant. Norris was sullen and savage both, looked the tiger, and spoke as snappishly as a lean cur over a beggarly bone, with two or three other companion curs, as lean as himself, watching, close at hand, for the opportunity to dart in and bear away the prize. The fellow's case was desperate, and he knew it! He had been taken *flagranté delicto;* and he had sufficient experience of law, when administered by a military man, to know that it was usually a matter singularly decisive and summary in all its processes.   He was a hardy ruffian; and, with *a gloomy sense of the danger that awaited him, his habitual mood now assumed the appearance of insolence and audacity.

But he was in the hands of those who had been accustomed to deal with all sorts of offenders.   Porgy awaited his approach with rare patience of demeanor.   His pistols, taken from his holsters, lay before him.   His sword, unbelted but sheathed, crossed his lap.   We are constrained to state the further fact, that our captain of partisans, in order to the more easy administration of justice, had unbuttoned coat, vest, and small-clothes, as far as he possibly could without actually discarding them; and his appearance was, accordingly, significant of a singular looseness of habit, which, we are pleased to say, did not by any means represent his usual moral character.   Let us add, also, that the act which gave him this peculiar laxity in dress, was studiously forborne until the carriage of the fair widow was quite out of sight.   Captain Porgy was one of that good old school, which, where ladies and gentlemen were concerned, was always carefully tender of the proprieties.   The school is somewhat out of fashion now, and is supposed to need its apologies; but we have not space enough for them in this place.

Lance Frampton stood a little on one side of the judge; but the latter, after the prisoner had been brought up, bade him be seated as one of the court.   Porgy was heedful of all details.

"You, sergeant," said he to Millhouse, "acting as sheriff, will be required to stand.   A certain degree of vigilance is necessary always, even when the court feels itself perfectly secure.   Ensign," to Lance, "take your seat more to the left; let the tree be a little between us—where you are now, we might both be ranged with a single rifle-shot; a fact which might tempt the rascal, yet in the woods, to let drive at us."

As this was spoken, the prisoner began to whistle.   The sounds were suddenly silenced by a smart blow from the stump of Sergeant Millhouse's game hand, who well understood the object of the whistle.

"Wait with your music till it's called for, my lark," quoth the vigilant sergeant.

The ruffian twitched violently at the cords by which his wrists were fastened, evidently desirous of resenting the indignity; and, failing in this, he plunged his head incontinently into the breast of the assailant, with bull-like ferocity. He was not tall enough to address his battering-ram at the face of the sergeant, or he might have done mischief to the mazzard of the veteran. The latter was taken by surprise, and almost lost his feet, as well as his breath, for a moment; but his huge and well-buttressed form was staggered only, not overthrown; and, recovering himself, he dropped his sword, and planted a settler in the nostrils of the outlaw, which laid him out like a log, the blood spurting, in a big stream, from the proboscis of the victim.

"Well delivered," quoth Porgy; "he will hardly try his horns upon you a second time, Mr. Sheriff. Help him to rise, boys." This was said to the negroes who hung around, quite delighted with the solemnity of the scene, and the action which had begun with so much spirit, and which promised to be so enlivening. Pomp, the fiddler, absolutely lost his propriety so far as to wave his fiddle aloft, while executing a sort of wild-colt movement upon his pins — a proceeding which was quickly arrested by an order of his master, to "box that fellow up till he's wanted." Pomp sank back demurely enough, and took especial care, during the rest of the scene, to attract no especial attention to himself: Tom, the cook, giving him first a gentle admonition, by a sharp sudden gripe about his weasand. This little episode occupied but a few moments. The outlaw Norris, half-stunned, was raised once more to his feet, the blood still dripping from his nostrils. Captain Porgy surveyed him very much as the Bow-street magistrate is said to examine the visages of old offenders, or those whom he thinks so; but he did not fall into the usual habit of that officer, of finding the offender always ill-looking. On the contrary, he had a different theory in such matters.

"But that you have spoiled his nose for a time," quoth Porgy, "the offender would be a good-looking fellow — even handsome, perhaps, stripped of his brush, and with a clean shirt on. Is it not curious that these rogues should be so commonly handsome? I don't remember one whom we have had to hang, who wouldn't be accounted quite a pretty fellow among the women! There was that fellow, Bryce, whom we left swinging at Four Holes; he was a fine-looking fellow, Lance. And old Echars, the Dutch-man, whom we dressed in tar and feathers at Monk's Corner, for stealing cattle, he was a beauty, though nearly sixty years of age. You see, my friend, that beauty is a snare. It makes many a poor fellow a rogue. I suppose, because it first makes him a fool. It turns his head; and when the head's turned, a fellow ceases to be a man, and goes to the devil like a beast. It is the head that keeps a man in position. Let him lose that balance, and he staggers, from right to left, with a sort of moral drunkenness. Talking of drunkenness, reminds me that a good sup of Jamaica would not be amiss after that little run we had, Sergeant Millhouse; but"—with a sigh—"we must now think of other matters! A handsome rascal, indeed! but"—addres-sing the prisoner abruptly—"well, my good fellow, how do you call yourself?"

Let us leave this examination for a moment, in order that all the parties to the scene should be properly shown up, each in his exact position, to the eye of the reader. Thus far, the whole progress of the affair had been witnessed, though imperfectly, at the distance of two or three hundred yards, more or less, by the out-lying squatter, Bostwick. Perfectly familiar with the ground and region, he had regulated his own course and move-ments entirely by those of the party which he no longer dared to assail. By crawling and creeping, crouching and winding— by stealthy movements, like those of the wild-cat and fox—by a sinuous progress like that of the serpent—he had wound his way from point to point, wherever he fancied that a good place could be had for surveying the proceedings of his enemies. In this progress he omitted no precaution, and none suspected how closely they were watched. It was the conviction of Porgy and the rest that the outlaws were completely dispersed; and that, terrified by the execution done among them—the death of no less than three of their number, and the captivity of a fourth— the two, escaping, had fled incontinently from the dangerous neighborhood.

But Bostwick had several reasons for lingering upon the ground, even after the chances of profit had wholly disappeared. He had a fellow-feeling for his captive comrade; and, as he had frequently done before, was prepared to follow the footsteps of his captors, in eager expectation of the moment when their vigilance would so relax as to enable him to effect his rescue, even at some hazard to himself. He was thus far faithful to the bond of brotherhood, which is said to be sacred even among thieves. He was prepared, as we shall see, for other necessities. He was not long permitted to remain in doubt as to the purposes of Captain Porgy and his associates; these, indeed, he readily divined. He naturally conjectured that the policy of the captors would prompt them to ascertain from the prisoner all the facts of the expedition—the parties by whom it was set on foot—the persons actually engaged in it, and the motives by which it was prompted. All the proceedings, as already described, confirmed him in his conjectures; and his interest and anxiety continued to increase, as he beheld the deliberation with which the party commenced the affair. He had got as near to the spot as he well dared, from that quarter of the woods which afforded him concealment, relying not less on the depth of cover which he occupied than upon the facility with which, in the event of danger, he could glide unseen into the recesses of the adjacent swamp.

Here he beheld the progress of affairs; saw Porgy let himself down deliberately at the base of the oak; beheld the prisoner brought up; heard the beginning of his whistle, and saw the summary manner in which he had been silenced by the game-hand of Sergeant Millhouse. The fierce assault of Norris, by which he had resented the blow, and the severe punishment which he had received in consequence, added to his excitement; and, but for the madness of such an act, he would have darted out to the succor of his comrade. He forebore; but it was with a feverish vexation, which kept him singularly fidgetty and restless. Not a syllable could he distinguish of what was said by either of the parties; but he could very well conjecture what was likely to be said. His disquiet greatly increased in consequence of his inability to hear. His interest was by no means an unselfish one. He knew that Norris was a stubborn scoundrel, hardened in sin, callous by repeated infamies; and one whom frequent hair-breadth escapes had rendered tenacious of his secret, and more than commonly confident of his gool luck in escape. But the squatter dreaded still, lest temptation and fear combined should finally get the better of his hardihood, and prompt those revelations which must be fatal to his own safety. Could he have heard the proceedings, he would have been more at ease, even though these should only tend to confirm his apprehensions.

With a mood that became momently more and more desperate from the very continuance of his doubts, Bostwick began, at length, to finger the lock of his rifle, scarcely conscious that he was doing so. He could scarcely resist the impulse which prompted him to send a bullet through the provoking abdomen of the captain of partisans, now rendered doubly offensive to the eye by the removal of the usual restraints of button, belt and buckle. At another moment his thought would be to single out, as a victim, the tall, erect, and raw-boned figure of the sergeant, acting as sheriff in the proceedings. Could he have got the three—the captain, ensign, and sergeant—in a range, or even two of them, he had never resisted the temptation. He had, under these exciting tendencies, continued to crawl and creep up within a hundred and thirty yards of the scene of trial, and at such a distance, with a rest, he had the most perfect faith in his own skill to make his mark, and the capacity of his rifle to speed the bullet home.

The disposition grew in his mind to adopt some such desperate course of action. He looked about him, accordingly, with regard to the means left him for escape, should he resolve to fire. This examination of the spot which he occupied, led him instantly to change it—a proceeding which involved, necessarily, some little loss of time. But he moved briskly, as well as stealthily, and at length found himself in a more satisfactory place of concealment and ambush, upon the edge of the swamp, where he was sheltered partly by the dense thicket of gall-bushes, of which we have already given some idea. Here, at his back, were all the facilities for flight, by a sinuous progress, and under cover all the way. Here ran a mighty cypress, half-buried in water, hidden from view by a wilderness of bushes, growing upon the tussocky ridge on the edge of which it had fallen. Farther on, a clump of bays, or dwarf-laurel, interposed to receive him. Beyond was a tract of the gall and hurrah-bushes, matted by vines, which seemed to enmesh their entire tops; beyond, the places of refuge spread away interminably, forming, even in daylight, an almost perfect shelter; but at nightfall, a questionless place of security. The region, which was called "Bear Castle" by the neighborhood, was one which he well knew. It yielded him, comparatively speaking, a perfectly safe mode of retreat from the point where he established himself, in the event of any necessity occurring for sudden flight. Here he found himself in a place altogether to his liking; one in which he might contrive to obtain a knowledge of what was going on among the partisans; overlook their proceedings, and interpose, if necessary, at the proper moment; yet one which he could leave at a short notice, and without embarrassment, for the deeper recesses of the swamp thicket.

"And now," said he to himself, "Dick Norris, it's jist as hell and you chooses! Ef you're the man to hold out, I'm the man to help you! You've been in as tight a fix afore now, and you know that I stuck by you then! Set your teeth hard, Dick, and I reckon we can scrape you through!"

This was all said in a whisper, though as if the person spoken to could hear. Bostwick now appeared more at his ease, was cooler and more composed; and, satisfied to have gained the required place of watch and safety, not much over a hundred yards from the place of trial, rifle in grasp, and *couteau de chasse* loosened in his belt, crouching beside a pine which grew upon a bank somewhat raised above the general level, before which stretched a little forest of gall-bushes and young myrtle, he peered keenly through the vistas of the wood, not losing a single movement among those he watched, while his comrade was undergoing "The Question."

CHAPTER XXV.

RAPID PROCESSES OF EXTEMPORE LAW.

"The Question," verily, in the sense usually given to the phrase in the times—which the silly world usually calls, "good old times,"—when state tyranny, and the Spanish Inquisition, were in *full blast,*—to use a vulgar idiom, but a very appropriate figure—did the trial of Norris, by our military court, promise in reality to be. Bostwick well knew the usual practice on all such occasions. He had some personal experience of "the question" himself. He had, as we had gathered from his words, been more than once instrumental in rescuing his comrade from its operation. He did by no means despair, accordingly; but kept himself in reserve for the chapter of accidents.

Our captain of partisans very well understood that one of the outlaws *might* be lurking about, and looking on; but he little dreamed how nigh, or with what purposes in his mind. He was proceeding with singular calmness in the trial, but with a solemnity of manner fully proper to the enormous offence of the prisoner. We have heard the inquiry with which he commenced the examination of Norris. It met with no answer. The fellow sullenly stood up, though with half-shut eyes, through which the latent ferocity could be seen still to flash out brightly, and showing that the devil was by no means subdued, though bruised sorely, and in tight bonds.

"Hark ye, fellow," said Porgy, repeating the question, "do you hear?—by what name are you known among your kindred?—who are you?—and what has prompted you to the commission of this outlawry? Be civil now—your safety depends somewhat upon your fully unburthening your conscience of all its secrets. Give an account of yourself to the court."

"Court! I don't see any court!" responded the prisoner, with a mixed air of contempt and defiance.

"Ah! you don't, eh! Well, but what if it makes you *feel*

it ? It strikes me there's something in *that !* Think better of it, my poor fellow, and answer the court with a decent sense of its power, if not of its authority."

"I'll answer when it suits me ! Time enough, when I'm raally before a court. You're none, I reckon. You're no more a j*e*dge than I am."

"I'm sorry you think so, my good fellow," said Porgy, mildly : "for your own sake, you'd better come to the conclusion that we *are* a court, having the power of life and death ; and prepare your defence accordingly. We give you a fair chance for your life. Tell the truth, the whole truth, and nothing but the truth, and you don't know what good it will do you — if not in this world, at all events in the next. Confess who set you on this expedition — who were your associates — where do they harbor — what are the names of those who survive ? Turn state's evidence as fast as you can, if you would be treated with indulgence."

"I don't see what you can do with me, but carry me to prison. There's no army ! Don't I know that the army is broken up, and all the British gone. And there's no courts y*i*t ; and if there was courts, you, I reckon, aint no J*e*dge, and these niggers aint no jury ! You kin only carry me to jail. That's the worst that you kin do ; and I ain't afeered of any jail I ever seed yit !"

And he chuckled, with the feeling of one who had been particularly smart, if not severe.

"You grieve me, my interesting fellow, by your imperfect knowledge of the law ! I am, at this moment, both judge and jury ; and my excellent friend, on the right, is my sheriff, and the executioner of my decrees ! These sons of Ethiopia are all good men and true, having an abiding sense of authority and justice. You will find them fully capable of understanding all the facts in your case ; and I feel myself equally able to expound to them the law upon it. As for the army, my friend, that is never broken up, so long as there are criminals, like yourself, to be broken in. The good citizens of a country must always constitute a standing army for the purposes of public justice and public security. Answer, therefore, as civilly and fully as possible, the questions I shall put to you, if you would secure for yourself the least indulgence. What may be your name ?"

"I sha'n't tell you !" was the insolent reply

"Well, perhaps that is not necessary. It is not necessary that we should know a man's name in order to hang him. In reporting our proceedings we shall, doubtless, find a name for you. For the present, we will consider you one John, or Tom, or Peter Nemo. Remember, Sergeant Millhouse, and you Pomp, and you, boys, generally, that the prisoner is called Peter Nemo, *alias* John Nemo, *alias* Nebuchadnessar Fish, *alias*——"

"I don't answer to any such names !"

"Silence gives consent ! You don't answer to any name, nor, it would seem, to any thing ! Don't deceive yourself, my pleasing prisoner. I don't care a straw whether you answer or not. That's just as you please. But we must go through certain forms, for your own sake ; and, for the same reason — simply to give you every chance — I must put some other questions to you. I don't want you to answer, if you don't think proper to do so. Who were your confederates, your allies, your associates, in this highway robbery ?"

"There's no highway robbery."

"Sorry that we must differ, my friend, in this matter. You are unfortunate that we found you in the act — in the full possession of the plunder. I am indulgent to you. I will repeat the question — who were your associates in the interesting enterprise in which I found you engaged ?"

"Nobody ! Ask me no questions. I sha'n't answer. Take me to jail, if you choose."

"Jail, my friend ! Impossible ! I don't approve of imprisonment. It degrades a freeman into the condition of a wild beast. I should think a man of your spirit would prefer death, a thousand times, to incarceration within stone walls, and iron bracelets. No ! no ! my friend, we will not punish you so cruelly. Your tortures, when your trial is over, shall be short. Who was the ringleader in this expedition ?"

"Oh ! be d——d ! Don't bother me with your axings. I ain't guine to answer nothing !"

"You are irreverent, my poor fellow ; you don't know the mischief you may do yourself ! Once more, let me know how many persons, and who, were concerned in this enterprise, which you will not allow was highway robbery. Who first set you upon it; who was your leader: and what was your scheme throughout?—Make a clean breast of it, my good fellow, that you may have 'well done' said to you for once in your life."

"Ax away, 'tell you're tired. You git no answer from me, old Porpoise!"

"The poor, d——d fool!" quoth Millhouse, in a whisper to Lance. "Every word he says is a-hitching him tighter and tighter!"

"That has a salt-water sound!" was the remark of Porgy, quietly made, but there was a sudden redness about the cheek and gills, as he spoke, that showed him beginning to be chafed at the outlaw's insolence. He restrained every ebullition of temper, however, in recognition of what he held to be the solemn unimpassioned character of his present duty; and continued to put his questions, in various shapes, until he had exhausted all the proper subjects of inquiry, and afforded the prisoner the fullest opportunity to reveal all that he knew. This done, and the answers being all equally unsatisfactory and insolent, our captain of partisans turned to Sergeant Millhouse.

"Mr. Sheriff, we have given our prisoner every chance; but he is wedded to his idols and vanities—he rejects every opportunity of mercy! There is a proverb, Mr. Sheriff, upon which we, in the army, are always prompt to act, and the expediency of which our experience has usually confirmed— 'The bird that can sing, and won't sing'—Eh! you remember, sergeant?"

"Must be made to *swing!*"

"Exactly!"

"I've been a-thinking, cappin, for a long time, that you was a'most forgitting our army practice. I've been a-wanting to clap a stopper on the fellow's muzzle ever sence you begun to ax him the questions."

"Ah! but a *muzzle* was not the thing exactly. To make him *unmuzzle*, was my object. Well, he would not do so to please us, we must now persuade him to do so to please himself! Give him a stretch, Sheriff! Appoint a couple of the Ethiopians, your deputies for the occasion, while you act as Provost Marshal, and"—looking about and above him—"there is a good large hickory upon the left which seems to have stretched out its arms for the very purpose the moment it was wanted. Let him be persuaded to that hickory!"

Millhouse seemed to have provided himself with due reference to the exigency. His single remaining hand produced a coil of slender rope from behind him. A running noose was found in it already; and, calling Pompey from the crowd, the fiddler was made to take the rope over his shoulder, and ascend the hickory. He stood on one of its outstretching boughs, and, having dropped the cord across the bough, sat quietly awaiting the prisoner.

"You see!" said Porgy to Norris.

The fellow refused to look up, but sat doggedly, with his head stuck on one side, as if with the most rigid determination.

"You hear!" continued Porgy. "Be warned, my poor fellow, and make a free confession. There is no good reason why your tongue should make your throat suffer. Speak freely, and don't make a figure of yourself."

No answer!

"Let him be persuaded to speak, Mr. Sheriff," said Porgy, in accents as mild as those of Ali Pacha in his most patriarchal moments. In an instant, and at a sign from Millhouse, a couple of the negroes seized upon the prisoner, and in their stalwart arms, it required but a moment to conduct him to the designated tree. Another moment sufficed to slip the noose about his neck; this done, the negroes took hold of the rope with alacrity, and, thus in readiness, they looked to the captain for his further orders.

"You feel?" said Porgy to the outlaw.

No answer.

"My friend," continued the captain of partisans, "I would not ruffle a single feather in the wing of so innocent a bird as yourself; but birds must be made to sing at the proper season. Will you sing for us?"

"No! d——n my liver if I do!"

"You have been a bad *liver*, my poor fellow. Whether you will die as you have lived, is a question for yourself! I give you time. I am, naturally, the most tender-hearted man in the

world; but tough rogues must be made tender also. Confess!
I would not be guilty of a cruelty to beast or man; but outlawry must be stopped; and thieving and murder are such offences, that indiscreet persons, like yourself, must be made to forbear them. Open your eyes to your danger, and empty your
bosom of its evil secrets. I will count one dozen, while you
meditate what to do. I will count slowly, that you may have
time for meditation; but, so sure as I am an honest judge, and
my sheriff a faithful officer, if, by the time I have said *twelve*,
you do not confess, you ride a nag that blacksmith never yet
tried to shoe."

And the captain of partisans began the tale with well measured deliberation; pausing, between the numbers, the length of
a colon at least—" one :" "two :" "three ;" and so-forth!

CHAPTER XXVI.

THE APPLICATION OF "THE QUESTION."

MEANWHILE, the squatter, Bostwick, had become quite sensible
of the danger of his comrade. He could not mistake his situation, or the nature of the experiment which was about to be
tried upon his firmness. Old experience had made him quite
familiar with the whole process. He was very well aware that
the purpose of the partisans would not be simply to execute
punishment upon him, except in degree; and simply to the extent which would insure the revelation of his secret. But this
was the very danger that he most dreaded. Were they to slay
the prisoner outright, the squatter would be much less disquieted.
But to force him to speak—to compel him to buy his life by
giving up his comrades—was a danger to himself, involving
many dangers, which he could by no means contemplate with
serenity. Agitated by various dark and savage feelings, he unconsciously advanced several paces from the spot where he had
sheltered himself. He advanced; but did not forget his caution.
His approach was still from cover to cover; his place of conceal-

ment being always made sure of before taking a single forward step. But he again receded—once more crouched into the thicket, and leaned against the tree; the big sweat coursing, in beaded drops, upon his swarthy forehead. But he still kept watch upon his unhappy comrade, and upon the proceedings of his judges. Sometimes, he muttered in brief spasmodic soliloquy, as if endeavoring to assure himself, in some such utterances as the following :—

"He will die game! He will not confess! Very well—all's right! Norris was always a tough fellow. He won't give up! I wish I could help him; but that's onpossible. But they won't carry it through! It's only to scare him! He knows *that!* He won't leak! He'll keep all close!—Ah!"

He again advanced, and a shudder went over his frame. He caught up his rifle, threw it out, and drew it to the range, as if in the act to fire, but in a moment after dropped it in the hollow of his arm again, while he murmured :—

"It's no use! It kin do no good! I might kill one on 'em, easy enough; but that wouldn't save him, and would only resk myself. Better he should die in the rope! Every man has his time. He must die some time or other. Ef I could help him, wouldn't I? But I can't! It's onpossible, me one, to do anything! Ah! they're at him! The bloody tigers! I know what they're arter!"

Meanwhile, at the signal of Millhouse, the culprit was drawn up slowly into the air. His hands were tied behind him. He could offer no resistance. He showed no submission—uttered no entreaty—submitted doggedly to the torture—impressed with the idea, no doubt, that the party would not proceed to extremities, and that the purpose was to scare him only. He accordingly remained firm! He bore without a groan or struggle the painful distension of his frame, and the stifling pressure of the cord about his throat—his face alternately whitening and reddening, and his breast heaving, with the voluminous effort of his lungs.

Porgy watched the effect with painful feeling. Practice had not indurated him, and, though satisfied of the outlaw's deserts, and fully sensible of the importance of procuring his confession, and not prepared to quarrel with a process which the practice of the army had fully justified—he was yet not insensible to the claims of humanity; and was disposed to spare the victim as much as possible. It is indeed highly probable, that, as was the conjecture of the prisoner himself, and of his ally the squatter, our captain of partisans did not really meditate anything beyond the wholesome fright which would compel the outlaw to disgorge his secrets. But the fellow remained obstinately silent, and his judges were disappointed.

"Ease him down, sergeant," was the order of the captain.

"Now, fellow," he continued, as soon as the criminal had somewhat recovered, "are you grown wiser? Do you begin to comprehend your danger? Are you ready to confess?"

The half-suffocated wretch answered with curses, and scorn, and defiance! In fact, from having been let down so soon, and having suffered so much less than he had anticipated, or had even endured before, he had grown more confident of his position, and more insolent accordingly. Porgy replied to him with real sympathy, but in his own manner.

"My poor fellow, you are trifling with your safety. You don't know your danger! Let me warn you. Do not force me to the last extremity."

A brutal oath was the only answer.

"Hoist away, boys," cried Millhouse, not waiting for the orders of his superior. Again the fellow was hauled up, again let down, but with the same result. Porgy began to grow restiff under the insolence of the outlaw, who, evidently suffering, was as insolent after recovering as ever. Time was accorded him, and new exhortations addressed to him.

"My poor fellow," said Porgy, "you must speak now or never! Your last chance is before you. If you go up again, you only come down to make a full confession, or you come down a dead man! You hear what I say? I am in earnest! You have shown yourself very much a fool as well as a robber. The time left you for growing wise is very short. The sun is near his setting! Confess your accomplices, and if we can catch and convict them by your evidence, we'll get you clear! Show yourself hardened, and you sleep to-night six feet under this tree. You have heard; will you deliver?"

"Do your d——dest! I ain't afear'd!"

This is quite enough of his answer, which exhibited greater brutality than before. We suppress the oaths with which he garnished every sentence. Again the executioners, at a signal from Millhouse, mutely drew the fellow up to the tree—this time with a swift motion and a somewhat rapid jerk. Millhouse had served as provost-marshal on other occasions. The outlaw now showed great distress. It was seen that his hands worked—opened and shut—as if giving signs; then he kicked desperately. His gasping, at length, grew into sounds like speech, and the party below at once understood the half-stifled assurance, that he would confess if let down. The miserable wretch succumbed the moment he began to fear that his judge was in earnest. His sufferings were of a sort to induce this change in his opinions. He could not have borne them much longer and lived. He was already black in the face, and his eyes seemed starting from their sockets. Porgy had already thwarted his own policy in the premature yieldings which he had shown. He was evidently unwilling to urge the torture beyond the degree necessary for his object. He had tried to maintain his apparent calmness; it was a matter of pride with him that he should do so; but he was not always successful; and now, as he witnessed the sufferings of the outlaw, he cried out quickly to Millhouse:—

"Let him down, sergeant. For God's sake, let him down!"

Millhouse hesitated, and ventured to expostulate.

"He's a mighty tough rascal, cap'n! 'Tain't tell the life gits a'most clean out of the body of such a rascal, that the honesty gits in! Don't be too easy with him, or we'll have to do it all over again."

"Let him down, I say, sergeant!"

"Very well; it's jest as you say. One thing's sartain. He's had a leetle bit of a warning this time; jest a sort of idee of what's the raal state of the argyment. He feels it too. He's not guine to crow agin to-day—and when a rogue stops to crow, why, you may look for him to sing as you want him!"

Millhouse was a tough customer even as a soldier. While he soliloquized, he motioned the negroes to let the outlaw descend slowly. When the fellow reached the ground, and the rope was relaxed, he sank down upon the earth exhausted, though apparently striving to speak. Lance Frampton promptly clapped a bottle to his mouth.

"Why, Lance, what's that?" inquired Porgy, with a new interest in the transaction. The youth slightly laughed.

"Jamaica, captain."

"Jamaica! Where did it come from?"

"The wagon, sir! This lark had been long enough in it to knock the bung out of a keg and try the liquor. It was open when they went to load the wagon, and Toby filled a bottle or two for us, thinking it might help us in sickness, or——"

"Ah! rascal—and you heard me sighing for this very stuff after our fatiguing services, and never gave signs of life!"

This was said very reproachfully.

" I knew the sort of work to be done, captain, and didn't know whether we ought to do any drinking in camp while the enemy was about us in the woods."

"You were right, boy! Many's the good fellow that has lost his scalp from taking too much heed to his swallow. But I am not the person, as you should know, to err thus—and I was almost fainting."

"Yes, sir, but if you had seen the bottle, the sergeant and Tom, sir, would have have seen it too, and——"

"Git out, you impartinent!" quoth Millhouse, interrupting him, with a slight kick—"and don't be choking him with an overdose."

He pushed him away from Norris as he spoke. The outlaw, meanwhile, had been made to swallow a few mouthfuls of the Jamaica, which had somewhat recovered him, though he looked about him vacantly, with blood-shot eyes, and seemed still very much stupefied. Porgy was disposed to be indulgent, and prepared to wait on the fellow for his revelations; but Millhouse thought this was altogether a mistaken pity. He looked out impatiently into the west, where the sun, himself no longer visible, was glinting the forest tops with faint horizontal fires.

" I'm a-thinking, cappin, we hain't got too much time to be wasting on this here rapscallion! Ef he's got to speak, let him speak! He kin make the music, or he kaint! Another h'ist will bring it out of him, I reckon. We've got a good eight miles to ride, and we'll be in the night."

Porgy looked at the outlaw forbearingly. The fellow had evidently suffered a good deal, and was still suffering, though his glances showed that he had fully understood all that had been said, and was not now insensible to his danger. He felt that Millhouse, at all events, a hard old soldier, was in downright earnest; and he might reasonably conclude that his suggestion would, in the end, influence the decision of his superior.

"It will not need many words," said Porgy. "We can ride in the night, sergeant, I think. We've done it a thousand times before, in worse weather, and with home much farther off. Nay, with no home at all to go to! Give the poor devil a chance to recover. We may have to hang him after all. But I hope not. He has had a strong taste of the tree, that last trial; and has probably come to his senses. Give him the needful time to get his wits together. When he does speak, it is only to answer some half-dozen questions, which will hardly need as many sentences. Meanwhile, let some of the boys be getting our horses ready."

Frampton gave the necessary orders, and two or three of the negroes proceeded to this duty. The horses captured from the outlaws were among the objects of their care. While they were thus employed, and Porgy and his companions waiting, with more or less impatience, upon the slowy recovering outlaw, how did the squatter, Bostwick, employ himself? His interest in the progress of the affair, we may be sure, has undergone no diminution. The proceedings, which we have thus far detailed, were all as evident to his understanding as they were apparent to his sight. He had beheld the sufferings of Norris, with feeling for which he could not easily find words; not pity exactly —the sentiment was one not likely to penetrate his bosom— but gratitude perhaps; at all events, with a conviction that the degree of endurance which the outlaw was required to show, was quite as important to *his* safety—though more remotely— as to that of the sufferer himself. Anxiety, the more predominant feeling, was naturally mixed up, accordingly, with a certain annoying sense of self-reproach, which gave bitterness to his moods, and made him eager to be doing something which might employ his rage against the persecutors of his colleague.

This sort of feeling, of mixed anxiety and rage, changed to

absolute terror when he saw the culprit let down from the tree for the *first* time.   Had he then consented to reveal his secret? Was he already frightened from his propriety? Beyond the torture of the process, Bostwick readily persuaded himself that there was no real danger to the victim. He had seen, from the slow and gradual manner in which the executioners worked, that the purpose was neither to strangle him nor to break his neck! When let down, accordingly, he rationally conjectured that this was done only to receive his confession. Such a conviction naturally filled his soul with fear. His brain throbbed. He advanced nervously, some ten steps nearer, with the most desperate impulses; but paused—relieved, in some degree, when he saw the executioner resume his cruel toils, and saw the culprit reascending. But his fears were aroused anew when, a second time, he saw him let down to the earth. A new relief was brought him when, a *third* time, he beheld the struggling figure of his comrade depending in empty air. The selfish nature of the ruffian actually rejoiced in the sufferings, so well endured, of the miserable wretch, as they seemed to promise him security for his secrets—as they testified to the hardy courage of the sufferer, and seemed to declare his determination to suffer the last extremities rather than betray his pledges, even to associates so unworthy of such fidelity. He could value this virtue in another, as it told for his own security. With a husky chuckle, he kept repeating to himself as he beheld the spectacle—

"Oh! he's all flint and iron! He's close as an eyester! You can't prize his jaws open, and make his tongue wag, however you kin fix it! Norris is a glorious chap. He's true blue! I always know'd him for a man! He'll die game! with a stiff upper lip! Poor Dick! Ef I *could* only help you, wouldn't you see the fur fly!"

Then, as he beheld the dangling figure again going up, he almost cried aloud—

"Hold on awhile longer, Dick! Hold on, and they'll hev' to give it up! *Shet* [shut] your teeth fast, Dick—jes' stand to it now, this one time, and they'll let you off. It's only to scare the truth out of you; but don't be scared; and I'm here to save you at the right time."

And, as if his comrade could hear every syllable he said, he proceeded with whispered assurances of succor.

"They'll carry you off to Porgy's house, and I'll follow. They ain't got no lock-up. I'll be close ahind them. I'll watch the proper chance for cutting in, and getting you out. It's only a sharp eye, and a light foot, and a bold heart, and a keen knife, and, maybe, a quick bullet, and we kin git you out of the hands of any one they puts to watch over you; and I'm here, a free man still, to help you, Dick; and you knows me, Dick—you knows Bostwick—he never desarts a friend so long as life's in him. Close, Dick, and don't you be scared!"

And all this, though spoken in a whisper, or at most a murmur, was accompanied with a restless, eager action, as if every syllable could reach the ears of the victim, and every movement of the speaker was apparent to his eyes. The encouragement thus spoken was really meant to reassure himself. For a moment, although the sweat covered his face and neck, it seemed to have the effect. His manner became calmer—his eye more steady—and with even step he stole back to the sheltering place from which he had advanced.

But when, the *third* time, he beheld the culprit swing aloft—when the distress of the victim was observed to be greater than before—when his hands were seen to work and twist, even in their gyves, and the legs were convulsively thrown out with spasmodic action—and the forms below were observed to be more than usually attentive, while the extended hand of Porgy seemed to promise indulgent mercy; and when, a moment after, the outlaw was let down suddenly, supported tenderly beneath the tree, and liquor brought to refresh him: then, the apprehensions of the squatter obtained full ascendency. He then knew all his danger. He felt that the revelation was about to be made. He understood the terms of mercy. He saw that the prisoner was let down, and those attentions shown him, only because of his promise of confession; and though, from the spot where he stood, he heard not a word that was spoken, he yet understood the new relations of the parties as thoroughly as if himself one of the nearest bystanders. His opinion of his comrade changed instantly from the favorable one which he had so recently expressed.

"The mean, miserable skunk!" he exclaimed. "He couldn't grin and keep it in, like a man! Ef I was only nigh him jes' to drive my knife into his jaws! The poor, mean, cowardly beast, with no more sperrit than a spider! But he mus'n't tell! Lord G—d! he mus'n't tell! He must shet up for ever. Ef he speaks, I'm gone! Let me see. They've lifted him again! Thar he stands up afore the inimy. I could put a bullet through jacket of either of them; but what's the use? I could kill one of 'em, I reckon; but that wouldn't help him! The niggers is there, and they've got we'pons too; and, with the other two white men, they'd soon be upon him, and finish him. They'd be upon me, too; but—looking around him—"I reckon 'twould be a cold trail they'd have a'ter me! I could put swamp enough a-tween us to laugh at all their s'arching. What's to be done? It *must* be done! Lord ha' mercy upon you, Dick Norris—you're a most bloody fool! But ef you're coward enough to blab, I ain't fool enough to let you, ef I kin help it."

The squatter now advanced a few paces. He moved confidently, as if his policy had been fully determined upon. He surveyed his ground very narrowly—saw that he had space for a run—calculated nicely the distance of the swamp thicket—the proximity of the cypress tree—the shelters, severally, of the gall and hurrah-bushes—and then deliberately wiped the perspiration from his brows with his sleeve. His head was stretched forward, as if, at the distance of a hundred yards or more, he could hear anything that was spoken, and in this attitude he appeared to listen. He seemed certainly disposed to wait a while on the proceedings of the partisans.

Meanwhile the outlaw, Norris, was recovering.

"You feel easier now, my good fellow," said Porgy, "and we've given you every indulgence. You've had time enough. Tell your story now; say who are your accomplices; who set you on this expedition, and what were its precise objects. A clean breast of it, my man, if you would hope for mercy; or you are run up for the last time!"

"I'll tell you all!" said Norris, utterly broken down.

"Good!" answered Porgy. "The sooner you set about it the better; for, though really willing to wait upon you, and be as indulgent as possible, time won't suffer it. We can't afford to lose the daylight; we must ride."

" Well, I'll tell you," began the outlaw. " There was six of us, you must know. We was got together in Charleston for this—"

Here he stopped suddenly, perforce. He was not permitted another syllable—arrested, at the very opening of his revelations, by a stroke, as if from the very bolt of fate. A rifle-bullet was in his brain! The report of the rifle and the effect of the shot were one. The victim was falling forward, among the group of listeners, at the very moment when the report of the gun was heard. The bullet was aimed with the truest skill. It had bored its way through the forehead, a little over the eyes, the region above both of which it completely traversed. The miserable wretch was dead before he fell!

A moment after, and Bostwick wheeled about for the swamp. He had but few words more of soliloquy.

" It had to be done, Dick Norris! Ef you had to speak for your life, I had to stop you for mine! I would ha' saved you, but you wouldn't let me! I'm mighty sorry, but it had to be done !"

The swamp thicket received him a moment after.

CHAPTER XXVII.

HOW THE FOX DOUBLES, WHILE THE HOUNDS PURSUE.

IT would be much more easy to imagine than to describe the confusion which ensued among our partisans and their followers by this unexpected catastrophe within their circle. For a moment all seemed paralyzed. The event was so strange, so startling, and so utterly unaccountable, particularly supposing it to be the act of one of the outlaws. Porgy was the first to recover, and to conceive the motive for the murder by the fellow's colleague. He started up, and cried aloud—

"One hundred guineas to him who shall take the murderer alive!"

One hundred guineas! Our captain of partisans was a person of most magnificent ideas. Porgy had not, himself, seen such an amount of cash, in one heap, during the last seven years! We have already been advised of the very moderate amount in guineas which he bore away with him at the disbanding of the army. But our captain always spoke in round numbers, such as could roll off trippingly from the tongue. He might have been good for five guineas, and no doubt he would have given this number cheerfully, though it drained him of every copper that he had; but a hundred! He laughed, somewhat bitterly, a moment after, at the audacity of his own imagination.

But it did not need any reward, so soon as the party had sufficiently recovered their faculties, to stimulate their pursuit of the murderer. But there was a decided pause for a brief space after the event. The negroes, at first, were terribly alarmed; some crouched closely to the earth, while others were disposed to scatter themselves in flight. All but Tom, the cook, who was an old soldier, and Pomp, the fiddler, who, flattered by recent distinctions, was ambitious to prove himself a young one — were utterly paralyzed by their terrors. A gulf, opening suddenly beneath their feet, could not have more suddenly swallowed up their courage than did the unexpected bullet of Bostwick. But with the voice of Porgy they looked up. Its clear, trumpet-tones cheered them, and satisfied them that they were not all slain. He rose to his feet, with surprising agility, as he cried aloud, and found Lieutenant Lance Frampton already on the alert, while Sergeant Millhouse, without a word, after giving a single glance to the stiffening body of the outlaw, proceeded, at monstrous long strides, in the direction whence came the bullet of the living one. Tom, the cook, and Pomp, the fiddler, both caught up weapons and darted after Millhouse. Frampton dashed off, also, pursuing another route. The negroes now, generally, encouraged by these demonstrations, took heart, and followed in pursuit and search. They were all more or less provided with weapons, which had been taken from the outlaws.

"Scatter yourselves, boys! scatter if you would search and

be safe!" was the cry of Porgy. He, too, was in motion, with an agility really astonishing in his case. He caught up sword and pistols in the twinkling of an eye, and started off at a moderate trot to gain the tree where his horse—that which he had taken from one of the slain outlaws—was fastened to a swinging limb. But he was not destined to reach it so easily, or in so short a space of time as he had allotted himself. He had forgotten certain embarrassments in his own case—forgotten that he had, in order to the more easy administration of justice, ungirthed and unbuttoned himself, when taking his seat under the royal oak. He was suddenly restored to recollection on this subject, and brought to an abrupt stand, by feeling himself fettered, with his nether garments clinging about his legs. The circumstances in which he found himself were utterly indescribable, but it will not be difficult to conjecture them. He was only brought to a full consciousness of his embarrassment by nearly measuring his full length upon the ground.

"What a devil of a fix!" quoth he, soliloquizing. "Were I now to hear the cry which aroused the Hebrew wrestler—'The Philistines are upon thee, Samson!' what should I do? I should be shot, and sabred, and scalped, before I could steady my legs for decently falling to the ground! I should go over in a heap like a bushel of terrapins! And what a figure I should make upon the earth! How dreadfully exposed! A most shameful condition for 'man and soldier!'"

And thus speaking, he deliberately laid down sword and pistols, and, looking about him cautiously, proceeded to draw up his inexpressibles, and to button, and belt up—a performance less easy than necessary.

"It's well the war is over," quoth he, as he labored to contract his waistbands over his enormous waste of waist, and to bring the strap and buckle of his belt to bear. "I am no longer fit for war. It's wonderful that I've escaped so long and so well! With such a territory to take care of, it's perfectly surprising there have been so few trespassers! I could not always have kept them off! They would have overcome me at last! They might have caught me at some such awkward moment, in some such awkward fix, as the present! Ah! There! It is done at last! The wilderness is under fence at last!"

And he breathed long and heavily, after such severe exertion! But he wasted no more time than was necessary. Porgy was no loiterer when duty was to be done. He skulked no task, shirked no obligations; and hence his greater merit, inclining, naturally, as he did, to the creature comforts, and a selfish desire for repose and luxury. He now reached his horse, and mounted in a few moments. He was a good horseman. It was much easier to raise than to lower himself—easier to get into the saddle, than to subside upon his leafy couch on the earth. Once in the saddle, he was a hard rider! The steed that carried him had a great deal to bear besides his weight. He used the spur freely, and was never more liberal in its use than now, when required to make up for lost time. Headlong, he drove into the thick cover of the forest, and for the swamp-fastnesses, where the outlaw, Bostwick, had taken refuge. Here, our partisan captain was soon found, making his way over log and through bog, in mire and water, through close thicket and tangled vine, in a wilderness from which the light was disappearing fast; and as far as horse could well go, where a career on horseback must be very soon arrested.

The pursuit was hotly urged. It was well that Bostwick had made his calculations so cunningly, and taken such deliberate precautions. He had to deal with old "swamp-suckers,"—hunters as keen and familiar with such places as himself. Had they been as well acquainted with this particular locality, he had never escaped. Nay, had there been one hour more of sunlight, his chances would have been very doubtful. As Porgy phrased it—

"But one inch of candle more, and we should have his hide."

As it was, the outlaw was more than once caught sight of in the chase. Millhouse once detected him, as a half-floating log turned with him in the water. Pompey cried out that he was going through the gall bushes in front; and Lance Frampton got a clear view of him, at long distance, crossing a tussock. He gave him both pistols as he sped—"bang! bang!" with scarce an interval between the two shots; but, at each fire, Bostwick was seen to duck his head instinctively; and, at length, he disappeared in a pond, rising up on the opposite side, amid a heap of drift wood. Here he paused, with his nose just out of water, and lay still, as he thought he lay unseen.

And he was in a place of safety. Night had come to his relief. He could hear the cries of his pursuers, but could no longer see them, and he felt that he was secure. It only required that he should keep still. The sounds of pursuit finally ceased; his enemies had all disappeared; and, like a great Newfoundland dog, shivering all over, he raised himself out of the alligator hole which had harbored him, and stood, savage and gloomy, upon the neighboring bank; the owl hooted overhead from the blasted cypress, and the sad stars coming out, one by one, and looking down like so many mysterious sentinels in Heaven, watchers over the guilty course of man on earth.

Bostwick shivered, as he looked up, with superstition as well as cold. He had certainly, that day, received a fearful lesson of the vicissitudes and terrors which wait upon evil deeds! The way of the transgressor is indeed hard! His comrades gone; not one to be seen! How many of the five who had set out with him on this expedition, now breathed the air of life with him? He knew not, at that moment, of *one!* He had been baffled in the purpose he had in view. Had lost everything — even his rifle, which, in the hottest of the pursuit, he had been compelled to cast away. But one thing he had saved — the box of the widow Eveleigh, containing the fifty guineas, and the papers which M'Kewn so much desired! He had concealed this box in a hiding-place in the swamp above, which he had no fear would be discovered. This was consolation in the recollection of those fifty guineas. He had other consolations when he thought of the papers and M'Kewn! For the latter, his present situation filled him with new bitterness.

"D—n him!" he muttered to himself. "He shall pay well for them afore he gits them! He shall make up to me all my losses! He shall pay for these poor fellows, and what they suffered. There will be a sweet bill of it, which he shall foot up every shilling, or there shall be no peace for him on this airth!"

Let us leave him, cowering and cursing in the swamp, and return to the partisans. They gave up the chase only when they found it no longer possible to see. Lance Frampton picked up, and brought in, the outlaw's rifle, which they all examined closely, in the hopes to identify it; but they had none of them seen it before in any hands. Three letters, evidently initials of a former owner's name, were cut rudely in the stock.

"M. T. C."

"Marcus Tullius Cicero!" quoth Porgy, very gravely.

"Who, captain? I never heard the name! Do you know him?" was the simple inquiry of the lieutenant.

"I ought to; for I received many a flogging, when a boy, that I might become intimate with him, and the old fellows he kept company with. And you may be sure the flogging did not make me love him or them any better! But I doubt if either Marcus or his companions owned this rifle. If they did, then the historians have suppressed many an interesting fact in science. But, let us push out of this wilderness, Lance, and get into the open road. Corporal, see to the negroes, and send them on ahead.—Let them get wood and have fire for us at least, when we reach home. It is getting monstrous chilly! Yes— we shall need a fire, even more than supper!"

Supper, indeed! thought Porgy. It was his philosophy only which preferred the fire.

Obedience was now pleasure. The whole party was well tired of the fruitless pursuit, and all began to feel the chillness of which the captain complained—and the hunger also, of which he did not think it necessary to complain.

"See that the negroes cover the dead bodies with leaves, Lance, until to-morrow, when we must borrow shovels from Mrs. Eveleigh, and have them buried. The buzzard and wild-cat will hardly find them in one night."

CHAPTER XXVIII.

THE OLD SOLDIER RETURNS TO A RUINED HOMESTEAD.

ALL was done as had been commanded. Tom's world of kitchen and camp baggage, was fairly divided among the ne groes, all of whom were now mounted on the captured horses of the outlaws, some of them riding double. The dead bodies were hidden away beneath the forest leaves and branches, as closely as it could possibly be done. The odds and ends of the party were carefully picked up; not a tin pan suffered to escape inquiry; and, under the growing starlight, the negroes took up the line of march, as a sort of advance, with Tom, the cook, for guide and leader; Porgy, Frampton, and Millhouse following at a less rapid pace. Of these three, the two latter were suffered to lead the way, our captain of partisans seeming disposed to linger in a manner that surprised Millhouse, who made it a subject of comment to his companion.

Frampton, through the sympathies which he entertained for his superior, could well understand the reason of his apparent apathy. Without much logic or knowledge—without being much a student of human nature—the genial temper of Frampton had taught him to conjecture the peculiar mood which now troubled the partisan. Besides, he had been enlightened measurably, that day, on the subject of Porgy's secret cares, by the long conversation between them which has been already reported, and, through which, the lieutenant had found clews to the captain's nature and difficulties, such as his buoyant temper had never before suffered him to betray. That the latter should now hesitate—now that he was almost at his own threshold—did not greatly surprise the youth, and reäwakened all his sympathies for his chief. He might well linger on the route, loath to approach scenes so precious once, so full of dear recollections, but now so full of gloomy aspects and discouraging auguries. From Porgy's own description, there could be no prospect half so cheerless as that of the ancient homestead which was about to receive him. Memory and thought might well be painfully busy in his mind. The one recalled a past which was full of sunshine and promise. The other reproached him with a profligacy which had measurably cast fortune from his arms; and bitterly rehearsed the recent history, in which events seemed to have studiously aided to consummate the ruin which his own erring youth had begun. The journey, from the camp of Marion, at the head of Cooper river, and which was now to terminate upon the Ashepoo, had afforded prospects, all along the route, well calculated to give the gloomiest color to the mind of the observer. Of this journey, we can not afford a better idea than to copy from Moultrie's memoirs, a few passages descriptive of what *he* saw, in a neighboring district of country, about the same period—in fact, the preceding summer—on his own return to his estates, which had suffered in like manner with most others.

"Soon after my being exchanged," writes the old general, "I prepared to set off, with my family, for South Carolina, and, early in April, left Philadelphia, and arrived at Waccamaw, in South Carolina; where I was informed that General Greene's army lay at Ashley river, quite inactive, and no military operation going on. I remained at Winyaw till late in September, at which time I paid a visit to General Greene. It was the most dull, melancholy, dreary ride that any one could possibly take, of about one hundred miles, through the woods of that country, which I had been accustomed to see abound with live stock, and wild fowl of every kind. It was now destitute of all. It had been so completely chequered by the different armies, that, not a part of it had been left unexplored; consequently, not a vestige of horses, cattle, hogs or deer, &c., was to be found. The squirrels and birds of every kind were totally destroyed. The dragoons told me, that, on their scouts, no living creature was to be seen, except a few camp-scavengers (turkey-buzzards) picking the bones of some unfortunate fellows, who had been cut or shot down, and left in the woods above ground. . . . . My plantation I found to be a desolate place; stock of every kind taken off; the furniture carried away, and my estate had been under sequestration."

This individual picture was equally true of all the country;

and the condition of Moultrie's estate, that of every man who had distinguished himself on either side, whether for, or against the revolutionary struggle. Very many had fared even worse —their negroes being wholly carried off, and their dwellings destroyed by fire. Though but a captain in the brigade of Marion, Porgy had been honored by a fair share of British hostility. His home, he knew, had escaped the torch of the incendiary, but his negroes had been stolen, and the plantation utterly laid waste. We have already seen what special additional causes of anxiety were at work to make him moody. Debt hung upon his fortunes like an incubus; and he possessed no conscious resources, within himself, by which to restore his property, or even to acquire the means of life. He rode forward, gloomy and comfortless, in spite of all his philosophy, scarcely exchanging a word with his companions.

Meanwhile, his negroes, under Tom's guidance, eager once more to regain their old homes, sped on, at a smart canter, which soon left their superiors behind. It was after ten o'clock at night, when the lights from a score of wild, gleaming torches, wavering in air, announced the approach to the avenue of "Glen-Eberly," which was the name of Porgy's ancient homestead—so named after a goodly grandmother by whom it had been entailed on her brother's children. Our captain of partisans was aroused to a consciousness of external things, by the loud shouts of the negroes who had preceded him, and who now hailed his approach after a fashion such as Moultrie describes in the same narrative from which we have already quoted.

"T'ank de Lord, here's maussa *git* to he own home at last! —B*r*ess de Lord, Maussa, you come! We all *berry* glad *for* see you, maussa—glad *too* much!"

And the same negroes who had been with him for several hours before, without so much as taking his hand, now rushed up and seized it, with loud cries, as if they were hosts, and welcoming a favorite guest. The tears stood in the eyes of our captain, though he suffered none of his companions to behold them; and he shook hands with, and spoke to them each in turn—few words, indeed, but they were uttered tremulously, and in low tones.

Fordham, the overseer of Mrs. Eveleigh, now made his appearance from the house. The wagon had departed, having left the supplies as the good widow had ordered. Porgy entered his house expecting to find it empty and cheerless. He was gratefully confounded to see the goods, blankets, drink, provisions, all around the hall, and shown to the best advantage under the ruddy gleams of a rousing fire in the chimney.

"Ah!" said he, " Fordham, Mrs. Eveleigh is a very noble lady. Make her my best respects and thanks. I shall soon ride over and make them in person."

"Well, my friends," said he to Frampton and Millhouse, when Fordham had departed, " I felt doubtful how to provide you your supper to-night; though, knowing this excellent lady as I did, I should not have doubted that she would contribute largely to it. See what she has done! Here are sugar and coffee; here are meal and bacon; here is a cheese; here—but look about you, and say what we shall have for supper. Supper we must have! I am famishing. Tom! Tom! where the d—l is that fellow! Does he think that he's free of *me*, because he's free of the army?—Tom! Tom!"

"Sah! yer, maussa! Wha' de debbil mek' [makes] you *holler* so loud, maussa, when I's jis' [just] at your elbow? You t'ink I hard o' hearing, 'cause I got hard maussa, I 'spose!"

"Hard maussa, you impertinent scamp! Another master would have roasted you alive long before this. See, and let us have something, in the twinkling of an eye. Look among these provisions, that Mrs. Eveleigh has sent us, and take out enough to give us all a good feed—*niggers* and all!"

"Miss Ebleigh! *He's* a bressed [blessed] woman, for sartin, for sen' we all sich good t'ings; de berry t'ings we bin want; and jis' when we want 'em. He's a mos' 'spectable pusson, is dat Miss Ebleigh. Ki! He's a'mos' [almost] ebbry t'ing for ge*m*pleman supper! Kah, me! dis da cheese, in dis tub! Pomp, you son ob a snail! why you day? Yer! [here] open dem bundle wha' b'long to me, in de piazza! bring fanner [a shallow winnowing basket] and bring bucket you will see day [there]. Hab out de t'ree knife and de four fork, for maussa, when he got comp'ny. See a'ter de hom'ny pot; and de coffee-pot; and look up some water for wash dem! Dere's no kitchen, maussa; he all bu'n down. We hab for cook de supper in de house, yer, or, maybe, we kin find fireplace down stairs in de brick part. Go see, Pomp—and Pomp, sen' out some of dem nigger for git lightwood, and bring water and udder t'ings."

We allow Tom to be thus prolix, not simply because he was so permitted by his master, but as he gives us a very correct idea of the condition of household affairs. The kitchen, as he states, was destroyed; the cooking was finally decreed to be carried on in the brick basement of the house hereafter, but, for this night, Tom made free with the fireplace of the *salle à manger*. The house was an ample one, of wood, on a brick basement. But it had been completely gutted. There was neither table nor chair; and our friends couched themselves upon the blankets of Mrs. Eveleigh, spread about the fireplace; and, accustomed as they had been to still harder, if not humbler seats, upon the naked ground, were not seriously conscious of any privations. Thus sitting, or reclining, they waited in comparative silence the preparations which Tom was making for supper.

That sable kitchen-despot had found employment for all the negroes, Pompey acting as a sort of lieutenant or orderly. Water and wood, in any quantity, were soon provided. Soon, the hominy was set to boil; the coffee-pot began to smoke; while the "hoe" and "johnny" cakes, spread upon sections of barrel heads, four or five in number, were seen facing the now brightly blazing fire. The chimney-place of the dining-room, though not quite so ample as that of a Southern plantation kitchen, was yet one of sufficiently large dimensions. What with the hominy and coffee-pots, the bread stuffs, and the frying-pan, hissing with broad but tender slices of ham—which the fork of the grand cuisinier shifted from side to side, as the occasion seemed to require—there was little space left in the premises, and no room suffered near them for mere idlers: in which rank, at this moment, we may consider the captain, himself, and his two companions in arms. But the fire was sufficient to warm the room, the shutters being closed in, though there was not a pane of glass left in one of the sashes. If the whites of the group were silent, Tom was not. The benefactions of

8*

Mrs. Eveleigh afforded him an ample theme for talk; and, while he stirred the hominy, and turned the ham and the hoe cakes, and pushed up the fire—keeping Pompey busy all the while—he maintained a running commentary on the blessings of life in the neighborhood of such an excellent woman—a woman so well conversant with her duties to her neighbors.

"Dis is fus' [first] rate *ole* bacon, maussa, dat Miss Ebleigh bin sen' we! And de grits [grist] is de bes' flint; an' dis flour is white like snow; and sich a bowl of coffee, as I guine gibe you to-night, wid sich sugar, you ain't bin see dis fi*b*e, t'ree, se*b*en years, maussa! Lord be praise, for all he mussies! When I bin riding 'long yer to-night, coming to we ole home, I bin say to myself, all 'long de way, wha' de debbil we guine fin' home yer for supper to-night! Enty I know, dem d—n British and tory bin skin de plantation ob ebbry t'ing? Hah! I say, der' will be heap o' growling 'tomachs yer to-night! An' I t'ink of de cole [cold] and de starbation, 'till I begin to shibber all ober like new sodger, jis when de inimy begin for shoot! But, de Lord be praise! Der's no cole, der's no 'tarbation! Yer's ebbry t'ing for las' we niggars, and you gemplemens mos' t'ree week!"

Tom had calculated nicely, as well as an experienced commissariat could have done. He had an eye to a man's dimensions. He continued:—

"Time 'nough t'ree week from now to consideration how for git more supper: and der's no knowing wha' guine tu'n [turn] up, in dat time, for gib us more hom'ny and bacon. De Lord is wid us! An' maussa, you ain't bin see dis bag o' rice, a good bushel I reckon, dat Miss Ebleigh bin sen' wid dem udder t'ings. Hab a pot o' rice to-morrow!"

Tom, when he declared it time enough to consider how to procure more food when the present supplies were fairly exhausted, dealt in genuine negro philosophy. Sambo seldom troubles himself to look out for the morrow. His doctrine somewhat tallied with that of Scripture. Instead of—"sufficient for the day, the evil thereof," he read, "sufficient for the day, the good thereof." Foresight and forethought are his remarkable deficiencies. He never houses his harvest in anticipation of the storm.

There was one virtue in Tom's philosophies. They never embarrassed, or delayed him, in his duties and performances; and it was not very long before he made the grateful annunciation to the hungering troopers that supper was ready to be served. Then followed the bustle. Then was Pomp conspicuous as head waiter, while Tom, as if satisfied with his share of the performance, already executed, drew up a keg to the fireside, and leisurely seated himself as a spectator—ready to take up the smoking dishes from the fire as soon as the cloth should be spread to receive them; but in no other way interested in the performance!

CHAPTER XXIX.

HOW A SUPPER MAY TAKE AWAY A DRAGOON'S APPETITE.

"Why you no spread de table-clot', Pomp?" was the snappish demand of Tom, seeing the other hesitate.

"I no see no clot' uncle Tom," replied the bewildered fiddler.

"Enty blanket is clot', you son ob a skunk! Is you lib so long in de worl', dat you neber l'arn wha' one t'ing is, and wha' nodder t'ing is—wha' is wood, and wha' is clot'! I reckon, boy, when we calls you to eat you' own supper, you wunt ax ef it's *dut* [dirt] you mus' eat, or hom'ny."

Pomp, humbled by his rebuke, possessed himself of one of the blankets, from the pile sent by the widow, but he still stood, vacantly looking about the apartment.

"Well," quoth our major domo, "wha' you 'tan' [stand] for, sucking in de whole room wid your eyes?"

"I no see any table, uncle Tom!"

"Don't you uncle me, you chucklehead! Lay de table on de floor! Who could b'lieb dat a pusson could lib so long and grow so big, and nebber l'arn nutting! Ha! boy, you bin in de army, you'd ha' l'arn all sort of t'ing at de sharp p'int ob de baggnet! De army's de place for mek' man ob sense out ob fool. Ax de gempleman's to git out ob de way, so you kin spread de table-clot'; dough gemplemans ought to hab **sense** 'nough, hese'f, for moob [move] widout axing!"

"Hear that impudent rascal!" quoth Porgy, moving good-naturedly, his example followed by Frampton and Millhouse. "Was ever fellow so completely spoiled?"

"I nebber *spile* supper, maussa!" responded Tom, with a toss of the head, as if to say—"nobody knows my qualities better than yourself."

"No, indeed, Tom, and you presume on your merits, some-what to their injury; but you will be taken down, you scamp, when you are required to find and hunt up the supper, as well as cook it."

"Ha! but you see, maussa, my business is cook—I knows um! It's maussa business to fin' de *bittle* [victuals]. Put de meat and bread yer, whay I kin put out my han' and git 'em, leff it to me to hab 'em ready for eat; but da's all I hab a right for do."

"Ah! indeed, my buck; but I'll persuade you, at the end of a hickory, that you have other rights."

"Wha' maussa; hick'ry for Tom! Nebber! Anybody else bin tell me sich a t'ing, I say, widout guine to be sassy—'he's a d—n fool for he trouble.'"

"Hear the fellow! Sergeant, do you want a negro—a cook?"

"I'll thank you, cappin, very much. Tom and myself agree very well together. I like his fries monstrous."

"You shall have him—when I'm done with him."

"You nebber guine done wid Tom, maussa! I 'tick to you ebbrywhere; you comp'ny good 'nough for Tom in any country, no matter whay you go."

"Thank you, Tom; but Tom, if you don't clap a hot iron to Pomp's haunches, he'll never have supper on table to-night."

"De boy will be de deat' ob me!" cried Tom, starting up, and administering a sudden whack to the ear of Pomp, with the flat of an amazingly rough hand. The lad reeled under the salutation. Pompey was more dexterous at the violin, than in the capacity of a house-servant. He had no idea of the novel duties he was required to perform; and, jerking him by the col-lar to the fireplace, Tom clapped the several dishes into his hand,

and proceeded, with the expertness of a veteran, to guide everything to its proper place. Under his administration, the table
was soon spread.

"Now you see, boy, how de t'ing is done. 'Member nex'
time, or you'll see sights ob hickory, wid de twigs all grow-
in' downwards. Now, tell de gemplemans dat supper is
a-waitin'."

And Tom resumed his seat upon the keg by the fire. Pomp
made the necessary signals, after a fashion of his own, and
Porgy, letting himself down upon one corner of the blanket,
which served as a table-cloth, invited his comrades in war to
follow his example. They did not wait for a second invitation,
but grouped themselves about the lowly board, occupying opposite places. Tom flung some fresh brands into the fire, which
blazed up ruddily, throwing a strong light over the great hall,
and showing, picturesquely, the group upon the floor, with Pomp
in waiting, and several sooty faces peering in through one of
the windows—from which a shutter had been torn—opening
upon the piazza.

The equipments of the board were quite as picturesque as the
group around them. The crockery closet of Captain Porgy
being utterly empty, the hominy-pot, black and smoking as it
was, had been lifted bodily from the fire, and now stood in the
centre, resting upon a barrel-head, into which its three legs
burned regular sockets. A pewter spoon was employed to scoop
up its white and well-boiled contents. The coffee-pot, a bat-
tered vessel that had been in the wars, occupied a similar rest-
ing-place; while the fried bacon was handed round, by Pomp,
to the several parties in a huge frying-pan, in which it had been
"done to a turn." This vessel bore proof, also, of serious service, having more than one flaw in the sides, while one half of
the handle had been carried away in actual conflict with the
keen sabre of a British dragoon. The partisans helped themselves to meat and gravy, in turn, from this sooty vessel, which
was then restored to the fireplace, the better to keep warm the
residue of the bacon. The hoe-cake, broken into good-sized
bits, was placed upon another section of a barrel-head, by the
hands of Porgy himself. At the side of each stood his tin cup
smoking with coffee, while the top of the coffee-pot was em-

ployed to hold sugar, and stood, conveniently for the use of all, in the centre of the group.

Thus served, our partisans were by no means slow in their performances. The edge of appetite was keen. They worked vigorously. The taste of the meats improved the moods of all parties, and opened hearts as well as jaws. The fullness of the mouth prompted the heart to speech; and, in the enjoyment of things of the flesh, Porgy soon began to forget the anxieties of the spirit. He smacked his lips over the luscious ham, exclaiming:—

"This may be called good, Tom—very good: in fact, I never tasted better. You have certainly lost none of your talent in consequence of your leaving the army."

"I bin good cook 'fore I ebber see de army."

"So you were, Tom; but your taste was matured in the army; particularly on the Pedee. But you were better at a broil, I think, before the war."

"Tom's jest as good, I'm a-thinking, at a fry as at a brile, cappin," quoth Millhouse, licking his chaps, while elevating a huge slice of his bacon into sight, upon the prongs of his fork.

"An' why you no say *bile*, too, Mass Millh'us'?" demanded Tom, apparently not satisfied that there should be any implied demerits in his case.

"En [and] so I mout [might]," answered the sergeant. "This here hominy now, to my thinking, is *biled* to a monstrous softness."

"An' de bake—de bread—wha' you say for him?" was the next exaction of Tom's vanity; and he handed up, as he queried, a fresh supply, from the fire, of a crisp, well-browned "Johnny-cake"—an article, by the way, which is too often served up, of most villanous manufacture, particularly at a *modern* barbecue; but which, in those days, might usually be commended, and which, in Tom's hands, was an achievement— a *chef-d'œuvre* of kitchen art.

"Well, Tom, I kin say with a mighty cl'ar conscience, that this is raal, gennywine bread. I only wish Miss Ebeleigh was here now, herself, jest to try a taste of it."

"Ha!" quoth Tom, heaving up—"I 'speck [expect] ef he bin yer, he would nebber le' maussa res', tell he beg me from 'em. He would want you to gib me to um, I tell you, maussa!"

"Give you, Tom! Give you to anybody? No! no! old fellow! I will neither give you, nor sell you, nor suffer you to be taken from me in any way, by Saint Shadrach! who was your blessed father in the flesh, and from whom you inherit your peculiar genius for the kitchen! Nothing but death shall ever part us, and even death shall not if I can help it. When I die, you shall be buried with me. We have fought and fed too long together, Tom, and I trust we love each other quite too well, to submit to separation. When *your* kitchen fire grows cold, Tom, I shall cease to eat; and you, Tom, will not have breath enough to blow up the fire when mine is out! I shall fight for you to the last, Tom, and you, I know, would fight to the last for me, as I am very sure that neither of us can long outlast the other."

"Fight for you, maussa! Ha! Jes' le' dem tory try we, maussa!" responded Tom, quite excited, and shaking his head with a dire significance. But Tom did not exactly conceive the tenor of his master's speech, or the direction of his thoughts. He did not conjecture that the earnestness with which the latter spoke, had its origin in his recent meditations; and these had regard to civil rather than military dangers—to the claws of the sheriff, rather than tory weapons! Once on this track, Porgy found relief in continuing, and in making himself better understood.

"They shall take *none* of you negroes, if I can help it! But they shall take *all* before they touch a hair of your head, Tom!"

"Da's it, maussa! I know you nebber guine part wid Tom!"

"Before they shall tear you from me, Tom——"

"Day [they] can't begin to come it, maussa! I 'tick to you, maussa, so long as fire bu'n!"

"But, it might be, Tom; the time might come; circumstances might arise; events might happen; I might be absent, or unable; and then, you might fall into the clutches of some of these d——d harpies, who take a malignant pleasure in making people uncomfortable. You have heard, Tom, of such an animal as a sheriff, or sheriff's deputy?"

"Enty I know? He's a sort of warmint! I knows 'em well! He come into de hen-house, cut chicken t'roat, drink de blood, and suck all de eggs! I know 'em, for sartain! Da him?"

"Yes, they are blood-suckers, and egg-suckers, and throat-cutters—that's true, Tom; vermin of the worst sort: but they still come in the shape of human beings. They are men after a fashion; men-weasels, verily, and they do the work of beasts! You will know them by their sly looks; their skulkings, peepings, watchings, and the snares they lay; by the great papers, with great seals, that they carry; and by their calling themselves sheriffs or constables, and speaking big about justice and the law. If any of you negroes happen to see any such lurking about the plantation, or within five miles, let me know. Don't let them lay hands on you, but make for the swamp, the moment they tell you 'stop.' You, Tom, in particular, beware of all such! Should they succeed in taking you, Tom—should I not be able to help you—should you find them carrying you off, to the city or elsewhere, to sell you to some other master——"

"Gor-a-mighty! maussa, wha' for you scare me so, t'inking ob sich t'ings?"

"Tom! sooner than have you taken off by these vermin, I will shoot you!"

"Me! shoot me! me, Tom! Shoot me, maussa!"

"Yes, Tom! you shall never leave me. I will put a brace of bullets through your abdomen, Tom, sooner than lose you! But, it may be, that I shall not have the opportunity. They may take advantage of my absence—they may *steal* you away—coming on you by surprise. If they should do so, Tom, I rely upon you to put *yourself* to death, sooner than abandon me and become the slave of another. Kill yourself, Tom, rather than let them carry you off. Put your knife into your ribs, anywhere, three inches deep, and you will effectually baffle the blood-hounds!"

"Wha', me, maussa! kill mese'f! Me, Tom! 'Tick knife t'ree inch in me rib, and dead! Nebber, in dis worl' [world] maussa! I no want for dead! I always good for cook! I good for fight—good for heap o' t'ing in dis life! No good 'nough for dead, maussa! No want for dead so long as der's plenty ob bile, and brile, and bake, and fry, for go sleep 'pon. Don't talk ob sich t'ing, maussa, jis' now, when de time is 'mos' [almost] come for me eat supper!"

"Tom!" exclaimed the captain of partisans, laying down his

knife and fork, and looking solemnly and sternly at the negro —
"I thought you were more of a man—that you had more affection for me. Is it possible that you could wish to live, if separated from me? Impossible, Tom! I will never believe it.
No, boy, you shall never leave me. We shall never part. You
shall be my cook, after death, in future worlds, even as you are
here. Should you suffer yourself to survive me, Tom—should
you be so hard-hearted—I will haunt you at meal-time always.
Breakfast, dinner, supper—at every meal—you shall hear my
voice. I will sit before you as soon as the broil is ready, and
you shall always help me first!"

The negro looked aghast. Porgy nodded his head solemnly.

"Remember! It shall be as I have said. If you are not
prepared to bury yourself in the same grave with me when I
die, I shall be with you in spirit, if not in flesh; and I shall
make you cook for me as now. At breakfast you will hear me
call out for ham and eggs, or a steak; at dinner, perhaps, for a
terrapin stew; at supper, Tom—when all is dark and dreary,
and there is nobody but yourself beside the fire—I shall cry
out, at your elbow, 'My coffee, Tom!' in a voice that shall
shake the very house!"

"Oh, maussa! nebber say sich t'ing! Ef you promise sich
t'ing, you hab for come!"

"To be sure;—so you see what you have to expect if you
dare to survive me!"

Tom turned gloomily to the fire, not a little bewildered. The
bravest negro is the slave of superstitious fancies, and Tom was
a devout believer in ghosts, and quite famous in the kitchen for
his own ghost experience.

"But to your own supper now, with what appetite you may,
and see that you feed the other negroes. I see that *we* have all
supped."

"Lor'-a-mighty, maussa, you tek' 'way all me appetite for
supper."

"You will soon enough find it, I fancy," quoth Porgy, coolly,
as he lighted his pipe. Millhouse followed the example, and,
accompanied by Lieutenant Frampton, the two adjourned to the
piazza. leaving the field to the negroes, who, at a given signal,
rushed eagerly in to the feast.

CHAPTER XXX.

SERGEANT MILLHOUSE DISCUSSES THE POLICY OF CAPTAIN PORGY.

IT has been said that the homestead of the old soldier was entirely swept of furniture. In emerging from the hall to the piazza, Porgy and his followers were without a chair upon which to sit. They paced the piazza, accordingly, puffing as they went. The floor of it shook beneath their steps. It needed repair. The bannisters were gone. The boards were half decayed. The steps by which they ascended to the house "were ticklish to the last degree," to employ the phrase of Porgy himself. The latter paused in his paces.

"This won't do," said he. "To smoke is to contemplate. Contemplation implies calm, repose, and an easy position for the body. With the pipe in my mouth, I must sit or lie. Let us go out and sit by that fire, boys."

The negroes had kindled a fire within fifty feet of the house, and on one side of the avenue. It was the customary camp-fire to the old soldiers, and there was no reluctance declared or felt to the proposition of the captain of partisans. He led the way, accordingly, and, with a grunt and some effort, let himself down beside the blaze. New brands were supplied by Frampton, and himself and Millhouse subsided upon the ground also, at respectful distances from their superior. Here they crouched for a while. Supper had done its work, in inducing a certain feeling of sluggishness. Change of circumstance was productive also of a mood which inclined rather to musing than to speech. The thoughts of all were more or less busy. The subject of Porgy's speculations may be easily conjectured. Those of Millhouse are not less easily definable, but they involved few anxieties on his own account. Lance Frampton was a young lover, who felt every hour an age which kept him away from his rustic beauty.   Of course his head and heart were filled with her image.   Not that he had not other thoughts more proper to his immediate associations.   His was a spirit of generous sym pathies, and, spite of all Porgy's selfishness of character, the young man, through an intercourse of three years, had learned to love and honor him for the really good points in his nature in spite of its egotism.   He mused quite as much upon the fortunes of his superior as upon his own.

For a time, accordingly, all were busy brooding each after his own fashion, and. all silent.   The pipes sent forth their volumes, adding not a little to the cloudy atmosphere by which they were surrounded.   The night was dark and raw, without being really cold.   The winds were low, and faintly sighed through the too scanty bit of wood which lay between our group and the north. The prospect promised rain by morning.   The weight of the atmosphere was felt, and, pressing back the smokes of the fire, kept the party enveloped in a white shroud of mist and vapor. A melancholy stillness overspread the scene, and the ear felt oppressed, as well as the eye, by the uniform absence of all provocation from without.   Not a star was to be seen.   A solid wall seemed to shut in the circle within thirty yards ; and inside of this circuit nothing was visible but the skeleton outlines of the trees, and the vague, faint white of the dwelling-house.   Our party felt the gloom of the prospect.   The captain and sergeant puffed with all their vigor, and very soon replenished their pipes. The former at length broke silence.

"We are to have rain by the morning; but this must not pre- vent us from putting those rascals out of sight"—(meaning the outlaws who had been slain).   "You must give instructions, Lance, to one of the negroes, to set off by daylight to Mrs. Eve- leigh, and borrow spades and shovels, or hoes, for the purpose of burying them.   I doubt if such things are to be found any- where on this place.   After that, Lance, I suspect you will de- sire to ride over and visit the widow Griffin.   It will be a day's visit only, I suspect, and you will be back at night.   But that's just as you and they think proper.   Of course, you know, my boy, that so long as I have house-room and enough for supper, you shall share it.   When you are married, you shall still do as you please.   You may bring your wife here, if it suits you, and her mother too. At all events, here is your home, so long as it is mine."

"Thank you, kindly, captain; and I hope you'll keep your plantation for ever. I expect to work for you here until I'm married, and after that we'll see. I reckon Mrs. Griffin will want Ellen and me to live with her when we are married, and to manage her little place."

"That is, if she herself does not marry."

"Oh! I don't think she's going to do that. She was mighty fond of her husband."

"Y-e-s!" quoth Porgy, taking out his pipe, and emptying the ashes. "Y-e-s! it may be so—and yet the widow is tolerably young, fresh, and good-looking. A dead husband is of no sort of use in this world, and that is the present question. When I have smoked out my pipe, and emptied the ashes, I am apt, after a little pause, to fill it with fresh tobacco. He who has smoked one pipe, will be apt to try another, and another, as long as he can smoke. That is, if the first has not sickened him. That the widow has found one husband grateful, is good reason why she should try another. Mrs. Griffin is a woman of sense, and has too many good qualities to remain single. She is a good housekeeper—everything is in trim about her. She takes care of everything, and herself neat. Besides, she makes a first-rate terrapin stew, quite as good as Tom; and her broil and fry will pass muster in any camp. I remember the blue cat, which she gave us on the Edisto, with a relish even now; and that reminds me, by the way, that we must get hooks and lines ready for the Ashepoo pretty soon. We shall have the spring upon us before we get our tackle ready."

"I'm a-thinking, cappin," said Millhouse, "that you'll have to be seeing about something besides blue cat and fishing lines. You'll want ploughs and hoes sooner than anything else. These niggers must go to work, mighty soon, ef I'm to have the managing of 'em."

"You, Millhouse! Do you mean to volunteer as overseer?"

"Don't I! I reckon that's pretty much all I'm good for. But it's lucky I do know something of rice planting; and I was never a slouch at making corn. I'm for breaking up land, and

and going to work, without so much as axing your leave or blessing."

"You shall do as you please, old fellow, for I don't know that I can teach you anything in these matters. I was always one of that large class of planters who reap thistles from their planting. I sowed wheat only to reap tares. I never had luck in planting."

"That's because you never trusted to luck, cappin. You was always a-thinking to do something better than other people, and you wouldn't let nater [nature] alone. You was always a-hurrying nater, tell you wore her out; jest like those foolish mothers who give their children physic—dose after dose—one dose fighting agin the other, and nara [neither] one gitting a chance to work. Now, I'm a-thinking that the true way is to put the ground in order, and at the right time plant the seed, and then jest lie by, and look on, and see what the warm sun and the rain's guine to do for it. But you, I reckon, warn't patient enough to wait. You was always for pulling up the corn to see if it had sprouted; and for planting over jest when it was beginning to grow. I've known a many of that sort of people, preticklarly among you wise people, and gentlemen born. It ain't reasonable to think that a man kin find new wisdom about everything; and them sort of people who talk so fine, and strange, and sensible, in a new way, about the business that has been practised ever since the world begun, they're always overdoing the business, and working agin nater. They're quite too knowing to give themselves a chance."

"That's philosophy, Millhouse."

"No, cappin, 'tain't philosophy, but it's mighty good sense. I kin make corn, and rice, I reckon, jest as good as any man; and you must leave it all to me. I'll work it all out, and you mus'n't meddle, cappin, except to do jest them things that I tell you."

"Good! I like that! I feel that I should greatly improve under a good sense keeper."

"'Zackly, cappin; that's the very thing you've been awanting all your life. Now, I've hearn you tell, how you used, when a-planting these same rice lands of your'n, to let the water off of the fields to catch the fish, ef so be some of your friends happen'd to come and dine with you. Sp'ile a whole field of fine rice, jest flooded, to catch a few *pairch!*"

"Ah! but, Millhouse, they were such beauties! You never saw such perch in your life."

"I reckon I've seed as fine pairch as ever you caught, cappin. But that ain't the thing, no how. Ef they were as fine fish as ever grow'd in water, it was a sin and shame to spile the rice to catch 'em; and, as sure as a gun, cappin, ef you had been rightly sarved, you'd ha' been tucked up to a swinging limb, and been dressed with a dozen hickories, tell you was made sensible and ashamed."

"Humph!" exclaimed Porgy, emptying the ashes from his pipe, and by no means delighted with the suggestion. But his self-esteem was less combative than usual, and he remained silent. Millhouse proceeded.

"Now, cappin, I've walunteered to be your sense-keeper, as you calls it, in all the plantation business, and you must jest let me have my own way, ef you want to git on sensible in the world. I'm overseer, and you mus'n't come between me and the niggers. I'll do my work and will make 'em do theirs. Ef there's any licking to be done, I'll lay it on. You may look on, but you mus'n't meddle. You may think what you please, but you mus'n't say nothing. We kin talk over the matter every night, and I'll show you the sense of what I've been doing in the day. You kin fish in the river when you please, and hunt in the woods when you please, and go riding and dining out where you please, and I won't meddle nor say nothing; but in the crop, cappin, you mus'n't put a finger to spile what I'm a-doing for your good."

"A very pretty arrangement."

"Ain't it, now?"

"Very! I have your permission to hunt, and fish, and dine abroad, if I think proper. These, then, are my duties?"

"'Zackly! but you are not to take hands and horses out of the crop, cappin, for your 'musements. You're not to carry a good plough-boy off to find bait for you when you're a-fishing; or horse and nigger to beat the woods when you're a-hunting. You must choose one horse for your own riding, cappin, and stick to that."

" You'll let me keep a dog or two, Millhouse ?"

" One, I reckon, ef he's a good one, cappin.   One good beagle is quite enough for these woods."

" But I shall want a pointer for birds."

" A p'inter !   I never could see the use of a p'inter !   I kin
find as many partridges, or doves, to shoot, in a pea country, as
any man can p'nt a gun at, and without any dog at all !   I've
shot, myself, a whole covey of partridges, sixteen, at a single
fire."

" Oh ! that was butchery, Millhouse.   Anybody can kill partridges upon the ground, or doves upon the tree.   But to do this
upon the wing, and to *bird* like a gentleman and a sportsman,
Millhouse, requires a dog to point and flush."

" Look you, cappin, them's all notions; and when a man's
wanting flesh for the pot, and meal for the hoe-cake, it's not
resonable that he should be a sportsman and a gentleman.   That's
a sort of extravagance that's not becoming to a free white man,
when he's under bonds to a sheriff."

" D—n the sheriff!   Don't mention such an animal in my
hearing."

" Well, d—n the sheriff!   I'm agreed to that.   I've no reason to love the animal any more than you; but when we can't
shake off the beast, the best way that I kin see is to draw his
teeth.   Now, the sort of life you wants to lead, cappin, will do
for a nigger gentleman, that ain't got nothing to lose; or for an
Ingin gentleman who's got nothing that a sheriff can put under
the hammer; but for you that's got edication, and has been a
soldier, the thing is different.   The difference between a white
man and a nigger, or an Ingin, is that a white man was made to
gather substance about him, and a nigger and an Ingin was made
to waste it.   That's the whole.   The Ingin was born to clear
the woods of the varmints for us; and the nigger to clean up
after we've eaten.   That's the philosophy."

" And very sensible philosophy too, Millhouse.   I had no idea
that you had such profound ideas.   I begin to think that you'll
save me from the sheriff if any one can."

" You must be doing something for yourself, cappin, besides
fishing and hunting; or, ef you will hunt, there's a sort of game
that, ef you kin take it, will always be sure to bring us meat

for the pot. That's the sort of game that you might hunt, and want no p'inter more than your own nose !"

"Unless yourself, Millhouse. Pray point out this profitable sort of game, if you please."

"Well, that ain't so hard a matter. And first, cappin, let me say you're a good-looking personable man, only a little over middle age. You hain't lost your uprightness. Your face is smooth. It hain't got a wrinkle on it. Your eyes is small, but of a mighty sweet sort of blue ; and though you're a leetle too fleshy to be *sprigh*, yet, Lord save me, you kin stand a mighty great deal of hard usage."

"And so———"

"And, therefore, cappin, you ought to git married !"

"As logical a conclusion as I ever heard in all my life. A man who can stand hard usage may safely venture upon matrimony. 'Pon my soul, Millhouse, your philosophy and logic improve together."

"I'm glad you think so, cappin," responded the other with increasing gravity. "I've been a-thinking what you ought to do ever sence I heer'd you talking of the bad state of your affairs. Now, says I to myself, what better kin the cappin do, than find some clever, good sort of woman, that's outlived all her girlishness and foolishness, and that's come to know the valley of a husband ! That won't be looking too closely at his figure, and thinking his paunch too big, and his legs too little— that won't be axing whether he's cut his eye-tooth or not ; but 'll jest consider that a man's a man in spite of his *gairth*, that a soldier's altogether the best sort of a man going in these times; and that'll pass over the sprinkle of gray in his head, in consideration of his sound teeth and good wind. Now, cappin, you does git a leetle out of wind, when you're pushed too hard ; but considering what a mortal weight of flesh you've got to carry, it's wonderful how much you *kin* stand. It's wonderful I say, and jest as surprising as wonderful. Well, now, considering all these things, what's to hender you from gitting to the right side of some good woman, with a smart chance of property, and proving your title to it, by the sensible way you come over her. I reckon there's more than a hundred such women here, in Carolina, now, that, when they come to consider how many of the handsome young fellows is cut off in the war, will be mighty glad to hev' you in spite of figger, and gray hairs. You ain't so old, cappin, but that you've a right to hev' a wife : and, under the sarcumstances, I say, a wife is the one thing needful; that is always providing she's got something of a property to go upon; for, onless you git a woman of substance, it'll only make your affairs harder to manage than ever. You must be thinking of a woman that'll way off that mortgage you talk about, and hev' something over. Then, we kin work the plantation to some purpose. Then you needn't fear the d——d warmint of a sheriff, and then, with God's blessing on our innocent disposition, we may all live here like fighting cocks."

All this, and much more, was said with a delightful gravity. Porgy was overwhelmed. He was so taken by surprise, by the coolness with which Millhouse analyzed himself and his affairs, and reported upon his shortness of wind, while he acknowledged the excellence of his teeth ;—the immensity of his girth, while he admitted the amiable cast of his eyes; his slenderness of leg, (or "shrunk shank," as Porgy muttered *sotto voce*) while recognising the smoothness of his cheeks—that he was absolutely *dumb-foundered,* and never once thought to interrupt him, letting him run to the end of his tether, which was by no means a short one. At length, the worthy sergeant came to a halt. He had reached his climax. What a soldier's idea of life —living " like a fighting cock"—properly must be, need only be left to the conjecture of the reader. Porgy evidently understood it.

" That would be something, indeed, Millhouse."

" Wouldn't it !" exclaimed the other.

" Yes, indeed ; as fighting militia man, we have seldom been allowed the privilege of living like fighting cocks, and I confess, for one, I should like to try it, for a season, if only by way of a change. But——"

Here the captain of partisans turned uneasily.

" Lance," said he to the lieutenant, " those negroes will never finish supper unless you stir them up ; and I begin to think that the house would be quite as a comfortable as the avenue. This mist is turning into rain. Get in, my lad, and see after them, and let them make a clearing for us !"

The youth disappeared in an instant.

"And so, Millhouse, you think I am still able to undergo the fatigues of matrimony?"

"It's the very thing for you, cappin."

"Well, you've thought so much upon the subject, I suppose you've even thought of some woman in particular, such as you describe, who has 'the needful,' and knows the value of a man. Pray, tell me, if such is the case."

"To be sure, I hev'! I've seed the very woman, and so hev' you."

"Ah! Well——"

"Well! it's jest the same lady, here, that we cut loose from the robbers—this widow Ebeleigh. When I seed the supplies in her wagon, and seed how liberal she was in giving; when I seed the bacon and the bread, the sugar and the coffee, and the old rum, cappin—says I to myself—'That's the woman for the cappin;' and I say it agin, cappin, she's a woman you kin stand. I wouldn't be consenting to your having any sort of a woman, but this here one is a beauty for a man at your time, who's a soldier, and knows what's good living in this world! And I'm a-thinking, cappin, that that's not far from her notion too. She looked on you amazin' sweet, I tell you."

"It is something to be thought of, Millhouse; but, as the widow isn't here, just now, suppose we try the rum? What do you say to a toddy?"

"Well, I say, that's quite a sensible and sodger-like idee."

"Your arm, my good fellow," quoth Porgy; and, with the help of the sergeant, he heaved his bulk into uprightness, and both of them passed into the house; from the hall of which Frampton had by this time expelled the negroes, sending them into the basement, Tom and Pompey alone remaining above, with the view to making proper arrangements for the night.

CHAPTER XXXI.

MUSINGS — MIDNIGHT ALARM.

" Tom," said Porgy, stirring his rum and sugar, and touching glasses with the sergeant (Frampton declined to drink)—" Tom, where are you going to spread my blankets to-night ?"

" Yer, maussa—yer by de fire. Yer's de place for you; de leftenant must lie dere, and de sarjint will ease he limbs yender, close by de sugar kag."

" 'Twon't do, Tom! I must sleep in my old room, you rascal, if it's habitable. You know this, but——"

" But dere's no fire dere, maussa."

" And why the d——l didn't you have a fire made there, you lazy rascal ? See to it at onée. Open the room, and if there's floor enough for my length and breadth, have it swept out in the twinkling of an eye. Set some of the fellows at once to work bringing in wood and kindling fire."

" You, Pomp——"

" Let Pomp alone. I want him here. Do it yourself, if you can find no one else."

Tom disappeared, and stirred up the negroes below stairs. The door of a chamber entering from the hall was thrown open, and a torch carried in.

" Is it habitable ?" was the demand of Porgy.

" Oh yes, maussa, when I done bresh 'em out, and mek de fire bu'n. One ob de floor-board is gone, but nuff lef for you lie 'pon."

" Very good. Bestir yourself. And now, men, for the order of the day to-morrow. We must get an early breakfast, and set out betimes for the burial of these rascals. Lance, did you instruct one of the fellows to ride over at daylight to Mrs. Eveleigh's for the shovels ?"

The reply was affirmative.

" Very good. And now, men, the sooner you take your rest

the better. To-morrow we must be stirring. There is much to be done. Tom, do you give out a blanket to each of the negroes; take one for yourself, and give Pomp another. Put the rest into my room. You, Tom and Pomp, will sleep in the shed-room, to be within call. See to the negroes below, before you lie down, that they do not crowd into the fire. If let alone, the blockheads will burn us all up. Have an eye to them. We must build a few pole-houses as soon as possible. And now to bed. Millhouse, will you take some more rum before you sleep ?"

"Not a drop, cappin."

"Help yourself, Tom, and put the rest safely away."

"T'ank you, maussa," and Tom helped himself with a liberal hand. Millhouse had already stretched himself out, and rolled in his blanket. Frampton lay upon his, resting upon his elbow, with his head upon his palm, and gazing demurely into the fire. Porgy cast a dubious glance around him, then gathering up his sword and holsters, was about to retire, when he turned and said :—

"Who has seen to the horses ?"

Frampton replied :—

"I have fastened them under the piazza, captain, and given them both corn and fodder. Mrs. Eveleigh's overseer brought over a supply to last a week."

"Ah !—all's right. Well, good night, men, and a good sleep to you—though I may as well tell you that the house is haunted."

Millhouse growled from within his blankets, with something of the tone of a bull-dog suspicious of a stranger. Frampton's eye brightened a little, but, except the "good night" with which he replied to the captain's, he said nothing. In a few moments, Porgy, Tom, and Pomp, having retired to their several lairs, the house was left in deep quiet, save from an occasional murmur that ascended from the negroes in the basement.

Our captain of partisans entered the chamber, and let himself down upon the pile of blankets which formed his couch. This was spread before the fireplace, and he sat with his feet to the blaze. He had disencumbered himself of his coat and small-clothes, his boots and stockings. His sword and pistols lay be-

side him, his saddle, over which one of the blankets was spread,
served him for a pillow. But for a long time he did not lie
down. His eyes were bent upon the fire, or slowly wandered
around the almost vacant chamber. It was a snug, but sufficiently capacious apartment, probably eighteen by twenty feet.
The walls still exhibited proof of a degree of pride and state,
which declared for a former wealth and taste, such as were
strangely inconsistent with the present fortunes of the possessor.
The panelling of wood over the fireplace still showed traces of
two landscape paintings in oil, done upon the panels with no
inconsiderable art. The framework around them consisted of
heavy carved work, and the pillars of the mantel-piece were
richly ornamented with carvings in similar style. About the
room still hung the dingy and shattered frames of pictures,
probably portraits, from which the canvass had been cut out.
It had probably been found useful for the meanest purposes, and
had been appropriated, with all other moveables of any value,
by the marauding British and tories. The glass was destroyed
in the sashes of all the windows. The shutters were mostly
torn from the hinges and carried off, probably destroyed for fire-
wood. One of the planks of the floor had been taken up, and
lay beside the opening, very much hewed and mangled by the
axe. The fragments of an ancient mahogany bedstead lay
piled up in one corner, but it was evidently no longer available
for use. It had been that on which Porgy had slept when a child:
it was the bedstead of his mother. A bit of green cord still de-
pended from a nail against the opposite wall. It had sustained
the picture of his mother; that portrait of a fair young woman,
taken when she was yet unmarried, whose sweet smiling features, in the active exercise of memory and fancy, seemed still
to be looking down upon him.

Porgy knew not that the big tears were gathering slowly in
his eyes, and gradually stealing down upon his cheeks. He had
reached his home, but it was a home no longer. The home is
made by the hopes which it generates, and he had survived all
those, of whatever sort, which came with youth and childhood.
The prospect before him was one of unmixed desolation. How
was he to redeem the mortgaged acres of his domain? How
was he to retain the poor remains of a once ample fortune?

What were his own resources for this task? What were left for him to do, and where was the agency, external to himself, by which to effect the difficult achievement. The embarrassing straits of his condition had made themselves apparent to him, most fully, on the moment of his return. But for the unexpected events of the day, and the generosity of Mrs. Eveleigh, he must have gone, himself, supperless to sleep, and witnessed the privations, in extreme, of his followers and slaves.

And the relief was temporary only. He must provide for these hereafter; and how? By incurring new embarrassments and obligations; by adding to the weight of former bonds and responsibilities; by endeavoring to establish a credit without being able to offer new securities. Was it probable that he could do this, in the unsettled condition of the colony? And what securities could he offer to the creditor? His lands were mortgaged to an amount five times their present value. A foreclosure of mortgage at the present juncture would not only sweep them away, but take his negroes also, and still leave him a debtor beyond all means of payment. Even if time were allowed him, could he hope, criminally ignorant as he was of all the arts requisite to the good planter, to recover himself and renovate his fortunes? These were the subjects of his meditations, and, chewing the bitter cud of thought and memory, his heart almost failed him.

He stretched himself out upon his blankets almost reproaching the merciful fate which had saved him from the bullet or bayonet of the enemy. His despondency for awhile, increased with his meditation, until he felt that it would not be difficult that very hour to die. To die, was to escape the cares, the troubles and the humiliations to which he felt himself unequal, and which he now felt to be inevitable from life, with such a prospect as now grew up, dark and distinct, before his mind. He would have found it at once easy and grateful to be roused that moment with the call to battle. He would have rejoiced to find a full finish to his cares, in a desperate onset, at the head of his corps of partisans. "But the wars were all over," and this refuge was denied him. He must live and how to live? The reflections that followed this inquiry, arrayed before him the small operations of his little force of half-a-dozen negroes in the rice fields, under the doubtful management of Sergeant Millhouse. True, the sergeant boasted of his merits as a rice planter, but was it so sure that he knew anything of the matter? True, rice was the most profitable crop then made in the country, but how much rice, even supposing the best management, and the most favoring seasons, could be made by his half-dozen negroes?

But then came up the last suggestion of the sanguine Millhouse. There was the widow Eveleigh? The widow was a woman of goodly form, of gracious manners, of fine and independent estates. The widow had experienced his friendly services; she had witnessed his valor in her cause; he had perilled life in her defence; he had, in all probability, saved herself from brutality, and her son from death. These were eminent services. She evidently felt them. Why should he not aspire to the widow? Was he not a man of person, portly, of commanding figure, of good features, and quite young enough for her. The captain stroked his chin with a sense of satisfaction as he reasoned thus. But, just then, occurred to him the somewhat disparaging reflection of the sergeant upon his legs. He looked down at the members, which were thus assumed to be impediments to progress, in direct conflict with their designed uses. Surely, they are not so slender—they are not shrunken at all; their dimensions are as great as ever. It is only in contrast with the mountainous abdomen, that they appear inferior. It was with some feeling of reproach and impatience that our captain fixed his eyes on the unnaturally distended member. By what malice of fate was it that it had so greatly grown at the expense of all the rest! But he was kept from quarrelling outright with the one region, by a timely recollection of the famous allegory of Menenius Agrippa.

"No! no!" quoth he to himself. "This will never do. I could wish my storehouse differently shaped and sized, if only for compactness and more easy carriage; but it has done good service in its time, and it is my own fault if I have used it a little too much, and the other members much too little. Had I worked them more, and it less—had I suffered them less to take their ease, I should now have nothing to complain of, either in respect to their deficiency or its excess. It has distributed as liberally as it could, according to my allowance; and they according to Agrippa, have received 'the flower of all,' leaving to the belly the bran only. Certainly, it is a monstrous necessity that I should be compelled thus to carry with me such a bag of bran. But what is to be done? It is an inheritance which one may not mortgage; a store-house of which no sheriff can deprive the possessor. This, at least, is a perfect right and indefeasible!" and he laid his hands rather affectionately on the region under description.

"At least!" he continued, "there is nothing insignificant about it. It may not be comely to the eye, but nobody can regard it as contemptible. It is not calculated to admit of the exhibition of grace; but what gentleman is ambitious of the renown of a dancing-master. Still, it is something on parade. Nobody finds fault with such a abdomen in a general. It embarrasses no man whose position requires that he should move with dignity. It guaranties the courage of the proprietor, since one is scarcely apt to run in battle, with such extensive stores to carry with him. No! no! sergeant, you shall not persuade me out of the faith that my parts are at all in the way of my person. But you may persuade me to the effort to place them properly in the way of other people. This widow is a noble creature—pleasing to the eye; amiable, I know; well off, in respect of fortune. She can redeem my acres. She can put me on my legs again, however heavy my incumbrance. And why should she not do so? She is young enough still for tastes and sensibilities, for which mere wealth can never suffice. She has tasted of matrimony, and does not seem to have suffered from the taste. We must think more closely of this matter."

He laid himself back upon his saddle, and mused awhile; rose again, and sitting, pushed up the brands, and drew the blanket over his legs. His meditations were now upon topics and details more immediately pressing.

"To-morrow, we will bury these scoundrels. It will take us till afternoon. We can do little more that day. The next I am to dine with the widow. Humph! After that I must set off for the city. We must have ploughs and hoes, and a hundred other things for the plantation. Millhouse must be pacified. The negroes set to work. We must work, that is clear, though the sheriff steps into the harvesting. Wagons, ploughs, hoes, axes, rope, furniture—I must have. By Jupiter! I am resolved to die in a feather-bed, if I can. Food—we must have some bacon for the negroes. I must have some wine for myself, and for a guest, and rum for the sergeant. Kitchen furniture—"

And he enumerated a score of other commodities.

" But, the d—l! How for the credit! I must counsel on the subject with the widow. A woman is never more flattered by a man than when he solicits her advice. She usually gives him more than he bargains for, but she not unfrequently gives herself into the bargain !"

The meditations of Porgy, mixed as they were, carried him late into the night. When every thing was still about the premises he was wakeful. As a thought would occur to him with any force, he would rise, fling a fresh brand into the fire, and sit up watching the blaze; lie down again for awhile, only to start up once more to meditation. But nature asserted her necessities at last, and his nostrils soon furnished audible echo to those sounds which he had heard at intervals issuing from the neighboring hall, and, as he assumed, from the proboscis of the sergeant. Deep thus continued for a season to call unto deep, without either paying much heed to their mutual responses. Once, it is true, a more than ordinary explosion from the sergeant's nose, seemed to disquiet the slumbers of the captain.

" Zounds !" quoth he, drowsing again. " How Millhouse does snore ! What an infirmity !—peculiar, I believe, only to the lower orders. Gentlemen never snore ! How is it with ladies ? Wonder if the widow Evel——"

And the conjecture remained unconcluded; and the mutual nostrils of captain and sergeant continued to respond to one another, without causing any annoyance to either party. But they were both destined to be aroused by an explosion of very different character. They had slept some hours, soundly, as was natural to men who had gone through such a day's work as that we have already described. It wore on toward morning— was, indeed, but a short hour to daybreak—when Porgy started up with a ringing and a rushing sound, seemingly immediately at his ears. Millhouse was awakened at the same moment. They were both upon their feet in an instant. But they were in the dark. The fire had burned down in both apartments, and Millhouse was stumbling in confusion over kegs and boxes, not knowing in which way to turn, or whence came the sounds of alarm which were still ringing in his ears. The captain wakened to instint consciousness of his situation. It was a pistol shot he had heard the moment after he was awakened. He detected a rush in the piazza, and fancied he could hear still the distant tramplings of a horse. He could also hear the soft dull pattering of the rain upon the roof of the piazza. There was evidently an alarm. His holsters were caught up, and the pistols detached in an instant. In another he was feeling his way into the hall, whither he made his way without any difficulty, the whole region being familiar to his childhood. Suddenly he encountered Millhouse. They grappled one another with a mutual instinct.

"Speak!" cried Porgy, "or I shoot."

"Is't you, cappin, is it?"

"What's the matter, Millhouse?"

"Dogs! I don't know! I jest heard bang! bang! and a shouting, and a noise of feet, and started up to make my way out, and heeled over one of these d——d kags! I've spilt some blood in the affair, though it's only from my nose."

"A part that may well spare it," replied Porgy, not willing to forego his jest at any season. "But, where's Lance?"

"I ha'n't seed him."

"Then it was his pistol. That fellow never sleeps. Stay! that window is open on the piazza. I see. He has jumped out there. Let me find the door. We must see after him. He's a sentinel among a thousand. Those d——d negroes haven't heard a word of the matter."

"Hain't turned over for a second nap, I reckon."

"Strike a light, Millhouse! Here's the fireplace, you know where you put the flint and tinder. I've got the door."

Saying these words, Porgy unfastened the door and stepped out into the piazza. All was still for a few moments. He could see nothing. The night was dismally dark. The rain fell in a settled shower. The wind sighed at a distance very mournfully. Porgy waited in silence. As the light kindled within, he drew the door to, that it might offer no aid to a random bullet. He stood thus, beginning, in his only half-dressed condition, to shiver with the chilling night wind, when he heard a footstep upon some decaying branches on the earth below.

"Who goes there ?"

"Lance !" was the reply, and the young lieutenant sprang up the steps, covered with mud, and soaking with water, with a pistol in each hand.

"What the d—l's the stir, Lance ?"

The youth's story was soon told. He was awakened by a trampling and seeming confusion among the horses below. He listened, and, as the stir continued, he rose, found his pistols, and was preparing to step out quietly, when he distinctly heard the free movements of a single steed, as if guided round the house. He immediately dashed open the shutter of the window under which he lay, jumped out into the piazza and challenged. Instead of an answer, the horse was put into instant motion down the avenue. He fired twice, at random, at the object which he fancied he could see, but he supposed without effect. He then darted down the steps, and down the avenue for a hundred yards, but without result. The fugitive, whoever he was, had succeeded in making his escape.

Of the mischief done, if any, nothing as yet was known. To this inquiry all parties now addressed themselves. Porgy hurried on his clothes. Millhouse, penetrating the shed-room where Tom, the cook, and Pomp, the fiddler, were doing any quantity of sleep, endeavored to arouse them both at the same moment, by punching them, as they lay side by side, with his sheathed sabre in his one hand, and with the stump of his remaining arm. His sword stirred Pomp into consciousness, while the stump of arm, pressing closely against Tom's cheek, was instinctively seized, by the sleeve, between the teeth of the negro, and held with a growl, which made the sergeant a little doubtful of his condition.

"Why, Tom," said he, "you're wolf-bit, and dog-bit too, I reckon, jedging by the sort of teeth you carry; but let loose, old fellow, or I'll be drawing your teeth out with a handspike."

"Who dat ?" quoth Tom.

"Git up, you varmint, and shake yourself."

"Gorrah ! I never guine git my sleep !"

" Sleep! You've had enough for a month. You sleeps like a bear in cold weather."

" Dis dah cold wedder 'nough for nigger. Ef I bin bear, Mass Millh'us, I nebber been let you go so easy. Wha' de matter now ? Wha' for you no let poor sodger nigger hab he leetle sleeps widout 'tir 'em up wid stump and swode ?"

" Why, we're robbed and killed here, you skunk; we've had a fight with the tories, and they've scalped Lance, and shot the cappin in three places, his head, his belly, and his witals."

" Lord ha' massy! Shoot maussa jes' as he git to he own home at last. I never b'lieb, eben ef I see em. Ho! maussa, I say, in der' !"

And, shouting as he went, followed by Pomp, Tom, the cook, now thoroughly awakened, hurried to join the group within the hall. Torches were kindled, and all armed, the party sallied out, having divided, one portion taking the front, the other the rear outlet. The house was circled, the avenue explored; horse-tracks were found going forth, freshly made in the mud; and an examination of the horses showed one of them to be missing.

" 'Tis de raw bone black, Pomp. De same *sawt* of hoss I bin see dat d—n Bossick ride."

The proceeding was a sufficiently daring one.

" The squatter, Bostwick ?" queried Porgy, looking to Tom.

" Da him, maussa, sure as a gun."

" It may be! Well!" compressing his lips. " He may ride one horse too much for his own comfort yet."

" The foal of an acorn!" said Millhouse. " I reckon it was sartain one of the chaps we fout with yesterday, whether you call him Bossick or what. And a mighty sassy fellow! Why, cappin, sich a thing hardly ever happened to us in all the campaigns."

" No, indeed !"

" It is a shame and a disgrace to us as sodgers."

" You forget that the war is over and we had no reason to expect attack. But it's no use talking. Well it's no worse. He might have taken all, but for Lance. Millhouse, you sleep like a tomb-stone, and snore like the seven sleepers. There's no more sleep for any of us to-night. It must be near day. Tom, turn in and have us some coffee. Lance, send off the fellow to the widow Eveleigh's for the spades and hoes. Tell him to go to the overseer's house, and be careful not to disturb the lady. Sergeant, will you take a little rum now, or wait for the coffee ?"

"Well, cappin, jest to be a-doing, I'll do both."

"You were born to be a soldier, sergeant," replied Porgy quietly, as he motioned to the liquor before him. Pomp was already at hand with a gourd of water. But Millhouse drank alone. Porgy had already turned to his usual resource, and was crowding fresh tobacco into his pipe. Day dawned within the hour, but very gloomily, and the rain, though slackened, still continued.

CHAPTER XXXII.

RETURN TO THE FIELD OF BATTLE.

THE day, as was expected, opened in gloom. The sun made no showings that morning. The skies were enveloped in unbroken cloud and vapor, relieved imperfectly by a constant fall of rain, which was of that cool, measured, deliberate sort, which indicates unfailing resource, and a quiet determination to have its own way. Our captain of partisans walked out into the piazza, front and rear, without any sense of relief from either quarter. The avenue in front exhibited a dreary aspect in spite of the fact that it was composed mostly of evergreens. The great oaks, grown together and arching above the track, each wore its heavy streamers of gray moss, which drooped almost to the earth with the great water-drops, like the old-fashioned pictures of winter, his big beard crested with icicles. Vacant fields on either hand, fenceless and wholly uncultivated, added vastly to the dreariness of the scene. Fog and cloud, vapor and rain, were present everywhere, and made everything as gloomy to the eyes of the spectator as it was to his thoughts. Those old fields, should he ever again see them smiling in corn ? The old house, whose timbers groaned beneath his tread, how long should he enjoy its shelter ? Should he ever, with any feeling of security, behold it gay with the joyous faces of his friends? Was not all the life-prospect before his mind as sombre and cheerless as that before his eyes? While he mused thus, perhaps with a wholesome bitterness, having in it no small degree of self-reproach, he was joined by Millhouse.

"These old fields, cappin," said the latter, extending the stump of his arm, as he spoke, to the indicated quarter, "these old fields will be sure to bring fine corn; they are all matted with weeds, and have been lying out so long. I reckon you kaint ricollect when they were planted last?"

"Not I!" was the answer.

"But you hev' seen 'em a-growing, cappin?"

"I suppose so; I can now see that they have been planted, and I suppose in my time; but really, my good sergeant, to say that I saw them in a crop, or ever saw the crop, of any kind, when I was professedly a planter, would be something of a rashness on my part. Pray believe that I was a very foolish, profligate person, who, in ceasing to be young, did not cease to be foolish, and continued his absurd vanities and excesses to the last. And I am telling you now, Millhouse, what has been but too commonly the case among our young men of fortune of my day. There were some exceptions, it is true; but the curse of my generation was that our fathers lived too well, were too rapidly prosperous, and though they did not neglect the exercise of a proper industry in themselves, they either did not know how to teach it to their children, or presumed on the absence of any necessity that they should learn. We were to be affluent in what they should leave us—enough, in God's name, if we could keep it—but it is very sure that the best way to teach one to value and to keep what he gets, is just to teach him how to get it himself. He who has not learned the one lesson will fail in the other, and is apt to waste what he did not work for. And now, my good fellow, don't say another word to me about the crops in past seasons. I have really no wish to confess my sins and follies to man as well as to myself and God. Turn in, if you are so disposed, and make your crops; you say you know how, and I am willing to believe you. I will assist you when I can——"

"But don't you meddle, cappin.'

"Oh, no! you shall have full swing for a season, at least, and I will second you—I will be *your* sergeant only. You shall have a fair share of the spoils at harvest-time, and we'll continue to live as decently as possible in the meanwhile. And that reminds me that it is time for breakfast. That rascal, Tom, because we broke his slumbers so suddenly this morning will be out of humor all day. Let's see to him."

Millhouse was not quite satisfied to have his mouth shut so summarily by the frank confession of the faults and follies on the part of his superior. He was not content that a general confession, however sweeping, should anticipate the details, one by one, of Porgy's short-comings. He had a sort of inquisitorial faculty for dragging out the truth, inch by inch, slowly from the criminal, so that he should not escape a single pang which was proper to his case; and his deliberate purpose had been to take the captain over his territories, field by field, and extort from him at each some admission of fault or ignorance. It was with a growl that he yielded to the very decided manner of his superior which at once closed the door against further "question."

The day, opened as we have seen with bustle and confusion, was destined to be a busy one. Breakfast was sullenly prepared by Tom, with whom the whole world had seemed to go wrong from the moment when the stump of Millhouse's arm that morning had made so free with his sensibilities; and Pomp, stupid rather than savage, was serving it up to our partisans, as he had done the supper the night before, when Fordham, the overseer, suddenly cantered up to the house. He had brought with him the negro who had gone for hoes and shovels, with some three or four others, similarly provided, for the purpose of assisting in the burial of the outlaws. This was due to the timely suggestion of the Widow Eveleigh, who, the night, before, had given the overseer his instructions, and who had expressed herself particularly anxious for the recovery of a certain mahogany box, which she urgently counselled him to look for in all the places in which the outlaws had been seen to harbor during the day of her adventure. She did not tell him of the contents of the box, and had been silent, so far as he was concerned, in respect to the paper which contained the memoranda of M'Kewn, and the signature of that amiable philanthropist. Fordham, accordingly, simply stated that a mahogany box was missing containing fifty guineas; and we may mention in this place that Porgy, his followers, and the negroes generally, all busied themselves in its search with as much anxiety as if the property had been their own. But the labor was unavailing, and the search was finally given up as hopeless, after a persevering scrutiny in swamp and thicket, hiding-place and hollow, wherever it seemed possible or plausible to think that the outlaws had penetrated. But to return.

Fordham was invited to share the breakfast, which he did with right good-will. He was now told of the alarm which the party had had, and the loss which they had suffered, of one of the captured horses.

"Which one, cappin?" demanded Fordham.

"A raw-bone black."

"Ah!"

"Da Bossick hoss, Mass Fordham," quoth Tom, putting in confidently. "Pomp say he know de hoss, and John Sylbester bin tell me de same t'ing."

"He look like hoss I bin see Bossick ride one time."

"But you ain't sartin, Pomp?" asked Fordham.

"He bin ride raw-bone black, one time."

"It may be," said Fordham. "Bostwick is not too good for any villany; and we have good reason to think it was by his means that your niggers and Mrs. Eveleigh's was carried off to the British. We don't know for sartin, but it's mighty like. Now, I have hearn of Bostwick riding a raw-bone black, but I don't know that I ever seed him on the critter in my life. He's a mighty cute fellow that never lets you git too near to him. I'm pretty sure he headed them rascals yesterday, yet I never seed one man more than another that I could lay finger on for him and be sart'in. Yet I could almost swear a Bible oath that he was one of them, and one of the worst. There was one on them that called Jenny, the nigger gal, by the right name; and I reckon he was the one. He know'd her well, and let the word slip *on*awar's."

"Does not the fellow live somewhere in this neighborhood still?" demanded Porgy.

"Well, thar's no telling if *he* lives anywhar. *He's* never to be seen in these parts. I haven't heard of him for a year, positive, from anybody that could sw'ar they seed him. He's got his family on the corner of Mrs. Ev'leigh's land, and not far from yours—jest in the swamp, and not a half a mile from the river; but I reckon he's hardly there once a year. The family never sees much of him, I'm sartin."

"But that is one of his quartering places. We must root 'em out, Fordham; his family is as bad as himself. Has he any sons?"

"A leetle boy, only, and two gals. The boy is just creeping about. The two gals are most half grown—one's about twelve, I reckon, the other ten. But, Lord love you, cappin, there's no rooting these people out. It would be the cruellest thing that you could do. They are so poor and miserable, and so humble, and the poor wife's so sad and heart-broken, and *on*happy, and the gal children is so sweet, and so mighty pretty, *pr*eticularly the oldest, who's a born beauty, jest like the darter of some great people. As for being as bad as himself, that's not so, cappin, axing your pardon. They're good people, working hard, night and day, and gitting none of the benefit of all that Bostwick *ai*rns or steals. He's hardly ever with 'em, and does nothing for 'em when he comes, *on*less for the oldest gal, and they tells me that he pets her a leetle, and according to his humors. It's a hard case for them that they have to do with sich a born rascal; but what's to help it? The poor wife can't get rid of *him* now; and the poor little children—they can only groan and cry together, when they're by themselves, and take what the marcy of God sends 'em, through the hands of their neighbors. You kain't think of rooting 'em out. Mrs. Ev'leigh knows jest as well as anybody what Bostwick is, but she has pity on the poor wife and children. She gives them spinning to do, and weaving, and the oldest darter is both mighty clever to work and willing; and it's through Mrs. Ev'leigh that they gits on at all: but for her, they'd starve; she feeds 'em, and physics 'em, and clothes 'em; and y*i*t that black-hearted scamp, Bostwick, has been about the worst inimy of her and her plantation, that she ever had in these parts."

"Well, Fordham, I'm sworn to do this poor woman and her children a greater charity than ever Mrs. Eveleigh has done—"

"Ah! you kain't do that easily, cappin."

" I will !"

" What's that ?"

" I've sworn by Acheron and Styx, to see Bostwick hung to the first good swinging limb within half an hour after I lay eyes upon him."

" And may God, in his marcy, grant you the strength and the chance, cappin, to keep your oath! That would be a great charity im consenting, to the poor woman and the little chicks; and I'm willing to take a hand in it, whenever you are ready to tree the critter. Ef she was free of him, she would do better. for he brings her no help, and I'm a-thinking takes away from her all she can airn. Besides, people's afear'd to hire her at their places, for fear they'll bring him about 'em. Ef he was dead and out of the way, she would be a thousand times better off."

" We must pay her a sudden visit to-day — try to ascertain if he has been there lately, and when. He would hardly visit the neighborhood without seeing them."

" That's as it happens, and seems *i*dvisable. He wouldn't resk a hair of his head on a visit to them at any time, though the niggers do say that he loves the oldest gal."

" And she's a beauty ?"

" A *raal* flower of the forest, cappin."

" Poor thing! Why don't Mrs. Eveleigh take her home ?"

" She's afear'd of the father's coming about the place; besides, the mother won't let her leave her. She says she's her only comfort, and I reckon she is. She's a *raal* sweet, smart, and beautiful little critter."

" We'll see them coming back. You can guide us, Fordham, for I pretty much forget all the routes in this quarter. And now, to horse."

" But what's the need for you to go, cappin?" demanded Fordham and Millhouse in the same breath. " We kin bury. these blackguards, and look up for the box without troubling you; and you see the rain keeps on."

" A fig for the rain! After soaking for seven years in rain, and, indeed, all sorts of liquors, to talk to me now of another soaking as a thing to skulk from. Shut up, my good fellows.

Pomp, my horse! Besides, how do I know but that you may have customers in the surviving robbers. A couple of stout rascals, in ambush, would easily settle twice their number, for your negroes could never be relied on. Ho! Pomp!"

"Wha' mek' you holler, maussa? Enty you see de hoss ready by de tree. All ready but you swode and pistols, and yer he is."

Thus Tom, with sword and holsters on his arm, expostulated with his master against his stentorian utterance. The sword was quietly girded about the waist of Porgy by Frampton, while Tom followed with the holsters. A few moments, and the party moved up the avenue, all mounted, even the negroes, who carried their hoes and shovels across their thighs, or up in air, as the Scythian and Cumanche robber carries his spear, and went forth better pleased with the idea of burying their dead, than with that of going into battle.

Their farther progress requires no detailed report. They reached the skirmishing ground in due season, and reviewed its aspects. The slain outlaws were found undisturbed where they had been left, and were buried where they lay. No coffin or shroud enwrapped the forms of those who had cast themselves off from social sympathies. Holes in the earth, some three feet deep, beyond the reach of wolf and wildcat, sufficed to hide them out of sight. And this was all. The negroes heaved up the earth in mounds above them, and a stake, cut from the woods, and driven down at the head of the grave, indicated to the wayfarer the place of human sepulture, in that wild spot, and remote from settlement or church, very much as the wayside cross in Spain denotes where the murdered traveller has perished. This duty done, and the search after the lost box of Mrs. Eveleigh proving ineffectual, our captain of partisans, some two hours after noon, proposed to his party to return. All assented but Lance Frampton, who seemed to hesitate, and, by his manner, ·reminded Porgy of the young man's obligations elsewhere.

"Ah! Lance, by the way," said he, "ride over and see Mrs. Griffin and her daughter. It is but two miles and a half from us where we stand, and a shorter distance, by twice that number, than if you go back with us, and then proceed. You can return at night, or not, as you think proper. Of course, we want you, if you can be spared, and will keep supper for you till bedtime. Go, my good boy, and present my best respects to the good widow. You remember, I spend the day, to-morrow, at Mrs. Eveleigh's, and shall wish you to accompany me. Mill-house will go, also, while Tom keeps watch at home. The next day, or soon after, I shall, probably, be compelled to set out for the city to get supplies. There now, my lad, you have all my plans for the present, and can make your own arrangements accordingly."

"Ef you are riding over to the widow Griffin's now, lieutenant," said Fordham, turning to the youth, "be so good as to say to her, that I'll send the peas and inyons [onions] over to her Saturday night—that's all."

And Lance Frampton rode off alone.

"And now, Fordham," said Porgy, "lead the way to the wigwam of the squatter. Let us see his family at all events, and find out, if we can, whether he has been there lately."

————————

CHAPTER XXXIII.

BOSTWICK, THE SQUATTER, AND HIS FAMILY.

It is time that we should return to the recesses of the swamp where we left the squatter, Bostwick, up to his neck in water. No condition could have appeared more hopeless—no situation more humbling or perplexing. It is, perhaps, the case commonly, that the habitual criminal is habitually an unthinking person, else how should the utter profitlessness, and certain perils of crime, fail to impress themselves upon the mind of him who toils in his vocation of sin, and is taught by the bitter experience of each day the terrible truth that the only wages he can earn, in this employment, is shame and scorn, and foes, and ignominy and death! What had been Bostwick's profits in his career? As he muttered more than once to himself, standing on the cold and gloomy hammock :—

"I have nothing to show! M'Kewn kin show, and Moncrieff

kin show; they've got the money and the goods; they're great men in the world and rich; but I—I've got nothing but the danger, and the cold, the resk and the exposure, the empty pockets, and the swinging limb! Empty pocket! No! not so bad as all that, either. The widow said there was fifty guineas in her box."

The miserable wretch found his temporary consolation in this reflection. His comrades had mostly perished. He had nearly shared their fate. The plunderers were stripped. They who went forth to shear, came home shorn. Even his horse and rifle had disappeared in the grasp of the partisans; and they were a class of people with whom long experience had taught him that it was very dangerous to meddle. But the recollection of the widow's strong box consoled him for the moment. That was safe. He had hidden it beyond the search and suspicion even of his comrades, and he chuckled to himself, even in that gloomy hour, at the cleverness with which he had succeeded in doing so. Fifty guineas were in that box. Fifty guineas! He began to calculate how long they were to last, according to the life of riot, drinking, and gaming, which he led. He made no appropriations of any portion to his family. They had no such need as himself. Fifty guineas! and the papers. They, too, must be in that box; and these papers, according to the inadvertent admissions of M'Kewn, were important to his safety.

"The d——d skinflint!" muttered Bostwick to himself. "He shall pay for them or hang! He talks of me hanging, and to my face, jest as ef he had any right to make me feel *oneasy*. But we'll see who has most right to hang. We'll see who's the rope guine to fit best. The mean, dirty scoundrel. I see what he's after; but I'll put a spoke in that wheel will upset his carriage, ef he don't walk a safe track with me. He's got property. He's a great man now-a-days. He's bought a plantation here jest alongside the widow's, and who but he, with his niggers and lands. Ha! well! He's played a mighty strong hand in the game, but there's a trump he ain't got, and ain't guine to git till he agrees to share the stakes. Let him try! He was quite a clever chap among the British. Lord! how they loved one another; and he's now to be quite a clever chap among the rebels! Well, it's for me to say, I reckon, how much love is to be lost atween 'em. Only wait! I'll wait—jest as long as it suits me. But now for the box."

And threading his way out of the swamp, with the ease of one who had never walked on freer or firmer ground, he proceeded to the spot in the woods above, not a hundred yards from the place where the widow's carriage had been brought to a halt, in which the box had been safely hid away.

He found it even where he sought. He held it up to the light of the stars. It was heavy, but it was locked. The key had never been taken from the possession of Mrs. Eveleigh. Her bunch still remained in her pocket. She had not been searched; but would have been, in all probability, but for the unexpected defeat of the enterprise of the outlaws. But the want of the key suggested no difficulty to our squatter. At one moment he had lifted up the box to dash it upon a stump, the short process being always the most grateful to the ruffian for attaining his object. But he arrested himself.

"The guineas will scatter, and I kain't afford to lose the ugliest on 'em."

He felt for his knife. It was gone—lost.

"Never mind!" he muttered, "I kin wait 'till I git to see Rachel."

Rachel—poor Rachel—his wife! He thought of her at that moment, not as one whom he loved or cared for, but as the creature from whom he might find service—obtain the implement which should give him access to a more precious treasure. He started off with the box under his arm. His swiftness of foot seemed undiminished by the day's fatigue. He was one of those sinewy, lean, elastic, beings of iron—hardihood and endurance —who seem never to have enjoyed life, yet are equal to all its requisitions. In training, like most people of the same description of life in the same region, he was an Indian—could outwind a horse in a day's journey, and never appear to suffer from thirst or hunger. He had short cuts through swamp and thicket, known to few besides himself, and in half the time occupied by our partisans on horse, he made his way, on foot, to the swamp margins of the plantations of Mrs. Eveleigh and Captain Porgy. Within half a mile stood the wigwam of his wretched family. It occupied a place half hidden in a little clump of woods, near which stretched a small cornfield of a few acres, the old decaying stalks crumbling over the spot where they had feebly grown. He again concealed his box, this time in the hollow of a cypress, when about to emerge from the cover of the swamp. He did not approach his own dwelling without the greatest caution. He knew not what sort of customers he was to encounter in the neighborhood. Winding about the woods wherever a cover could be found, he gradually drew nigh to the rear of the habitation which he skirted cautiously. The hum of the spinning-wheel alone reached his ears from within. He stole up to the habitation and peeped through a crevice between the logs. We will follow his example.

The wigwam was one of the meanest sort of log-houses, not more than sixteen by twenty feet — built of slender pine poles, which were already greatly decayed. The spaces had been closed with clay, but this had mostly fallen out. Originally, the house had been *clap-boarded* (a large, coarse, and inferior shingle) with split pine, and fastened down by wooded pegs. Much of the roofing had decayed, and the openings were thatched with broom-grass and pine-straw — a very slight and imperfect shelter for the encounter with our March and September winds. But there was an additional protection in a great live oak, of a thousand generations, which overspread the roof on the northern side, the branches resting upon it, and, when stirred by the wind, making such a strange scraping along the clap-boards — as if a score of wild cats were striving to scratch their way — as would have startled one, not familiar with the noise, with a thousand staggering apprehensions — particularly at midnight. But our squatter's family heard nothing, or if they did, the sounds had become companionable, and thus agreeable. We are not sure that the wife of the squatter did not find it a great relief to listen to the disordered branches, in the long, weary hours of the night, when the children were all asleep, but when the blessing of sleep was denied her eyes. The poor, subdued, faint-spirited woman, she sat within, knitting her worsted and cotton into thick stockings for the ungrateful wretch who peered, unsuspected, between the logs, and beheld her occupation.

She was a thin, frail, pale-faced body, with fair complexion still, of soft, sad eyes, the only remains of a once girlish beauty.

Her look almost vacant, was fixed upon the fire. Her dress was of the plainest sort of blue homespun—her own manufacture—but it was scrupulously neat and clean. She seemed to work unconsciously, as if from habit; yet her fingers traversed the needles and passed the threads with the rapidity of one whose whole soul was in the task. At the other corner of the fireplace, stood her eldest daughter, whom she called Dory. Her proper name was Dorothy. It was her spinning-wheel whose song saluted the ears of Bostwick as he approached the house. Dory, although still but twelve years old, was an adept at all her labors. Nobody—it was her mother's boast—could spin better than Dory, a finer or a stronger thread. And Dory could weave also, quite as well as her mother. The child was nearly as strong. Indeed, responsibilities, at an early period, had matured her mind and body very equally. They grew together, and therefore both grew strong. The child might have passed for a girl of fifteen, so well was she developed. When you looked at her face she seemed still older—there was such a sad, settled, and profound expression in the sweet symmetrical and chastened features. She was very fair, though she bore the fuel from the woods, and the water from the spring. She was tall, and, moving to and fro about the spinning-wheel, she exhibited a natural grace such as an humble life like her's seldom displays. Her hair, a rich auburn, curled and floated free in long silken tresses, having escaped from the massy folds in which she commonly kept it bound. She, too, was clad in the simplest homespun, and her naked feet and ankles, in consequence of the scantiness of her dress, were conspicuous upon the floor. But the floor was kept tidily clean. If there was poverty in the dwelling, there was evidently a natural purity also, which reconciled the spectator to the scene.

The other children of the squatter, were asleep in a pallet in one corner of the room. There was no separate apartment. Dory slept with her mother in the father's absence, and when he came home she crouched in with Bet, her younger sister, and Benny, the infant boy. The mother's bedstead, was a rude frame work of pine, clumsily executed by a country carpenter. There was a single pine table in the room, and four chairs, bottomed with cowhide. This was all the furniture. A

few gourds containing seeds and spices hung against the walls.
A shelf outside sustained the water bucket. In a corner of the
fireplace was an iron pot, and in a nook of the chamber was
leaned a frying-pan. The fragment of a mirror, without frame,
a trimmed bit of glass, of a few inches at most each way, was
fastened by pegs against one of the logs over the fireplace.

Such was the picture, lightened up fully by the blaze from
half-dozen pine knots, which hissed and sparkled in the hearth,
giving light and heat equally. The very poor, in all the south,
rarely use candles, or those of their own making only. The
squatter's wife had hers, it is true, a small supply, made of
tallow and myrtle wax, but these were to be used only on
particular occasions. They were made by Dory, and were too
precious to be wasted. But this was not a consideration with
Bostwick. He consumed them whenever he came home, with
little heed to the poor child whose means were so small, and
whose labors were so heavy. Yet the miserable wretch loved
this child as well as he could love any human being—infinitely
more than he loved the mother. He was sensible of her beauty
—her eye sensibly impressed him. To her he was never brutal,
seldom harsh. To all others of the family he was cold or trucu-
lent. Something in her glance seemed to impress him with
respect, if not awe. She did not shrink from, yet did not seek
to conciliate him. She felt, and resented by her withdrawal,
his brutalities to her mother. She submitted to his endearments,
yet never returned them. Her instincts—shall we not say her
thoughts—were all at war with his nature, and the habits in which
he indulged. She had courage, too, and, never once forgetting
that he was her father, she could yet venture upon terms of
rebuke and reproach, at moments when his excesses revolted
her, such as became singularly impressive, spoken by the lips
of a child, and in the unsophisticated language of the heart.
Still he loved her, after a fashion—loved her with a sort of reverence, as she represented to his eyes that higher phase of society to which he felt that he himself could never aspire, and to
which, as is commonly the case with the class to which he be
longed, he looked ever with feelings of envy and desire.

He announced his presence to the inmates of the hovel, by a
peculiar whistle through the logs. The girl looked quietly at

her mother, but said nothing. The woman started up, all in a terror, and hastened to draw the bolt of the door and give him entrance.

"What! Bostwick! You've come?"

"Don't you see me? Well, Dory, hev' you got nothing to say to me?"

"Howdye, father," and the wheel was stopped, and she offered her hand. He kissed her, but not the mother; and frequent repulses had taught the latter not to attempt to bestow her kisses upon him.

"You're all well, I reckon?"

"Yes!" faintly answered the woman, as she resumed her seat by the fire, and her knitting, after drawing a chair for him. Dory resumed her spinning at the same time.

"What! the d—l," said he, "a'n't you guine to git me some supper?"

And he flung himself into the chair, and looked fiercely at the wife.

"We hain't got much," replied the woman, meekly, rising at the same moment and proceeding to one side of the chimney where some clothes were hanging, forming a sort of curtain.

"Much or leetle, let's hev' it; I'm hungry to kill. Got any-thing to drink?"

"Not a drop, but I'll make you some coffee, Sam, ef you'll wait for it."

"Wait! Humph! Git it! But first, let me hev' a big knife, ef you've got one, and your tinder-box and steel."

"Why, what's become of yours, Sam?"

"What's that to you? It's lost somewhere."

"And you've been in the water, Sam!"

"Yes? hev' you got any dry clothes for me?"

"There's the old scarlet breeches of the officer, and the coat, Sam——"

"Won't do; scarlet won't do for my wearing now. That time's gone. You must dye them clothes, before I can wear 'em. Dye 'em blue or green, either."

"You come on foot, father?" queried Dory.

"Well, ef I did, Dory, I reckon foot was given me to come on."

"But you hev'n't sold Black Ball?"

"Sold him! Yes! Perhaps! a sort of mortgage, I reckon; but what's the matter? Suppose I hev' sold him, who's to ax about the bargain? Mind your own business, child."

The girl looked at him, quietly, and the brute turned his eyes upon the fire. He somehow couldn't meet her glance. The mother, spreading the table the while, with a rare inexperience, took up the inquisition.

"And where's your rifle, Sam? You didn't bring it with you?"

"Look you, woman, I didn't come here to answer questions. Suppose I left horse and rifle in the swamp, it's what I've had to do a thousand times, and I had my reasons for it; only do you recollect, keep your tongue close when you talks to other people about my horse and rifle, and about me, too, ef you please. You don't know how soon you may be axed. And look you, Rachel, when you've got to answer, see that you do it yourself. Don't leave it to Dory. You kain't trust her. She don't love her father enough, to say what may save him from the inimy."

"But you've got no inimy now, father. Why should you have an inimy? Don't they say its peace, now?"

"Peace! As ef there was any peace for me! I tell you the whole country's sworn agin me, only because I wants to git my living out of it. But that's neither here nor there. You 'member, now, you don't know nothing about me :—ef you're axed, you reckon I've left the country. I hain't been here. I've got no black horse—remember that in prcticklar! That's enough! Where's the knife I axed you for?"

"It's here!" said the mother, handing him a clumsy blade, set in a common wooden handle. He looked at it scornfully.

"It's the best we've got," said the woman, apologetically.

"And good enough, too, for all you want with it. Now, git the coffee ready by the time I git back."

With these words, grasping knife, flint, steel, and tinder-box, he rose and hurriedly left the dwelling. The moment he had disappeared, the mother said—

"I wonder what he's after now. I'm afraid it's no good. Lord, ef he'd only stay quiet at home, and make corn for his family; but there's no such comfort for us, Dory, I'm afear'd. He's got the habit of going off, and doing God knows what; and we must only work as we kin, to keep from starvation."

The girl was silent for a space, and the mother, in the meantime, spread the table, got out some cold meat, and kneaded the dough into a hoe-cake, which was set promptly before the fire to bake. She had resumed her seat, when Dory, pausing at her wheel, remarked quietly and gently, but with that air of certainty which truth, simplicity, and earnest conviction will inspire, at all times, even in a child, and which crown its words with a degree of authority:—

"I wouldn't be asking father any more questions, mother. It does no good, and only makes him angry. He don't mind what we say, and we can't help it when he loses anything. He's always losing, and coming home poor and wanting; and he don't like to tell us how he came to lose. He's in some great trouble now, and you'd better not speak to him about it. I reckon he's not going to stay now he's come; but I wouldn't ask him."

"Ah, Dory, it's easy for *you* to talk so; but when I know — when I know——"

Here the mother sobbed and wiped her eyes with her apron. What did she know? and why did she forbear to declare it? The girl had no answer and no inquiry. The wheel whizzed round more rapidly than ever. The mother spoke again.

"It's fifteen years a'most sence we were married. Then he was so fond of keeping at home. Then he wasn't so fierce and fretful as he is now. Then he didn't drink, and there wasn't a more active person in the world, in the cornfield. Oh! it was a cruel day when he fell into the hands of Dick Jeffords—a cruel day. He's never been the same man sence. Dick Jeffords taught him all that he knows of wickedness—taught him to drink—taught him to——"

Another pause, and sobbing and wiping of the eyes.

"But Dick Jeffords is dead, mother," said the girl. "Don't you talk so of him."

"And why shouldn't I talk of him, when he was the cause of all the mischief——"

"Hush! mother!" with a warning finger, said the child,

pointing toward the door. Her keen ears had distinguished the light footsteps of the squatter. The mother stooped to turn her hoe-cake, and the wheel continued it's evolutions even more rapidly than ever.

CHAPTER XXXIV.

THE SQUATTER'S TREASURES, KNOWN AND UNKNOWN.

THE squatter, meanwhile, armed with knife and tinder-box, hurried away to the edge of the swamp, eager to examine his casket of ill-gotten treasures. He drew the box of Mrs. Eveleigh from the hollow of the cypress, and, upon a little bank in the swamp, surrounded by a wall of forest and swamp, thicket, shrubs, vines and trees, he proceeded to strike a light. It required but a few moments after this, to pry open the cover of the box, which was much better suited to a lady's toilet, than for the purpose of keeping or securing a treasure. The guineas were the first objects that compelled his attention. They were contained in a small linen bag. He counted them religiously, and then proceeded to turn over the rest of the contents of the box, which was pretty closely packed with papers. He was able neither to read nor write. He took for granted that the paper, which M'Kewn so much desired, was among them, but the point was one beyond his capacity to determine.

"It's here, I reckon, safe with the rest; but won't he pay for it when he gits it."

His curiosity was satisfied, if not his cupidity. One would suppose that his first act would be to convey to his wife and children a small portion, at least, of the golden spoils in his possession. But he was too selfish and too wary for that. His cunning did not suffer him to risk, in their hands, any proof that might facilitate his detection. It seems that some suggestion did arise in his mind, prompting him to detach a guinea, to be given to Dory. He spoke of her affectionately, and turned the glittering coin, separated from "his pile," between thumb and forefinger.

"But where's the use," he muttered, "and ef they was to ax where she got it, what is she guine to say?"

He restored it to the heap, restored the bag to the box, with all the papers, and restored the box to the hollow of the cypress, the base of which was encircled by a thick shrubbery. This done, he made his way back to the cottage, where his supper of bacon, corn-bread and coffee, already awaited him. He flung the knife down upon the table, and proceeded to eat, but had scarcely begun, when he commanded that the spinning-wheel should stop.

"The blasted noise keeps a body from hearing anything. Ef an inimy was at the door, nobody could know tell they *bursted* in."

The girl obeyed, put her cotton into the basket, and removed the wheel to a corner of the room. She then disappeared behind the curtain of clothes, and when she again came forth, and drew near the fire, he perceived that she had a book in her hand. Dory had been taught to read by her mother, and loved her book. The eyes of the squatter did not suffer her long from sight.

"A book!" said he, "and what sort of book is it, you've got?"

"It's the Holy Bible, father."

"The Holy Bible; and what do you know about the Holy Bible, and where did you get it, I want to know? You hain't been spending money, or your airnings, upon a thing that's no account, hev' you?"

"No, father, 'twas given to me by Mrs. Eveleigh."

"Well, she might hev' given you something to be more useful to you. She's rich; she might hev' given you some good clothes, I'm a-thinking, ef she'd ha' wanted to do a good thing for you. But these great rich folk are all as mean as h--ll!"

"Mrs. Eveleigh ain't mean, father; and she *has* given me clothes," replied the child.

"She has, has she? what! the frock you've got on, I reckon."

"No, I made that myself. She's given me good clothes, to wear when I go out, and on a Sunday."

"Sunday! as ef there ever was a Sunday for a poor man! Let me look at the book."

She handed it to him without a word, and he turned it over curiously. It was not a costly book; had it been—had the edges been of gold, and the back richly adorned with the same metal —it is quite probable that the perverse wretch would have been tempted to throw it into the fire. As it was, he thrust it back into the child's hands, saying:—

"And what's the good of it to you? You kain't understand it even ef you reads it."

"Oh? yes I can, father."

"Let me hear you read some—thar', jest where the paper's been turned down. I'll see ef you ain't been reading how to curse your own daddy."

The child gave him but a single look, but it made him restless. He could not meet the clear, calm glance fixed upon his own. He turned his gaze upon the fire, but repeated—

"Read, I say—let's hear what sort of bible l'arning you're a-gitting. Read where you've put the mark. That a man's own children should turn agin him!"

The child gave him another look, so simple, so expressive— of a calm, unspeaking, submissive sorrow, the most touching of all sorts of reproach: then, turning to the book she began to read from the New Testament, the Acts of the Apostles, the first chapter, just where the leaf had been turned down; but scarcely had she got through three paragraphs, when the squatter started up, having by this time finished eating, and, swallowing a pint of coffee at a gulph, he cried out:—

"That's enough! It's mighty good, what you're reading, I'm a-thinking, for a gal child. But it's no use. There's no apostles, now-a-days. At least, I never hear tell of any merracles now, or I reckon I might have a chance of being saved myself. But, without a merracle, I'm pretty much past saving, so it's no use to try. Shut up, Dory; you kin read to your mammy after I'm gone. I must be off."

"What!" cried the poor mother, "you're not a guine, Sam, at this late time o' night."

"And what should I stay for? Don't I know there's none of you hev' any love to spare for me here."

"Oh! don't say so, Sammy; don't!"

"Pooh! Git out! Don't suppose I'm fool as well as scamp. You're too full of good books and good women here, to have any likings for sich as me. Kiss me, Dory, you're a good child for a gal. I don't say you shan't read the book the widow give you, only I don't care. You may read, for the good 'twill do you. 'Twon't do me none. Blast all the gifts of your rich people. They only burn the heart out. What's good you kin git out of them, is what you kin take! I'm off; and look you, Rachel, mind what I say. Ef you're axed, you don't know nothing about me. You ain't seed me you don't know when, and, as for a horse, you don't reckon I've had one for a year, not sence the blasted men of Harden carried off my bay trotter. Blast all their two legs for ever for it. Don't you let Dory say nothing. She don't know how to speak sensible in such cases. Good-by, Dory."

And he was gone—gone out into the darkness—lost to sight as to hope. Not another word of kindness or farewell. None, in fact, to the poor woman who followed him to the door, as if entreating for it. Not even a glance to the poor children sleeping on the pallet, the eldest of whom, awakened by the unusual voice, raised herself up in the bed, and looked, but did not dare to make herself heard. She had old experience of blows, suddenly and sharply administered, to admonish her against any childlike and loving forwardnesses. Besides, the watchful mother had seen, and pushed her back, under the scanty covering, with—

"Lie still, Bet, it's pappy!"

Dreadful sound with which to quiet the baby! the baby was quiet for the rest of the night. But he was gone, and then the woman sat down and wept over the fireplace.

"Ef he had only shaken hands, Dory, and told me good-by, my child; but no! He wouldn't care ef I was on my cooling board to-morrow."

The girl began quietly to read the chapter in the Acts which she had attempted at her father's bidding, and her low, soft voice, still that of a child, delivered the inspired sentences in good time, and with very tolerable discretion, but without emphasis, and with the simplicity of one who did not fully comprehend what she was reading. When she had finished and put away the book, the mother said—

"I know it's good to hear and to read the blessed book, but my heart ain't in it. I don't feel it at all. I feel only that I am a very great sinner, very poor and miserable."

"We must pray now, mother, you know."

And the two dropped upon their knees, while the child alone audibly uttered "Our Father."

Let us leave them to such sleep as God vouchsafes to the sufferer, more sinned against than sinning, and follow the footsteps of the squatter, reckless of the peace he outrages, and quite incapable of conceiving the purity he leaves behind him.

"Acts of the Apostles," quoth he, as he darted forward in the direction of the highlands. "They sarved for their time. There's no Apostles now, I reckon, to do any more acts for poor people. Sich as preaches to us now, don't help much. Lord! what warmints. I've hearn a hundred that hadn't any more sense, and I reckon, warn't no better, ef the truth was known, than myself. They talk and they talk, about it and about it, and all what they says, don't consarn us at all, and don't suit. One speaks mighty big about luxuries and fine linen, yit I never seed one yit that warnt ready to swig the best of liquors at a rich man's table, and to eat ontell he was ready to burst; and which of 'em ever refused the best of English broadcloth for his back. There was Joe Downs, and Ephraim Sparkin, and Jake Frisbie, and a hundred more I've know'd, that was all jest too lazy for any work, and so they set up to be apostles; living from house to house, never paying for nothing; never refusing good feed and liquor, and jest talking things they didn't onderstand. No! the days for Apostles is at an *eend*, and men does jest what act suits 'em best. So I does mine. 'Taint so good as it mout be, but ef I can git back the old Black, with fifty gould guineas in hand, and what I kin squeeze out of M'Kewn, I'll do for awhile yit. It's a resk to try, but what's to be done? I shan't walk when I kin ride, and ef I take, it's only my own.

Such were the meditations which led to the attempt of the squatter. We have seen how it succeeded. Once mounted, though with the pistol bullets of Lance Frampton whistling about his ears, and he felt his strength and courage equally increase.

He never thought to return to the cottage. He felt very sure that it would soon have a score of visiters. He had striven hard for disguise and concealment, but his instinct taught him that he would be suspected. The neighborhood would be quite too hot, in a few hours, for his safety. He gave it a wide berth, accordingly, and making a circuit, which carried him far above the miserable hovel which his family occupied, he proceeded to descend the country, making an oblique progress toward the Edisto. —Let us return to Porgy and his party.

CHAPTER XXXV.

HOW MILLHOUSE REBUKES THE EXTRAVAGANCE OF PORGY.

THE poor woman, the wife of the squatter, was half-scared to death when she saw the squad of our partisans approach her dwelling. She at once conjectured that the squatter had been at his old tricks, and that the enemy was upon his footsteps. Cadaverously pale, trembling in every limb, she staggered to her bedside, and sank upon it, faintly exclaiming as they approached the house—

"Oh! Dory, they've come after him."

"Lie down, mother, and let me speak to the gentlemen," said the little girl.

"You, Dory! oh, no! You remember he told me, you were not to speak at all. Come back from the door, I tell you. Don't you say a word."

"But you musn't look so scared, mother. They'll think something wrong if you're so pale and trembling. Don't be afeard. —We haven't done anything wrong, and we don't know anything of father's doings."

"Hush, child, you musn't be talking. There they come. Oh! my God, what is to become of us?"

"Don't be afeard mother! God won't let them hurt us."

"Oh! how do you know, Dory?"

"I believe, mother."

"Believe! oh! yes, you'll believe anything, even though the soldiers kill us and carry us to prison. Come back from the door, I tell you. I'll open it. I'll answer all they ax."

The child drew away, and rested her elbows upon the table, as the party approached the house. A rather heavy knock, thrice repeated, threw the mother into a new passion of terror. She wrung her hands.

"Lord have mercy! What shall we do?"

"Open the door, mother, or let me do it. I'm sure these people ain't going to hurt us. One of them is Mr. Fordham, and he's a good man, you know."

"Mr. Fordham, is it?" in a whisper, and, somewhat reassured, rising and smoothing her apron. "To be sure, Mr. Fordham's always been our friend."

Another knock, and the voice of Fordham —

"It's me — it's a friend, Mrs. Bostwick."

The poor woman took courage. The door was opened, and Fordham, without, stood in front of the party. He had alighted from his steed, and held him by the bridle. Porgy was in the act of letting himself down; a performance, with him, usually to be classed among his most deliberate acts. Millhouse kept his saddle. The negroes were grouped in the rear. It was a most formidable party, still, in the eyes of the squatter's wife. The girl, Dory, looked on with some curiosity, but with the saddest possible look of resignation. Porgy and Fordham threw the bridles of their steeds to the negroes, and proceeded to enter the dwelling at the invitation of the hostess, who was tremulous with solicitude.

"This is Captain Porgy, Mrs. Bostwick — perhaps you may remember him before he went into the army."

"I've seed the captain," said she humbly, "but can't say that I should recollect him."

"Very likely, my dear madam," responded the captain courteously, taking off his cap, and entering. "In the last five years I've grown out of my own knowledge — one of the few men of the army, madam, who fattened on starvation. Your daughter, Mrs Bostwick."

"Dory, sir, my oldest."

"Dory! Is that her name?"

" For short, captain. Her given name is Dorothy.'

Porgy took the offered hand of the child, and looked to Fordham significantly. Fordham nodded his apparent affirmation.—
Porgy, still holding the child's hand, proceeded to seat himself
on a chair which the officious hands of Mrs. Bostwick put beside
him. Dory had already perused the lines of his countenance,
which, not wanting in manly beauty, though with some defects,
was at the same time benevolent and even tender in expression.
His eyes, small, but full of life, were also distinguished by good
nature, and his mouth was similarly marked. The child felt at
ease as she surveyed his face. A single glance sufficed for this.
He was no ruffian, that she felt sure; that he was a gentleman
by birth and education, her instincts at once assured her. The
fact was sufficiently proved by the ease with which he inspired
confidence in both mother and daughter. Our captain was quite
as observant of Dory's features as she had been of his. The
singular beauty of the child struck him at a glance, and compelled consideration. She resembled her mother very little.
Who could she resemble? Was her father's face like hers?
Could that ruffian and outlaw wear anything in his countenance,
like the serene sweetness, the ethereal loveliness that formed the
life of that pale but glowing aspect? The thing was impossible.
The conjecture was expelled from his thought the moment it
sought to enter.

Meanwhile, Fordham had broached the special object of their
visitation to the anxious woman, by asking for the whereabouts
of her husband. Her apprehensions were renewed; her tremors
became visible. Dory struggled out of the hands of Porgy, and
immediately placed herself beside her mother. The action and
its motive, so prompt and so instinctive, at once afforded to our
captain a clew to the strong moral courage and propriety of the
child. The question of Fordham showed the visit to be one of
quasi hostility. The party was to be confronted, not embraced.
The mother, in her moment of danger, must have the full support of her children. They were not to give countenance to
those who threatened a father's safety, however erring. Of
course, such thoughts as these formed no argument for the un-
ripened mind of the child; but the unerring instincts of a rightly
placed, and rightly sympathetic heart, sufficed to bring about

the instant conviction just as certainly as if it had been produced by thought and reason.   Porgy saw it all.

"Come back to me, Dory," said he mildly, extending his hand. "You are not afraid of me?"

She looked into his face, and immediately returned to him. Confidence was reinspired in consequence of the sudden activity of other instincts; and the captain had her again, a moment after, seated upon his knee.   In the meanwhile, it was apparent that Mrs. Bostwick either would not, or could not, give any account of her husband.   She was evidently greatly frightened, answered wildly, and was seemingly so much distressed, that Porgy interposed for her relief.

"It does not matter, Fordham.   Mrs. Bostwick evidently knows nothing of her husband — and we know nothing, Mrs. Bostwick; but we thought it possible that he might, from his knowledge of the people of the country, and the country itself, put us on the track of a band of outlaws who were guilty of a great outrage yesterday."

"Yesterday, captain?" asked the woman in renewed terror, and looking wildly to Dory.

"Yes, madam, yesterday!   They waylaid that excellent lady, Mrs. Eveleigh, her son and Mr. Fordham; seized them; tied the lady to her carriage, captured her wagon, and no doubt would have robbed and killed all the party, if I had not providentially come to their rescue, with a few friends, at the last moment."

"Lord save us! and yesterday!"

"We defeated the ruffians, and four of them were slain."

"Oh! my God!   Did I ever——!"

"We captured their horses; yet, such was the audacity of the surviving ruffians, that they ventured, one or more of them, even to my dwelling last night, and carried off one of the best of the captured horses."

"You don't say?"

"Yes, madam; a large raw-boned black!"

"A black!" and the conscious mother grew paler, and looked to Dory.   The child was pale also, but the features were motionless.   They said nothing.

"Now, Mrs. Bostwick, we thought that your husband might possibly———"

"Oh! I'm sure, captain, he don't know nothing about it. He's had no horse for a year, that I've seed, and where he is, there's no telling. It ain't often we sees him at home. He's away all the time, ontell his own children hardly knows him when he comes."

Porgy looked into Dory's face with an expression that won the child's sympathies at once. His look, involuntarily seemed to say, "Can it be possible that he is indifferent to such a dear innocent, such a pure, bright bud of the wilderness as this." But he said nothing, and suffered the mother to proceed in a series of rambling denials and disclosures which only served, to prove to both Porgy and Fordham, that the woman really knew more of the husband and his recent operations than she so solemnly declared. Of course, neither of them suspected her of any share in his proceedings, or any sympathy with them. Fordham had already put our partisan right in his estimate of the existing relations between husband and wife, and of the humble heart and honest character of the latter.

The overseer, baffled in his effort to ascertain from the mother anything with regard to the recent visits of the squatter, now addressed himself to the daughter.

"And when did you see your daddy last, Dory ?"

The child turned her eyes quietly to the querist, but before she could reply, Porgy exclaimed—

"No! no! Fordham! That won't do! Enough! If Mrs. Bostwick don't know, and hasn't seen, how should the little girl ? But I have some questions to ask you, Dory, and you must answer me.

And he looked into her eyes with a look which taught her that there was no snare, no danger.

"You spin, I hear, Dory, and weave, and knit, and sew, and do a great many clever things. Now I'm in great want of sewing, spinning, weaving, and knitting. I want woollen cloth, and cotton cloth, and thread, Dory, and a great supply of stockings. See what a big foot I've got—*two* feet, you see, and both of them are in great straits for want of clothing. Will you knit for me, Dory, and spin for me, when I beg you ? I shall want

both you and your mother's help in fitting up my poor establishment. I am no longer a soldier; and am about to become a
planter again, and you know what a planter wants. Now, my
dear, to begin — I must have as many pair of stockings as mam-
ma and yourself can knit for me between this and July. And you
must let me pay you for them in advance, that I may make
sure that you will do the work. Here, take this, Dory," thurst-
ing a guinea into her hand, "and here is a kiss by way of seal
to the contract."

The little girl took the money without a word, but her eyes
instantly filled with tears, and she suffered her head to decline
on Porgy's shoulder. He kissed her again, and put her down,
and she immediately walked across the room to her mother, and
laid the guinea in her lap, and stood, during the rest of the visit,
with her hand leaning on her mother's chair. The good woman
was loud in her acknowledgments.

"God bless you, sir," she said, "you're very good to us.
Dory shall work for you; she kin knit jest as well as I."

"*She* must do my stockings," quoth Porgy, "only she. You
mus'n't touch them. I must have the satisfaction, when I wear
them, of knowing that she made them. I shall find work for
you, too, Mrs. Bostwick. You shall hear from me when I want
you. Good-by, ma'am; you are a good woman, and ought to
be more comfortable in the world. Good-by, Dory; don't
forget me."

The child came up, and offered him her hand, which he took,
then stooping, kissed her again, took a respectful leave of the
mother, and led the way out of the house. Fordham followed,
but not before the wife of the squatter contrived to say :—

"Oh! Mr. Fordham, tell Mrs. Eveleigh, that I'm so sorry she
was robbed and troubled on the road. I'm so very sorry."

And she looked as if she felt that she herself was greatly to
blame in the matter; thus satisfying the shrewd overseer that
she was well aware of, or at least suspected, her husband's share
in the transaction. When they had mounted their horses, and
were out of hearing of the house, Fordham said to Porgy :—

"Ef you hadn't stopped me, captain, I reckon we'd ha' got
out o' Dory all about her father's coming, ef so be he had been
there."

"Yes," answered Porgy, "or she would have been made to lie about it, and would thus have spoiled the prettiest mouth in the world. No! no! Fordham. We must not demand of the child the evidence against the parent. I was not unwilling that you should ask the mother; though after the thing was begun, I felt that there was a degree of meanness about it, which made me feel a little ashamed. Still it was desirable to have the truth, and the wife of such a husband, might be supposed to be somewhat used to lying for him, and to be a little blunted in her sensibilities. But that child. She is the very picture of innocence as well as loveliness. Isn't it a wonderful thing that such a child should be born to such parents. How strangely will the perfect plant, the most beautiful flower, exquisite in excellence, and admirable in hues, spring up on the common dunghill. She ought to be plucked from it with all haste, and reared in a garden to herself.

Fordham could not altogether perceive the propriety of Porgy's refinements. He thought his philosophy a little too strained for common use, but he was silenced by it. But Porgy was not to get off so easily. He was now grappled with by no less a person than his sergeant, Millhouse, who, sitting on horseback, at the entrance, throughout the interview, had been a curious but silent spectator of the scene. He suddenly turned upon his superior, and said :—

"Cappin, you gin a guinea to the gal to make you stockings! a whole guinea!"

"To be sure! Well! what of it, Millhouse?"

"Why, Lord love you, cappin, that ought to buy stockings enough for a regiment. Why four shillings would git you as many for your own wear, as would last you from now to Christmas."

"Very likely, Millhouse. But, in truth, I did not give the guinea for the stockings. I gave it for the child to buy her own stockings, if need be, or whatever else she needs. I gave it from my heart, Millhouse, and not from my pocket."

"Oh! ay! I see! It was a sort of charity then, cappin."

"Well, I suppose you may call it so."

"Of course, there's no *eend* to the supply where that came from! Lord be marciful to them who ain't marciful to themselves! You'll want all of them guineas before long. But I reckon you've had jist sich a dream as poor 'Lisha Dayton, that s'arved with us at Georgetown, and was killed at that blasted skrimmage at Quinby, where we lost so many good fellows."

"And what sort of dream had Elisha?"

"Why you see, 'Lisha was always dreaming of good luck and finding fortunes, though poor fellow, he had precious small chances of luck at any time that ever I heard tell of. But when we were at camp 'pon the High Hills, he somehow got hold of a pair of pretty good boots, a leetle worn only, that he tuk from a British ensign that he brought down with a bullet on a scout. The boots was too fine for 'Lisha to wear, so he agreed to sell them to Lieutenant Withers for nine shillings, in the raal silver. The boots were worth a great deal more, but that was all the money the lieutenant had, and there was nobody else about that had any. So 'Lisha 'greed to take the nine shillings; and with that money jingling in his pockets, the poor fellow thought he'd got the world itself in a string, and the two eends of the string both in his own fingers. He thought so much about it that he was constantly dreaming of buried money and all sorts of great discoveries. One day he come to me; says he—'Millhouse, I've had the same dream three nights running. It must be true. I'm sure on it. It's of a great heap of money buried on the Block House Hill. I seed the hill in my dream, and the very trees, jest how they stand, above the place where the money lies. I wants you to go with me and git it.' Says I, 'I don't b'lieve in dreams.' Says he, 'But this is a true one. I'd take bible oath on it, I'm sure. And ef you'll go with me and help dig, and let nobody else know, I'll give you a whole quarter of the pile, and the pile is a mighty big one.' Says I, ''Lisha, them dreams is only making a great fool of you.' And then he swore, and he was so sart'in sure of it, and he begged so hard with me to go and help him, that I concluded to go; but says I, ''Lisha, as I tell you, I don't b'lieve in dreams, and if you'll agree to give me them nine shillings, in hand, that you're a jingling in your pocket now, I'll give up the quarter that you offer me out of the buried pile.' When he heard that, he was a leetle slow to answer. 'Then,' says I, ' you don't b'lieve in your own dreams 'arter all.'

Then he swore a most outrageous big oath, and he said, 'It's a bargain.' So I made him give up the shillings, and I jingled 'em in my pockets all the way we went; and he pushed fora'd, pretty fast ahead, for now he didn't seem to like the sound the shillings made when they were in my pocket and not his own. We had both of us pick and shovels, and sure enough he led 'zactly to the place as he seed it in his dream; and the 'tarnal fool had gone there before mid-day by his own self. 'Well,' says I, ' 'Lisha, where shill we strike ?' 'Thar,' said he, 'that's the 'zact place.' And into it I went with the pick. And into it he went, like a strong man. And we picked the earth loose, and the roots, and we shovelled and threw out the naked yellow clay, jest as God had put it there, maybe, a million of hundred years before, until we both sweated like an overseer's horse in fly-time. At the eend of two of the longest hours I ever know'd in my life, 'Lisha jumped out of the hole, and says he with a laugh, 'What a blasted fool I am to b'lieve in a d——d dream !' 'So you are,' says I. 'It's no use,' says he, 'there's no pile to share. I see it now. And so, as there's no treasure, Millhouse,' says he—the bloody fool !—'you must give me back my shillings.' And as he said, I jest dropped pick and spade, and put my fingers to the corner of my eyes, and I said, 'Look here, 'Lisha, ef you sees gooseberries any where in them two eyes.' 'Why,' says he, 'as we hain't found any money, you ain't guine to keep my shillings ?' 'Ain't I then,' says I. 'The speculation in the dream, was your own, 'Lisha, and I worked only for the sartainty of the thing. You kin keep the pile when you find it, but I'll keep the pile I've found already; and I confess to you, 'Lisha, I'm better pleased to dig for my money in a fool's pocket, than in the side of a d——d hard clay hill like this !' Lord ! how he did rip and tear, curse and swear; but 'twant no use. I had the shillings, and he soon l'arned that it would call for bigger curses than was in his body, to draw the shiners out of my pockets. He gin it up at last, and then I said to him 'you ain't fit to keep money, 'Lisha, but I won't be hard upon you. Here's three of your shillings back, jest enough for you to jingle. They'll make all the music you desarves to hear."

And, at the close, the recollection of his achievement prompted a glorious burst of cacchination from the throat of our military financier.

"A good story, Millhouse, and excellently told," quoth Porgy; "and, pray, how will you apply it to our present purpose?"

"Why, easy enough, cappin! Don't you see, ef you've got a dream like 'Lishe Dayton, of a pile of treasure somewhar' to be got only for the diggin', t'wont be *on*reasonable or *on*righteous, if you let me jingle in my pockets the rest of them guineas in your'n."

"Humph!" muttered Porgy; "it would, perhaps, be just as well, Millhouse, if I did; but, with your permission, I'll wait for the dream. Be sure of this, my good fellow, that while you wield pick and shovel, in getting in my treasure, you shall be quite welcome to share my shillings, nor shall I envy you their jingle."

"Don't I know that, cappin? 'Taint for myself I'm a-speaking, but jest for you and your gettings, I'm afeard you'll want every guinea that you waste."

"Don't mistake, Millhouse. I waste no guineas. When I give money, it is only that I may get a good interest for it. The true man, Millhouse does not live by money, nor by that which money will always buy—bread and meat. There is still better food than that for which I more hunger; and yet I know not the man living who has a better appetite for good living than myself."

Fordham had been a quiet listener to this conversation, and seemingly quite an interested one, but he now arrested it by recurring to what had been one of the objects of the expedition—to find, if possible, the route which the outlaw had taken who had carried off the horse.

"There's no tracks," said he, "about the cabin, only those made by our own horses. I reckon he hain't been to see his family on horseback; though I'm thinking his old woman has seed him sence the attack yisterday. She show'd it by the scare we gin her. He's not gone back after he got the horse. He's too 'cute for that. We shan't see him back, in these parts, I'm a-thinking, till its all pretty much blown over."

Still the search was made. The party traversed the region, along all the avenues which it was possible for the outlaw to pursue, assuming him to have steered for the cottage. But they found no traces. And this was no vague search. Nobody, who does not know the woodman of the South, can conceive the excellence of his eye in discovering the slightest traces upon the ground, or through the forest, of the objects which he pursues. On horseback, at a smart canter, he will pull up, dismount, and show you where the deer or turkey has gone by, perhaps the night before. He can, with very great approach to certainty, say what interval has elapsed since the passage of the prey. His instincts are those of the Indian. Taught in the same school, his eye and ear are wonderfully keen, quick, and discriminating. Knowing the qualities of our woodmen, the report of Fordham, Frampton, or Millhouse, on matters of this sort, would always be quite conclusive to our captain of partisans. But it was sunset before the scouting was arrested. A little after that period, they reached the dwelling of Porgy, and Fordham was readily persuaded to stay to supper.

CHAPTER XXXVI.

PLAY AND PAY.

It does not need that we should accompany the Squatter, Bostwick, on his course to and along the Edisto, pursuing the downward route until it brought him within sight of the ocean. Enough that we find him there in safety after a little interval of time.— But there was one adventure, however, which occurred to him on the road, and within seven or eight miles only of the spot where he had engaged to meet with M'Kewn, and to bring the negroes and the papers, should he prove successful in his attempt upon the cavalcade of the widow Eveleigh. Stopping at a hovel on the roadside, for refreshment, he was surprised to come upon the fellow, Tony Hines, the only other surviving member of the gang which he led on that occasion. Tony, it will be remembered, had succeeded in saving himself, when pursued by Porgy and Corporal Millhouse, by taking to the swamp fastnesses before the two partisans had got within striking distance. His terrors in the flight had been such as to prompt him to such desperate efforts as to kill his horse; when he resumed farther flight on foot, never stopping on his downward route until it became physically impossible to proceed farther.

Flight, fatigue, the want of food, and perhaps an already diseased condition of the body, had resulted in a burning fever, and, in utter exhaustion, he had sought shelter and succor in a cabin whose inmates could afford but little of either. It was here that Bostwick found him stretched on a miserable pallet of straw in a state of extreme suffering. Physic and physicians were not to be had in that sparsely-settled region. The patient died or lived according to the strength of his constitution, or the decree of Providence. "Yairb [herb] tea," was the only remedy of the poor and simple population, and of this sylvan remedy, the good woman of the hovel was willing to provide any quantity, and did pour it down the throat of the sick man, till he turned from her with loathing; and he hailed the appearance of Bostwick with a yell of delight, as it seemed to promise him what the old people had denied—a draught of cold water. Bostwick would have supplied him from the bucket, but the old woman interposed with hands and tongue.

"It'll be the death of him, stranger. It'll chéck the perspiration, and give him a chill to kill him."

"Let my old woman alone," quoth the husband; "she knows how to doctor fever."

And the squatter withheld the beverage from the burning lips of the patient.

"But what in the world's name brought you here, Tony?" Bostwick curiously demanded. Rogues are naturally suspicious of each other, and, finding the fugitive directly on the route to the secret place of meeting with M'Kewn, and only a few miles from it, the squatter began to conjecture that there had been some connection between the two, which had been withheld from him.—M'Kewn, so far as he knew, had never seen Tony. He had also been earnest in his injunctions to keep his creatures from all knowledge of the party by whom he had been employed. The squatter, fully assured of the dishonest and deceitful character of M'Kewn, now strove by a series of circuitous inquiries to

probe the fugitive outlaw, and it was only after a long cross-exam-
ination, carried on with very excellent skill, that he arrived at
the conclusion, that in taking the route which he had pursued,
Tony had no other purpose than that of throwing as much
breadth of swamp and forest between himself and his pursuers,
as was possible, and that he really knew nothing of the Scotchman.

Satisfied finally of this, the squatter promised to do for him
what he could; to try and procure physic and assistance; and,
commending him to nature and the old people who sheltered
him, left him to the chapter of accidents. We must not suppose
that he abandoned him indifferently. It was not in his power,
in fact, to give him either help or consolation. He knew of no
remedies, being one of that class of persons who never had leisure
for sickness. Nor, even if succor could have been bought, had
he the means in money for the purchase. He had left behind
him, in his cypress hollow, the strong-box of Mrs. Eveleigh, with
all his ill-gotten treasure, as well as the much-valued paper. A
few shillings sufficed him for the expenses of the route, and he
looked for the replenishing of his purse to the meeting with
M'Kewn. He left his comrade accordingly, but not without
promising to bring him medicine and money on his return, which
he told him would not be long delayed. When he got to the
place appointed for his meeting with M'Kewn, the latter had not
yet made his appearance; but he was soon joined by Barton and
Drummond, persons of the brotherhood, who acted as agents for
M'Kewn, and who shared his spoils. They reported the transport sloop to be in waiting, standing off and on, and to be brought
in, in a couple of hours, by a signal which had been agreed on
with the captain.

"But where's the niggers, Bostwick?" demanded Drummond.

"Niggers?"

"Yes; M'Kewn expected you to bring down fifteen or twenty."

"M'Kewn expects other men to do things he kaint do himself."

"Why, that's pretty much the way with most people. But
have you got any?"

"Well, we must talk over them things another time. I must
eat and drink now. I'm a'most famished. I haint had a decent
mouthful of anything for three days."

"The devil! Well, we can provide you. We're well off here. Plenty of the good stuff—raal Jamaica, and as much grub as would feed a regiment. Let's be off to the castle."

"Castle!"

"Ay, what you may call a castle, it's to hard to be got at; but if you look for anything better than a canvass tent, in a deep swamp, you're dreaming to no purpose. Come along. Barton will stay here and meet M'Kewn, and bring him along. He'll be here after nightfall."

Drummond, one of the confederates, was the speaker, and he led the way, on foot, to his swamp castle, which lay deeply imbedded in tangled thickets near one of the mouths of the Edisto. —Bostwick kept on horseback as long as he could. A few minutes riding lost them the cool, fresh breezes of the sea. Soon, they were buried in a dense region in which the air seemed to sleep like a lake in the hollows of the mountains. But the change was not a disagreeable one at that season of the year. In a little while, ignorant of the locality, you would have fancied yourself anywhere but near the ocean, all was so still, so utterly confined and shut in, and with the horizon within finger-reach. A blind path showed the way imperfectly, winding circuitously through lagune and thicket. At length, the two ascended a slight elevation, and, through the shrubbery, Bostwick caught glimpses of the dingy canvass which formed the tent of the confederates. They were now within the walls of "the castle;" a castle, indeed, of a magnificence such as the works of art, in the hands of man, has never yet displayed. The bank upon which the tent stood was crowned with aged oaks, that spread themselves out like great green canopies, covering all within their reach, their white beards trailing to the earth, or sweeping in the wind, like those of the Druid Bards, howling their songs of hate and death in the ears of the tyrant Edward, as described in the much undervalued ode of Gray—a production very far superior, in all poetic respects, to the over-lauded elegy of the same writer. Our live oaks are certainly patriarchal presences when we find them of an age beyond the memory of man. These, in the castled keep of our confederates, almost within sight of the ocean, and within the influence of its salt atmosphere, would have thrown into comparative insignificance, the "castled crags of

Drachenfell's," placed in close neighborhood with them. But they were not alone. If the oak is the Druid priest, the ancient patriarch, the Magnolia is the crowned king of the forest. There were three of these sovereign forms within thirty feet of each other, and alternating among the oaks, on the bank where the tent of the outlaws—for such, in fact, they were—had been raised. Not one of these trees was less than a hundred and fifty feet in height, their great shafts rising up like columns, straight as an arrow, and bare of foliage for more than a hundred feet, then swelling into a mighty crown of green, darkly bright, which the hands of May would enliven, not enrich, with the purest of her great white flowers. Myrtle and cane, the honeysuckle and jessamine, and dog-wood, not yet in bloom, or even brightening, grew, and were gladdened in the shadow of these protecting potentates; while the billows of the sea, at the height of the tide, wound in among the creeks, and freshened the hollows, even to the roots of these princes of the forest, whom they were insidiously to undermine in season.

But the squatter had no eye for these objects. With him, as with most of the ignorant, a tree is a tree only; and in a region which boasts of such a wilderness of trees, the most noble is but little valued—is cut down and cast into the fire without remorse on the smallest occasion. Bostwick regarded the natural aspects of the spot only with reference to their uses for the shelter of the fugitive. He was not insensible to this feature of the 'castle.'— But the tent and what it contained more certainly appealed to his tastes. He was conducted into it by Drummond. Here they found an old negro woman, a withered crone of sixty, who appeared to busy herself in cleaning pots and rinsing kettles. Of these utensils there may have been half-a-dozen strewed about. There was no table, or chair, or bed in the tent, but one or two boxes, and a pile of cloaks and blankets, served to show how the inmates garmented themselves for sleeping. A capacious jug was visible, standing on the ground, which Drummond bade the old woman replenish with fresh water. A neighboring spring enabled her to do this in a few seconds, for the woman was brisk though old, and moved about with very juvenile celerity. Whether through love or terror, her rulers had taught her equal docility and activity. When she returned with the water, Drummond threw open the box, and revealed several huge square bottles of Jamaica,—the great liquor of the low country during this period, and for a goodly time after.

To drink, was a thing of course. It was the initiatory process in those days of all society, high and low, of the palace and the hovel. Bostwick enjoyed the double advantage of an incorrigible head and an eager taste. He was one not easily satisfied, and not easily suffering. Drummond was by no means a milk-sop either, and the draught was repeated no less than three times in the half hour which the two employed, cast upon the earth, and chatting together, we may suppose, of the joys of knavery, and the luxury of sin. After a while, Barton made his appearance, just about dark. He was followed by a couple of sailors bringing in fish. Candles were lighted within the tent, and a fire was kindled without. Around this, the woman proceeded to prepare supper.

"I wonder what keeps M'Kewn?" queried Bostwick.

"Oh! he'll be here directly. 'Taint time for him yet. But let's be doing something till supper is ready."

"Well, I'm consenting," replied Bostwick, readily comprehending what the something meant. "Hev' you any *books?*"

Books meant cards in the vernacular of the forest.

"We'd be without our salvation if we hadn't," was the answer of Barton. Drummond, meanwhile, pulled out from the fathomless bowels of the box, a paper containing several well-thumbed packs.

It is curious that all primitive periods, in all countries, are distinguished by the passions for gaming and drinking, and by such a degree of invention as will enable men to gratify both. The fact illustrates the necessity of the race for mental exercise, and for the excitement of the nervous system. And this is in what we vulgarly and ignorantly call a state of nature, as if man, who is a born creature of art, ever knew such a condition, in the sense in which nature is commonly understood. But we must not philosophize, having to deal with our present company.

"What shall be the *marks?*" demanded Drummond, throwing himself down beside the two, and spreading the cards before them.

"Ontell I see M'Kewn, and git some money, I shill have to run upon mighty small marks, I tell you," was Bostwick's answer, drawing forth the few shillings that remained in his pocket, and detaching a single one from the rest.

"Well, *it is* a small p'int," quoth Barton.

"But when a man kaint run, you must let him walk," answered Bostwick, taking up the cards and proceeding to shuffle. The other two put up their shillings. In those days the moral and philosophical games of brag and poker, now the favorites where the shillings are forthcoming, were not known among the people. It had not then been reduced to a science, the study of one's moods at play — a study upon which success at Brag and Poker so much depends. The ordinary game with the "little dogs," was one still known and still reasonably practised among this class under the several names of old-sledge, seven-up, all-fours, &c.; and on the present occasion it was adopted tacitly, not a word being said to decide the point on either hand. The squatter, like most of his class, was an adept at this play; not only knew the game well, but had little adroitnesses which increased the *science*, and sometimes remedied the deficiencies of fortune. He could make the trump, and cut the jack — when not too impertinently watched — almost at his pleasure. The only qualification to this merit, was in the fact that it was shared in pretty nearly the same degree, by his associates. They were well matched, and, this being the case, but little room was left to either *to play the knave*, out of his turn. They were in the midst of the play when M'Kewn entered.

"I'm mighty glad you've come, M'Kewn," was the abrupt and somewhat irreverent address of the squatter, " es I'm jest in want of the shillings. These chaps here hev' pretty nigh *dreaned* me of all I had."

"And a small *all* at that," laughed Drummond.

"A man's *all* is enough for him to lose at any time," muttered the squatter, as Drummond took up his last shilling. "I'm a-looking to you, M'Kewn?"—and he extended his open palm. His manner was such as to impress the Scotchman with the notion that his more important game had been successful; and, though the familiarity of the squatter had now began to grate upon his sense of the more dignified position to which he was rising in the world, he yet, with a good-natured sarcasm, handing him some money as he spoke, replied—

"I should like to know, Bostwick, when you'll cease to look to me ?"

"Well, there's no knowing; when I've done with you I reckon."

"Or I with you," responded the other, *sotto voce ;* and the look which spoke to the squatter at the same time, seemed to say that there should be no long delay in cutting the connection, the present affairs being finally adjusted. Bostwick grinned. The parties knew one another and were fairly matched.

"Why, what's this, M'Kewn ?" growled the squatter, as he looked at the handful of coin, which the former had given him. "Nothing but silver, and pretty much shillings and sixpences all."

"What would you have, man ? You're betting shillings only."

"That's only bekase I had nothing better, and I must make up my losses by tall betting. Give us some gould, kain't you ?"

The humor of the request did not seem favorably to impress M'Kewn ; but it was one which he was not prepared to combat openly at present. Nay, the very confidence with which the application was made, seemed to say—I know how largely you owe me for my services.—He handed the squatter three guineas.

"'Twon't do, now, M'Kewn. Make it ten. Don't be splitting the hoecake too thin."

"Wait till you lose them before you ask for more."

"But I ain't a-guine to lose 'em ; and its bekase I'm guine to win now, that I want to go to tall betting.—There !" said he to Drummond and Barton, and clapping down the handful of small silver that he had received from M'Kewn, "plank down agin the heap, both on you."

The money was counted, and each of the challenged parties faced it with a like sum. M'Kewn, gazing on the squatter, could not keep from showing, in his face, the feeling of scorn and disgust which he entertained for him. The latter saw the expression of his countenance, and read its full meaning. His own glance, in reply, was one of mixed bitterness and derision. The play, meanwhile went on. The parties played as unconcernedly as if nothing were at stake. Practice had indurated them. Barton was drowsy, to all appearance, but keenly vigilant. Drummond was gay and garrulous, but not a point of the game escaped him ; while the squatter, seemingly reckless and indifferent at the same time, was saying to himself, " These skunks would steal the eyes out of a body's head if he'd let 'em. But I knows 'em." M'Kewn seated himself upon the chest, and gazed upon the three in silence. In a few minutes Drummond cried out—

"Seven up! That's into you, Bost!" and he raked up the two piles with the coolness of one spooning up his uncooled broth. The action was followed by the squatter casting down the three gold pieces which he had just got from M'Kewn. The latter started up.

"What!" cried he, "you don't mean to stake the three upon the game?"

"Why not, Squar?" answered the squatter.

"The devil! And you expect my pockets to keep you supplied?"

"In course!" was the cool rejoinder.

The Scotchman jumped up, hurried to the entrance of the tent, walked out, was gone a moment, then returned and took his seat upon the chest. It was not long before Barton gathered up the stakes.

"Luck's ag'in me," quoth Bostwick, "but every road I ever seed has a turn somewhere. I must hev' the guineas, M'Kewn."

And, without looking round, he extended his open palm to the person he addressed.

<hr>

CHAPTER XXXVII.

BREWAGE OF BITTER BEVERAGE AMONG THE BRETHREN.

M'Kewn started to his feet.

"What, the devil?" he exclaimed, "do you suppose I'm made out of gold?"

"If you was, how I should like the k'ining of you," responded the squatter with a rare coolness.

"Hark ye, Bostwick, do you mean that I'm to find you guineas for you to stake by the handful on a rascally game of cards?"

"In course! But old-sledge ain't a rascally game, M'Kewn. It's a mighty fine game, I tell you, and takes a mighty smart sort of person to play it now. I reckon, ef so be luck wasn't always agin me, I could beat you from Monday morning to Sunday night, and never stop once to pray. Fork over now, sensible, M'Kewn, and don't keep the boys waiting. Five guineas will do."

"I must see you first."

"Oh! there's no seeing about it. I'm here. You see me, I reckon. I'm alive and kicking—pretty sprigh too, all things considerent. I've been a-working in your business; that's enough. Hand up the gould, and shet up."

M'Kewn seemed disposed to show obduracy. He rose and again sat down, and, all the while, the hand of the squatter was stretched out before him, the fingers working toward the palm. Bostwick was playing more games than one. It was with the most desperate reluctance that M'Kewn conceded the demand, and flung down five pieces of gold upon the ground between the players.

"Let it lie thar'," quoth Bostwick, "and kiver it, boys, if you dare!"

M'Kewn started up, almost furious.

"Bostwick, I warn you."

"Oh! warn be d——d! I know's what I'm about, M'Kewn. It's my money now, and I've the right to use it jest as I chooses. Are you down, honeys?"

"Faced, full point, Bost," answered Drummond. And fifteen guineas formed the pile. M'Kewn tried to look on, but couldn't endure it long. He darted up, and sallied out of the tent. When he returned, the whole pile belonged to the squatter, and his opponents were compelled to plead for a mitigation of stakes. The stakes were now of silver.

"It feels so mean!" quoth the squatter, "to git back to white money, after ye've had sich a pleasant feel of the yallow. But I'm agreeable to anything."

And he dealt out the cards, threw up a knave, and ran out the game in a jiffy, gathering up the sixpences with the air of a man who is half disposed to regard the act as more troublesome than compensative. A stop was put to the game by a call to supper. Suppose this performance to be achieved, and the parties satisfied, and the things removed.

"Well, honeys," said the squatter, with still increasing audacity, "whenever the feeling of old-sledge comes strong upon you, I'm the man to say, h'ist away! I don't want to be carrying off your gould chickens, ef you're the men to call 'em back to the old roost."

"Work before play," interposed M'Kewn. "We've got something to do, I think, and the sooner we set about it the better."

"Well! I don't know what *you've* got to do, M'Kewn," coolly rejoined the squatter, "but ef you hev' anything on hand to trouble you, the sooner you get at it, the better. But my work's done for this time, I reckon, and I'll play tell all splits,—ontell I kin get another job that's profitable."

"You forget, you have not made your report about the last job. ·You want your pay without performance. But you don't get another stiver from me until I know what's been done. I must be satisfied."

"And so you sh*ll*, soon enough, ef anything kin satisfy you. But there's time enough. Let us play awhile. I'm in for luck now, and I ain't guine to lose the chance."

"Let him git rid of his guineas, M'Kewn," quoth Drummond. "They burn in his pocket. He won't be easy till he empties it."

"And then he'll not be easy till he fills it again," answered M'Kewn angrily. "Don't I know him?"

"Ef you does, you knows a man that, when he's done his work, must hev' his rest," answered the squatter, with an air of savage doggedness. "Look you, M'Kewn, when you knows all, you'll wonder I ain't a tiger, or, it mout be, some worser wild beast than that."

"Eh!" exclaimed M'Kewn, with a stare.

"Yes! You may say 'eh!' and look wild. But I've seed sights to make a man think of hell, and worse places."

"Come out with me, Bostwick, and tell me all!"

"I ain't guine to talk about it 'tell I'm ready. Wait awhile.— Let's play,—all of us."

"Play!" said M'Kewn. "I'm in no humor for play."

"*E*n I'm in no humor for work," retorted the squatter.

"We'll play awhile," said Drummond to M'Kewn, with an appealing look; at the same time, turning to the chest, he motioned

M'Kewn to rise, and drew from it a huge black bottle of Jamaica.
"A drink all round before we play."

"I'm agreeable to that!" answered the squatter; and the cups
were filled in a twinkling. Bostwick drained the fiery liquid in
its native state, disdaining the qualifying aid of water. All drank,
M'Kewn barely tasting the beverage. His one virtue of sobriety,
by the way, served to increase greatly the potency of his vices.
—He still refused to play, but sat down sullenly observing the
others.

"I'm for small points," said Barton, putting up a single guinea.
"I'll not drain my pockets in one fling to pleasure any man."

"Scared!" grinned the squatter.

"Well, a man might jest as well be, dealing with such a born
devil for gambling as you, Bostwick."

The squatter's self-esteem was gratified. He gave a chuckle;
and, hauling out all his guineas, raised them in a pile beside him.
One of them was put up to suit the resources of his comrades.
They played. Luck still attended him; and he was the winner
of game after game, until, at a significant glance from M'Kewn,
Drummond and Barton both declared themselves penniless.

"Git more!" roared the squatter. "Borrow! Thar's M'Kewn."

"I don't lend a penny!" shouted the Scotchman.

"And I won't borrow," said Drummond, governed by the evident wishes of M'Kewn, rather than by any scruples of his own.

"Nor I!" echoed Barton. "It's only to lose. You've sold
your soul to the devil, Bostwick."

"And a devilish bad bargain the devil has made of it," muttered M'Kewn, "if he gave five shillings for the stuff."

"I reckon that's jest the price you put on your own soul, M'-
Kewn," was the sarcasm of the squatter; and, growing more audacious, he added, "and ef old Satan be the cunning chap that
people thinks him, he'd not be apt to buy it any price. It'll
come to him some day, of its own free will, at no cost at all."

M'Kewn looked more and more savage. His face had actually
grown livid as he listened to the increasing insolence of the
squatter. Hitherto, the creature, though apt sometimes to say
an impertinent thing, had never shown any such consistent purpose of doing so. M'Kewn could only account for it, by supposing such a degree of success, on the part of the squatter, in

his late operations, as had stimulated his *amour propre* to a degree even beyond the control of his fears or judgment. This being the case, M'Kewn was willing to tolerate a great deal; but his pride chafed greatly at the necessity of doing so, and what was contempt before, in the feeling which he entertained for the miserable wretch whom his cupidity had employed, was rising absolutely into a sentiment of hatred. Unconsciously, vague purposes of resentment and revenge were beginning to work into his mind, to ripen into performances as soon as occasion should offer opportunity for their due exercise. Either Bostwick did not suspect the feeling he inspired, or was regardless of it. He continued to play the reckless insolent; cool, savage, scornful and satirical in all that he said, as far as it lay within his capacity to be so. And, with all his vulgarity and his educational inferiority, he was still capable of making himself felt. That he should presume at all, was a sufficient cause of offence to M'Kewn, whose social pride was growing in due degree with the acquisition of wealth.

Bostwick, stimulated by a sudden and unusual run of luck, was vexed at being arrested in it. He was acute enough to couple the refusal of Drummond and Barton to play any longer, with the obvious wish of M'Kewn, and he so expressed himself as to make the parties understand that he saw through them all. He knew that Drummond and Barton had money enough for play, and felt sure that, if they had not, and desired it, they could command, with even more facility than himself, the requisite loans from the Scotchman.

"Well," said he, looking round him with a scorn that might be really entertained—"Well, I'm about as poor a dog as ever gnaw'd a bone; but, by Jiminy! I'm not so poor a dog as to let any man say whether I shill bark or not, jest as it pleased him!—No! Ef I'm to hev' a master, I'll choose one that'll let me run or sleep when I wants to, and not rout me up because it suits him only, and set me to barking ag'in, when I've lost all tongue a'ready in a long day's hunt. In some things, I knows I'm worse than a nigger, but bad as I am, I reckon I'll never let any man put his collar round my neck."

"And who does that?" demanded Barton and Drummond in a breath.

"Why, you, both on you. You aint half a man between you. Here I knows you both wants to play, and will take to cards as an old sarpent to a young frog: but, jest because M'Kewn here has given you a look out of his gimblet eyes, you shet up, and put on a righteous face, and swear agin your very souls, that you're tired and don't want to play, and hain't got any more money, and I don't know what other 'scuses. That aint being a man and a gentleman, any way. It's more like being a dog and a slave, I say!"

"Don't you call me a dog and a slave, Bostwick, or I'll hurt you!" growled Barton. Drummond only laughed merrily.

"Hurt will you? Who's afear'd? You're barking up the wrong tree, Barton, if you thinks to scare me with your tongue. I could take the starch out of your jacket any day in three minutes, ef you wants to try."

"Pshaw!" put in M'Kewn, "no more of this! Be still, Barton; and you, Bostwick, don't be a fool! If you're fool enough to play together, and gamble away your money when you ought both to be earning it, at least don't be such fools as to quarrel when your profits can only grow from your working together. You, Barton, set off, and see about the schooner. The tide serves, and she's either up or coming. See to her, and make stowage of what you've got, and that's a matter about which we must talk together, Bostwick. You, Drummond, go with Barton, and see that everything's right."

The two rose without a word. The squatter then —

"Well, ef we're to hev' a talk of it, jest you put out the Jamaica, Drummond, that we shan't hev' a dry time of it. M'Kewn is mighty apt to git thirsty when he talks of business, and I work so hard to listen that it makes my throat mighty dry too. Heave out the liquor, will you?"

"Plenty's the word," answered Drummond, doing as he had been asked. The portly black bottle, square and capacious, was put within reach. The negro woman just then brought in a bucket of water from the spring. She was dismissed, and Drummond and Barton soon disappeared, leaving the squatter and his employer in sole possession of the tent.

11*

CHAPTER XXXVIII.

BLOOD MONEY.

Scarcely had the other parties all disappeared, when M'Kewn began—

"I don't know what to make of your conduct, Bostwick, to-night. It's rather unusual, I must say, and quite different from what, I think I have a right to expect. You have treated me pretty much as if I were one of those ruffians that you have sometimes employed; and seemed to forget, my good fellow, that it is I who am your employer; not you mine!"

"Forgit it, you say! No! by Jiminy! not a bit of forgitting with me in that business," was the reply; "but before I begin, I'll try the Jamaica. It'll take more than you kin find for me, M'Kewn, to make me forgitful of you and your business."

This was said in tones of singular bitterness, and with such a look of scornful superiority as quite confounded the listener.— Meanwhile, the squatter resorted to the bottle, and poured out the Jamaica, and dashed it with water, with as much deliberation, as if there were no other objects before him for consideration. At all events, he showed no regard whatever to the obvious impatience of his companion. At length, having drank, and struck down the cup upon the chest, he turned to M'Kewn, and confronted him.

"And now for it," said he. "You wants to know about the business, and how we got on, and what we've got, and where's the niggers and the papers, eh! Well, now, look you, M'Kewn, ef, before I told you the leetlest word in the world about the matter, I was jest to take this knife, and drive it up to the handle in that rotten heart of your'n, I'd make the right sort of beginning for sich a story as I've got to tell!"

He suited the action, in some degree, to the words; flourishing the blade of his *couteau de chasse*, in singular proximity to the eyes of his auditor. M'Kewn was no imbecile. He was a

cool, firm man; not a hero, perhaps—possessed of none of that
sort of bravery which springs tumultuously into appetite and action on the merest show of provocation—but he could fight
when need required, and could look calmly the ordinary danger
in the face. But the proceeding of the squatter was so entirely
unexpected—the fellow had so uniformly shown himself the
submissive creature, to be bought and used at pleasure, by the
agency of drink or money—and there was now in his face, such
an expression of vindictive hate and ferocious frenzy, that, if
the Scotchman did not actually quail with terror, he was certainly most terribly confounded.

We do not pretend to say from what sources sprang this new
exhibition of conduct, on the part of the squatter, to one who
hitherto had been allowed to appear quite as much his master
as employer. It may have been the dictate of a cunning policy
to inspire the emotion of fear, the better to exercise future control over the person from whom he was otherwise to derive but
little future service. The temper of the squatter, who had his
pride and vanity also, may have been driven to this degree of
desperation by the unconcealed contempt, and the too frequently
studied insolence of M'Kewn. The rum he had been drinking
might have had something to do with his ebullition;—or, it
might be, that the scenes through which he had gone, his own
narrow escape, the death of four of his associates, the necessity
which he had felt of putting one of them to death with his own
hand—these, together, may have combined to work upon his
brain, so as utterly to deprive him, for the time, of all the restraints of judgment.

It is very probable that all the reasons above suggested were,
in degree, at the bottom of the novel demonstration which he
had made; and that policy prompted him (for he had sufficient
sagacity to fathom the character of his associates) to employ his
natural and mixed emotions with a certain regard to his own future interests. Whatever the source of his speech and conduct,
they produced the effect of paralyzing, for a moment, the cold-
blooded scoundrel, in whose hands, hitherto, had rested the reins
of full authority over the creature who now seemed to threaten
him. The picture appeared strangely to realize that German
fancy which represents the devil as serving, for a long time, in

perfect submission, the conceited mortal out of whose hands he one day wrenches the staff, only to break with it the head of his astonished master. M‘Kewn absolutely gasped. He could not summon words to answer; and the squatter seemed to rise even into dignity, as he certainly did into superiority, as, with a calm and steady eye, he watched scornfully the effect which he had produced upon the meagre, vacant countenance, and the trembling frame of his confederate.

"Yes," said he, "M‘Kewn, ef I was jest now to stick my knife into the softest part of your heart, and work it there with a heavy hand, it would be only the right way to begin the telling of my story."

M‘Kewn gathered strength to say—but still in gasping accents—

"Why, you wouldn't kill me, Bostwick."

"I don't know but I ought to. 'Twould be a mighty good sarvice done to good people. I ought to, M‘Kewn, and ef I was a good man myself, I'd do it soon as eat."

"Why, what have I done, to put you in such a fury?"

"Done! Listen! Of the five men that went with me on this infernal expedition, there's only one now living on this mortal airth!"

"What! Four!" recovering himself—his terror changing into astonishment. "You don't say that four men have been killed?"

"Every man but two on us swallowed his bullet; Bill Sykes, Dick Norris, Rafe Burke and Jeff Brydges. Of all them good fellows, there's not one on 'em, but's a-lying in the woods, and all the ice in nater' couldn't make 'em feel cold. You, and you only, have been the death of them four fellows."

"Pshaw!" exclaimed M‘Kewn, in husky and half-choking accents, "that's all nonsense! I had nothing to do with their living or dying. But how was the affair—how did it happen? —What was done?"

"Oh! you're mighty curious to know ef we got the niggers and the papers! You don't mind much ef we was all killed and sculped, so that you had your eends sarved. I know you, M‘Kewn, and it's bekase I know how little you care what comes of us, that I feel it in my heart to find my way with this knife into your'n. But I ain't guine to kill you yit; 'kase you see, I'm wanting more of your money."

The Scotchman laughed feebly, and with effort.

"You laughs, does you, and I'm telling you of four stout lads all convarted to carrion in your business."

"But that's no fault of mine."

"Whose, then ? Wasn't it your business ?"

"Yes ; but I did not expect—I did not wish—that anybody should be killed on my account."

"Ambushes, when men's got we'pons in their hands, is very likely to hurt people, and prehaps to kill 'em. These fellows are killed, I tell you, four on 'em a-lying stark in the cold night, and looking up, and never once seeing the stairs. And we did our best. There's but one, of all of us six, alive now, beside myself, and the d——l knows how long he's to be allowed to keep in the open daylight. I seed him not four hours ago, only seven miles from here, with a fever on him hot enough to burn his brains to a cinder."

"Who is he ?"

"Tony Hines."

"And he has a fever, and but seven miles from here ? And what did you do for him ?"

"What could I do ? It's all in the hands of nater. I'm no doctor; I've got no physic; he must die or live, as it happens."

"We must do something for him. But seven miles. Where does he lie ?"

"At old Ephraim Smyzer's, the Dutchman. But we needn't talk of him. Ev you've not any physic to do him good, give it to me, and I'll carry it in the morning. Let's talk of the other matter."

He filled himself another cup of the Jamaica, sipped a little, and, while M'Kewn tried to compose himself, and prepared to listen, the squatter, though with evident dislike of the subject, proceeded to unfold his history, in his own manner.

"We set the trap, and the widow walked fairly into it. The carriage was ahead of the wagon half a mile or more, and Fordham and the young fellow was on horseback. They rid ahead, and when the overseer stopped to water at the branch, with the young fellow on t'other side of him, Bill Sykes lent him the butt-eend of his rifle, and tumbled him into the branch. Onfortunate, Bill Sykes made no account of the lad, seeing he was more a

boy than a man; but the chap's as quick a varmint as ever looked through a green bush, and the moment he seed Fordham
down, and the man that down'd him, the little fellow, setting on
his horse, let fly at Bill with his pistols, first one shot, then t'other,
though the first bullet was enough. Bill hadn't a word to say
arter that for any of his friends on airth. Then the young devil
wheeled about, and went off like a streak. But a shot from one
of our boys tumbled the lad's pony, and we captivitated him and
tied him down. Fordham tried to git up, and he had two pistols,
but we put in, seasonable, and stunted him with another touch of
the rifle-butt, and he lay quiet enough while we tied him down.
The widow Ebleigh we took out of the carriage, and gave her a
hitch too——"

"Did you tie *her?*"

"Yes, 'twas a needcessity, for the s'arch, and the rest of the
business. Then we stopt the wagon, and made at the niggers.
They scattered, and we caught only seven of them——"

"You got seven, then?" said M'Kewn, feeling a little relieved.

"Got h—ll! We took 'em, but couldn't keep 'em. For,
meantime, a nigger gal, name Jinny—I know her well—slipped
out somehow from the carriage, and hid in the bushes, and, when
we was a-running down the niggers, what does she do, but cuts
her missis loose, and cuts Fordham and young Arthur loose, and
they gits possession of their own we'pons, and the rifle of Bill
Sykes, and takes the woods on us.

"Now, Fordham is a great fellow in the woods, and where they
harbored we couldn't say.—At last they got a crack at Dick
Norris, and bark'd his limb with a bullet, but not to do much hurt.
Then our work was to begin. It's a long story to tell how we
snaked and foxed through the bushes, to git upon their rear. At
last, Rafe Burke, like a bloody fool, got into a passion, and showed his teeth to the widow, and his fool head to her son, and draw'd
his bullet, I reckon from a rest, for it laid him out flat as a sarcumstance. So you see, thar was two fine fellows tumbled by a brat
of a boy. But he's a quick chap as ever lived, and ef he grows·
to be a man, he'll make somebody see sights. But I reckon we'd
ha' fixed 'em all at last, for we was marching off the seven niggers, we captivitated under Tony Hines and Jeff Brydges, when,
all of a sudden, who should bolt in upon them and us, but that

bloody fat cappin, Porgy, with half-a-dozen dragoons at his heels. They cut down Jeff Brydges in his tracks; they run Tony Hines into the swamps, where, what with cold, and scare, and hunger, he's got the fever; and they tuk Dick Norris in the wagon, and hitched him to a swinging limb, putting a knot in the rope jest under his left ear, that's made him careful never to speak a word sence."

" Good God ! is it possible ! Did he confess ?"

" I reckon he didn't hev' a chance. Dick's a good fellow, and he disapp'inted them. He died too sudden to say much. They gin me a hard chase, so close that I had to throw away my rifle. I've lost rifle, horse, and everything; and four fine fellows shet up for ever; and one p*r*haps, a-dying now, and the other here, as you sees, before you, purty desperate, M'Kewn and jest as willing to knife himself, and you, and a'most anybody that crooks a finger at him, as to sup this Jamaica."

"What a shocking affair! How your fellows must have bung-led !"

" Bungled ! By the Etarnal ! don't say that agin. A man what pays for his bungling with his life, has a right to hev' the decent thing said about him. It was no bungling, but a clever piece of business, mighty well done; but a man's not able for everything, and who was to know that them d——d hard-riding men of Marion was to come down sudden upon us."

" But you admit that the negro-girl, Jenny, escaped your ob-servation, and it was she, you say, that cut Fordham and the young man loose."

" Yes, 'twas she; but ef it hadn't been for your business, 'twouldn't hev' happened; but you was so set upon heving them bloody papers, that I made for s'arching the carriage arter them my own self. Ef I hadn't done so, but let them go to ——, and jest seen to the captivating of the party, and not trusted to the other fellows, I reckon all would ha' gone right. But 'twas the blasted papers that you talked so much about."

" Did you get them at last—the papers?" demanded M'Kewn, eagerly.

" Yes! 'twas all I got out of the affair."—The squatter thought of the fifty guineas as he spoke, but without compunctions of any sort. "Yes! I got 'em; I got all the papers the widow had in

the carriage, a good sized box full, and yours, I reckon, is among
'em. I seed two papers jest like what you show'd me, and tell'd
me about."

"Let me see them"—eagerly—"I can tell."

"No! no! M‘Kewn! that cock won't fight tell he's well fed.
Them papers, ef they're so vallyable to you, are jest as vallyable
to me. You've got to pay for them papers afore you git 'em.—
They're worth a sight of money. They're worth them four fine
fellows that got knock'd in the head to git 'em. They're worth
my horse, my rifle, my trouble, my danger, and the *orful* fright,
and hurry, and run, and confusion I've had. Them papers must
pay for all."

"Well, but Bostwick, I have not refused to reward you for what
you have done. I've paid you punctually for all your services."

"Paid me? And whar's the pay? What am I the better for
it? It come in driblets and it couldn't last no time. Sich re-
wardings! 'Twon't do to talk of what you've paid me, M‘Kewn;
it's now that I'm to show you what you've got to pay. I must
hev' one hundred guineas in hand, bright and yellow here"—
touching his palms—"before you gits them papers into your'n."

"A hundred guineas! Why man, you're mad. A hundred
guineas for a sheet of paper!"

"It's a paper that kin hang you, M‘Kewn."

"And you, too, my good fellow."

"I'll be ready for the rope when they're a stringing you. I
jest don't care for nothing now except my comforts; and my
comforts is to be bought with guineas; and ef the guineas ain't
there to buy the comforts, why I don't care how soon the eend
of the rope is worked into a slip knot for both our necks. Thar!
Them's my principles. Make the most you kin out of them. A
hundred guineas is the least I'll take for them bloody papers, I
tell you."

M‘Kewn changed his tactics.

"But my good fellow, you don't expect me to pay a hundred
guineas for the papers without seeing them. What evidence have
I that you have really got them?"

"The word of a rascal to a rascal, ef you please, and I ain‘t
guine to give you better evidence; for I kain't. Take that or
none at all."

The face of M'Kewn, naturally of a cadaverous cast, flushed instantly to crimson. The space between himself and the squatter had diminished wonderfully in a single week. But he had no remedy. The man who weighs his own life at so small a value, has that of his enemy always at his girdle. He had only to temporize.

"But, as we know each other so well," said M'Kewn, "pray what security shall I have, when I have paid this money, that you will then deliver the papers? How do I know but you will still keep them, and still be calling upon me for more money."

"Well, that sartainly would be a good way to do business. I hadn't thought of that. You're more cute than me, M'Kewn."

"You see for yourself. My only security is in your delivering the papers, at least, when I am prepared to pay the money."

"Kaint be did, M'Kewn, even ef I was willing, which I aint. The box of papers is hid away, where all h—ll couldn't find them."

"Ah!"

"Yes! You might take a thousand rigiments and s'arch from Christmas to Christmas, and never once come within nosing distance of their hiding place. It'll take me three days good riding to bring 'em here; and them guineas, one hundred on em, I must hev' before we part to-morrow."

A cloud passed over the brow of M'Kewn. His forehead was contracted. He mused in silence for a moment, then said—

"Well, I must think of it to-night. One hundred guineas!— I must think of it."

With these words, he abruptly left the tent, while the squatter proceeded to replenish his cup with the convenient Jamaica.

CHAPTER XXXIX.

KNAVES PAIRING OFF.

M‘KEWN had suddenly been enlightened by a new idea. He walked out into the woods, taking a *blind* path with which he appeared quite familiar, and which gradually conducted him to the near neighborhood of the river, or rather that arm of the sea which afforded harborage to the brigantines, or transport vessels, to which, he and others, engaged in illicit trade, were about to furnish stolen cargo. But, though approaching this neighborhood, he was not yet disposed to show himself to his confederates. He had to solve his problems, in secret meditation, before he required their cooperation. Exercising our peculiar privilege, we, however, are enabled to report the subject of his thoughts and the conclusions to which they conducted him. As might be expected, his meditations all related to the squatter, Bostwick, and the embarassments which threatened him from that quarter.

" Either," he said to himself, " this fellow has the paper or he has not. Whether he has, or not, his object is to impress me with the fact of his possessing it, and, through my fears, on that subject, to extort money from me. He will never surrender the paper as long as he can do this. He will hold it over me, *in terrorem*, for ever. I must disarm him of this power. I doubt that he has this paper. If he has obtained it, he has secreted it, as he boasts, where I can never lay hands on it without his consent. I know the scoundrel so well, that, supposing he has it, I could swear that it now lies hidden in some hollow tree, in some unfathomable swamp. He will confide the secret to nobody else. What then ? If I can keep him from it, it is secure from all other persons. It will moulder and rot in its burial place. It can never rise against me. But, even if he has not this paper, his own evidence may trouble me hereafter. He will still want money— will always be full of wants—so long as he can threaten me.

I must get rid of him! I will do it. This very skirmish with Porgy and his followers increases the danger, and makes it doubly important that Bostwick should be out of the way. I see! I have it. Drummond can manage *that!* But, in the meanwhile, I will see this associate of his—this fellow, Hines. It is possible that he has the paper, and only awaits Bostwick's orders on the subject. He is sick with fever—that may be true or not. I must, at all events, find out what I can—all that he knows, and whether he knows more than is becoming for our safety. Eight miles! I can see him and return in four hours. It must be done!"

Having reached this conclusion, he emerged from the thicket, and moved rapidly toward the bluff which usually formed the landing-place for the brigantine. The tide was making rapidly into the creek on which it stood. Three persons were already there, who, on his approach, proved to be Drummond, Barton, and a burly, broad-shouldered, and excessively short person, partly in the habit of a sailor. He was in fact, the master of the brigantine. His name was Forbes. These three were in waiting for the vessel. She was approaching under a fair breeze, cutting directly across the inner bay, having been concealed, for several days already, against the opposite shore; her tall rakish masts mingling naturally with the great trees of the forest, which, in that quarter, hung directly over the river. She was guided in her progress by signal lights just over the heads of our party—three lanterns, in a triangle, suspended from a cypress pole. By daylight she was signalled by three separate smokes. M'Kewn joined the group who awaited her, and they spoke together on the subject of their affairs in general. Various matters were discussed among them which need not tax our attention, but scarcely a word was said of the squatter; Forbes only remarked—

"Bostwick, it seems, came empty handed. It's not often that he fails."

"He was probably drunk or he would not have failed this time."

"Is there any chance that he will mend the matter?" was the inquiry of Forbes.

"Scarcely in season for you. You have a pretty fair cargo, however, and there's no policy in waiting upon him."

"No, indeed! I shall try to be off by day-peep. We have a hundred and seventy-one. I am prepared to take two hundred, if they were ready; but there's quite too much risk in waiting. Some French vessels-of-war went by yesterday, going north, and close in shore. Every day will add to their number, and they are enough now along the route, to keep us watching with all our eyes."

"I want some physic out of your chest, captain," said M'Kewn somewhat suddenly changing the subject.

"What's the matter? You're not going to take physic?"

"It's not for myself."

"We have a good supply. You can have what you please. For my part I don't see the good of it, in our hands at least. When a sailor's to die, it makes no sort of difference whether you physic him or not. Die he will, and the physic only keeps him from dying easily."

"It's very different with a backwoodsman. He believes in physic, and relishes large doses. He'll hardly think himself well, unless he has taken physic. The old women, half of them, feed on it, and learn to like it as well as coffee and sugar."

"That's when it's mixed with alcohol," quoth Drummond. But who's it for, M'Kewn?"

"A fellow named Hines, a friend of Bostwick, who has been taken sick some eight miles above, at the cabin of an old man named Smyzer. Do you know anything about him?"

"What, old Ephraim? To be sure, I do, and his old wife, too — a pair of turtles that might be owls for the good looks between 'em. But how are you to get the physic there?"

"Carry it myself."

"What! to-night?"

"Yes; as soon as possible. You can direct me as to the road."

"Oh! that's plain enough. It's a short eight miles. Hardly more than seven, I think; good enough for a man on horseback. I can tell you all about it. But you're getting wondrous charitable of late. Time was, the man might have died and gone to the devil, and you'd never have crossed a creature to carry him physic though you had only a mile to travel. What's in the wind?"

M'Kewn answered by a glance only, but that was sufficiently

significant for all who saw it. They readily comprehended that their confederate was busy in the common cause. It was not necessary to ask or answer questions where the parties were satisfied with each other.

Meanwhile, the rattling of bolt and cordage announced the approach of the vessel. Soon she plunged ahead and shot into the little harborage. A brief delay, and the confederates boarded her; the contents of the medicine chest were overhauled, and M'Kewn selected a small supply of such medicines as, in that day, were mostly resorted to in cases of fever. Provided with them, he wasted no time on matters not absolutely essential to the objects of the party. He quickly returned to the land, having first called Drummond aside. He led him into the wood, and at once proceeded to unfold his further designs.

" I do not see that this fellow, Bostwick, can be of any further use to us here, Drummond. On the contrary, he may be troublesome. He promises to be so, as you see. We must get rid of him. He has been a good woodman; he may become a good seaman. Forbes is short-handed, and will have no objection to a sharp, lithe active fellow who will soon learn to run up a rope, as he has run up a tree. You must get him employment in the transport."

" But will Bostwick be willing ?"

" By no means! These fellows rarely know what is best for them. We must help him against himself. Give him a good berth whether he wishes it or not. Get him on board to-night, on some pretext, and take him off with you. Invite him to a match at cards. His love of money, and his passion for gaming will make it an easy matter to do this, particularly if he is well fuddled. If, however, you can't persuade him, hoist him on board, and make sail. He will be reconciled to it after a while and when you have given him a taste of your sea pleasures— nightly drinking and gaming. When ashore at Jamaica, leave him there. It is to him a sort of rum and sugar paradise, where he may be well content to stay. At all events, there will be no policy in bringing him back. See to it. I shall ride at once to see this fellow, Hines. Try and have it all over before I return. I do not care to see him again. He is already half drunk. Go back to the tent, and resume the cards. Bet as highly as he may desire. Let him win for awhile. You can recover all your losses on the voyage. Above all, and to effect all, keep him well soaked. The rum will make all easy."

Drummond liked the project. He offered no objections. Without having any motive so grave as that of M'Kewn—without, indeed, having any knowledge of the particular reason which the latter had for getting the squatter out of the way—he yet saw that the proceeding, might, in some degree, contribute to the common cause. Besides, Drummond had a passion for fun, and the abduction of the squatter promised ample store for merriment.

"It will be comical," said he, "when the fellow wakes and finds himself out of sight of land. Won't he look wild?"

The plan being properly understood, the parties separated, M'Kewn at once taking horse, without showing himself at the tent, and speeding, with all possible haste, toward the cabin of old Ephraim Smyzer. Two hours as he had calculated, brought him to the place. The family had retired for the night; but M'Kewn's business was urgent and he prepared to rout them up. His entrance into the enclosure brought upon him the fierce assault of a couple of hounds, the attentions of which made him rather slow to dismount; but he kept them off with his whip, and made his way to the steps of the house, which consisted of three huge pine blocks leading to a low piazza, into which, as there was no railing around it, he alighted directly from the saddle. Fastening his horse to one of the columns, he thundered at the door, keeping close watch upon the dogs, which had ascended the piazza also, but hung about the steps, seeming in some degree, to respect the house, if not the intruder. But they did not spare their tongues if they did their teeth. Their clamors were incessant, and between their music, and the tune kept upon the door by M'Kewn's stick, the inmates of the hovel were soon aroused.

"Who's thar?" was the demand, in a female voice.

"It's the doctor," answered M'Kewn, promptly. His cue had been adopted long before, by which he included himself among the faculty. "You've got a sick man here, haven't you?"

"Yes; I reckon; and I'm sick myself," answered the old woman, opening the door, and displaying herself in her night dress

—a very short one—with a ragged blanket over her shoulders, and a blazing torch of lightwood in her hand.

"Won't you come in, doctor," she said. "I'm mighty glad to see you. The poor man's got the fever yit, and a mighty hot fever it is."

"Where is he?" was the eager inquiry which M'Kewn made, pushing in as he spoke.

"Well, now, jest set down a bit, doctor, while I light the fire;" and the good woman squatted down to the occupation on the hearth. A grunt from the bed in one corner, drew M'Kewn's attention to that quarter.

"Is it Doctor Ferney?" asked old Ephraim.

"No; I'm Doctor Warley."

"Yis! I hearn of you,—somewhar' about Dorchester, I'm a-thinking. Well, doctor, I'm mighty glad you're come to do something for the poor man what's sick here; and something for all on us. I'm sick myself with an awful bad turn of rheumatiz—one whole side of me is a'most useless, doctor; I kain't well straighten myself these times. Kain't you give me something to do me good?"

The fire by this time was kindled, and the old woman interposed with her complaints which were chronic also, like those of her husband. We spare her narration. M'Kewn was not unprepared for any emergency. He knew the people, their usual ailments, and the faith which they had in professional art. But he was too anxious about the patient he had come to see, to suffer any delays of the interview.

"Well," said he, "as this poor fellow has a hot fever, his case is the most pressing. We'll see what his condition is first, and then attend to yours."

He was conducted accordingly to the shed-room where Hines lay. The patient was awake, and welcomed the supposed physician with profound satisfaction. Dr. Warley—as he called himself—sat down upon the pallet by the sick man, and grasped his wrist with a professional promptness that would have done honor to the regular faculty—then shook his head slowly with a very deliberative nod. Mrs. Smyzer was disposed to linger and to mingle in the conference; but this by no means suited our medico.

"Leave us, my good woman! The secrets of the sick are to

be respected. I will see to your ailments, and those of your old man, when I have got through with the case of Mr. Hines."

The good woman retired.

"You knows me, then?" quoth Hines.

"To be sure! Bostwick is an old patient of mine. He's done many a pretty turn for me, and I've saved him many a time when he was on his back. He begged me ride here to-night. I'd have done it for no other man. But, in truth, I know all about his affairs and yours. He counsels with me about other things than physic."

"Oh! ho!" said Hines,—and he straight began to suspect that his worthy physician had been the employer of the party on its late expedition—a secret which Bostwick had studiously kept to himself. The next thought with the sick outlaw, was to ascertain what had been the reward which had tempted the squatter. His cupidity taught him to suspect that Bostwick had monopolized the lion's share, as is too common in all such cases.

"I'll pump him about it," was the almost spoken resolve of Tony. The two parties, it will thus be seen, had each a covert object to be gained, in each case demanding some exercise of ingenuity. As the very being a rogue always implies some degree of ingenuity, it is needless for us to say that the hopeful pair were quite equal to the objects entertained. We shall be compelled, however, to omit many of the details, and much of the dialogue between them, and report results rather than the process by which they were reached. It was M'Kewn's object to appear quite familiar with the squatter's affairs. It was the policy of Tony to show the doctor that he had a sufficient inkling of the relations existing between the parties.

"You have a very hot fever, Tony; but you owe it as much as anything else, to the scenes through which you have gone.— You've had a hard time of it. But Bostwick don't spare his men. I warned him to be careful of what he was about."

"He didn't mind you much, doctor. Bost is too quick a leetle He don't look about him enough. But you paid him too well, doctor, that was it! He was so keen for his pay, and he didn't watch both *eends* of the road close enough."

"I paid him!—oh! yes! as you say, he was too quick for his pay to do his work properly. And that's the reason of all the misfortune. He bungled badly, and lost all he came for. But he got the box and papers, eh?"

"Box and papers!"

"Yes; didn't he? He made sure of that? Of course, you know."

"Know? I reckon I do. But about the box and papers——"

"He got them from the carriage!"

"He did?"

"He says so; of course he did! Didn't you help search the carriage?"

"No! dern his liver, I didn't! That was what he was arter then! We helped knock down the driver, and tie the fellows and the woman, but 'twas him that s'arched the carriage."

"Well, didn't you know what he found there—the box, the money, and the papers?"

"Box of money! No, there was no money. I axed him, and Morris axed him, but he swore there wasn't no money."

"Oh! you surely forget. Bostwick's an honest fellow. He wouldn't cheat me—wouldn't tell me a lie, I'm sure. He found the box, I'm sure."

"Honest, you say! Well, I reckon he is, and I reckon every man's honest tell he's found out. Ef there was a box I never seed it, and ef he got any money out of the carriage, then he told us all a-most etarnal lie, for he swor he couldn't find nothing."

"All was in the box. You saw *that!*"

"No, I didn't."

"Is it possible? Why how could he have hidden it? You all helped to stop the carriage, to tie the women and the men, and you must have seen."

"Yes; we did help, but you see, the dern'd fox of a fellow— now I see it all—he s'arched the carriage first, by his one self, and kept us at a distance to see after the men gone ahead and the wagon behind, so that he had all the chances."

"But, if he got it, how could he hide it from you, so that you shouldn't see even the box?"

"Easy enough! He kept us all busy, and he kept pretty much with the woman. Ef anybody seed the box and money besides himself, 'twas Rafe Burke, and he's not able to say any-thing about it now. Bostwick swore he found nothing."

"Oh! he didn't think of the box at the time. But I'm sure he got it. He says so now. He's hid it somewhere, he says——"

"In the swamp! He had chance enough for it, for we divided, you see, one set agin the carriage, one agin the overseer and boy, and another agin the wagon. He kept the carriage and the woman to himself, and was a long time about 'em. But he swore there was no money."

"But did you believe the story? Did you suppose that the widow, who is so rich, would go to the country and take no money with her—even if it were only a stocking full of shillings for chicken money. I shouldn't wonder if she had a hundred guineas in that box!"

"A hundred guineas! The etarnal cheat! And you paid him so well, too."

"I!—oh! we wont say what hand I had in the matter, seeing that it's turned out nothing. The box might be worth something now, if we had it."

"Dern the box, I say; and dern that fox of a fellow that kept his mouth shet all the while about the box. Now, look you, I kin jest show the chance he had for gutting the carriage and hiding a dozen boxes"—and he proceeded to give such a full account of the whole adventure, as served to confirm the story, told by Bostwick, and to satisfy M'Kewn that the squatter, in all probability, had secured the papers. The sick ruffian aroused himself at the squatter's appropriation of the spoil, allowed himself no reserve, and went into particulars which supplied many gaps in the narrative as given by the latter. M'Kewn listened coolly, egging the fellow on by a word thrown in, now and then, at the right moment. He now recalled certain studious efforts of Bostwick to send all his confederates out of sight, and, in fact, accounted for the failure to secure the negro-girl, by the solicitude of the squatter to put the mysterious box out of sight.

"Well, I'm sorry I told you of the box and the hundred guineas; but I really supposed you all knew what was done. Bostwick didn't speak of it as any secret, and I reckon he'll give you your share of the money. He only forgot."

"Forgot! D—n him! He forgot a-purpose! Now, of all the money you gin him in this business——"

"Who? I!—oh! no! I suppose somebody employed him and paid him well, but I am only his friend when he's in trouble."

"Hem! oh! yes! I onderstand! It's only right not to say too much. But I reckon he got famous pay beforehand."

"Very likely. Hundreds, no doubt!"

"What! guineas!"

"To be sure—guineas. To do such a business as you went on must have called for a round pocket full. Bostwick is not the man to look at such work for less than a hundred for himself."

"End you gin him? You think he got so much as that?"

"Not a shilling less!"

"The 'tarnal rascal! Look you, doctor, give me the physic and let me get out of this fodder. I longs to jest call the dern'd fellow out into the bushes, and ax him for a showing of his pockets."

"Oh! you musn't quarrel. I'm sorry I told you. He'll make it all right, I'm sure."

"Jest you make me well, doctor. I longs to be at him. I'll go into him with a mighty sharp tooth."

The "doctor" again felt the pulse of the patient, now somewhat heightened, and proceeded to prescribe for him. An enormous dose of Glauber's salts was poured into a tumbler, and the old woman was called on for Virginia snake-root. Of this root the country is everywhere full, and all the peasantry is well acquainted with it. A grain of tartar was deposited among the salts.

"It will disquiet him to some purpose," quoth M'Kewn, to himself, as he mixed the medicines, "and that is all, perhaps, that physic ought to be expected to do."

There were other words between himself and patient, and when he left him, he bestowed a reasonable time upon the old couple, for whose ailments he left other medicines, possibly as wisely chosen, with reference to the intended object, as the salts, tartar and snake-root. This done, our *soi-disant* doctor did not unnecessarily delay his departure. As he rode away, on his return, he stated his own conclusion to himself, thus—

"He has got box and papers! But this fellow knows nothing of them, and he is the only other survivor. Bostwick has hidden them from his confederates, which is pretty much like hiding them from all the world. What more do I want? If he hides them from all others, I am quite as well satisfied that he should hide them from me. Let them rot in their hiding-place, and let him rot in Jamaica or——in a hotter region! He shall trouble me no more!"

CHAPTER XL.

THE HAZARDS OF THE DIE.

While M'Kewn was playing the physician, his confederates, Drummond and Barton, had made their way back to the tent where the squatter had been left, prepared to put in practice the policy which the first-mentioned person had suggested. They found Bostwick stretched at length upon the ground, with his head and shoulders resting against the chest, the cup of Jamaica and bottle by his side, and a pipe in his mouth, from which an occasional puff only, betrayed the half-drowsy state of the smoker. He roused himself up as they came in, but it was evident, from his flushed face and the wildness of his eyes, that he had been exceedingly frequent in his potations, and was now, as Drummond phrased it, in a whisper to his associate, "rather the worse for wear." This was a condition that promised them much facility in performing the duty confided to their hands. That Bostwick suffered from the effects of the liquor was not, however, favorable to his amiableness and sweetness of temper. His natural sullenness had become savageness, and he abruptly asked—

"Where's M'Kewn?"

"He's about somewhere. He'll be in directly."

"Well, he'd better. I kain't wait too long. I wants money!"

"Why, you've *got* money, man! Where's all that you won from us, and what you had before?"

"That!" said he, thrusting his hands into his pockets, and drawing forth and displaying the contents—"What's that! I tell you I wants a hundred guineas from M'Kewn—not a guinea less—and I must hev' it!"

" A hundred guineas !" exclaimed Barton in unaffected astonishment. " Why, what the devil does he owe you a hundred
guineas for ?"

" What ! But that's my business ! He owes me a great deal
more, ef the right was known, and I'll make him know it afore
I'm done with him. He's too mean a rascal, by thunder, to be a
white man !"

" Look you, Bostwick, that's not the way to speak of a person
that's finding you the grub you eat !" said Barton. Drummond
nudged his companion, and in a whisper said—

" Don't answer the drunken fool, or answer him according to
the folly and the liquor."

" Grub ! Find me ! And who the h–ll tells you that I owes
sich a fellow as M'Kewn any thanks for anything. It's he owes
me ; and he shall pay me, too, or sweat for it. I say he's as
dirty a dog as ever run without a nose ; and ef you don't like
what I say, jest try your hand to make me speak more agreeable ; and see what'll come of that. I'm a man *eeny* day for my
inches against the inches of *eeny* other man !"

" Pshaw ! what are you both mouthing about ? You're both of
you drunk, I reckon, or so near on the road to staggers that you'll
never reach it together. Shut up both of you, and let's have a
drink all round. I'm as thirsty after work as a bull-frog after
a dry-shower. Come, Bostwick, my boy, you don't mean to soak
up all the Jamaica in your own sponge."

" Thar it is ;—I'm not onreasonable with *eeny* man, and will
jine you, ef drinking's the word and no offence meant. But that
don't make me onsay what I've said of M'Kewn. He's as mean
as gar-broth, and a rascal to boot !"

" Well, that's just as you and he pleases. We shan't fight for
either of you. You're both of you able to do your own fighting,
I reckon."

" He fight !" quoth the squatter. " Never ! onless with your
we'pon or mine. He'll use our fingers for the skrimmage always,
yet always forgit to pile our hands when its done. I say he owes
me *more* than a hundred guineas, ef I'm to git my rights ; and
I'd like to see the white man that says 'lie' to me !"

This was said rising, and with a fierce look at Barton. Drummond again nudged his companion, in order to check any ebulli-

tion of defiance which he might be disposed to offer; a necessary precaution, as Barton was one of that irritable race who too frequently smelt the fire, when there was really nothing to be found but smoke.

"Psho!" interposed the peace-maker, Drummond. "Why the devil do you talk of fight, when I talk of drink. None but a fool fights so long as the liquor lasts. Here, hand up the bottle, Bost, if you're sober enough for it, and empty your cup. I go for a full swallow all round, fresh from the fountain. Come, Barton, smooth off your rough-dry visage, and suck. You shall drink first, if not too bashful; and if you are that, leave it to me to show you how the thing may be done. Quick with the cup, Bostwick, there's no time to be lost. I want to get at the pictures. I want to win back some of my money."

"Or put a leetle more into the heap," answered the squatter, as he carried the cup to his lips, and emptied it.

"Now fill," quoth Drummond.

"After you first."

"Well, there's no use taking up precious time making faces; here, boys, is good luck to all good fellows. The world's made up of two sorts of people—those who live for other people, and those who live by other people. I'm one of the last, but I don't complain or quarrel with the first, seeing that we can't exactly do without 'em. I'm for live and let live."

"That's what I'm a thinking. It's only jest right and nateral," responded the squatter, warmly. "I aint, anyhow, an onreasonable man. You first, Mr. Barton," he continued with amiable tone, but with something ceremonious in his manner.

"Drink yourself," said Barton, "I aint in a hurry."

"And I aint in no hurry neither," answered the squatter. "I aint such a dog when I'm a-tharsting, that I must jump right into the pond."

This was said doggedly. He had not been sufficiently reconciled to the other, not to misconstrue everything that he said. Barton saw his error.

"Oh! I didn't mean that, Bostwick; so don't be wolfish. I'll drink and have done with it; so, fill up for me, Drummond. Your health, men, and good profits always to good fellowship."

"And righteous pay when the work is done," added Bostwick.

" Amen!" quoth Drummond. " That's good doctrine! And now, boys, as we've got no more to do to-night much, any of us, shall we turn up the pictures. I'm ready to face you with the goldfinches, Bostwick. I got a small supply from Forbes."

" Forbes! who's he ?"

" The captain of the schooner, and a fellow you're born to like."

" I doesn't know him."

" But you will. And that reminds me. What say you to going aboard ? We can play there better than here, and there's one more man with money in his pockets."

" Who—the captain ?"

" Yes; to be sure—Forbes; a fine fellow as ever tripped an anchor, and, I reckon, with guineas enough to buy and sell us all. He hasn't been sailing between Charlestown and Jamaica these five years not to have crammed more than one sea-chest to bursting."

" Let him come here," said Bostwick.

" He can't! Can't leave the vessel. But he'll be infernal glad to see us aboard, and will give us the best of liquors, a good table, good lights, and a supper after it,—all much better than we can get here. What say you ?"

" I'm willing," answered Barton.

" I ain't," was the reply of the squatter. " I don't like the smell of the sea and the smell of the ship. It always hurts me, and makes me feel oneasy. Give me the feel of the solid airth under my foot. It's a sort of tempting of Providence to try to ride or walk on a shifting thing like the water. The Jamaica is good enough for me, jest here, and I've found it a good thing without any water at all."

Barton would have argued the case with the squatter, but Drummond, the better politician, yielded the point at the proper moment, and before the victim should have suspected the hook concealed in the untaken bait. He made a merit of necessity, and declared himself quite satisfied with any arrangement, particularly if it called for no delay.

" We are enough for fun," said he, " and have gold enough for a smart fight till the small hours. Whether I lose or win, I shall sleep sound enough when the time comes for it. Square yourself round, Barton, and haul up your legs. Bost, throw a few lightwood knots into the fire. Let's see what we're doing. And now put up your pennies. How do we begin — small or large — white or yellow ?"

"When I've once had the feeling of the yellow, I don't like to touch the white," quoth Bostwick, "but we'll begin small, ef it pleases you." And he put up a single guinea. The others did the same. The cut was made for the deal, which fell to Barton, and the hands were dealt round.

"Let's liquor before we begin," cried Drummond, laying down his cards.

"I'm agreeable," said Bostwick, reaching round for the cup and bottle. Again they drank ; the sly Drummond barely dashing the water with the rum, and Barton imitating his forbearance. The squatter always drank in good faith ; his own tastes never allowing him to suppose that his associates, in order to circumvent another, would ever deny themselves. He was further deceived by Drummond's eloquent declarations in favor of good liquor. It was his frequent topic, and he even volunteered a dithyrambic, of rude fashion — probably his own — the burden of which gave a most glowing picture of the glory of the bacchanalian, and a most melancholy one of the sorrows of temperance,—which was fiercely chorussed —

> "'Tis the milk-sop that withers in autumn,
> And shakes, in the winter, with chill,
> Not he who dives down in the bottle,
> And grows warm by the fire of the still !"

"A mighty good song that, Drummond ; ef I could sing, I'd larn it. 'Twould be good to sing when a fellow had no liquor. 'Twould almost warm him of itself ; jest as one feels warm if he only smells at the empty jug where the Jamaica has been kept. Spade's trump,—and there's a lead for you."

The devil ! The ace !" cried Barton, throwing down the ten of the same suit.

"Heh ! I had you then !" cried the squatter, with a chuckle. "I wonder ef there's no more purties in danger, standing without any company. I'll fish for 'em."

And the ace was followed by the king.

"Dickins ! why, you're a witch, Bost !" was the cry of Drummond, as he yielded his knave to the lead.

"It's luck only—it's time I had some, I'm a-thinking. Count up. I've one to go."

In a few minutes more the squatter gathered up the stakes.

"We'll double!" said Barton, pushing up two guineas.

"Ditto!" quoth Drummond, doing likewise.

"I'm agreeable to anything when the luck's with me," was the response of the squatter, and the game was resumed with new interest. Other games followed, and the fortunes of the squatter were rising.

"Let's liquor, boys. It may change the luck," was again the proposition of Drummond, carried *nem. diss.*, and the parties drank.

"I wonder where M'Kewn is!—d—n his splinters!" cried Bostwick, as Barton now gathered up the stakes.

"Be here directly. He's at the vessel, I reckon. If you're tired, we'll go there."

"Tired! I'd like to see the man what could tire me out at this business. Push on, Barton. We're a-waiting."

"It'll come soon enough, Bostwick, for you; for I reckon luck's changing, and I mean to root you out to-night."

"Kaint be did, by any man of your timbers, I'm a-thinking. What's that?"

"A diamond."

"Throw on more lightwood—there's no seeing what one's got."

"That's only because you've got so little, I suppose. What do you do?"

"Stand, by jingo! Play to that!" flinging down a card.

"So I will, and one you wont be liking much."

"The devil! You hed the ace!"

"Yes; and the deuce too!"

"Jimini! that's what I call mighty bad fortin. I stood on king and tray."

"Cut on both ends, high and low; and look at that and that!" flinging down knave and ten.

"Criki—Lord! what an etarnal hand!"

"Scared, Bost?"

"Skear'd, never!—see by that, if I'm skear'd!" And he now thrust up five guineas, and demanded that they should be covered.

"You're sworn to make a short night of it, Bost!" said Drummond. "At that rate, the time of some of us will be short, too!"

"Out loose!" cried the squatter—"I'm the old sarpent now. I'll wind you up."

"I must have another sup of Jamaica, boys, to give me heart to begin," said Drummond. "There's too much to lose, on an empty stomach. Who says for a sup?"

"I'm consenting!" was the pliant answer of Bostwick. "But where the d—l is M'Kewn?"

"He's about! He'll be here directly. And now, boys—the bold better, the honest winner, and to him who can keep what he gits."

"It's a wise man to be all three, I'm a-thinking, but I drinks it with a whoop! Whoop! whoop! hurrah! for the first horse and the best shot! Whoop! whoop! hurrah! and the devil take M'Kewn!"

"Amen!" quoth Drummond, echoing the pious adjuration—then, in a whisper to Barton—"The snake's bitten him fairly. It's time that we should win, *now*. When his gold's all gone he'll probably be willing to go too."

"Whoop, old fellows, and at your p'inters! I'm the old sarpent, I tell you, and am going into you with a horn. Whar's the gould! oh! thar! It's fifteen guineas I'm to take up."

"If you can."

"Ef I kin! Ef be hang'd! I'm the man to take 'ef' by the collar, and make him work in my harness. 'Ef's' no master of mine, and never was! I kin send him to the right about with a whoop! whoop! whoop! hurrah! and into the shiners!"

The cards were to be dealt by the squatter; but he had so many ejaculations to make, and a pause accompanying each, that the process was a slow one.

"Three to you, Drummond!—whoop, old fellow, I likes you."

"And, thus speaking, he threw the arm, with the card hand, about the neck of the preferred companions, and drew him lovingly over into his lap.

"I always thought you a good fellow, Bostwick, of a most tender heart."

"And who says I ain't? I'm as tender as a gal child. Oh! ef you could only see my Dory."

"Your what!" asked Drummond.

"I didn't say '*what!*' I said Dory! Dory's my oldest gal child, and a beauty of the forest, and nobody shall say anything onrespec'ful about her."

"To be sure not. She is a beauty."

"I know'd you'd say so. You're a man of sense and a gentleman, Drummond. You shall see Dory some of these days. She's a gal child to please a gentleman. Well!—but why don't you play?"

"Deal out the cards, then," said Barton, who was yearning to restore some of his lost gold to his pocket.

"Deal!—well, I swow! but I hev' the pictars in my own hand. That's strange. How's that!"

"Why, to be sure—you're dealing, and you've given me three. Go on to Barton."

"Three to you, Barton, and three to me."

The deal was finished after some further maudlin delay. Bostwick picked up his cards, and the habit of play contended successfully for awhile with his drunkenness. He absolutely won the game. Barton became captious, and was kept in check only by the vigilance of Drummond. The latter, finding that the squatter was still able to play his cards with habitual skill, proposed another draught of Jamaica; but Bostwick had undergone a new phase of drunkenness and feeling. He refused doggedly. The maudlin had given place to the sullen.

"No! I'm blister'd ef I do! I'll not drink agin jest now. Drink yerself, ef you likes it. I don't. It don't do me no good. I'm a-thinking of my children. Jest now, I talked of Dory, and you didn't know what I meant. And when I wanted to deal, I forgot all about it. That makes me know I've had jest enough for a sober man. Jamaica ain't a sensible liquor ef you takes too much of it. I've had my share for this drinking."

"You're right!" quoth Drummond. "I proposed as a matter of course, seeing I wanted a drink myself, but it's true, Bost, I thought you had a dose large enough for your business half an hour ago."

"You don't mean to say I'm drunk!"

"No! not exactly drunk, but a little in the fog, that's all!"

"In the fog! It's a sign of fog is it, when I've been doing all the winning."

"Psho!" said Barton. "That's all luck—luck don't ask if a man's drunk or sober when she turns on his side."

"You think so! It's luck! well! we'll try luck a leetle more. You don't mind fattening the sheep?"

"How much?"

"Oh! it don't matter; put down your gould, as much as you wants to see kivered. That's all I ax!"

The pile was soon raised. The cards dealt; the game played and the prize won. Drummond was the successful gamester. His success continued until the last guinea of the squatter was put up. It was lost also. Bostwick was once more reduced to his shillings, and pretty well sobered by the reverse of fortune. The shillings, in turn, became the prize of his opponents, and, starting to his feet, he seized the bottle, and swallowed a fearful draught of the fiery liquor.

"Where is that bloody satan, M'Kewn?"

"Can you get more gold from him, think you?" demanded Drummond, with a pleasant sneer upon his countenance.

"Kin I?" he answered. "Ef I let him off with less than a hundred guineas, may I never taste a drop agin."

"Let us seek him at the vessel. I have no doubt we shall find him there. I'll go with you as long as there is any hope of the guineas."

"Come then! Blast his liver, he's a-dodging me. But he don't know me yit. I'll feel the bottom of his pockets, or the bottom of his heart, this time, ef he's got any."

"Another draught before we start!" cried Drummond, rising to his feet. The others joined him in his potations. Then they all proceeded to the river bank, against which, almost touching it, lay the vessel.

"You'll go with us on board?"

"No! You go, Drummond, and bring him out. I'll wait for you here."

Barton would have tried to persuade him, but Drummond again interposed.

"No," said he, "there's no use. If he gets more money, he'll only want to go back to the tent to play."

And the two went on board the vessel, which lay quiet, rocking with the tide, nobody visible on her decks, and everything silent around. They soon disappeared from the sight of the squatter, who threw himself down on the grass to await their return with M'Kewn. While he lay there, half stupid, yet full of secret rages, three men left the brigantine and approached him. He noted their appearance, and concluded them to be the two persons who had just left him, returning with M'Kewn. They had reached him, when he discovered that they were strangers and all sailors.

" Where's M'Kewn," said he, rising to his feet.

" In the cabin," was the reply of one of them, " and the captain's spinning a long yarn. He says you must come to him."

" I'll see him d—d first. Tell him to come to me."

" Oh! that's all gammon, my hearty. You must go to him."

With these words the spokesman laid a hand on Bostwick's shoulder, lightly and without any show of violence; but a something in the tone and manner of the fellow seemed to alarm the squatter; he pushed him off, recoiled, and clapped his hand to his side for his knife. It was gone. He was disarmed. Not a moment was allowed for parley. He was at once grappled by all the three, lifted off his legs in a moment, and, struggling all the while, was carried on board the vessel. Suddenly, he was let down into the dark but open hold, and slid down and away, as he thought, into the bottomless depths of the sea. But he soon encountered a solid object. He rolled over a pile of rice barrels; and grasped at them with the hold of one in mortal dread of sinking. The stars, for a single instant, were visible overhead. But a single instant. The opening was then darkened by the figures of his captors. He strove to rise and shrieked to them in question, appeals and curses; but, with rude laughter, they clapped down the hatches, and left him in unmitigated darkness.

The hours went by wearily, and, in utter exhaustion, the captive slept. When he awakened, he almost swooned with the sickness which he felt. The billows were rocking beneath him. He was already out at sea. When suffered to appear on deck, the land was a mere riband along the verge of the ocean. He was flying, perforce, from his familiar swamps and fastnesses, his woman and her children.

"Oh! Dory! Dory!" he cried, as this conviction forced itself upon him. "I'm aguine from you, the Lord only knows wh*ar'*, and maybe won't never see you no more!"

"One danger disposed of," said M'Kewn, to himself, as he left the cabin—for he had been there at the moment when the squatter was brought on board—"and if Forbes and Drummond can take a hint, the impudent scoundrel will give his secrets to the sea rather than the air. His mouth is stopped for ever!"

Not so fast, M'Kewn. The sea has been known to give up its secrets as well as its dead. We shall see in due time what is to come of all this!

CHAPTER XLI.

PORGY'S NOTIONS OF THE USEFUL.

As we have no particular motive, just now at least, for following the fortunes of the squatter upon the seas, let us return to the dry land, and, with all speed, to the ruined homestead of Glen-Eberley. We left Captain Porgy and his two companions, Millhouse and Fordham, about to console themselves with supper, after the fatigues of the fruitless search after Bostwick. Lance Frampton had gone to see his sweetheart, and the party of three proved quite adequate to the supper in his absence. Tom, the cook, had recovered his good humor; Pomp, the waiter, after a frequent lessoning from the flat broad hands of his senior, had improved in knowledge of his duties, and activity in their performance; and the evening repast had been enjoyed with an equal degree of satisfaction by all parties. Fordham did not long remain after supper, but took his leave while Porgy and Millhouse were lighting pipes. While he remained, however, he was an amused listener to the guardian councils of the latter whose self-esteem found grateful exercise in suffering the guest to see how strictly he held the reins of authority in his grasp, and with what judgment he could rebuke the want of it in his superior. He had employed himself in twitting the captain with all the thoughtless, profligate and expensive performances of which he had been guilty, and not only throughout his campaigns, but, as far as he had acquired a knowledge of them, during all his life previous. The subject had been brought up by a repeated allusion to the guinea bestowed upon the squatter's child.

"It's the weakness of the cappin, Mr. Fordham," quoth he — "his wery worst infarmity. I'm a most thinking its the only one he's got — but it's a mighty bad one for a man that wants everything on his plantation for the working of a crop. Sich a man has no right to be ginerous. It's a sort of cutting off one's own life to lengthen other people's. Now, all through the war 'twas jest the same thing. He'd be a giving, whenever he had it, and to all sorts of people. And he was always a giving to them persons from whom there was no sort of reason to ixpect to git anything back again. Now, you know, there's no sort of charity in doing for people who kain't do nothing for you. The proper sense of charity is always to git back for it a leetle more and a leetle better than you give. But Cappin Porgy could never, so far as I see, git the right sense of charity and ginerosity. He was always a wasting himself on people who hadn't nothing, and warn't in the way to git anything. Ef there was a poor camp woman that had lost her man in a skrimmage, the cappin was the first to empty his pockets into her lap. I've seed him do it a dozen times. Now, that was all great foolishness. Ef he had given her a matter of three or four English shillings, or we'll say five or ten or twenty pounds continental currency, after it had got so plentiful that one might work with a pack of it, and not airn his potatoes after all — why there mout have been a justifying of his doings; but to fling the guineas away, the raal grit, all yellow jackets, three, five, ten — jest as many as he had — when the shillings would have done as well — that was the sin and the foolishness of the business. And the cappin has been very foolish and a great sinner in that way. Then he'd waste himself on the sort of company he kept. Now, cappin, what did you ever see in that blasted longshanks, Oakenberg — that called himself a doctor — a fellow that sickened and killed more good fellows with his yarbs and poultices than he'll ever meet in heaven — what did you see in that skunk of a fellow to make you do for him what you did? Why, Mr. Fordham, would you believe it, the cappin let that fellow who was next door neighbor to a born *ee*diot, set at his mess and feed daily, when Oakenberg couldn't neither bring in food nor game; couldn't work nor fight; was the skeariest chap you ever seed, and could only talk conceited about snakes, and how to be safe in fighting in the army. That fellow lived on the cappin, and though the cappin dispised the fellow, and poked all sorts of fun at him, yet he gin him money, and clothes, and food, when he wanted them all for himself. At a famous scrimmage we had here with Fraser at Parker's Ferry, the cappin mounted a British officer, and told him to deliver, and wanted to make him prisoner, but the red coat was either mighty drunk or mighty sassy, and when there was no sense in it, for he couldn't git off, he run his horse close agin the cappin's, and flashed his pistol in his face. Ef the dirty leetle we'pon hadn't a-missed fire I reckon he'd ha' killed him. Well, the cappin fired up furious, and cut down the poor fellow at a jerk — cut him clean through his skull to his chin. Tom run in — Tom 'members all — don't you, Tom?"

"To be sure I 'member," quoth Tom, "wha' for hender? Maussa owe me for dat ossifer coat, and breeches, and boots, he gee way to de doctor, to dis day."

"That's it!" exclaimed Millhouse. "That's it! Tom ran in, stripped the officer, coat, breeches, boots and all, and ginerously offered 'em to his master, the cappin there, after all the fighting was over. What do you think? Jest at that moment he sees Dr. Oakenberg, with his long shanks and high shoulders pretty nigh naked, and he kicks the whole pile over to Oakenberg."

"Das' true, mass Millh'us! Jes' I see dat, I make a grab at de close; — de doctor hab no right for tak 'em; — and maussa tu'n round short and kick me over. Maussa promise for pay me guinea for em, but I nebber see de shine of dat guinea face to dis day."

"It's all true, Mr. Fordham, as Tom tells you; he kills the red coat with his own hands, — and when Tom strips him he gives his rigimentals, — first rate broadcloth coat, hat, boots and breeches to the meanest and most undesarving skunk in the whole army."

"Oh! Millhouse," quoth Porgy, "had you seen the wistful eyes of poor Oakenberg, as he saw those breeches, and looked down at his own bare legs ———"

"D—n his bare legs! He had the meanest looking legs in the army——"

"The very reason why they should be covered out of sight," quoth Porgy.

"But not at your cost and ixpense!"

"Why, Millhouse, listen to Tom, and he will tell you that it was at *his* cost and expense. There was the double beauty of my procedure; I not only clothed the naked, but compelled that selfish scoundrel, Tom, to become charitable."

"Psho! don't I know that you'll pay Tom yit! Don't I know, and don't he know, that he'll git more than he bargained for——"

"What! more kicks than coppers?"

"No! more goulden guineas than you promised. The truth is, cappin, that you're never so foolish as when you've got money. You don't know any decent way to git rid of it. There, you was always for having that fellow, Dennison, about you, eating the 'lowance of other men, and drinking more than his share of the Jamaica always—and for what? What could he do? He warn't a reasonable, useful man. He couldn't cook a steak, or bake a loaf, or, sew his own breeches, or do nothing. He could only joke, sing, and tell redickilous stories, and make them foolish po'tries —tink-it-a-tank, tink-it-a-tank—one word knocking agin another at the eend of the line, as I may say, agin natur,—for where do you hear decent, sensible people talking with a bell ringing in their ears all the time? That fellow couldn't keep anything— money, clothes, hat, shoes,—everything went, somehow, and yit the fellow was such a blasted fool that he never seemed to care about it at all, and would jest keep on, laughing and singing, and making his tink-it-a-tanks, and think-it-a-thanks, with a sort of looseness that was vexatious."

"Come! come! Millhouse! you must not be running down my poet. Dennison is a great fellow and has frequently saved me from suicide. More than once, when we were starving in the swamps, I should have cut my throat, or yours, Millhouse, but for the consolation which Dennison brought me in his verses and songs; and Oakenberg, though as you say, a great fool, was yet a fool with a relish. He had the virtue of making himself laughed at, and that afforded relief to sensible people. He had his uses, and you must think better of him. I shouldn't be at all surprised to see both Dennison and Oakenberg here before long. I asked them both to come and see me."

"The d—l you did! You don't say, cappin."

"Ay, but I do! you may look for them both some of these days."

The sergeant threw up hands and eyes in horror.

"Thar it is! The old way! Thar is no eend to the flinging away of some men's guineas. Why, Lord bless you, cappin, ef once they git here, you'll never git shet of them. They're people to stick like a pitch plaster, and to draw like a mustard."

"Well, they must stick then! Poor devils, they must stick somewhere. The world owes them a living, and they must have it. They were born to a certain amount of sunshine, and if they can find it at Glen-Eberley, while I'm master of it, they're welcome."

"Why, save you, cappin! They'll do nothing here for a living. They kain't work and they won't."

"Well, if they can't work here, they can work nowhere, sergeant."

"That's true! Let 'em starve then and be —— !"

"No! no! You don't say that from your heart—only from your head, sergeant, and your brains, just now, have got into a *kink*, in consequence of the care and anxiety which you feel about my fortunes. But don't be afflicted. Oakenberg and Dennison, should they come here, will both work for me, though perhaps not in the fields."

"I'd jest like to onderstand how, cappin."

"How!" quoth Porgy, emptying his pipe,—then looking up and around him, with a somewhat vacant gaze, silent the while, as if listening—after a few moments of pause he said—

"Do I not hear a bird? a mock-bird, singing? Hark! do you not hear it now?"

All parties appeared to listen; at length, says Millhouse—

"It's the singing of the fire, I reckon, cappin. I don't hear nothing. It's too soon in the season for mocking birds to sing."

"No! not when the weather is good. I have heard them, years ago, in all the trees around the house, singing through the winter, and frequently at night, and all night. They attach themselves to old and well settled habitations, and will rear their generations for a thousand years in the same trees, if left undisturbed. They belong to man. I am disposed to think they were created for him, and to do this particular duty. You like their music, Mr. Fordham, do you not?"

" Well, cappin, I can't say that I ever hears 'em much, onless when somebody tells me to listen. As for liking their music, I confess, cappin, I'd much rather hear a good fiddle."

" And so would I," quoth Millhouse, " though I don't count fiddle music as much either. A good horn is my music, and I count a boat horn on the river as the sweetest of all kinds of music. I kin listen to that hafe a night, that is, when I ain't too much tired and hungry."

" I like that too, Millhouse, and I can relish a good fiddle in a crowd. But what would you think of a person who should tell you that he didn't relish the boat horn, Millhouse."

" Why, I'd say he might as well be stone deaf and blind too."

" At least, you wouldn't suppose he was any the better man for not having an ear for the music of the horn."

" No! I'd be thinking he was rather the worse for it."

" Precisely! well, you'll permit me to feel the music of a bird's song and not think me very foolish or wicked perhaps, if I say I like to hear it very much."

" Well, I s'pose not! Every man to his own liking, I reckon there's a sort of natur in every man's liking."

" Exactly! That's the very word. There is a nature in it; and it was to feed this nature, and to work upon it in a mysterious way, that God appointed the birds to build their nests in the trees that surround a man's dwelling. Now, you must know, that it is a fact, however curious, that singing birds never harbor in uninhabited countries. In our great forests, you never hear birds. The smaller birds would become the prey of the larger ones, and they shelter themselves in places which are inhabited in order to be safe. And they reward man for his protection, by their songs, and by the destruction of insects. Now, Millhouse, Dennison is one of my song birds. He sings for me when I am sad. He makes music for me which I love. It is soul music which I owe to him, which finds its way to the ear of the heart, and seems to fill it with sunshine. Now, I call that being very useful to me."

"I could see how 'twas useful ef he was to eat up the grubs and insects, jest like the birds, but ——"

"And so he does, Millhouse. The grubs and insects of the heart are its cares, its anxieties, its sorrows, its bad feelings, and vexatious passions. He drives them away—he destroys them. He is appointed for this very purpose, and if men were wise, they would rejoice when they could have such a bird of the soul under their roof trees. It would prove that they *had* souls, if they could show that they have an ear for his music. Now, you are not any *better*, sergeant, because you want an ear for soul-music. It is your misfortune, Millhouse, and you ought to be sorry for yourself, not angry with the musician, whose songs you can't understand. You should pray for the proper understanding, and work for it, too; for you must know that an ear for music of all sorts is to be acquired; and the ear opens so as to correspond with the growing wishes of the heart, and the growing wisdom of the mind. You hear a great deal said, perhaps, of education. Everybody seems to wish for education. I have heard you deploring, very frequently, the fact that you had no schooling. Now, schooling and education are meant for this very purpose, to give us an ear for music—the music of birds as well as men, the music of the soul, as well as of the throat—music which fills the heart as well as the ear—music which is not only sweet, but wise—which not only pleases but makes good; for, after all, the great secret of education is to open all the ears—which we call *senses*—of a man, so that he can drink in all the harmonies of that world of music, which we commonly call life!—Do not, my dear sergeant, suppose you are any better because you do not comprehend such music as George Dennison makes; and do not suppose that George is any worse man because he is too apt to give away, and perhaps waste, the things which he needs himself, quite as much as the person to whom he gives them. George finds it profitable to give away —to waste! If you knew the satisfaction which he feels at making other people happy, you might be even more extravagant. He may be wrong, sometimes, in his giving; but you are not altogether right in judging him so harshly. He values certain things too little; you, perhaps, value the same things too much. You both may be forgiven your offences, which are due to a want of proper education, provided you are modest enough never to censure the music which you do not understand."

Porgy lighted his pipe after this long speech. Millhouse scratched his head and looked dubious for a while; but after a brief pause, he resumed the subject in this fashion:—

"Well, cappin, all that may be very wise and sensible, though there's some of it I don't 'zackly onderstand; but I'm willing to let it pass this time. But supposing all you say of George Dennison is true, and I reckon there's some reason in it, I'd like to know what sort of music you gits out of Doctor Oakenberg."

"Millhouse, do you remember a little Frenchman, named Pelot, that joined us when we were making the forced march after Gainey, toward the Great Pedee?"

"In course I do."

"Well, do you remember a reel in a bottle that he had, that amused half the soldiers, and was too much for all of them to get out of the bottle without breaking it."

"Yes, I tried it many a time myself."

"You knew that it was put into the bottle after the bottle was made, and that it could be taken out in the same manner."

"In course."

"Well, did you ever hear that reel sing, or speak, while in the bottle?"

"Lord love you, no! How could it?"

"Did you ever see it come out of the bottle and dance?"

"Diccance! no!"

"And you never saw it hoe, or cut wood, or kill game, or cook food, or make clothes, or fight the enemy, or do anything which you consider useful."

"Never!"

"Yet, you were curious about it. You tried many a time to find out the secret. It employed you—it interested you—it interested most of the soldiers; yet, in itself, it was perfectly worthless. It could neither sow nor spin, it could not even grow —it was of no sort of value to anybody in camp."

"That's true, cappin, though I never thought about it."

"Doctor Oakenberg is my reel in a bottle. His soul is my puzzle; how it got into his carcass—where it does nothing useful—where it does not even grow—is the problem which amuses me. Now, Millhouse, whatever interests a man is valuable, though it neither works nor sings. Whatever may amuse a man is an important agent in his education. Whatever exercises the ingenuity of man, though it be a fool's brains, or a reel in a bottle, is worthy of his care and consideration. I assure you that should George Dennison, or Doctor Oakenberg, pay me a visit, they shall both be welcome. I shall find use in both of them."

Millhouse muttered something which was inaudible closing with —

"Well, cappin, ef they once comes, they sticks. You will never git rid of them."

"Be it so ; the more helpless they are the more they pay for the shelter."

"How's that, when they've got nothing."

"God is good security for all the debts of the poor!"

Millhouse fidgetted ; Fordham rose to depart. Porgy did not rise, but extended his hand from the fireside.

"Excuse me, Mr. Fordham. Sergeant"—in a whisper— "the Jamaica."

The hint was taken, and the two overseers hob-and-nobbed after the prescribed fashion. Our captain of partisans reminded Fordham of his intention to visit Mrs. Eveleigh next day, accompanied by his *subs*, and sent a courteous message to the lady, to that effect. When Fordham withdrew, Millhouse accompanied him into the piazza and down the steps, to his horse, which was fastened to a swinging limb in front.

"You hear what *redick'lous* notions the cappin's got about these here things ; and a most wasteful man would he be, ef there wa'n't somebody to keep a tight rein over him ;" and he made the motion, with his one hand, of pulling in the steed.—"I does it where I kin, but it stands to reason I kaint go too far, seeing as how he was my commanding officer, so long. But I gives it to him pretty plain, and right for'ad sometimes. But I aint the pusson altogether for it. In fact, Mr. Fordham, ef anything's to be done with the cappin, it must be by a woman—some raal lady that'll take his case in hand, and guide him right in his driving. Now, he's a raal good man, but a leetle shy of the womenkind. I'm a-thinking, though its strange it should be, seeing how long he's been a sodger, that he's sort o' bashful. Ef he could git a fine woman now for a wife, a raal lady, I reckon it would be a wonderful good thing for both on 'em. See what a fine plantation he's got here, agoin' to ruin headlong in his hands onless I kin save it--and I'll try my best,—but I'd be sure of saving him and it too, ef so be he had a wife to back me in the business. So long as he's got no wife, you see, he'll be run down by these idle rascals of the army, that aint fit to do nothing but eat double 'lowance of grub, and swallow any quantity of Jamaica. You hear what he says of this fellow Oakenberg, who is a sort of yarb doctor, and a most extremelous fool,—and this George Dennison, who makes jingling stories,—that keeps a sort of time with every now and then, a tink-it-a-tank, tink-it-a-tank. Well, these chaps never works; they'll come here and eat us out of house and home, and all bekaise the cappin haint got a good sensible woman to back me when I wants her, and keep the cappin in order. You see, arter all, it's a good woman and a wife that he wants to make all things right ag'in on this plantation."

Fordham admitted the wisdom of this opinion.

"As for these idle fellows, they gits no incouragement from me. Ef I have the leetlest chance, I'll send both on 'em off, and all on 'em that comes, with a flea in their ears. I aint gwine let the cappin waste himself and his substance upon sich wagrints. I'll have to keep a strict line upon him, for ef he once gits the bit betwixt his teeth, there's no stopping him, and he'll smash and tear everything to pieces. 'Taint bekase he's naterally vicious, but so long as he's been living in the world, he aint grown bridle wise; but Lord bless you, a woman could manage him to prefection. It's the only saving of him and this fine property, and I'm glad you 'gree with me about it, Mr. Fordham."

Fordham shook himself free with difficulty. The sergeant had many last words, the burden of which invariably led to the repetition of the one opinion, that a wife was the one thing needful to the wants and safety of his superior.

CHAPTER XLII.

MILLHOUSE ON THE UTILITARIAN PHILOSOPHY.

" CAPPIN," says the sergeant, returning to the hall, where Porgy still sat, half drowsing, amidst voluminous wreaths of smoke which poured from his pipe, — "Cappin, you must 'scuse what I'm guine to say ef I speaks to you mighty free, for you see, I'm your friend to sarve, and I reckon jest about as good a friend for honest, upright and downright sense and sarvice, that ever you had in all your born days. I don't mean to say that I love you better than some others, — say, the Ensign, and Tom, the cook, but I'm bold to detarmine, that I love you more sensible, and for sarving and helping sarvice, than a'most *eeny* other person, let 'em bé as wise as they please. That being the case, I say you must 'scuse me, ef I make free to put you right in the way you've got to go, and show you how you've got to put your foot down for the rest of your journey in this life. You must 'scuse me, I say, ef I roughs a leetle too hard sometimes along the tender places."

" Excuse you, Millhouse ? oh ! surely, my good fellow. You are usually so very modest and forbearing, tender and scrupulous, that you may well be permitted a little occasional roughness in helping a friend through the world."

" 'Zackly, cappin, you're right ; you takes the right look at the thing as it ought to be, — sensible as I wants you."

" You are always tender, Millhouse, even in dealing with your enemies. I remember seeing you hew a fellow half in two with your sabre, then, as he was falling, drive the iron handle into his mouth, breaking every tooth in his head. Certainly, his teeth would only be a mortification to him, after he had lost all capacity to eat ; — and yet, Millhouse, I should like to be buried in possession of a good mouthful of them. Your tenderness in my case, is of a like fashion always ; and if, as a good surgeon, you should occasionally be compelled to be a little rough — probing wounds already healed, or such as are absolutely incurable, in order to satisfy yourself that there *are* some sensibilities yet remaining to the patient—I am clearly of opinion that you should be allowed the privilege of doing so, if only that the humanities of your nature should be kept lively, and in becoming exercise."

"Jest so; and I must say for you, cappin, that sometimes you're quite sensible, and have a good onderstanding of what's right and proper in affairs of business. Ef you didn't so much love sich company as George Dennison and Oakenburg, there's no telling, how knowing you'd be; and ef you'd only shet up, and not talk about things no common-sense pusson can onder-stand, it would be a great deal the better for you. Now, you don't think that this good fellow, Fordham, know'd what you meant to say when you was a-going it about Dennison's po'try, and soul music, and all sich fly-away matters? I could onder-stand it all, bekaise I've hearn you at it, day and night, through-out the campaigns.—But how was he to l'arn it? You might jest as well hev' talked it to the man in the moon. And what was the use of it, ef he did onderstand? Why, he wouldn't valley it a continental d—n, which everybody knows won't buy a calabash of skim milk. Now, as you don't know nothing about farming, or rice-planting, and as you hevn't any sober idee about any sort of business except fighting,—and I say it, myself, you're prime good at that—I'm a-thinking that you'd better shet up quite, when goin it in company with men of business like Ford-ham and me, and jest listen to what we're a saying. You'll l'arn something by it, I tell you."

"Do you really think so, sergeant?"

"I swow, but I does. It's the only way to l'arn."

"It looks reasonable. Leave off talking myself and listen to you and Fordham."

"Jest so! and ef there was any other sensible white man, of *business*, you might listen to him too; for *onder*stand me, I'm not pretending that Fordham and me are the only people having a right sense of things in this world.—There's other people, I reckon, that have learned something of business; though they're rather scarce in these pa*i*rts."

"It's possible! Well."

"But there's a time when you might open, and hev' your say

cappin; that's when you gits among people who has likings like yourself; young fellows who aint got ixperence in the world,—women folks,—and sich like."

"You think I may venture to talk among the women, then?"

"Edzactly, cappin; women are weak vessels that aint expected to be reasonable, and things will tickle their ears that are only foolishness in the ears of a sensible man. They will listen to sich stuff as po'try and music, and all the time they're a losing the profits. They're made to sing, and to dance, and to dress up, and make themselves sweet to please the men when the day's work's over; and Lord, cappin, you kaint say hardly anything amiss, in the way of wanity and foolishness, ef so be you says it lovingly, and with a sawt of fondness in your eyes all the time. Now, I've hearn you talk to women, and you knows pretty much what the critters loves to hear. You kin talk it to them, by long stretches, and make it smooth travelling all the way. It's when you gits among them that I'm willing for you to open."

"You are certainly indulgent, sergeant. I am to understand then, that, whenever there are ladies in the presence, I have permission to speak."

"Premission aint the word, cappin, for you see, you're your own master, and kin speak always, whenever you're a mind to, no matter whose in company."

"Oh! Ah!"

"It's jest, you see, as I'm idvising you, for your own good. 'Taint bekase I've got any power to shet or open your mouth, but I wants you to see, for your own self, what's best for your own benefit. You see your ixperence is jest none at all in the way of business. You don't know what's useful in the world. You only know what's pleasant, and amusing, and ridickilous, and what belongs to music, and poetry, and the soul; and not about the wisdom that makes crops grow, and drives a keen bargain, and swells the money-box, and keeps the kiver down. Now, I reckon, you'd always git the worst of it at a horse-swap. You'd be cheated with a blind horse, or a spavin'd, and you'd go off on three legs, though you come on four. Now, ef there's wisdom in this world—that is *raal* wisdom—it is in making a crop, driving a bargain, gitting the whip hand in a trade, and always falling, like a cat, on one's legs. As for music and po'try

and them things, it's all flummery. They don't make the pot
bile. I likes the fiddle when there's a crowd, and after the day's
work's done, and the horses fed; but ef there's one music in the
world that's more sweet than another to the ears of a man of
sense, it's the music that keeps tune to the money coming in.
I'm minded of what was said by a man up on the Edisto, not
very far from Orangeburg, who was jest about the most sensible
white man of all that country. He was one time at a sort of
ball, or party, in the village, and there was a lady who was
playing on the ha'psichord and singing, and she said to him,
'Squire, does you love music?' then he up and said—'Music,
ma'am! kaint say that I does, 'cept one kind.' And says she,
'What kind's that, Squire?' Says he—'Ma'am, that's the
music of my mills on the Edisto; they keeps a grinding and a
sawing night and day, and all the time they seems to be a singing
in my ears—"Dollar! dollar! dollar, oh! dollar! dollar! dollar,
oh!" That's the music for me, ma'am!' and sure enough, that
was what I call useful, business, mercantile music. He made a
fortin by it, and died worth, Lord knows how much, but they did
say, a'most four hundred thousand dollars! But any other kind
of music is apt to draw the money out; not bring it in; and that's
the sin of it. It is, I say, a sinful practice that's always a drean-
ing the pockets, and never putting anything in."

"It is clear, Millhouse, that you have studied the philosophy
of music with great closeness. You are evidently well prepared
to be a teacher. You counsel me to speak as much about poetry
and music to the ladies, as I please, but to avoid it wholly among
men of sense, unless, indeed, I have something to say about mercantile music."

"That's it! For, look you, cappin, jest give a look round to
the world—" and here the sergeant rose, and stretched his one
arm out with measured movement, circling the hall, as if grasping
the poles—"look round at all the world, and wherever you look
you see that the great needcessity everywhere is the gitting of
bread. When I says, gitting of bread, I means, of course, gitting
of bread and meat, and drink, clothes to wear, and the tools to
work with. But bread and meat is the first and greatest needcessity; for without it, there would be no world, nor no men, nor

no women. Now, then, what does I larn from that. Jest answer me that."

"Well, sergeant, what *you* would learn from it, it might be difficult for me to say; you have studied the subject so profoundly that it is not easy to follow you."

"Well, cappin, it *ought* to be cl'ar to you, but I'll show you. I larn from all that that the great business of men on this airth is eating—that is to say, eating and drinking, and clothing—fighting agin starvation and thirst and cold weather."

"It is certainly a business that is done pretty extensively—universally I suppose, since I have never known a man or woman refuse to eat at proper hours."

"And onproper hours too, and at all hours, cappin; that is ef they hev' it. And the business of life is to hev' it. Now, ef that be the great business of life, it stands to reason that them ocky-pations what don't bring in bread and meat and drink, or the money to buy it, is *on*reasonable, *on*natural, and *on*respectable ockypations.   Aint it cl'ar to you so?"

"I'm afraid, sergeant, if I make any farther admissions you'll be for knocking George Dennison on the head."

"Accordin' to the argyment, he and Oakenberg, and all of them worthless sawt of people, that only makes music and not bread, ought to be knock'd on the head; as Scriptur says of the tree that don't bring fruit, 'hew it down and cast it into the fire.' Well, the laws of the land don't follow out the laws of God. Ef we was to cut down them idle fellows that sing and make varses when they ought to be at the plough tail, we'd be hung a'most without jedge or jury, jest as ef we'd been doing agin the laws of Scriptur, instead of following them out rightly. The men that makes the laws of man, cappin, I'm jubous, are mighty poor followers of the laws of God.   Ef they wasn't, we'd git rid of a mighty great deal of rubbish."

"Well, but, sergeant, when a man has earned all the bread and meat, and drink, and clothing, that he needs, is he to be satisfied?"

"Satisfied! no! He's to work on, and on, and what he's got over and above his wants, he's to send to market and sell, and git all the money for it he kin."

"Ah! well,—what is he to do with that money?"

" Why, increase his force, and his land, to be sure."

" Why, that will only increase his money !"

" To be sure ; and that's what he's to aim at.   He's to go on gitting, and gitting, and gitting, to the end of the season, outill Death gits him.   As he gits, he kin increase his comforts—git better bread, more meat, pass from apple and peach brandy to old Jamaica—ef he likes it, git wine,—though I never seed the wine yet that could shine the same day in the face of good Jamaica :—git better clothing ; hev' his horse to ride ; prehaps his carriage, and jist make himself a sort of king, in the way of comforts."

" Well, these got,—should he spend his money on nothing else ?"

" Nothing, that I kin see.   He's got all that's needful.   Then he's for gitting as good bargains as he kin—then he's for gitting to be a ruler ef he kin—gitting to be a colonel or a gineral in the militia ; gitting to be a representative and a senator in the legislatur ; gitting to be a justus of the peace ; gitting to be a sawt of king over the people, and making them all feel that he's got the money to buy and sell 'em, every mother's son of 'em, ef he pleases."

" Well, that must be a very delightful sensation.   But would you not use some of this money for charity—would you not give Oakenberg his living, if only to catch snakes and make a collection ?   Would you not help Dennison to his dinner ?"

" Not a copper on your singing birds and idlers.   They should starve for me.   Not a fellow that wouldn't work would I feed."

" But, Millhouse, you would do something for religion, wouldn't you ?"

" Why, to be sure.   It's expected of a rich man that he'll go rigilar to church and set a good example, and help pay for the preacher, and put something every month in the charity box, and be decent and rigilar, jist that he mayn't lose by it, sence people respects religion, and it might be onprofitable, and hurtful to one's business, ef he didn't make good signs that people should see.   To be sure, I go for religion that's right, and every right religion's bound to uphold the man who is rich and helps to pay ixpenses."

" You have admirably grasped the whole subject of profitable duty, sergeant. I should not have answered exactly as you have done, on the subject of charity and religion; but I have no doubt that you have answered as correctly and fully as the most profound utilitarian philosophers would have done. And now, what say you to a little Jamaica? It's a part of your system to drink as well as eat."

"It's the needful, cappin."

The Jamaica and water were brought by Pompey, and when their cups were filled, quoth Porgy—

" Well, Millhouse, considering the lesson you've been giving me, suppose we drink to the man who is wise enough to open his mouth only in the proper company."

" That's it, cappin; jist you mind what I've been telling you, and you'll work upward yit into cl'ar water. You're quick to l'arn, I see; and only you give up this foolish po'try and soul music, 'cept when you're among the women—and listen with good will to what men of business and sense is a telling you, and there's no saying how sensible you'll grow in time. Here's your health—and the Lord presarve you, cappin, and git you into a strong position agin the approaches of the sheriff."

<hr>

CHAPTER XLIII.

MILLHOUSE TREATETH TOUGHLY OF THE TENDER GENDER.

Suddenly the barking of a dog was heard without.

" It's a dog!" quoth Millhouse. " Some nigger dog, I reckon. I'll kill every nigger dog I see on the place. You hear that, Tom! you hear Pomp! 'member it, boys. I don't 'low nigger dogs on any place where I'm manager. I knows what's the natur of a nigger dog, cappin, and what they're kept for."

" But, won't that be rather hard, sergeant? a negro likes coon and possum. Ask Tom there about possum."

" Possum better than pig, maussa."

" We almost learned to think so ourselves, sergeant, in the army. How often should we have gone without meat but from dogs bringing in coon and possum."

"All coon dogs, on this place, cappin, must be owned by a white man; by you, by me, or by the lieutenant. A nigger dog is a *hog-dog* by nater; and where the nigger eats one possum, he eats five pigs. It's the infarmity of a nigger's dog and a nigger too, that a fat pig makes his eyes run water. No nigger dog here, cappin, onless you says so."

"But, sergeant, even if it be, as you say, that a negro dog is always a hog dog, and I'm perfectly prepared to believe the as·sertion, still there would be no harm in having such an animal at Glen-Eberley, since it will be wonderful if a solitary pig is to be found on the premises."

There was no gainsaying this humiliating fact, and it took the sergeant all aback for a moment, but only for a moment. He was a man of resources and prompt reply.

"But they'll come, cappin; pigs will hev' to come! You'll hev' to git half a dozen brood sows with your first money, and begin to stock the plantation."

"Well, corporal, wont it be quite time enough then to get rid of the dogs?"

"It's a shorter way not to let 'em begin to harbor here. Lay down the law at the beginning. That's my way wherever I manages, and then there's no mistake."

The barking of the dog now became more audible without, the sounds alternating with sundry lively blasts of a bugle.

"It's Lance Frampton," said the captain; and the tread of horse's hoofs succeeded to the words. In a few moments the young lieutenant entered the apartment, accompanied by a good-looking dog of a somewhat mongrel aspect, a sort of cross of wolf, cur, and beagle—which shrunk back timidly toward the entrance, on finding himself confronted with so many strange faces—or, he might possibly have seen something in the looks of the sergeant to inspire him with a proper caution.

"Where did you get your dog, Lance?"

"From Mrs. Griffin, captain. She had two and only wants one, and she tells me this is a famous fine coon dog, which is no use to her as she can't hunt, so she gave it to me. We want fresh meat, captain, and I'm for a hunt this very night, if I can get some of the boys to go."

Pomp, who was in attendance, began to grow fidgety.

"There's a volunteer already," quoth Porgy, pointing to Pomp; "he has shifted his carcass from one leg to the other a dozen times since the dog made his appearance. Do you want to take a coon to-night, Pomp?"

"T'ank you, maussa, I berry happy, ef you please."

"To be sure, old fellow. I'm quite pleased if you can make yourself happy by the performance."

"I guine too," exclaimed Tom, the cook, who had just at that moment thrust his oily face into the apartment. "I too hungry arter coon. I usen to been know all 'bout de coon and possum quarters on dis place; and I tell you, ef dere's anybody yer wid sense to find de fattest warmints yer he am!—me, Tom."

"They'll all go ef you let 'em," growled the sergeant. "They'll hunt all night and won't be worth a cuss to work to-morrow. Look you, Tom, don't carry off all the hands with you; let 'em sleep. You and Pomp are quite enough, or you may take one other fellow with you. Three on you ought to empty the woods of all the possums in 'em."

"I yeddy [sometimes *yerry*, otherwise 'hear you'] mass Mill-h'us," answered Tom impatiently, and by no means seeming to relish the voice of authority from that quarter: "Tom know berry well wha' for do in he maussa business. Coon and possum mus' be ketch in de time when der's no fresh meat for de pot.—So!—Pomp!—Look at me, boy!"

"I da look, uncle Tom," said Pomp reverently.

"Tom berry quick for march, boy, but you hab for larn some ting fuss. You bin in camp ebber, you'd ha' been larn at de rope's *eend*. Tek' dat bucket, boy, and run to de spring and git de water. Spose maussa want for drink when you gone and der's no water? Spose gemplemans, ossifers and ginerals, happen for come in when you gone and maussa hab for ax 'em to swallow de raw rum—enty you'll feel mean 'nough when you yer 'bout it! Git de water, boy; 'tir [stir] you' stumps, and help Peter git de lightwood. Der mus' be coon fight to-night, ef dem tory rascal aint eat de country out."

This was said pretty much in such an aside to Pomp as the stage tolerates. Meanwhile, Frampton was making his report to the captain, of his day's visit, and of certain friendly messages of Mrs. Griffin and daughter, in response to those with which

Porgy had commissioned his lieutenant.   The former appeared
to take quite an interest in these particulars; a circumstance that
seem to produce some uneasiness in the sergeant.   After a while
he interposed with —

"You're making a mighty long story of it, lieutenant, and I'm
a-thinking you're a burning daylight.   Ef you are to hunt the
coons, the sooner you're off the better—the sooner you'll be
back, and the niggers git their sleep and be ready for a good
day's work to-morrow."

Frampton quietly took the counsel, whistled his dog down the
steps of the piazza into the court where Tom was already busied
in hewing lightwood for the necessary torches.   So soon as he
had disappeared, Porgy said—

"Why, what the d—l sort of work can you put the negroes at
to-morrow, Millhouse?   What's to be done?"

"A hundred things; rails to be split; fences to be made;
poles to be got out for nigger houses; land to be broke up for
planting; ditches to be cut; banks *im*paired;—there's no saying
how much is to be done!"

"But where are the tools, my good fellow, the hoes, shovels,
axes, ploughs——"

"Don't you mind, cappin.   I'm overseer, aint I?   Well, I've
seed to all that.   *On*der the piazza is all them spades, and shovels we've been a using to-day; and Mr. Fordham told me, without my axing, that he could spare me a few ploughs and axes,
and other little matters, *on*till you could lay in supplies in town.
He said 'twas the orders of Madam Eb'leigh that I should
hev' 'em."

"Mrs. Eveleigh is certainly as provident as she is liberal!"
remarked the captain.

"And it's them very vartues, cappin, that you're a-wanting
here to make the pot bile, and to see that it don't bile over.   Ef
you'll keep your eyes right, cappin, you won't let the chaince
slip of getting yourself into good quarters.   It's cl'ar to me that
Mrs. Eb'leigh's giving you the right sort of signs, and you'll be
the blindest sawt of a sarcumstance of a white man, ef you don't
take the right motion from what she shows.   A nod's as good as
a wink to a blind horse, and the man that wants more than the
pull of a sleeve, from a fine woman, to understand what she

wants, why I'm a thinking he aint the valley of a dead dog with three buzzards pulling different ways at his carkiss. I'm considerate of you, cappin, and your sarcumstances, and I'm cl'ar to say that the charitablest thing you kin do, when you see how the cat wants to jump, is jest to open the window, and give her a cl'ar track. Don't you be waiting upon Providence tell some wiser man walks in and takes the fat turkey off the nest. I'd be at her, bright and airly, to-morrow, and I wouldn't wait a week, ef she's willing, before I brought her home to your own roost."

"You're quick on trigger, sergeant. Does it not sometimes occur to you that you're a very rapid man?"

"I reckon 'tis bekaise I was born in a hurry. I came into the world in a hurry, and never waited for the midwife. I grow'd up in a hurry, and in all sawts of wickedness. I reckon no person ever l'arned his vices so quick as me. I never seemed to want book or teacher. Lord love you, I charged into 'em, jist as I charged among the inimy's baggage, and held on to 'em as loving as if they was so many army stores, with the money chist in the middle. If I had any vartues, they come slower, but I was pretty fast with them too; and fast motion is a vartue by itself, when you've got to do with man or woman, friend or inimy. For, what's the truth, cappin? Lord love you, there aint much time 'lowed to a man in this life. What he's got to do, he's got to do in a hurry, ef it's to be done at all. Ef he pokes and saunters, grim Death gobbles him up afore he gits to the eend of his journey. Well, this courtin' of a woman is jist the sawt of business that calls for fast usage. It's a sawt of race where the hindmost wins nothing but loses. You kaint stop to look behind you. You must go ahead, jist as if the d—l had you on an eend, and you had no chaince to git on and off, but by bolting like a mad bull, even though you should lose your skairts in the run. And a woman of ixperance likes a man the better if he gives her no time for long thinking. Courtin' is like storming an inimy's batteries. Women expects naterally to be taken by storm. They likes a good ixcuse for surrenderin'. You must go it with a rush, sword in hand, looking mighty fierce, and ready to smite and tear everything to splinters; and jist then she drops into your arms and stops the massacree by an honest givin' in. 'You're too strong for me, I see,' says she, when she surrenders—'so' she goes on, 'only spare my life and take everything I've got;' and she gives herself in into the bargain; —what we sodgers calls a surrinder at discretion. But you must jest show her that you are detarmined to conquer; that you kain't be marciful; that you must hev' everything or lose everything; and that your name's 'master' from the beginning."

"Really, sergeant, you must have enjoyed a wonderful experience among the sex."

"It's hard to say what I hevn't seed in my time, among all sorts of people; an' it's hard to say where my ixperance eends in dealing with people—man and woman. I'm showing you, cappin, by the teachin' I'm a-giving you."

"You are a sage, grave counsellor, Millhouse, and I am bound to suppose—being myself inexperienced, particularly among women—that you counsel wisely. But have you only a single rule for your operations? Is it possible that you recognise no difference among women, and that you use the same policy with all?"

"Lord love you, no! In course, you're to *on*derstand that man is the born master; but every master knows that you manage hands differently, each one accordin' to his natur. But woman is born with a knowing that some day she's got to find a master. That makes her ready for him when he comes. But it skears some, them in perticklar that haint got no ixperence. With a woman of ixperence, storming's the way;—and a fort, you know, that's been once stormed knows all about it, and kin be easily stormed agin. But the fort that's never been taken, is to be managed different. You don't let sich a fort see all your strength at once. You don't show all your sodgers in front. You manœuvres, and marches and countermarches. You don't let the garrison see where you're guine to make the attack. You approaches cautious, cappin, and you works by sap. But I needn't tell you of what's needful in works of war. I only mean to show by a sawt of picter which you onderstand, how you're to work with women. The young gal you captures by insinivations, but the widow Eb'leigh's no young gal. She's had ixperence of things; and you're to conquer her jest by storming and 'scalade. Put on your biggest thunder now, cappin, and go to the attack with a shout and a rush, and dang my peepers ef she don't surrender at the first summons."

"Certainly, you hold forth a very encouraging prospect. But, sergeant, marriage is a very serious business. To a man who has been free all his life, has had nobody to restrain his conduct, outgoings and incomings, there is something positively frightful in the kind of bondage which it makes. It sometimes happens that instead of the woman getting a master, the man gets a mistress. There's a great part of this in most marriages. To reconcile one to the danger, I suppose, the passion of love was invented——"

"Love! Oh! Lord, don't talk of sich child's play as that, I beg you! Marriage is business; 'taint love. It's airnest work; 'taint sport! Nobody, I reckon, marries for the sport of the thing, ef he's once cut his eye-teeth. Your boy and gal marriages is a sort of baby house-business. When we talks to grown men and women about the thing, we means an argyment, and a reason, and a sense, and a needcessity. You aint surely guine to tell me of likes and dislikes in the business. Nobody ixpects you at your time o' life, to have any sich child feeling of love, sich as works upon infant young fellows, that's just begun to l'arn the run of the woods."

"But I confess, sergeant, if I am to marry, I should like to consult my tastes in the matter. I confess that I believe myself not a bit too old to have an affection."

"'Fections mustn't stand in the way of business. How's the case? You're bad off in plantation sarcumstances. You want everything, and kaint, by your own self, keep what you've got. Well, jest beside you there stands a rich widow. She's well off in plantation sarcumstances. She kin save everything for you. Isn't the case cl'ar enough to a person with only ha*fe* an onderstanding."

"Still, I am for having a certain feeling satisfied—call it taste, or affection, love or what you will, sergeant, if I'm to marry and lose my liberty, I must know that my jailor is a lovely one."

"Oh! Lord, cappin, don't be foolish and ridickilous. I've no patience with such etarnal throat-cutting sentiments. Don't you resk the best chance in the country on sich foolish idees. What right hev' you, at your time of day, and in your sarcumstances, to talk about sich boy and gal sentiments. Here you're at forty-five, with your head gitting as grey as ef 'twas rolled over in a meal bag;—with your body all of a heap in the middle, and the pins mighty slender for sich a weight to go upon; and your sarcumstances all in a kink, and knotted upon with the fingers of that etarnal warmint, the sheriff;—and yet you're a-talking of love, and sentiments, and defections, jest as ef you knowd no more of human natur than a lad of seventeen, who's jest beginning to spread sail for a breeze. I kaint let you talk sich foolish idees, cappin! 'Twont do, I tell you. I wont hev' it! You shan't throw away the good fortin', jest as it's a-tumbling, ripe into your mouth, ef I kin help it. 'Twould be a sort of right that your friends would have to give you a good choking first."

"Ah!" said Porgy, drily,—"such friendship as you describe is somewhat rare, sergeant."

"As I'm a living man, cappin, I'd be the man to do the thing ef 'twas for your good and to save you; and I'd do it jest as free and bold as your own self when you surgined my arm to the saving of my life—I would!"

"Thank you, sergeant, thank you! I acknowledge the peculiar frankness of your friendship, but trust never to make it necessary for my friends to choke me, in order to make me take my medicine."

"Fruit, not physic, cappin."

"Well, fruit!—But suppose there are other fruits that I happen to like better than that which you offer me. Suppose, to speak more to the point, there should happen to be another woman whom I happen to like better than Mrs. Eveleigh?"

"Ha! is it that? Well, the only thing to ax—is the other woman in the same sarcumstances as Mrs. Eb'leigh,—ready and able to help you out of the halter of the sheriff?"

"Don't name the animal quite so often, sergeant, if you please."

"Well, I wont; but I ax agin—is the other woman as well off as the widow Eb'leigh? Has she as many goulden guineas, as many niggers?—"

"Not a stiver that I know of—not the hair of a negro."

"Can't be, cappin, you're thinking of the widow Griffin?" exclaimed the sergeant, rising to his feet and confronting Porgy with a look of blank astonishment—"

"Griffin is a prettier woman than Mrs. Eveleigh."

"Diccance! cappin! what hev' you got to do with purty women. What's a purty woman to a man in your sarcumstances?"

"Why, Millhouse, do you suppose, because a man wants money,
he must also want good taste."

"Taste!—that's another of them foolish idees! I thought I
had given you a right notion of all sich things. A man what's
poor and in danger of the sheriff has no right to hev' a taste."

"But suppose he can't help it, sergeant—suppose he *has* the
taste whether he wills or no?"

"Then the Lord have marcy on his *sarcumstances*. But, cappin, you kaint afford to hev' a taste for the widow Griffin. She's
a mighty comely woman, I confess; but comely in a woman is
as comely brings. It's not what a woman looks, but what she
owns, that makes the comely; and you kaint afford to encourage
her ixpectations, ef she's got any. Your business is with widow
Eb'leigh, and you kaint git over the needcessity afore you, try
it as you may. It's a law of natur, in your sarcumstances, that
you marries her, and nobody else!"

Porgy was silent, looking thoughtfully into the fire, his pipe
hanging over his knee, forgotten in his grasp. Millhouse rose, at
the close of the last speech, in which he had uttered his decree
as emphatically as if it had been that of the Medes and Persians,
and motioned with his one arm to the Jamaica

"Aint you thirsty, cappin?"

"No, sergeant, but I am sure that *you* are very *dry*. Help
yourself, and don't wait on me."

"It's a bad sign when a travelling horse won't drink, cappin."

"True, sergeant, but though one man may carry a horse to
water, ten can't make him drink, when he's not willing."

"Why, Lord, love you cappin, there oughtn't to be any great
onwillingness for you to marry the widow Eb'leigh. She's got
a mighty sweet face."

"True."

"And a mighty plump figure."

"True."

"And the whitest skin, cl'ar red and white; and sich a soft
blue eye, and sich sweet lips, so red and ripe like;" and the
sergeant swallowed half the contents of the cup, and smacked

his lips as heartily as if in the actual encounter with those of the widow.

"And she's young for her age, and with sich a nice, full figger; not a bit too stout, not over fat, but jest right. Why, cappin, ef taste, as you call it, was to decide, and the taste was a downright honest, good sodger taste, why it would choose the widow Eb'leigh a thousand times before the widow Griffin."

"I will drink, sergeant," said Porgy, rising and approaching the barrel, on the head of which the water jug, the Jamaica and the cup, found a temporary asylum. He filled, and when about to drink, he said:

"You are a philosopher, sergeant, such as the world everywhere respects. But though your philosophy succeeds pretty generally, in the world, *you* never would."

"*En'* why not, cappin?"

"Because the chief secret of the success of such a philosophy as yours is that it never vaunteth itself. It's professors never publish their virtues as you do. They are content to practise in secret what you mistakenly praise. They *do* what you *preach*, and *preach* against what they themselves *do*. Pride thus discourseth of humility with moist lips; selfishness thus becomes eloquent in its exhortations to self-sacrifice; and the good preacher will possess himself of the fattest ewe lamb of the flock while insisting on the beauties of a perpetual lent. But what say you to bed? It will be some hours, I fancy, before the lieutenant and the boys get back from their coon hunt, and we may enjoy a good sleep meanwhile. We must also rise soon in the morning, that we may see what we are to wear to-morrow. There must be some patching of my garments, before I shall be able perfectly to appear at the widow's table; and you too, in all probability, will need some adhesive plasters, front and rear."

"I'm glad you're a-thinking of that, cappin. You must put on your best front, and put your best foot for'ad, for, jest hev' what tastes and idees you think proper, you kaint git off from marrying that widow."

CHAPTER XLIV.

THE GHOST AT GLEN-EBERLEY EMBRACES THE SERGEANT
vi et armis.

WHEN Porgy had retired, Millhouse mixed for himself another cup of Jamaica, with water, laid it down before the fire, drew a blanket up to the hearth, squatted upon it, pulled off his shoes, and exposed his naked feet to the blaze, He replenished his pipe, drew a keg near his back, leaned against it with the air of a man who was about to enjoy life philosophically, and, with a few vigorous puffs, encircled his head with a becoming atmosphere of cloud and vapor. With the momentary removal of the pipe from his jaws, he moistened his lips with the Jamaica. He again dried them with a puff, and again moistened them with the provided beverage. The philosophic mood thus properly stimulated, he began, *sotto voce*, to soliloquize upon affairs and things around him, his reflections prompted by the conviction that he had been gratefully opening the eyes of his superior to truths and a wisdom which the other was slow to arrive at.

"He's down in the mouth! He aint in good sperrits. It's a needcessity to make him see how the matter stands, and what he's got to do in his *per*dicaments. Well, to say truth, for a wise man, and a smart man, and a man what's seen sarvice, the cappin is jest about as foolish as a young person of sixteen. And it's mighty strange at his age, he should be so bashful. Here, it's cl'ar to every man what's got an eye to anything, that this here rich widow is ready with the bridal garmints. She's to be had for the axing. I watched her mighty close when they war a-talking together, and ef ever a woman's eye said, 'Look at me, I'm at your sarvice, stranger,' her eye said that same thing to the cappin. Yet, for all that, his cussed bashfulness won't see and believe it. But he shan't want for the incouragings to make him come up to the rack and taste the fodder. It's good fodder,

well-cured fodder, and a plentiful armful of it too ; and there's
good corn where the fodder comes from, and he shall crack that
corn, ef he's got a tooth in his head, and ef he haint, I'll hev' it
ground for him. But eat it he sh*ll ! Don't I see the woman
likes him to kill. And he aint an onlikely pusson in any woman's sight. Ef 'twarn for his almighty gairth, he'd be a figure
to go through an army of women, and take his pick as he went.
I'll take a hand at gitting her to-morrow, and I'll see that Tom
takes in his belt a few holes closer. He must be made to look
his best. Ef he had some new clothes now ! His old buffs are
mighty full of stains. 'Twont do to wash buff breeches in
swamp water no how, and to dust 'em with swamp mud hurts
their complexion more than the water. But with good brushing
we kin make 'em pass. A-most everything in the way of clothes
will pass where a woman's eye's already quite full of the pusson
himself."

Putting the pipe into his mouth, he drew it, fiercely, and send
forth several enormous jets of smoke, which kept up the due philosophic consistency in the atmosphere, then taking another sup
of the Jamaica in order to maintain his own mental consistency,
he proceeded, still in under-tones, to soliloquize in respect to his
superior.

"Talk of Mrs. Griffin ! What kin Mrs. Griffin do for him ?
Whas kin he do for Mrs. Griffin ? Why it's jest the same as ef
we tied both of 'em in a poke together, and gin em to the sheriff
to sell at public cry ! And who'd buy ? The price they'd bring
wouldn't pay for the cost of selling. The woman's good looking
enough — mighty good looking I'd say, and jest the sort of woman to suit *me*, ef there was any sense in *my* marrying at
all. Whether I'd be wanting a wife would a-most altogether
depend on the sort of eencome I could git out of it. She's got
a small place, nice farm enough, a good comfortable house
upon it, with a horse and a cow, and a few pigs and chickens ;
and ef there was nobody but her one, — why it might be no
bad sence for me to be 'greeable and take her ; but there's her
marriageable da'ter, guine to be married too, to the Lieutenant,
and leetle enough there'll be for the three to feed on. 'Twont
do ! a sensible marriage, for a man, means the bettering of his
sa*r*cumstances, and there's no bettering in sich a buisness.

When one marries, it's the sarcumstances that he's got to consider, and not the woman that hangs on to 'em. It's neither for me nor the cappin to think of the widow Griffin, though ef it's to be done by either on us, why it's for me to do it. It's the t'other woman's sarcumstances that he's got to consider, and he'll hev' to come to the scratch whether he wants to or no."

A renewed puffing at the pipe was followed by another sip of the Jamaica, and the utilitarian philosopher proceeded, still *sotto voce*, to consider " the sarcumstances."

"Everything 'pends on what he does and says to-morrow. I'll be thar, and I'll push him for'ad. I'll make the chance for him and the argyment too, ef so be I sees him playing shilly-shally. It's mighty fortinit for the cappin that she axed me to go too. I reckon she seed for herself, that I know'd something that aint to be larned in books, and it's fortinit for the cappin that I'm his friend, that aint guine to see him lose a good game without telling him when it's the right time to fling down trumps! I must put the lieutenant up to help me, and Tom kin throw in a word, seasonable, to strengthen the argyment. And may I be etarnally squashed under a mountain of swamp, fenced in with alligators, ef we don't git possession of that widow and all she's got."

Another succession of fierce puffs at the pipe, and then a renewed moistening of the lips with the Jamaica. The soliloquy was then resumed: —

"She's got more than a hundred niggers, I reckon. That's Tom's thinking. She aint got no debts to pay, and aint afeared of no sheriff. She must divide them niggers betwixt the two places, hafe here and hafe there; and then we'll see which makes the best crops, Fordham or me! Fordham's a good enough chap I'm a-thinking; but he aint had the benefit of seeing the world in the army. I made good rice, I reckon, 'fore ever Fordham seed backwater. When a man lives always in one place he he don't know much and kaint l'arn nothing. I'll show him the good of army life for bringing sense into a family. As for the drill among the niggers, I reckon I'll make him open his eyes wider than ever any tarrapin lying on the flat of his back, and the water biling fast for him to thicken. Ef I don't beat him at a crap, then my daddy had no right to his own son!"

The sergeant continued to muse and speculate, for two goodly hours after his worldly fashion. Porgy's chamber was silent. He probably slept. So thought Millhouse. Frampton was still absent on his coon and possum hunt; on which enterprise he had been accompanied by Tom, Pomp, and several other negroes, all eager to procure a supply of fresh meat, and to renew sports which always brought them pleasure. It might be hours still before they would return, since it requires, sometimes, a large circuit of woodland and swamp before the dog scents his prey. Millhouse, in the meantime, had ceased to soliloquize. He had been kept wakeful a long time, in consequence of the singular variety and activity of his scheming fancies; but he was beginning to succumb to drowsiness. He had emptied his pipe of its ashes, swallowed the last drop of the Jamaica, and pushing away the keg from his back, prepared to roll himself up in his blankets, when he fancied he heard a footfall in the back piazza. In half listless mood he listened. The step ceased, and he drowsed. Then he was awakened by what he thought a rustling against the door. He raised himself up, threw a brand on the fire, which was beginning to sink, and saw it kindle and blaze up brightly. Remembering the robbery of the previous night, he kept his eyes keenly fixed upon the door. He was afraid to rise for his pistols, which lay in the opposite corner, lest he should frighten off the intruder, and he was too anxious to get at him to suffer this, if possible. He resolved, accordingly, to wait till the last moment. All on a sudden, while he looked and listened, the door was pushed open, and a tall female figure stood before him in the dusky opening. There was evidently female drapery —*that* he could distinguish—but all else was undiscernable He remembered, for the first time, that the captain had told him, the night previous, that the house was haunted; and the thought now seized him that this was the ghost. The sergeant was brave enough, as the world goes, but he could not prevent a strange uncomfortable shudder from passing through him. He did not will to believe in ghosts, but what else could be the intruder?

"Who's it?" he cried out, after a pause, in accents somewhat less confident and formidable than those in which he had discoursed to Porgy of the proper philosophy.

"Who's thar?" he demanded; and the stranger advanced into

the room,—a tall, slender form in a sort of loose, dingy white garment, the draping of which seemed somewhat to confine its movements. It happened, vexatiously enough, that the fire upon the hearth, which had blazed up brightly enough but a moment before, seemed almost to expire; a circumstance so aptly associated with the presence of the stranger as somewhat to confirm the fancy of the sergeant that she was certainly the household ghost. He remembered, in an instant, what he had heard in his young days of the lights burning dimly and blue, in the presence of the spectre, and he could conceive of no less influence which could so effectually, and in an instant, deprive 'fat lightwood' of its proper inflammable virtues. He began to feel more and more disquieted, while the silence of the intruder added to his doubts. Again he cried out, this time raising his head, if not his voice,—and speaking with prodigious effort—

"Who's it thar, I say?"

The answer dispelled his apprehensions immediately.

"Da you, my chile?"

The voice was that of a negro as well as a female.

"Who's afraid of a nigger ghost!" exclaimed the sergeant aloud —and rising to a sitting posture.

"Who's you! I say! and what hev' you come for."

"It's me, my chile! It's you own ole woman—Sappho! Enty you member de ole woman—you own nuss,—de same Sappho wha' bin mind you a t'ousand times. De Lawd be praise for bring you back—dat de ole woman kin hug he chile once more, fore he dead for ebber."

With these words the speaker darted forward, and, falling upon her knees upon the blankets of the sergeant, seized him in her firm embrace, and before he could recover from his surprise, and extricate himself, hugged him closely to her bosom, and bestowed upon his cheeks, a flood of kisses from a toothless mouth!

"Git out! Oh! thunder—Oh!—Hello! I say! What the splinters are you after! Whoo! D——!"

Thus, half suffocated for a moment, the sergeant vented his horror and surprise. He struggled fiercely, with his one arm, to push her away; but she had him at great advantage. He was in a sitting posture, swathed half in blankets; and, kneeling beside him, the ghost had grappled him about the neck, and in the ardor of her kisses had almost succeeded in pressing him over upon the floor.

"My own chile!" she sobbed ever as she kissed.

"But I aint! Git out, I say! Lord, old woman, who the h–l kin you be, and what's you after! Child be d——d! Me a child!"

"My belubbed infant! I hab you in my arms agin, 'fore I dead! De Lawd be praise!"

"Infant, be ———!"

"Oh, my chile!"

"Child! you old fool! What's you thinking about!"

"Dat old Sappho should ebber lib for see dis day! I kin dead happy now; the Lawd be praise!"

"Dead! I wish you was, and the old d—l had you!"

"My chile—my bes' belubbed son!" and she blubbered aloud.

"D—n my splinters, old woman, ef I don't be the death of you for sartain. I'll knock you into the leetle eend of a sarcumstance ef you don't let go."

"It's you own ole Sappho, my chile! You no know you own nuss; you own good ole woman, old Sappho, my son! Wha' you push me 'way for? I bin nuss you in dese arms a t'ousand times, and I lub you better dan all de worl'. Don't push me 'way!—I lub you too much for leff you; I wunt le' you go!"

"We'll see that! Lord! that I should live to be squeezed to death by a nigger, and suffickated in the arms of a raw-head and bloody bones like this! You old scout of satan, you—I'll——!"

The sergeant, swearing, and almost shouting in his rage, at length succeeded in extricating himself from the blankets; then, throwing off the loving intruder who had evidently mistaken her man, he managed to gain his feet, and to stand erect, with his one arm extended, the fist being now doubled until it wore the appearance of an awful maul, such as the rail splitter employs in driving home his wedges. The strange woman, singularly named after the tender-hearted wanton who flung herself away for love of the phlegmatic Phaon, had by this time arisen also; and, recoiling from the person she had so closely grappled but a moment before, she stood some five paces off, curiously regarding him, now satisfied of her error, and quite as much confounded as he was wrothy. It was at this moment, when the sergeant, fully persuaded that, if a ghost, the person before him was sufficiently substantial to feel the force of arguments such as it was in his power to deliver from his knuckles, was preparing to fall upon the intruder, tooth and nail, that the captain of partisans, aroused by the voices and the struggle, made his appearance in his night-clothes, but with a blanket over his shoulders, and interposed between the parties.

"Who's this, Millhouse? What's the matter?"

Before the sergeant could answer, the woman pushed beside him with a cry.

"Dis dah him! Dis dah my own chile!" and with sobs of joy she threw her arms about the neck of Porgy as she had done about that of Millhouse.

"Why, hello! my good woman! Who do you take me for? You are quite too free in your affections."

Porgy endeavored to extricate himself, but the effort was as difficult in his case as in that of Millhouse. Millhouse witnessed the effort, and chuckled outright.

"It's your turn now, cappin, and your right by nater!"

"My chile! my chile! You no know you mudder nuss,—you own Sappho, wha' bin min' you when you bin leetle baby, only big like my han'."

"Sappho!" cried Porgy,—"what Sappho, is it you, my poor old mauma!—my good old woman!"

"Dah him! Dah me! my chile! my chile!"

"And a pretty sizeable sarcumstance of a child he is!" cried the sergeant, laughing at the spectacle.

"There, Sappho, my good old woman, that will do now," said Porgy—"come into my room and let us sit down where I can hear you."

"Da's it, my son! Oh! how I wants for tell you ebbry ting what's pass and gone;" and clinging to his arm the old woman accompanied the captain to his chamber.

"I'll bring you some lightwood, cappin," quoth the sergeant, "you'll be wanting to see, I reckon, the sawt of pusson you're a-talking to."

The lightwood was brought, the fire soon put into a blaze, and seating himself on one corner of his blankets, the captain, with some difficulty, persuaded the old woman to deposite herself on another. The sergeant with his blanket wrapped about his shoulders, took his stand beside the mantlepiece, his stump-arm resting upon it, while he looked curiously upon the group, and listened with interest to what was said. The spectacle was, indeed, a sufficiently curious one.

Porgy, as we already know, is somewhat of a spectacle himself, particularly with a toilet incomplete. But his companion, now, is one in admirable contrast with himself. She was very tall and thin—a mere skeleton, in fact—her garments loose and light, rather hanging about than fastened to her person. She was about seventy-five years old, or more. The successive wrinkles of her face, drooping together at last, hung about her cheeks and chin, like a once well filled, but long emptied purse. Her teeth were entirely gone; the lips, unusually thin, finding no resistance upon pressure, had sunk in, making a deep valley across the face, the nose on one hand and the chin on the other, both prominent and sharp, rising up like peaks of Teneriffe. The scant hairs which thinly covered her head, and escaped beneath the old handkerchief which wrapped it, were gray as the moss upon the old oak, and not much unlike it in texture and curl. But her eyes were as bright, shining out in the general blackness, as two fiery little stars, preparing for battle. They were small and deeply set, but as intense in their gaze as if the proprietor were fifteen only. Toothless wholly, the old woman was not tongueless. The tongue, indeed, seemed to find it necessary to do double duty in consequence of the deficiency of the teeth; and eager, yet mumbling the words the while, the ancient woman ran on, all the while, with little or no pause, ejaculating her thanks to heaven which had vouchsafed that she should see "her chile agin!"

"But you no know me, my chile. You bin fo'git old Sappho! Enty I know. You kaint tell me. Hah! das de way wid de world. You back tu'n, you gone, you in de ground, de berry chile you bin carry in you' arms, he fo'git all 'bout you!"

"But I didn't forget you, mauma! As soon as I saw you fairly, I knew you; and I only wonder I didn't know you by your voice."

"It's de teet', my chile! De teet' gone! De old snag drop

out,—de berry las' ob 'em drop out de beginning ob dis winter. *Nary* one [never a one] leff now for me chaw 'pon. Ah! de ole woman is a-gwine fas', my chile. It's de preticklar blessing ob de Lawd dat I leff for see you git back to you' own home and people. De Lawd be praise for all he mussies!"

"Well, mauma, I'm truly happy to see you once more alive. It reminds me so much of everything—of my mother—of the old wagon—of the little bay ponies, and the rides we had together down to uncle Dick's. Why, how could you think, Sappho, that I should ever forget *you?*"

"It's de way ob de worl', my chile! an' I was afear'd dat when you git out in de worl' fair, an' see de people, an' git mix up wid de sodgers, you would shame for 'tink 'bout poor ole woman, da's a nigger, too."

"Never, Sappho! I have thought of you a thousand times, and I'm more glad to see you now, still living, and still able to see and to speak, than I should be at meeting with the best white friend I have. But, Sappho, you must tell me about everything. I want to know how you escaped in the general sack and confusion. When I sent Tom out here once to see how things went on, he could find nothing of you, and hear nothing. He only gathered that the British and tories had been here, had gutted the plantation and carried off all the people. You were believed to be dead, Sappho, and though not much given to weeping, I shed some tears for you, mauma. You may believe me, old woman, for I remembered you not only for yourself, but for others who were very precious to me."

"Enty I blieb's you, my chile. It do de ole woman heart good to blieb you. I knows you got a good heart, yourse'f, my chile, and dough, I knows, you lub much better to laugh dan to cry, I knows too you kin cry when dare's 'casion for it. But, yerry [hear ye] my chile. I gwine tell you all about wha' happen sence you bin gone."

And the old woman smoothed her garments in front, laid her hands crosswise on her lap, then beginning a regular swinging, or see-saw motion of the body, to and fro, proceeded with a long and somewhat tedious, but clear and intelligible account of plantation affairs up to the moment when the negroes were dispersed or carried off by the enemy. We will not afflict the reader with this narration. But preserve only such portions of it as particularly arrested the attention of Sergeant Millhouse. As he stands somewhat in the relation of a third party, it is possible that what impressed his regards, will not be unworthy of the attention of other persons, the more particularly, indeed, as the matter was of some importance to the pecuniary affairs of Captain Porgy.

"Soon as I yerry, my chile, dat de red coats bin 'pon Gillon place, an' bin carry off de people, dat berry time I scare. Den I say to meself—wha' for hender 'em come yer, an' carry off we people too? Je's I bin tink dat ting, I begin gedder [gather] up for de swamp. Pot, kettle, pan; I tie 'em up in de blanket. I say to Cæsar—boy, clap 'em on you back; den I say to Cha'lot, my biggest da'ter;—he marry Cromanty Ben, my chile, you 'member—"

"Yes! yes!"

"Well, I say to him, pick up you tings. Do like you see me do. I tell de same ting to Betty, my second da'ter. He bin marry Eli, you 'member."

"Yes! yes!"

"He hab he four chillen [children] tree gal chile an' one boy; Cha'lot only hab two chillen; he loss two wid 'fection ob de bowels;—well, I say to Betty, pick up you chillen and tings, chile, we hab for hide, I see. An' I make him go right off to he husban' wha' bin a-work down in de big pine fiel', and tell 'em for drop he hoe, and pull foot dis way. My t'ird da'ter, Cinda [Lucinda], you 'member, I 'tir him up too and make 'em gedder up he chillen. He hab tree, but he husband dead dis two year. Den we tell Edisto Jenny, and scal' arm Sally, and leetle Jupe—de boy wha' hab de bow leg, you 'member, and he two sister—all ob 'em hab bow leg—we tell 'em wha's de trouble coming—an' we would ha' bin tell all our people, but, you see, day [they] was scatter, some in de cowpen fiel', some in de long tater [potato] fiel', wha' jine 'pon Miss Ebleigh; some one way, some tudder [t'other] an' dere's [there's] no time for loss, an' we kaint see dem. So we people start by our own se'f [selves], me, an' my tree da'ters, Cha'lot, and Betty, and Cinda, wid my gran' chillen, Liz and Mart'a, Cha'lot chile; an' Bob, an' Rachel, an' Clough, Betty chillen; an' Scip, an' Andra, an'

14

Harry, Cinda chillen; dem's all my ginerations wha' I bin carry in de swamp; but Cromanty Ben, Cha'lot' husban', an' Eli, Betty husban'—day gone wid us too, and four udder women, Edisto Jenny, an' scal' arm Sally, an' Sukey and Pussy, sisteren of Jupe—and Jupe hese'f—all ob dem wid de bow legs—all ob dem gone wid us—an' dem's all the ginerations ob de chillen ob Adam, my chile, dat git off wid us in de swamp, when we yerry de red coats is a-coming. An' we carry ebbry ting we kin lay hands 'pon, an' carry 'em safe an' easy—de pot an' de pan, an' de blanket, an' de clo'es, an' de axe, an' de hatchet, an' de knife—wha' ebber tings we kin pick up in de hurry, we carry dem off wid us clean. An', time for us do so, my chile, for when we peep out de swamp, de whole nigger quarter da bu'n, an' wha' ebber dem udder people bin leff dere, he bu'n to cinders an' ashes 'for you kin say t'ree prayer to de Lawd for all he mussies."

The sergeant had shown himself very restless during all this narration. He shifted his position from side to side of the mantlepiece; crossed over; now stood behind the captain; now beside the old woman, and, at moments, had his eyes and hand lifted up as if in meditation; or, as the fingers of his one hand were crooked and elevated successively, it might be in computation. When the old lady had reached what seemed a natural pause in her relation, the sergeant, as if unable to contain himself, cried out, over Porgy's shoulders—

"Why, old lady, you don't mean to say that you've got all these niggers in the swamp now ?"

"De Lawd be praise, sah, day's all libbing [living], 'cept little Jupe, de bow-leg, wha' dead by break he neck; he fall from tree he bin climb one night for catch possum, and nebber kick arter he touch de 'airth."

"All living but leetle Jupe !" quoth the sergeant, lifting his surviving hand, and separately displaying the fingers sundry times before his own eyes, muttering all the while the tale to himself, with eager rapidity.

"Ef that's the case, ole woman, 'cording to my count, you've got in the swamp, not counting you, jest eighteen niggers. There's your da'ter Charlotte, and her two children—that's three—her husband makes four; Betty and her husband, and four children, that's six, in all ten; then Cinda, her three children and her husband—"

"Cinda husban' dead, sah!"

"Ah! yes! that's true; well, Cinda and her three children, making four, put to the other ten, is fourteen, by all counts; then there's two other women, that's sixteen, and two bow-legged gals, is eighteen! Eighteen niggers and most of 'em women! And you mean to say, old lady, that all these people are jest now in the swamp a-hiding?"

"As de Lord is mussiful to me, sah, day's all dere, 'cept Jupe, as I bin tell you, wha' bre'k he neck, by fall from de tree when he hunt possum!"

"Jimini! that's great intelligence, cappin. And how many of these is grown niggers, old lady—how many of 'em good to take up the hoe now, and—"

"No matter, sergeant," said Captain Porgy, who had been sitting silent, rather sad, indeed, listening to his ancient nurse,— "there are other more necessary questions—

"Sappho, have these people any clothing? Your own garments, mauma, are thin enough."

"Ah! my chile, we bin see berry hard times; de cloding [clothing] is moss in rag; an' we try for keep warm by de fire; an' we aint feed so well, my son; an' when Cromanty Ben come into de swamp last night an' say to me, "Mammy, dere's a smoke coming out ob maussa house windows; I wonder who day in maussa house?'—'I say de Lawd be praise ef my chile is come home to git his people clo'es and blanket.' Den day all 'gree dat I must come out and see; dey all 'fear'd for come, for fear de tories an' de red-coats grab 'em. Day knows dat day nebber gwine carry off poor wort'less old woman like Sappho. So I come, maussa, an' dis de trute ob all my gineration's in de swamp."

"Jiminy! captain! But that makes the force quite expectable. We'll do. But we'll be a-wanting more hoes and axes; more supplies; you must make a bigger list, cappin; we must make a main fine crap this year, in spite of sarcumstances."

And the sergeant strode the room to and fro; his one hand waving at intervals; his fingers still crooking and extending in occasional computations; and his form rising up into unusual erectness, while, though walking in his stockings only, he made the floor quiver with the solemnity of his tread. The old woman had more to say, and Porgy more to ask, but, the interruptions of the sergeant were too frequent to suffer other parties much liberty, and these interruptions were the more frequent and more impatient as Millhouse fancied that Porgy dealt in much very irrelevant matter. The latter, accordingly, put a very sudden close to all further talk that night, by saying :—

"Well, old lady, it's time now that we should sleep. We are very weary, and you, at your time of life, must not sit up too late. Let me give you something to make you strong. Sergeant, we must take a sup of Jamaica, with my old nurse."

"Won't I, cappin! She's a sensible old woman, and I like her. The way she dodged them tories and red-coats, and saved them niggers for us, is desarving of a drink. And I took you for a ghost, old lady, would you believe it, and ef you hadn't a-hugged and kissed so close, I'd mout be ha' b'lieved it to the very last."

"'Scuse me, sah; but I t'ought it was my own chile, all de time."

"Oh! you're 'scusable enough, under the sarcumstances. But let's have the drink all round."

The Jamaica was broached, and the cup which Porgy poured out he handed to the old woman.

"Drink that, Sappho, it'll help to strengthen your old limbs."

"T'ank you, my chile. The Lawd is good. God bress you for ebber, a t'ousand times, my son! may you nebber see trouble in de house ag'in!"

And she drank.

"Ha! it makes me feel warm to de heart. It's a good physic for ole people, my chile."

"And for young ones too, old lady," quoth Millhouse, emptying the cup at a swallow. Porgy drank, then giving Sappho a blanket, he conducted her into the shed room which had been assigned to Tom.

"Here, mauma, you will sleep to-night. To-morrow we'll see what's to be done for the people in the swamp. Lie down now, old lady, and take your sleep. Good night."

When the captain returned to the hall, the sergeant seized his arm—

"By the powers, cappin, luck's with us. We'll do. We have a force now that begins to tell—twenty-five niggers, and all, I reckon, able to hoe a task."

"Let us sleep now, sergeant!" said Porgy.

"Sleep! May I be squashed unconvartibly for ever, ef I shall be able to shut an eye to-night. I'll have to think over everything what's to be done with these other niggers."

"As you please, sergeant; but you will suffer me to sleep if you please." And Porgy disappeared. Millhouse threw himself down by the fire—

"Sich a man! he's got no more ambition than a dirt-eater with agy [ague] on him. He kaint even shake, he's so wanting in the proper sperrit!"

Let us drop the curtain for the present.

CHAPTER XLV.

THE SERGEANT IN A MAZE.—HE RETORTS UPON THE GHOST.

SOMETIME after midnight, Lance Frampton and his sooty companions returned from their nocturnal hunt. They had been tolerably successful, having bagged three possums and a coon. The dog had proved his merits, having had a severe fight with the coon, who was a well-grown monster, and gave in only after a long contest; yielding without a cry—to the great disappointment of Pompey, who was particularly anxious to extort this sort of acknowledgment from the victim. Frampton soon folded himself up for sleep in his blankets, not disturbing Millhouse, who slept soundly in spite of his own convictions to the contrary. He muttered and turned in his sleep, evidently dreaming earnestly; Frampton being able to distinguish a few broken sentences, in which the sergeant seemed to be still busy in a difficult but interesting arithmetic—

"Eighteen and seven—twenty-five;—seven women—no, nine—and—two—and the boys—and—boo!—boo!—boo!—"

The speech was swallowed in the snore. Our friend Tom, the cook, accompanied by Pomp, was somewhat surprised to find his chamber partly occupied, and by a woman; but Sappho awakened at his entry—indeed, the old woman had scarcely slept—age never sleeps very soundly—and she made herself known to him in few words, and soon put him in possession of all the history as it is already known to us. This was done in low tones so as not to disturb the household. Pomp was soon as oblivious of the outer world as a stone, and Tom finally entreated the ancient lady to forbear all further revelations for the night.

"Kaise, you sees, aunt Sappho, dis 'ere boy, you humble sarbant, he's a-most breck down wid tire. Ef you bin know all wha' he bin do to-day, and dis 'ere coon hunt to-night, you gwine say youse'f, de chile better hab he sleeps. I glad for see you, aunt Sappho, berry much glad for see you; kaise you bin ole fellow sarbant wid me, and I bin yer you bin dead. But you aint dead, I see, and I hopes berry much you aint gwine for dead, long time, and so, aunt Sappho, as I bin said—a-ye-ho-he-yo he-me, ya-ya-ya!" (yawning with open jaws, wide as those of the great cave of Kentucky); "I must hab some sleeps now! and de Lord bress you, aunt Sappho—an' I'll tank you to shet up now!"

"Tek' you sleeps, my son; I sees you wants 'em. I terra [tell-a] you ebbry t'ing nudder time. You kin sleep now, I done!"

"Da's a good aunty! nudder time will do!" And Tom soon followed the example of Pompey, and save for an occasional growl from Frampton's dog, and a more regular succession of noises, scarcely so pleasant, from sundry nasal eminences growing upright in several parts of the household, all would have been entirely quiet. There was no further disturbance during the night.

Bright and early, Sergeant Millhouse was afoot. His dreaming and waking thoughts had greatly contributed to his power and importance. He scarcely gave himself time to get his clothes on, before he presented himself at the entrance of the little shed room to which Sappho had been consigned.

"Hello! old lady—Sapphy, in there—come out, and let's have a good look at you by daylight."

There was no answer. He repeated the summons. It was

still unnoticed. He grew impatient, and, with a single kick at the door, sent it open, and penetrated the chamber. It was dark. He threw open the window—the room was empty. There was no sleeper, male or female, in the apartment, and—which surprised our sergeant still more—no signs of bed or blanket.

"Why, what the d—l! Who'd ha' thought an old skillyton of a woman like that would ha' bin out and off so early! I reckon she's down stairs among the niggers."

Down he goes to see. The negroes were just turning out, only half wakened.

"Hello! there? where's the ole woman, ole Sapphy?'

"Sapphy! Ole woman! Dar's no ole woman yer, mass sergeant."

"No ole woman! Why, where kin she be? Ah! she's gone to see her chile, the cappin! Mighty fine child, I'm a-thinking. A leetle too large for his petticoats, by reason that he grows so fast."

And with a glorious chuckle at his own wit, the sergeant ascended to the captain's chamber and broke in without ceremony. Porgy was already up and at the window shaving. He had been up for some time, had heard the sergeant's inquiries below, and knowing thoroughly the sort of person with whom he dealt, could very well understand the motive of his anxiety. Porgy had seen old Sappho already that morning, and spoken with her at the window. The old woman, with her blanket around her by way of a cloak, was already moving off to join, and make her report to her "ginerations" in the swamp. She had but few words with her foster child—for such Porgy had been—and they were such as the reader can readily conceive from what has been shown already. As the sergeant thundered up the steps and entered the piazza, our captain of partisans readily conjectured that the next visit of Millhouse would be to himself. He prepared to disquiet him.

"Hello! cappin; would you think it, that old skillyton of a woman's off a'ready?"

"What woman do you mean, Millhouse?"

"What woman! Why old Sapphy, to be sure, that I tuk for a ghost—that come in upon me last night, and gin me such a huggin', and a-kissin', and all on your account."

"I really don't know what you're talking about, sergeant."

"Don't know what I'm a-talking about!" quoth Millhouse, in amazement—"Don't know, cappin! Why, Lord love you, the old woman, your nuss, that calls you her child, that hugged and kissed both of us till we was a-most choked and smothered—the one that's got the niggers in the swamp, seven ginerations and more, making in all eighteen good hoe hands. Lord save us, how kin you forgit sich a matter!"

"Forget! How should I remember a matter which I never heard of before. You're certainly dreaming, sergeant."

"Dreaming, cappin! Ef I thought so, I'd be mighty apt to bust my brains out agin the fireplace; but you're a-joking only. Sartainly, you kaint forgit the skin-dried old skillyton of a woman that slept in here last night; and we kim [came] into your room, both on us; and you was a-setting thar, jest on the edge of the b'anket, and she was setting thar jest on t'other edge; and I stood up thar jest agin the fireplace; and how she told us of her gitting away from the red-coats and the tories; she and her three da'ters—I 'member all their names perfectly; there was Charlotte, and Betty, and Cinda—I kaint forget—and Charlotte had two children, and Betty four, and Cinda three, and two on 'em had husbands living, though I kaint be sartain which, all on 'em in the swamp, and there were two bow-legged gals, and there was a bow-legged boy, and his name was Jupe—and, you kaint forgit that! Jupe fell from a tree, climbing a'ter coon, and jest broke his neck outright; and there was other niggers, making eighteen in all, not counting old skillyton Sapphy her-self; I counted 'em all up last night, and ranged 'em off for working, soon as they come in, so far as I could, not having seed any on 'em. You must 'member all that matter, cappin."

"Not a syllable! It's all news to me, sergeant!" And Porgy gazed on him with a well-affected amazement of stare that provoked the most natural consternation in the world in the features of the other.

"The d—l you say! But, Lord, cappin, you kaint be forgit-ting your own ole nuss, Sapphy."

"I never to my knowledge, Millhouse, had a nurse with such a name, which seems to be that of a heathen goddess."

"Heathen h–ll! cappin; she set thar, I tell you."

"Impossible, sergeant."

"And she warnt in your room last night?"

"Not that I know of."

"Lord help me, ef I shan't go crazy! And I warnt in your room last night?"

"It may be that you were. You know best. If you were, it was while I slept."

"Slept! By the powers, cappin, you was wide-awake as a black fish; and when the talk was over, we all kim out, and swallowed a little Jamaiky by way of medicine. And we gin the old nigger a cup for the good news she brought, and then you gin her a blanket, and you showed her yourself whar to sleep in Tom's room, and thar we left her."

"This is a strange delusion of yours, sergeant. But why not go to the room and find her there, if you say you saw her go there to sleep?"

"Lord save me, but you put her thar yourself."

"There you are mistaken! But, if such is your notion, go and seek her there."

"I've been thar, and she's not thar!" cried the sergeant, in a state of approaching perspiration.

"I thought so!" muttered the captain of partisans, in subdued tones, but sufficiently loud to be heard, and he touched his head significantly—

"Millhouse, your suppers are too heavy. I would counsel you against much meat at night. A single bit of that broiled ham—the slices thin—is quite enough for any decent white man. And in eating your hoe-cake, take my counsel to reject the softer parts; confine yourself entirely to the crisp portions, the crust. Besides, coffee is a wonderful stimulant of the brain. Don't go over a pint hereafter at night; and, perhaps, it will be well to deny yourself the freedom of the Jamaica after a certain hour. Say, a single glass after smoking your last pipe, and then to sleep. Believe me, my good fellow, by observing these simple forbearances, you will escape the visitation of the nightmare. She has evidently given you a fearful hug last night."

"'Twas the old skillyton nigger, I tell you—'twas Sapphy, your nuss, and not any nightmar'. Lord, cappin, ef you wouldn't drive me 'stracted, don't you go on so. Warnt that old nigger here, that nuss of yourn, as skinny as a dry peach-skin — all skin and bone — warnt she setting thar for a good hour, a-telling us of her da'ters in the swamp, and their children, and their husbands, and of the boy Jupe, that broke his neck a'ter the coon, and them two bow-legged gals, his sisters. Now, jest be sensible, cappin, and tell all about it, as I seed and heard it my own self."

"I can tell you nothing more, sergeant. You've certainly had a very lively dream last night, which I should greatly like to see realized."

"A dream! Lord! Lord! I shill go crazy and outright *re-stracted*! And you hadn't a nuss named Sapphy?"

"Never!"

"Oh! Lord, what shall I be thinking!"

"Don't eat so much at night again, sergeant."

"It *kaint* be a dream! —"

"Leave off the coffee in particular!"

"I swow! it warnt no dream!"

"One drink only of Jamaica, after your last pipe."

"Ef 'twas a dream it was as much like the *raal* and living life as I ever seed it."

"That's always the case with pleasant dreams, sergeant; but they always lead to disappointment. What a glorious crop you could make if your dream of those eighteen negroes were true?"

"Lord, yes! and I had jest set my heart on beating Fordham out of sight. But O! stai*rs*, cappin, it ought to be true and it must be true."

Just then Tom was heard below, calling to Pomp.

"Thar's Tom! He must ha' seed her ef she was thar. I'll ax him."

"Do so," says Porgy, "and satisfy yourself. It will do you some good and make you less certain of your dreams hereafter."

Millhouse sallied out, and Porgy darting to the window, caught the eye of Tom, ascending the stairs to the piazza, and motioned with his hands to him. At that moment Millhouse from the hall cried out to him —

"Look you, Tom, where's the old nigger-woman what slept in your room last night?"

Porgy shook his head negatively to the cook. Tom was quick

to conceive, and knew thoroughly the habits of the captain of partisans, as a practical joker. He immediately conjectured what was required of him, and his answer was as prompt as if dictated by the very mother of the truth.

" Wha' womans you talk 'bout, mass Millh'us ? I aint see *nary* old nor young woman 'pon dis place !"

"The h–ll you aint! The Lord be marciful to my poor senses."

" Somet'ing seem for trouble you, mass Millh'us ; may be you is berry much hungry for you breakus."

"D—n the breakfust! Oh ! thar's Pomp ! I recken he must ha' seed the old woman."

Pomp was beginning to ascend the steps leading to the back piazza, at the head of which Tom stood. Tom replied for Pomp, in tones loud enough for the other to hear.

"Wha', Pomp! How kin he see ole woman in my room, ef me, Tom, no bin see 'em ? Heh! Pomp? Speak, boy,—you *no* bin see no ole woman in de room whay we sleeps las' night?"

Tom's tone, and the fierce scowl which he put on while speaking to the boy, effectually taught the latter what sort of answer was required from him, and he responded without hesitation—

" Nebber see ole woman in de room, uncle Tom."

"Da's wha' I say, mass Millh'us. You muss ha' bin dream 'bout dat old woman."

"Dream ! Lord ! Lord ! and here am I a loser of eighteen niggers, fus' rate fiel' hands, and nobody seems to care about it. Lord ha' marcy upon you, cappin !" returning, as he spoke, to Porgy's room—" but you don't seem as ef you had any feeling for your own losses. Now, I 'member—ef 'twas a dream I had of that skillyton nigger wench,—I thought it mighty strange you show'd so little consarn when I told you about putting the eighteen niggers to work, and what they'd hev' to do. I thought it mighty onnatural, of you last night ; but I feel its mighty onnatural, now, as it looks to me this morning. Eighteen able bodied niggers gone, as I may say, in the snapping of a finger. I does feel so mean. Tom, old fellow, do let's have breakfus' mighty soon. We are gwine to see Mrs. Eb'leigh to-day, and must fix up for it. Lord ! Lord ! ef I could only ha' told her 'bout them eighteen niggers out of the swamp, added on to the

poor seven we've got now! How could I ha' dreamed a thing
so natural, and seed the old woman so cl'ar in the firelight, and
felt her a-hugging me, and a-kissing me, with her nose and chin
poking into my face all the time. 'Twarn't no dream, I swow,
cappin—'twarn't no dream. 'Twas too natural for a dream! I
kaint help but b'lieve it all, try the best I kin!"

At that moment, a strange voice was heard without. Millhouse
started and prick'd up his ears. In the next moment, Porgy saw
him dart forward, with a shriek of delight. The captain of
partisans looked out of the window upon the piazza, and there
the spectacle of the night was reversed. It was old Sappho,
who was, this time, nearly suffocated in the embrace of the sergeant!

CHAPTER XLVI.

NEAR APPROACHES TO SANS-CULOTTISM.

"God bless you, my beautyful old nigger. I'll love you tell
my heart drops out of my body for this visit. You're jest as
beautiful now, to my eyes, as ef you'd dropt out of heaven, and
brought all the bright stairs along with you. But, Lord, old woman, what a scare you've given me. I thought you had ruined
me for ever. To lose eighteen niggers, without a minute's warning, aint so easy to be stood, I tells you; and I begun mightily
to feel as ef you had done me that same dissarvice; made me a
rich man first, only to make me poorer than ga' broth arterwards!
Lord! with what an etarnal honest face, the cappin kin lie; and
lie so bodily;—lying through the whole melon, and never choking at the rine [rind]. But I forgive him! The Lord be praised!
old lady, I must give you another hug. I'm so spontinaciously
nappy."

"Tank 'e, maussa," answered old Sappho, quietly, and without
any struggling to extricate herself—"but I tinks you wasn't so
glad to hug de ole woman las' night!"

"Thar' you hev' me, old lady. That was kaise I didn't know
you then. 'Member, you kim in like a sperrit, and you tuk me,

by supprise a leetle. 'Twas onawares you tuk me. I warnt
scared, but I felt as ef I didn't know you, and to be squeezed up
lovingly by a body one dont know, and pretty much in the dark
as we was, is mighty apt to make a pusson feel jubous and on-
sartin what to say or do. But now that I knows you, and what
you come for, I'm your well-wisher, and friend, and off'cer, and
I takes you continentally, as I may say, into the ranks."

"Are you still dreaming, sergeant?" cried Porgy, emerging
from his chamber, and coming out into the piazza.

"You're jest about the fattest sinner living, cappin, and can
jest now lie as easy as ef a conscience warn't no sort of trouble
to you at all. En, how did you put up that black faced satan,
Tom, there, and Pomp, to back your lying for you? Lord! how
nateral they did it. As sure as a gun you'll all go to the devil
together, and not one soul of you miss the road."

"When that time comes, sergeant, you will be found leading
the forlorn hope!—Well, Sappho, my good old woman, you are
as sprightly as a girl of sixteen. You've done more work than
all of us together. And these are my poor people. Charlotte,
and Betty, and Cinda, I remember; and Ben—"

"An' Eli, maussa; you 'member Eli, enty?"
was the interruption of Betty's husband who now ascended
the steps, leading the way for the group, and grappled the captain
by the hand. His example was followed by all the rest; and
numberless and sufficiently various were the exclamations of rejoicing on every hand.

"De Lord be praise, maussa, you come home at las'!" "Tanks
be to de Fader!" "Oh! I so happy, aunty!" and—"Maumy,
maussa come! Enty you glad?" "Glad for cry, my chile."

But we need not multiply the phrases. The character of the
catalogue may be sufficiently conjectured from these samples.
But he who knows what a Carolina plantation is—one of the
old school—one of an ancient settlement—where father and
son, for successive generations, have grown up, indissolubly
mingled with the proprietor and his children for a hundred years,
may follow out the progress, and repaint the picture for himself.
Porgy had few words, but his sympathies were more clearly expressed, to the eyes of all the slaves, than if he had spoken them
in the best chosen language. As the several groups passed up

the steps, and gave way for each other, the men with their wives and their children, the calculating sergeant could not contain his joy. Now he strode up and down the piazza, counting with the fingers of his solitary hand. Anon, he paused to take with an affectionate grasp, some one girl or boy by the shoulder, according as the development showed a desirable strength.

"Eighteen, by the powers, and every one of them a fuss rate for the field. Dream, indeed! Did I dream! Lord, how some people will lie. Cappin, I'll never forgive you that trick. I b'lieve its made some of my hairs turn gray."

Porgy, meanwhile, gave the negroes a brief talk. He should soon visit the city and find them in clothes and blankets, hats and shoes. In truth, these were all greatly needed. Nothing but the abundant stores of lightwood, which the country afforded, could possibly have kept the poor wretches from freezing, even in a Carolina winter. Affectionately welcomed, and assured of proper provisions, they were all dismissed to the basement rooms for the present, except old Sappho, for whom the captain was resolved to provide elsewhere.

"And now," said he, "here is Pomp signalling us for break-fast. I trust, Millhouse, that your dreams have not spoiled your appetite."

"No thanks to you, that it haint. Ef the dream hadn't ha' come true, I'd ha' hardly eaten to-day. But ef I don't eat now, it's only bekaise I'm still busy a-dreaming.

Breakfast was soon despatched, when Sappho was called in to take her portion from the table. This duty over, another of much more embarrassing character was to be attended to — the examination of the several wardrobes of our partisans, in order to a proper exhibition at the dinner party of the widow Eveleigh.

The entire stock of clothing possessed by Captain Porgy (that portion excepted which he wore in common) was carried in a rude deerskin portmanteau or valise, of camp manufacture, — the workmanship of a common soldier. Beyond a single dress-suit, that is for dress parade, our partisan had but very little to boast. There may have been a change of small-clothes, — two pair, in brief, one of buff and one of blue, — that which he wore belonging to neither color. It might have been blue once, possible gray, but time, and sun, and rain, and wind, and frequent intercourse with the soil, had left the original ground-work very questionable, and, to be safe, we will call it neutral. When the portmanteau, which had never known the safe virtues of a lock, was unstrapped, and the contents displayed, uppermost appeared the two articles already mentioned. The blue small clothes were first examined. As at first opened, they suggested the idea of an enormous sack, such as might now serve to take in a bale of long cottons. Capacious as they seemed, however, the experience of the captain had determined that they were by no means sufficiently ample to afford him the degree of freedom which he required when dining out. To the eye, the blues were the least questionable of his small-clothes, in consequence of the fact that they had been, on several occasions, — as they seemed to need it — redipped in a decoction of the native indigo. But even these wore a suspicious whiteness in certain spots, which, unless he wore his hunting frock, by which they were covered, were apt to obtrude themselves rather boldly upon the sight of the spectators. Though faded, here and there, however, the blues were intact — there were no awkward rents or patches; and no places so much worn as to keep the wearer in constant apprehension of an explosion. Porgy, with the help of Tom and Pomp, subjected them to a severe scrutiny, and they were then laid aside for a moment.

"They're the best," quoth Porgy, musingly, "if they were not so atrociously contracted about the hips and waist. I'm always in dread lest I should burst them."

"Day strong, maussa."

"Yes, Tom! But not strong enough for everything. and the widow will, no doubt, give us a first-rate dinner, and I am in honor bound to do justice to it. There will be wines, too, and I must drink, — I *will* drink, and try every variety that's offered. By Bacchus! the very idea of wine inspires me. It's long since I've smacked my lips upon the tears of the vineyard. Lift up the buffs, Pomp."

The garment thus described dangled in the air from the extending finger of Pompey.

"They would do well, in respect to size ; but these d—d patches, Tom."

"Day mighty broad in de face, maussa."

"As the full moon, Tom, though less bright of complexion."

"Ef you puts on dese, maussa, you hab for wear de shirt [hunting]. De pigeon-tail nebber guine to cubber [cover] 'em."

The hurts of the garment were chiefly in the rear. Porgy always seated himself with emphasis. Sometimes, indeed, he came to the ground, though letting himself down never so easily, with something of a shock. The results always told fearfully on his small-clothes. The buffs had particularly suffered, and in this special region. The consequence was that it had become necessary, on more than one occasion, to "put a plaister on them,"— using Millhouse's descriptive phraseology. Now, this plaister or patch, or pair of patches—for Porgy wore his clothes with some uniformity—at least in wearing them *out*,—were, for two sufficient reasons, supplied with buckskin, dressed in camp, and with sufficient rudeness. Nothing but buckskin, it was thought, could possibly endure the constant strain and pressure in the ailing region. But, besides this, the buff was not to be found in camp. The art which was available in that region, was not of a sort to make the boundary line of patch assimilate naturally with the original continent of cloth; and though, from use, the buff and buckskin had gradually grown to look alike, as loving wife and husband are said to do after certain seasons,—yet it needed no critical eye to discover that there were ridges, rising almost into promontories, by which the lines of union, or demarcation, were at once distinguished. A frequent renewal of the stitch had increased the deformity, and upon present inspection it was found that the craft of the tailor was even now necessary to reünite the parts, and renew the integrity of the bonds that held them together.

"He tear out yer, maussa."

"Torn!" with some horror.

"Yes, he breck out, and der's leetle hole working yer, in de middle ob de ledder [leather]. Lor, a mighty, massa, you's too hard 'pon you breeches! 'Taint decent and like gemplemans, de way you wear you clo'es."

"Get out, you rascal, and get ready to sew them up at once. Get your needle and thread; or see Sappho, and see if some of these young grand-daughters of hers can't do the work less clumsily. I reckon she's taught some of them to sew."

The girl was found, and squat upon the floor, provided with all Tom's stock in trade as a tailor, she was soon busy with the garment.

"Ef you wears the buffs, maussa, you hab for wear de shirt."

"Yes! yet the dress coat is more in style," said Porgy, with something of a sigh, lifting both coats up at the same moment, and holding them apart for survey, in separate hands. The hunting-shirt was a blue homespun; the dress-coat was a faint approach to the proper army-uniform of a captain in those days. It was of broadcloth, originally red, but thrice dyed in blue. The latter color, however, had somewhat faded, and the red, or a most unnatural phase of it, was about to reappear through the subsequent dye.

"Ef we had some indigo to gee dat coat a dip now," quoth Tom, himself rather preferring the garment on account of its texture and brighter buttons.

"Still I couldn't wear it with the buffs. No! no! I must wear the shirt. It helps to cover the territory requiring to be concealed, and to hide these wornout acres."

"He's acre for true," growled Tom, looking at the patches which the negro girl was repairing. "He big like de skairt ob saddle."

"They must do, nevertheless," muttered Porgy, with a doleful visage. "Examine the coat, Tom, the hunting shirt, and see if it's sound."

"Hab breck under the arm, maussa."

"Throw it to Pussy, and let her sew it up. Now, Pomp, unroll me that homespun bundle. We must see for shirts and stockings."

"Ha! Shirt and stockin'. I 'speek dem guine gee you trouble 'nuff for fin'."

Pomp unrolled the bundle. The stockings appeared—well saved—the dress pair,—used by the captain only on state occasions—of thick white cotton. They had been a present from the widow Griffin.

"He all gone at de heel and toes, maussa."

"Fortunatly those parts are buried in the shoes. What of the shirt, Pomp?"

Pomp proceeded to unfold it. There was but one.

"Tenderly, you rascal; do you think you're handling a side of leather. Are your hands clean, you monkey. Look at the fellow, Tom; take it from him. He will have it in rags without a warning."

"Ha! maussa, only le' um 'lone, he tumble into rags hese'f."

"But we musn't let it alone, you rascal, and we must be careful that it does not tumble into rags until this day's business is over. It was once the best of Irish linen. It is the last of six dozen. Six dozen! Heavens! was I indeed the owner of six dozen shirts at one time!"

"Ha! ef that was the only 'stravagance and foolishness, maussa. You le' de sergeant know you bin once hab six dozen shu't, all de same time, he gee you h–ll ob a sarmon 'bout you 'stravagance! But, de Lord sabe us, maussa, de shu't aint all yer [here]! All de skairt ob de back is gone." And Tom displayed the ill-conditioned garment outright.

"The skirt gone! How! Where?—True, by Jupiter. That infernal savage. It was Indian Bet that washed it last. The catamount. She has torn it out and carried off the fragment. Look in the portmanteau for the piece!"

"Ingin Bet nebber bin carried 'em off in dis worl'. Wha, he carry 'em for? He too rotten. Ingin Bet good hand for tief, but he nebber guine tief rotten shu't. Look, Pomp, I 'speck he must be in de bottom day [there]!"

The search was vain. And Porgy stood aghast at the spectacle.

"What's to be done, Tom!"

"Is de buzzum good in de front?"

"Yes."

"Well! easy 'nuff. De coat cubber de back, you know. See yer! yer's de hole for put you head t'rough. When you guine dress, I 'tan behin' you and slip de shu't ober, and when you hab 'em on, I get t'read [thread] and make Pussy 'titch [stitch] two t'ree, sebben, five 'titch cross de back for hold de two side togedder. Da's de way for do 'em; I see. I guine fix em."

A white vest was found in the valise; a leather stock, a pair of yellow buckskin gloves; and, after a fashion, Porgy succeeded in displaying, ready for use, the entire habit which he was to wear that day. This done, he proceeded, with the help of Tom and Pomp, to put himself in harness.

Talk of the iron garments of ancient chivalry! Never did the closing of rivets on the part of the knights of the English Harrys and Edwards, on the eve of battle, require more time and painstaking, or cause more anxiety to pages and squires, and armor-bearers and armorers, then did the costuming of their master, that day, occasion to his two sable attendants. Such gingerly handling of coat, and vest, and shirt, and small-clothes, was, perhaps, scarcely ever beheld before. The adjustment of the captain's linen, was especially a subject of some solicitude. While he sat upon a keg, Tom, standing on one side, and Pomp on the other, the former quietly dropped the garment, shorn of its fair proportions, over his neck.

While Porgy buttoned it at the throat, and slipped his arms into the sleeves, the two attendants seized the skirts at a signal, and drawing the sundered sides as nearly together as they dared, Pussy, the girl, with a dozen successive stitches, united the reluctant skirts, but not so as to cover a large waste of territory between, which, until Porgy could get his vest and coat on, remained as bare in back as a Pict in full armor. Porgy sat erect during the operation, never daring even to move, until Tom gave him permission by telling him —

"You kin feel yourse'f a leetle now, maussa; but tek kear how you ben' you back, and 'tretch out you' arm, tell you git on you coat and weckset. Dis here shu't nebber guine tan' pull and jerk, mek' 'em easy as you kin."

"*Feel* myself *a little*, indeed! I certainly should like to feel myself less? — Hand me those shoes, Pomp!"

"Ha! Hello! Boy! — Wha' dis? You never bin brush you maussa shoes ebber sence he bin trabble in all dat mud wid 'em?"

"I no see any brush, uncle Tom!"

"Ha! you no see any brush, you bull eye nigger! I tek' hole' ob you, I show you brush on de back wid sights ob hick'ry. Git out, and fin' piece ob clot', and see you rub off de mud from dem boot' fore I kin crook my elbow. Clot' is brush, you warmint, ef you use 'em so."

Pomp was off, and Porgy resigned himself patiently on the keg, which sufficed him for a chair, until his inexperienced "*valley de sham*" could re-appear. Meanwhile, Tom handed him his hunting-shirt.

"Look you, maussa," said the cook, as he helped his master on with the coat—"You hab for walk 'traight in dis coat. He aint so 'trong arter all. You mus' tek' care and no t'row youse'f 'bout when you at Miss Ebleigh's. Ef you forgit, sometime, and t'row out you arm too wide, you'll breck somewhere, I know; in de sleeb, or under de arm, or mout be in de back; an' ef once he begin for go, dere's no stopping 'em. You'll breck all side, I tell you, and de breeches will be for busting out too; and dat won't do no how, when you da 'stan' [stand] 'fore de ladies. Min' wha' I tell you, maussa, and walk 'traight track. Be berry preticklar, jis' when you's gitting off de hoss; and when you's a-walking up de steps, don't you 'tretch out for hol' de bannister; and when you's a-talking big wid de lady, you mustn't tink for raise up you arm to de heabens, as ef you was a-calling de sun, and de moon to be witness for wha' you say. 'Twon't do: —you'll be breck out ebbry side ef you guine try for do all dem mighty t'ings. Set down easy in de chair, and don't you go for 'traddle you legs too wide. I no 'pen' [depend] 'pon dese breeches 't all."

"It's come to a pretty pass, indeed, when such a sooty scamp as you are, Tom, undertakes to teach me how to carry myself in a lady's presence."

"Enty I know?"

"So, you think I had better not lift my leg unadvisedly so—"

"Top, maussa; you sure for bu'st dem breeches."

"Or throw out my arms, right or left,—so!"

"Lawd! maussa, don't you now! De coat is ready for pop ebbry way."

"I feel it, Tom! I shall be cautious for my own sake, not less than for decency's. But, be off; send Pomp to me with the shoes, old fellow, and see what you can do toward fixing up the lieutenant and the sergeant. They'll need quite as much help as myself, I fancy, in preparing themselves for this visit."

Tom disappeared. The shoes were soon brought by Pomp, and drawn on with a degree of care and deliberation which showed that our captain of partisans was as duly sensible as Tom of the danger which might follow any extraordinary efforts of muscle on his part. He felt himself, at length, completed for his visit, all but cap and sword. The sword, however absurd it might seem, was still an essential in his present habit, which was wholly military. It was still justified, in use, by the unsettled condition of the country, and we must not be surprised to see him, on his departure for the city, not only wearing his sabre, but carrying his holsters and pistols; and this, chiefly, with due regard to propriety of costume. But we must not anticipate. To buckle on his sabre, and don his well-worn coonskin cap, was the work of a moment. The horses had been already saddled, and were in waiting in the court below. The voice of Millhouse was heard calling, and the heavy tread of himself and Frampton were echoing loudly in the hall. They were evidently ready, and Porgy joined them.

"Let's look at you, cappin," quoth Millhouse, "and see how you're a-looking." And he walked round his superior, scrutinizing him at every point.

"Your sk*a*irt's *rether* short," quoth he.

"Do you see the blisters—the leather patches—sergeant?" demanded Porgy, quickly.

"N—o!" answered the sergeant slowly, peering about curiously the while; "but as you love your life, cappin, you mustn't bend for'ad the leetlest, for you aint got any *skairts* to spare. Your gairth is so mighty big that it draws up the gairments monstrous high."

"To horse!" cried Porgy, with something very emphatic in his tones, leading the way.

"Stop a bit!" said the sergeant, "while I take in another hole in your belt. It'll better your figger a leetle; though 'taint easy to help it much."

"D—n the figure!" exclaimed the indignant captain, breaking away, without suffering the intended service.

"Look you, cappin, ef you splurges about in that sort of style you'll resk mightily the security of all your fixins."

We shall say nothing about the costume of the captain's subordinates. Enough that they partook of the deficiencies, and provoked the same sort of embarrassments, which we have seen troubling their superior. They had done their best to prepare for the eyes of the lady, and they, at least, had no misgivings, as troubled with no expectations. A word to Tom, and another word to old Sappho, who could not sufficiently admire the wonderful dimensions, the great sword, and the fearful looking pistols of her child, and the three cantered off at a free pace, in the direction of the widow Eveleigh's. When approaching the avenue, the sergeant suddenly drew up, and entreated the attention of the captain for a moment.

"Cappin," says he, "now's the time. Head's up! Off'cers to the front. Cappin! It all *im*pends upon you now! One thing I've got to say: a widow aint like a young gal. She's *got* ixperence. 'Taint any needeessity, when you 'tacks a widow, to be guine all about it, and about it. They don't aix that of you. They onderstands. 'Taint any use to ride round to the gate; jest pull down the fence and ride in. What did I say to you afore? A widow's jest like a fort that's used to surrenderin'. It's only to summon it and say here we are to make a breach, or run over the walls. Jest show yourself ready to scale and storm, and what does the commander of the garrison say? Why, says he—let's make good *tai*rms and that's all we're axing—and that's what the widow'll say; but I wouldn't make the *tai*rms too easy, cappin. You're needing a mighty deal of assistance. Hold her to it. Give her no chaince, and when she finds you ready to seize, she'll give in. She kain't help herself. Only, don't you be mealy-mouthed, cappin! Go it, like a charge!"

Porgy surveyed the speaker for a moment in the most perfect silence. Then quietly, with a smile, he said, clapping spurs to his horse—

"Millhouse, you were surely born to be a general!"

In another moment the party was pacing up the noble avenue of ancient oaks conducting to the mansion of the wealthy widow.

CHAPTER XLVII.

THE SERGEANT PUTS THE CAPTAIN FAVORABLY FORWARD.

THE plantation of Mrs. Eveleigh was one of the finest and best kept along the Ashepoo. The widow had been fortunate in the circumstances which secured her equally against the hostility of both parties during the late war. She had friends at court, no matter who was sovereign for the season. Her husband had been a popular officer in his British majesty's army, and, when not on service, had been a favorite among his neighbors. The widow shared his popularity, possessing, in eminent degree, those qualities of character by which he had secured it. Her estate, accordingly, had escaped that harrying process, by which so many of those around her had been devastated; and the excellence of the land, the skill, sobriety and integrity of her overseer; good seasons, profitable staple (rice) and her own judicious economy, had resulted in a constant increase, by which she had become one of the wealthiest persons of this region of country. She lived, during the greater portion of the year, upon her estate, and this had been an additional secret of her prosperity. Her presence had served, not only to promote the success but the charm and beauty of her plantation. Her fields were well distributed, always kept clean and under good fences; the grounds were well laid out; the undergrowth kept down; the woods trimmed up; the groves, whether of oak or other forest-trees, such as wooed the wandering footstep, and appealed sweetly to the musing fancies. Long shadowy avenues, on three sides, conducted to her dwelling which stood among sheltering clumps of a growth extending far beyond all human memory; while the house itself, of ample dimensions, and built in a style at once tasteful and simple, was furnished with all the attractions which, in that day, distinguished the mansions of American refinement.

The morning was a mild and bright one. As Captain Porgy and his two companions cantered up the avenue, Mrs. Eveleigh might be seen, with her son, sitting in the open piazza.

"They're on the look out for us, cappin," said the sergeant, with an air of triumph. "She's mighty airnest to see you, I tell you. Now, cappin, 'member what I've said. Now's the time. All the signs is favorable. Don't you let the chaince slip through your fingers. No man gits a widow by being bashful about it. It's the bold heart, a'ter all, that gits the good things of this life. When the fruit's ripe it's only to shake the tree. You needn't climb, but jest take hold, like a man, with a detarmination like, never to let go, 'till your eend's answered. That's all. Now go ahead."

With the air of a man who has given the last words of counsel to a young beginner, when sending him forward to the fight, our sergeant waved his one hand, and suffered his superior to ride ahead. Porgy answered only with a faint smile. He seemed uneasy, if not chafed at the pertinacious conceit of his follower; while Lance Frampton, when Millhouse had fallen back and joined him, took occasion to school the veteran in unexpected style, and with some warmth.

"Look you, sergeant, 'twont do for you to be talking to the captain as if he was a boy, and you was his teacher. You'd better be quiet now before you make him angry. He knows you're his friend, and that makes him stand a good deal from you; but what can you teach him about fine people, and high life, and the sort of behavior he's to behave when he's in company with rich ladies in their own houses. He knows more of such people than you and I ever saw, and don't want any education how to do when he gets among 'em. You'd better shut up now in all these matters. I see he don't like it, and you'll some day go one step too far, and you'll rouse him."

Millhouse glared upon the lieutenant with mixed looks of surprise and indignation. When he recovered himself, he said:—

"And don't I know what's good for him, and don't I see what's needful to save him from the cussed sheriff. He must marry this rich widow, I tell you; that's his only chaince."

"Well, he won't, I'm thinking."

"Why won't he! She's eager enough, I see, to ax him herself."

"I don't believe a word of it; I don't believe she'll have him, and you're just doing wrong now, to put such ideas into his head."

"She won't!—Lord, Lance? as ef you had any ixperence to know. Why, look what she's done for him a'ready; and look at her axing you and me to come and spend the day and take dinner. Don't you know, as well as me, that these people never yet axed people of our sort into their houses, or let 'em set at their table. It's only bekaise we're friends of the cappin that she axes us."

"It's because we helped to save her son's life and her own It's because she's grateful; and if you're right-minded, you'll just be quiet all to-day while in her house, and be respectful, and listen only, and answer when you're spoken to, and just say as little as y 'u can in civility; for we ain't asked to be heard; it's only because she wants to be grateful. Now, I must say, sergeant, you've too great an ambition to be a-talking. The less you talk, the better; for though you're a sensible man enough, in actual service, yet you're not the person to speak the sort of things that the great people likes to hear."

"Well, I must say, there's no eend to the conceitedness of young people. Here, Lance, you, only a brat of a boy, as I may say—though a very good one—you're a-teaching me; and me old enough to be your gran' fayther. I wonder ef you won't, some day, show me how to work my way into my egg, by telling me to crack it at the butt, and on the eend of the table. Jest you don't consarn yourself, my boy, in this business of the cappin, and ef I don't help him to git this rich widow, then poke your finger at my eyes whenever I goes to talk."

"Take care! That's all, sergeant. You'll be burning your fingers, some day, by a fire that you won't see till you're in it and can't back out."

The warning was in low tones. The party was quite too nigh the house to admit of more. Captain Porgy was already dismounting—a performance executed with less deliberation than usual, yet more effort. Let us add that it was successful; whatever the peril to his garments, they survived it; and he proceeded to ascend the steps of the dwelling, conducting to the piazza. Young Arthur Eveleigh descended to meet him, catching his hand and welcoming him with a warm and hearty grasp, which declared the impulsive and generous nature of the boy. Mrs. Eveleigh stood at the head of the steps with her hand extended in welcome also. Her manner, simple and unaffected, genial and friendly, was that of the accomplished lady, well versed in the proper graces of society. Arthur Eveleigh remained on the steps to receive the followers of the partisan. These were welcomed up also; and a gracious bow was accorded them by the widow, when they reached the piazza. Here, they all seated themselves, following the example of the lady and the captain.

"The day is so mild and genial," said the widow, "that we have suffered the fire to go out. But you soldiers scarcely need a fire; and Arthur and myself, since breakfast, have not felt the want of one. We have been talking of you and your brave followers, captain, all the morning;—going, for the twentieth time, over all the details of that fearful day, from the perils of which you rescued us."

"Too happy you will believe, my dear Mrs. Eveleigh, in being of the slightest service to you," was the gallant answer of the captain.

"That was a most bloody leetle skirmage," put in the sergeant. "Them rascals gin you a most awful hitch, ma'am; and ef twarnt for the cappin thar, there's no telling what might have happen'd in the long run. It's the cappin, ma'am, that's about the best man, I ever seed, to fight for the women folk. He was born, I may say, to be their sav'or and purtector!"

Porgy glared sternly at the speaker, who, fancying he had been making a highly profitable, yet delicate suggestion, leered first at the widow, then at the captain while he spoke, with the manner of one who seems to say, "I have set the ball in motion —see that it don't come to the ground between you."

Mrs. Eveleigh answered the sergeant with a kind manner, saying—

"We owe him a great deal, certainly, sir, but we owe equally our gratitude to yourself and your young companion. My son, I am sure, will always regard you both as his friends, and if I do not adequately acknowledge your help, it is only because all language must fail to do so. I feel that, but for your arrival and timely and judicious succor, my son and all of us would have been murdered."

"That you would, ma'am! Them villains warn't a bit too good to sculp you in the bargain; but they've got their sass and dressing, and some on 'em will never trouble the high roads of this airth agin. For them that got off, it's jest enough to know that the cappin's in these quarters, and they'll be mighty cu'rous how they keeps out of them. I don't think they'll be the pussons to break into any henroosts in this part of the country. Ef there was any man in this world born to be the nateral protector of a plantation, it's the cappin thar."

Porgy twitched uneasily in his chair, while the sergeant proceeded —

"Lawd, ma'am, to think that a pusson that can cut his way through an inimy's bloody bagnets, a whole rigiment, should be so tender at the same time, and sich a purtector of poor, trembling, dangerous wimmin! To think how a pusson that shouts so furious when he's at a charge — how soft he kin make his voice when it's to a woman he's got to speak! It's a-most wonderful, and not to be calkilated, the difference 'twixt the same man, when he's at them different dealings!"

Porgy could stand it no longer. He broke out —

"Why, Millhouse, Mrs. Eveleigh will suppose that I have employed you especially as my trumpeter, and not as my overseer. Shut up! my good fellow, or speak of your own valor and your own tenderness, if you please. As I have no apprehensions that I shall be suspected of any deficiency when either is needed it is no policy to insist upon them now, lest both of them becomes suspected."

The widow saw the captain's uneasiness and smiled pleasantly, as she said —

"The problem seems to puzzle Sergeant Miller —"

"Mill*house*, ma'am, ef you please."

"Millhouse — Sergeant Millhouse —"

"There was a Sergeant Mil*ler*, ma'am, that b'longed to the Pennsylvany rigiment, and he went over to the innimy on that bloody affair when they wanted to sell Gineral Greene — you remember, I reckon; that time when the gineral sent off full speed to call the old fox, and we poor malitia men to keep his continentallers in order."

"I remember, sergeant. I am glad you corrected my error.

It must be an unpleasant thing to be confounded, even by mistake, with a traitor."

"That's it, ma'am; you're sensible on the subject."

"Was there ever such a bullheaded monster!" quoth Porgy *sotto voce.* "You were remarking, Mrs. Eveleigh—"

"Upon the problem that seemed to puzzle Sergeant Mill*house*," emphasizing the last syllable duly. "Yet, it seems to have been proverbial that the most brave-hearted are also the most tender-hearted, always, captain."

"The effect has commonly shown itself in the number of wars which have been occasioned by the sex, Mrs. Eveleigh. It is proverbial, also, that, when all other arguments fail to inspire the man with the proper courage, you have only to goad him in the presence of the lady whom he most admires."

"Ef anything will make him fight, ma'am, that will," put in the sergeant. "It's jest what you sees daily with these common dunghill fowls. They hain't got much heart for fighting at any time, yet, jest let the hen be nigh, when one's a-coming; and the other, though he run before, will dash up, and Lord, how he will make the feathers fly!—It's natur! and it shows the valley of the women in keeping up a good breed of sodgers in a country. And I do say that the women folks had as much to do in making our people fight the innimy as anything beside, and all besides. I 'member well, when I went out with Gineral Middleton agin the Cherokees. Well, you know thar was Grant, with his British rig'lars, along with us; and no great shakes they was, I tell you, in an Ingin skrimmage. Well, it used to make my very blood bile in my body, to see how them red coats made free with our young women at the farmhouses. Why, ma'am, they made no more ado of chucking the gals under the chin, and smacking at their lips, jest wherever they found 'em, than I would at kissing my own wife — ef 'taint ondecent for me to speak of my wife when I ain't got one, and never ixpect to have. But that ain't to pervent other people, what's more personable and better off, from getting a wife, I'm thinking."

And here the sergeant looked, with a leer the most significant and complacent, to the captain of partisans, whose disquiet was duly increasing. Mrs. Eveleigh, too, began to comprehend that there was something latent in the sergeant's speeches; but she had no notion of his real purpose, and ascribed whatever was queer in his manner and words, to some eccentricity of character. Meanwhile, Arthur Eveleigh had attached himself to Lance Frampton, and the two young men had gone out to the stables. The widow felt the call to be elsewhere, but could not leave the parties at the moment; and the conversation proceeded, the lady opening upon another topic which was necessarily addressed wholly to the captain.

"You find everything in disorder, Captain Porgy. You have been a special sufferer, I know. You are probably not aware that I am in possession of some of your property."

"Indeed!"

"Yes. As an old friend of your family and self, when I heard of certain bands of loyalists about, knowing the practices of which they were guilty, I sent over several of my hands, and, with the aid of your servants, brought over to my house such of your furniture as had been left after their first foray. One Grainger had been before me, and had destroyed the family pictures, and made a fire, I was told, of certain pieces of furniture. As soon as he disappeared with his band, I secured your sideboard, a couple of chests of drawers, a few chairs and tables, a pair of fine old steel mirrors, and a variety of other articles, including knife-case, with knives and forks, decanters, glasses, and sundry small things, such as you will find useful. There was no plate that we could find—"

"It was all melted down in camp, Mrs. Eveleigh. We have been living on it in part—"

"Ah! I conjectured that; though, by the way, the report is that your own overseer, Halford, helped to spoil you, and would have effectually done so, but that he was accidentally killed at a great muster of the loyalists, near Coosawhatchie."

"He turned out to be a great scoundrel; went over to the British after serving a campaign with us. I suspected him before that event, and my discoveries probably led to his treachery. But I had not supposed that anything had been saved from the wreck of my furniture. My debt to you increases every hour, Mrs. Eveleigh."

"By no means, captain. I shall owe you a debt which my whole life could not repay."

"That's it!" cried Millhouse, slapping his thigh with his one hand. "That's it! I know'd it."

Porgy gave him a single stern look—then turning to the widow, said—

"Do not talk of any debt to me, my dear Mrs. Eveleigh; you owe me none. What was done for your rescue, by myself and my companions, would have been done in behalf of the poorest creature of the country—"

"Let me interrupt you, captain, by saying that, in like manner, what I have done for the saving of your chattels, in your absence, would have been done for any other neighbor. But, the better course would be to say nothing of these mutual services, however much we feel them."

"Edzactly—but the *feeling!*—" and the sergeant closed. The widow proceeded—

"I am rejoiced that I shall have you again for a neighbor!"

"And *nara* [never a] better *pur*tector of wimmen could be found!" quoth the sergeant, with an emphatic slap of his one hand upon his thigh. The lady did not seem to observe him, but proceeded.—

"And if in any respects I can be of service to you, particularly at the present moment, you have only to let me know, and—"

"There's a want of *everything*, I may say, ma'am, from plough to shovel. You see, ma'am, I'm to manage for the cappin, who's got some of the finest rice lands on this river."

"He has, indeed. I know them," said the widow.

"That's it, ma'am! You're right! It's so! I seed 'em; and they've had a long rest. They'll bring *all*fired fine crops; and I'll make 'em do it. Ef we had *your* force on them lands, now, Madam Eb'leigh, there's no telling what I could do! No, ma'am! There's no telling, 'twould be so magnisifent! But we've got only a mighty small force of *twenty-five* niggers!—"

This was said with a wave of the one hand and a twitching of the mouth, and a turning up of the nose, as if nothing could be more contemptible in the sight of the speaker. The air was that of one, who, born to command armies, was reduced to the necessity of expending his genius upon a corporal's guard. But the widow's surprise was at the number, not at their insignificance.

" Twenty-five !"

" A second instance of good fortune, my dear Mrs. Eveleigh.
When I encountered you, I knew not that I had a negro in the
world, besides Tom. You restored me seven; last night, my
old nurse, Sappho, who has survived the wars and starvation for
three years in the swamp, came in, and reported all her children
and grand children as with her. She brought them in this
morning, eighteen in number—"

" And who knows ma'am but there may he a hundred more
where them come from," interposed Millhouse, dilating again
into great dignity.

" Not likely! I fancy these are all I possess, Mrs. Eveleigh;
they are more than I expected, and much more, perhaps than
I deserve."

" It's not onpossible, ma'am, that there's a hundred. How
should the cappin know? He's quite onknowing of all his sarcumstances, and for that matter, aint altogether the best pusson
in the world to be looking a'ter them. That's what I tells him.
Leave it all to me, cappin. He knows I'm right. He ecknowl-
edges I'm his sense-keeper; and *I am*, in all business that
b'longs to the making of a crap—"

" In all other matters too, it would appear. But, for the present, Millhouse, suffer me to be my own sense-keeper."

" You kaint, cappin, 'taint in you. Why, Madam Eb'leigh,
he's the most wasteful and perfligit pusson in this heathen
world. With, perhaps, not more than a hundred guineas in his
pocket, he don't stop to throw one or two on 'em away, at a single lift, upon a beggar child, in charity like."

" A hundred guineas, sergeant? Why what are you talking
about?" said Porgy, indignantly. " He has certainly the most
overwhelming imagination! He has converted these eight or
ten pieces into a treasure!"— With the words, Porgy drew forth
the few gold pieces which he had, from his pocket, and exposed
them in his palm to view.

" This is all that I possess in the shape of money."

The sergeant wheeled about, indignant at the exposure, drawing up every feature in vexation, and tossing his one hand in air
as if everything were lost. The widow saw the action, and began to understand his character. She looked to Porgy with a

smile. He strove to smile in reply, but the effort was a feeble one, and the result only a faint and counterfeit presentment. He was disquieted the more, as he began to fear, from the widow's looks, that she not only saw into Millhouse's character, but suspected his desires. It was, accordingly, something of a relief to both the parties when Arthur Eveleigh, just at this moment, reappeared with the lieutenant. Mrs. Eveleigh seized the occasion to invite her guests to take refreshment, and led the way for them into the dwelling. As Porgy followed, Millhouse nudged him with his elbow.

"How could you do it?" he murmured—"Show jest that leetle heap when I was a-spreading you out?"

"Pshaw, fool!" was the muttered thunder which saluted the sergeant in reply, the captain fiercely pressing forward, and completely covering the entrance as he did so.

"Fool!" growled the sergeant to himself. "Well, that's for sarving a pusson what don't desarve it."

"Here is some old Madeira, captain, and some Jamaica. Please show the way to your friends—my son does not drink."

"Why, ma'am," quoth Millhouse, possessing himself of a beaker, and approaching the widow—"you don't mean to let the young man go without a sodger's edication."

"His father was a soldier, sir, yet it was his dying injunction that Arthur should never drink."

"Well, that's mighty strange, I swow!   'Twouldn't ha' done in *our* sarvice, where the only way to forgit that you had nothing to eat, was to git r'yal drunk on what you had. Here's your health, ma'am, and my sarvice to you, ma'am, for ever."

The lady bowed, and Porgy, having refreshed himself with such a glass of Madeira as he had not often enjoyed for years, withdrew, at a motion from Mrs. Eveleigh, to an adjoining room.

"Why, whar's the cappin!" cried Millhouse, who had been lingering over his liquor.

"And whar's the widow, too?" looking around him. Young Arthur stared at this familiarity, but his glance was not remarked by the speaker, "Ah! I see!" he continued, with a chuckle. "All's right! Lawd, ef people only had the sense to see the thing what's afore 'em."

"What did you say, sir!" said young Arthur, addressing our

soliloquist — and evidently somewhat dubious that there was something offensive in what he had spoken; forming this conjecture rather from the expression of Millhouse's face than from anything in his words.

"Oh! it's you, young master! So, you're not to drink while you live! Well, to a man whose nater is usen'd to the thing, like mine, that would be mighty hard! But you don't feel the hardship yit; and you're young. But it's a darn'd sight better, let me tell you, never to l'arn to like it, than to long for it arterwards when it's not to be got. That's a feeling, let me tell you, for I've had it, jest as much like the devil having you on an eend and no help for it, as anything on this etarnal airth. But, Lord, to know as how you kaint drink makes me a leetle thirsty, and ef it's your pleasure, I'll score me down two."

"If you please, sir," answered the young man; an assent for which the veteran did not wait. He had already prepared the Jamaica. Lifting the draught which he had mixed, he pointed to Lance Frampton — "Now," said he — "thar's one that makes his own law agin liquor. He won't taste a bit, but only to pleasure company, and then he takes it most like as ef 'twas physic. There's something wrong in one's natur, when you see that. It's a sign he aint got nateral good taste and good sense. And he aint. He's good at a scout and he kin shoot like blazes, rifle or Ingin bow; and he's not afear'd of Samson and Zebeedee, the Philistians; but, Lord, that's all; he aint the sense; he kaint see; kaint see some things when they're jest onder his nose, and a' axing him to look and be satisfied."

Frampton laughed, and Arthur Eveleigh followed his example. The latter now began narrowly to consider Millhouse as a study. The sergeant, finding that he had secured attention, strode the floor, glass in hand, sipping and dilating as he went. At last, finishing his glass, he said to Arthur:—

"Your ma! she's out with the cappin somewhere, eh! They've got some sly talking to do together?"

There was a grin on his face as he spoke, which young Eveleigh could not comprehend, and which he did not by any means relish. He simply bowed affirmatively.

"Ha!" said Millhouse laying his one hand on the youth's shoulder,—"the cappin's the man to show you fine things. He's a most wonderful man, and you'll l'arn to like him famous,—to love him I may say—to love him as ef he was a born friend, and brother, an uncle, and a son,—as ef he was your own born father. Eeny young man on this airth might be happy to have him for a father!"

"Is he drunk?" queried Arthur, when he and Lance again got out together, which they did soon after.

"No!" said the other—"it's only a strange way he's got of talking foolish things—he don't know much what."

———

CHAPTER XLVIII.

PORGY FINDS A BANKER.

THE widow motioned the captain to a seat, and took one near him. Her manner was full of the sweetest frankness, and an easy familiarity. With a smile, as soon as he had seated himself, she said—

"Captain Porgy, I am about to take a liberty with you, which you must excuse on the score of old acquaintance, near neighborhood, the interest I feel in your prosperity, and the gratitude which I owe you for the great service which you have so lately rendered me."

"Do not speak of that, Mrs. Eveleigh——"

"Oh! but I must speak of it, captain, in some degree to justify myself, if only *to* myself, for the freedom which I take with you."

"Ah! madam," with a courtly bow and expressive smile, "you can have no sufficient idea of the extent of your own privileges, where I am concerned."

"Thank you," answered the lady, quietly; "I am disposed to presume upon them, and will say what I have to deliver without further apologies."

"Pray do so, my dear madam."

"Briefly, then, captain, I am not ignorant of the embarrassments which environ you, and the difficulties in the way of your
success. I know how much you have been a loser by the war,
and how great were your obligations before the war began."

"Ah! madam, do not, I pray, remind me how greatly I have
been the profligate."

"I will not, unnecessarily. You have only committed a too
common error of our people in these parishes; allowing hospitality and good fellowship to fling prudence out of the windows.
Of course, you have to pay the usual penalties; but it is due to
you that your friends should see that you do not suffer too greatly.
At this moment, what is left to you of your property can only
be made of profit to you, by the help of a little ready money;
and of this commodity I suspect, you have not been able to find
enough in the army chest of General Marion to pay up your account against the country. You have got but little pay at the
close of the war."

"Not a copper, ma'am! A few guineas,—as you have seen
—the loan of a friend, enough to pay my way for a week in the
city——"

"I thought so. Now you will want supplies for the plantation;
clothes for the negroes; provisions, utensils; a thousand things
which it should be your policy to buy *for cash*, at this moment
when money is scarce, and the stock in the city is necessarily
large. With provisions, I can supply you on an easy credit;
implements and utensils for working the crop, I can lend you for
present use; I have a wagon to spare you for a season; and——"

"Ah! my dear madam, you overwhelm me!"

"Hear me out, captain! With all these things I can supply
you without the slightest inconvenience myself; nay, driving a
good bargain with you all the while. Oh! you will see that I
am sufficiently selfish. True, I can *lend* you second-hand ploughs
and shovels, hoes and axes, cart and wagon; but I mean to sell
you corn and bacon at a good price——"

"But the pay!"

"Oh! I know you have no money, but you have credit——"

"I don't know——"

"Yes, you have; with *me*, at least, captain, and you must use
it. You shall have corn and fodder, rice and bacon, on loan, or

on a credit, as you think proper. If you make a good crop this season, return me what you borrow, *if you can;* if not, you shall pay me, *when able,* at the present rates for these articles."

"You are very indulgent, my dear madam, but—"

"Hear me a little farther. I must have no 'buts.' You will need money in the city. You might borrow it there, *possibly;* though that is very doubtful at this moment. But it is fortunate that I can help you to a sum adequate to your necessities and wants."

"My dear Mrs. Eveleigh—"

"Stop, captain, let me do the talking for awhile, if only in the assertion of my feminine privilege. Wait till I confess to the exhaustion of *my* budget, and you can then proceed to show the contents of yours. I have some money not only to spare, but some that I desire to lend. I wish it out at interest. I wish it safely invested. It is no great deal, yet I should not like to lose it. It will be safe in your hands. I can let you have five hundred guineas."

Porgy's face saddened. His head drooped into his palms. For a moment he was silent. Then raising his head, he said—

"This is a great kindness, Mrs. Eveleigh, which is more precious to me by far than the possession of all your wealth. It touches me, my dear madam, to the soul. It takes from me the power to answer. How shall I answer—how declare my thoughts, my thanks, my gratitude—"

"It is my turn now to employ your own language. Not a word of gratitude. Let us speak of this only in the way of business. It is a business transaction simply. I have money to put out at interest, and you would borrow money. You shall have mine—"

"Here, again, my dear madam, I must falter. I certainly do need money, but it will be at the lender's peril that he lends. I have no security to offer."

"What! With one of the best rice-plantations along the river, and twenty-five negroes?"

"Ah! madam, you know not half of my ill-fortune. You do not know that my plantation is mortgaged to a voracious creditor, for thrice its value, and that this mortgage pressed, at this juncture, will swallow every negro that I own."

" I know the whole—the worst! I know that you are at the
mercy of one M'Kewn, a person who is supposed to show no
mercy if a selfish policy prompts the other way ; I know that he
has a lien upon your plantation, to a far greater amount than the
place will sell for; but I also understand, captain, that he has no
lien upon your negroes—"

" Ah ! madam, how is that ?"

" These are not mortgaged. They will become liable for your
debt to M'Kewn should he obtain a judgment against you, and a
part of my scheme is to make you indebted *to me*, that we may
save these negroes *from him*. You shall *borrow* my money, *buy*
my corn and bacon, and give *me* a mortgage upon the negroes,
which shall at all events secure them from him."

" You are my saving angel. By Jove, my dear madam, you
take me from out of the depths. I have been desponding, in
the very slough of despair, for a week past. You hold me up
by the locks while drowning. I accept your offer. Now that I
can give you security, I will take your loan. God bless you,
my dear Mrs. Eveleigh, you have made my heart of a sudden
very light."

The captain caught the widow's hand, carried it to his lips,
and kissed it fervently. At that moment, he thought it the
prettiest and whitest hand he had ever seen. When he looked
up, the widow saw the moisture in his eyes, but, like a considerate
lady, took no heed of it. She proceeded without seeming conscious of his raptures.

" This understood, captain, let us see how the arrangement can
be carried out. In anticipation of your acceptance of my proposition, I had prepared these letters. Here is one for Saunders &
Dart, which will procure for you five hundred guineas, or even
more should you need it, on your giving a mortgage upon a sufficient number of your slaves, their value to be estimated at the
present market prices."

" You shall have a mortgage upon them all, my dear madam."

The widow smiled.

" Not so, captain. You forget that twenty-five negroes are
worth a great deal more."

" True ; but I prefer that they should be secured to you, lest
they fall into worse hands."

"But, my dear sir, suppose I were to die, what would be your security? My lien would be a valid one."

"My security is in your son. You have only to confide to him the transaction. I have every confidence that a son, trained by you, must be a youth of honor."

The widow looked at the speaker with affectionate gravity.

"Be it so," she said; "I will, however, see that there shall be a legal security which shall protect you, even from my son. Here is another letter which I should suppose scarcely necessary, since you, yourself, must know the party to whom it is addressed."

Porgy read the address—

"'Charles Cotesworth Pinckney!'—surely, I know him well. We have served together! I knew him well before the war."

"Nevertheless, take the letter, and confide your legal difficulties to him. He must save you from M'Kewn, if possible. He can do so, if anybody can. I have already spoken to him of your affairs; do you get him to revise your accounts with M'Kewn. There are some particulars, in respect to this man, which move me to suspect him of great frauds in your case and that of other persons. At present, I will say nothing of what I know or suspect; but if I could recover the box which was stolen from me the other day by these outlaws, I could show you a paper which, I think, would give us a hold upon this person, M'Kewn, by which we should compel him to come to reasonable terms. But it is needless that we should speak of this now. Here are the letters. I have said all that I have to say."

"You have saved me, Mrs. Eveleigh. What woman would have done for me what you have done?"

"Many, I trust; knowing the circumstances, and in the same condition to serve you."

The captain shook his head, and, taking her hand, said—

"You are a wonder of a widow! You have the soul of a man!"

She smiled.

"I suppose I must take such a speech as a compliment, coming from one of the masculine gender."

"Ah!" said he, "you know what I mean! You are not a girl —not a child—not frivolous or feeble. You *have* a soul! You have earnestness and simplicity, and these make sincerity of character. You have faith, too, and—"

"Which, by the way, captain, is not often a manly virtue.—There, I fancy, is where our sex has the advantage of yours. You, perhaps, are an exception. Here, for example, you are willing to trust me and my boy, with all your property, without any security."

"Ah, madam, I could cheerfully give it to you both, did you need it. The pleasurable feeling of sweet faith and confidence, and generouse unreserve, and liberal sympathy, which you have this day shown me, is more grateful to me than any amount of wealth or money. I now know where I can confide. I feel, too, that there is one, at least, who can confide in me. We do not watch each other as victims, or as birds of prey; seeking to devour, fearing to be devoured. Madam, if you will permit me, I will be your friend—your friend."

She gave him her hand.

"No more now, captain; let us go to the hall. I hear the dinner signal."

They rose; she led the way out, but paused at the door.

"By the way, captain, your one-armed soldier seems a very queer creature."

The captain seemed annoyed, and peered into the eyes of the widow, as if to fathom the extent of her discoveries or her suspicions.

"Yes," said he, "a very queer creature. He will say many things to surprise you. Army life sometimes spoils a good fellow, who, if he remained humble, might be a favorite. Don't heed him, I pray you. He is good enough in his way—devoted to me—imprudently devoted, I may say; and sometimes officious enough to save me against my will."

"Surely, you should not complain of such officiousness."

"I don't know! One would have a vote in these matters. The sergeant's friendship is not sufficiently indulgent. Still, he is devoted to me—would die for me, without a murmur, and fight for me to the last; but the scoundrel wants to *think* for me, also; and that is an offence—if the thing were not so ridiculous—that I should not much tolerate. His misfortune is not to know how much a simpleton he is."

"Simpleton! I should suppose him rather shrewd than simple," said the widow, with a smile.

"Yes; he is shrewd after a fashion—shrewd in all those respects which belong to his mode of life, and the narrow range of his intellect. He is shrewd, like the beaver or the possum: knows how to find a shelter for his hide, and can find, by instinct, where the corn and acorn may be gathered. He will house and hive, while I should freeze and starve, perhaps. It is his misfortune that his sharpness has stimulated his self-esteem, as is usually the case with persons of his class who prove successful. If, for example he should drive a great bargain in rice or butter, he would just as lief explain the law to Cotesworth Pinckney, as to Tom, my cook. Ten to one should he see you at the harpsichord, he will give you a lesson in music."

"I shall be careful how I afford him the chance."

"He is only a grub, a human grub, with a monstrous instinct for acquisition and saving; no more; but withal useful, and to be cherished—at a distance. I have suffered him to come too near, and familiarity has somewhat blunted me to his obtrusiveness. I see the evil of it only when he comes in contact with others. He has been faithful, however, and I can not cast him off. As long as I have a home, he must share it."

"Fordham tells me that he is to be your overseer."

"He volunteered; insists that he knows all about it; and has set his heart so completely upon it, that, even if I wished it otherwise, I could not well deny him. At all events, I will give him a fair trial this season."

"Fordham will cheerfully assist him."

"Oh! bless you, he fancies he can teach Fordham his business. I tell you he is a simpleton."

"But he must not be suffered to ruin your crop."

"Fordham shall assist *me*, with a hint, should there be any reason to suspect this danger. Meantime, dear madam, please give the fellow no heed. He will say many things that will startle, if not offend. But the blockhead means no evil.—Will you take my arm?"

CHAPTER XLIX.

THE SERGEANT PUTS A SPOKE IN THE CAPTAIN'S WHEEL.

As the captain and the widow emerged from the inner room into the hall, they discovered the sergeant pacing to and fro, around the apartment. As soon as he saw them, he exclaimed, almost loud enough for everybody to hear—

"Arm in arm, by the pipers. Lord! how the world moves!"

And he advanced to them, bowing, with the most complacent grin.

"Dinner is a-waiting, I'm a-thinking; but Lord! there's some business that mus'n't be hurried. A man must take his time, ma'am, in *some* things, even though the roast-beef is a-cooling on the dish. Eh, cappin!"

And, wheeling to leeward of the captain, as he spoke, he thrust the stump of his game-arm into the ribs of his superior. Porgy turned quickly, and gave the subordinate a look speaking daggers; but the other only grinned.

"All right, I see!" said he, "thar's the track. Go ahead!—Dinner below! I've been down a'ready to see how it's laid out. Things look mighty nice. Good management in this house.—Roast-beef for dinner;—a round of corn-beef—*also!* Tongue! cabbage! potatoes! Seen 'em all in the kitchen. Woman cook! Had a talk with her. Good cook enough; but scolds like thunder, and lays on with a double fist when the boy don't fly.—Hem!—How she kin laugh! It's a sensible woman that laughs out free. Sign there ain't no vinegar in the nater."

Such—as the widow and Porgy led the way into the basement—was the running fire of speech which the sergeant kept up audible to all. The widow laughed outright as she listened, and, though somewhat startled by the merry peal which he heard, we yet see that the reflections which it provoked in the mind of the old soldier were not of a disagreeable nature. Lance Frampton and young Eveleigh followed; the latter wondering, as well he might, at the speech and conduct of Millhouse; but satisfied to think, with Frampton, that he was simply silly and with no harm in him. The dinner-table was spread as the parties entered the saloon. The sergeant has already given us a notion of the viands put before them. The widow took her seat at one end of the table; her son at the other; Porgy occupied a side to himself, while the lieutenant and sergeant took the other. A couple of liveried servants were in waiting. The lady herself pronounced a grace, and the proceedings began. Porgy was in good spirits. His mind was somewhat relieved of its troubles, and the sight of dinner was calculated always to give it animation. The return to well-known aspects of civilization, so different from his camp experience, was also a source of unspeakable satisfaction.

"Ah! madam!" said he, "I feel, as I look around me, that I may once more become a gentleman. I have been little more than a savage for the last five years. The camp makes sad havoc in the tastes of a gentleman. Rough fare, rough usage, the bare earth for a table, lean beef, bad soup, no bread, frequently no salt, and bad cooking—these are enough to endanger any man's humanity. Talk of patriotism as you will, but, truth to speak, we pay a monstrous high price for it in such conditions as we have been subjected to in this warfare."

"But it does so sweeten the heart, cappin, when we gits a good dinner like this here, at the last. Now, this is what I calls a raal good dinner, Madam Eb'leigh. That roast is done jest to a right brownness; though I was beginning to git mighty jubous that it would be overdone, a-waiting for you and the cappin. I was beginning to think that you was a-sarving the cook onjustly. Now, you've got a mighty good cook, for a woman. She ain't edzactly up to our Tom, I'm a-thinking; but then Tom's a merracle of a cook, and at stew, roast, brile or bake, he ain't got his match, I've a notion, in the whole country. But your cook'll do. She's monstrous cross and ugly. I hed a talk with her in the kitchen afore dinner—but she knows how to do a thing, and the way she makes the leetle niggers fly, is a sensible sight for any man that wants to know how a nigger ought to be managed. Now, ef she was about six months under our Tom, he'd make her fuss-rate."

The sergeant made this long speech while waiting upon Frampton, who, on *public* occasions, like the present, officiated as his carver. This duty was not often needful in camp where one grasped his bannock in one hand and his slice of bacon in the other; where the carver was as frequently the broadsword as the knife, and the fingers supplied all deficiency of forks. Mrs. Eveleigh smiled as she answered—

"Old Peggy would scarcely tolerate being sent to school at this time of day, even to such a proficient as the captain's Tom. She has as rare an opinion of her own merits as a cook, as if she had graduated with all the honors fifty years ago. But I have no doubt of Tom's superior merits. Colonel Singleton has been frequent in his praises, and Cotesworth Pinckney insists upon him as beyond all comparison in a terrapin stew."

"Pinckney knows," said Porgy, "if any man. He has a proper taste for the creature comforts, and has done me the honor, frequently, to discuss with me Tom's performances in this preparation. But 'old Peggy' needn't fear comparison with anybody. This beef is excellent. Pray, Mrs. Eveleigh, how did you save your cattle from the marauders."

"As I saved everything else, captain, by having friends on both sides of the question. The leading whigs were personally friendly; while the rank and position of my husband, in the British army, secured me protection on that quarter. He was intimate, besides, with General Leslie, and this was of great importance to my interests. Since the general has been in command, I have lost nothing. The result, I confess, has made me somewhat unpatriotic. I supplied the enemy with aid and comfort, but always, in the phrase of the tradesmen, for a *consideration*. I sold cattle and rice to the commissaries, and always got the first prices. I thought it better wisdom to do this, than make enemies by refusing, and have my cattle driven off, and my houses burnt. The war, accordingly, which has ruined so many has made my fortune."

"Well, ma'am, ef you'll jest listen to me, you'll be axing how you're to keep the fortin! It's a mighty deal easier to make a fortin than to keep it. I reckon thar's few women that kin keep what they makes. It's for them to find out the right sort of hands to put it in. Ef they trusts themselves, it's a-most always sure to slip through their fingers. All women ought to have a guardeen, by law and natur'. And the guardeen, in course, ought to be a man-body. Now the nateral needcessity of a woman, I may say, jest so soon as she gits old enough, is to git a husband. A husband is the only nateral guardeen of a grown woman; and when she's so foolish that she hems and haws about it, the law, or, if thar's no law, the gov'nor, the gineral, or whatever's the off'cer in command, he ought to look through the ranks, and pick her out the right sawt of a man. That's what I say ought to be the way in every well-regilated family or country."

Having made this significant and philosophical speech, the sergeant plied his fork in his plate and gave his tongue a brief respite. The lady looked at the captain, whose consternation and chagrin, apparent in his face, gave it the most lugubrious expression; she smiled, and her blue eyes twinkled merrily; and he, unable to control the sudden impulse, laid down knife and fork, and burst into an uncontrollable fit of laughter. The widow felt the contagious influence and yielded to it. She laughed with the frank, hearty, impulsive spirit of girlhood. Arthur Eveleigh looked at both bewildered; but Lance Frampton, catching faint glimpses of the sergeant's impudent absurdities, and taking his cue from his superiors, chuckled in under tones, as in due respect for the company. Millhouse looked up with astonishment, fork in hand, prongs upward, and a huge gobbet of roast-beef hanging from them at the opening doorways of his jaws.

"Well, I'd jest like to know what's the fun about! I kain't see edzactly, but I reckon, now, it's something I've been a-saying, and I don't see what I've said so cur'ous. What's it? I only said that a grown woman, with a fortin, ought to hev' a guardeen, and I says that it's only nateral she should; and who's to be her guardeen, but a man-body, what kin take care of her and her property; and what man-body but her husband. An' what's to laugh at in all that, is what I don't edzactly see."

"That's good logic, sergeant, whatever we may say for the philosophy," quoth Porgy.

"Well, I don't mean it for any logic or philos'phy; but I mean it for the *nateral* law in the case; the straight fora'd up and down, *sense* and the religion and the reason of the thing;

and if it ain't all them, why I ain't fit to know nothing about man and woman in this breathing world, that's so full of them. I've sarved, Madam Eb'leigh, in many sitiwations, and that's why I've l'arned to know more things than other pussons; and what I say to you that's strange to your way of feeling and thinking, is, prehaps, only bekase you hain't seed so much of this airth, and the people in it, as I've seed and know'd. But what I says, I don't mean for no offence, ma'am, though, moutbe, the wisdom of the thing is what you hain't quite come up to, being a woman body, and not having an equal chance with we men pussons."

"Oh! no offence, sergeant; on the contrary, I am very much pleased at the novelty of your suggestions. They are, certainly, rather new to me——"

"I reckon'd as how they would be, ma'am. I hain't often found the pusson, man or woman, that know'd quite as much as me, and that's maybe, bekase they hain't had the chaince. You ladies, hain't much chaince in this world to l'arn much about it, seeing as how you lives pretty much to yourselves; and bekase when men talks to you, they us'ally talks about foolish things; music and dancing, and dress, and how people looks and talks, and what they says of one another and themselves. But, I don't *improve*, no how, of that way of talking. I don't see, bekaise a woman's a woman, that she shouldn't l'arn to be sensible like us men. But ef what I says is onpleasant to you, I'll stop. I don't mean no offence, no how, as I'm a free white pusson, and a sodger of liberty."

"Surely, no offence, sergeant; I beg that you will go on. I like to hear your views of these subjects."

Porgy gave the widow an appealing look, but her eyes twinkled back with glances of mischievous merriment. The worthy captain, by way of a diversion, seized the decanter.

"Mrs. Eveleigh, may I take wine with you?"

The widow graciously accorded the desired permission, and the parties bowed and sipped.

"Help yourself with wine, Lieutenant Frampton; Sergeant Miller, perhaps——"

"Mill-*house*, ma'am, ef you please."

"Pardon me, sergeant——"

"Oh! no offence, ma'am; only you see, there was one Miller, of the Pennsylvany Line, that was hung up for lying and stealing and sich like treasonable offences. He was a sort of Gineral Arnold for rapscalties, and I don't like to have my name called after him."

"I'm very sorry, Sergean Mill-*house;* but perhaps, you will join Lieutenant Frampton."

"Thank you, ma'am; but ef you please, I'd much prefer to hev' *you* for a partner; and, ef you'd let me, I'd rether try *my* liquor out of this here diccanter"—touching the Jamaica. "This old rum seems the nateral drink of a sodger. The wine is a trifling sort of liquor that's made, I'm a-thinking, most for the use of women."

"As you please, sergeant. Your good health, sir, and much happiness."

"The same to you, ma'am. A lady of your fortin' desarves all sorts of happiness, but, as I've been saying, thar's no safety for the fortin', and I may say thar's but leetle chaince for happiness, to any grown woman, onless she has a nateral guardeen, and that guardeen ought to be a good husband; and ef I was the woman, Madam Eb'leigh, to choose, I'd be for taking my husband out of the army. A sodger, who is an off'cer, is about the best of guardeens for a woman. He's naterally use to command, you see, and he'll keep all things straight. Ef so be you was invaded, why, here he is on the spot to defend the post, and rigilate the garrison, and train the troops, even though they be only nigger troops; and to carry 'em into battle with a hollering and a whooping that'll make the inimy trimble. Lord, ma'am, thar's no telling the vartues of such a guardeen in a family. He'll fight the enemy till all smokes ag'in, and, same time, he'll keep the garrison in right order, ready, at the word of command whether it's to fight or run. I wish you, ma'am, a nateral guardeen, from the line of the army, for the *pur*tection of your family and fortin'!"

Thus speaking, the sergeant waved his glass to the lady, and swallowed the contents of the tumbler at one gulph.—His eyes next sought the countenance of his captain, and he was taken aback by the mixed look of horror and anger which he there beheld. He could not understand the expression at all. He fancied he had been doing the thing most handsomely, and that he should thereby secure the captain's eternal gratitude. He had somehow received the impression that Porgy was rather a bashful person among women, and he felt that it was a ·becoming duty on his part, to help him forward, and make the way clear before him. That he should have only annoyed and mortified him never occurred to him for a single moment; and he did not even now, while he watched the looks of his superior, fancy for a second that he had given any cause for the expression of countenance which he saw him wear. He rather thought that the captain labored under some sudden indisposition.

"Air you sick, cappin? You look so. Somethin's disagreed with you, I reckon."

"I should think so!" answered Porgy, with an audible groan.

"Take some of that Jamaica," cried the veteran, pushing the decanter across the table. "It's that Frenchified stuff you've been a-drinking. I never did hev' any opinion of that sort of washy liquor. Try the Jamaica."

"Not a drop, sir!" answered the captain, sternly, pushing the bottle from him. "Not a drop. You cannot know what's the matter, sir; if you could——"

Porgy arrested himself. Speech and look were equally tending to an explosion. Millhouse very complacently responded—

"Well, thar's mighty few cases of trouble in the body, that I kain't know what to do for. There's the stomach and the liver, and the witals,—why, cappin, for any trouble in either of them, there's no physic like Jamaica. Sometimes it's an inside, sometimes it's an outside, epplication; but every way it's a-most always good. I don't mean to say, Madam Eb'leigh, that it's so good as Madara for troubles of women as for the troubles of men; but I'd rether resk my chainces on Jamaica, than on eeny other physic I ever seed. It's most powerful vartious in curing me of my troubles. Why, ma'am, when it's the bowels, we'll say—"

"Sergeant Millhouse!" cried Porgy, in a voice of thunder.

"Cappin!"

"Silence in the ranks, sir!"

"I'm shet up!" responded, *sotto voce*, the military martinet, now satisfied that the captain had misconceived some of those suggestions which he had put forth for his good. He pitied his inexperience, looked at him with a respectful sort of sorrow, then dashed his fork into the meats of his plate, and proceeded to give his teeth double exercise for the rigorous inactivity imposed upon his tongue. .Meanwhile Porgy groaned again aloud, in utter vexation of spirit. He could eat no more. His appetite was utterly gone, and as he gazed upon the untasted good things before him, which he had no longer the disposition to touch, he felt that he could never forgive the offender.

"You do not eat, captain," said the widow, with interest, the pleasant light still in her eye, in which the worthy captain of partisans read enough for his discomfiture. He fancied that the widow comprehended the whole game of the sergeant, and naturally dreaded lest she should suspect how greatly she had been the subject of their conferences and calculations. Her late generous treatment of him and sympathy in his affairs, rendered the doubt trebly oppressive and painful. At all events, Millhouse was silenced, though the result was reached by a process which, sufficiently legitimate in camp, was hardly to be justified at the dinner-table, and in the presence of a lady. The widow felt very much like protesting against the assertion of military rule at her board, and by one of her guests; and was half tempted by the spirit of mischief to set the sergeant again free, by provoking him to farther revelations of his peculiar philosophy. But she felt that the annoyance of Porgy had been sufficient, and was rather apprehensive that, with so blunt a speaker as Millhouse, whose experience was so various, and whose knowledge was so universal, she, herself, might come in for a share of the disquiet which oppressed the captain. But she employed her art, successfully, in dissipating the cloud about her company, and Porgy recovered after awhile, sufficiently to unite with her in the effort. It was of no small importance to the object, that Millhouse did not lose his appetite; and a full enjoyment of the feast, made him soon forgetful of the tempest he had provoked.

"I hain't eat such a dinner, Madame Eb'leigh, sence I don't know when!" was his grateful acknowledgment, as he pushed away his emptied plate, and proceeded to replenish his tumbler from the portly decanter of Jamaica.

"I'm glad that you've the appetite, sergeant, which rarely allows any sort of dinner to be unsatisfactory."

"Thank ye, ma'am; but ef you think I'd lay in as I've been a-doing, with nothing better afore me, than the or'nary rations of the camp-kettle, even with our Tom's cooking, you're very much out. It's the good things you've gin us, ma'am, that's made me dewour enough to sarve seventeen red-skins on a scout. I'm a-most ashamed to see what I've been a-doing; pretickilarly as it don't seem to me that other people have been a-doing anything to speak of it in the same way. The cappin thar' has a-most eaten nothin'."

The captain eyed him with such a glance as the hyena might be supposed to bestow upon the beast which had somehow deprived him of his prey; but he said nothing. We need not show how the rest of the day was spent. The widow was cordial to the close. Millhouse was invited to see Fordham for what he wanted, in his capacity as overseer; and the details were fully explained and understood, by which the implements for working, the hoes, shovels, ploughs, and wagon, were to be transferred, and when, from the one plantation to the other. Porgy had again some words in private with the widow, a fact which again extorted shows of undisguised delight and exultation on the part of the sergeant. Lance Frampton made engagements for a deer hunt with Arthur Eveleigh, the two youths seeming equally well pleased with each other; and after friendly adieus, the guests rode away; Porgy clapping spurs to his steed, and going ahead with a haste which declared for the continued irritation of his mood, and which disquieted the sergeant a little to keep up with; as he declared that, "efter sich a dinner, one don't like to hurry about nither!" When the two followers did reach their leader, he did not seem in the humor to notice either; but Millhouse was not satisfied that his exertions should go without acknowledgment.

"Well, cappin," says he, "it's a good beginning of the war. We've broke ground fairly in the inimy's country, and we've come off well after the first skrimmage. What a dinner she gin us!—And then how lib'ral she offered everything. Ef ever I seed a better chaince for a straight up and down courtship than this, I kaint jest now call it to mind. She gin you a mighty fine chaince, cappin, them two times when you hed her all alone by her oneself; and the first time you was with her, I reckon more'n an hour. I'm only hoping you warn't mealy-mouthed, seeing you had to deal with a widow. The cards was in your hand, and a famous game you hed to play, cappin, ef you know'd what you was about."

It was with singular deliberation, drawing up his horse, and looking at the speaker with a savage sort of smile, that Porgy answered—

"I suppose, Sergeant Millhouse, that you fancy you have helped this game wonderfully."

"Reckon I hev'! I show'd you whar the trump cards laid.— I've put a good spoke into your wheel."

"A spoke indeed! Hereafter, sergeant, let me put in my own spokes, will you. Let me play my own game, if you please; I need no assistance."

And the splenetic captain, driving spurs into his horse, went off at a pace, that left the two followers far behind him.

"The cappin's mighty snappish to-day," quoth Millhouse to his companion.

"And a right to be so. If he had snapped off your head, he'd have served you right. What business have you to be meddling with his courtings, if so be it's that he's after."

"Why, Lord, that was to help him only."

"He don't want your help, I reckon. He's a full-grown man, I suppose. Besides, it's enough to ruin a man, seeing the way you go to work. I don't know much about women folks, but I'm pretty sure, any woman of sense, will be mighty apt to sicken of a man if she sees he gits his courting done by another."

"Teach your grandmother how to suck eggs. As ef I didn't know about the matter; but that's your foolishness. There's no sich thing as a woman of sense, you see; they ain't made for it. It's according to nater that man is to find them all the sense they've got any use for. Talk to me about wimmen! Why, Lance, I've kissed more purty gals than you ever seed, and never seed the woman yit that I couldn't hev' had for the axing."

"Oh! that's your conceit only. You think so because you're so conceited."

"I know so, my lad; and that's perhaps the reason jest why I never married eeny. 'T would ha' seemed like a surrenderin' to the inimy at the first summons, and I'm not that sort of sodger."

"Well, sergeant," quoth the lieutenant, "I'm just willing to say that you're about the conceitedest person that ever served in the army; and, moreover, I'm a-thinking from all you say, that a woman is, just of all animals, the hardest for you to understand. You haven't begun to know 'em; and the way you talked to Madam Eveleigh to-day — you thought it mighty fine — was just such foolishness as ought to hang a man.   Even her son, Arthur, thought you was insulting to his mother, and I had to tell him that you was a very foolish sort of person, and that it was a fool way you had of talking about things you don't understand; and he musn't mind you."

"You told him I was a fool, did you?"

"That I did!"

"You did!"

"Yes, indeed!"

"Me a fool!   That I should be called a fool by such a hop-o'-my-thumb as you — you long-bodied snipe — you snake without a head — you leetle eend of a sarcumstance!   Lord! how I could thump you now.   I jest feel like tumbling you from your critter.   Me a fool!   Well, I'll tell that to the cappin.   Ef I don't, p'int your finger at me and say 'squash!'   Me, a fool! Mighty good, indeed!   Mighty good!"

Frampton rode on coolly, never heeding him and never answering.   When they reached Glen-Eberley, Captain Porgy was already there, alighted, and seated, pipe in his mouth, in his piazza.

Millhouse knew quite enough of his superior to take care not to disturb him in his mood.   Though obtuse and presumptuous, he had been taught to observe the features and deportment of the captain, so as to time his approaches.   His recent blunderings were the result of an unusual condition of elevation, which blinded his ordinary faculties.   But the captain's manner and Frampton's suggestions had opened his eyes.   Accordingly, specially avoiding speech, he entered the house, filled his pipe, and going down to the basement story, seated himself beneath the piazza where Porgy was giving voluminous breath to his chibouque.— With no offences to atone for, Lance Frampton forebore, in like manner, to obtrude upon the sultan. He busied himself about the horses and the negroes, and found employment out of doors for the rest of the evening.

Meanwhile, the clouds gradually cleared away, and, by the time supper was ready, Porgy had recovered his good humor. His bowl of coffee was enjoyed with satisfaction and composure, and his irritation being subdued, he had leisure to reflect upon the improved prospects in his affairs, which were due to the widow's liberality. It was not in his nature to suppress or conceal his good tidings from his companions, and when the supper things had been removed, Millhouse, somewhat humbled, Frampton, as usual, quiet, Tom and Pomp rather loitering about than in attendance, the captain proceeded to unfold his budget, and put his followers in possession of the facts in his good fortune. They were all overjoyed. Tom was the first to speak.

"Hah! enty I bin know. Da's good woman, Miss Eb'leigh. He hab sense. He no like dem fool woman wha' don't know how to 'habe [behave] to gemplemans. He hab 'spect [respect] for gemplemans. He hab 'spect for me, Tom. He shak' han' wid Tom. He say 'Tom, I yer [hear] 'bout you. You maussa is my frien'.' He's a lady, ebbry inch ob 'em. You mus' tak' he money, maussa, ef it's only to 'blige [oblige] 'em, and mak' 'em feel easy. Da's it!"

Frampton said not a word, but he rose during the captain's recital, came closer to him, and when he had finished his statement, grasped his hand and wrung it warmly. Millhouse, once more set free to speak, launched into the most superb eulogium on the virtues of the lady, which we need not report, concluding with the opinion that "sich a good woman, with sich a fortin, ought to have a guardcen out of the line of the army."

Porgy only looked at him, with half closed but flashing eye, then, as if speaking rather to himself than to his companions, he said musingly—

"And it is such a noble woman, that I was to select as the subject of a matrimonial speculation!"

"And who better?" quoth Millhouse. "She's the very sawt of pusson There's no speckilating upon a poor pusson. Whar's the profit in it? And ef the pusson's rich, but happens to be mean and stingy, why, Lord! even the money ain't guine to make it agreeable to hev' transactions with her. But when the woman has the good heart and the good fortin together, then it's a good speckilation. By thunder, cappin, now's the time to make a push into that market, and buy out the business. But I reckon you hev'n't been sleeping all the time you two was together."

"Sergeant Millhouse," said Porgy, with great composure, "you are no doubt, in some things, as shrewd and sensible a person as any I know, but I think there are a few subjects upon which you had better not expend your time and labor."

"Which on 'em, cappin? I'd like to know."

"I think, for example, that when you go to heaven, which I trust you will do some day—"

"Arter a time, cappin; but Lord love you, I ain't in any hurry to leave this airth."

"In your own time, sergeant; but when you do go, I think it will not be altogether proper to undertake to show the angels, Gabriel, Michael, Raphael, or any others with whom you may become familiar, in what way they ought to use their wings. I have no doubt you have some very wise notions as to how birds and beasts may fly; but the angels, perhaps, have more experience than you, if not more wisdom, and it will require that you should see much flying done among them, before you can venture to give them any lessons."

"Why, cappin, I reckon you're jest a-laughing at me now, out of the corner of your eye. I ain't sich a bloody fool as to do them things."

"Perhaps not! But when a man is so wise as you are on so many subjects, he is apt to think himself wise in all."

"Well, that's nateral and reasonable too, I'm a-thinking."

"Natural enough, no doubt, but not so certainly reasonable, my good fellow. If you were suddenly to find yourself among bears and buffaloes, you might reasonably undertake to show them how to find their food or prey; if among snakes, I have no doubt you could teach them superior modes of beguiling young frogs into their jaws; as a dweller among hawks and owls, or minks and weasels, you might open new views to them of the processes by which they might empty all the hen-houses in the country; and, teaching squirrels, they might be grateful to you for new lessons in the art of gathering corn out of the fields, and cracking hickory-nuts;—but I doubt if these capacities of yours should entitle you to think yourself appointed to teach young oysters how to swim, or young angels how to fly; and I am even doubtful how far they should justify you in an endeavor to set yourself up as a teacher of love and courtship. Of one thing let me assure you, before I stop, that if ever you undertake to make love to any woman on my account, again, and in my presence, by the Lord that liveth, sergeant, I will fling you from the windows, though the house were as high as the tower of Babel. Be warned in season;—and now let us have a sup of Jamaica, before sleeping for the night."

"I told you so,—" said Frampton, brushing by the sergeant as the latter stood up, in silence, to drink with his superior.

"Well, thar's no *on*derstanding it," muttered the sergeant, after the captain had retired. "Thar's some people so cross-grained in the world, they won't let you make 'em smooth."

Tom, the cook, had his comment also.

"Hah! mass Millhouse, you yer! Look out! when maussa talk so, he's in dead airnest! Ef he tell you he guine fling you out de window, he do 'em for true. And you know, for all you see 'em look and walk so lazy, he strong as a harricane when he git in a passion. He will, sure as a gun, brek' you neck out de window, ef he promise!"

"Thar's no onderstanding it!" was the only response of the sergeant to those suggestions. "And all the time I was a-doing the best,—jest a making his wheel run smooth!"

CHAPTER L.

THE BACHELOR'S EMBARRASSMENTS.

WE must suppose an interval of several weeks since the occurrences of the last chapter. Meanwhile, Captain Porgy, charged with his letters of credit and introduction, has visited Charleston; has obtained the five hundred guineas of the widow; has executed to her a mortgage of all his negroes, with the exception of Tom; has procured and sent to the plantation all necessary supplies; has conferred upon the state of his affairs with Charles Cotesworth Pinckney; has received his counsel; has endeavored, but in vain, to see his creditor, M'Kewn, who was absent from the city, no one knew where; and has returned to his plantation, where he has ever since remained.

During this period his subordinates have not been idle; but have proceeded, with proper energy, to the prosecution of affairs at home. Millhouse, in his capacity as overseer, and Lance Frampton, as a temporary assistant, have stripped to their tasks and done wonders. The lands have been broken up for planting; the negro-houses have been run up as if by magic; rails have been split, and fences raised; and the usual labors of several months have been compressed into as many weeks. The negroes, glad once more to find themselves in possession of a homestead, certain provisions, and the protection of a white man, have worked with a hearty will and cheerfulness which have amply made up for lost time. If Millhouse was vain of his prowess as an overseer, he was not without good reasons for his vanity. He himself thought it a merit to be boastful.

"I likes to hear a man brag," said he, "of what he kin do; for then, ef he aint about the meanest skunk in all creation, he must be a-doing, and a-doing well, to carry a decent face among white people. Wanity is a wartue when it makes a fellow work."

And this philosophy Captain Porgy did not dispute.

Lance Frampton took special charge of the buildings,—saw to and assisted at the erection of the stables; did all the birding and squirrel shooting; prepared lines for fishing; and, with so much success did he pursue his field-sports, that it was very rare indeed that the family went without fresh meat for dinner. In these pursuits, Captain Porgy took sufficient part. Squirrels were bagged in abundance; once or twice, hunting with Arthur Eveleigh's hounds, a stout buck was tumbled in his track, and, on one occasion, a brown bear was badgered in the swamps with so much ingenuity, that he finally rendered up his hide in return for a few charges of rifle bullets and gunpowder. Young Eveleigh found his new associates at Glen-Eberley particularly good company, and was hunting, or birding, with Porgy or Frampton, or both, every other day in the week. At his coming, always, the sergeant could he heard to whistle with exultation; be seen to loll out his tongue as if in the enjoyment of a sweet morsel, and to wave his one arm abroad, as if grasping some very enviable possession. Sometimes he ventured to mutter, in Porgy's hearing, the hopes which were still active in him, in phrases peculiar to himself;—as for example—

"The poor young fellow feels the want of a pappy! It's a sad needcessity, ef so be he kaint find the right one. But his nose p'ints out the right way. He looks straight to the line of the army. Well! I wont say much;—but what's to be will be. The Lord's over all, and he'll bring all things straight in time."

Porgy, at such speeches, would give him a look of warning, which usually arrested his eloquence before it broke bounds.

Meanwhile, the visits were not all on one side. Porgy rode over to the widow's, on an average twice a week, dining there usually when he went. He did not ask the companionship of his followers, on such occasions, nor did they receive any more invitations from the lady. Millhouse was content. If he was not to be permitted to assist in the courtship, he was quite willing to be absent from the scene of it. He would sometimes mutter his apprehensions to Frampton, that things did not advance with sufficient rapidity, and that his services would yet be needed. On which occasions, the lieutenant, reüttering what had been said by Porgy, would suggest to the overseer, the propriety of his making an early call upon the arch-angels, Gabriel, Michael and Raphael, to see how they were getting on:—a suggestion that usually sent Millhouse to the right-about.

At the widow Eveleigh's, Porgy was received on the most friendly and familiar footing. He was well read, of contemplative mind, had been trained in good society, and, though somewhat wanting in the precision of the courtier, in consequence of the loose, free and easy manner which he had acquired in camp, he was yet capable of curbing himself, when the impulse strove within him; and this done, he could minister to the social tastes of his fair companion, with an ease, grace, and vivacity, that made him always a very grateful visiter. Mrs. Eveleigh was almost wholly free from affectations; was frank and ever gay of mood; always cheerful; always ingenuous, and never labored at the concealment of her sympathies. She laughed at the good things of the captain and freely pardoned his familiarities. There was a freshness and a saliency about his peculiar humor which pleased her, and when he chose to be serious, he could rise into provinces of thought, generalizing from the abstract to the familiar, and thus coupling the most remote affinities and associations, in a strain of expression at once graceful and expressive. He quickly discovered in what respects he could most successfully address her ear, and he naturally availed himself of his discovery. Porgy, before entering the army, was well read in Shakspere, Milton, Dryden, and the best of the then current English writers. It must be admitted, we fear, that he had also drank freely of fountains less undefiled; had dipped largely into the subsequent pages of the Wycherlys, the Vanbrughs, the Congreves, the Wilmots, Ethereges, and Rochesters, of a far less intellectual, and therefore less moral, period. But the taste of the latter had not spoiled him for the just appreciation of the former; had perhaps heightened his estimate of them by force of contrast; and the fruit of his familiarity with both classes of writers, was a knowledge, not then commonly possessed— scarcely now, indeed,—of materials for graceful conversation, illustrated with frequent happy quotations, which particularly commended him to a woman who was, herself, at once refined and intellectual. We can readily understand how interesting was the intercourse between the parties, in a region which, sparsely settled, and wanting in books, left so many wearisome hours, and wanting moods, which no plantation employments could satisfy or supply.

We do not mean to say that the widow regarded Porgy in any other aspect than that of a very agreeable companion. But we are constrained to admit on behalf of the captain, that he soon became seriously interested in the widow. That he should respect her heart, and love it, because of the liberality she had shown him, was natural enough;—but when he came to know her mind; the sweet graces of her intellect; her quiet, gentle, always just and wholesome habit of thought; the pleasant animation of her fancies; the liveliness of her conversation, enriched by the anecdotes of a very large and varied experience, as well in England as America, he began to admire her on other grounds, so that frequent association with her became almost a necessity. Still, there was a something wanting to the perfect sway of the widow over her admirer; something which he felt, but could not explain, or account for, to himself. She was a fine-looking woman, "fair, fat, and forty,"—but he found himself occasionally objecting to "the fat." The very fact that he was, himself, too much so, was enough to make him quarrel with her possessions of the same sort. He asked himself repeatedly the question: "Do I—can I love this woman?—as a woman *ought* to be loved; as a man ought to love;—as she deserves to be loved by any husband, and especially by me?"

Millhouse, could he have heard this question, would have answered it without a moment's hesitation; but Porgy never broached the subject in his ears, and now, studiously, since the memorable dinner, checked every approach to it which the former made.

"Yet," quoth the soliloquizing captain, "am I not shaping this passion of love into a bug-bear for my own fright and disappointment? Does it need that either the widow or myself should experience all the paroxysms and fancies of eighteen, in order to feel secure of the force of our attachment. Is it natural or reasonable, that, at forty-five, I at least, should need, or expect, to recall my youthful frenzies, before venturing upon the married condition? Is not the sort of love which we require now, that which belongs rather to the deliberate consent of the mind than the warm impulses of the blood and fancy? Is it necessary with us, that, in addition to the cool conviction of the thought, in favor of the propriety of this union, there should be a nervous and excitable upspringing in the heart, of tumultuous emotions, indefinable, intense, passionate, eager—which reject reason, which baffle thought, which seem to be guided rather by dreams than by right reason—and which ask none of the securities, by which thought would shelter faith—which is, in fact, a faith itself, beyond any of the help or the convictions of the understanding? My judgment is perfectly satisfied with the widow Eveleigh. She is vastly superior, as a lady—as a woman of sense and sweetness—grace and intelligence—to any that I know. She thinks well and kindly of me; that is evident. We harmonize admirably together. She listens with pleasure to my speech, and I am willing to listen gladly when she speaks in turn. She is a noble-looking woman—a little too stout, I admit—but of fine figure nevertheless, and a face that is at once sweet and commanding. She has wealth; but, by Jupiter, I reject that as a consideration. Her money shall not enter into the estimate. Her other attractions are surely quite sufficient. Yet, *are* they sufficient? *Am* I satisfied? Why do I ask myself so doubtingly whether I can bind myself to her, for life, and feel no lack, no deficiency—no weight in the bonds I carry?"

The captain ended the soliloquy with a sigh. He strode the chamber impatiently, and paused finally before the fireplace, in which the fire smouldered rather than gave forth light and heat. At that moment the form of the widow Griffin rose vividly before his eyes.

"Why is it?" he muttered to himself, "that, whenever I try to meditate this question of the widow Eveleigh, the image of Mrs. Griffin starts up before me. *She* is a fine woman undoubtedly; good, gentle, humble, affectionate; and has no doubt been very beautiful;—is still very sweet to look upon;—but she can not compare with the widow Eveleigh! She is not wise; not learned; is really very ignorant; has no manners, no eloquence; is simply humble and adhesive;—*she* is rather thin than stout, that is true, her figure is good;—she has still a face of exquisite sweetness, but she is no associate for me ;—she has no resources, no thoughts, no information; has seen nothing, knows nothing! They are not to be spoken of in the same moment. The widow Eveleigh is far superior in *all* but simply personal respects! Yet, Griffin does move about with a delightful grace; so soft, so modest. In household affairs she is admirable. I don't know that I ever saw Mrs. Eveleigh attending to household affairs at all. Her servants are numerous and well trained. She has only to command. Yet, on a small scale, considering her inadequate resources, it is wonderful with what skill Griffin manages; with how little noise, how little effort. Poor woman, what a lonesome life she leads. It is abominable that I have only been to see her once since I have been from town. I will certainly ride over to-morrow."

And he did so; and he dined with Mrs. Griffin; and a very nice extempore dinner did she give him. There were some cold baked meats; there was a beautiful broiled steak, a stripe from a quarter of beef which she had received as a present the day before from Mrs. Eveleigh; the breadstuffs of Mrs. Griffin were inimitable; her butter was the best in the parish, and a cool draught of her buttermilk, fresh from the churn, was welcomed by Porgy with all the enthusiasm of a citizen escaping, for the first time, from dusty walks and walls, to the elysium of green fields and forest shelter.

Notions of arcadian felicity crept into Porgy's mind. Everything seemed perfect, and perfectly delightful about the humble cottage of the widow Griffin. The trees had a fresher look; the grounds seemed to shelter the most seductive recesses; even the dog lying down in the piazza, and the cow ruminating under the old Pride of India before the door, seemed to enjoy dreams of a happier sort than usually come to dog and cow in ordinary life. The skies above the cottage appeared to wear looks of superior mildness and beauty, and to impart a something kindred to the looks of the beings who dwelt under their favoring auspices. What a sweet, smiling, modest creature was Ellen Griffin, whom our Lieutenant Frampton was shortly to take to his bosom. And how like her still—how nearly as youthful—how quite as meek, and gentle, and devoted—was the mother.

Porgy was delighted with the part of the day spent with this

little family. His incertitude, in matrimonial respects, increased
the more he surveyed her. Griffin made her impressions, differing much from those of the widow Eveleigh, but in their way
not less strong; perhaps, stronger, since it was certain that
Captain Porgy showed himself much more at ease with the one
lady than the other. There was no doubt, indeed, that the superior social position of Mrs. Eveleigh, her equal grace and dignity of bearing, the calm, natural manner with which she met
his approaches, all joined, in some degree, to restrain our hero
— to lessen, somewhat, his own ease; to make him less assured
on the subject of his own dignity. He was sometimes warned
by the lady, that the *brusquerie* of his army habits, would not
altogether answer—that he must be on the watch against himself, to check his involuntary *escapades*, and never to be forgetful of the fact that the time had come when, to play somewhat
with the language of the poet—"arms must give way to
the *gown !*"

It was this feeling of constraint which chiefly qualified the
pleasure of his intercourse with the widow Eveleigh; which made
him hesitate to give her the preference; and which, on the other
hand, assisted to increase the favorable impressions which a previous association had given him of the fair widow Griffin. With
her, easily awed, conscious of social inferiority, looking up with
great reverence to the captain of partisans, as her late husband's
superior, he felt under few restraints of mere language and deportment. He did not dare to swear in the presence of Mrs.
Eveleigh; that would have been a terrible violation of the rules
of good society in that day. Yet our captain had an infirmity
of this sort, and so inveterate was his habit, that he had only
been able to check himself, at times, when in the widow's presence, by arresting the unlucky oath upon his lips by a manual
operation; by clapping his broad palm entirely over his own
mouth. Now, he did not feel the same sort of necessity when
in the presence of the widow Griffin. Her social standards were
less exacting. Her social experiences were more adapted to his
own later habits, and the feeling of ease which he enjoyed in
her presence, was such, that, without deliberately weighing the
claims of the two ladies against each other, he rated it as a something almost compensative for the surrender of the graceful, in-

tellectual attractions of the wealthy widow. He could smoke his pipe in the presence of the widow Griffin, which he had not dared to do at Mrs. Eveleigh's. The former when he had dined with her, filled his pipe, herself, from a store of tobacco which might have been a hoard of her late husband, and dropped, with her own hands, the little coal of fire, from the tongs, into it. It was like a coal from the altars of Cupid, upon the heart of the partisan; and while he sat in the piazza, after dinner, his chair resting solely on its hind legs, his own thrown over the bannisters, his head thrown back, at a declination almost the proper one for sleep, and sent up cloud after cloud, by way of tribute to the heavens, his half-shut eyes watched with a growing sense of the grace and beauties of the widow, her gliding and unobtrusive figure, as she busied herself about the hall and table; assisted Ellen to move the table back, brushed up her hearth with a fairy-like besom of broom straw, and finally drew her knitting to the doorway, and sat down in silent and submissive companionship. Porgy mused and said to himself:—

" One does not want an equal, but an ally in marriage. A man ought to be wise enough for his wife and himself. To get a woman who shall best comprehend one is the sufficient secret; and no woman can properly comprehend her husband, who is not prepared to recognise his full superiority. When it is otherwise, there are constant disputes. The woman is for ever setting up for herself. She is not only unwilling that you should be her master, but she sets up to be your mistress. Why, if she has the mind, should she not use it; and if she has mind enough for the household, what's the use of yours? Clearly, there can not be peace in any planet which acknowledges two masters."

How long the pleasant surveys and soliloquies of the captain might have continued, it is not possible to say. They were interrupted by the sudden riding up of Mr. Fordham, the overseer of Mrs. Eveleigh. He made a respectful bow to the captain, taking off his hat, and offering his hand as he did so; and entered the house, shaking hands with the widow and daughter with all the frankness of an old acquaintance. After a while, the captain's horse was brought out, Fordham volunteering to do the service. Porgy left the overseer behind him. As he rode off, the thought suddenly occurred to him—

"Can it be possible that this fellow, Fordham, is thinking of the widow?—Humph!"

And the suggestion led to a prolonged fit of musing which was only arrested when he found himself within his own avenue.

CHAPTER LI.

DEBTOR AND CREDITOR.

THE next day Porgy rode over to see the wife of the squatter, from whom he had received a supply of stockings, and some cloth of her own and daughter's weaving. It was fortunate that he did not suffer Millhouse to know that he dropped three guineas into the hands of little Dory when one would have sufficed for payment. He gave other commissions to the humble family, and noted with pleasure the improvements and acquisitions in the little household, the fruits of his own liberality and that of Mrs. Eveleigh. While sitting in the porch of the hovel, with Dory quietly nestling in his lap, he was surprised to see the widow and her son ride up on horseback. Of course, the interview was a pleasant one all round, though our captain felt a little awkward, at the first blush, when caught in his paternal relation with the little girl. She, too, by some strange instinct, started up at the coming of the new visiters and retreated to the side of her mother.

"I had a call yesterday, captain," said Mrs. Eveleigh, "from Mr. M'Kewn. You have heard that he is now a resident at the plantation adjoining me, which he owns. He is making the rounds of the neighborhood, and you may soon look to see him, I suppose."

"Too soon, I fear," answered the captain, looking disquieted.

"Well," said she, "we must hope for the best.—If I could recover that box—" she added, half to herself, but here she stopped, and the captain could only look curious.

"You have heard nothing of your husband yet, Mrs. Bostwick?" asked the widow of the poor woman.

"Not a word, ma'am, and I don't know what to think. I'm dub'ous something's happened to him."

To this the widow said nothing. After a pause, however, she proceeded to give a commission for a quantity of homespun cloth, and concluded with asking that Dory might go home and spend a week with her. Dory looked earnestly toward her mother, and the latter, with eyes filling, and with some reluctance in her manner, gave her consent that she should go over the next day. Porgy accompanied the widow and her son, when they took their departure, though he did not attend them home. He was quite too full of serious thoughts, which naturally came up with the statement made respecting M'Kewn. He *had* heard of that person's arrival in the neighborhood; but the sympathizing manner of the widow was calculated to impress him more seriously than his own thoughts, in respect to the legal relations in which he stood with the Scotchman, and the danger with which he might expect very soon to be threatened. This danger he well knew could not long be evaded. The trial of strength must soon come on, and when he reflected upon those suspicions in regard to M'Kewn, which the remarks of Mrs. Eveleigh had imparted to his mind, upon the facts in connection with the abduction of his slaves, and her conjectures in respect to the share which M'Kewn had taken in the affair, he felt very much like making the conflict a personal one. Our partisan would greatly have relished any circumstances which would authorize a transfer of the proceedings from the courts of law to those of arms. But we need not anticipate his reflections, particularly as we shall soon hear from his own lips, what are his feelings and resolves in the matter.

The very next day M'Kewn made his appearance at Glen-Eberley. Porgy was alone in his piazza, as the former rode up the avenue. Millhouse'was somewhere in the rice-fields; Lance Frampton had ridden over to see Ellen Griffin, his marriage with whom was very shortly to take place; and, except Tom, the cook, and Pomp, the fiddler, there was no one present to witness the interview between the parties. Porgy had been smoking, and the pipe was still in his mouth as M'Kewn came in sight. As soon as he was recognised by our partisan, the latter betrayed his emotions by a single movement, which, taking the pipe from his mouth, shivered it over the railing of the piazza. This done, he remained comparatively cool; at all events he preserved his external composure. Pomp took the horse of the visiter, who, at once, in a free and easy way, ascended to where Porgy still maintained his seat. As he reached the floor, the latter rose, and with calm and courtly gravity, said :—

"Mr. M'Kewn, I believe."

"At your service, captain. I'm very glad to see you safe, sir, after the war. It's a long time since I've had the pleasure of seeing you."

"Pleasure!" quoth Porgy—then motioning to a chair—"take a seat, sir."

The Scotchman accepted the reluctant invitation, laid his hat down beside him, drew off his gloves, rubbed his hands, and looked about him with the air of a man resolved on putting himself on the easiest possible terms with his host. Porgy looked on with the stern calmness of one who compels himself to submit, with as much composure as possible, to an unpleasant necessity which he sees not well how to escape. His visiter, meanwhile, began with a repetition of his congratulations; that the war was over, that the country had achieved its independence, that old friends were safe, that old associations were to be renewed, and so forth. Porgy heard him for a while in silence and great gravity of aspect, until getting weary and impatient of the commonplace preliminaries which the other had employed, he himself broke ground in relation to the only subject of real interest between the parties.

"To make a long story short, Mr. M'Kewn, I owe you a considerable amount of money, which, no doubt, you desire should be paid."

"Very true, captain, a very considerable amount indeed, out of which I have been lying for several years, and which I certainly am very much in need of."

"You are secured I think, sir, however, by bond and mortgage?"

"Secured, sir? No, indeed! My mortgage covers the lands of Glen-Eberley, but if these were all sold to-morrow, at present prices, they wouldn't pay one half of the debt for which they

are bound. And you know, sir, there is a considerable unliquidated debt besides, sir; some thousand pounds, sir—"

"Ah! yes! Well, Mr. M'Kewn, you certainly do not expect
that I should have any money so soon after the war. You sufficiently appreciate the patriotism which called us into the field
and kept us in the ranks for so many years, without any com-
pensation."

"True, sir, true! Nobody honors more than I do the patriotism that achieved our independence; but, sir, it is not for a single person like myself to do more than his share in such a conflict. I have made a great many sacrifices, and lost a great deal
myself in the cause; and you will admit that a credit of more
than five years—"

"Is no credit at all, sir, under the present circumstances, unless, perhaps, continued for as many years more."

"Oh! that is quite impossible, Captain Porgy. I am greatly
in want of money, now. Buying this plantation and negroes, it
has stripped me quite and left me considerably in debt myself."

"I don't see how I am to help you. You can not possibly
suppose that I have any money."

"Well, captain, I don't know," was the answer, with a significant smile. "Report says that you have money, and in considerable amount. You have been purchasing largely in the city
—and the rumor is——" here a pause, and an increased significance of smile.

"Well, sir, what of rumor?"

"Why, sir, the rumor goes, that Captain Porgy, returning
from the field of Mars with laurels, has been welcomed to those
of Love, and—"

"Stop, sir!—Mr. M'Kewn, I am willing that you should repeat what rumor may have reported, but I must warn you by
no means to attempt any invention of your own."

"Inventions, sir!" And M'Kewn looked a little angrily—"I
have no invention, Captain Porgy. I only state what others
have said to me, or in my hearing."

"Well, sir; confine yourself to that, if you please."

"It is briefly said, Captain Porgy. The rumor is, that a certain wealthy widow of this neighborhood is prepared to honor the
laurels of the soldier, and supply all his deficiencies of fortune—"

"Enough, Mr. M'Kewn," said Porgy, arresting him—with a stern aspect, and warning finger uplifted. "You have said what you have heard, I suppose, and now hear what I say. If, hereafter, I hear any man repeating this story, I shall slit his tongue for him. The lady in question is one whom I greatly honor, and of whom I will not hear anybody speak in disparagement. There was that in your tone and manner, Mr. M'Kewn, just now, which I did not relish. Be pleased to take warning."

M'Kewn was somewhat taken aback, but recovering himself, he said—

"I do not know, Captain Porgy, why I should take warning in particular. I am hardly apprehensive that anybody will slit my tongue for anything I say, though I am not the man to give any provocation to violence on the part of anybody. Let me add, sir, that I see no harm in the report which I mentioned—no harm, certainly, in saying that a certain brave officer of our armies has been distinguished by the favor of a certain lovely and wealthy widow of our county."

"There is harm, sir, because there is great indelicacy and great injustice in it. I am the proper authority in this matter, and I tell you, sir, in answer to this rumor, that the intercourse between Mrs. Eveleigh and myself is that simply of friendship, occasioned perhaps, wholly, by a service which I had the good fortune to render."

"Well, but, captain, there is no good reason why friendship, in such a case, should not ripen into—"

"No more, sir! The subject is one upon which I can suffer no jesting. That upon which we have to speak simply concerns money. I owe you money;—you want your money you say."

"I do sir; I have been kept out of it long enough, Captain Porgy."

"Do you mean to intimate, sir, that I have perversely and willingly kept you out of your money ?"

"I state nothing, sir, but the absolute fact, that the money is due me, has been due too long, and that I certainly expect it to be paid, and paid very soon."

"Very good, sir! Such then is your expectation. Now, sir, hear me. I shall expect from you a full statement of our accounts, with all items of charge particularly stated."

"Why, sir, you've had the accounts rendered you in full, six years ago."

"No, sir; such is not the case. It is true, I was improvident enough not to demand them, and to take your summary statements when I should have had a full bill of particulars. I require them now, sir."

"In the case of the bond and mortgage, sir, the requisition need not be answered. That is a liquidated claim, acknowledged under seal, and, sir, according to law—"

"You are something of a lawyer, I perceive, Mr. M'Kewn, and I claim to know nothing about law. Still, I have some hope of justice, and, in the case of bond given and mortgage sealed and signed, under circumstances of error or fraud——"

"Do you mean to impute fraud to me, Captain Porgy?" demanded M'Kewn with some fierceness of aspect.

"And if I did, sir, do you suppose I should value a fig your hectoring looks? Keep your temper within bounds, Mr. M'Kewn; for you would try to bully me in vain; and to let you understand this more fully, let me tell you that I *do* impute fraud to you—"

"Ha!" rising from his seat.

"Yes, sir! I think you at once a great and a little rascal. Since you demand my opinion, you shall have it. I believe you have cheated me in these accounts, for the satisfaction of which, in my blind confidence and folly, I gave you a lien upon my property. I shall require a thorough overhauling of your accounts, from the beginning, sir, and fancy that I shall be able to find, in some process of law, a means by which to arrive at the awards of justice!"

"Very well, sir; very well, sir," gathering up hat and gloves—and shaking them in both hands with nervous fury—"If it's law you want, sir, you shall have it. You shall have enough to remember it all your life."

And he wheeled about to descend the steps. Here he encountered Millhouse, at whose back stood Tom, the cook, and Pomp the fiddler.

"Say the word, cappin." quoth Millhouse, "and I'll give the fellow a h'ist."

"Say de wud, maussa; da's all," echoed Tom, his sleeves

already rolled up; while Pomp threw himself into an attitude, claws extended as if about to grapple with a bear. M'Kewn looked at the enemies in his path, and drew up with recovering dignity.

"Am I to be assaulted in your house, Captain Porgy?"

"Let him go, Millhouse! Let him pass."

The three made way for him, reluctantly, Millhouse muttering—

"I feel mighty *on*pleasant at parting with the critter, without giving him jest one squeeze!—I reckon that's the fellow they calls M'Kewn."

The creditor, by this time, was on horseback. He looked back with gleaming eyes upon the group, then dashed up the avenue at full gallop.

"It's cl'ar, cappin, that the war's declared atween you!"

"Yes, Millhouse, and the army-chest nearly empty."

"Well, we'll do the fighting all for love; eh, Tom!"

"Hah! da's jist de way for fight, kaise you lubs it! But how you guine fight? Da' bucrah ain't de sawt of pusson to lub yer [hear] de bullet whistle."

"Ah! Tom! there's not the sort of fighting that he intends. He makes the sheriff do his fighting. Do you remember what I told you about the sheriff?"

"Enty, I 'member, maussa? He's a warmint, you bin tell me!"

"Yes, indeed, and now, how to keep you all from falling into his clutches."

A long consultation followed between the captain and sergeant, to which Tom occasionally contributed a characteristic suggestion. Lance Frampton returned at night to share in the discussion. Neither of the parties, however, could throw much light upon the difficulty which embarrassed them, and Captain Porgy, while he reflected, felt that he had perhaps brought on the conflict of strength rather prematurely, and that prudence should have prompted more forbearance; but whenever he recalled the references made by M'Kewn to the widow Eveleigh, he became reconciled to his own rashness.

"No! d—n the fellow! whatever happens I shall never regret what I said to him. Better break at once with such a scoundrel, than have him perpetually about you; now fawning, now threatening; always vexing your soul, and, whatever the delay, destroying you at last. I can face all the evil that he threatens with a stout heart, but can't, with any heart of contentment, suffer him to face me with his scoundrel countenance!"

CHAPTER LII.

THE RANDOM SHAFT.

THE news soon got abroad of what had taken place at Glen-Eberley, between its proprietor and creditor. M'Kewn's own rage forced him to tell the story to various persons, and Millhouse conveyed the substance of it to Fordham, the very night that it took place. The two overseers had met that night, in the basement of the dwelling at Glen-Eberley; Millhouse having taken one of the lower rooms to himself, while that adjoining had been assigned to Frampton. Porgy was suffered to live in loftier state, above stairs, to himself. The parties met always at the same table in the dining-room, and would sit together usually of an evening; but Millhouse had his own circle, of whom Fordham was one, whom he received only in his own domain. The two overseers went over together the whole history of the relations of our partisan with M'Kewn, as far as they knew it, and discussed with some anxiety the modes of escape for their superior from so voracious a person. It need not be stated here, that the united wisdom of the two was scarcely of a sort to help them very greatly in the encounter with the difficulty. The substance of all Fordham learned was conveyed the next day to Mrs. Eveleigh, whose interest in the affairs of Captain Porgy was no secret to him. He, himself, felt a great sympathy for our partisan, and found it impossible to avoid talking over the matter, and meditating the modes of escape. Of course the widow saw at a glance, that none of the suggestions of her overseer or of the captain's, could avail for any useful purpose. The next day she wrote a note to Porgy, requesting him to visit her; a summons which he promptly obeyed. Her son, Arthur, brought the invitation and the captain accompanied him on his return.

The two, however widely removed by years and experience, had become pretty close intimates, and Arthur had learned to relish the eccentricities of his senior, particularly as he always found something in his conversation which sensibly compelled his thoughts in a novel direction. Porgy loved the society of the young and framed his conversation to suit their tastes and impulses. He was playful as well as thoughtful, could happily unite the playful with the thoughtful, as is the case usually with the contemplative mind; and, what with narratives of the stirring events of the army, anecdotes of persons and performances, a lively satirical vein, and a frank humor, he contrived, without much effort, to make himself highly attractive to the youth, who frequently rode over to Glen-Eberley to sit, as well as *bird* with him, and who, for a time, became quite enthusiastic in his admiration of the partisan. He frequently amused his mother with a recital of the subject-matter of conversation between them, and learned to repeat the good things of the captain, as if they were his own.

Porgy, who liked the grace and spirit of the youth, was pleased with the admiration which he displayed, and was at some pains to secure it. Arthur possessed a pair of foils, left by his father; Porgy gave him lessons in fencing, and was equally delighted with his rapidity of improvement, and the grace and ease of his address in swordmanship. In brief, the veteran and the youth were on terms of the most cordial intimacy; and the latter, as soon as he heard the particulars, became, of course, deeply concerned in the legal embarrassments of the former. We need not say that he could give no help by his counsels in the matter, though he rather inclined to the opinion of Millhouse that the better method was to contrive some way of fighting through the difficulty, and it was with a modest earnestness that he whispered to the overseer his perfect willingness to serve as a volunteer in any expedition which should contemplate this method of squaring accounts with Porgy's creditor.

He listened with curious interest, and possibly some dissatisfaction, when he heard his mother gravely rebuke the captain for suffering himself to get angry with M'Kewn.

"You ought to have conciliated him as far as possible. Your policy should be to gain time. There is none in precipitating the event. Doubtless, you had provocation, but—"

"Very great!" muttered Porgy, but he could not venture to tell her that she herself had been the subject.

"We must still gain time, captain—gain as much as possible. There are now no courts in session. There will be none till the fall. I don't know much of business, but I suppose M'Kewn can scarcely proceed till then—"

"I don't know that," said Porgy. "I know very little of the law, but I believe there are certain processes which, even before judgment, will enable a creditor to bind or seize a debtor's property."

"We must consult with Pinckney. In the meantime, there is a matter which concerns this person M'Kewn, in connection with both of us, which, perhaps, ought to be known to you, though, as affairs at present show themselves, I do not see that the possession of my statement merely, will be of any avail to your relief."

She proceeded to tell of the papers which she had appropriated from the desk of Moncrieff, but suddenly arrested herself to say to her son—

"Arthur, remember, this matter must not be whispered by you to anybody. It may do mischief if repeated, particularly under impulse or excitement, and without the means to prove what I say."

She then went on to speak of the missing box, and manuscripts, and to describe the contents of the latter, giving particulars, of which we are already in possession. Porgy saw at once the importance of the statement could the writings be recovered.

"My dear widow," said he, "could we recover the papers, and prove this fellow's handwriting, which I could do easily, we should have him at our mercy."

"This was the opinion of Mr. Parsons; it is also the opinion of Colonel Pinckney. I have consulted both; and but for the unfortunate loss of that box—"

"It must be found. I will find it," cried Porgy.—"That fellow Bostwick must be forthcoming."

"Has nothing been heard of him?"

"Nothing for two months. I have sworn to hang him to the first tree, should I lay hands on him, if only for the benefit of his wife and children."

"Stay!" said Mrs. Eveleigh, putting her finger on her lips, "here comes little Dory."

And the little girl came into the piazza at the moment, and entered the hall, passing promptly forward to the captain, and putting her little white hand into his. He looked at her with surprise. Such a change as a few days had wrought in her appearance. She was newly clad, in better quality of clothes, made in better style. It was Cinderella, the drudge, converted by fairy hands, into Cinderella the princess. The little thing, beautiful in all her obscurity, was singularly so, emerged from the cloud. She smiled consciously, as she saw the captain perusing the change. He kissed her between the eyes, and with a bound she darted away.

Scarcely had she gone when Arthur Eveleigh showed himself a little restiff. In a few moments he disappeared also, leaving the captain and his mother to conclude their conference without witnesses. It is not our cue to pursue it further. Enough that Porgy left the widow with the increasing conviction that he was destined, in some way, to owe his safety and relief to her. They had agreed upon certain matters together. They were both to write to Colonel Pinckney, while Porgy was to renew his efforts at recovering the missing box. When Arthur Eveleigh returned to the house which he had left, on some pretext of looking after dogs and birds, he seemed a little disappointed that Porgy was gone, and at once resolved to ride after him. But he gave up the resolution in a moment after, and contented himself with taking up his rifle, calling up one of his squirrel dogs, and setting forth on a tramp into the pine woods.

His route led him directly down the avenue leading to the high road. He had scarcely emerged into this, before he encountered, on horseback, the very person of whose secret scoundrelism he had heard so much said only an hour before. M'Kewn, the Scotchman, was making his way directly toward the widow's. Arthur would have avoided him, by burying himself in the woods, but it was too late to escape unseen, and M'Kewn seemed determined to prevent it. He saw, in the aspect of the young man, the prejudices and suspicions of the mother. His policy was to disarm them both. We have seen that he had already called upon the widow. The rifle on the lad's shoulder, and the dog beside him, at once afforded him a clew by which to conciliate the son.

"Good morning, master Arthur," said he, as he approached; "good morning. You are for a squirrel-hunt, I perceive. Well, if you will take my woods you will find them in greater abundance than in any other part of the country. I do believe my fox-squirrels are the most magnificent of size that can be found anywhere. One of them can easily eat up half a dozen ears of corn at a sitting. Do me the favor to hunt them up and make as familiar acquaintance with them as possible. My grounds are always free to you, and you will find them full of other game. If you want a deer-hunt at any time, let me hear the night before, and I will secure you a shot; and, as for doves and partridges, you can scarcely skirt the fields anywhere without stumbling over them."

Arthur thanked him, but received the overture with coldness.

"Your mother's at home, I suppose. I see she has recently had a visiter."

Here he smiled significantly, looking up the road. The youth bowed.

"Captain Porgy is a frequent visiter at your house."

"Yes, sir; he comes sometimes, and we are always glad to see him."

"I suppose so,—I suppose so; the captain is no doubt a great gallant—most military men are. The ladies usually find them invincible. But the wars are now over, master Arthur, and the gown they tell us, when that is the case, soon gets the better of the sword. It is the captain's misfortune that he does not sufficiently credit this fact. I barely reminded him of the fact that he owed me a certain and very considerable debt, and he was for fighting me on the spot. Ha! ha! what do you think of such a mode of settling a debt?"

Arthur only looked at his rifle but said nothing.

"You say your mother's at home, master Arthur."

"Yes, sir."

"Well, I am about to visit her. I will not carry you back with me, knowing you had much rather be at better sport. But see to my fox-squirrels, will you, and remember, whenever you would have a crack at a buck, I can certainly give you one always."

The youth again thanked him, and hurried into the woods. M'Kewn looked after him as he disappeared, and muttered— "The cub has had his warning. They are all against me. But!—" and he gave his horse the spur, and was soon cantering up the avenue to the widow's dwelling. She received him very civilly, and after a few preliminary flourishes, he began—

"I have called to see you, Mrs. Eveleigh, as a neighbor whom I very much respect, in order that your mind may not be abused by anything that you may have heard respecting a late affair with Captain Porgy. I believe, my dear madam, I have as much desire to keep on good terms with my neighbors, as anybody in the country, and, I am sure, if there be any difference between us, the fault is not likely to be mine. You must know, Mrs. Eveleigh, that I am, and for years have been, a large creditor of the captain, and I hold a mortgage upon his lands. But this mortgage does not half secure me, and I called upon the captain, intending only to ask him for additional securities, when he fell into a passion with me, without any sort of provocation, imputed fraud to me, and I know not what, and so we parted. Now, as you may hear of this matter, from other sources, I wish to put you in the right as to the particulars. I have too much desire of your good opinion to be willing that you should hear of the affair from anybody but myself, and I am anxious to assure you that, as a new-comer into the neighborhood, it is neither my policy nor my wish to have any quarrel with anybody."

He said a great deal more than this, all in the most conciliatory vein. He had his own objects in keeping on good terms, especially with the widow, and in fact he was glad of any occasion which would justify his frequent visits. He was a bachelor and she was a fine woman, having a fine fortune. But, apart from this, he still entertained some lurking apprehensions that he might be somewhat in her power. Thinking that she had possessed herself of the missing papers between himself and Moncrieff, yet not quite sure that Bostwick had obtained them, there was a lurking anxiety which troubled him and made him quite solicitous to make the most favorable impression upon her.

M'Kewn was a hard but not ill-looking man, and he had seen enough of good society to carry himself fairly in the presence of the sex. We must not forget to mention that everything about him was in the first style of fashion. He wore the best clothes, and did not stint himself in decorations of his person. His fingers shone with rings. A large jewel blazed in the pin which secured the ruffles of his shirt. The frills at his wrist were of the finest lace. His boots would have satisfied the Bond or Broad street dandy; the equipment of his horse would have won admiration on the race-course; and all his domestic arrangements contemplated the best defined standards of the existing fashions. M'Kewn was emulous of the best social position, and, so far as money might be expected to secure it for him, it was used without stint or limit. The lady heard him with quiet composure to the end.

"I thank you for your complimentary wishes in regard to myself, but I should prefer not to be required to sit in judgment on this difficulty between yourself and Captain Porgy."

"Ah! madam, but that I have reason to know that the captain has been beforehand with me in his revelations, and the fear that you might be prejudiced in the matter—"

"Even if this were the case," said the lady, "I do not see, Mr. M'Kewn, how the matter will affect the interests of either of you."

"Ah! madam, I am not unaware of the interest which you have taken in the captain's affairs. I am not ignorant that it is to you, and your friendly loans, that he owes the restoration of his establishment,—and—"

"This, Mr. M'Kewn, it appears to me, is a business which need not provoke the concern of any third person."

"I beg pardon, madam;—you are right—I simply stated what was the notorious fact."

"It is one of those facts, sir, in respect to which there has been no privacy. Captain Porgy was in want of money, and I had money to lend. I lent him money on good security. I have a mortgage on all his negroes."

"But," with a smile, "that mortgage will scarcely cover them all. At present prices, five hundred guineas will scarcely buy twenty-five negroes, or the half of them."

M'Kewn had evidently been a shrewd inquirer into the affairs of the parties.

"Perhaps not, sir, and that is not the idea I mean to convey. It is enough that my loan is quite secure in order to justify me in making it, though I am not aware that my conduct in the transaction needs any justification."

"By no means, madam; do not suppose me guilty of any intention to convey such an idea."

The lady proceeded.

"One word, Mr. M'Kewn. Captain Porgy is a gentleman by birth and education, who has been doing good service to his country, for several years, without pay or reward, and to the grievous injury of his own fortune. It seems to me that he deserves every indulgence that can be accorded him by those who are grateful to Heaven for those blessings of independence which he has helped to win. I am at a loss to see what motive there can be for urging him to a satisfaction of these debts which can only be paid now by the entire sacrifice of his property.

"I understand you, madam; and I may say that I should have been pleased to indulge Captain Porgy, but he is a person who won't let you serve him; and when he insolently called my honor in question, he determined me to give him no indulgence. In brief, Mrs. Eveleigh, Captain Porgy is, with all his education, a mere ruffian, a coarse brutal soldier, who thinks to carry it with violence and a high hand against the laws. But he shall see. His personal insolence to me, madam, is beyond forgiveness."

"Really, Mr. M'Kewn, I do not understand you. Am I to understand that your mode of resenting a personal indignity is to clothe yourself with the terrors of the creditor, instead of—"

The lady paused. She felt that, in uttering this sarcasm, she had gone too far; she was doing mischief to the cause which she wished to help; and that her policy, on the part of Porgy, and as she had been counselling him, ought to be conciliatory only. She was conscious of error on other grounds. She had suffered local associations, and the current practice of the times to usurp place in her judgment, at the expense of her religion. She was ·

tacitly exhorting or goading the creditor to resort for his redress to the duello. She stopped herself suddenly, and apologized—

"Pardon me, Mr. M'Kewn, I am wrong. I did not mean this. Perhaps you are quite right in the assertion of your claims by established legal methods. That I should have thought, or suggested otherwise, only shows that the subject is one that should not properly concern me. Let me simply repeat the wish, that you should accord as much favor to a brave man,—not a ruffian, sir,—one whom, perhaps, you have somewhat ruffled,—as may be consistent with your interests. It will do you no hurt, but rather much good in the neighborhood, if you forbear as long as possible toward one who is such a general favorite."

"Nay, madam. One who is evidently a *particular* favorite," he answered with a sneering smile. The cheeks of the lady flushed and her eyes flashed fiercely.

"I am hardly prepared to understand you, Mr. M'Kewn, though it is evident from your looks and manner, that you designed something very sarcastic and offensive—"

"By no means, Mrs. Eveleigh—"

"Let me say, sir, by way of protecting myself, that I have been a soldier's wife; and I have learned some lessons from his feelings and opinions, which I may not advocate, or argue, or defend in any way, but the force of which I acknowledge, and the laws of which I obey. I am a woman, sir, it is true; but if it needs, for the assertion of my womanly dignity, that I should lift the weapon of the man, I shall feel no womanly fears in doing so. If you have any scruples, sir, in resenting personal indignities as men are apt to do, I have none; and though I have many friends, sir, who would cheerfully do battle in my cause, I would not suffer one of them to incur any peril of life or limb, while I am able to stand and confront the insolent, myself. I trust you understand me. Here, if you please, our conference must end."

She had risen when these things were to be said, and M'Kewn had risen also. Her tall and portly form, her commanding attitude, her sharp, clear voice, the indignant fires in her eye, breathing equal scorn and nobleness, were a study for the dramatic painter. She was Boadicea at the head of her Britons. She was Zenobia at the moment of her greatest confidence, when she defied all the strength of Rome. M'Kewn was awed. He stammered some inconsequential apologies, which only caused her lip to curl with increasing scorn.

"Go, sir," she said, " no more!—and yet, one word, sir. There was a person, one Bostwick, a squatter for many years on my lands, whom I had the fortune to encounter at Colonel Moncrieff's when you and he were in conference together. Do you know, sir, what has become of that man Bostwick?"

It was a mere instinct—a somewhat savage one—that prompted the widow to sent that shaft at random, seeking the proper victim. It struck him. M'Kewn, awed before, was now shocked, almost paralyzed. His face grew pale as death, his lips parted but not for speech. He stood for a moment vacantly gazing upon the inquirer, as still erect, with finger pointing directly to him, she seemed to await his answer. With a prodigious effort he at length gave it—only a single sentence, uttered with a gasp.

" I know nothing of the man."

" Ah !—well !—enough !"

She said no more, and, with a faint " good morning, madam," he hurried from the apartment.

CHAPTER LIII.

LANCE FRAMPTON GOES OFF SUDDENLY.

M'Kewn rode home with scarcely a consciousness of his progress. It was some time before he recovered from the Parthian shaft of the widow. He saw at a glance whither her suspicions tended, and it was only after a long interval, that he reflected that hers were suspicions only ; and so long as the missing papers were not forthcoming, no matter what suspicions were entertained, they could in no respect avail against him. But were the papers missing ? Had not Bostwick deceived him ? Was there not some reason for supposing, from the course taken by the widow, that she was still in possession of her proofs ? But a little calm reflection satisfied him to the contrary.

"If she had them, she never, with such a feeling toward me, and with such a passionate nature, could have kept quiet so long. It is her passion that speaks now. Had I not provoked her, she never would have let out so much. I'm glad that I stung her into the showing of her secret. It is now clear to me that Bostwick got the papers; and he—I trust that he is in the sea, or in ——, it matters not where, so he keeps away from this! Yet, she saw the rascal in that one glimpse at Moncrieff's? She has the eye of a hawk! She would fight too! Sword or pistols, five paces even, and never wink an eye! She should have been a man! She would have been a famous one! As a woman she would never suit *me*. She might undertake to horsewhip me in my own household. Will she marry this mammoth Porgy? No, indeed! She has been to long free to seek or suffer another master, now! D—n him, unless she marries, she shall not save him! I will strip and beggar him, if there be law or lawyer in the land."

Leaving him in this amiable determination, which underwent no modification with the progress of time, it is proper that we should glance at the affairs of other and subordinate parties in our true life-history. The appointed period had arrived when Lance Frampton should be united to Ellen Griffin. The wedding was to take place the very night of the day when Captain Porgy made his last visit, as briefly described, to Mrs. Eveleigh. When he returned home, not having remained to dine as usual with the widow, he found the lieutenant already making his preparations. His wedding-clothes were spread out; Pomp was brushing his boots; one of the negro-girls was mending his suspenders; and the youth himself, busy about a dozen different things, was in such a state of nervous excitement that he really knew not what he was doing. Somewhat forgetting his own affairs, the captain jested with him merrily, after his style of humor, upon the event which was approaching. Porgy, of course, had been invited to attend; so was Millhouse; Tom, the cook, without being asked, notified the young man that he would be present.

"You's one ob de family, Mass Lance, an' I muss' see how you guine through de ezaction [transaction]. It's wuss to some people, dis getting married, dan guine into de fight. Dey feels all ober wid a sawt ob cold sweat; and dey trimbles jest as ef dey was a-feelin' de push of the inimy's bagnets. Now, Mass Lance, le' me tell you wha' for do. Jes' before you hab for 'tan up before de passon, tek' a stiff pull at de Jamaica. He will help mek' you 'trong.—Ef you skear, nebber le' Miss Ellen see you skear; for womans always will tak' de vantage of man wha' dey see is skear. You mus' 'tan up 'traight, hole up your head, and jes' you keep t'inking all de time, ef you no kill de inimy, he guine to kill you.—Da's it ! and when you t'ink dat, you will shet your teet' close, an' fling out wid all you 'stren'th as ef you yer de cry all 'bout you, ' Ta'lton Qua'ters !' Ef you no feel 'trong dat time, when yon t'ink you y'er dat cry, you loss de battle, and de woman will be you maussa for ebber arter, for t'ree t'ousan' yers [years], an' all de season's guine to be winter ! Yerry wha' I say, and feel youse'f 'strong, 'fore de time for de fight come on.''

The sergeant contented himself with saying that, '' Marriage is good for some people. 'Twould do for the cappin, ef so be he got hold of the right pusson; but what sich a fellow as you, should git a wife for, thar's no seeing. You've got nothing, and she's got nothing, and two nothings put together, make a housefull of ixpenses, and not a shilling of profit. 'Twouldn't ha' done you eeny harm, Lance, ef you'd waited tell you was forty-five, like the cappin, and then died a bachelor, onless you could git the right sort of pusson,—one that had something to put to your nothing, my lad. But that's not saying that Ellen ain't a mighty nice gal, Lance; she is, and a purty, and I reckon it's that mostly what has taken you. But to be purty ain't enough, and when you marries so soon, you don't give yourself hafe a chaince.''

But these cold-water speeches did not discourage our lieutenant. They only served to increase his anxiety to have the affair over. An hour before sunset found the whole cavalcade ready for departure aud in the saddle, Porgy taking the lead, Lance and Millhouse riding together, just behind him, and Tom and Pomp bringing up the rear. Pomp had his violin slung about his neck. In his blue jacket, with red facings, his glazed cap, and white homespun breeches, Pomp felt that he had made a large stride in dignity since the period of his rescue from the British hulks. We owe it to the captain not to omit stating that he had sent off a cart a couple of hours before, with a demijohn of Jamaica, a gallon of wine, and some other small creature comforts, designed to help out the merry-making. He had also some presents for the bride in the shape of dresses and ornament, and a box and barrel, also conveyed by the cart, contained a pretty little contribution to the future housekeeping of the young couple. Millhouse saw these things put up to be sent, with no cordial feelings, though the subject was one upon which he dared not openly say a single word. But, in secret soliloquy, he deplored the captain's profligacy.

"They doesn't stand in need of all them things, and it's jest nothing better than waste. Waste breeds want; and the Lord knows how soon he'll be a-wanting everything himself. Then what's the look out? It runs from him, when he's got it, jest like water from the mill, when the dam's broke down in a fresh. Lord! how he does want a strick master over him!"

It was sunset when the party reached Mrs. Griffin's, and the company was already beginning to assemble. There were several young people of both sexes whom the captain did not know, and one of the girls, all of whom had walked, had got a tub of water in front of the house and was coolly washing her feet. Fordham, the overseer, was already present, and it struck Porgy that he seemed very much at home. He was assisting Mrs. Griffin in spreading and arranging tables. The captain thought he appeared officious rather than polite, particularly as he saw him disposing the tippet upon the widow's shoulders, which had been disordered by her exertions. There was much good-humored talk, and some mirth, in under tones between them, which put the overseer in a more obtrusive and less agreeable point of view than he had hitherto shown himself to Porgy's eyes. But the affair was one of a sort to render all parties free and easy, and our captain was persuaded that the customs of the country, and the class, with which he did not claim to be very familiar, might possibly justify all these freedoms. He was the more readily disposed to think thus when the widow Griffin, approaching him with the profoundest deference, and full of smiles, entreated him to come and take a seat which she had placed and prepared entirely for him, where he could be at ease, in one of the best positions for witnessing the ceremony, and on a capacious cushion which she herself had made especially for his use, and of which she entreated his acceptance. The captain was easily persuaded. The seat was a good one.—The cushion gave him the notion of a new luxury. He forgot very soon all his misgivings, while she sat beside him, listening with the most deferential manner to all he had to say, and Fordham civilly contented himself with making merry with the young people in the porch.

Candles and torches were lighted. The parson had arrived; the guests crowded into the hall, and pretty soon filled it. A decent interval, and the parson asked after the young lady. And soon she appeared attended by one bridesmaid. Ellen Griffin certainly looked very pretty in her simple white muslin frock, with one bright flower stuck in her silken ringlets, contrasting not more with them than with the delicate paleness of her cheeks. At her approach, Millhouse clapped Frampton on his shoulder, and murmured pretty loudly in his ears—

"Now, don't be skear'd. As Tom says, jest you think you're a-charging the inimy, and stand up stout for the crossing of bag'-nets. Don't you forgit the cappin is a-looking on you."

And the youth stood up, and his fingers met and twined in with those of the damsel, and the parson confronted them, and the ceremony was begun. Millhouse stood up in the rear of the lieutenant. But the occasional push in the ribs, and whispers which he gave him, did not seem to inspirit the youth, whose head continued to hang down bashfully, until, in the midst of the ceremony, the voice of the sergeant became audible—"Heads up, and the Lord be with you!"—to the consternation of the parson and half of the assembly. The youth was more prompt and decided in his demonstrations when he was instructed to salute the bride, which he did with a resounding smack that gave satisfactory testimony to the ears of the sergeant, who exclaimed—

"Well, that's doing it something like. Nobody kin say now it isn't done!"

The parson followed the example of the bridegroom, and Capt. Porgy followed him. The captain did not rest content until he bestowed a similar compliment, very suddenly, upon the widow Griffin herself, who stood provokingly nigh to Ellen; but he was confounded, a moment after, to find the overseer, Fordham, taking a similarly extempore liberty.

"He's surely been tasting the Jamaica!" muttered Porgy *sotto voce*; but Millhouse, who overheard the speech, promptly rejoined—

"He's after the sperrit and the flesh, both! Lord! I swow! but I should like to eat a leetle off the same plate! The widow looks like a mighty nice eatable!"

Porgy turned away from the speaker as in some displeasure, and resumed his seat upon the cushioned chair. The ceremony was fairly over; it had not been a long one; and merry was the uproar that followed. The company adjourned to the piazza, to dance, leaving the hall mostly vacant, and to the free use of those who were to arrange the supper. Porgy had his chair wheeled out to the porch. In those days, the parson, like any person of flesh and blood, waited for the frolic and the feast; and he and Porgy, while the fiddle of Pomp began to speak up, engaged in a warm controversy as to the merits of matrimony; both being upon the same side throughout, but differing in the philosophies by which the subject was approached. The fiddle of Pomp called up many guests who had not been invited. The negroes of a dozen plantations filled the yard in front, already practising in "Juba" and "double shuffle." Suddenly, Millhouse discovered that the whole regiment of Glen-Eberley was among the crowd. Here was a palpable infraction of the laws. Here was treachery and insubordination. The sergeant was in great commotion.

"I won't stand it, cappin, I'll be into 'em like a troop of dragoons. They must pack, every rascal among 'em, man and woman, or hickories don't grow in this country."

"Psho!" growled Tom, the cook, "wha' for you make so much bodderation, Mass Millhouse, when der's no use? De nigger done he w*u*k [work], he mus' hab he play! Enty you see dis dah wedding time, when ebb'rybody, wha' aint git marry hese'f, kin hab he fun?"

"Tom's right," quoth Porgy, "let the negroes stay, Millhouse, and enjoy themselves."

"They won't be worth a copper for work to-morrow, cappin."

"Then we must give them holyday. But that's all a mistake. They will work better for a little play to-night."

" Das a trute, maussa," said Tom. " De sergeant is too foolish preticklar. I don't t'ink he want nigger for sleep as much. Sleeping and dance is de t'ing for mek' nigger wuk like a gempleman, and keep him from tief. When he dance, he sweat out all he badness. Den he good, lub he maussa, an' 'tan' up to he wuk, like a sodger 'g'in de inimy. I wonder, Mass Millhouse, ef you nebber 'lows youse'f any pleasure ?"

" Do you ever see me at it, Tom ? Do you ever see me dancing ?"

" Da's kaise you kain't. You got only one arm for swing, when you shakes you leg, an' you goes over the wrong side. But nigger wha' got he two arm, aud he two leg, him kin dance an' feel he sperrit joyful! Look a' dem two boy, yonder, wha' dance Juba! Enty he do 'em great. Dem fellows is de most righteous young fellows, in Juba, I bin see, for t'ousand ye'rs! See how de leetle one shuffle he right leg, while t'udder one dey sleep. See how he's a-slapping he t'ighs [thighs] wid bot' he hand, jes' in time wid de fiddle, le' de fiddle jump about in wha' tune he please. And de fellow look, all de time, as ef he bin sleep; he eyes shut, and he face wid no more 'spression in 'em, dan a greasy punkin. And de udder fellow, wha' keep he eye so open bright, and look so keen 'pon de leetle fellow, see how he manage 'em! How he mek' um do jest de berry t'ing he want. Now he go quick, now he go slow, now he go quick and slow togedder, till de berry bones seem a-guine to fall out ob de breeches. Ha! de t'ing is a most extonishing, won'ersome t'ing, Mass Millh'us. Dem two boys is mak' for not'ng in dis worl' but to dance Juba."

" Ef they were mine, Tom, I'd find out, at the end of a hickory, ef they wasn't good for something besides Juba. I'd tickle 'em to another sort of music in the cornfield, I tell you."

" Psho !" muttered Tom, turning away, and giving the benefit of his response to his master. " De sergeant is too cussed foolish! He don't comprehend nigger nater 't all! He's always a-talking 'bout wuk, as ef der's no play in de worl'; and always a-talking 'bout hick'ries, as ef de airth was nebber mek' to raise any better t'ings! • Da's always de way wid dem poor buckrah, wha's got no nigger ob he own. He's always a-wanting to wuk de niggers ob udder gempleman's tell he bones come out ob he skin. Hah! he hab leetle touch on he own shoulder, ebbry morning, from hard maussa, jes' for tek de stiffness out ob um, he hab better comperhension ob nigger nater."

This taste may suffice; white and black danced till midnight. The former in the piazza and hall, the latter in the open grounds beneath the trees. Solid was the supper that followed, and strong the drink; and wild enough the scampering, great the shouting, hard the riding, when each party took its way homeward, somewhere about the dawn. Lance Frampton's wedding was an event which is still remembered upon the Ashepoo!

CHAPTER LIV.

SUMMARY OF THE EVENTS OF THE SUMMER.

THE summer was passing rapidly. Captain Porgy lived pretty much after the old fashion. He spent a day, occasionally, at Mrs. Eveleigh's; sometimes took his dinner at the widow Griffin's, where Lance Frampton had taken up his abode with his young wife. The time passed without much excitement, and with no absolute embarrassments. It was in the future that the clouds lowered threateningly, and the philosophy of Porgy was not to look in their direction. Whenever the subject of M'Kewn and his claims was forced upon him by the pertinacious Millhouse, he thundered and lightened for awhile, and finally thought upon the widow Eveleigh. She was his one particular bright star of hope, and one whom the policy of the sergeant for ever sought to place before his sight, as far as he dared do so after the stern warnings which he had received. The captain's own musings brought up her image with sufficient frequency to his eyes. He found himself perpetually arguing her virtues, her excellences, her charms, all of which he acknowledged freely to himself. But a sigh would usually close these meditations. There was still a something wanting to her perfections—he could not say what—or a something in excess, which left him always unwilling to pursue the subject to any definite result. It was through the medium of his own infirmity that he saw this deficiency, or excess, in the widow Eveleigh; and it was because he looked through this medium only, that he failed to determine in what it consisted. We are better prepared to see, and to resolve it, than himself. His infirmity was self-esteem; and the veneration of the widow had been qualified and moderated by a long intercourse with those higher walks of society in which faith is not apt to flourish. Convention is very much the foe to hero-worship.

When dissatisfied with his meditations in respect to the widow Eveleigh, Porgy found, invariably, that his thoughts turned for relief in the direction of the simpler widow, Griffin. There was something so meek, and artless about this lady—something so little imposing and yet so grateful—that his mood became soothed while he contemplated her. She rose before his mind's eye in an always gracious attitude, and with a most gracious aspect. He remembered her slight form with pleasure, and contrasted it with that of the widow Eveleigh. The latter, in all such comparisons, appeared to him to be quite too masculine. The former seemed the very embodiment of feminine perfection. His ideas of woman were those of a period when the sex had not yet determined to set up for itself; though wielding a most potent sway in society, and even in politics, particularly in Carolina. His models, accordingly, required absolute dependence in the woman, though without meaning to abridge any of her claims as a woman, or to subjugate, unjustly, her individuality. He never dreamed of denying her any of her rights, when he required that she should recognise the lordship in the hands of the man. There was something assured in the position and the endowments of Mrs. Eveleigh, that startled his sense of authority. Her very virtues had a manly air which girded his pride; her very wealth, and its importance to his own case, seemed to humble him in his relations with her; and, when he admitted to himself, as he was forced to do, that this wealth was really a consideration in the case, the effect was to lessen the attractions of the lady, which were yet intrinsically very great in his eyes. Had she been poor, and were there no Mrs. Griffin in the field, we venture the opinion that Porgy would never have fancied any other woman. As the case stood, there were times when he decidedly gave her the preference, and fancied that his heart was absorbed wholly with her attractions;—when he believed that his affections demanded her sympathies, and would be satisfied with nothing less; and, so feeling and thinking, he would resolve to ride over, after an early breastfast, or *to* an early breakfast, the next morning, and bring his cogitations to the final issue, and his doubts along with them. But a sound night's rest, with probably, some faint, shadowy vision of the widow Griffin in his dreams, seemed to act as a sudden sedative to his passion for the wealthier widow, and the purpose would dissipate into thin air, while his meditations would become more dubious, yet more intense than ever.

His admiration of, or attachment to, Mrs. Griffin, was not without its qualifications also. He could not fail to be disquieted as he reviewed her intellectual inferiority. In this respect, she was the weakest vessel in the world. She had no intelligent conversation; no education; no experience; no natural endowment; no mother wit; and, though her sweet temper, gentle bearing, and implicit deference, were all agreeable to his self-esteem, he could not but ask himself whether something more was not requisite to the one whom he should choose as a companion in life. While the war lasted, and when the life of the camp rendered most of the desires sensual, he would not have vexed himself with any such inquiry. He then thought only of the excellent management of the housekeeper; her skill in soups and stews; the culinary art which would convert a vegetable into a meat, a wing of chicken into a fish; and at such like magical and charming transmutation, viewed through this medium only, Mrs. Griffin was incomparable.

To a certain extent, Porgy still examined his object through these endowments. But his media of study had become multiplied. Released from the camp, and its necessities, old tastes had been resumed; ancient refinements were recalled; long banished, or subdued tastes, had been once more lifting their heads; and his sensual nature had been gradually taking some golden and amber hues and tints from the recovering vigor of his mind and fancy. Griffin, was, in certain respects, therefore, as difficult a case as Eveleigh; and the captain of partisans, sitting, pipe in mouth, at Glen-Eberley, and looking alternately to the fair widows on either hand, might be likened to that sagacious animal (whose length of ears has been unkindly made his reproach) who sees, on each side of him, a goodly bundle of sweet fresh hay which, drawing both ways with equal strength, will suffer him honestly to approach neither. The struggle, occasioned by this embarrassment of taste and need, was such as sometimes to affect the appetite of the captain. He evidently grew thinner as the summer and his meditations grew together. There was no such amplitude of waist to be girded in, as formerly, when he toiled, and travelled, and fought, daily and nightly in the army. He now took in several more inches in his belt, and, not unfrequently, the sergeant drew his attention, with great concern, to his diminishing dimensions.

"It's the heat of this infernal summer," said Porgy.

"It's the want of a fondelsome wife, cappin, as I've been a-telling you all along—a woman of substance, that'll help you drive off that d——d sheriff, and put the idee that troubles you out of your head."

"How the devil should I get the sheriff out of my head when you are constantly thrusting the monster in at my ears?"

This outbreak usually terminated such a discussion. Meanwhile, M'Kewn, like some great political spider, sat in the centre of his web of meshes, and waited for the moment when, in the exhausted state of the victim, he should fall an easy prey. He was not altogether quiet, though seemingly so. The lawyers were at work in the city. Documents, with great seals, were in preparation. Vile inventions, vulgarly denominated writs and declarations, were getting in readiness. Malice was keen in its work, and law, with solemn brow and sable gown, was pliant—ready to give the demon all necessary help. Stately and serious letters had been brought to Porgy, from dignitaries yclept attorneys-at-law. He, too, had written solemn, serious, stately letters, to the same class of persons. These parties had benevolently arrayed themselves on both sides of the question, in order, perhaps, that justice, like any other fat body trying two stools, should fall equally between; and Porgy, on the one hand, and M'Kewn on the other, were looking to what was termed, "The Fall Term," for results more serious than any fall of the leaves known to either. M'Kewn confidently calculated on having his claims, in cash and character, equally satisfied; but he had moments of misgiving and apprehension, which were usually betrayed by brief and expressive oaths, and adjurations, at the expense of persons of both the sexes.

"That d——d prying widow! If I only knew! That rascally ruffian, Bostwick—were I sure that he is feeding the sharks at the bottom of the sea!"

Unfortunately, the sea refused thus far to give up its secrets, and the prying widow was quite as close as she was curious. She seemed quite able to keep hers! The Scotchman got nothing by his curses. Whether, like chickens, they were destined to return home for roosting, is yet to be seen.

In certain respects, the summer was auspicious to all the parties. M'Kewn's overseer made him a good crop; Fordham did the same thing for the widow Eveleigh; while Millhouse, as if fate had studied to justify all his boasts, succeeded in beating both of them, in proportion to the force he managed. Never had such a crop been seen at Glen-Eberley. The season had been a very favorable one, and Millhouse had shown indefatigable industry, and a very correct judgment; but he probably owed a good deal to the fact that the lands of Glen-Eberley had been so long rested. Harvest-time came on under good auspices, and the sheaves were heavy with the golden grain. Great was the *swangering* of Sergeant Millhouse, as, with his brother overseers, he reviewed the result. He had engaged in a friendly contest with Fordham and Blythewood (the overseer of M'Kewn), and they yielded the palm of victory to the sergeant, with good humor, and literally "acknowledged the corn." Porgy was pleased, of course; and Millhouse required him to acknowledge his satisfaction, and do justice to his particular genius, almost nightly. But, even the sergeant's pride and pleasure bore no sort of proportion to the same feelings in the bosoms of his negroes. They showed their triumph in greater degree than any other parties. It was their labor that had brought out the genius of Millhouse —it was their crop that had put to shame the negroes of the rival plantations. Porgy gave them a great pork supper after the harvesting, while the bets of the sergeant, with his opponents, resulted in his obtaining one also, at their expense, in which Jamaica occupied a place as distinguished as pork, and which kept busy the party of a dozen—the number present— through the hours of a goodly Saturday night; the dawn of

Sunday looking in upon them at their feast, before they were quite satisfied to think it finished.

The profits of Captain Porgy afforded no satisfaction to M'Kewn, except so far as they promised better spoils when they should fall into his clutches. If he rejoiced in the result, it was with no benevolent feeling; but rather with the vindictive thought of the deeper disappointment and mortification of his victim, whom he should thus topple and overthrow from a greater height and hope, which this good fortune should encourage. He felt secure of his prey, unless in one event, and this he labored in a secret way to defeat. This subject of his apprehension was the marriage of Porgy with the widow Eveleigh. He was quite aware of the frequent visits of the captain to the widow, and he conjectured the object of these visits with much more certainty than Porgy could determine it. He, himself, would have had no objection to taking the widow to wife; but he had common sense enough to see that, with her present prejudices against him, the thing was impossible. But he was a hopeful person, and did not despair, if time were allowed him, of removing these prejudices. At all events, it was his policy to prevent the success of the captain. To this he addressed himself in sundry ways, one of which, and the most likely to be successful, was through her son, Arthur.

We have seen that his first approaches to the young man had been unsuccessful. For a time they continued so; but perseverance will remove mountains quite as certainly as faith; youth is flexible, indulgent, and easily persuaded, where much solicitude is shown to gain it; and gradually M'Kewn found his way to the ears of Arthur. He contrived, without seeming effort, to meet the lad frequently, when he rode out or rambled in the woods. He was always particularly deferential to him, and thus adroitly appealed to the vanities of youth. Gradually, the slight barriers which the mother's prejudices had raised up in his mind, against his neighbor, were broken down. Finally, M'Kewn persuaded him to accept a beautiful English pointer. The widow was greatly chagrined that he did so, and Arthur himself was disposed to regret it, when he found his mother so much fretted; but the thing was done; and the result was, that the son, after a while, began to combat the prejudices of his mother against the

Scotchman, and to declare that he always found him a marvellous proper man. The widow became a little angry, and the young man a little insubordinate. Unfortunately, she could not venture to convey all her suspicions to him, of M'Kewn's agency with the outlaws, and with the robbery of her negroes, so that all she could exhibit was her naked and, seemingly, unreasoning hostility, which Arthur was old enough to see lacked obvious justification. It was additionally unlucky that, recently, the cares and anxieties of Porgy had rendered him a somewhat cloudy companion for the young man, while the marriage and withdrawal of Lance Frampton, had taken from him one of the chief inducements for his visits to Glen-Eberley.

Under these circumstances, M'Kewn enjoyed favorable opportunities which he never allowed to escape him. Gradually, and when in some measure he had won the ears of the youth, he suffered himself to speak of the affairs of Porgy — of his recklessness of character, and his associates; his debts; and went so far as to indulge in some sneers at his mammoth dimensions, his amplitude of abdomen, and the enormous appetite in which he was supposed to indulge. When he found, after a while, that these jests and sneers, provoked the young man's smiles, he felt encouraged. His next labor — a more delicate one, but which he pursued with as much art as diligence — was to convey to the youth a notion of what he supposed to be the object of Porgy in his visits to his mother. He insinuated the idea, so formidable to a young man of self-esteem, of a despotic father-in-law; then hinted at the waste of property to supply the appetite, or repair the ruined fortunes of a profligate; and then, in immediate sequence, he would turn to Porgy, and make a ludicrous portrait of his unwieldy figure.

The youth was slow to receive the revelation so gradually made; but, at length, it unfolded itself fully before the eyes of his mind, and, then, a great many things, hitherto strange in his past experience, became clear to his understanding. He could now comprehend the impudent language and manner of Millhouse, when the party dined with his mother, already described, and which then provoked his wonder. As a matter of course, his indignation was aroused, and, the chief force of it fell upon the captain. But the suggestions of M'Kewn, as they were designed, led him farther—led him to think somewhat harshly of his mother, and suspiciously of her motives in aiding the captain. That she should sympathize with Porgy, encourage his visits, aid him with loans of money, receive him with so much welcome, show herself so solicitous of his comforts, were all ascribed to her own secret attachment to the man, and argued the probability that she would finally lift him into the lordship of the household; an idea which Arthur Eveleigh found quite insupportable. The moment that this apprehension was forced upon him, he hurried home full of aroused feelings which he neither could, nor desired to, suppress. This happened at a moment of some importance. He found Captain Porgy closeted with his mother, evidently discussing some matter, which seemed of mutual interest. Perhaps it may be well to account for the present interview.

As we have shown, the time was ripening fast for the consummation of M'Kewn's legal projects for the ruin of his debtor. The summer had past: the fatal "Fall Term" had come; the courts were in session; and at length there were decrees, and judgments. Porgy was advised by his lawyers that danger was at hand; and that he might soon reasonably look to see hawks abroad. He had been warned also that his case could not be helped, that judgment could not long be averted. He, accordingly, prepared himself, as well as he could, to fold his robes about him and die with decency. There were some preliminary performances which he felt to be absolutely necessary to his peace of mind. In order to attend to one of these, he summoned Tom to his presence.

"Tom," said he, "put on your best clothes. I want you to ride over with me to Mrs. Eveleigh."

Tom was soon becomingly equipped. The master and man were soon mounted; and, on the way, the captain opened the business upon which he was bent, to his favorite *cuisineur*.

"Tom."

"Sah!"

"You are still a tolerably young fellow."

"Ha! maussa, enty I bin know dat."

"You have no wife, but you will be thinking of one some of these days."

"Lawd ha' mussy; we does we bes', but who kin tell wha' guine happen to um next day and to-morrow?"

"True, Tom, who knows! You will get a wife, you will probably have a family, and you might be happy for a great many years, if your life were spared so long."

"Da's true, maussa."

"I don't wish to shorten your life, Tom—"

"Wha' maussa!"

"I wish to see you live as long as God will let you—"

"To be sure; t'ank you, maussa!"

"But, Tom, if I am to see you live as the slave of that scoundrel, M'Kewn, I should rather you were dead. Now, Tom, I must either sell you to Mrs. Eveleigh, or shoot you."

"Shoot me Tom! Oh! git out, maussa, da's all only you' ole foolish talk. Tom aint for shoot."

"Then I must sell you, Tom, or M'Kewn will have you."

"Ha! I tek' de swamp fuss! I nebber guine lib wid dat crook-eye Scotchman."

"Better live with Mrs. Eveleigh."

"I no so much lub for lib wid womau, nodder, maussa. Woman, maussa, is a most too hard 'pon nigger. Wha' for I must be sell?"

"I owe M'Kewn money—the sheriff will seize you if you belong to me. I wish Mrs. Eveleigh to buy you, to keep you out of his clutches; and if I am ever able to buy you back from her, I will do so. Meanwhile, I will hire you from Mrs. Eveleigh."

Such was Porgy's scheme, by which to save his favorite. Tom, for a long time, failed to see the merits of it; but, silenced at length, if not satisfied, he followed his master, with a very gloomy aspect, to the residence and the presence of the widow. There, our captain of partisans made a frank showing of his fears, his wishes—Tom being in the presence all the while.

"Pinckney writes that nothing can be done to avert this judgment—that it must take effect—that the lien upon the lands is perfect—that judgment upon the unliquidated accounts, once entered, will bind all the slave property and moveables, subject only to your mortgage, and that that mortgage will not prevent the sale. Tom, Mrs. Eveleigh, is the only one of my negroes not covered by your mortgage. I hesitated to forego my entire control over his destinies, as it was my purpose always that Tom should never be the slave of any man but myself. I should free him this hour, if this were possible; but Pinckney writes that such grant of freedom would not avail against existing debts and creditors. But I may make a *bona-fide* sale of him, Mrs. Eveleigh, and I propose to do so to you. You will give me a hundred guineas for him, with the understanding between us that I am to hire him from you at fair wages, and that you will sell him back to me, on the same terms, whenever I shall feel able to repurchase him. Should I never do this, my dear madam, I shall still feel some consolation that I have kept my vow—to sell him to no other man—and, in selling him to a woman, I sell him to one whom I esteem the very first among her sex."

Here Tom put in.

"You buy me, Miss Eb'leigh, I good sarbant to yer. You's a lady. Yer wha' maussa say. He's berry much trouble dese times, and don't know wha' for do! You kin help 'em. Help 'em, an' I berry much 'blige to you, ma'am. Ef you buy me, I promise you I guine tek' care ob you, same as I tek' care ob maussa.—When Tom say he guine be good sarbent, you kin do no better dan buy 'um."

"I believe you, Tom," said the lady, kindly, "and I think I may safely promise you to be an indulgent mistress. You may go home now, Tom, and consider yourself as belonging to me. I shall arrange all with your master."

"T'ank you, missis, and de Lawd pour down he blessing 'pon you 'tell you beg him for stop, you own se'f. God bress you, missis, an' a berry good mornin' to you."

"Thank you, Tom. Good-by to ye."

And with a grasp of the hand of his late master, and a bow to his new mistress, Tom disappeared, and proceeded to canter back to Glen-Eberley.

Porgy had prepared and brought with him the necessary bill of sale. He had signed it in the presence of Lance Frampton, the night before. The widow asked if he did not desire any written engagement, from her, to resell the negro to him, according to their private understanding; but, with his usual indifference to his own securities, the captain declined it. The lady

gave him an order upon the city for a hundred guineas, and received, and put away, the bill of sale. The wages of Tom,
while he remained in the service of his former owner were then
easily adjusted; and the parties were still engaged in conversation, the captain very low in spirits, and the lady, with a justi-
cious delicacy, striving to soothe and conciliate him, when Arthur
Eveleigh bounced into the room.

CHAPTER LV.

THE WIDOW AND HER SON.

A SINGLE glance at the young man sufficed to show that he
was greatly out of humor. He spoke with bare civility, and no
cordiality, to his ancient friend, the captain. The widow regarded her son with anxious and reproachful eyes, which he retorted
with such looks of evident suspicion and bad feeling as to con-
found and disquiet her. Porgy saw that something was wrong,
but had no notion that he was a party to the provocation. He
spoke to Arthur in the old language of familiarity and affection,
but without perceiving any very grateful effect from it. The
young man had come in with his fowling-piece and birding equipments, which suggested to Porgy the proper subject for talking
with him.

"Why do you not look for your birds at Glen-Eberley, Arthur?
It is a full month since you have paid me a visit. The partridges
are in abundance. You can scarcely walk anywhere without
flushing them."

"I need not go off the place here, sir, to seek for birds; when
I do, I find them in as much abundance, at Mr. M'Kewn's, as I
desire."

"M'Kewn!" said Porgy and was silent.

"I wish, my son," remarked the lady, "that you would seek
your birds in any other quarter."

"And I don't see why, mother. Mr. M'Kewn is very civil to
me."

" There are some civilities which I am half inclined to regard as injuries !" said the lady gravely; " but it should be enough for *you*, my son, that I have expressed my wishes. My objections to this man—"

" Unless there be *good* reasons for them, mother—"

"Of the goodness of my reasons, my son, you should allow me to be the judge, without requiring me to show what they are. It ought to be sufficient for you that I have expressed my wishes—"

" Your wishes ! Ah ! but have you expressed them ?" was the pert response, and something of a sneer upon his lips.

" I do not understand you, Arthur. You certainly have heard from me the repeated wish that you should have as little communion with this man, as was not absolutely unavoidable."

" And I don't see why, mother. Mr. M'Kewn seems quite as much of the gentleman as most men I've seen," replied the youth petulantly, and looking at Porgy.

" You have been unfortunate, my son ; or, which is more likely, you are scarcely yet a sufficient judge of the subject, or a sufficient discriminator of persons."

" Perhaps not," said the fiery youth, his face reddening ; " but mother—!"

Here he paused abruptly and with evident effort restrained himself. Porgy at this moment rose. His manner was mild, calm, and dignified ; a little touched with sorrow. He felt that he was in at the beginning of something like a scene, and he had no taste for it, or curiosity to witness its close.

" Mrs. Eveleigh, suffer me once more to thank you for your kindness. I shall remember with gratitude what you have done for me. I will trespass no longer. Good-by, ma'am—good-by;" and he shook her hand warmly. " Arthur, I am half tempted to regret that you can find your birds at any other point than Glen-Eberley. We can afford you *friends* there as well as birds; and such friends as will never desert you when the battle's coming on."

To this the youth had no answer. He gave his hand sullenly to the captain, who looked at him kindly and curiously, but with a smile that seemed to say, " I understand all your difficulty, my boy," but, beyond his farewell, he had no more words to say. The widow would have persuaded him to stay to dinner, but, glancing significantly from her to her son, he declined the invitation. He did instinctively understand the case of Arthur Eveleigh. Riding out of the avenue, he muttered to himself—"The foolish boy; that scoundrel, M'Kewn, has been poisoning his ears. I should not be surprised if the rascal had been telling him that I was courting his mother."

He meditated sadly as he rode. "What a pitfall, what a thing of snares, of serpents, and sorrows, is this miserable life. How the devil hangs upon the footsteps of innocence, turn whither it will, ready to delude, to defraud, to degrade, to destroy. Here is this youth, just as he begins to drink of the better and purer sweets of life, the fiend drops his malignant poison into the bowl; embittering the taste as well as the draught—and shaping the whole future career for sin and sorrow. I had taken a great liking to that boy. He could have made a noble fellow. But, he looks upon me as an enemy. He looks upon his own mother with suspicion. It has needed but a mean cunning on the part of this miserable wretch, M'Kewn, to make him turn upon his natural and best allies. Heaven help us, for with the devil at our elbow, with foes among those who surround us, and the vices and vanities at our own hearts to second their labors, unless Heaven help us in season, and with all its angels, hope and humanity stand but a poor chance for happiness."

The subject offered a fruitful matter for reflection after he got home, which a draught of Jamaica with the sergeant, and a long dissertation from that person, *de omnibus rebus*, &c., failed wholly to arrest or dissipate. We must leave him to its indulgence while we return to the widow's, curious to see that issue between herself and son, which Porgy preferred to escape. She was not slow to approach the subject.

"My son you have behaved very strangely, very coldly, almost rudely, to Captain Porgy. May I know what he has done to occasion this treatment?"

"I don't see that he deserves any other," was the dogged reply.

"Indeed, Arthur, this is a very singular change of feeling and opinion. A month or two ago, you were so perpetually over at Glen-Eberley, that I feared you might wear out the welcome you received; now—"

" I went then to hunt with Lieutenant Frampton."

" But you also hunted with the captain, and your report was always singularly favorable in respect to *him*. You have evidently nothing kind or cordial in your feelings toward him, now; and, as I trust you will never allow yourself to be guilty of any mean evasion of the truth, I hope that you will frankly inform me as to what has caused that change in your conduct, which is sufficiently apparent to him as well as to me."

" But I want to know, mother, why it is that you are so anxious that I should be on good terms with this Captain Porgy."

" I am anxious that you should be just and honorable, my son; not mean, or captious; not capricious and unprincipled."

" I don't see how I should be either, only because I do not like him."

" Unless you have a good reason to justify your dislike, you must be all of these, Arthur. We owe Captain Porgy a great and vital service—"

" We owe just as much to Lieutenant Frampton, and the one-fisted sergeant, mother."

" That may be, but that doesn't lessen our obligations to him."

" At least, *they* do not *presume* upon *their* services."

" I am yet to know that *he* does."

" What does he come here so frequently for, then ?"

" I suppose he finds some pleasure in doing so."

" Ah ! and you find pleasure in it, too, mother ?"

There was an increasing color in the widow's cheeks, as she met the gaze and heard the significant inquiry of the forward boy, but she answered him very quietly—

" Certainly; I find Captain Porgy a very pleasant associate. I know few gentlemen whose conversation is so sensible and interesting."

" Gentleman ! he looks very much like a gentleman with that great paunch of his, large as a rice-barrel."

" Stop, Arthur; I must not suffer this sort of language in my hearing. You forget yourself, my son; you forget what is due to me, and to this worthy, but unfortunate man. I shall say no more of what we owe him for saving your mother from indignity, and possibly from death, since you do not seem sufficiently to comprehend the extent or value of this service. It is enough that I require you to forbear such rude language of one whom I am pleased to honor as my friend and neighbor."

"Is he going to be content, mother, with being friend and neighbor? Does he aim at nothing farther? Is he not borrowing all your money to pay for his extravagances? Is he not—"

"Stop, once more, my son! Am I to understand, Arthur, that you suppose *yourself* likely to lose the money which I lend to Captain Porgy?"

"I don't see what else will follow, living as he does, and having to pay off his old debts."

"You have been listening to an enemy, Arthur. But let me disabuse you. It is not possible that you or I shall lose anything by the loans made to Captain Porgy. These are all sufficiently secured by mortgage; the papers drawn up by Colonel Pinckney, who assures me that the debt is perfectly secure. We get legal interest on the money, and, so far, Captain Porgy is, perhaps, less under obligations to me than I am to him. If your cause of disquiet contemplates nothing beyond this, you may reasonably dismiss it from your mind; but there is something farther, Arthur. The evil spirit who has found his way to your ear, has never been content with so meagre a scheme of doing mischief. Let me hear all that disturbs you, my son; keep nothing back; I would rather you should pain me directly to the core, than leave me to apprehend that you entertain thoughts and feelings in secret, which you dare not unfold to your mother."

The youth seemed for a moment uneasy. He strode hurriedly off to a window, and seemed to look out. The widow calmly awaited him, without seeming to observe his motions. After a pause, he wheeled about suddenly, approached her, and, as if he had brought himself to the proper point of determination, he said :—

"I ask you, mother, if you think that Captain Porgy comes here only when he wants company or money? I want you to tell me if you think he has not some other purpose? Speak candidly, mother, as you ought to speak to me, and as I have a right to expect that you will speak."

The mother almost sternly surveyed the youth; then, with rigid lips, she answered—

"We may think differently, Arthur, about our mutual rights.

I certainly ought not to be required to account for the secret motives of action of Capt. Porgy or of any other man. Your challenge of my candor, unless you have some imputation upon it, is only a gratuitous offence, my son. At your age and mine, there may be cases when it would not be proper to unfold to you all my thoughts or opinions. Where these contemplate the character or motives of other persons, I should be wrong in doing so. If you have any *particular* question to put to me, Arthur Eveleigh, which would seem to be the case from what you do say, let me hear it, and if it is proper for me to answer, and if my son has a right to make the question, let him be assured that I shall answer with the utmost readiness."

The youth hastily strode the chamber. He was evidently reluctant, half-ashamed, to betray the lurking suspicions in his mind. But, at length, as if vexed at his own weakness, he paused, stood erect, and pointing to a splendid, full length of Major Eveleigh, which hung against the wall—a noble figure, in the prime of manhood, and garbed in the rich military costume of Britain,—he cried out with a burst of passion—

"That is my father, mother, as he looked, as he lived. Can it be possible that you mean to fill his place with such a person as this Captain Porgy ?"

And the boy looked noble, erect, manly, almost magnificent, like his father, as he uttered the passionate inquiry. Had there been sufficient cause for his question,—had the widow shown herself weak, frivolous, wanton, easily accessible, and inclining to fling herself away upon a worthless person—there would have been something very admirable in his bearing and position. The mother looked at him a moment, her face pale with indignation, and the tears gushed, all at once, in a flood from her eyes. Through them she spoke, with impetuous anger.

" Arthur Eveleigh, you have been listening to that devil of mischief, M'Kewn. You have suffered this vile Scotchman to fill your ears with venomous discourse. You have meanly permitted him to whisper to you a scandal of your own mother. You have basely suffered him to fill your heart with evil thoughts of one to whom your mother owes her life and honor. And you have suffered this wittingly. You were warned against this evil-minded wretch. You were taught to regard him as an object of suspicion and dislike.　You have preferred his counsels to those of your mother—to those of your friend.　You have been used by him as a despicable tool against friend and mother.　Leave me for the present, Arthur Eveleigh.　I can neither speak to you, nor look on you, with a proper calm of temper.　Leave me."

"But mother—"

The young man was aghast.　He had never seen his mother so fearfully aroused—had never so aroused her himself,—and now began to feel that he had unwisely and unbecomingly trespassed.

"Yet stay," she said, "and hear farther, Arthur Eveleigh.—While I acknowledge my responsibilities to you, as your mother, and the representative of your father, I still hold an independent relation to you in all matters which concern myself.　On these, I will submit to no dictation.　I shall be the mistress of my own thoughts, feelings, and sympathies, as far as it lies in my power to be so.　I shall account to you in no respect, unless I am pleased and prefer to do so.　While I shall never feel the relations between your late father and myself to be other than sacred and very precious, if it should seem to me wise, and right, and grateful to take another husband, it shall be my own will that I shall consult in the matter.　It may be that your own conduct shall compel me to this, where I would not choose.　I must have affections and sympathies—I must have devotion and society—I must love, Arthur, and must be beloved—at all events, I must be confided in.　If my own son abandons me for the stranger—if he prefers the counsel of the serpent against which I have warned him, and offends me with the rude insolence of his suspicions, I must seek succor elsewhere.　You have heard me.　It is for you to determine.　Go now; yet hear me: go not to this man, M'Kewn.　I tell you, Arthur Eveleigh, that you must make your choice between this evil genius and your mother.　I must cease to trust you, if I find you put any trust in him."

"Mother, dear mother!"

He rushed, with a cry, and threw his arms around her.

"Forgive me, dear mother, forgive me!"

He clung to her, sobbing his regrets and repentance aloud.—She folded him fondly to her arms.

"Oh! Arthur, you know not how rude a blow you have struck my heart."

Just then, the little Dory came in, and with looks of equal ter
ror and sympathy, darted to them both. The widow laid one
hand upon the head of the child, kissed her son, and freeing herself from his grasp, hurried out of the chamber.

"Oh! Arthur, what is the matter?"

"Only I have been very foolish, Dory, and have made my
mother vexed."

"But you are sorry, Arthur?"

"Very sorry, very."

"Then God will forgive you, Arthur."

"Ah! if I could only forgive myself, Dory."

"But you will, Arthur, for my sake."

"For your sake, Dory?—well, for your sake, I will try,—but
I have been very, very foolish. I have made my mother very
angry."

"She will forgive you, Arthur.   Go to her now, and beg her."

"Not now."

"Oh! yes, now! I want her to forgive you before I go. I
am going home this evening, you know   Mother wants me."

"What can she want you for? You are better here, Dory.
I can't do without you, you know. You must stay with me."

"No, Arthur, I *must* go and work for mother."

"Work! Well, I will go home with you and help you. I'd
rather go away for a week, Dory; I'm so ashamed to meet my
mother!"

CHAPTER LVI.

THE SHERIFF IN LIMBO.

EVENTS continued to ripen fast. Porgy's visage grew gloomier
with their progress, and a stern expression settled upon his features. He smoked and drank more freely than ever. His conversation grew more and more brief daily, He 'heard the sergeant without heed, and seldom responded, except by a brief sarcasm, to his prolix exhortations. He was apprized from the city
that his danger could not be any longer averted; that there was

no longer any barrier between him and the sheriff. Col. Pinckney wrote him an affectionate letter, full of sympathy, but cutting him off from all farther hope of escape. Pinckney did not stop at this. He sought the sheriff, who was a well-known army man, of good nature, something of a humorist, indeed, and with quite a friendly regard for Porgy, whom he had met more than once during the war, and whom he very well knew. The object of Pinckney now was to persuade the sheriff to as much indulgence as possible. To "do his spiriting gently." To this the latter was naturally inclined. But, on the other hand, there was the impatient creditor, M'Kewn, urging the rapid execution of the proceedings. The law! The law! He claimed the benefit of the law in its utmost rigor, and waited, with intense appetite for the news of the execution of his processes, the sale of the lands of Porgy, and the seizure of the negroes. Pinckney wrote the captain all these particulars. He had tried the inflexible creditor in vain. He was resolved on his pound of flesh, and as much blood as he could draw along with it.

Porgy read the letter to Millhouse. The latter, by a private despatch, summoned Lance Frampton to the council. He came over to Glen-Eberley armed to the teeth, with rifle on his shoulder, sabre at his side, pistols in holster, just as he had gone through the wars. The requisitions of the sergeant had been to this effect. He had expressly enjoined the lieutenant to come in war-fashion. He met him at the entrance, armed in like manner though not on horseback; and with an ominous shaking of the head and the hand, in answer to Frampton's inquiries, he said—

"The inimy is in motion, lieutenant; we've got to stand an assault, maybe a siege, and I know'd you warn't aguine to stand by and see the cappin bombarded and invaded, without being ready to jine at the first sound of the trumpet. You'll see the cappin's mightily changed in the last week. He's more down in the mouth than I ever seed him. He kain't talk, and when a man kain't talk, that's been so used to it, it's about the worst sign in his sarcumstances. But, don't you say nothing of what you sees. Jest you listen to me, and when I pushes on one p'int, be ready to follow up the push. We must purtect the property from the inimy. Ef they gits the place, thar's not much use for the niggers, and ef they gits the niggers, thar's not much use for the place. The two stands together pretty much like gun and gunpowder. What's the use of the gunpowder if thar's no gun, and what's the use of the gun if thar's no powder? You sees! Now, we must purtect the niggers and plantation against siege and storm. That's the first needcessity; the next is to open the cappin's eyes to the needcessity of marrying the widow. His sarcumstances ain't to be put off any longer. We must, both on us, argufy him into the sense of this needcessity."

Having, as he thought, sufficiently given the lieutenant his cue, the latter was allowed to enter the dwelling, and to see his old commander. He found Porgy sombre enough, but glad to see him. He put on a cheerful countenance when he beheld the youth, gave him his hand, and, for a little while, seemed to recover his spirits. But Frampton remarked that, though he entered the room, armed *cap-a-pie*, the captain never seemed to observe it; and that, even while he spoke to him of familiar things, and with a smile upon his face, his mind yet seemed to wander. After a while, he lapsed into moody silence, never once taking the pipe from his mouth in the course of half an hour, even though its fires had gone out. The lieutenant took his place in the household quietly, as if he had never left it. He had his bed there that night. After supper, Tom being warned to be in attendance as an auxiliary, the sergeant opened by degrees upon the subject of embarrassment before them.

"Ef you has no dejection, cappin, I wish you'd read to the lieutenant that 'ere letter of Col. Pinckney."

"Oh! to be sure. You've not heard, Lance, that the Philistines are about to descend upon us. Writs are out, and executions, levies, and arrests, Ca Sa's and Fi Fa's and I suppose *ne exeats*, and whatever other diabolical inventions of the law can be brought to bear upon a man whom the devil has determined to destroy. I told you of my fears before we got home. I was then better prepared for the disaster than I am now. The respite I have had, the restoration of my negroes, and the help in money afforded me by Mrs. Eveleigh, have helped to spoil me for vicissitudes; and, in getting a new taste of my old mode of life, I am much more reluctant than ever to give it up. But the thing seems inevitable now. This letter of Colonel Pinckney, which I will read to you, will show you how the land lies, and from what quarter, and in what force, the enemy will probably make his approaches."

And he read the letter.

"The case you see, is hopeless. The wolves will have their victim. Nothing can be done."

"Well, cappin, I doesn't edzactly see that. Here's Lance, and me both, and Tom, all ready to have a fight on it, and beat off the inimy, ef they don't come on us too many at once. We three, and you, cappin—"

"Pooh, pooh, sergeant! That's all nonsense. There's no fighting to be done in the matter, and no flying, that I can see. All `that is left to me now, or is likely to be left to me, is my philosophy, and that of my little Frenchman. I am trying to school myself to the trial with the best grace in the world, though by the powers, if a good fight would help the matter, I'd be pretty quick to man the fortress; but that's out of the question. The notion of the sergeant is simply absurd. The case, look whichever way you please, is absolutely hopeless."

"You're clean wrong; jest bekaise you refuses to look the right way. Now, I've been seeing, a mighty long while past, that thar was a way of saving all, and blocking the game on the inimy, and that, you see, was jes' by coming down upon the widow Eb'leigh, and storming her premises. I show'd you, long ago, how a widow was a sort of post which had been afore taken by the inimy, and so was to be taken ag'in; and where the storming was conducted by a good off'cer, from the line of the army, that the thing mout be done easily. This widow Eb'leigh, now—"

"Hush up, Millhouse. No more of that. It must not be thought of. How will it look for me—I who have been borrowing the widow's money — to propose to pay my debts to her, by making her my wife?"

"And the most ixcellentest way for settling a debt that ever was invented on this airth."

"Why, man, I've gone to her as a beggar. I owe her six hundred guineas. Shall I go to her and offer her payment in a bankrupt husband?"

"But ef she likes you, cappin, won't she jump at it?"

"Ah! but that is all very doubtful."

"A man what's doubtful, I may say, is a'most d——d a'ready. Thar must not be no doubt when you're a-guine to storm a fortress. Now, I see that this here widow is a'most ready to surrender at the first blow of the bugle. I knows it, cappin; I sees it in everything she does for you, and in every look she gives you; and the best thing you kin do is jest to make a trial of the sarcumstances of the case."

Porgy shook his head.

"Now, don't you be a-shaking of your head as ef thar was nothing in it. But jest you hear what I'm guine to ax you.—S'pose, now, the thing is jest as I'm a-saying it. S'pose she's ready to give in the moment you are ready to make the attack? Won't you be a most bloody fool—pardon me, cappin; I doesn't mean to be onrespectful—but I ax, won't you be a bloody fool, not to give her a chaince to surrender handsome, and save her feelin's, and save this fine property, and save your niggers, only bekaise you are so mealy-mouthed. Won't you feel most mean and vicious, and onhappy, ef so be you keeps hanging off, and she has to come and pop the question to you? I declar', cappin, it seems a most pitiful and cruel thing for you not to help her out a leetle, by jest axing her in time to save her feelin's."

"Ha! ha! ha! Delightful! 'Pon my soul, Millhouse, you put the case in quite a new and striking point of view. You think I should speak in time to prevent the widow from addressing me, and so spare her blushes."

"In course, I does! That's jest the thing—spar' her blushes!"

"But, suppose she were to propose to me, and I were to—refuse her?"

"Lord love you, cappin, and be merciful to your onderstanding; but you wouldn't be so onkind and outright redickilous, as to do that—and after all that's she's been a-doing for you."

"It would be rather hard-hearted, I confess."

"'Twould be most monstrous redickilous! But, cappin, you mus'n't wait for her to do the axing. It mout-be she'd come arter awhile, and when she couldn't stan' keepin' in her feelin's any longer; but then it mout-be—it would be—too late, then, to help your sarcumstances. Ef the property was to be sold by the sheriff, what would it bring, I want to know, now, when thar's so little money guine about. Not enough, by half, to pay this warmint, M‘Kewn. But, ef 'twas only on account of the lady, it's your business to speak quick. The man has no right to keep the poor woman a-waiting on him. He has no right to keep a-thinking, with pipe in his mouth, while she's a weeping and pining away a-most to nothin'."

"But I don't see that Mrs. Eveleigh shows any such signs of suffering, Millhouse."

"It's all innard, cappin. She's got too proud a stomach, to show outside, in her flesh and sperrits, how much she suffers innardly. Many's the woman that's looked fat and hearty, while her heart's been a-breaking in her buzzum. I don't mean to say that the widow Eb'leigh is so far gone, cappin, 'kaise, you see, she's had ixper'ence in heart affairs, being a widow; but she's got her feelin's and sufferin's, cappin, in the heart, that keeps it sore and bleedin' all over, though it's too strong to break. She oughtn't to hev' any sufferin's and bleedin's at all, ef so be you kin help her; and I say, and I'm sure on it, that you *kin* help her, jes' by the same thing that helps you'self. I'll leave it to the lieutenant here, and to Tom, ef they don't 'gree with me, that the widow Eb'leigh has a nateral right to marry you, considerin' your sarcumstances."

Tom nodded his head affirmatively.

"You hab for marry 'em, maussa. He bin too much good to you, maussa. You can't 'scuse 'em—you can't 'fuse [refuse] 'em. You hab for do it, den we all t'ree b'long to one anudder, maussa."

Frampton was of opinion that the proceeding would certainly relieve the captain of all his present difficulties, and was for this reason quite advisable.

"That's it, cappin! considerin' the sarcumstances! It's the sarcumstances you've got to consider; and I say it again, considerin' them, and the sarcumstances of the widow, she's got a nateral right to marry you."

"But have I any natural right to marry her?"

"In course! Ef she's got a right to you, thar's no help for it, and you must jine your right to her'n. You've got no right to refuse to hev' *her*, seein' it's her needcessity to hev' *you*; and the true way for an honest man, and a gentleman, and a good sodger, is to put it to her manful, at once, and not keep her a-waiting, and a longing and a sorrowin', till the poor woman gits sick from her needcessity.''

"Really, Millhouse, you make a new case of it. You are making it clearly a duty and a charity that I should marry a lady of fortune, and so save myself from the sheriff.''

"That's the how! That's the very thing.''

"Now, Millhouse, if I could only be sure that the excellent lady whom you so freely discuss, labored under any such feelings as you describe—''

"Aix Lance—aix Tom!'' responded the sergeant, appealing to each of them in turn.

Lance certainly had seen the very favorable glances, which the widow had cast upon the captain.

"Sheep's eyes, they calls 'em, cappin,'' quoth the sergeant.

Tom gave his opinion with solemnity and confidence.

"Miss Eb'leigh hab eyes, enty, for see, maussa? Well, who dat say maussa ain't man 'nough for please any woman? Da's it! I see 'em how he look at maussa. He fire up, he mouth 'tan' open and sweet, and when he talk to 'em, it's jest like any bud [bird] dah sing to 'nudder but, and axing 'em wha' for we kain't buil' nest togedder dis spring?''

"Well,'' said the more liberal sergeant, "'twould be all mighty great nonsense to talk of building nests in spring, when here we are jest on the edge, as I may say, of winter. But what Tom says would be quite right, ef he'd make the nest buildin' together about Christmas. I like a marriage, Christmas time, better than any other; and ef the cappin does the right thing, like a man, we'll have a raal blow-out this coming Christmas. You've hearn, cappin. Me, and the lieutenant, and Tom, all agrees that the widow looks on you with mighty sweet eyes; and I say she's got a nateral right to you, and you've got a nateral right to her; and you must jine your rights, and give us a blow-out this Christmas; and ef the sheriff, or M'Kewn, or any other warmint, comes shark-ing about these primises, I've got a nateral right to give him a h–ll of a licking, and I'll hev' my rights, by blazes, whenever I gits a chaince!''

We are not prepared to say that the captain was convinced by this argument, which was continued for sometime after this, and

was wound up by a stoup of Jamaica, when the parties all retired for the night. Millhouse congratulated himself and companions
that a favorable impression had been made, but Frampton was
doubtful. His sympathies had thought him better how to see
into the captain's heart, and to comprehend his mysteries. The
sergeant judged only of what *should* be the effect of arguments,
and an eloquence, so potent as his own.

The next morning, at sunrise, found the two subordinates
astir. Frampton and Millhouse went forth together in consultation, the latter looking exceedingly ominous, like some great
bull-dog on duty, and having a keen-scent in his nostrils of some
intruder. At breakfast, the subject of the last night was resumed by the sergeant, but the captain made no response. He expressed no surprise to see Frampton linger away from his young
wife. The lieutenant said nothing of the object of his visit, or
of the summons which induced it, but quietly assumed the air
and attitude of one on duty. The good youth, accustomed to
military authority, and trained up in great measure by Porgy,
was prepared to obey at every peril. Of law, he had only vague
notions. So far as his experience went, civil authority had been
only a name—a venerable thing, perhaps—but which men every
where plucked by the beard, without fear, and with impunity.
He had yet to learn that it could prove more potent now than
during the seven years previous, when each man did the thing
that was best in his own sight, and when there were no judges
in the land, however numerous might be the executioners. He
had come to stand up beside, and for, his feudal lord—such was
really the sort of relation between the parties—and to break
spear for him, and peril life, against all comers. It is possible
that Porgy understood the purport of his visit, but he forebore
all remark upon it. The youth was simply welcomed, as of old;
and, as of old, he went at once on duty. The sergeant soon
showed him that the duty was to be a vigilant one, and was quite
necessary. The two mounted guard alternately. Certain favorite negroes were selected as scouts and videttes, who watched
all the approaches to the plantation. One was chosen to ascend
through the scuttle to the housetop, and keep his eyes at once
on every point of the compass. And thus matters stood, without

any event to excite alarm, until the third day after Frampton's arrival.

On this day, some little after noon, and just when Porgy was beginning to think of dinner, the scouts came in bringing intelligence of the approach, in the direction of Glen-Eberley, of a very stylish looking gentleman, in black habit, driving the vehicle, then in fashionable use for one or two persons, called the "chaise," a heavy lumbering sort of gig, with a capacious top to it. This *was* the sheriff, the well-known, amiable, graceful and accomplished Colonel ——, whose solicitude to do an unpleasant duty pleasantly, had prompted him to undertake a task which is now-a-days commonly confided to a deputy. At the gate of the avenue of Glen-Eberley, the sheriff found himself suddenly arrested by a person in military habit. Before he knew where he was, a huge horseman's pistol was clapped to his head, and he was required to give an account of himself. The sheriff was confounded.

"Why, young man," said he, "what does all this mean? Why are you armed to the teeth, and why am I arrested with violence on the peaceful highway? Who are you, and what do you take me for?"

"For a person that's after no good, stranger!" was the answer of Lance Frampton. "We hear that there's some enemies of Captain Porgy after him, who want to seize him and his negroes, and we are jest here to see that they do no such thing!"

"Why, who is there to take his property?"

"Who! I don't know; but they are enemies, and varmints, sheriffs, and such like tory people!"

Frampton's mode of cataloguing, showed considerable inexperience, by which the sheriff was amused rather than annoyed.

"You do not mean to say, my friend, that you would resist a sheriff in the execution of his lawful duties?"

"Let him only try it here!" was the indignant answer.

"Well, my good friend, my business here is to see Captain Porgy."

"But you're not the sheriff?"

"Sheriff, indeed! I'm Col. ——, formerly of the army. I know Captain Porgy well. He'll be glad to see me, I've no doubt."

"And you're not one of the sheriff's fellows, then ?" demanded Frampton, doubtfully.

"Do I look like any one's fellow ?" asked the sheriff, laughing.

"I don't know! I'm on duty here to see that no sheriff, or any of his fellows, get into the place ; and I'm bound to examine closely. But I'll take you in, where you can see another person that's on duty, and that knows better what's to be done than I do. Get out boy"—to the sheriff's driver—"get up behind."

In a moment, Frampton had changed places with the negro.— This done, he took the reins, saying as he drove —

"If you were to drive up this avenue, stranger, except under my charge, you'd be most like to have a bullet through your jacket."

"The devil! You have then converted Glen-Eberley into a fortified place ?"

"Yes, indeed! And we can make a pretty stiff fight against a good troop of sheriffs."

"Humph! The captain's at home, I suppose ?"

"Yes indeed! But it's a chance you won't get a sight of him. It all depends upon Sergeant Millhouse. He's the officer on duty. You must make it all clear to him, that you don't come for any evil, before he'll let you 'light."

"Indeed !" and, with his secret meditations, the sheriff smiled pleasantly enough ; but his smiles were arrested as suddenly as he himself had been before, as, almost in the middle of the avenue, Frampton drew up the horses.

"Here's the sergeant !" said he.

The sheriff, at the same moment, saw approaching, from the head of the horses, a stalwart figure, with pistols in belt, and sabre waving in his left hand. A cap made of the skins of a pair of gray-squirrels, with the tails flapping on both sides, covered his head. His uniform was of strange military mixture, altogether indescribable, but propriety requires that we should describe it as a uniform. His eye was fiercely suspicious, and his mouth was compressed with most rigid determination.

"Who's he ?" was the stern demand of the sergeant as the vehicle was stopped, and he presented himself, waving his sabre, in front of the visiter.

"He calls himself Col. ——, of the army ; says he's not the sheriff, or any of his fellows, and wants to see the captain."

The sergeant glared at him with eyes of piercing inquiry; and, after a moment's pause, said—

"Take off your hat, stranger, that I may see what sort of a head you've got of your own!"

The sheriff, smilingly civil, complied with the requisition.

"He looks onharmful enough, Lance, but there's no knowing. I never haird of any Col. —— in the army; I've hearn of a cappin with some sich name, but I never haird that he did anything much. He warn't no great shakes. You say, stranger, that our cappin knows you?"

"Yes!" said the sheriff, meekly, beginning to feel somewhat dubious of his securities.

"Well, hev' you any way to let him hear from you, by any writing or letter. For, as for seeing him afore he hears all about you, that's onpossible!"

The sheriff produced a pencil, tore off a bit of paper, from a letter, wrote his name upon it, and offered it to the sergeant.

"Stick it on the eend of my sabre," said the wary soldier, not knowing how such a talisman, taken into his hands, might compromise his relations with the captain or the enemy.

"Now, Lance, git out, and take out the horse; then you carry this paper, jest as it stands, to the cappin; I'll keep guard on this pusson, in the meantime, when you're gone."

A few moments sufficed for this performance, and Frampton set off, bearing the missive at the point of the sword, and leaving Millhouse, pistol in hand, confronting the visiter. The latter made a movement as if to get out; but the sergeant, with a horrid voice of war, cried out—

"Don't you stir a peg, onless you wants me to blow a winder through your buzzum! Jes' keep quiet whar you air, ef you wants an easy time of it!"

And he followed up the terrible threat by a wilful obtrusion of the huge pistol, jaws wide open, full into the gaping jaws of the doubtful visiter. The sheriff recoiled, as well he might. He was half afraid now to move a limb, although, just then, it occurred to him that the ends of certain legal documents, of considerable size, were peering too conspicuously from a breast pocket; and he feared, if remarked, it would scarcely be possible for him to escape the imputation of being the much-hated officer for the hostile reception of whom these men were in arms. He finally attempted the thing once, but, as he lifted his hand to his bosom, Millhouse mistook it for an attempt to get at his weapons, and he instantly applied his own. Again was the huge muzzle of the pistol clapped to the sheriff's head with an awful injunction—

"Ef you lifts a hand, or stirs a peg, stranger, you swallows a bullet that no white man can chaw. I've been in the army, too long, my friend, to let the inimy git his hand fairly into his buzzum. Jest you try it ef you wants to see how I manages in sich a case. Jest you try it, ef you'd see blazes to shet up both your eyes."

The sheriff resigned himself submissively to the necessity. The sergeant, clearly, was not a sentinel to be trifled with; and the prisoner, beginning honestly to wish himself well out of the present predicament, was now afraid to relax the stiffened limb, to ease out leg or arm, knee or elbow, lest he should incur the sudden penalty of blow or bullet. He remained thus in a most uneasy state of rest, which was anything but repose, waiting, with anxiety, for the return of the more civil of his two captors.

———————————

CHAPTER LVII.

COUP DE THEATRE.

When Lance Frampton entered the house with the paper of the sheriff, addressed to Porgy, and which contained only the name of the former, the captain of partisans was preparing himself for dinner, which Tom, the cook, was himself about to place upon the table.

"Where's Pomp, Tom?" demanded the captain.

"Pomp dey somewhere; dey tak' care ob hese'f, I 'speck," replied Tom, with a significant jerk of the head.

"Somewhere! Taking care of himself! Why, what the d—l is he after, and why don't you call him in to his duty? You should see, Tom, that the scamp does not skulk too frequently He has too much taste for it, as is, perhaps, the case with all fiddlers. Halloo for the scamp, and see that he is at his post. Take care of himself, indeed! I'll see that he takes care of me."

"He no guine yer holler dis time, maussa!" answered Tom. "Nebber you min' maussa; he will come jis when we wants 'em; only jis now, he sca'ce [scarce]!"

"But we want him *now!*"

"Can't come *now*, maussa! Pomp in de swamp, safe shet up. Nobody for sh'um [see him]!"

"In the swamp! What the d——l is he after in the swamp?"

But the farther dialogue was arrested by the appearance of Frampton, very much to Tom's relief, since he could not much longer have evaded the direct demands of his master, while Millhouse had enjoined upon him silence. To let the reader into a secret, all the negroes had taken to the swamp, except Tom, from the moment when the sheriff's chaise had been arrested at the entrance of the avenue!

"Well, Lance; in armor still? What's the matter?"

"We've captured a man here, captain, who calls himself Col. ——, and says you know him. He sends you this."

Porgy read the slip.

"Col. ——; and you've captured him, you say? How?— Why?"

Frampton told his story briefly.

"Why, you see, we're on duty; and we thought he was the sheriff, and so we took him into captivity. The sergeant's standing guard over him, while I brought you the paper."

"Captured him! And where is he?"

"In the avenue. You can see him through the window, where the sergeant has him under guard."

Porgy looked out, and burst into an uncontrollable fit of laughter.

"Ha! ha! ha! Good, i'faith! excellent! The captor in captivity! Ha! ha! ha! Well, this is promising! The game begins well. We shall have a laugh on our side, at least, whether we lose or not in the long run. Ha! ha! ha!"

The captain made the lieutenant repeat the details—the dialogue—every particular; and the merriment of the captain was renewed. The whole thing struck him amusingly. It appealed to his leading passion for practical jokes. He determined to humor it to the end.

"So, you thought Col. —— the sheriff did you? Ha! ha! ha! admirable! What a story to tell! But, I will go out to him. I must only put a few extra dishes on the table. Here, Tom!—And now, Lance, step out to the sergeant; tell him to watch his prisoner closely. I will come out and see if he is really the colonel, whom I know very well! We must not be imposed upon, Lance! By no means! Ha! ha! ha! The captor in captivity! Very good, by Mercury, very good!"

Lance Frampton disappeared; perfectly satisfied that the captain approved of all his proceedings; a matter of which he had not been quite sure previously. When he was gone, Porgy, with Tom's assistance, proceeded to put himself in caparison of war. His uniform was hastily hustled on, his belt girded about his waist, sword slung at his side, pistols stuck in his belt, and in his hand he carried a long rifle. This done, he proceeded to arrange certain mysteriously-covered dishes upon the table. Tom was also made to equip himself in armor—that is, with a light tomahawk over his shoulder, a huge *couteau de chasse* in one side of his belt, and a great horseman's pistol in the other. Porgy gave him some final-directions, and then sallied forth to examine the prisoner.

Before he appeared, the sheriff had begun to meditate the propriety of declaring his indignation, in very strong language, at the treatment he received; but, at the approach of Porgy, looking swords, bayonets, and blunderbusses, his purpose changed.—Was the captain crazy? Could he really mean to defy the laws? The colonel began to have his doubts. He had heard of the mad freaks of which Porgy had been occasionally guilty; he had heard that he was very free in his potations; he saw nothing but savage defiance in the features of Millhouse, and nothing but sober soldier resolution, and dogged adherence to authority, in the aspect of Frampton. The gown began to tremble in the presence of the sword. "I must temporize!" was the unspoken decision of the sheriff, "I must see how the land lies first! Who knows what desperate actions these mad fellows may not commit."

Porgy came on slowly, as became his size and state. As he approached, the sheriff made a movement as if to rise.

"Not a step, stranger!" cried the vigilant Millhouse, holding up the yawning pistols. "Wait tell the cappin gives the word."

The captain seemed slow to give the word. He drew nigh with the air of a man who felt that he might, at any moment, be required to pull trigger. His rifle was held in readiness, his finger near the trigger. He walked up to Millhouse, and looked suspiciously at the vehicle.

"Who have you got here, sergeant?"

The sergeant saluted, in military style, flourishing the pistol instead of the sword, as he answered—

"A fellow who calls himself Col. ——, but I don't know. He mout-be, and mout-be not, the colonel. But he says he knows you, and you knows him."

Porgy advanced a pace, and peered suspiciously into the vehicle, still keeping a very deliberate step, and a severe suspicious aspect. The sheriff cried out—

"What, Capt. Porgy, don't you know me?"

"Bless me, so it is! It is Col. ——. My dear colonel, I am truly rejoiced to see you, and greatly regret that my fellows should have subjected you to 'durance vile' for a single moment. It was all a mistake. Get out, if you please. They took you for some d——d harpy of the law—the sheriff or some one of his vile myrmidons. Get out, my dear fellow, and let us hurry in to dinner. You are just in pudding-time."

"He evidently does not know that I have been made sheriff," was the silent whisper of the colonel to himself, as, accepting the invitation, he descended from the vehicle, which Porgy immediately told Frampton to drive up to the house.

"We have but one single negro on the place," said Porgy; "at sight of you, supposing you the sheriff, every two-legged animal, of dark complexion, took to the swamp. You gave them a scare, I assure you. But come, I am really glad to see you at Glen-Eberley, and just at this moment."

And he shook hands with the sheriff, with the cordial army shake, which threatened to dislocate a member in order to compel remembrance. The sheriff felt a little relieved, even while the usage was so rough. They walked toward the house arm in arm.

" Let me carry your rifle, captain," said the sheriff.

" My rifle ! No, indeed, colonel, no ! I never part with it. I know not at what moment I may have to use it. There is a skunk of a Scotchman in my neighborhood, who may cross my path some day, and, as I tell you, I am in momentary expectation of the visits of the sheriff, or some of his satellite harpies."

" But you certainly would not draw trigger upon an officer of the law ?"

" Would I not !" exclaimed the captain, suddenly stopping in his march, withdrawing his own arm from that of the other, and confronting him with a stern expression. " Would I not ?--Will I consent, after fighting the battles of my country for seven years, to be driven from my estates by a d——d civilian—a fellow, probably, who never smelt gunpowder in his life. No! indeed! I will die in harness and in *possession!* They may conquer me —I suppose they will, in time ; but I will hold on while I can, do battle to the last, and when they do take possession, they shall walk into it only over my dead body."

" And here's the man to baick you, cappin, by the Lord Harry !"

Such was the speech, delivered with stentor-lungs, from the rear ; the sergeant at the same moment amusing himself with thrusting back his sabre into the steel sheath, with such an emphasis, as to make it ring again. The sheriff was startled from his propriety, for a moment, by the sudden illustration which followed the captain's fierce determination.

" They are all mad together," he again whispered to himself ; and it might be observed that his deportment became more conciliatory than ever.

" Come, colonel, let us in, now, and see what dinner we shall find awaiting us. A stoup of Jamaica will refresh you after your ride, and me after my scare. The very idea of a sheriff makes me thirst ; and to be relieved of this idea, I must drink. Come! In !"

And the captain seized his guest good-naturedly by the arm, and the two ascended to the piazza, the sergeant thundering with heavy tread behind, his sabre sheath rattling against the steps at every stride, and reminding the sheriff, momently, of the military nature of the escort. When in the house, he threw off his hat, and Porgy discarded his military cap; the squirrel-skin covering of Millhouse was doffed also, and the three joined in a devout draught of Jamaica. But neither of the two latter laid aside his weapons. The swords still swinging at their sides, and the pistols at their belts.

Meanwhile, dinner was announced, and the captain of partisans motioned the sheriff to a seat at one end of the table, he preparing to take the place opposite. The sergeant sank into a seat on one side. Once seated, the captain unsheathed his sabre, which he laid across the table, the hilt convenient to his grasp. The sergeant followed the example, only substituting his lap for the table. Lance Frampton came in at this moment, took a place opposite the sergeant, and, seeing what the latter had done with his weapon, made a similar disposition of his own.

The sheriff saw these proceedings, which seemed habitual, with increasing surprise. "Certainly," he again whispered himself, "these people are all mad!" The reflection increased his observances, and made him studious to maintain the utmost propriety of demeanor. He looked about him, and curiously surveyed all that came within the range of his vision. We have not hitherto thought it necessary to mention that, with the borrowed money of Mrs. Eveleigh, the captain had succeeded in furnishing his house with some regard equally to comfort and display. The want of money in the city when he entered the market, and the number of families who were selling out, had enabled him to procure a complete outfit at small cost. He no longer dined upon the floor, carpeted with blanket. He had now ample supplies of chairs and tables; there were mirrors against his walls, and fine linen upon his table. There was no display of plate, it is true, beyond the necessary allowance of spoons, but his china was quite imposing, and would be considered so now. His decanters and tumblers were of cut-glass, and the covers to his dishes were of very handsome plating.

When the dishes were uncovered, it was with increasing surprise that the sheriff beheld one, within reach of Porgy, containing a pair of highly-polished pistols. He attempted something of a jest when he saw them.

"Really, captain, you can not design that dish for the digestion of any visiter."

"The digestion must depend upon himself," was the cool reply; "but there *are* parties, who might sometimes intrude upon me, for whose special feeding they are provided."

"What! the sheriff, eh?" with a faint chuckle.

"Exactly! Shall I help you to soup, colonel?"

"If you please."

"Bouillé?"

"Thank you—a little."

"You will find it more manageable than bullet."

"Yes, indeed!"

"Try a little of that Madeira with your soup. It improves it wonderfully to my taste. Tom!"—tasting—"you have not put quite enough salt in your soup?"

"Who say so? Enty I know? Tas'e 'em 'gen, maussa! I 'speck you fin' salt 'nough in 'em next time. Heh! Ef I ain't know, by dis time, how for salt de soup, I t'row 'way heap of my life for not'ing."

"Hear the rascal. He knows that he doesn't belong to me, or he would never be so impudent. How are negroes selling now, colonel? I got a hundred guineas for that fellow."

"You were well paid, captain. At his time of life, unless a fellow had some rare qualities, he could scarcely command more than half that money."

"Tom *has* rare qualities. He *can* cook a good dinner; can make and season soup to perfection, and would have done so to-day—would certainly never have thrown in too little salt—but that he heard some talk of the sheriff, and in his agitation and the hurry with which he armed himself with his favorite weapons—see the knife and the hatchet—he has been careless with his salt—has probably spilt half of that in the fire which he intended for the soup. How does it taste to you, colonel?"

"Right, sir; very good soup, and well seasoned. I should say that your cook has salted it sufficiently."

"T'ank you, sah," quoth Tom. "I mos' bin 'fear'd I spill some ob de salt, when I yer 'bout dem warmint, de sheriff; but ef you tas'e 'em, da's 'nough. Salt mus'n't be too sharp in soup for he good seas'ning."

From the soups they passed to the solids. There was a round of beef. There was a pair of wild ducks. The sheriff began to recover his confidence with his appetite, and to praise Tom's cooking. Porgy watched and listened to him with a grim pleasure. Occasionally, the sergeant put in, with some of his philosophies, whenever anything particularly provocative had been said, but it may be stated that he was particularly taciturn that day. The fact is, the conduct of the captain was somewhat mysterious. The guest was inoffensive—was clearly not the sheriff—yet he saw that Porgy was playing out a game upon him—whether for the purpose of alarming the stranger's fears, or amusing himself, he could not determine; but the doubt kept him fiercely suspicious, and watchful of every look and movement of the guest.

The sheriff noted the man's air and manner, and was impressed accordingly. The conduct of Lance Frampton, who was singularly quiet, was yet of a sort to fix his attention. In this young man he beheld a fixed confidence in his superior, and a readiness to obey orders, which showed that, at a wink, he would be prepared to act, and without any regard to responsibilities. After awhile the wine began to circulate, though the sergeant still confined himself to the Jamaica. Even when, at the summons of the captain, he emptied his glass of Madeira, he was sure to swallow a good mouthful of the rum after it, as if to prevent any evil consequences from the more aristocratic liquor. The dishes were cleared away, and Tom gave the party a rice-pudding, which was voted good on all hands. Its removal was followed by the introduction of raisins, ground-nuts (*peanuts* or *pindars*). and black walnuts. Over the wine and walnuts, the chat grew more and more lively. It passed from topic to topic; the town and country; the camp and court; civil life and that of the soldier; but there was one lurking trouble in the mind of the sheriff which invariably brought him back to the peculiar condition in which he found the household.

"Really," said he, "captain, I find it impossible to realize the assurance that you make me, that you are all armed and equipped here to resist the operations of the law."

"Indeed!" said Porgy, looking grave. "You find it difficult to understand, and why? Is it so strange that I should be unwilling to surrender all my possessions, at the first demand, and without a struggle."

" But you could scarcely expect to make resistance to the laws of the land. The sheriff is armed with a sovereign power for the time. How would you hope to hold out against him ?"

" You mean to say that he would overwhelm me with the *pos-se comitatus ?*"

" Ay, and if need, call out the military !"

" To be sure he may, and certainly there is a power to which my own must succumb. What then ? If I am to yield up all the goods of life, why not life also ? What is life to me ? You know my tastes and habits. You know how I have lived and how I still live. Some men will tell you that I am a glutton, others, that I imbue my appetites equally with my taste and philosophies ; all agree that I am, essentially, a good deal of an animal — that I was profligate in youth that I might enjoy life, and that in the good things of this life, I find life itself. I won't deny the charge. Be it so. Am I to survive the good things, and yet cherish the life ? Wherefore ? What does Shylock say — whom, by-the-way, I take to be a very shrewd and sensible fellow, and a greatly ill-used rascal —

——' You take my life
When you do take the means whereby I live !'

And, when I have perilled my life a thousand times for the benefit of other people's goods, shall I not venture it for the protection of my own ?"

" But, my dear captain, there is a material difference between doing a thing with the sanction of the law, and in defiance of it."

"None to me ! Don't you see, my dear colonel, that I am prepared to sacrifice my life with my property, and that law can in no way, exact a higher forfeit ? But d—n the law ! We've had enough of it for the present. Fill up your glass. You will find that Madeira prime. It is from an ancient cellar !"

" Thank you ! [Fills.] Well, my dear captain, suffer me to hope for you an escape from the clutches of the law by legitimate means !"

" I'm obliged to you, my dear colonel ; but we army men don't care much about the means, so that we effect the escape. I am for stratagem or fight, sap or storm, just as the best policy councils. Life, after all, is a constant warfare. Rogues are only enemies in lambskins, or ermine. They do not care to cut my throat so long as I have a purse to cut; they will not care to drive me to desperation, so long as it is profitable to them that I should live. I know them! I defy them! I can die without a grunt to-morrow. I have neither wife, nor child, nor mother, nor sister, to deplore my fate, or to profit by my departure. I am, with the exception of these two faithful comrades of mine, utterly alone in the world. They shall live with me while I live. They would die for me to-morrow. Were a man but to lift a finger against me, to assail my life, or my meanest fortunes, they would be into him with bullet and bayonet, and need not a signal from me."

"That's a rightious truth, by the Hokies!" exclaimed the sergeant, with his one fist thundering down upon the table. The lieutenant's eyes brightened keenly, and he looked to the captain, but he said nothing.

"I have no doubt they are true and faithful friends, captain," said the sheriff; "but suppose now, only suppose, I say, the sheriff was suddenly to appear among you, just as I am here now, and were to—"

He was stopped! Stopped in an instant, as by a thunderbolt, by the prompt reply and action of Porgy.

"Suppose the sheriff in you! Ha! suppose the rest for yourself.—See!"

And with the wild but determined look and action of a desperate man, he seized both pistols lying in the dish before him, stood up, reached as far over the table as he could, and covered the figure of the amiable but indiscreet sheriff with both muzzles cocking the weapons as he did so. The sheriff involuntarily dodged and threw up his hands. At the same instant, and as soon as the purpose of the superior had been understood by Millhouse and the lieutenant, they were both upon their feet—the sergeant swinging his sabre over the head of the supposed offender; while Frampton, more silent, but quite as decided, while he swung his sword aloft with one hand, grasped with the other the well-powdered shock of the sheriff, in an attitude very like that which we see employed by the ferocious Blue Beard in the opera, when the poor wife is tremblingly crying out for

her brother.   Here was an unpremeditated *coup de theatre!*
Two swords crossed in air above the victim,—two pistols, with
each broad muzzle almost jammed against his own; every eye
savagely fixed upon him, and all parties seeming to await only
the farther word of provocation from his lips.   Nothing had been
more instantaneous.   The subordinates were machines, to whom
Porgy furnished all the impulse.   Their action followed his will,
as soon as it was expressed.   There was no questioning it, and
the amiable sheriff was so much paralyzed by the display, that
it was only with much effort that he could cry out—"But, my
dear captain, don't suppose me the enemy—the assailant—the
d——d sheriff or any of his myrmidons."

"By no means, colonel; but you supposed a case in order to
see whether, and how, we were prepared for it; and it was essential that you should have a proper demonstration.   You have
seen; be easy; fill up your glass, my dear sir, and forgive my
merry men here for the earnestness with which they performed
their parts.   They had no reason, indeed, to suppose that I was
not serious.   You see what chance a *bona-fide* sheriff would
stand, if he aimed at any showing here!"

Porgy had resumed his seat, and restored the pistols to the
dish as coolly as the actor, who takes his brandy and water, equal
parts, after strangling his wife, stabbing the traitor, and dying
famously in the person of Othello.   It was not so easy for Millhouse to throw off his tragic aspect.   He resumed his seat slowly,
never once taking his eyes from the colonel's face, as he did so;
and during the whole progress of the feast, he continued to
regard him with only half-reconciled senses.

CHAPTER LVIII.

LEGAL REGIMEN.

THE excellent sheriff no longer felt any call to trespass in experiments upon the legal antipathies of the captain of partisans and his observant follower. He steered wide of all allusions from thenceforth to the officer of the law, and his possible appearance in the precincts. He felt really impressed with the danger of any one who should, with *malice prepense*, do so, in the evidently diseased condition of mind and mood prevailing at Glen-Eberley. That he should thus forbear, however, was by no means agreeable to his self-esteem or his sense of duty. He was uncomfortable when he thought of his official station, and the sealed documents in his pockets. He had come there to make a levy on land and negroes, without dreaming that he should encounter any opposition. Resistance, with force of arms, was entirely beyond his imaginings; and to depart, having done nothing was at once a *lachesse* of duty and a personal mortification. More than once he felt like plucking up his drowning courage, and perilling his life upon his manhood — boldly challenging the danger, and facing it with folded arms of defiance; but, on all such occasions, as if Porgy and his followers knew, by instinct, his emotions, there would occur some explosion, or some symptom of explosion, which would remind him vividly of the smouldering volcano upon which he sat. For example, he once made an allusion, deliberately designed, to M'Kewn; and Millhouse flared up, and fumbled his sabre, and gnashed his teeth, even as the Frenchman when he cries, "Sacre!" through his mustache, or the Spaniard when he growls "Demonios!" and flourishes his dagger. Frampton showed similar signs of impatience — while Porgy exclaimed aloud, striking his fist down upon the table : —

"Don't mention that scoundrel's name in my hearing, colonel! I feel wolfish when I hear of him. Let him but cross my path;

let any of his myrmidons but put themselves in my way, and if I do not crop their ears, close to the head, then there's no edge to any weapon in my household."

"But is he not a neighbor, captain?"

"Neighbor!　Well, sir, I suppose you may call him a neighbor, even as the devil is a neighbor, and is said to take free lodgings in every man's dwelling; but such neighborhood does not prevent us from flinging the wretch out of the windows, whenever our good saints give us the necessary succor. Don't speak of such a scoundrel to my ears, or I may do you the injustice to suppose you are his friend."

The sheriff took the warning, and M'Kewn was dropped, and all subjects were dropped which were likely to stir up the bile and black blood in the bosoms of the host and his companions. The sheriff resigned himself to his fate, and to the policy of doing nothing with as much grace as possible. He was not only frightened from the purpose for which he came, but the feeling of good fellowship momently grew stronger with the circulation of the wine, and the excellent spirits of the captain. The latter, in all respects, except the one, was on his best behavior, and in most amiable temper. He never showed himself more really humorous and delightful as a companion in all his life. The sheriff was charmed and listened. He was soothed and satisfied. His philosophy came into the support of his necessity. He reasoned thus, accordingly : —

"There is no need to push the matter! Porgy's estate is good, at any moment, for this debt. Every day increases the value of both lands and negroes. Were I to seize and sell now, the property would be sacrificed. It would pay the debt, but leave nothing over to the good fellow, who has been serving his country in a long and honorable warfare. D—n the fellow! I like him, and he shall have indulgence as long as I can grant it!"

As soon as he had reached this conclusion, and resolved that his visit should no longer have a professional object, the play was easy. He yielded himself up to the society in which he found himself. He felt the charm of his host's fun and philosophy; and he, too, had good things in his keeping. When he had once resolved to sink the sheriff, he gave himself free scope, let himself out, and became, what he was known to be in the army, a really good fellow, of no savage inclinations, fond of a jovial circle, and capable of making himself the life of it. The day passed and the party of four had not left the table. They had raised their clouds around it; all being smokers except the lieutenant. Coffee was served by Tom, in the midst of the cloud. When the coffee disappeared, the Jamaica and the Madeira were restored. Cards followed, and at twelve o'clock at night, the sheriff rose a loser of some thirty shillings to sergeant Millhouse, who played through the hands of Frampton, and who became more and more reconciled to the suspicious guest with every shilling which the latter yielded. When, next morning, after the colonel's departure,—which took place soon after an early breakfast—he was discoursing of his good qualities, his companionable virtues, and so forth, the captain of partisans laid his hand on his shoulder—

"Ah! Millhouse, but you don't know the man."

"What! he's Col. ———, aint he ?"

"Yes."

"And a main good fellow, I say."

"Well enough;—well enough; but—your ear, sergeant."

The latter yielded it; the captain stooped as if to whisper—then in deep, solemn accents, as if drawn up from immeasurable depths, he cried out :—

"The Colonel is the sheriff !"

The sergeant made but one bounce, and was across the room; his countenance wo-begone with surprise amounting to terror. His involuntary utterance, occasioned equally by what he had heard, and the tone of voice employed in telling it, was characteristic of his early attention when at church service.

"Hark from the tombs! The sheriff, cappin !"

"The sheriff !"

"What! *our* sheriff, what's a-coming a'ter *our* goods and chattels."

"The same !"

"Oh! ef I'd ha' knowed it !—I'll be a'ter him !—Lance !"

"No! Do nothing of the kind ! We've got off, thus far, very well. The joke is a good one, upon which I can feed fat with laughter for a month. I must ride over and tell the widow. How her sides will shake !"

"The sheriff! It's *on*possible, cappin! And he 'haved himself so civil and sensible, and never said a thing about the d—d execution!"

"No, indeed! the pistols looked too full of *executions* of a more serious sort, to say nothing of your two-foot sabre, and your monstrous ferocity of visage, sergeant."

"Ha! ha! ha!—ho! ho! ho!—haw! haw! haw!"

The whole story became very slowly apparent to Millhouse; but when he did receive it fully, the house was made to shake with his wild yells of laughter. Lance Frampton was perhaps more keenly sensible to the force of the jest, but he permitted himself, at best, a quiet chuckle only in a corner. It was in the midst of a torrent of Millhouse's yells, that Porgy had his horse saddled, and rode over to the widow Eveleigh, to whom he recounted the little drama, from the first scene to the last, with inimitable effect. The widow did laugh; dignity, in those days, did not deny the privileges of an honest cachination even to nobility; and, we are constrained to admit, as had been predicted by Porgy, that her sides did shake; but not vulgarly, or with too ostentatious a display of the commotion within and without. It was a lady-like show of shaking which did not discredit, in the least, the social claims and bearing of the fair widow. But when she recovered herself from the shaking of the sides, she shook her head, and, with becoming gravity, said :—

"But, captain, is not this flying in the face of the law? Will this not compromise you seriously?"

"By no means, my dear widow," he answered merrily; "the law never showed its face to us for a moment. We have treated it with no discourtesy."

"But its messenger, the sheriff!"

"He never showed himself in that character."

"But that was due to your course—"

"Perhaps; but that course was not illegal. There is nothing penal in the case. If he allowed his apprehensions to get the better of his sense of duty, the more fool he. He has no right to complain and will be ashamed to do so. As for the law, we have done nothing against which the law can shake a finger."

"But the matter does not end here. The sheriff will of course come again, and—"

"I shall play out the play, my dear Mrs. Eveleigh, as it has begun. I must have the fun in full; and for the rest,—why, I will content myself with the proverb of the patriarch—'Sufficient for the day is the evil thereof.' It will be time enough to look out for the bolt when we hear the thunder."

"Too late—the flash!"

"Precisely, my dear widow, precisely that! It is because the case is one against which no precautions can avail, that I choose to look out for the bolt after it strikes and not before. But, good-by, I must ride back and write to Pinckney all about this matter. He must share the fun. He will relish it, I know. I would he had been a spectator! The thing is indescribable;—only to be seen in the visages of Millhouse, Lance, and the sheriff, as the two crossed weapons over his head, and I faced him out of countenance with my unmuzzled bull-dogs. My dear widow, would you believe it, the innocent pups that looked so fiercely in the eyes of the sheriff, were toothless. There was no load in either. But, good-by; God bless you! I must get back in a hurry. I rode over only that you should enjoy the story."

The story, indeed, was quite too good a one to be quiet in any bosom. That very night Millhouse gave an entertainment to Fordham and the overseer of M'Kewn himself, when the narrative was given at length. M'Kewn's man relished it quite as much as did Fordham; and the next day, when M'Kewn sauntered out to his stables, he was duly enlightened upon the events occurring in his neighborhood. He had expected the sheriff at his house after or before the levy, and had he made it, the probability is that the night would have been spent with M'Kewn instead of Porgy. The former listened to his overseer without comment. He saw that the latter watched him furtively, to see what effect would be produced by the revelation. But he was disappointed. M'Kewn maintained the utmost immobility of countenance. He said nothing, spent the day as usual, but the very next, he had his carriage got and started off on a visit to the officer of the law. The sheriff was by no means surprised to see him enter his office; but the visit disquieted him.

"Have you proceeded in that business, colonel?—M'Kewn *versus* Porgy."

"Not yet, Mr. M'Kewn."

"But did you not visit Glen-Eberley for the express purpose, colonel ?"

"No — not exactly! I wished to look about me, and judge of the securities. As I saw that the property would bring the money at any moment, I did not see the necessity of forcing it into the market, where it would be only sacrificed."

M'Kewn smiled significantly. The sheriff saw the smile. He understood it, and blushed to the ears. He saw that the secret of his reception had got abroad. He, at once, felt all the mortification to which it would expose him. He longed for M'Kewn to give him occasion of quarrel. He needed somebody on whom to expend his anger and vexation. But the Scotchman was too wary for this. He quietly said —

"I can not leave this matter to the discretion of anybody, colonel, however excellent his judgment. I must have my money; and I must require you to realize it as soon as it is practicable."

"But, Mr. M'Kewn, it will be the ruin of Captain Porgy!"

"That is his lookout, not mine; — not to realize *my* money, may be *my* ruin, colonel; I must require you to do your duty, sir. From this moment I shall look to you."

"Be it so, sir. There is a deputy. He shall be despatched at once upon the business."

M'Kewn looked round upon the person designated, and nodded his head approvingly. He knew Crooks — Absalom Crooks — of old, and respected him as one of the very best bull-terriers of the law — a broad shouldered, stout, short, little fellow, with no crook about him except in his legs, which were bowed, so as to render the space between a very happy oval; while his arms hung out from his body at large range. He had a red head, red face, red whiskers, red waistcoat, and was tolerably well read in the law. M'Kewn knew his man and approved him.

"Crooks," said he — taking the deputy aside — "see well to this business; — get the negroes into your custody, and bring them right away with you. It shall be worth to you five guineas extra, as soon as the money is realized."

Crooks crooked the pregnant hinges of the knee, at these pregnant words, and promised solemnly.

"Hark you, Crooks; you are dealing with cunning fellows,

who will try all ways to scare you out of your duties; but don't
allow yourself to be frightened."

"Frightened!" exclaimed Crooks,—"don't know how to be
frightened, sir,—never learnt, sir—couldn't take that sort of
education. Frightened! I'd like to see."

And Crooks looked his fiercest. In truth, he was not the man
to be very easily made afraid. He was a fiery little fellow, all
combustible; as ready to fight as eat, at any time, and though
continually getting drubbed, as continually forgetting the event
in the encounter with a new assailant. He readily undertook the
mission, and felt a sort of personal pique against Porgy and his
men, as they were supposed capable of inspiring such a person
as himself with fear. The sheriff saw the deputy depart under
secret instructions from M'Kewn, with well founded apprehensions. But he could do nothing to avert the danger. He had
only to look anxiously for the progress of events. Of course, he
was somehow curious to see how Crooks would fare at Glen-
Eberley. He knew that the fellow had no fear, and his mind
was distracted betwixt two points—

"Either he will succeed by boldness, where I failed through
timidity, or Porgy and his fellows will do him serious harm.—
In either case, should the facts about my visit be blown, what
the d—l will be said of me?"

We must leave him to these annoying reflections, and accompany our deputy to Glen-Eberley. Mounted on a stout hackney
accustomed to official dignity, Crooks made his way, with all
diligence, to the scene of his anticipated labors. The documents
were in his pocket, and, once armed with a formidable parchment,
well scored with Gothic characters, and made terrific with seals
of state, Crooks felt no sort of doubt of the uniform reverence
which he should everywhere command. Crooks had never
served in the wars, though pugnacious enough for all sorts of
struggle; and he had no notion of any power which, for a
moment, could gainsay or run counter to that of the law. The
courts of law were, to his mind, scenes of far more imposing
graudeur than any he had conceived of in earth or in heaven—
a judge, in gowned black, was a more potent personage to him
than was Rhadamanthus to the superstitious among the ancients;
and, for a sheriff (the ambition of a deputy, or a constable, in

those days, never dared look so high as this office for himself; it was a stretch quite beyond the vulgar imagination in the first days of the republic), Crooks held him in as much veneration, or more, than he could hold any general of the army—unless, indeed, General Washington. He was yet to become familiar with a feudal baron, and to comprehend the extent of his authority.

He was encountered at the entrance of the avenue, precisely as his principal had been, by a man in armor. His first salutation was a seizure. He, who had done the seizing hitherto, was, in turn, seized upon. His hackney was suddenly brought up, by a short jerk, from a man springing out of the covert beside the gate of the avenue.

"Who are you?" was the unexpected demand, as the horse was backed upon his haunches, and a pistol held toward the head of the rider.

"Who am I?—I'll let you know before you like it. Let go my horse!"

"No fooling! Who are you? What are you after here? What's your business!"

"My business is my business, and you'll know it soon enongh. By what right do you stop me? Do you want to rob me, you rascal."

The words were scarcely out of his mouth before a blow of the fist tumbled him out of the saddle. The horse bounced; the deputy rolled over for a moment; and Lance Frampton, for it was he, seized the opportunity to turn the steed into the enclosure. He thus obeyed the instinct of the partisan. He had captured a horse, and his first measure was to secure it. The next moment he looked after his prisoner. It was time; Crooks was already on his feet and making toward him. Frampton confronted him with his pistols. Crooks had nothing but his riding whip. This, he shook at his assailant, at a moderate distance.

"You shall sweat for this, you rascal. I am an officer of the law. I represent the county. I stand here in the sheriff's shoes, and resistance to an officer—an assault upon an officer—*vi at armis*,—with swords, pistols, dagger, knife, rifle, blunderbuss and gun, you rascal—is outlawry,—and you shall sweat for it. I tell you I stand here in the shoes of the sheriff.

" You do, do you? and if you stood in the jacket of the sheriff it wouldn't help you much. Turn in to the avenue, or I'll put a bullet into you. You're my prisoner."

" *Your* prisoner! Was ever the like? and me a deputy sheriff!"

"Get in, I tell you; you shall have a fair trial."

"Trial! Try me! Who the h–ll are you, sir?"

"Never you mind. Get in, and ask your questions of the captain."

"The captain! What! you mean Captain Porgy."

"Yes! Who else here?"

"The very man I want to see. I'll go in. It's not because I'm afraid of your pistols, young fellow; I don't care that for 'em [snapping his fingers], and you shall sweat for showing 'em to me; but I go in to see Captain Porgy. He's my man.

"Get in! I don't care what you go for, so that you go!"

Lance Frampton sounded his bugle, as the deputy entered the gate. Crooks went · forward, venting his indignation at every step. He was suddenly stopped, midway in the avenue, by another man in armor. Lance and the new-comer saluted, and the prisoner was formally transferred from the former to the latter. Frampton proceeded toward the house. Crooks, staring at the gigantic figure, and frowning aspect of the new-comer, and greatly bewildered at the odd accumulation of uniform and armor about him, was, however, about to press forward, following his late assailant, when the sergeant suddenly arrested him.

" Stand where you are, fellow, or I'll be into you with something sharper than a baggonet."

And he flourished his sabre directly in front of the person of the deputy.

"The devil! What do you stop me for? Do you know who I am and what I've come for?"

" I've a notion," answered the sergeant, looking more fierce than ever.

" Do you know I am here for the sheriff; sent here to make a levy of all the lands, rights, titles, hereditaments, goods and chattels, niggers and stock, furniture and apparel, carts, wagons, ploughs, hoes, shovels, and all and every the implements of this plantation, to take and hold thereof, and make sale thereof, in satisfaction of the judgment in the case of M‘Kewn *v.* Porgy. Do you hear? Do you understand? And do you dare to arrest and stop me in the prosecution of this, my lawful duty."

"I thought as much!" said Millhouse, with an awful lowering of the brows, and a lurid smile in his eyes.—"I thought as much. And it is sich a little mean copper-headed son of a skunk, that has the impudence to come here and to seize the rightful property of a gentleman—and one too, who is a rigilar off'cer in the line of the army. I've most a mind to take hold of you and lace your jacket with hickories—I hev'!"

"Lace my jacket! Hickories! I dare you. Do your best. But you shall sweat for it. You shall, ef there's any law in this land."

"Don't provocate me with your law!" was the reply—"the very word 'law' makes me feel wolfish—the hair all growing innardly. Law, indeed! Shet up, you little polecat, or I'll mount you with sich a spur as will take all the red blood out of your hide in no time."

"I dare you! I defy you! You can't scare me with your big words and your bullets. Give me one of your pistols, and I'm willing to try a crack with you on the spot."

"You ain't! Well, ef you warn't a prisoner, I'd let you; but thar's no sense in granting we'pons to a prisoner."

"By what right do you make me a prisoner? By what right do you deprive me of my liberty, and stop me in the prosecution of my duty? Answer me?"

"Oh! shet up! When did you ever hear that the prisoner was to ax the questions? It's you that's to answer, and here comes the lieutenant. He'll tell you what the cappin says and what's to be done with you."

"Very well! I'll hear."

"You'll hev' a fair trial, I promise you."

"Trial! Who's to try me? I won't go! I'll not submit to any but a lawful court."

"And who's to ax you! Well, lieutenant?"

"The captain says bring the fellow before him."

"Come, copper-head! march!" and Millhouse, planting himself on one side of the captive, Frampton took his place on the other.

"I'll not march! I'll not go! Let the captain come here to me, if he wants me. I'm far enough on this place for what I've got to execute, and I charge and command you both, and all who hear me, as good citizens——"

"Shet up, you bawling warmint!" cried the sergeant, and he accompanied the words by thrusting the rough handle of his sabre quite across the jaws of the deputy. The other turned upon him fiercely, but was brought back, with a jerk, by the hand of Frampton, who, with a shove, forcibly bade him—"go ahead—on!" At the same moment, he was pricked keenly in the flanks by the tip of Millhouse's sword, and, looking to the lieutenant, he saw that of the latter ready to enforce his progress by similar arguments. This was sharp practice, and quite new to Crooks, The sweat stood full on the face of the little fellow; but he still cried out, with a tough spirit, burning with fury:—

"Oh! *you* shall both *sweat* for all this."

"Oh! very well! That's as it happens. Every man must hev' his turn. But it's for you to sweat first," and a renewed pricking of the sergeant's sabre threatened something worse than sweating.

"Oh!" groaned the deputy, as he obeyed the impulse and went forward. Several times he paused, making a new endeavor to hold his ground, and as often was he made to feel the spur. When he reached the house, he was forced up the steps, through the piazza, into the hall, then thrust down into a chair, with a hand of each of his attendants upon his shoulder.

"We've got him, cappin!" cried out Millhouse to Porgy in his chamber. The captain of partisans had been reaping the stubble field, the autumnal harvests of his chin, which were quite too grisly to be suffered to offend his own or other eyes. He came forth with coat off, sleeves rolled up, neck bare, and razor in his grasp. The moment he beheld the deputy, he cried out—

"Heavens! What a monster! What a horrible looking creature! What a beard. Coppery-red; a perfect jingle, and full, no doubt, of all sorts of diminutive beasts. Sergeant, we must have that fellow's beard off."

Millhouse absolutely shouted at the idea.

"Tom!" roared the captain. Tom appeared at the door. "Quick, Tom, soap and napkin; and take off that horrid beard."

Crooks would have bounded from his seat. He prided himself on his beard. It's coppery red, apparently so offensive to all about him, was to him the perfection of beauty, It's red he held to be that of roses, and as for the amplitude of it, its wild, wide-spread bushy dimensions, these he stroked a thousand times a day with an affection which may be imagined. To lose his beard, even in jest, was almost as bad as to lose his scalp. He now began feverishly to apprehend, that with such companions, he should lose both. He leaped up, but was immediately thrust back into his seat by the ready hands of his attendants.

"I won't submit to this. I tell you—I warn you—I am an officer of justice. I'm here under the great seal of the state. I'm on official duties. I'm under the sacred protection of the law."

"How horribly he shouts! But, with such a beard, what mortal man can talk like a human being. You don't understand a word he says, sergeant ?"

"Not a word! I reckon it's a sort of nigger speech from Africa."

"Do you understand the savage creature, Lance ?"

"I reckon's he's crazy, captain," answered Lance.

"Truly, I think so. He will need a strait jacket. But there's no judging rightly his condition till we take off that brush."

"Let's burn it off, cappin."

"No! no! he may be human, and that might hurt him. We'll shave it off, and then see what he really is. I suspect he belongs to the monkey species—he's an orang-outang ;—you know what that is, sergeant."

"Hafe man, hafe horse, and two parts alligator, I reckin."

"You're very nigh the mark. Hurrah, Tom! make haste."

Tom made his appearance with basin, towel, soap, &c. The deputy seeing his danger, and that the affair was looking serious, made another effort to escape from the clutches in which he was held, and accompanied the effort by a fearful outcry, touching the terrors of the law. But in vain.

"Tie him down. Handkerchief, there, Tom. Secure him, so that he may not do himself harm. He is certainly very wild. He must have been only lately caught. Somebody must have put these clothes on him by force."

While the captain thus dilated, his assistants busied themselves in securing the deputy to his seat. His arms were tethered to the back of the chair, which was one of those massive mahogany receptacles so common at that period, and representing a much earlier period in the history of English civilization. The chair was, in fact, modelled upon the times of Elizabeth. Thus secured, with his head held back, the napkin tucked beneath his chin, Tom approached and proceeded to lay on the lather. The thick soapy mass was thurst *ad libitum* into mouth and nostrils. The deputy yelled, but as the soap made fearful progress into his jaws at every opening, he was, perforce, content to sputter, and sneeze, and kick and writhe. All efforts were unavailing. His captors were resolute in their fun. "Law!" he cried. "Lather!" cried Porgy; and Tom obeyed. Half suffocated, though more furious than ever, Crooks finally yielded, and Tom proceeded to apply the razor. Tom had acquired, in camp, the arts of the barber, as well as the cook. He was not so dextrous as determined. Crooks saw that it was at his own peril that he writhed, or twisted, or reared his head, or stuck out his chin unnecessarily. Tom would say quietly:—

"You only guine to wussen youse'f, buckrah—ef you is a buckrah—wid you kickings and cawortings. Better you keep youself easy, ef you don't want me for slice off you nose."

Here was a new peril. Slice off his nose! The loss of the petted beard was a great evil—but to lose his nose also, was such as it made him doubly sweat to meditate.

"Don't cut off his nose, Tom," cried Porgy, with a great air of concern. "This class of animals seldom have much to spare; and the loss of such a member, would really disfigure the face terribly."

"Lord, cappin, nothing could make such a critter more ugly than he is," answered Millhouse; "but he could lose an inch of snout and never miss it. Why, Lord, he's got a nose like a baggonet and a most hafe as long!"

Tom, meanwhile, prosecuted his labor with diligence. He was a bold cutter. It was all army practice with him—swift, slashing, reckless, not easily stopped by trifling impediments. At every swoop, Crooks found a wide waste of forest growth removed; huge tracts of warm furze disappeared, as the prairie

grass in autumn, under the fire.   Soon, the entire wilderness of
brush was cleaned up.   The territory was now smooth, and the
light let in upon a region that had not seen the day for half a
dozen years.   Crooks was no longer the same man; he felt cold
about the chin; but his chill greatly increased when he heard
Tom ask—

"Must tek' off he hair now, maussa?   He look berry bad and
ugly.   I reckin he must be full of warmints."

Porgy seemed for a moment to meditate the matter; but he
waived Tom off.

"No! that's enough, Tom, for the present.   I think we may
now make out the species of the animal."

" I'm the deputy sheriff—my name's Crooks."

" A well-known warmint, cappin.   I reckon you mout as well
skin him altogether.   Jest you take off the scalp now, and we'll
be sure to know him next time."

"No! no!   It is not so much that we may know him, as that
he may know us hereafter.   I see what he is.   Let him go now.
I reckon he's tame enough for the present.   Now, let him have
a swallow of Jamaica."

" I drink nothing in this house!" cried the deputy rising to
his feet.

" Then you lose the taste of a mighty good dram of liquor."

" And I warn you all—all three of you—that you shall answer for this assault and battery.   You, Captain Porgy—I know
you—and you, and you, I will have it all out of you three, if
there's any law in the land."

"You won't drink," said Porgy.

" Not a drop with you, or in this house."

" Will you eat ?"

" Not a mouthful!"

" Then we've done all that we can do for you, unless you desire
that Tom should take off that shock.   It is unnecessarily thick
and long.   Can that be hair?"

" Look you, Captain Porgy, I've submitted to your assaults
and batteries because I could not help myself."

" A mighty good reason too!"

" But I will have redress.   Now, sir, I will do my duty, and
here I give you notice, that in the character of the Sheriff of—"

"Boo! woo! woo! woo!   Shall I muzzle him, cappin?"

"No! let him go.   Depart, my good fellow, while your bones are whole.   We have done for you the best we could."

"I'll not go until I have made a levy upon all the lands and negroes, the goods and chattels of this estate of Glen-Eberley, under the authority of the papers which I now carry, and which I will read for the benefit—"

By this time he had drawn the documents out of his pocket.

" Beware how you attempt to read any of those vile heathen documents here," said Porgy, assuming an air of great sternness.

"State of South Carolina!" began the deputy.

" As surely as you attempt to read that paper, I will make you eat it!"

" Eat it! I'll eat nothing in this house!"

" We'll see to that."

" State of South Carolina—" resumed the deputy.

" Seize him," cried Porgy—" seize him!"

And, in the twinkling of an eye, Frampton caught Crooks in his embrace, and Millhouse set his enormous thumb and forefinger about his neck, and the deputy was forced back into his chair.   The paper was snatched by the lieutenant from his hand.

" In the name of the state!" screamed the deputy.

" Feed him with it!" shouted Porgy.

" I levy and seize, distrein and take possession—" began the deputy at a rapid rate, but his mouth was suddenly filled with his documents.   The execution was crammed into his jaws—a part of it at least; and the voice of the sergeant, in accents too clear and loud to be misunderstood, advised him what to do with it.

" Feed or suffocate, you skunk."

" You're choking me to death!"

" Feed, then! Chaw! Swallow!"   And, at every word, the sergeant plied the unhappy deputy, with a fragment of the execution.   It was in vain that he flounced and floundered, strove, kicked, and scuffled with his persecutor.   The iron arm of Millhouse was seconded with an equally iron will, and, perforce, the victim was compelled to chew and mouth the musty document.

" My God! do you mean to kill me?"

" Not unless good feeding will do it. You love the law, you live on it, and ought to be able to digest it. Give him another mouthful, sergeant. It must all be eaten. It is not too much for one meal."

With every bit offered, and finally forced upon the deputy, the same struggle followed, the same unavailing resistance. He was compelled to eat. Nothing but the seal remained. This was not then the fiction which it is in recent times. It was not then thought quite sufficient to write '*locus sigilli*,' and withhold the seal itself. In the present case this was a goodly circular plate of red wax, of some dimensions. It was now offered to the unwilling feeder. At the sight of it the fellow cried out with horror—"I can't eat that! It'll be the death of me. It's got poison in it."

"Ah! ha! is it so? And do you bring p'ison into a gentleman's family, and try to sarve it on him. Well, it's only your own medicine, my honey; you must eat it with the rest. The physic of a law paper kaint be good onless the seal goes with it. Bite! Eat! or I'll——"

But for the interposition of the captain, the sergeant would have persisted in testing to the utmost the capacities of Crooks' stomach. Fortunately, the former was disposed to more indulgence.

"Let him off," said he, "he's had enough. Now give him some Jamaica;—or, perhaps, you'll prefer an emetic, my good fellow, to produce reaction. I can have you a little tartar in a second."

"No! no!" cried Crooks with choking accents—"The rum! the rum!"

The liquor was poured out for him, and the glass put into his hands; as he was about to drink, Millhouse exclaimed—

"Ha! ha! I know'd you'd hev' to come to it at last. You swore you wouldn't eat or drink in this house. You've done both!"

The taunt was enough. The deputy dashed down the untasted liquor, smashing the glass upon the floor.

"Curse the house!" he cried, "and all that's in it!" and shaking his hand in fury, he broke through all restraint, and disappeared from the apartment.

"After him, boys, and see that he clears out. Attend him to the outposts, Lance! He will hardly venture back with other documents."

CHAPTER LIX.

M'KEWN AT HOME, AND THE SPECTRE THAT SIPPED HIS PUNCH.

THE captain had not fairly lost sight of the deputy before he began to reflect upon the enormity of the offence which he had sanctioned and committed. It was not so much that he had outraged the laws of the land, as that he had violated those of humanity. He began to feel ashamed of this, for, when not carried away by impulse, he would have revolted at everything like brutality, unless, as in the case of actual conflict in war, it took the form of a necessity. His successful jest with the sheriff, which had proved harmless, had prompted a renewal of the experiment; and, once committed to the joke, he had been hurried on by his first impulse, long after the matter had ceased to be mirthful. Though he said nothing of his misgivings to his companions, he yet felt very much ashamed of the affair, when the time had come for reflection. We may add that he did not, on this occasion, ride over to report the adventure to the fair widow. He would rather, indeed, that it should not reach her ears from any lips. But it got abroad nevertheless.

Crooks, as soon as he could mount his horse hurried at full speed over to M'Kewn's, to whom, boiling with fury, he described the whole affair. It did not need the exaggerations of language to render it hideous. M'Kewn was secretly pleased at the occurrence. It fastened an odium upon our partisan, whose patriotic services had otherwise made him popular. It left him more at the mercy of his creditor, by depriving him of those sympathies which his distresses would certainly have secured for him. But, M'Kewn did not suffer his secret thoughts, on this head, to reach the ears of the deputy. His indignation at the treatment which he had suffered, was expressed in language as warm and violent almost as his own, and, giving him a douceur of five guineas, he despatched him, the next day, with a letter to the sheriff, renewing his demand upon him for the immediate compliance with his duties.

The sheriff was naturally angry at the ill usage of his deputy. There was a great sensation in the city. Pinckney and Parsons, the friends and lawyers of Porgy, were in much confusion. They endeavored all they could at the arts of soothing. The shaving of the deputy they made very light of. Indeed, they affirmed it to be an act of kindness. The procedure, they insisted, had greatly improved Crooks's appearance; but the matter was quite too serious to be laughed out of court; and such a suggestion made Crooks, himself, more angry than ever. They found it politic, accordingly, to forbear this mode of treating the affair. The compulsory feeding to which the deputy had been subjected —the utter scorn and defiance of the law which had been shown by Porgy and his followers —were serious offences against the peace and dignity of the country, which most persons were inclined to resent. The sheriff talked of immediate processes of arrest — of the *posse comitatus,*— of a military force, — and of terrible penalties, forfeitures, and imprisonments!

To gain time was now the object with Porgy's friends, until the public indignation should subside; and they brought every possible influence to bear, which might, in any way, effect their purpose. It happened, fortunately, that Marion and Colonel Singleton were both in the city, and both anxiously busied themselves to rescue an old favorite and follower from his difficulties. They appealed to the sheriff for delay, at least until the affair could be inquired into peaceably. M'Kewn's debt must be satisfied, of course;—for this several parties were prepared to pledge themselves; — and it was supposed that the hurts of Crooks might all be cured by a sufficient salve in the guise of hush-money. These matters arranged, the irritated self-esteem of the sheriff might be soothed, and the damage done to the dignity of the laws might be repaired — as is commonly the case in a good democracy — by taking no sort of notice of it. With us, you may pull the nose of the law, at pleasure, but you must be prepared to pay well for any such liberty taken with the nose of its officer. Crooks, as yet, was quite unapproachable on the subject of his wrongs and injuries. It was supposed by Pinckney that he would continue unapproachable, until beard and whiskers had once more grown out to their former ravishing dimensions. Meanwhile, all proper efforts should be made to mollify him;

and, to effect this, Pinckney himself prepared to run up to Asheepoo, and see the captain, in order to bring him to reasonable apologies.

These negotiations necessarily occupied some time, during which Glen-Eberley was left free of molestation. The sergeant congratulated himself that a victory had been obtained. Porgy was less sure and satisfied. He had sobered down from his late excitement, and could see the state of affairs through the proper medium. He saw that the time would come when he should pay for his frolic; but, like most persons of his temperament, he preferred to postpone the consideration of the affair till the last moment—until, indeed it was forced upon him. Winter, meanwhile, was advancing rapidly. The nights of November were becoming very cold. Our captain of partisans was now in the full enjoyment of field sports, and was proving himself quite a Nimrod. His corpulence did not seem to lessen his appetite, or his vigor in the chase. Arthur Eveleigh, sensible of his fault, had become measurably reconciled to the captain, and he and Lance Frampton met at Glen-Eberley, once a week at least, to hunt. Porgy's sports, however, in the field, did not lessen the number of his visits to the two widows. He was still, as before—not to speak disparagingly of the sex in our comparisons—betwixt hawk and buzzard. This homely figure was one frequently in the mouth of the sergeant, in reference to the attitude of his superior, though he did not venture to obtrude it upon the ears of the captain. Both widows still seemed very gracious, and their looks of favor increased the impatience of Millhouse to effect his long cherished object.

"You might have either on 'em, I reckon, for the axing," quoth the sergeant; "though it's cl'ar that the widow Eb'leigh is the most loving critter of the two. It's a needcessity, cappin, that she should hev' you."

The frequent iteration of this assurance, finally made its impression upon our captain;—but, though half persuaded only, that Mrs. Eveleigh labored under the "needcessity" aforesaid, he felt, as a man of honor, that he could not approach her as a suitor, until he had paid her his debt—at all events, having extricated himself from the meshes of the law. "Then,"—he thought;—but it is proper we should not anticipate!

Meanwhile, what of the inexorable creditor, M'Kewn? Housed at his plantation like the great black spider, to which we have already likened him, surrounded by subtle snares of policy, and sly devices, and meshes of cunning, for taking in and securing the thoughtless flies of humanity—for making prey of all he could—he crouched in seeming quiet, most of the time unbeheld, in secret crevice, and when seen, seeming only to drowse, in the central circle of his innocent encampment. He was pleasantly satisfied with his progresses. What, with his own art, and Porgy's rash impulses, he felt that he had fairly involved that greatest of all his flies in a mesh from which there was no escape. All of his schemes appeared to prosper. Other victims were in his snares. His money bred as if under the direct management of Mammon—as if Mammon had become his private banker, and determined his loans and enterprises. He had made a good crop, and rice was rising in the market. He had bought, at moderate prices, a lot of *new* negroes, from the coast of Guinea, from a virtuous puritan captain, of Rhode Island, who had gleaned wonderfully from the gold coast, and whose great grand-son, by-the-way, has since shown himself a virtuous abolitionist in the senate of the United States, breathing hate and horror toward the descendants of the very people to whom his philanthropic grand-sire sold the stolen negroes. All M'Kewn's speculations seemed to be prosperous. All his apprehensions of Mrs. Eveleigh were relaxed in her continued silence. He had got over his fears of her, in the conviction which he felt that the seas rolled for ever between himself and the squatter Bostwick—perhaps, rolled *over* him; a fate which he preferred for his enemy, and which he rather thought he must have suffered, since he had no reason to doubt of the sagacity and fidelity of his creatures, Forbes, Drummond, and Barton.

Thus, with all his fears at rest, all his fortunes prosperous, all his victims in his meshes, all his enemies *hors de combat*, M'Kewn yielded himself up to his pleasures. Shall not his soul take its peace at last; shall he not reward himself for long abstinence and self-denial; shall he not feel himself in his place and power, in due self-atonement for a long and tedious career of sycophancy, and base submission to the moods of others? M'Kewn's best mode of reasoning taught him no higher aim or nobler philosophy than this. He was prepared now to take his ease at his inn! He was preparing to look about him for a wife, such as a fortune, great as his, might reasonably command. He would have been pleased to lift the widow Eveleigh into that honored station; but the last interview which he had enjoyed with that lady, taught him the utter hopelessness of that object—taught him farther, that, though she could by no means establish the truth legally against him, she was yet morally possessed of evidence the most conclusive of his guilt. He kept heedfully from her sight accordingly; while, under a new impulse, young Arthur, whom he had labored industriously to corrupt, kept as heedfully from his.

Thus, apparently secure, thus measurably happy—satisfied with himself and his successes, or striving to be so—M‘Kewn took his ease at his plantation, or wore, to other eyes, the appearance of one who did so. He lived well, sought the neighboring planters, emulated their hospitality, was frequently a visiter abroad, and as frequently entertained his guests at home. He gave good dinners, indulged in choice wines, and, being a man of the world, who had enjoyed a considerable experience, and was naturally intelligent, he proved, in most cases, a very excellent companion among the persons whom he was pleased to seek.

It was a cold and cloudy day, late in November, when a party dined with him. They were all good fellows, the dinner was served up in excellent style, the wines were fine, the dessert in good taste, and the enjoyment of all parties extreme. They sat late—they drank freely. It was a bachelor's establishment, and song and story spelled the intervals between the several pledges. Soon, the wines gave way to stronger liquors. Old rum and fiery French brandy and genuine Scotch whiskey took the place, upon the board, of more courtly spirits. M‘Kewn was famous at hot whiskey punch, and felt a sort of national pride and pleasure, presiding, with an antique Scottish bowl before him, of immense size, and the wooden ladle of curious carving in his grasp, and the little silver tankard smoking before each guest, while their lips smacked with delight, and their tongues grew thick with the language of unintelligible compliment—the more grateful as unintelligible. The company dispersed at a tolerably late hour, going home with no consciousness of dark or danger, shouting as they went, and fortunate in drivers, or horses, who had enjoyed no such pleasant privileges of punch as themselves. M'Kewn was left alone to his own fancies. He summoned the servants, ordered that the remains of the vessel of punch should be taken into his chamber, and, a fire having been already kindled there, repaired thither himself.

The night was dark and cold, but the room was bright and warm. Too bright, was the thought of M'Kewn, since he extinguished the wax candles both, which the negro had left burning, satisfied with the sufficient blaze of the lightwood brands cast upon the fire, and of which an adequate supply stood ready always in a box upon the hearth. M'Kewn sat in front of the fire, his slippered feet presented to the blaze. His sensations were decidedly comfortable. He was in affluence; his health was good; he was yet a comparatively young man; at least on the sunny side of fifty. He might reasonably calculate, according to existing probabilities, upon a long term of enjoyment. In spite of the awkward doubts in certain quarters, he was able to command good society. If he could not claim entrance into one circle, he had a very tolerable refuge in another. He had wealth, and wealth can always buy society, though it may command neither real respect, nor affection, for its possessor. The people who had spent the day with him were all people of excellent standing. Good fellowship made them flexible. They sneered at M'Kewn himself; but they entertained a very genuine respect for his dinners. There were some of them who aimed at something beyond his dinners—who, perhaps, would scarcely have permitted themselves to dine with him but for their occult objects. These persons had maiden sisters or daughters, of a rare and virtuous antiquity, whom, for their especial claims to admiration, they desired to see framed in settings of gold. They patronized M'Kewn to this end—no more. The Scotchman readily saw through their schemes, grinned in secret over their absurdities, but did not discourage those hopes by which he secured himself in *good* society. Sitting by his now solitary hearth, he mused with great complacency, thinking upon these and other matters. The affair of Porgy and the deputy sheriff had been brought upon the *tapis* during the day, and had been discussed with great frankness on both sides of the question, as is the way commonly with our impulsive planters of the parish country. Some of them, most desirous of conciliating M‘Kewn, were loud in their denunciation of the violent and illegal proceedings of the captain of partisans. Others chuckled over it as a rare and admirable jest which furnished quite an excellent example to all future creditors. Others went further, and, moved by very earnest sympathies with the debtor, professed to regard any innovation of a man's household, on the part of a creditor, or his legal representative, to be a most impertinent intrusion, justifying any severity of treatment. M‘Kewn heard all, and smiled in all directions, satisfied, at the close, to say, in a costive manner—

"Let him settle with the sheriff as he may, gentlemen; he will have to settle with me! He may struggle, but can't escape me. In three months, at least, there will be an end of him, and the jest will be on the other side. They always laugh who win; and if the loser has the mood to laugh, why, we may safely suffer him to indulge it."

And it was with this conviction of ultimate conquest,—the final overthrow of his insolent debtor—that M‘Kewn would chuckle to himself, sipping at his whiskey-punch the while. Of this popular beverage, whose virtues lie always below the surface, and penetrate much more than skin deep, M‘Kewn had a snug silver pitcher, long necked, of vase fashion, and silver lidded, standing conveniently beside him on a table;—moderate measures were poured out as he wanted it, into the tumbler beside him. He stirred and sipped, and, tumbler still in hand, drew nigher to the blaze; and, after a little while, and as his feet began too much to warm before the fire, he threw them up against the mantelpiece, throwing them wide apart, so that the whole panorama of the fire, the smouldering ruins, the blazing piles, were all present to his eye through the frame work of his parted thighs. His head was cast back, the lids of his eyes drawn down; he watched the fire as through a microscope, taking in its small details. His chair, a heavy one of mahogany, with a great back, was nicely balanced on its hind legs. The tumbler, half filled with the grateful beverage, was as nicely balanced in his hands. His mind had reached that condition of repose which brings about pleasant reveries. M‘Kewn saw his future through a magic medium. His enemies were overthrown, his course was triumphant, his wealth underwent hourly increase, the magnates of the land were subservient, he himself had become a magnate; and his eye had only to determine which of the several beauties at his service, he should choose, to make his world an Eden.

Happy M'Kewn! The fates are busy always to beguile with pleasant auguries those whom they would involve beyond their depths. Sometimes, a speck would appear suddenly on the face of his magic mirror, a slight cloud pass over it, a lurid flash, and he could fancy distant thunder—in other words, images of Porgy and the widow Eveleigh, and the hateful Bostwick, and other persons, would recall to him suddenly a train of subjects suggestive of fear or difficulty; but M'Kewn found it easy to disperse these obtrusive shadows, simply by a renewed appeal to the warm whiskey-punch beside him. It was surprising how soon, after this application, the speck and cloud would disappear from the magic mirror which his fancy had polished so well for his contemplation.

Thus sitting, musing, dreaming, in that doubtful sort of consciousness which seems to be equally distant from absolute sleep or waking, M'Kewn thought he beheld the waving of an arm and hand before his half-shut eye. He fancied that some one had taken up the beaker of punch which, having sipped a little of the contents, he had just set down. But his energies were fast yielding beneath the sluggish happiness of his dreamy mood, and, though somewhat conscious of a movement, and even of a sound, he dismissed it as a natural suggestion of his revery itself, and never turned his head. A moment may have elapsed, or more, when, suddenly, a hand was laid heavily upon his shoulder. He unclosed his eyes, and stared. He was paralyzed. Was it true—was it a dream? Did he really behold the infernal squatter, Bostwick, once more?—or was it his drowned, thrice damned, and ever haunted and haunting ghost, emerging from the depths of the green sea, and following him on the mission of the furies! Was it the hand of a spectre or a living man that still rested upon his shoulder. Was there mortal speculation in those fiery red eyes that now stared terrifically down into his?

CHAPTER LX.

HOW THE SQUATTER MADE THE VOYAGE TO THE WEST INDIES,

IN the sight of M'Kewn nothing could be more distinct, more life-like than the spectre. He looked just as he had seen him a thousand times before; the same great red staring eyes, the same expression in the face, of a mixed savage and cunning nature sly at once and desperate; the same small but sinewy figure; the same lounging, slovenly carriage; the same person altogether, except, perhaps, that each vicious quality of his face was exaggerated; the grin upon his mouth was more satyr-like; his eyes were blood-shot; his cheeks mottled with the long continued habit of intemperance: his skin bronzed to a copper, yet flushed as with the hues of a warm sunset. Was he indeed a spectre? Had the grave given up the dead? Had the seas thrown up their victim? Did the spectator really dream or not?

M'Kewn closed his eyes, and again opened them, thinking the fearful presence might then be gone. There it stood, and he could no longer doubt the solid pressure of its grasp upon his shoulder. The Scotchman was paralyzed. Dead or living, the appearance of Bostwick was now a terror. M'Kewn was almost in a state of collapse. The cold sweat had silently streamed out upon his face, his neck, his breast, his whole body. His feet, thrown up against the mantelpiece, sank down to the floor nerveless; his lips parted, but not for speech; only in silent consternation. But his frozen gaze never once fell from that of his fearful visiter. There, in utter silence, the one stood, the other sat, gazing full upon each other. Bostwick seemed to take a malignant pleasure in fixing and fastening the other's eyes, as if with a serpent's fascination. After a little while he slowly withdrew his hand, and coolly turning to the table, filled himself a stoup of the whiskey-punch from the silver vessel, into the tumbler which M'Kewn had used, and swallowed the contents at a single gulph. He laid the tumbler down, then extended his open palm—

"That hundred guineas, M'Kewn!"

The spell was broken as he spoke. M'Kewn began to recover.

"Why, where have you been all this time, Bostwick?"

"Where did you reckon I was? In the bottom of the sea?— In h–ll's blazes, didn't you, and warn't you mighty glad to think so? But h–ll ain't hot enough for either on us yit, and when I had my last talk with the devil, he promised me, as how, when he did come for me, he'd take you at the same time. But he don't want us yit. He's got more work for both on us, on this airth. You was intirely wrong, M'Kewn, in trying to git rid of me. You kaint do without me, no more than I kin do without you. We're born for each other, and we've got to work together a long time to come?"

"But where have you been?"

Better not aix! Not edzactly whar you wanted me to go, but jest on the edge, as I may say. I looked in at the door, didn't like the looks of it, the 'commydations they offered me, and turned short round. It was a question whether I should go in or your friends, Drummond, and Barton, and Forbes, the cappin, or me. I reckon'd the lodgin's would better suit them than me, so I let them take my place. They're gone with the despatches you made out for me."

"What do you mean? What despatches?"

"Oh!" you knows jest as well as me, what it was you meant them to do for me. But the devil, he come to my help, and made the sarvice cl'ar. They got the preference, and I gin up my place to 'em."

"What place? Where are they?"

"In h–ll, ef you wants to know; they'll never trouble you nor me no more. The devil put the ch'ice afore me—either them to burn or me to drown, and I didn't want three minutes to consider. I know'd they'd have to git usen to fire in time to come, so I thought the sooner they began to l'arn the feel of it, the better for them."

"In the name of God, Bostwick, what do you mean? What have you done?"

" You're mighty slow to onderstand, these times. That's from heving such a world of money. What should I mean? Your friends took me out to sea—"

" Is it possible! Took you to sea!"

" Shet up, and don't lie to me. 'Tain't no use, M'Kewn. I know you like a book. We knows one another. 'Twarn't on sea that they were the good fellows they was on land. When we was in the ' castle,' and under the green trees, we was friends, and all on equal tairms. We played cards together, and some-times they dreaned me, and sometimes I dreaned them. At sea the natur' changed. I was a man of the woods; they made me a man of the sea. I could climb trees; they made me climb ropes. It was no play thar; all work; they didn't wait to win my money, by a fair seven-up. They tuk it from me by main strength of hand.—Then I got the cat! The cat! You knows, I reckon, what they calls the cat?"

M'Kewn professed to be ignorant.

" You've got to l'arn it. I've promised Old Nick to do his work, on the very condition that, when he gits us both, he lets me treat you to the cat every night; so that you may lie down with a sartain softness in your feelin's, that ain't altogether sweetness. That cat which they gin to me has left its claw-marks on every inch of my back and body. But that warn't enough for 'em. When they got right off the place called Bar-badoes, they holds a counciltation over me. What's to be done with me—what's to be done for *you*—and they 'grees 'mong their three selves, that the best things for both on us, is to send me over into the sea, to look after the great whale that swal-lowed Jony, the Philistian prophet—"

" Impossible! Did they really mean to—"

" Oh! shet up. Lying won't do 'twixt us, 'kaise, you see, we knows one another, M'Kewn, and we've got to work togeth-er, by solemn contractings, for the old horned Satan. Well, thar was the land, jest off thar; and the night was a-coming' on, and the sea was deep, and the shirks was a-playing about, and look-ing upward to the ship with all-fired hungry noses. And the counciltation of Forbes, and Drummond, and Barton, went on; and they said these poor shirks must be fed; and this poor Bost-wick will give 'em mighty good feeding for a time; and when he's gone, we'll get the hundred guineas from M'Kewn in place of him, and we must git shet of him to-night: and so the counciltation went on. But the devil stood my friend, and he hid me where I could hear all the counciltation; and when they had done, he said to me—'Now, Bost, whether you're to drown, or they to burn. It's for you to choose. Thar's the sea, and them's the shirks a-waiting for your supper; and the moon goes down about midnight, and then it's for you to try the cold feel of the water, and see how deep it is, and find out ef thar's any big whale to take you in, like Jony, the Philistian prophet, and save you from the shirks. Ef you waits to choose ontell the midnight, the water's your portion, and the bottom of the sea, whar thar's no bottom. And when the brigantine goes up to the town in the morning, they'll report one Bostwick, fell overboard last night and lost, from taking too much liquor.' It's a blessing that they gin me none, and I was sharp as a bag'net. Says the devil —'thar's one way to git out of danger.' And he showed me three kegs of gunpowder where they were stowed away; and he told me, what was mighty cur'ous to me to l'arn, that ef that gunpowder only happen'd to git the leetlest taste of the fire, it would fly like old blazes, and carry everybody up into heaven. That was mighty cur'ous, I thought; and he show'd me further, how a thing mout be managed, called ' a train,' and how a man setting in a boat outside of the ship, might jest touch the fire to the train, push off, and see the ship sail up in the air, much quicker than she ever sailed through the water. Well, you see, I thought that was better sport than to take the water myself, and s'arch after Jony's whale; and, with the help of Old Horny I tried it; and, sure enough, off she went, ship and all, and the three counsulters, and a small chaince of pussons more; and the people found me on the beach, and who knows how I got thar? They said I was blowed thar by the gunpowder;—and now, M'Kewn, that ere hundred guineas!"

CHAPTER LXI.

THAT HUNDRED GUINEAS!

It was easy for M'Kewn, even with this hurried and imperfect statement of the squatter, to gather the whole history of his enforced voyage, and the horrible catastrophe by which it was terminated. The cool and savage deliberation with which it was delivered, did not, however, produce any of those revolting and crushing sensations in the mind of the hearer, which might have arisen in that of any person of sensibility. M'Kewn, like his companion, was callous and cold-blooded; of so rank a selfishness, that sensibility had long since ceased to oppose any barriers to cupidity; and whose shows of humanity—shows only— were simply employed in deference to society, and with the view the better to promote the objects of his desire. Instead of shuddering and shrinking at what he heard, he was employed in recovering the subdued and scattered forces of his mind, in order to encounter the struggle which the reappearance of the squatter necessarily threatened. He knew the fellow too well to suppose that he should get off without a conflict, and felt that he was too well understood by him, to render available any of the ordinary arts of imposition. The terms upon which they stood, in regard to each other, were such that neither found it of any use to affect virtues which he did not possess. They had only to treat of crime and its reward, as of any matter of legitimate business. Any declarations of surprise, any avowals of good faith, or sympathy, would, he well knew, be utterly wasted on the ears of a person who knew him quite too well to be imposed upon any longer. Accordingly, with a manner the most unconcerned, M'Kewn, after a brief pause, remarked—

"And that was the way you got rid of them?"

"Yes; jest so. It was short and quick, and we had no quarrel. It was a private counciltation on both sides, them three on one side, and Old Horny and me on t'other. They were three to two, but we were a little too much of a match for 'em. It turned out famous well for me. The people of Barbadoes raised a su'scription for me, and that filled my pockets, and I got home with a free passage, and didn't hev' any much work to do; though I did a leetle to please the cappin. 'Tain't quite four days sence I got to Charleston, and I pushed up here knowing you'd be mighty glad to hear of your friends, and how you wouldn't hev' to fill their pouches any more. I reckon it's a great gain to you, the loss of them men."

"Gain! It's a loss to me of thousands. I owned one third of that vessel and cargo. I owned sixty-nine of the negroes in her."

"Diccance! I'll hev' to 'low their valley out of the amount you owes me, then. It's only fair! Let me see: thar's what you owed me afore I went to sea; we'll reckon that at a thousand guineas; thar's the carrying me to sea agin my will, and only to pleasure you; that I vallies at five thousand guineas more, and cheap at that, I tell you; but we'll say five thousand —that's six thousand. Then, thar's the scare I had from the shirks and the drowning, all on your account; that ought to be a thousand guineas more; then, thar's the selling my soul to the Old Horny, to get out of the hands of them fellows. A free white man's soul ought to be worth something, and we'll call it a thousand guineas more; that makes eight thousand; then, thar's the onhappiness I had to skyrocket them three good fellows to heaven; that was a great onhappiness, and I valley my sufferin's mighty high; but we'll say two thousand guineas more; and that, in round numbers, will be ten thousand guineas; and, out of that, I'm to 'low for them sixty-nine niggers of your'n that went up in the skyrocketing. I reckon they mout be vallied at fifty guineas apiece :—how much is that in all? Count up, M'Kewn, I'm guine to 'low for all."

"Pshaw! What are you talking about?"

"What em I talking about? I'll tell you, and you may jest pick your ears that you may hear it plain. Thar's an account of life and death to settle atween us, M'Kewn, that may be settled up with money, ef you've the sense to onderstand what's best for you. You'll pay it out of your pocket, ef you're sensible; ef you're a fool, it comes out of your heart. To pay for it in money, won't drean your pocket; to pay for it in blood, will go nigh to drean your body of all it's got. I knows what I says. I knows that I kin hang you jest when I pleases, and I don't owe you any love that I should keep my hands off. But I kin sell my hate and my love together. Everything I've got is to sell, ef so be I'm well paid for it; and you must buy from me at my prices, or I'll bankcorrupt you, as they calls it. You'll hev' to feed me and find me, me and my fam'ly, my wife and my children, jest so long as you lives and we lives; and you'll hev' to feed us well; and to begin, I'm a-wanting jest one hundred guineas to-night, and next week, I'll be a-wanting, prehaps, a hundred more. I'm guine to buy property; I'm guine into a speckilation for the good of my fam'ly. You hear it all. I put it plain before you. It's jest for you to say whether it's peace or war; fair tarms or foul; money or blood!"

This was all plain enough, delivered in a manner the most downright and direct, the squatter confronting the Scotchman at the distance of a single pace, and his hand flourishing at moments in the very face of the latter. When he had finished speaking, he again turned to the whiskey punch, unasked, and repeated his draught.

M'Kewn listened with chilled sensations. He understood but too well the existing terms between himself and his enemy. He saw that nothing had been exaggerated in the speech of the squatter. The latter truly had him at his mercy; and he felt that he was destined to continue exactions, so long as Bostwick or himself should live. There was no evasion of the incumbrance, and the time was gone by, utterly, when the employee could be put off or deceived. He had no remaining subterfuges against a foe so wily, and so well-informed in respect to his character. Meanwhile, the squatter seemed to amuse himself surveying the apartment, which was large, lofty, highly finished, richly hung with drapery, and with fine pictures hanging against the walls. A sabre, between a pair of silver-mounted pistols, was among these decorations. The squatter's eye took in all.

"You're a-living like a fighting cock, M'Kewn," said he, with a *dégagée* air that was quite distressing to the Scotchman, and served to increase his irritation. "Now, I'm a-wanting to live easy and like a fighting cock, too, but don't you think I'm a-wanting to hev' sich fine things in my cabin. They doesn't suit sich as me, and agin, I doesn't care to hev' em. What I wants is a sartainty for myself, and for Dory. That's all; and the sartainty must be a respectable one. A nice little house and farm, and, prehaps, two or three niggers to work in the field, and an old woman to cook, and a gal to be a sort of waiting-maid to little Dory."

To this, M'Kewn only answered with an "Ah!—Well!—Yes!" but his eyes followed the movements of the squatter with an intensity of interest which gave them a wild expression.—Meanwhile, though stalking about, with an air of inebriate hardihood and indifference, that seemed to be heedful of nothing, the squatter might be seen to keep a furtive watch on the Scotchman, which never suffered the slightest movement to escape him; but this was not perceptible to M'Kewn. Highly excited by his own reflections upon the desperate bondage in which he felt himself placed, the usual vigilance of this cool and subtle strategist was greatly lessened. His passions served to bind him somewhat at the very moment when every faculty should have been most acutely sharpened and observant. His thoughts, under the influence of these passions, were of a sort to madden him. Was there no escape from the arrogance of this enemy? Was he to be plagued perpetually without any hope of relief? Was he for ever to be made to fear for his secret, particularly now, when, this danger quieted, his position in life was so grateful, and might become altogether triumphant.

It was past midnight. The house was quiet. The servants were all retired and asleep. Nobody had seen the squatter enter. Nobody knew of his visit. The rain was now falling heavily; the winds beat sullenly against the shutter. Night and storm were auxiliaries to a deed of blood. Why should he not quiet the foe for ever, by a single blow? Why not, by one sudden, desperate deed, relieve himself for ever from this haunting, harrowing arrogance; this perpetual danger, which promised never to suffer him to repose in security? His eye rested upon the pistols which hung upon the wall. They were both loaded, he knew—charged with a brace of bullets. They were such as he could well rely on. The suggestion coursed rapidly through his mind. It grew in force; it ripened to conclusion; it became a resolution. In a moment, he sprang to his feet, whirled aside the great chair upon which he had been sitting, and darted toward the pistols.

But, resolute as was his determination, secret and sudden of purpose, and prompt of execution, he was too late. The squatter knew his man, had suffered none of his movements to escape him, and when M‘Kewn stretched out his hand to grasp the weapons upon the wall, he encountered the squatter. Bostwick stood between, and, instead of arming himself, M‘Kewn found a pistol at his own breast.

"Keep quiet, now, M‘Kewn, and git back to your easy chair. It is not your time yit, nor is it mine. I don't want to hurt you, but I knows you, and will jest keep a p'inter upon your motions, tell I has my axings."

"Devil! Would you murder me? Would you drive me to madness?"

"Well, twarn't good sense in me to be doing either one, so long as I gits what I wants by easy means. But, rether than not git it, I'd kill you soon enough, and drive you to the devil, and to madness, and eny whar' you choose, and not sp'ile my appetite in doing it. Set you down, I tell you, and don't be making yourself a redickilous figger!"

"What is it you want?" was the demand of M‘Kewn, half-moved to rush upon the fellow in defiance of the pistol.

"Well, that's a foolish question arter all I've been a-telling you. I wants a leetle of my rights. To begin—a hundred guineas, which I must hev' this very night."

"That's impossible. I don't keep money in the country!"

"That's nothing to me. You must find it. I don't quit you, M‘Kewn, till I gits the gould guineas, one hundred on 'em, in this very hand. Set you down quiet, and think over the different draws, or holes, whar' you hides away your yallow-birds. As for gitting at the pistols, while I has a pair on 'em myself, crammed to the muzzle with bullets, that's onpossible, and you knows it. Set down quiet, and think over what you hev' to do. I'll give you time for the thinking."

M‘Kewn drew back submissively, and sank into the seat again. As he did so, the squatter took down the pistols from the wall and stuck them into his belt.

"It's only a removing the temptation from your eyes."

This done, he began to pace the room languidly as before, at times humming the words and air of a song of vulgar independence, then quite popular among the whigs, but the words of which have only in part descended to our times.

> " I've no money, I've no lands,
> Yet I carry fearless hands,
> And I fear no lord's commands.
>   Let him thunder as he may,
> I've the strength to do my part,
> Strong of arm, and stout of heart,
> And I do not care ————''

Here M'Kewn's voice broke in upon that of the singer.

"And if I give you this hundred guineas, Bostwick, are you prepared to deliver up those papers in the box of Mrs. Eveleigh?"

" Not edzactly! You don't git them delivered, M'Kewn, tell you plank down one hundred more guineas, on the nail, and I'll ixpect you to do that very thing by the middle of next week."

The Scotchman again started up in a fury.

"Easy, M'Kewn; take it easy, and it'll be so much the better for your narves. You're flurried and thar's no use for it. Don't you see, now, that you hev' to come to it. Thar's no gitting off."

M'Kewn groaned aloud; then turning to the silver flagon which had held the punch, he proceeded, with trembling hands, to pour its contents into a tumbler.

" That's right! It'll steady your narves. I'm only afear'd I've left you too small a sup!"

"Yes!" quoth M'Kewn, quickly. "I'll step down stairs and get a fresh supply. You'll be wanting more also."

" Quiet, M'Kewn. You doesn't leave this room ontell I gits my guineas."

And, with the words, the squatter coolly locked the door, and put the key into his pocket.

" Damnation, man! Do you mean to make me a prisoner in my own house?"

" Oh! psho! shet up! What made it your house any more than mine? Only bekaise you had better skill in roguery. Ef I goes out here onsatisfied, M'Kewn, your house goes to the devil and you 'long with it! Don't you onderstand yit, that I kin tear you out of it, by the hands of Johnny Ketch, the born rope-stretcher. Be sensible, and git the guineas; and then you may git the drink."

M'Kewn resumed his seat, and sternly regarded his persecutor, no longer concealing, or seeking to conceal, the venomous hatred of his heart, betraying itself, without disguise, in every feature of his face.

"Well," said Bostwick, "you're looking now more honest-like than I've seed you for many a day. You'll be letting me hev' those guineas, I see. That's the right sense. You hev' no chaince, M'Kewn. I'm a-top of you this time!"

The words were those of truth and soberness, however strange, coming from such lips. M'Kewn felt them to be so. He had been put in check at every point of the game, and to avoid check-mate it was necessary to sacrifice a few pawns. However reluc-tant to receive this conviction, it came to him at last.

"You shall have the guineas; but I must have the box of papers."

"All in good time! It'll take a hundred guineas more, I tell you, M'Kewn, afore you gets them papers."

"And when am I to have them?"

"Next week, when I wants the other hundred guineas."

"And then?"

"Well! What then?"

"Am I then to be rid of you for ever?"

"For ever's a long time, M'Kewn, and I kain't quite answer; but I rether think you'll never be rid of me; for, as I tell'd you, Old Horny has promised that we shall keep together all the time, work together on this airth, and go to him together; and when thar"—pointing downward—"I'm to give you a little taste of that same cat that has left its claw marks all over my mortal body."

"Pshaw!"

"You may 'pshaw' as much as you please, but I tell you— whether I seed or haird, or only dreamed it, I kaint say—but as I'm a living sinner, *I think*, I seed the devil in his own nateral shape; something more than a human, something less than a beast—a mighty fearsome sort of cross between a big man and a wild animal, *nara* one nor t'other edzactly, and looking a heap like both, and talking like a man, so that I could *on*derstand;

and he tell'd me the same words I tell you, which was—'Bostwick, when I comes for you, I'll call for M'Kewn at the same time. You're bound to come together.' Thar! believe it as you choose, only git me the guineas!"

"And if I now give you a hundred guineas—"

"Next week another hundred."

"You will then give me up the papers, and rid me for ever of your presence?"

"That last thing, M'Kewn, you see, ef the devil speaks truth at all, is quite *on*possible; and I ain't the man to fly in the face of the devil, and say I won't see any of his friends. I reckon I'll hev' to see you whenever I wants money; but after them two hundred guineas, I'll give you a long rest—may be for six months or more."

M'Kewn reflected, and determined to leave the promised security, for the present, to the chapter of chances. To gain time is the great object with every politician whom stubborn necessity threatens to gravel. M'Kewn had a faith in a sort of devil providence. He meditated to himself—

"If I can get the papers out of him, and be sure of six months forbearance, much may be done—much may happen in that time. I shall not always be locked up and weaponless, in a close room. The pistols need not always be upon the wall. He may be found napping in turn. In that is my hope." Aloud—

"You shall have your hundred guineas Bostwick, now; and next week, when you bring me the papers, you shall have another hundred."

"That's being sensible, I say."

"But I must then be rid of you. Remember that!"

"Well! That's jest as it happens, M'Kewn. I'm sure it's not you I wants to see any time, and ef you kin find out the way to fill my hand with the gould chickens when I wants 'em, I'd never darken your door in a hundred years of Sundays. But quieck, M'Kewn; I've got a stretch of bad riding to do yit before daypeep."

"The money is in that chest," said the Scotchman, as if to himself. He crossed the room toward the chest with stood in the opposite corner, stooped, and prepared to open it. The squatter's vigilance did not desert him. His reflections were of this sort—unuttered, of course.

"He's got other we'pons in that chist, prehaps; other pistols, loaded with double bullets. He don't catch this weasel asleep this time!"

M'Kewn opened the chest, which contained a variety of things. There was money—gold and silver in an open box;—there were trinkets of value, several large pieces of plate—and, sure enough, conspicuous over all, a splendid pair of pistols, easy at hand, ready for use. The hand of M'Kewn hung indecisively over the open chest. There was the gold on one side, there the pistols on the other. The fingers clutched one of the pistols. He raised his head cautiously, and cast his eyes upward. The squatter stood immediately over him, with the muzzle of his own formidable pistol staring him in the face. Bostwick, stealthy as a wild cat, had crept behind him, weapon in hand, and was peering down into the chest, ready for any event. He laughed aloud, as he saw the action of the Scotchman.

"T'wont do, M'Kewn! This weasel never sleeps when he's in the fowl-house."

M'Kewn quietly laid down the weapon he had grasped, and gathered up the gold. The signs in his horoscope were not then friendly. He must wait events—have patience, and look to another shuffle of the cards. The money was counted out, paid and received.

"Look for me next week, M'Kewn, and be ready with the other hundred."

"And see that you bring the papers; for I tell you, Bostwick, if I die for it, you get not another shilling till I have the papers."

"You shill hev 'em, and the account will then be squared between us, of all that happened before you shipped me for the shirks. But after that, we must have new reckonings."

"D—n his reckonings!" exclaimed M'Kewn, after he was gone. "Once deprived of those papers, and I do not fear him. *His* evidence will not be worth a straw in any court."

The squatter again popped his head suddenly into the chamber:

"I'll leave your pistols for you, M'Kewn, outside the door, down stairs. But shan't we hev a sup of that same liquor together afore I leave you."

"Begone—no!" The squatter grinned only—

"Well, good night, M'Kewn; what's left of it!"

CHAPTER LXII.

THE SQUATTER IN HIS CABIN.

THE squatter did not show himself to any other eyes that night. He did not proceed to the cabin where his wife and children dwelt. He housed himself in the swamp with his secret treasure. He found this safe. His fastnesses had not been found out; his box of guineas and papers had been undisturbed, in the same condition as when he left it. Crouched in the hollow of the cypress, he slept over it, and did not emerge the next day till the sun was high in the heavens. Then he issued forth, and stood still, in the shelter of the woods, but upon the dry land. He made his way to the spring which, about a quarter of a mile from his dwelling, supplied his family with water. This was one of those sweet, secret, unobtrusive basins, issuing modestly from the earth just on the edges of the swamp, such as form a peculiar feature in our forest country; a little hollow, with clear white sand at the bottom, and a grassy fringe all about it, with the waters gushing out silently from a couple of small eyes in the bankside. Shaded by great trees of the forest, it was always cool, and with a tolerably rapid course to the swamp, it was always clear and pure. The squatter knew where to look for the *calabash*, the cup of gourd, hanging from a bough of the tree just over it. He dipped and drank—drank deeply of the delicious waters—then stooping, bathed·his head and neck in the running stream. This done, he threw himself down among the trees beside it, with an air of exhaustion and languor quite unwonted in his usual habit.

In truth, his appearance was that of a diseased and almost deranged man. His face burned with fever, his eyes were bloodshot and prominent, almost seeming to start from his head; his mouth lay open, and he panted with the least exertion. As he walked, his motion was unsteady, and his limbs tottered beneath him. He rose, after a little while, again drank, and again dipped his head into the waters. Scarcely had he left them, once more retiring among the trees, when his keen ear detected the sound of approaching voices. His instincts at once prompted him to hide himself; which he did without effort, among the shrubs near at hand. Very soon he beheld the persons of the intruders. These were no other than young Arthur Eveleigh attending his own pretty daughter.

Dory, whom he had not seen before now, since his return, was wonderfully improved. She had grown evidently taller in six months. She was now at that interesting period of life when the girl may be said to glide into the woman. She was precocious, and her air and manner were in advance of her years. She had caught up quickly, in her occasional visits to Mrs. Eveleigh, the graces of a higher sphere of life than that to which she belonged, and it was with a natural pride that the eye of the squatter beheld the mixed ease, simplicity, and animation of her movements. Her features were as beautiful as ever; her form showed to more advantage in the better costume which the widow had provided her; the lively flashing of her eye, and the clear, silvery, flute-like accents of her voice, declared a pure happiness of the heart, such as she had seldom before betrayed in the sight of her father.

At the first sight of his child, the heart of the squatter bounded within him, with a pleasurable and exulting sensation. She was *his!* She was the only one, perhaps, of all his household, who had somehow found the way to his rugged and spasmodic affections. But, after a few moments, the natural selfishness of a bad heart suggested that the girl had improved in grace, beauty, health, and showed improved fortunes, and joy, and hope, and animation, though he the father had been a wanderer—though he had been tossed about wearily in distant lands, in dread, and strife, and danger — and, for all she knew, might be dead, drowned, or sacrificed with brutal ferocity to the vengeance of his enemies.

For a while the bitter feeling inspired by this reflection predominated over all others. But this disappeared when he looked upon Arthur Eveleigh, and witnessed the lively interest which that young man seemed to take in his beautiful child. Dory carried a bucket, with which she designed to bring water from the spring. It was not a large or weighty vessel, but Arthur would have snatched it from her, and carried it himself, but she refused and jerked it away, and, laughing sportively at his attempts, darted from him, flying like a fawn, and, reaching the spring before him. He, of course, pursued, and a playful struggle took place at the spring as to who should fill the bucket.

"Not you, Arthur!" said the child, keeping always in mind the superior social position of her companion.

"But why not, Dory? I'm the ablest, the strongest, and it's not right that a girl like you should do such things. I will fill it."

"Well, you may help me. I'll fill it half, and you shall fill the other."

"Very well; but I want some to drink, Dory. You fill the calabash for me, and I'll fill it then for you. You want to drink, I suppose?"

"Yes! I'll do that! There!" and she handed him the simple gourd filled with the sweet and sparkling waters.

He insisted that she should drink, but she refused resolutely, and he did not press it, but satisfied his thirst, threw away the water remaining in the cup, stooped, rinsed it in the running stream, then dipped up a fresh supply of water. His carriage was gently solicitous, fond and playful, but studiously considerate and respectful. Between them the bucket was filled finally, but not in the shortest possible time. They prattled, the girl and boy, over every gourd of water which they lifted up; and when they were done, Arthur seized upon the bucket and proceeded to bear it off.

"Oh! you mustn't, Arthur; mother will be vexed if she sees you doing such work."

"Work, indeed! why it's nothing to me, Dory, to carry it."

"Yes, but I can't let you; mother will think it's unwothy of you." And she seized upon the handle, but Arthur refused to yield it.

In pulling opposite ways, the water began to spill; then, as by mutual consent, the two set the vessel down, and suddenly, before Dory could suspect his purpose, Arthur had seized her about the waist, and bestowed a sudden kiss upon her burning lips.

"Oh! Arthur, you promised me you wouldn't do so again."

"Well, why did you fight with me for the bucket, Dory," was the pert reply of the boy.

"I didn't fight with you. You know I ought to carry it. Mother—"

"Oh! don't tell me about your mother. You are always talking as if she was the greatest scold in the world. Now I know she never scolds you at all. So, no more of that, Dory. You take one side of the handle, and I'll take the other, and we'll carry the bucket so together."

The compromise was acceptable, and the two disappeared with their burden, prattling away all the secrets of their young hearts, never once dreaming who had been the listener. When they were gone, the squatter fell into a fit of musing, in spite of his feverish and suffering condition, for he now, himself, felt that he was really ill.

"Ef he would marry her now, she'd desarve it. She's a most beautiful and blessed looking child as I ever did see. She's beautiful and sweet enough to be the wife of any man. But 'tain't possible that sich a thing could happen. His mother would be agin it. When he grow'd a little older and more knowing, he'd be agin it. People would talk. He'd hear 'em speak of the Squatter Bostwick. He'd hear 'em tell of how she was the child of a poor man, that lived in a cabin; and who was, altogether, a most bad man, and a rascal. And how could he stand that? No! he couldn't stand it. He couldn't marry her: and so there must be no love doings betwixt 'em. I must take care of that! Dory is too blessed a child to hev a man fooling about her when he can't never marry her: and I must take care of her; and I must take care of him; and ef I finds him at eny mischief, I'll put a knife into him jest as soon as I would stick a pig, and a great deal sooner too."

Again the squatter moved down to the spring, and drank. He was really suffering. He lounged or lay about in the woods for some hours. Why he still kept away from his cabin and his family, it would be difficult to conjecture. But he only drew nigh to it at-night; and then, under a sense of suffering which rendered him inaccessible to the sense of fear. He found his way in at last, and immediately took to his bed. His illness increased. His wife gave him some simple medicines, but they afforded him no relief.   For several days he lay upon a couch of pain, without succor, the excitement of his mind increasing with the increase of fever.   At length he called Dory to his bedside.

"Dory, you must go to M'Kewn for me.   You know M'Kewn. You know where he lives ?"

"Yes, father !   I saw him when I was staying with Mrs. Eveleigh."

"What ! you staying with Mrs. Eb'leigh ?   But never mind that now.   You must go to M'Kewn, and tell him to come to me to-night; I wants him.   I must see him here; and don't you take any 'scuses, you hear !   He must come.   Tell him I'll fix the thing for him.   He shall hev the papers, but tell him be sure to bring the gould.   And look you, Dory, don't you let anybody see you.   Take the short cut through the woods ; and don't you be guine now to the widow's and don't you let anybody know nothing of who sent you, and whar you're a guine.   Now, you *on*derstand ?"

"Yes, father."

"Well, let me hear what you've got to do and say."

She repeated his instructions.

"Very well; and now be off as soon as you kin.   I'm in a hurry, you see."

The girl obeyed.   Of what nature was the hurry of which the squatter spoke, he, perhaps, had no certain consciousness ; but he soon made it apparent to his wife that his mind was unsettled. He called her up, as soon as Dory was gone, and said : —

"When M'Kewn comes here to-night, you must cl'ar out with the children.   You kin hev a fire made up in the woods, and keep warm while we're a talking together.   We've got a long talk to do together.   We've got a heap of business.   I'm a guine to buy a farm for Dory, and you and the children can live with her when she's married.   I'm guine to buy her some niggers, and fix her up handsome in the world.   She shan't be a beggar child *eny* longer.   You hear to that, and ef you takes the right care of her it'll be all the better for you.   Do you hear to that ? Give me some water to drink.   I'm consuming thairsty,"

She gave him the water.   He drank, and rose from the bed ; but staggered from weakness.   The wife urged him to lie down again, but he replied sharply—

"Git out, and don't meddle whar you don't *onderstand.* Go along now, and put yourself on the road leading to the pinelands, and see ef thar's nobody about, and come and tell me quick."

She did so, and during her absence he proceeded to dress himself, which he did with evident effort. He was feeble, had taken little or no nourishment, and was sustained only by the excitement of fever, and a will that would not suffer him to admit, even to himself, the extent of his sufferings. By the time that he had finished dressing himself, his wife returned. The road was clear; there was nobody to be seen. He prepared to go forth.

You're not going out ?" she asked.

"What's it to you ef I am ? Mind your own business."

He disappeared, and was absent a full hour. When he returned, he brought with him, wrapped up in the folds of his cloak, the box of Mrs. Eveleigh, containing the papers and the stolen treasure, with the hundred guineas additional he had received from M'Kewn. The wife saw that he carried something with him, but she was not permitted to know what. He concealed it beneath the bed-clothes where he lay, sinking upon the couch in utter exhaustion as he did so. The day passed. In due season Dory returned, bringing a message from M'Kewn, who promised to come as required.

"Good !" said the squatter, languidly smiling upon the child. "You're a beauty of the forest, Dory, and I love you, and you shill hev a farm of your own, Dory, and niggers to work for you, and a nice little waiting-maid servant of your own—all of your own."

"Thank ye, father; and, father, I want you to let me read to you now, out of this book."

"The Bible ! no, none of that now; for I've got dealings with the devil to-night, or one that's a born brother of the devil, and I don't want any good lessons when I've got to deal with such sorts of persons. Shet it up, Dory, and jest you sit by me now, and sing for me some soft sweet little bit of a song. But, first, give me some water."

"Father, oughtn't you to take physic ?"

"Well, ef I know'd what physic to take, Dory; but I don't."

"There's a Doctor ———"

"Jest stop, now, and don't you tell me of doctors, now. I

hev'nt got money to give to doctors. I'll want all to buy your farm and niggers."

"Oh! don't mind that, father, but send for Doctor ————."

"Shet up! You don't know what you're a saying. I must mind that. I've got nothing else but that to mind. I'm aguine to make you a lady, Dory, so that you shill be able to marry a fine great gentleman some day."

"But, father —"

"Shet up, and jest sing, that's all."

The child obeyed, and she sang for him a well-known rustic ditty. He shut his eyes, and seemed to slumber; and sometimes watching him, sometimes singing to him, and answering his calls for water, the day sped away, and the still watches of the night come on. As the wife lighted her dipped candles in the chamber, the squatter started up.

"It's night, and that devil M'Kewn's not come."

"It's just dark, father, I reckon he'll be here."

As she spoke, the hoofs of a horse were heard.

"That's him, I knows," said the squatter. "And now," he continued, addressing his wife, "do you cl'ar out, as I told you, and take Dory and the children with you, and make up a fire in the woods, and don't be poking about here to listen, for when a man's got to talk with the devil and his angels, he don't want eny body to hear the bargain he makes."

In a few minutes M'Kewn tapped at the door, was admitted, and the wife, with her children, disappeared. The door was carefully fastened, and the two criminals, colleagues no longer, were alone together.

CHAPTER LXII.

THE SKRIMMAGE AT GLEN-EBERLEY, AND HOW IT ENDED.

FROM the cabin of the squatter to the mansion of the planter is, with us now, as it frequently is in fact, only a stone's throw. Let us pass from one to the other. The bolt has descended. Captain Porgy is in tribulation. The sheriff, with the *posse comitatus*, is at Glen-Eberley. There is great confusion in the garrison. It is a garrison, however, well defended. The doors are all barred and bolted. From the upper windows, Sergeant Millhouse and Tom, the cook, are keeping watch, armed to the teeth. The captain is moving from chamber to chamber, breathing defiance. There is warrant out for his arrest. He swears that his person shall never be dishonored by the touch of the sheriff. Meanwhile, that officer, with his myrmidons, has environed the dwelling. They have failed to capture the negroes, who are all off. Tom, and that antique mother of many " ginerations," old Sappho, only excepted. Apprized of the approach of the enemy, Lance Frampton was deputed by Millhouse to take charge of the negroes, and house them in the swamp. This duty done, he was to act as a scouting party, making proper efforts to relieve the garrison, by throwing in provisions, whenever opportunity should offer.

The sheriff, meanwhile, sustained by Crooks, the much-suffering deputy, who tenaciously sought his own revenge, with some half dozen auxiliary bull-dogs of the courts, was yet bewildered with the difficulties of his situation; provoked by the perverse and utterly useless obstinacy of Porgy, yet half-laughing at the military resolve to convert his house into a castle at a period when the mailed coat of the soldier was in duty bound to give place to the gown of the civilian. The sheriff's natural good humor and love of good fellowship, were in conflict with his official dignities and duties. And, now, under the trees in the avenue, he sat in consultation with his forces. They did not dare to venture within a hundred yards. They had already tried the defences and were warned off; sullen looking rifle-muzzles protruding from port-holes cut in the shuttered windows, and pistols swaying out significantly through broken panes of glass in the upper story.

While thus they sat, in front of the strong and well-manned garrison which they had summoned in vain to surrender, they were threatened by unexpected dangers in the rear. Lance Frampton, having securely housed the fugitive negroes, was making the circuit of the plantation, when he beheld two strange-looking persons approaching. One was an exceeding tall man, something over fifty, lean, lank, long; of dry, withered aspect; simple as skinny of visage, but with something in his face that pronounced him a character. His companion was altogether a different person, of middle size, well built without being stout, of a full, frank, fair countenance, fine complexion, light blue eye, which twinkled merrily when he spoke, and a joyous laugh, like the ringing of a bird note, that you could hear a mile off. Both of them carried rifles, and, with their arms, equipments and dress, were altogether just such persons in appearance as were Captain Porgy and his comrades, as we beheld them when, homeward bound, they first left the camp of Marion.

It was Frampton's present duty to overhaul these strangers. They might be additional forces of the sheriff whom he was bound to cut off. He resumed all the strategic practice that he had acquired in the war; tied his horse in the woods and stole under cover toward the strangers, who were both on foot. One of them, by the way, the tall man, carried an enormous sack upon his shoulders, which stuck out in every direction; the other bore a little wallet, of leather, which hung out upon the end of his rifle. When they approached sufficiently nigh, Frampton leaped out with a joyful cry to meet them. He knew them at a glance.

"What, George?" he cried, to the younger of the two,—"Is it you?" and, "Doctor, I am really glad to see you."

The parties have been, more than once, subjects of remark in our narrative. They were old followers of Porgy;—the one, Doctor Oakenburg, a culler of simples and catcher of snakes of both of which his sack was now full; tumbled in, in old confusion, with shirts and breeches, and other body-gear;—the other was no less a person than George Dennison, the poet of the partisans, of whom Porgy had been always very fond, and whom he was required to defend very frequently against the utilitarian philosophies of Millhouse. The meeting on both sides was very joyous; the welcome of Frampton was delivered in earnest. These were auxiliaries, allies, whom he took for granted, would readily side with him against the sheriff. Upon Dennison he could put reliance. Oakenburg was one who had no relish for danger; and now, when told of the predicament in which Porgy stood, and asked if he would not co-operate for his relief, he avowed his readiness to do so only on condition that he was required to "act in a situation which should be *one of perfect security.*" The phrase was one to which all his associates had been accustomed for years; and yet, though stipulating thus always, he had gone through several campaigns without absolutely skulking from any fight. His professional *rôle* was something of a protection, it is true; but it was notorious that a patient was never in more danger than when Oakenburg promised to save him. Dennison was delighted with the notions of circumventing the sheriff, and readily fell into all the plans which Lance presented. His scheme was suddenly to fall upon the party of the sheriff in the rear, and by giving a proper signal to the garrison, effect a simultaneous movement, by which the two parties, pushing forward at the same moment, might utterly surprise and capture the myrmidons of the law together, at one single swoop. It was calculated that a mere demonstration from front and rear, at the same moment, would enable them to succeed in their object without shedding a drop of blood. Our partisans, it will be seen from this, had but very little notion of the valor of those who had served only in the chambers of the law.

Frampton's plans were soon completed. His companions were both armed, as we have said. They submitted to his directions. He brought them down, under cover all the way, until they lay *perdu,* each with the bead of his rifle prepared to tell upon an enemy's button. To establish a communication with the garrison was the next object. To effect this — having given Dennison full instructions as to what he and Oakenburg should do, and at what moment—Frampton stole away, and they lost sight of him for half an hour. In this time, he made his way, unseen by those without, to the dwelling, and by signals previously agreed upon with Millhouse, found admittance. His scheme was duly reported, rapidly considered, and eagerly resolved upon. Porgy was now in such a state of excitement, that he never stopped to reason upon any portion of the affair but the probability of its success. An enterprise of this nature carried him back to the familiar stimulants of several exciting years. He thought of the sortie, its beauties, its *modus operandi;* the sally, the shout, the triumph;—never once of THE LAW; the sacred character of the sheriff—the awful powers of the courts; the state and its enraged dignities!

Frampton had now disappeared, and the garrison beat to arms. Porgy appeared in the hall in full armor; Millhouse was there, with his sabre waving in air; Tom carried a sabre also; a rifle was slung upon his shoulder, as upon his master's; and there were pistols in everybody's belt. We must not forget to mention one fact, however, that, wild as was our captain of partisans, he took special care that none of the weapons should be charged with ball. Good heavy charges of powder, well-wadded, were thrust into the guns and pistols; but nothing more heavy. Our captain's aim was to surprise, to scare, and to capture or disperse his enemy. He made Lance Frampton and Millhouse understand this matter clearly; and was particularly heedful that they should see, that, however willing to violate the laws in some respects, he was yet scrupulous that no blood should be shed.

We are not prepared to say that he felt no anxieties on this head, since any encounter of the sort must necessarily, even with the best purposes of forbearance, on the side of one of the parties, be of doubtful accidents; but, in truth, his own excited temper did not suffer him very profoundly to meditate the possibilities of the experiment. The watch above stairs, meanwhile, duly reported progress. Signals were momently expected, and our garrison stole down the inner stairs to the basement, prepared to rush from under the porch upon the sheriff's party, as soon as Frampton could be heard from. He, meanwhile, made his way to his new allies, Dennison and Oakenburg. The better to encourage the latter to audacity, the lieutenant described the affair as a furious jest only. The withdrawal of the bullets from all their weapons seemed to confirm this.

"But," says the lieutenant—"you must look as if in earnest, and behave just as if it was all real and serious fighting. That's the only way to scare off these fellows. They ain't used to fighting, and a few random shots, and a good big shouting, will be pretty sure to do their business, particularly when they see us, on one side, and the captain and his men on t'other, rushing on like mad, and flourishing pistols and broadswords. That's all we shall have to do."

Dennison was eager for the fun, and, now that it seemed so innocent, Oakenburg was not unready. Quietly, the three stole toward the sheriff's party, in silence the most profound, as long as they could possibly approach without discovery. Frampton, on this progress, had separated from the two, and taken another direction, which enabled him to act between the several parties. He was to give the signal, discharging a pistol, and rushing into sight, though at a greater distance from the enemy than either of the other parties. This, after a little interval, he did.

His pistol-shot, his fierce halloo, and his rush, from out the covert, was followed in a few seconds by a terrible uproar from the court of the dwelling; and, directly after, from Dennison and his companion : Oakenburg had famous lungs, if his courage was wanting in firmness. He could roar like an alligator, and his bellowings shook the wood. The sheriff and his party were at once on their feet. They were environed with dangers. They knew not which way to turn. Their consternation was evident at a glance. The sheriff was firm, but surprised; his immediate ally, Crooks, whose own revenges were ever uppermost in his mind, was ready for battle, so far as appetite was concerned; but he was divided between three fires. The one great bully, whom they had brought with them, and who had never in his life shrunk from fist or bludgeon, now showed a very different spirit, when pistols and rifles were introduced into the discussion. He had a very wholesome reluctance to an atmosphere about to be impregnated with gunpowder. At the very first shout and shot (which came together) he started off at a run, and was knocked down by the furious Crooks, as he was making off. He scarcely stirred again until the affair was over—until the firing had fairly ceased.

Meanwhile, the several parties performed their separate duties with admirable concert. On a sudden, the corpulent might of Captain Porgy, like a young buffalo, might be seen emerging from the cover of his piazza. He came forward, swelling and *splurging*—to employ the phrase by which Millhouse frequently described his assault afterward—his eyes glaring like meteors, his voice yelling a terrific slogan; his broad-sword waving like the broad tail of a fiery comet, at the advent of an earthquake. Porgy could not exactly rush or run, but he could roll forward with wonderful effect, and his lungs were good. His strength was great when he once set hands upon his victim. He looked in terrible earnest as he came. While his right grasped the broad-sword, his left carried a pistol. As he advanced, he fired with deliberate aim at the enemy, then dropping the one pistol drew another, still advanced, still took deadly aim, fired and hurried onward with a shout.

Millhouse did likewise. So Frampton from his quarter; so Dennison and Oakenburg from theirs; so Tom, the cook, following close in the wake of his master; and finally, so Sappho, the ancient, whose screams from toothless jaws were absolutely most awful of all to hear. Can you wonder at the result. Can you doubt that the sheriff's party was discomfited, even before a blow was struck. His men fled incontinently from the field, all but Crooks, who stood bravely beside his chief, with bludgeon in hand, and looked the danger in the face with tolerable composure.

The sheriff drew his small-sword with the air of a nobleman in a conflict with a crowd of *canaille*, who sees that he must perish, and takes the proper attitude at once to die with grace and dignity, and do something *wicked* while falling. But he was allowed no chance. Half a dozen pistols flashed pretty near his face and that of Crooks, utterly blinding them. They both concluded themselves slain, though doubtful at the moment where to locate their hurts; and while the sheriff, with the despair of a dying man, darted forward and thrust out his sword in the direction of Porgy's abdominal demonstration, Tom, the cook, rushed upon him from behind, dexterously dived between his parted legs, lifted him fairly from the ground, and, while his sword furiously but fruitlessly slashed away in air, hurried him off to the house a prisoner.

Crooks was captured—nay, ridden down—by Oakenburg, who, with immensely long legs, seeing a terrier-like little man before him, with his back turned, deliberately cast his leg over his shoulder, curled the limb completely about his neck, and thus brought him down to earth; when Millhouse took him into keeping, by leisurely letting himself down upon the captive, whose bristles of chin and cheek he curiously examined; feeling them with his one hand, while commenting upon the wonderful rapidity with which red or copper-colored beards shoot out. Crooks struggled fiercely, but it required the slightest effort in the world on the part of the sergeant, to suffer his fingers to slip from the chin to the throat of his captive. A gripe of the weasand, by such steely prongs as Millhouse wore by way of fingers, soon subdued all the bristles of the deputy, whether of wrath or whisker.

While this was going on, Porgy was engaged in rescuing the sheriff from Tom's clutches; a not easy matter. Our excellent cook, assuming that he should certainly be permitted to strip, if not to slay his prisoner,—as had been his custom in battle,— was not willing to deliver the captive until his master promised to account to him for his garments; when he suffered the discomfited sheriff to feel the solid earth once more. Porgy came up and clapped the knight of the shire upon his shoulder—

"Shall there be peace between us, colonel?"

"Peace!—Captain Porgy, you have dishonored me! You have still your sword in hand, and I have mine. I appeal to your sense of honor, that we cross blades."

"Pooh! pooh! my dear fellow, there's no need of that. You are already conquered; don't you see."

"You will pay dreadfully for this! You have killed several of my people."

"Not a man of them, unless the scare shall have done so. For, look you, my dear colonel, we went into the fight with powder only. Not a pistol or gun was shotted!"

This made the sheriff furious. He cried—

"Bid your fellows stand off, while we fight.   There is no sham in steel."

" And no shame to you, my dear colonel, in being shot at with empty pistols.   Pooh! pooh! man, can't you relish a good army-joke, now that you're a peace officer.   Put up your sword, and let us all in and have a stoup of Jamaica.   I am in a lather of perspiration."

But the sheriff was not so easily appeased, and the dispute went on, and, in spite of Porgy's good humor—which, now that he had gained the victory and enjoyed his jest—was of the most genial description, there is no saying what might have been the upshot of the business; when suddenly the tread of horses, and the wheels of a carriage, were heard rumbling toward them. And soon the cumbrous vehicle drew nigh, drawn, as was frequently the fashion in those days, by four horses.   Then a voice, well known to both of the parties, cried out from the carriage—

"Halloo!   There!   My brave fellows, what have you been about?"

The new-comer was the gallant and highly popular Charles Cotesworth Pinckney—a man, who, but for the curse of party, would have been subsequently made president of the United States.

"Ha! my dear Pinckney," answered Porgy, "you have come in the nick of time to keep the peace.   I have won a victory, but because I have been merciful, I can not quiet those whom I should have slain."

Pinckney got out of the carriage, stepped between the parties, and heard the story.   He had sped, by the way, with all haste after the sheriff, to prevent difficulties.   The latter, goaded by M'Kewn, and somewhat mortified by the stories spread about at his expense, touching his former fortune—stories very much exaggerated—had evaded the friends of Porgy, and set out for his arrest, and to effect the levy, without their knowledge.   As soon, however, as the fact was known, Pinckney started in pursuit.   He came too late; and the difficulties of his mission were increased.   But he was not the person to despair.   He had that twofold capacity, at once of persuasion and command, which rarely suffered him to fail in influencing the minds of men.

"What, colonel," he said to the sheriff,—"angry still, after what you hear. This must not be. We must reconcile you to our friend, who, as we all know, will have his jest though he dies for it."

"Not at my expense—at least."

"Surely not," said Pinckney, "and he will atone for every hurt of honor that he has inflicted. I promise you this, my dear fellow, *on my honor;* and now let us into his dwelling, and see with what sort of hospitality he will receive us."

"In with you all,—good friends, all!" cried Porgy; "and if nothing short of Glen-Eberley will suffice to satisfy you, Mr. Sheriff, why, it is at your service. There's my hand on it,— and now in!"

The sheriff was somewhat reluctant still; but Porgy seized his hand and shook it with vehemence, and Pinckney repeated his assurance that every atonement should he made. The knight of the shire was forced to yield. Crooks, the deputy, now relieved from the incumbent weight of Millhouse's body, was not so easily pacified,—but, when Pinckney becoming impatient, told the sergeant to resume his captive, and the seat which he had occupied with such effect, the little fellow cooled off, and followed the rest into the house. Here, for the first time, Porgy was enabled to welcome his old associates, George Dennison and Oakenburg, which he did with a hearty satisfaction that quite disturbed the sergeant. He muttered *sotto voce:*—

"Lord ha' marcy! now they're here, they'll stick, and *nara* one of 'em able to airn the salt to his hominy!"

Let us suppose the efforts of Pinckney to be successful in reconciling the conflicting parties, and persuading the sheriff to receive the apologies of Porgy, for all that had been personally offensive between them; apologies which Porgy gave without a moment's scruple. But Crooks was to be hushed with other coin. His hurts of honor were to be settled by some regard to his pocket; and, after a little while, an exact estimate was made, in money, of the amount of injury done to his self-esteem and honor. These affairs once adjusted, the question next was confined wholly to the satisfaction of the judgment in the case of *M'Kewn* v. *Porgy*—a matter of more difficult arrangement. We will leave the three prominent persons, Pinckney, the sheriff,

and Porgy, engaged in this discussion, in the parlor, after supper was over; while Sergeant Millhouse, well supplied with
pipes and Jamaica, did the honors below stairs to the other guests.
Frampton had suddenly disappeared after the "skrimmage."
He excused himself only to George Dennison, and to no other
parties did his absence occasion any surprise. It was probably
two hours after nightfall when he reappeared, and, suddenly
making his way into the parlor where the three principal persons were yet engaged in the discussion, he called Porgy out to
the piazza, and said:—

"Beg pardon, captain, for troubling you just now, but you see
the matter is important. There's the squatter, Bostwick, he's
got back to his family. Pomp saw him in the swamp, and when
he told me, I put Pomp and another to watch the squatter's
house. They saw little Dory go out, and one of them watched
her all the way to M'Kewn's; and to-night, a little after dark,
M'Kewn went in to the squatter's cabin. He's with him now,
and they both may be caught together. I'm a thinking that if
you was to seize upon the squatter, right away, and give him a
good scare with the rope or the hickories, you would get back
that mahogany box of the widow Eveleigh, and find out all about
your missing property, and the attack on the widow."

Lance Frampton was a brief, comprehensive speaker. He
hardly employed more words than these in making this revelation.
Porgy felt its vast importance, and rightly estimated the utility
of prompt proceedings. He, at once, took Lance into the parlor and communicated his intelligence to his associates. Pinckney was at once upon his feet.

"We must act *instanter*. The squatter must be seized; but
legally. Here's the proper officer. I can take your lieutenant's
affidavit and yours, embodying your suspicions, and issue the
warrants, which will suffice to get one or both these parties into
custody—the rest may follow; but rope or hickory, unless by
the proper hands, must not be thought of. Call your deputies,
—a couple of them, Mr. Sheriff,—while I prepare the papers."

Five minutes sufficed for this. The parties, Pinckney at their
head, prepared to set forth; Porgy was about to accompany them,
but Pinckney objected.

"Better not you, Porgy. Your entanglements are quite sufficient already, and you'll be for grappling this fellow M'Kewn on the spot, and pulling his nose, or doing some outrageous thing. Besides, your debt to him makes your appearance, at the time of his answer to such charges, a rather delicate proceeding."

"If I don't go with you, may I be ——!" was the reply of the doughty captain, putting his pistols in his belt.

"Obstinate as ever! But, as you will. How far is it? Do we ride!"

"The horses are ready now, sir," was the reply of the prompt lieutenant—"Better ride to Cattle Branch, captain, and then get down and walk."

"Right, Lance, right! we must take the rascals by surprise. Gentlemen, to saddle."

CHAPTER LXIV.

THE BOX OF PAPERS, AND HOW PAID FOR.

UNDER the guidance of Lance Frampton, the party proceeded to the Cattle Branch. Here, they alighted, fastened their horses in the shelter of a bit of wood, and went forward on foot. Attracted by the gleam of fire in the forest, Lance Frampton stole away to see by what it was occasioned, and, without allowing himself to be seen, he found the wife of the squatter, little Dory, and the two other children, cowering about the blaze of a fire which they had kindled about two hundred yards from the house of the squatter. Here, wrapped in blankets, and housing themselves as well as they could against the night wind, they waited the conclusion of the conference between the confederates in the cabin.—Having ascertained, scout-fashion, all the necessary particulars in the case, Frampton rejoined his party and made his report. They went forward, stealthily, toward the house, and imitating the precautions of their guide, succeeded in approaching it without disturbing the inmates. Through chinks between the logs, from which the clay-plastering had fallen out, and by the light of a couple of tallow-candles which burned in the chamber of the squatter, they could see pretty much all that took place within. Using our privilege, we can witness the proceedings on easier terms, and are able to report them from the beginning.

Once in the chamber, the family shut out, and secure, as he thought, against surveillance, M‘Kewn approached the bedside of the squatter, who raised himself up in the bed to receive him.

"What's made you sick, Bostwick?" said the visiter.

"Sick! O! I aint much sick; aint too sick to do business. Business always make me well ag'in. The sight of the gould a-coming in, is always a cure for me, no matter what's the sort of ailment a troubling me. Hev' you brought the gould, M‘Kewn?"

"But you are sick, Bostwick, and very sick too," said M‘Kewn, seeing the fiery eyes, the blotched features, and feeling the burning hand of the patient. "You have a scorching fever, and look ill out of the eyes."

"Oh! don't you mind about the eyes. I tell you, ef they once sees the guineas, and a smart chaince of 'em, they'll git well, and I'll git well directly. Hev' you brought them guineas? I must hev' 'em, and a great count of 'em too, M‘Kewn."

"Guineas! Why, man, you need physic now, rather than guineas. I must send you some to cure this fever."

"You! Send me physic! You! Never! I'll not take any physic of *your* mixing, M‘Kewn. You're not the one that I'll app'int to bile my gruel."

"Why, you don't think I'd poison you, do you?"

"That's jest what I'd be afear'd of, M‘Kewn. You see, I knows you, and you knows me, and I tell you, there's only one sort of physic I'm willing to take out of your hands, and that's *gould* physic, M‘Kewn. *Hev'* you brought them guineas?"

"I have! There are a hundred guineas here, in this bag; but I'll not give you one of them, Bostwick, until I see that box of papers—until I get it delivered into my own hands."

"You won't, you say?"

"No! I will not!"

"Then, you don't git 'em, that's all!" and the sick man hustled the pillow, and a portion of the bed-clothes, in a heap beneath his head, with an appearance of care which did not escape the observation of his visiter. "Look you, M‘Kewn," continued the squatter; "you don't hev' them papers onless I gits *five* hundred guineas."

"Five hundred guineas! Why, you're mad."

"No I aint; I'm only sensible. I'm in want of a *heap* of gould. I'm a-guine to buy a farm and seven niggers for Dory. —I'm a-guine to set her up, and make a lady of her. And she shill be fine; and shill hev' fine clothes, silk and velvet: and shill hev' niggers to work for her in the corn-field, and a maid-sarvant to wait upon her, and help put on her clothes; and you're to pay for all."

"The devil, I am!"

"Yes! The devil you air! and bekaise you air a born devil, and bekaise, jest now, I'm your master, and kin make you work for me, I'll make my child a lady of fortin'. So you'll hev' to fork up the money, and do it han'some. Ef I kain't git her settled, han'some, out of my airnings, I'd like to know what's the use of all my rapscalities. Five hundred guineas is little enough to aix you; that is, after the hundred guineas you've got in the bag.—Them you must leave with me, and go and git jest five hundred more, and when I sees them counted out, fair before me, ten piles and fifty in every one on them, then you shill hev' the box of papers; and not a minute before."

And here the squatter grasped the heap beneath his pillow, with the air of a man making sure of his possessions. The keen eye of M'Kewn again observed the action, and his mind drew instantly the proper inference from it. He observed, also, that the excitement of the squatter was increasing. His eyes, now more accustomed to the degree of light in the chamber, M'Kewn was enabled to see that Bostwick was really much more an invalid than he had thought him at first; though, even the first glance had shown him that the man was very ill. He now began to suspect that his mind was wandering. This conjecture was reached, not so much because of the extravagance of his demands, as from the wild and glittering terror of his eyes, which were dilating, as if about to burst out of their sockets, and shone like coals of fire; from the fitfulness of his voice, and the spasmodic action which accompanied his utterance. To temporize with such a patient was his present policy.

"Well, but Bostwick, you surely can't expect me to pay this money until I see the box of papers."

"It's that very thing you hev' to do! You hev' to trust me to the eend of the business. I *knows* what I've got, and knows its valley to you. I knows you kain't do without them papers; and I knows what'll happen ef them papers gits away from my hands to another pusson's. Kin you guess what would happen ef the widow Ev'legh got 'em, or Cappin Porgy, or eeny other honest white man—that knows *you*, and how you stands? What's the valley to them? Ef 'taint five hundred guineas, I'll give 'em for nothin'. *You* shan't have 'em for a shilling less!"

"Well, Bostwick, I don't say that they will not be worth the money, but I say that you must let me see them *first*, that I may be sure of it."

"You don't see 'em, M'Kewn, tell the money's on the nail. You *shill* trust me, and I *won't* trust *you;* for I knows you, and you're a born rascal, and I'll hang you, M'Kewn, for the pleasure of the thing, ef so be you don't fork out."

"How long will it take you to get the papers, after I bring the money?"

"How long? How short, rether! You kin hev' 'em arter that, as quick as you kin cry Jack Robinson."

"Ah! and if I bring you five hundred guineas this very night?"

"Then you kin git the papers this very night! And you better bring 'em, M'Kewn, for you see, Dory must be a lady. I must make her rich as a queen; she must be able to carry as high a head as the widow Ev'leigh, and then she kin marry young Arthur, the widow's son; and he likes her, and is guine to marry her, jest so soon as I makes a lady of her, and gives her a fortin' of niggers and a farm; and you shall be at the wedding, M'Kewn, though, by blisters, I should like to see you hanging up, with your feet upon nothing, only the minute arter. But, bring the guineas, and make haste about it. Lord! How my head aches and jumps. How my eyes burn! Bring the guineas; I'm a-longing to git shet of you, and to call in Dory, and make her a lady. Be quick, and you shill hev' the cussed papers, and ef you aint quick, I'll be a hanging you like a brute warmint. Oh! the head, how its a-busting!"

He sank upon the pillow as he ended, with an evident show of increased suffering.

"If I were quite sure, Bostwick, that you could produce the papers as soon as I brought the money! But you told me that they were hid away in the swamp where nobody could find them."

"Swamp—h–ll! So they were, hid in the swamp once upon a time; but, hain't I been thar' sence I got back; hain't I got 'em *here*, in this very house, whar' I kin put hands on 'em jest when I wants them? Git the guineas, I say, and don't be foolish with your questions; and when I sees Dory a lady of fortin', with her farm and niggers, then you shill hev' the box, and much good may it do you."

Again the squatter sank back upon the pillow, with his hands feebly and nervously feeling about it, as if to make himself secure of his possession. M'Kewn now varied his game.

"I don't believe a word you say, Bostwick, and now, let me tell you, I saw the fellow, Tony Hines, at Smyzer's, he told me that you had got no box, no papers—"

"Ha! Yes! Don't I know that you saw Tony Hines, at Smyzer's; and don't I know that you gin him physic, and called yourself a doctor; and you p'isoned him with your physic, and killed him. Don't I know? Does anything you do hide itself from me?   I tracked you, like a sarpent, sence I got back; and I knows all your doings, sence I've been gone, as well as before. That's another thing agin you; — your p'isoning of Tony Hines."

"He's not dead, is he?"

"Sure as you handled him! I seed old Smyzer, and hairn all about you. But don't be aggravatin' me, I tell you, for I kain't stand it. My head is jest a busting now. Ef you aggravates me, I'll hang you! I'll git my gould from another pusson, I'll sell you in the market; I'll send off for Cappin Porgy to come to me. You hear, do you?"—almost screaming. "And now fork out the money, and let me see Dory a lady, with a fortin'. It's as much as your neck's worth ef she don't git it right away."

"You shall have the money, Bostwick. There *are five* hundred guineas, not *one*, in this bag."

"Let me feel it—it don't look big enough for so much. You're a lying to me, now; I knows you."

"No! let me see your box of papers. Hold it in your own hands, while I count out the money."

"Well! I'll do *that.*"

And the sick squatter made an effort to rise and turn about, while one of his hands began to remove the bed-clothes from about the pillow. M'Kewn eagerly watched him, the bag suspended in his hand. The squatter suddenly paused, looked round at this moment, and caught the glance of the Scotchman's eye.

"You're a great scamp, M'Kewn. I knows you. Oh! you're a warmint! You don't see the box till I sees the money counted out. It's here, you born thief, and rapscallion, but I won't trust you so much as to let you see it, ontell the money's put down here, the yellow birds, all a-flying about me, on the white bed-clothes, where I kin count 'em. Plank 'em down, and when I sees 'em, then you shill see the papers."

Once more the squatter sank back exhausted, muttering spasmodically —

"Plank 'em down—all for Dory—lady, fine fortin'—Arthur Ev'leigh. Ha! ha! ha! Don't I see? Don't I know it'll be? Dora Ev'leigh. *Mrs.* Dorothy Ev'leigh."

M'Kewn was apparently disposed to do as he was required — to open his bag of guineas, and to count them out upon the bed; and the squatter, though sinking back exhausted, was yet keenly observant of all the movements of his associate. But, either the demonstration was not seriously begun by the Scotchman, or his purpose suddenly underwent a change. While he looked upon the seemingly faint and feeble condition of the squatter, other purposes, which he had already contemplated, rapidly ripened for performance in his brain. The thoughts occurred to him —

"Shall I continue at the mercy of this miserable wretch, when a little determination is all that is needful to extricate myself from his power. He has the box of papers beneath his pillow. Of his possession of it, no one knows but myself. He can give no evidence of its contents. No one sees us. The family is all away. Why should I not possess myself of this testimony and destroy it? He can not oppose me. He has not strength for it. In a moment it is mine. In another moment I give it to the flames. I were a fool to hesitate—to suffer this auspicious moment to escape me!"

The stillness of the scene—the loneliness of the neighborhood—night and silence—the feebleness of the squatter—his own necessities and apprehensions—all conspired to persuade M'Kewn to seize upon the desired possession. He saw directly where it lay, and, though the head of the squatter rested upon it, no great effort would be required, he thought, to tear it from under him. The temptation was irresistible; and while Bostwick was looking to see the bag of gold laid bare before him, M'Kewn suddenly thrust it back into the pocket of the great overcoat he wore, and, in the same instant, seized upon the pile of bed-clothes which covered the box, beneath the pillow, and, with a violent grasp, tore it away upon the floor. The head of the squatter, in consequence of the jerk, was thrown off, with the pillow, from the box. The desired treasure was exposed, fairly, before the eyes of the Scotchman. He seized it eagerly; but before he could drag it from its place, the squatter had grappled with it also; screaming out his fury, at the same time, in the wildest accents.

"Ha! you born thief, en' that's your game, is it? But two kin play at that game, my honey; and we'll see who's the best man."

The squatter was now up in bed. Even in this situation, and sick, M'Kewn found him no easy customer. Lithe, active, and accustomed to every sort of toil and encounter, his strength was really surprising. For awhile the parties struggled for the box; but soon the squatter, more accustomed to the emergencies of such a strife, suddenly relaxed his hold upon the object of contention, and caught hold of M'Kewn himself. His fingers were soon about the throat of the Scotchman. The latter found it no slight matter to break away from the tenacious grasp of his opponent. But, still grasping the box, he finally succeeded in doing so. But he was not thus to escape in triumph. Bostwick bounded after him, out of the bed, and fastened upon him again with the claws of a young tiger. The fearful conflict was renewed. After awhile M'Kewn bore him back successfully, and thurst him again upon the bed; but even then he failed to throw him off. The squatter clung to him with a spasmodic energy, which seemed to increase his powers; and, desperate by the opposition he encountered, M'Kewn fiercely smote him upon the head with the box, twice, thrice — holding it in both hands — the blows coming down with a heavy, dull sound, as if upon a bank of earth.

With a howl, rather than a cry, Bostwick seized his assailant with a new hold; taking him now with both arms, about the neck, and drawing him down upon him, where he lay. Here, while almost fainting from his hurts, and the exhaustion of such a struggle, he strove, with his last wolfish instincts, to bite and rend, with his teeth, the enemy whom he could no longer injure with his hands. At this stage of the proceedings, and before either of the combatants could conjecture the proximity of other persons, Porgy burst open the door of the hovel with a single stroke of his feet, and rushed into the room, followed closely by Pinckney, the sheriff, and the rest of the party.

They did not appear a moment too soon. The head of the squatter was bleeding freely from several hurts; his teeth were already sunk with the ferocious passion of the wild beast, into the throat of his assailant. So fast was the hold which he had taken, that it was difficult to tear M'Kewn from his grasp. The effort to do so dragged the squatter from his bed upon the floor, where he lay like a baffled and wounded panther, writhing and shrieking in his agony and disappointment.

M'Kewn lost all presence of mind, all strength, the moment he found himself in the presence of other parties. He had been fearfully breathed in the violent struggle through which he had gone; but it was mental paralysis from which he now suffered A complete collapse of all the energies followed the exposure. The box fell from his nerveless grasp, and was instantly picked up by Lance Frampton. He staggered back toward the bed, upon which he sank; his jaws fell; and his strength seemed barely enough to allow him to cover his face with his hands. In a single instant he became conscious that all was lost; and that he was self-delivered into the hands of his most powerful enemies.

"You are my prisoner!" said the sheriff to M'Kewn, laying his hand on his shoulder.

He had not a word to answer; thoroughly overwhelmed by

the circumstances of his situation, and the fact that he had been caught *flagranti delicto*.

"That's it! that's right!" cried the squatter, whose loss of blood had brought him fairly to his senses, and who now, quite as promptly as the Scotchman, appreciated all the difficulties of his situation. "Take him prisoner," he cried—"I'm the witness agin him, the infernal thief and tory, and murderer and villain; that stole your niggers, Cappin Porgy; I carried him forty-three on em that never kin git back—all off your place—and he sold 'em to Moncrieff; and many more besides; but here's the box; it's got the pretickilar papers to convict him and to hang him, the villain, and the nigger thief, and murderer. You seed him how he wanted to murder me in my own bed, and all to git the papers, and to hush up my evidence; but he'll hev' the justice done to him at last, and I'll be a witness agin him ef they'll let me go free, and pardon me for what I did for him. I did it only for him."

"You are not forced to speak," said the sheriff. "It is just as you please—to be silent, or tell all that you know."

"I'll tell all I know! I'm ready and willing, of my own free consent."

"Stop!" said Pinckney; "let him be sworn. I have a reason for it. Is there a bible in the house?"

Porgy was able to find one. He knew where Dory kept it. It was produced. Pinckney administered the oath; and the squatter, in the hearing of the man he accused, made a tolerably clean breast of it. He furnished a long and fearful history, the character of which we can well conjecture from the portions already put into our possession. The statements were all taken down as delivered. M'Kewn sank upon the bed utterly prostrate, and incapable even of denial. The miserable criminal absolutely swooned under the prospect of discovery and conviction.

"And now," cried the squatter, when he was done, "you'll git me my pardon, won't you? I've told all! Them papers in the box will tell you something, too. He set me on to do what I did, and he's got all the profit, the etarnal villain, that wanted to murder me in my own bed, and me a sick man. You'll git me off, cappin; and you, Colonel Pinckney—I knows you, colonel! You'll git me my pardon, from the gov'nor, when I tells all afore the court?"

"You must seek your pardon of heaven, my poor fellow," was the answer of Pinckney, made with proper solemnity. "The only court which you will now be summoned before, is that of the Eternal Judge of the world. Humble yourself before him with all the haste you can, and repent your sins, and pray for the mediation of Christ in your behalf. I deem it only proper to tell you that you are even now a dying man! Gentlemen, the sooner the most of you leave this room, the better; this unhappy man is dying of the small-pox!"

<hr>

CHAPTER LXV.

CATASTROPHE.

THOSE only who know the terrors inspired by the small-pox, at the period of which we write, can properly appreciate the panic which was occasioned by the speech of Pinckney. Among the people of the country, in particular, this scourge of humanity was held a worse danger than the plague of the East. Men who would fearlessly brave the field of battle, fled, at the bare mention of this pest, without once looking behind them. It was so on this occasion. Our excellent captain of partisans was among the first to find his way out of the hovel. He was followed by all but Pinckney, the sheriff, his deputy, and the prisoner M'Kewn. These, as citizens, were more accustomed to the pest, and had, we suppose, been all inoculated. They remained in the farther prosecution of the work before them. At the door, Pinckney proceeded to suggest to Porgy the course to be pursued in respect to coincident matters.

"You must see to this man's family, captain. Have them bestowed in safety, in some place where they can not come in contact with persons not inoculated. If you or Mrs. Eveleigh have any servants who have had the disease, send them here to attend upon this wretched creature. He will scarcely live another day; but send for Dr. Warley, and, in the meantime, let him have some cooling medicines, and proper food. But see that you keep his wife away, unless she has been inoculated—which I suppose very unlikely."

Porgy undertook all the necessary commissions. We will leave him to execute them, which, we may add, in this place, he did with equal diligence and effect. Returning to the chamber of the squatter, Pinckney found him raving.

" The small-pox!" he cried. "Don't you tell me sich d——d foolishness. 'Taint no small-pox, I tell you! It's only fever— it's a mighty hot fever, I know, and this fight with that etarnal villain thar, has only made it worser and hotter;—but 'taint no small-pox. Whar was I to git the small-pox, I wants to know; me living in the swamps and here. 'Spose I was in town! was that to give me small-pox, when I was thar a day only? I know better! I know 'taint small-pox, and I've got the strength of a horse; yet you tell me I'm a dying man—me a dying man, and sich a mortal sinner! Lord God! ef I'm so sick as all that, send for the doctor. Thar's gould to pay him—thar, in that box. Thar's a hundred and fifty guineas in that box. Mind you, it's Dory's money; and thar's a bag of guineas in that bloody villain's pocket, and by rights that's Dory's money too. Re- member Dory! Lord, whar's Dory? Don't you let her come nigh to me, ef it's small-pox I've got; but send for my wife to nuss me. She's somewhar about in the woods. You'll see by the fire. Send her here? What's she doing in the woods when I'm a wanting her here. Oh! Lord, that I should come to this; and thar you stand, and a doing nothing for me, and yet you says I'm a dying of the small-pox. Yet, don't I know it's a lie. It's only done to skear me! And what does you want to skear me for eny more? Hevn't I told you all I know about that bloody scamp. Ef you wants me to tell about the skrim- mage, and how I had to shoot Dick Norris, you're clean mis- taken. I won't say a word; I'll shet up, and you shall never pry betwixt my teeth to see what's under my tongue. No! nor you shaint know about the blowing up of the vessel. She blow'd up, and what hed I to do with it. Thar was a train—I knows that—and it ended in the three kags of gunpowder; but who seed me put fire to it, I wants to know? Whar's the pusson here kin say he seed it, I'd like to know! No! thar's no pusson;

and why should I hev the small-pox ontell you prove agin me all these things. The small pox, indeed! That's mighty foolish. What should give me, a strong man, usen to the city, the blasted small-pox? I laughs at it, I tell you! I laughs! Ha! ha! ha? and I snaps my fingers at it. Does that look like a dying man. A dying man! Lord God, hev marcy ef so be its true what these men says! Oh! my God, hev marcy upon me a sinner. I know I'm a black sinner, and blasted through and through with the p'ison of sin; but ef I am, air you guine to let me die without a doctor, and arter I tel'd you everything I know'd about that murdering villain thar? Oh! Lord, send for the doctor. Don't leave me to die. I kaint die! I won't die. I hev a heap to do, to buy the niggers and the farm, and to see Dory a lady of fortin! Small-pox be d——d! 'Taint no small-pox! It's a hot fever only. Give me some water. Oh! how it burns. I'm a burning up. I'm all blisters, and nobody to help me. Take him away, that bloody villain thar; I'm all afire so long as I sees him. Take him away and hitch him up. Ef I'm to die, I know who's to hang. We goes together. The old Horny swore it should be so, and I tel'd him! Oh! the black villain, he's got to hang, and that's the satisfaction I'll hev at the last. I knows it, and he knows it too! He shall hang, like Dick Norris, and nobody to save his neck from cracking, by a bullet through the head. He don't desarve a friend. He don't. But, oh! Lord, the fire in my witals. Whar's that woman— whar's my wife—to give me drink? The small-pox! But don't you let Dory come. Even ef I dies, she's to be a lady of fortin. Thar's the money. It's all for her!"

We need not listen farther to these ravings, though they were still, for some time longer, poured into the ears of Pinckney and the sheriff, with unceasing volume, and wonderful rapidity. The fever was rapidly increasing in the brain. The disease was doing its work with fearful speed and vigor. The terrible secrets of a life of crime were delivered without a consciousness, and the strong men shuddered as they heard, hardly deeming it possible, from their previous experience, that society should possess an individual capable of such a revelation of evil deeds, the performance of his own hands.

After a brief consultation with the sheriff, the latter, with a couple of his assistants, took M‘Kewn away. The latter was passive in the hands of his guards. They conducted him to his own house, and securing him in his chamber they put watches upon the apartment, so that he could not escape. Porgy, meanwhile, conveyed the wife of the squatter, with Dory and the two other children, to his own dwelling, in which he asigned them the best apartments. Lance Frampton went after Doctor Warley, the ablest and nearest physician upon the river, while a couple of elderly slaves, both of whom had passed through the fearful disease which was consuming the life of the squatter, were sent by Mrs. Eveleigh to attend upon him. Cooling medicines, beverages, and delicacies, such as might be thought calculated to alleviate the sufferings, or meet the wants of the patient, were provided, and, by dawn the next day, he was in as good hands, and as carefully attended, as was possible under the circumstances. Doctor Warley was soon with him; but, the first glance at the patient showed that all efforts would be made in vain. The type of the disease was singularly malignant; and exposure in the swamps, violent passions, and vexing strifes and anxieties, had added fearfully to its virulence. Within the time predicted by Pinckney, he was a corpse.

A conference ensued between Pinckney, the sheriff and M‘Kewn, at the house of the latter. He was still in close keeping. The charges against him were of a sufficiently serious character, involving not simple his fortune but his life. He felt all the dangers of his situation. In the first feeling of utter hopelessness, he humbly entreated the mercy and forbearance of the prosecutors. The better to secure this, he produced the bond and mortgage of Porgy—he entered satisfaction upon them, and upon the judgments which he also held against the rest of his debtor's property. He confessed to a participation in the sale of the forty-three slaves abducted from the captain's plantation, as charged by the squatter, and as confirmed by the documents, now open before them, from the box of the widow. There was, perhaps, no confession necessary. The conviction would be quite complete without it. But M'Kewn's policy was to make a merit of necessity. As he began to recover his confidence—removed from the fearful sights and scenes in the cottage of the squatter —he ventured to urge upon Pinckney and the sheriff, the concessions he had voluntarily made as a plea for some indulgence. He tendered bail, but neither of them was authorized to receive it. He pleaded for a mitigation of the rigors of his confinement; but, on this point, Pinckney referred the matter wholly to the sheriff, who, thereupon, instead of lessening the sharpness of his watch, increased it, leaving one of his most trusty deputies within the chamber of the criminal. This man, M'Kewn attempted to bribe with a large amount of money in gold. But the deputy was invincible. The criminal opened the chest within his chamber,—the contents of which we have already seen, when the squatter was permitted the same privilege,—and drew forth a pile of the glittering treasure, so dazzling to greedy eyes and drowsy consciences.

"You shall have it all," said he, in a husky whisper, "only secure the fellow in the passage until I can get off. You can both make off with it—with all that you can carry,—and you need not then dread exposure."

The amount thus proffered was a severe temptation for a poor man; but this one,—who, by the way, had not the courage to stand the threatened lead of Captain Porgy and his veterans,— had yet the firmness to say to the tempter—"Get thee behind me." It might be that his virtue was governed by his fears, and by the knowledge that there were other watchers besides himself, but we prefer, for the sake of humanity, to believe in the fellow's virtue. We continually do mischief to morals, by assuming too low a standard of virtue for the poor.

Deceived and baffled, M'Kewn grew morose. Food was brought him at the proper hour. He refused to eat. The dinner-hour passed. Night came on. He would take no supper. But he drank, if he did not eat. He drank till his cheeks were flushed, and his eyes wore a ferocious and glazed expression, which the deputy dreaded very much to behold. About an hour after night, the sheriff entered the chamber, and said—

"This man Bostwick, is evidently dying. Dr. Warley thinks he can not live through the night."

The teeth of M'Kewn gnashed fiercely.

"What is that to me! Let him die and—"

The sentence remained unfinished. The sheriff readily gues-
·sed the words with which he would have supplied the blank.
He turned away and left the prisoner; but, seeing his condition,
and suspecting in some degree the cause, he removed the decanter of Jamaica which stood upon the table. M'Kewn saw the
act but said nothing. He possibly felt that it would be useless
to expostulate. At twelve that night, the squatter died, howling, in the wildest agonies, physical and mental, with horrible
curses on his lips. An imprecation upon the head of M'Kewn,
while his fingers seemed to grapple and rend something in air
before him, finished the awful scene, which Pinckney witnessed
with the physician. Glad to escape into fresh air, he mounted
his horse, the moment the scene was over, and galloped off to
Glen-Eberley. Here supper awaited him, and the partisan, and
sheriff, with their companions. They had scarcely seated themselves and begun to partake, when they heard the tramplings
of a horse at full speed, and, a moment after, one of the deputies,
left in charge of M'Kewn, bounded into the room, his cheeks
pale, and his eyes wild with fright.

"How now, my good fellow, what's the matter?" demanded
the sheriff. "What has scared you?"

"Oh! Sir, the prisoner's blowed his brains out."

All the party started to their feet.

"Have the horses got, Lance!" said Porgy promptly.

"How was it?" demanded the sheriff. The deputy's story
ran as follows:—

It appears that the moody sullenness of M'Kewn continued.
He demanded more drink. It was denied him, according to the
instructions of the sheriff. He suddenly supplied himself with
more from a closet, and his keeper did not think himself authorized to take it from him by force. As the night advanced his
potations increased in frequency, and his sullenness and ferocity
were succeeded by a fit of extreme nervous susceptibility. He
would start up and exclaim passionately, then sink down in his
chair and cover his face with his hands; but he could not continue long in this or any other position. At length, he suddenly
confronted the keeper.

"Let me out," said he, "I must go and see Bostwick. He has sent for me to come. He calls for me. I hear him."

The keeper refused.

"Will you go to him then for me? I will pay you. See. Look here. You shall have all this, if you will go to him with a message."

And he opened the chest and, kneeling by it, took up several pieces of gold, which he counted from one palm to the other. The keeper still refusing, he flung the gold back into the chest, —and seemed about to rise, when he suddenly exclaimed—

"Don't you hear him? He is there! He is here! He hales me to him. I must go!"

And he seemed to follow with his eyes the motion of a person unseen. Then he threw himself into an attitude, still over the chest, as if about to struggle with a foe.

"I will never go," he cried. "To the gallows, yourself, wretch; but you do not carry me. No! No! I defy you. The devil, you say! The devil! Pshaw! I am not to be frightened in that way."

Then, as if suddenly filled with terror, he crouched and buried his head in the chest — crying out—

"He hales me away — he is too strong! Help! Help! I can not stand it!" and, rising, with a cry, from the chest, the deputy, for the first time, saw that he had a pistol in each hand. With these he seemed to confront some unseen enemy. He made no demonstrations upon the guard, who did not dare to approach him, thus weaponed. At length, as if about to be overcome, he retreated to the opposite side of the room, crying out—

"Do not press me to the wall. If you do,—if you dare— Oh! my God—my God! He will come!"

With these words, he discharged one of the pistols at the imaginary object, then cried, while every limb trembled with horror—

"It went through him, and he does not fall. He comes still. Oh!" with a choking cry—"His fingers are upon my throat! Oh! God, have mercy!"

Thus speaking, he clapped the other pistol to his own head, and, with the crash of the report, sank down in a heap upon the floor, utterly lifeless, with his forehead entirely blown away.

Such was the story told by the guard. According to the statement of time, there could not have been five minutes between the death of the two miserable criminals. Enough!

> "Draw the curtain close,
> And let us in to meditation."

CHAPTER LXVI.

THE GRAPES ARE SOUR!

IT was a remarkable proof of providential interposition—so thought in those days at least—that not one of the persons who came in contact with the squatter in his last illness, caught the small-pox from him. Yet his wife, little Dory, and the two other children, had been, for three days at least, constantly in the sick man's chamber. This was held a wonderful proof of God's gracious favor; and to those who knew the contagious character of that malignant pest, it was certainly a very remarkable circumstance.

After a proper interval, the humble family was again permitted to commune with its former patrons. Mrs. Eveleigh took Dory into her house, and the united appropriations of the widow and our captain, made ample provision for the future comfort of the mother and the other children, in a little farm of her own, where she dwelt for ever after, in a condition of humble comfort, which left her little to desire. Porgy gave her an old negro, and the widow Eveleigh a young one. Little Dory had a teacher provided for her, and, in a superior society, and with proper education, the native talents and graces of the child, daily exhibited new blooms, and the sweetest developments. In process of time, when she grew to womanhood, her charms made themselves felt in every heart with which her own came in contact, until—but let us not anticipate. Let us return to our principal parties.

Glen-Eberley, by the events recorded in our last chapter, was made secure to its proprietor. Our captain of partisans was relieved of all his embarrassments. His debt to Mrs. Eveleigh was not of this order. The profits of the plantation were quite adequate, with a few years of indulgence, to liquidate this, and all other obligations of a pecuniary nature. Porgy, at last, found shelter beneath his fig-tree, with none to make him afraid. He had his friends about him, his singing-bird, and his puzzle in a bottle. George Dennison and Doctor Oakenburg, much to the disquiet of Millhouse, became portions of the establishment. The one furnished the ballads for the evening fireside; the other was content to provoke the wit of others, without possessing a spark of it, himself. The sergeant still delivered the law from his self-established tripod. He was still an oracle who suffered no dog, to bark. Lance Frampton was a frequent visiter, and so once more, was Arthur Eveleigh, satisfied to seek good fellowship, and piquant matter of remark, though still occasionally suspicious of the captain's inclinings to his mother. On this subject, however, he no longer ventured to exhibit his boyish petulance. The one stern rebuke of his otherwise gentle and affectionate mother, had proved quite sufficient to curb, at least for the present, the young tiger striving within him; and, to sum up in a word, Glen-Eberley presented to the eye the condition of a well-managed household, in which the parties were all at peace with themselves and one another.

The same thing might be said of the neighborhood. The genial moods prevailing in the one household radiated in all directions. Glen-Eberley became a sort of centre for the parish civilization. The charm was great—a sort of salient attraction—which drew the gentry, all around, within the sphere of its genial, yet provocative influences. Free of anxiety, Porgy resumed his ancient spirit. The piquancy of his society, was everywhere acknowledged; and, with the sergeant and Doctor Oakenburg as his foils, the humor of our captain of partisans was irresistible. Fun and philosophy were strangely mingled in him, and they wrought together in unison. To rise from a practical jest into fields of fanciful speculation, was an habitual exercise with our camp philosopher. To narrate the experiences through which he had gone, delivering history and biography, anecdote and opinion, with the ease of a well-bred gentleman over his wine and walnuts, was to him an art familiar as the adjustment of his neck-cloth.— And these things were all delivered with a spirit and a quaintness, giving them wonderful relish, and which was peculiarly his own.

Thus the days glided by as if all were winged with sunshine.—
Thus the nights escaped all efforts to delay them, too brief for
the enjoyment which they brought. It may be that we shall
some days depict these happy times, the "Humors of Glen-
Eberley," even as they were well remembered by many, thirty
years ago, in all that cluster of parishes which lie between the
Ashley and the eastern margin of the Savannah; but, at present,
we can refer to them only. Enough, that peace reigned in the
household, under the strong will, and the happy temperament of
its chief; that the dangers which threatened from without, were
all overcome, in consequence of the events already recorded; the
sheriff had been soothed by ample apologies from Porgy, to which
Pinckney easily persuaded him; and Crooks, the deputy, sea-
sonably sauced with good words and hush-money, was easily persuaded to believe that his digestion was totally unhurt by the unnatural sort of repast which he had been made to swallow by the
lawless partisans. Tom, we may here mention, was bought back
from the widow Eveleigh, and received a gift of himself, from
Porgy, which he cunningly rejected.

"No! no! maussa," he cried, with a sly shake of the head,
"I kain't t'ink ob letting you off dis way. Ef *I* doesn't b'long
to *you*, *you* b'longs to *me!* You hab for keep dis nigger long as
he lib; and him for keep you. You hab for fin' he dinner, and
Tom hab for cook 'em. Free nigger no hab any body for fin'
'em he bittle [victuals]; and de man wha' hab sense and good
maussa, at de same time, he's a d—n pretickilar great big fool,
for let he maussa off from keep 'em and fin' 'em. I no guine to
be free no way you kin fix it; so, maussa, don't you bodder me
wid dis nonsense t'ing 'bout free paper any more. I's well off
whar' I is I tell you; and I much rudder [rather] b'long to good
maussa, wha' I lub, dan be my own maussa and quarrel wid
mese'f ebbry day. Da's it! You yerry now? I say de wud
for all! *You* b'longs to *me* Tom, jes' as much as me Tom
b'long to *you;* and you nebber guine git *you* free paper from me
long as you lib."

Thus the matter was settled, and Tom continued to the end
of the chapter, the cook and proprietor of his master.

It was probably three months after his emancipation from the bond of the sheriff, that Captain Porgy, one morning, made his appearance at breakfast in full dress. His toilet had been prepared with a much nicer care than usual. His beard, which, we shame of confess, was sometimes allowed to grow wild for a week, was now carefully pruned down, leaving the smoothest possible surface of chin and cheek. He wore his buff small clothes, and his new blue coat, with great shining buttons. His neck-cloth was a sky blue silk, which had before been worn. His silk stockings were of the most irreproachable flesh color, and Pompey had done his best to polish his shoes, so as to make them emulate, in some degree, the glittering shine of the fine patent leather of the present day. The whole appearance of our captain was so fresh and so unique, that his presence caused an immediate sensation. The improvement in his toilet struck all parties. Millhouse could not forbear an exclamation, and even Oakenburg opened his eyes as he might have done at the discovery of a new and hitherto unsuspected species of rattlesnake or viper. Dennison only smiled, and said something touching the premature coming of the spring.

"We shall soon be looking for the swallows, captain."

"One would think that we had them here already," replied the captain, glancing obliquely at the enormous bowls of coffee which Pomp was pouring out at the moment. No more was said. But when, after breakfast, Porgy ordered his horse, the sergeant immediately became enlightened on the subject. The disappearance of the captain, opened the fountains of his speech.

"I knowed it," quoth the overseer—"It's to happen at last. Well, its all right. It mout ha' been done, a year ago, and 'twould ha' saved some trouble. But it's never too late. I see I'll have to open new lands."

"What's to happen?" demanded Dennison.

"Don't you see. He's gone a-courting."

"A courting?"

"Yes! he's gone off now, I'm main sartin, to pop the question to the widow. Well, she's got a smart chaince of niggers, and when they gits hitched fairly, my force will be something worth counting. I'll begin to cl'ar up my gum land to-morrow. I'll put in a hundred more acres this season. Lord! what we mout ha' done a year ago, ef the cappin hadn't been so mealy mouthed."

"And you think he's gone to be married!" demanded Oakenburg—"a wife."

"To be sure! What else! I knows it—a wife it is! and sich a wife. She's got more than a hundred niggers, and I'll hev' to manage 'em all. But, I'll tell you what,—she'll manage you. She'll not hev' you idle fellers about the premises. A wife that's been a wife before, and's had the managing of her own affairs so long, she aint gwine to hev' her house filled up with warmin. She'll hev' a clearing, I tell you both. Singing-birds and snake-catchers aint gwine to eat her out of house and home. She'll find out what's the wartues of work in you, or she'll make you pack. Sich a broom as she'll bring with her when she comes, will sweep away all the rubbish."

The communication caused Oakenburg to look blank. Dennison, with that rare disregard of to-morrow, which is supposed to mark the poetical nature, only laughed, and went off, humming an old English ditty about stirring housewives and fairy besoms. Meanwhile, Porgy pursued his way, as the sergeant had truly conjectured, to the dwelling of the widow Eveleigh. The sergeant had no less truly divined his object in the visit. For some time past, the captain had been meditating the obligations which he owed the widow. He reflected upon what Millhouse had repeatedly suggested to him, in respect to the tender sort of interest which she was supposed to feel for himself. This might be a well-founded suggestion. Repeated examinations of the matter, in his own mind, had not persuaded him that the interest of the widow was anything more than that of a friend. Still, it was possible; and if it were really the case that she entertained any stronger sentiment in his favor, it would certainly, as the sergeant had said—"be a most cruelsome thing that she shouldn't hev' the man she wanted, pretickilarly when she had done so much for his sarcumstances." Porgy felt the ingratitude of any such neglect, on his part, supposing any such feeling on hers, and gratitude furnished a crutch where love might have faltered lamely and failed in his approaches. Repeated meditations had brought the captain to a definite conclusion; and he had armed himself to "come to the sticking point," in other words, to make her a formal offer, of hand and heart, and household.

Fortunately for his purposes he found her at home and alone. Dory had gone on a visit to her mother.—Arthur had set forth on a deer hunt with Frampton and some other young men. This was probably known to Porgy when he chose this day for his demonstrations. He found the widow as kind, and frank, lively and agreeable, as ever; and, after chatting on a variety of topics, he gradually brought the one subject in particular to bear. He was very nice, and as he thought, very judicious in his preliminaries. He discoursed of marriage in the abstract as a beautiful and admirably-conceived condition for human beings; he discoursed of his own wants in particular. Of course, he forbore any allusion to what might be supposed her wants also. He was pleading, and humble and solicitous, and reasonable and reverential, and touching and truthful;—and, in short, without throwing himself absolutely at her feet, he declared himself so, and without actually taking her in his arms, he avowed his great anxiety to do so;—and this, we are bound to say, in the best possible style, with proper modesty and misgiving.

The widow, with a sweet smile, laid her hand upon his own, and said as gently and tenderly, but as calmly, as possible:—

"My dear captain, why is it that men and women can not maintain an intercourse, as friends, without seeking any other relation. Is it not astonishing that such a thing should seem impossible to everybody? Now, why should not you and I be true friends, loving friends, trusting each other with the utmost confidence, coming and going when we please—welcomed when we come, regretted when we have to depart—and never perilling the intimacy of friendship by the fetters of matrimony. Can't it be so with us, my dear captain—and why not? I confess I think—I feel—that we may be very dear friends, captain, for all our lives; glad in each other's society, doing each other kindly and affectionate offices—faithful always and always confiding, as friends, and—nothing more."

The captain answered confusedly. The widow proceeded.

"The fact is, captain, if you look at the matter properly, you will see that it is quite impossible that we should marry. We should risk much and gain little by such a tie. I confess to you

that were I again to marry, I know no person to whom I should
be more willing to trust my happiness than yourself."

The captain squeezed her hand.

"But, captain, I am willing to trust myself to nobody again.
I have been too long my own mistress to submit to authority.
I have a certain spice of independence in my temper, which
would argue no security for the rule which seeks to restrain me;
and you, if I am any judge of men, have a certain imperative
mood which would make you very despotic, should you meet
with resistance. There would be peace and friendship between
us, my dear captain — nay love — so long as we maintain our
separate independence; and, in this faith, I am unwilling to risk
anything by any change in our relations. Let there be peace,
and friendship, and love between us, — but never a word more
of marriage. There is my hand, captain, in pledge of my good
faith, my friendship, my affectionate interest in yourself and
fortunes — my pleasure in your society — and you must be content with that. Will you, captain? For my sake, let me entreat,
and please say no more of other matters."

Porgy took her hand and carried it to his lips.

"God bless you, my dear widow, and believe me grateful for
what you are willing to bestow. I must be content — will be —
assured of such a friendship as your heart is capable of. You
are right, perhaps, and yet—"

"No doubt I am right. We know each other, and there shall
be no misunderstanding between us. You must stay to dinner
with me to-day, that I may be sure you feel no impatience with
me."

And he stayed.

But the idea of marriage had, for the time, taken particular
possession of the brain of our captain. Three days after, he
rode over to see the widow Griffin; but, on this occasion, he did
not take the same pains with his costume as when he visited the
other widow. His dress was less pretending, and more sombre
of hue. The captain knew, before he started, that the widow
was alone. Lance Frampton had gone on a visit with his wife
to Dorchester, the scene of some of his own exploits during the

war, and where he had some relatives. Porgy found the widow in good health and trim, and especially in good spirits. Her welcome was always genial, and she looked particularly charming, though in ordinary household gear. She was at her spinning-wheel when he came. A basket of carded cotton stood beside her, and as she drew off the threads from the wheel, approached it and retired, he thought her as graceful as a young damsel of sixteen. For the first time in his life, he fancied that spinning was a particularly picturesque performance, and wondered that he had not seen it more frequently delineated in pictures.

Mrs. Griffin was very lively and good-humored, and the captain gradually became more and more gallant. After awhile, he officiated somewhat in her operations. Now, he drew the basket of cotton to her side. Anon, when she desired to move the wheel, he caught up one end of it, while she took the other. It.was thus borne into the piazza, the better to afford room for her proceedings. In the obscure situation of the cottage, off the public road, and surrounded by great shady evergreens, the piazza was scarcely less private than the hall. The feeling of privacy had its effect on Porgy. Soon, he became more frequent in the little helps he gave the widow, and, at length, when putting aside her spinning, she proceeded to reel off a pile of yarn, the captain forced away the reel, and gallantly thrust his own arms through the hanks. It was in vain that the good, simple Griffin, wondering in discomfiture at this self-humiliation on the part of the captain, strove against it. He gave her a fierce smack upon the lips with his own, and thus put an end to all her efforts to repossess herself of the thread.

Then he placed himself before her in a great chair, his arms extended to the uttermost, his eyes surveying her tenderly, while she, with downcast looks, proceeded, as the sultan ruled, to reel off the threads as well as she might from the digits of her awkward auxiliary. The picture was a sufficiently ludicrous one, but it may be better fancied than described. Griffin might have seen—probably did see,—the grotesque absurdity of the scene; but Porgy was in his Arcadian mood, and certain feelings which he had in reserve, made him obtuse in respect to the queer figure which he cut in this novel employment.

He was startled into a full consciousness of his ridiculous situation, by the sudden appearance, in front of the house, on horseback, of the widow Eveleigh and her son Arthur. In the chat which the captain had kept up, tender and sentimental, and perhaps a little saucy, neither Griffin nor himself had heard the the sound of the horses, until escape was impossible. The parties were fairly caught. The first thought of the captain, when he looked up at the sudden noise and saw who were the visiters, was to fling the yarn over Griffin's head; at all events to fling it from his arms; but the mischievous threads adhered tenaciously to the broadcloth, and caught upon the buttons at his wrist, and tangled itself about his fingers, as if each thread were a spirit of disorder, sent especially for his discomfort and defeat. When he sought to rise, it fell in a mass upon his feet, and when he strove to kick it off, the feet got involved within the meshes, so that he dared not take a step forward lest he should lay himself out, at full length, along the piazza. As for the yarn, before he got out of its meshes, it was one inextricable mass of disorder, which filled the eyes of Griffin with consternation to behold.

The pair were really in most pitiable plight; an awkward consciousness of the ludicrousness of the picture they afforded to the new-comers, striking them both irresistibly for the first time. But Porgy's consciousness was particularly vexing upon other grounds. To be seen in such a relation to the one widow, after seeking *such* a relation with the other! As the poor captain meditated upon the matter, which he did in a single instant of time, his face streamed with perspiration, though the month of March, when the event happened, is considered a tolerably cool one, even in a Carolina climate.

Porgy hardly dared encounter the eye of the widow Eveleigh, who had alighted with her son, and now entered. But he strove to pluck up courage, and, in seeking to appear lively, he simply showed himself nervous. When he did catch the eyes of the widow, he saw them filled with a significantly smiling speech, which added to his confusion. She gave him her hand, however, very frankly observing, as she did so —

"What, in our times, Hercules subdued to the distaff!"

"Ah! my dear widow, it is only woman that finds the hero weak. That *you* should have seen me at this folly!"

This was said in somethimg of a whisper.

"Do not count it folly," answered the widow. "It is through the weaknesses of the man that we known his proper strength. That one is able to forget his dignities, only shows that his heart has not been forgotten. But, truth to speak, my dear captain, the picture was an amusing one."

"Funny! very! It must have been." This was said with a ludicrous attempt to smile, which resulted in a grin. Porgy's plan of courtship was exploded for that day, and for a goodly week afterward. But the purpose was not abandoned.

It was about ten days after, when the captain took occasion to revisit the widow Griffin. Frampton and his wife were still absent. Millhouse, Arthur Eveleigh, and George Dennison, were off on a deer hunt somewhere down the river; and Porgy having smoked his after-dinner pipe, and feeling dull, if not drowsy, having dined alone, resolved briefly the desolateness of his state, and, under a sudden call to change it, ordered his horse, determined to woo the widow Griffin after the most lion-like fashion. To confess another of our captain's weaknesses, he had but little doubt of success in his present quest. Griffin had been so docile, so gentle, so solicitous of his ease and comfort, that he really persuaded himself he had but to seek to secure. And so he rode.

A pretty smart canter soon brought him to her door, where the spectacle that confounded him was even more astonishing to his sight, than the situation could have been to the widow Eveleigh, when she caught himself. He could scarce belief his eyes. There, in the piazza, stood the fair Griffin, clasped close in the arms of the overseer, Fordham, and that audacious personage was actually engaged in tasting of her lips, as a sort of dessert after dinner. The situation was apparent as the noonday sun. The facts were beyond all question or denial. The parties were fairly caught, and so conscious was the wicked widow of the sinfulness of suffering herself to be caught, that, not able to face the captain, she broke away from the arms of Fordham, and rushed headlong into the house. Porgy was swallowed up in astonishment. He was about to wheel his horse around, and ride off, at greater speed than that which brought him, when Fordham sallied out, and asked him to alight, and with the coolest manner in the world said—

"Well, cappin, you've caught us at it; but no harm done, I hope. The widow and me hev' struck hands on a bargain, and I reckon we'll be mighty soon man and wife; and I hope, cappin, to see you at the wedding."

"The d—l you do!" was the only response of the captain, as, looking fiercely indignant at such cold-blooded audacity, he wheeled his horse, clapped spurs to his sides, and sent him homeward at full gallop.

"Mighty strange!" quoth Fordham. "The cappin doesn't seem to like it!"

Simple-minded Fordham, to suppose that a man should like to see his neighbor feeding on the very fruit he had thought to gather for himself.

With the defeat of these attempts, Captain Porgy gave up all notion of marriage.

"Woman!" quoth he, "woman!" and there his soliloquy ended; but the one word, repeated, was full of significance. When at length his comrades were again assembled about the board, and the cheerful fires were blazing on the hearth, and the philosophic cloud wreaths floated about the apartment, and the tankards were filled with potent floods of sunny liquor, Porgy said suddenly to his companions—

" My good fellows, there have been moments when I thought of deserting you,—that is, I sometimes meditated bringing in upon you a fearful influence, which might have lessened your happiness, and destroyed the harmony which prevails among us. I have had various notions of taking a wife—"

"A wife!" cried Dennison. "Oh! hush, captain, and don't frighten a body so! A wife! What madness prompted such a thought?"

" A wife !" cried Oakenburg,—"the Lord deliver us !"

"Ef she'd ha' come, she'd ha' delivered you mighty soon,' quoth Millhouse; "I don't see what's to skear a body in a wife, pervided she's in proper sarcumstances, and is kept strik, by a man usen to army rigilations."

" Maussa better widout 'em," quoth Tom ; "I nebber kin 'tan for be happy in house whar woman's is de maussa."

" Well, you will all be pleased to hear, then, that I have determined to live a bachelor for your sakes. I sacrifice my happiness for your own. I renounce the temptations of the flesh. It has been a pang to me, gentlemen, to do so for beauty is precious in my sight. There are women whom I could love. There are charms which persuade my very eyes to sin. There are sweets which make my mouth water. But, for your sakes, I renounce them all. I shall life for you only. You could not well do without me; I will not suffer myself to do without you. You shall be mine always—I shall be yours. To woman, except as friend or companion, I say depart! I renounce ye! Avoid, ye sweet tempters to mortal weakness—ye beguile me with your charms no more! For your sakes, dear comrades, there shall be no mistress, while I live, at Glen-Eberley."

" And may you live for ever!" was the cry from all but Millhouse. He only muttered in the ears of Dennison—

"I sees it all! He disowns the women bekaise he kaint help himself. The grapes is sour!"

THE END.

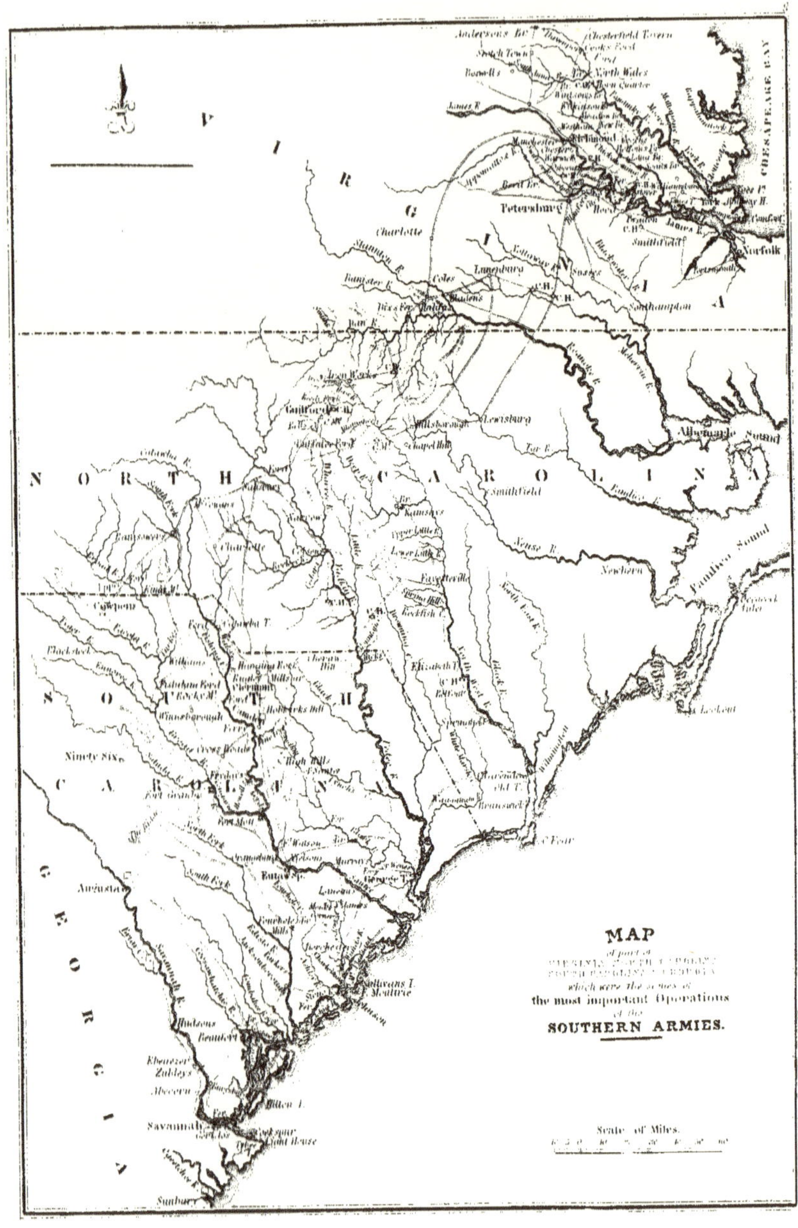

From the S. Lewis engraving, Plate VIII of the Atlas accompanying
John Marshall's *The Life of George Washington* (1807).

EXPLANATORY NOTES

by

George F. Hayhoe

These notes are intended to identify persons, places, events, quotations and obscure or archaic words and terms in the text of *Woodcraft*. Special emphasis has been placed upon the Revolutionary War history in this novel, including, when possible, the identification of Simms' sources and his departures from them.

[3]. Dedication "JOSEPH JOHNSON, M.D.": Johnson (1776-1862) was a native of Charleston, where he practiced medicine. His earliest years spanned most of the period of the Revolutionary War, and his father, William Johnson, had been an ardent patriot. He was the author of *Traditions and Reminiscences Chiefly of the American Revolution in the South* (1851).

[3].5-7 "The humorists . . . fanciful localities": "Humorists" here is probably used in the sense of "comic characters." While Simms maintains that all of the major characters of the book are based on actual persons disguised in fiction, definite sources have been discovered for only a few. It is possible that, although Simms used published anecdotes and traditions such as Johnson's as the basis for some of his characters, he modeled others on figures he had heard Johnson and others talk about.

4.1-2 "I owe so much . . . your own researches": Simms occasionally mentions his friend Johnson in his correspondence with others and recommends him as a source of information on the Revolution. Simms wrote to Evert A. Duyckinck in 1854 that Johnson was "one of the best living reminiscents" whose book contains "instructive & interesting material" *(Letters of William Gilmore Simms* [1952-1956], III, 343).

5.1-5 "The provisional articles . . . December": The provisional articles of peace, which recognized the thirteen states as "free, sovereign and independent," were signed in Paris on 30 November 1782. Simms made the same error about the date in his *History of South Carolina* (1860), p. 388. Word of the signing reached Charleston soon after the British had departed. The final treaty was signed 3 September 1783. Although the British had announced plans to evacuate Charleston on 7 August 1782, they did not finally withdraw until 14 December. The fleet which was to assist in this operation arrived in early September (see note 6.14-15), but it took more than three months to complete the process of transporting troops and equipment.

5.8-9 "a cordon . . . to break": After the Battle of Eutaw Springs (8 September 1781), the British were no longer able to control any part of the state except the Charleston peninsula. The Americans, both Continental Army and militia, were able to contain the British in this area, but were unable to take the city since the British still controlled access to it by the sea. The British ventured out of their enclave only in armed foraging parties. The surrender of Cornwallis at Yorktown (19 October 1781) should have brought an end to the war in South Carolina, as it did elsewhere; nonetheless, many small skirmishes were fought in the state until the British finally withdrew.

5.14 "not wisdom, or a better state of feeling": Although the British withdrawal was certain, they persisted in seizing slaves in retaliation for the confiscation acts, and in encouraging loyalist raids into the countryside. The Americans forced the British forays by refusing to sell them supplies. As a result, many men were needlessly killed on both sides in what D. D. Wallace aptly calls "an insane game with human life" (*History of South Carolina* [1934], II, 315).

5.17-19 "For more . . . the enemy": The British took control of Charleston on 12 May 1780, and remained until the evacuation. See also note 5.8-9 on the decline of British control in the rest of the state. In this passage Simms is drawing on William Johnson's *Life of Greene* (1822), II, 367.

5.22-23 "the Americans . . . to come in": In July the Continental Army had camped on the west side of the Ashley a few miles from the farthest British outposts at Shubrick's farm, which was three miles from the city. The American soldiers were quartered about twelve miles from Charleston at Middleton Place and at the adjacent plantation, Ashley Hall, which belonged to Commodore Alexander Gillon.

5.23-6.2 "commissioners from both . . . soil": The Jacksonborough Assembly (which convened in January 1782), the first meeting of the state legislature since the fall of Charleston, had passed laws calling for the confiscation of the estates of 239 persons who had been active allies of the British, and the amercing of the estates of forty-seven others who had denied their services to the state. The British protested this action and retaliated by seizing the slaves of known whigs. In order to deal with these and other problems resulting from the forthcoming British withdrawal, commissioners were appointed by both sides.

On 10 October Benjamin Guerard and Edward Rutledge for the state
and Alexander Wright and James Johnson for the loyalists agreed to
articles intended to return most slaves to their former owners, to
guarantee British merchants from retaliation by the whigs after the
evacuation and to ensure that no violence or insults would be directed
toward the exiles or their families. Two whigs, Edward Blake and Roger
Parker Saunders, were permitted to live in Charleston to deliver slaves
to their owners in the country. However, they soon discovered that the
British refused to cooperate under the terms of the articles and were
thus forced to abandon their efforts to recover slaves on 19 October
(see note 8.18-20). Why Simms should have chosen to ignore the fact
that the attempt to recover slaves ended quickly and unsuccessfully
is unknown.

6.4-5 "The latter . . . ancient brethren": Due to the precedents of
whig retaliation against the loyalists since the beginning of the war,
loyalists faced the dilemma of deciding whether to emigrate with the
British or risk the possibility of violence or economic reprisals if they
remained. General Leslie gave many loyalists a good occasion to solve
their problem when he ordered those supporting the whigs to leave
the city lest they be arrested as spies. A large number of loyalists took
advantage of this opportunity, made their peace with the state and
were welcomed by the whigs.

6.9-11 "twenty-five thousand slaves . . . West India Islands": Modern
historians have remarked that this figure, taken from David Ramsay's
History of the Revolution of South-Carolina (1785), is probably
inflated.

6.11-12 "there were yet other thousands waiting": 5333 blacks boarded
ships in Charleston harbor on 13 and 14 December.

6.14-15 "transport-ships . . . provided for passengers": Sir Samuel
Hood's fleet arrived in Charleston on 6 September 1782 to begin con-
voying personnel and goods out of the city.

6.23-24 "Colonel Moncrieff": James Moncrieff (1744-1793) was a
Scot who had served as an officer in America and the West Indies since
1762. As a military engineer, he was partially responsible for the
success of the defense of Savannah in 1779 and the Siege of Charleston
in 1780. Negroes from sequestered estates were put to work under
Moncrieff's supervision, and in March 1782 Colonel Balfour suggested
to Sir Henry Clinton that Moncrieff should lead a brigade of blacks
against the whigs. According to several sources, Moncrieff shipped 800
of these slaves from Charleston to the West Indies where he sold them
as his own property, though slaves were to be taken only to protect
them from angry whig masters or to be given their freedom. Such

exportation of slaves was illegal but was such a common offense that Cornwallis had issued orders forbidding it without his express permission on 2 August 1780.

7.35-36 "General Leslie": Alexander Leslie (d. 1784) had led the British into the city when it was taken on 12 May 1780; he replaced Cornwallis as commander of the military garrison of the city in October 1781, while Colonel Nesbit Balfour remained as head of the civil department. Leslie requested to be relieved of his command due to illness in May 1782, but his request was denied.

7.36-38 "My name is Eveleigh . . . now hold": In his *Traditions*, Johnson describes "a widow lady of great respectability,—'fair, fat, and forty,'—who entertained" the troops, and of one young officer who flattered himself that he might acquire her wealth by marrying her (p. 408). This description is quite probably the germ of the novel, especially because it incorporates the phrase which served as the book's original subtitle (see note 370.20). While the name Eveleigh seems to have been rather common in the state at the time, no specific person has been identified as the source of either Simms' Mrs. Eveleigh or as the subject of Johnson's anecdote.

8.18-20 "we have been delivering . . . American commissioners": The plan was for Blake and Saunders in Charleston to send the Negroes to Thomas Fergusson and Thomas Waring at Accabee Plantation, on the west bank of the Ashley, where they could be recovered by their owners. However, the American commissioners were not allowed to examine any of the ships bearing the king's ensign, but were supposed to take the commander's word that all slaves on board would be returned if their masters were seeking them. In the first group of ships to embark, the commissioners found and claimed 136 slaves, but only seventy-three were returned. The commissioners were then informed by Leslie that no further slaves would be delivered until the Americans returned three captured British soldiers. On 19 October, Governor Mathews wrote to Leslie saying that he could not interfere with General Greene's military plans. Thus, the attempt to restore slaves to their masters ended unsuccessfully. See also note 5.23-6.2.

8.36 "In the old hulk, sir, at Market dock": Many British prisoners were housed in the dungeon of the Provost under miserable conditions; still others were held on prison ships in the harbor. Although there is no evidence that slaves were held on these ships, Moncrieff may be hiding them there to circumvent the prohibition against illegal exportation (see note 6.23-24). Market dock was located on the East Bay at Market Street.

9.10-12 "my late husband . . . in this contest": Such a position was extremely common in Charleston and elsewhere in the state, for sometimes family ties and loyalties imposed obligations which, for those involved, were far more important than politics. Mrs. Eveleigh's position was somewhat unusual since, for her husband's sake and because she refrained from publicly espousing the whig cause, her property was spared by the British, with the exception of the slaves carried off.

9.20-21 "The commissioners are employed only to represent the *absent*": See note 5.23-6.2. Planters whose slaves had been seized by the British were represented by Blake and Saunders in the attempt to recover their property. Presumably, anyone living in Charleston could deal with the British personally if he dared. From Moncrieff's surprise, we can probably assume that such an act was unusual.

10.5 "M'Kewn": James McKloun was one of the addressors of Clinton who was not subsequently banished by the whigs; nothing further has been discovered about him. Major Thomas Fraser first engaged in the lumber business on the Edisto River and then became a merchant in Charleston. He did not seem to prosper and was disliked by the whigs. These two men are representative of the many Scottish loyalists remaining in the state after the war on whom Simms might have modeled this character.

10.17 "undress coats": Dress or uniforms worn on ordinary occasions, as distinguished from full or service dress.

10.18 "carpet-knight": There is no evidence that this disparaging term could be justly applied to Moncrieff historically; indeed, his service record seems to have been a distinguished one.

12.38 "squatter": Bostwick has apparently been living on Mrs. Eveleigh's property without authorization, and has not been required to move.

13.25 "Hessian": For a discussion of the Hessians, see note 21.20-21.

14.5 "a fleet of three hundred vessels": William Moultrie in his *Memoirs of the American Revolution* (1802) estimates the number of the fleet as "upwards of three hundred" (II, 360).

14.22 "the 'Tartar'": A British frigate by this name was involved in naval operations in America during the war, but it has not been determined if the *Tartar* was part of the fleet in Charleston at the time of the evacuation.

15.15-16 "get into his majesty's transport": That is, leave the city with the British.

16.38 "the king's stores": Apparently much of the payment that changed hands for these stolen slaves was in the form of goods themselves probably stolen or otherwise misappropriated from the British.

17.18 "They are monstrously in need of clothes": There are many references to the sorry physical state of American troops, both regular and militia. Ramsay says of the Continental troops, "their tattered rags were so completely worn out, that seven hundred of them were as naked as they were born, excepting a small slip of cloth about their waists" (II, 258).

19.3-19 "I have seen . . . . fitting harmonies": Major John André (1751-1780) was a British officer who was arrested and hanged by the Americans as a spy for his part in arranging for Benedict Arnold's betrayal of West Point. There is an unconfirmed legend recorded in Johnson's *Traditions* (pp. 255-257) that, during the Siege of Charleston, André entered the city as a spy. It is known that André accompanied Sir Henry Clinton as Clinton's aide and deputy adjutant general, and resided in Charleston for several weeks. While in the city with the British, André was involved in gaining intelligence from slaves, in dealing with other problems related to slaves, and in preparing a report on prisoners taken by the British. In a letter to John Laurens after André's execution, published as *The Fate of Major André* (1916), Alexander Hamilton wrote, "he possessed a pretty taste for the fine arts, and had himself attained some proficiency in poetry, music, and painting" (p. 18). Some of André's poems still survive (*e.g.*, Johnson's *Traditions*, pp. 204-206).

19.29 "fearless": André's fearlessness in the face of his own execution elicited the admiration of many Americans.

19.36 "We exchanged swords": No record has come to light that André and Moncrieff actually did exchange swords. However, since both men were concerned with the employment of slaves in Charleston, they were undoubtedly at least well-acquainted.

20.7-8 "just when he was . . . with Sir Henry": Henry Clinton (c. 1738-1795) was British Commander-in-Chief in America during the Revolution, and led the British forces during the Siege of Charleston. Clinton left the city to return to New York on 5 June 1780.

20.26 "Captain Porgy": Porgy, who appears as a secondary character in *The Partisan, Mellichampe, Katharine Walton, The Forayers,* and *Eutaw,* is the central character in *Woodcraft.* Various theories have been advanced regarding Simms' sources for this figure, who undoubtedly ranks as one of his most memorable creations; Paula Dean summarizes most of these in her 1971 Auburn University dissertation, "Revisions in the Revolutionary War Novels of William Gilmore Simms" (pp. 191-198). While Porgy bears some resemblance to Shakespeare's Falstaff (1 and 2 *Henry IV, Henry V, The Merry Wives of Windsor*) and other literary characters, it is likely that much of the inspiration for Simms' portrait of Porgy is derived from the sketch of Dr. Alexander Skinner of Lee's

Legion in Alexander Garden's *Anecdotes of the Revolutionary War in America* (1822). Garden describes Skinner as "an honest fellow, just as ready to fight as eat" (p. 136) and points out his "strong resemblance to the character of Falstaff" as well as to Sancho Panza in Cervantes' *Don Quixote*. Garden adds that, although Skinner was unsuccessful in attempting to court Mrs. Charles Elliott, the mistress of Sandy Hill, "a kind invitation to feel himself at home, in the most hospitable mansion in the State, made Skinner the proudest and happiest of men" (p. 138).

20.26 "the Ashepoo": The Ashepoo River is located in St. Bartholomew's Parish, in what is now Colleton County, and is southwest of and runs roughly parallel to the Edisto River.

20.39 "the gang of Marion": General Francis Marion (1732-1795) was a commander of South Carolina partisans noted for his success with guerrilla tactics. Known as the "Swamp Fox," Marion and his men usually emerged from the swamps to harass the enemy and then quickly returned to their hidden camps. Marion plays an important secondary role in all of Simms' Revolutionary romances except *Joscelyn,* and is also the subject of a biography by Simms (1844), who considered him the South Carolina partisan *"par excellence"* (*Life of Francis Marion,* p. 9) and a soldier of unimpeachable honor. Lord Cornwallis, however, wrote: "Colonel Marion has so wrought on the minds of the people, partly by the terror of his threats and cruelty of his punishments, and partly by the promise of plunder, that there was scarcely an inhabitant between the Santee and Pedee, that was not in arms against us" (Tarleton, *History of the Campaigns* [1787], p. 200).

21.20-21 "Hessians . . . in the world": "Hessian" was the name applied to the approximately 30,000 troops whose services were purchased by Britain from the German principalities of Hesse-Kassel, Hesse-Hanau, and others. General Howe's secretary called them cruel and cowardly, and they were often considered lazy drunkards and inefficient soldiers, as well as frequent deserters. There were at least three regiments and three other battalions of German troops in Charleston at the time of the evacuation, and many of these men deserted and hid until the British had left the city.

21.24 "Church street": A Charleston street running north and south, one block east of Meeting Street.

21.25-26 "The Merchants are all our friends": This pun operates on the fact that many of the Charleston merchants at this time were loyalists.

23.20-24 "the costume . . . or militia": People in the back country, as well as the poorer classes of city-dwellers, almost always wore homespun clothing, and blue was an easily accessible dye since indigo was a staple crop in South Carolina. The militia frequently wore hunting shirts as a uniform; see note 37.19.

24.8 "Jamaica": Jamaican rum, an extremely popular drink in America at the time.

25.38 "'up the path'": "Up the path," a commonly used local expression, refers to the old Indian footpath which was the predecessor of Highway 17 leading north out of the city.

26.12 "May the foul fiend deliver us": This appears to be a combination of the expressions "deliver us from evil" (Matthew 6:13) and "defy the foul fiend" (Shakespeare, *King Lear*, III, iv).

27.20-23 "It will suffice . . . to their owners": Only seventy-three slaves were recovered by the American commissioners in Charleston. Sir Guy Carleton later maintained that all slaves under British control when the provisional articles of peace were signed could be disposed of as the crown saw fit, and that the British were not obliged to return them.

30.8-9 "half-a-dozen of the fellows of Huck's gang": Captain Christian Huck was a Philadelphia loyalist lawyer who led a band of militia notorious for their cruelty. He and many of his men were killed by the whigs on 12 July 1780 at Williamson's Plantation; the survivors were pursued by the whigs for thirteen or fourteen miles. It is possible that some of the survivors could have returned to Charleston by 1782, but no evidence of this has been found.

30.13-14 "transport sloop . . . next two weeks": The mouth of the Edisto River is about thirty miles from the city, far enough to have hidden a ship safely for a time. Though no record exists indicating that British evacuation ships lingered in Carolina waters after they left Charleston, it is quite possible that a clandestine trade in slaves and other booty was carried on between Carolina and the Caribbean Islands by privateers.

30.16 "breaking up the rice land": Rice was grown primarily in the inland swamp areas of the state where irrigation could be easily provided. Fields were usually plowed in December before the ground froze and planted in winter wheat or oats; the rice would be planted beginning in mid-March.

31.6 "my mortgage covers his land": Porgy's situation at the end of the war was similar to that of many planters, even those as wealthy as Charles Cotesworth Pinckney. Not only had Porgy's home been nearly destroyed by the British and his slaves carried away, but he was in debt to M'Kewn, his own countryman. Creditors like M'Kewn were eager to recover outstanding debts, frequently in order to pay their own debts, or to force forfeiture of land title for non-payment. The severity of the situation was compounded by the inflation of Continental paper currency and the shortage of gold and silver.

31.7 "Gillon's": It has not been discovered whether this plantation belonged to Commodore Alexander Gillon (see note 5.22-23) or to someone else of the same name.

31.20-23 "Saturday . . . two days": Simms here paraphrases Moultrie's *Memoirs*, II, 358.

33.1-2 "purple chamber of aristocracy": A child of the imperial family of Constantinople was born in the *Porphyra* or purple chamber; hence, the home of anyone born of a noble or wealthy family.

33.26-28 "a contractor . . . unforgivable offence": M'Kewn has apparently been supplying the British force in Charleston. On 23 May 1782 Leslie had offered to buy provisions from General Greene, but Greene refused and attempted to restrain trade between the city and surrounding countryside as much as possible. The addressers of Sir Henry were 210 Charleston loyalists who had written a public letter congratulating Clinton and Admiral Arbuthnot on the surrender of the city. The Jacksonborough Assembly ordered them and other active loyalists banished and their property confiscated.

34.25 "to ride a wooden horse": That is, to be hanged on a gallows.

35.6 "a plan": Leslie had suggested mutual safeguards to General Greene (see note 35.8-11); in return for a pledge from Greene not to attack the rear guard of the British, Leslie promised not to injure the city.

35.8 "General Greene": Nathanael Greene (1742-1786) succeeded Gates as commander of the Continental Army in the South in December 1780.

35.8-11 "the British . . . to the wharves": Under the agreement between Leslie and Greene, the British were to leave their farthest outpost at Shubrick's farm three miles from the city (near the site of what is now Magnolia Cemetery) at 7 a.m. They moved down the King Street Road through the city to Gadsden's wharf at the foot of what is now Calhoun Street, where they boarded the ships waiting in the harbor. Details regarding the number and specific units of British and Hessian troops embarking from Charleston on 13 and 14 December are contained in "Evacuation of Charleston, S.C., 1782" in the *Magazine of American History* (December 1882), 826-830. According to the article, one of the docks from which the troops boarded was named Eveleigh's Wharf.

35.12 "General Wayne": Anthony Wayne (1745-1796), nicknamed "Mad Anthony" by a deserter, joined Greene after the Siege of Yorktown. Wayne had not fought in South Carolina, and many Carolinians afterward resented the role he played in the repossession of Charleston.

35.13-14 "follow slowly upon their footsteps": Leslie had requested that the Americans follow about two hundred yards behind the British (Moultrie, II, 359).

35.15-18 "The fleet ... Five Fathom Hole": Simms has taken this information about the British fleet in the harbor from Moultrie, II, 359-360. Fort Johnson, the first fortification to protect Charleston Harbor, was originally built on the northwest point of James Island in 1704 and improved and enlarged in 1759. Five Fathom Hole is located just inside the main channel of the harbor, between the bar and Morris Island, and provides a point where large ships can anchor safely at low tide.

35.18-19 "'It was a grand and pleasing sight,' says old Moultrie": This quotation is taken from Moultrie, II, 359-360. Moultrie was captured when the British took Charleston in 1780 and was paroled on 19 February 1782. He was invited by Greene to participate in the triumphal re-entry. Moultrie's *Memoirs* served as one of Simms' major historical sources for this chapter in *Woodcraft*.

35.20-27 "Not less pleasing ... of the other": Simms has taken the details of the welcome of the American troops from Moultrie, II, 360. William Johnson in his *Life of Greene* says that the residents of the city watched the entry of Greene's army in "mute thankfulness" (II, 367), not with cheers. Leslie had ordered the inhabitants of the city to remain quietly indoors until the British troops had all embarked, probably in order to prevent abusive demonstrations by whig Charlestonians. It is difficult to determine which of the two sources is accurate.

35.27-30 "an early hour ... centre of the city": It took nearly four hours (7-11 a.m.) for the troops to march the three miles from Shubrick's farm to the city (see note 35.8-11). They had to proceed slowly because they were being loaded onto ships in the harbor.

35.30-32 "Wayne's detachment ... Lee's cavalry": Simms has probably taken the figures for Wayne's detachment and Lee's cavalry from Moultrie, II, 358; the same numbers are provided in Johnson's *Life of Greene*, II, 366-367. Henry ("Light-Horse Harry") Lee (1756-1818) was a Virginian and officer of Continental Cavalry who served in South Carolina in 1781-1782. He was disliked by Marion and Sumter because he sometimes took credit for engagements they had won. Six-pounders are field pieces which take a six pound ball.

36.1-4 "'This must not be,' ... call a halt": Simms is here dramatizing a more general description of several such incidents which Moultrie records (II, 359). See note 35.27-30.

36.6 "palmetto banners": After the taking of Fort Johnson in 1775, the Council of Safety directed then-Colonel Moultrie to design a flag. He chose a silver crescent on a field of blue to commemorate the uniform of the 1st and 2nd Regiments which defended the fort. After the defense of the palmetto fort in 1776 (later renamed Fort Moultrie), a palmetto tree was added, and this has remained the state flag to the present day.

36.19 "near Chalmers, in Meeting street": Meeting Street is one of the main north-south thoroughfares in Charleston; Chalmers Street, one of the oldest in the city, runs east to west between Meeting and State streets, and is one block north of Broad Street.

36.36 "Major Barry": Captain Henry Barry (1750-1822) served in Charleston during the occupation and had been aide and secretary to Lord Rawdon. At this time he was deputy adjutant general to Leslie. He also appears in *Katharine Walton*, *The Forayers* and *Eutaw*.

37.16 "the rich scarlet uniforms of the British": British troops wore a red uniform with colored facings identifying the regiment they belonged to. Once in America, replacement uniforms were hard to find and many soldiers had to make do with whatever was available.

37.17 "Broat street": Broad Street (the misspelling is obviously due to a typographical error) was the main east-west street in Charleston.

37.19 "blue coats": Blue was adopted as the official Continental Army uniform color in October 1779. Prior to that date, green and brown had been the predominant colors of American uniforms. American troops, both Continental and militia, more often than not fought in work and hunting clothes; at one point, George Washington suggested that the hunting shirt be made the standard uniform for the soldier.

37.24-29 "At 3 P.M. . . . Bank of South Carolina": Simms' source for this passage is Moultrie, II, 359. John Mathews (1744-1802) was elected governor by the Jacksonborough Assembly in 1782 (see note 5.23-6.2) after Christopher Gadsden declined the office on account of illness and advanced age. The council of state consisted of advisors to the governor. Mordecai Gist (1743-1792), a Marylander, served with Gates and Greene in the South during the last years of the Revolution. The Bank of South Carolina building still stands on Broad Street.

38.22-26 "stately cavaliers . . . fiery Wayne": Many of the members of Greene's army came from the Middle Atlantic States. The Old North state is North Carolina. Before returning to South Carolina, Wayne had just finished a Georgia campaign to force the British to abandon that state.

39.3 "Mrs. W——": Although Simms seems to be disguising an actual name, this woman has not been identified.

39.19 "Scotch merchant": Many of the merchants in Charleston at the time were Scots, some of whom left the city after the evacuation.

39.23-24 "one of the few . . . during the war": Simms notes in his *History of South Carolina* that Scottish, English and German immigrants were more likely to become loyalists at the time of the Revolution, while native-born persons, Irish immigrants and people in the low country were usually whigs. The position of the Scots resulted from the British attempt to compensate them after the Battle of Culloden in 1746 by offering them opportunities for positions and land in the southern colonies of America. Thus Scots settlers who owed their land and livelihoods to the generosity of the crown were likely to feel a sense of allegiance to the king.

39.27-29 "He has been . . . state of affairs": Marion actually did employ spies as a means of obtaining information from occupied Charleston. According to Johnson's *Traditions*, Marion "encouraged the aged, the timid and the wavering, to take protection, remain at home . . . and be a source of information to him, of the various manoeuvres and advances of the British and armed tories" (p. 283).

40.3-4 "a very celebrated Carolina lawyer": This person is almost certainly Charles Cotesworth Pinckney, who appears later as a character in the novel; see note 350.13.

40.27-28 "Government is only nominally established": The Jacksonborough Assembly (see note 5.23-6.2) represented the first step in reestablishing the civil government of the state. This was a slow process, however, and according to Simms' *History* "It required many years before the wild passions which had been stimulated by . . . the Revolution, could be restrained by the arm of law . . ." (p. 395). Although civil courts were reconstituted in 1783, desire for revenge on loyalists sometimes prevailed over the execution of justice. In Ninety Six shortly after the war, Judge Aedanus Burke acquitted a notorious loyalist plunderer and murderer on a charge of horse-stealing, but an angry mob seized the man from the courtroom and hanged him outside. Burke could not intervene for fear that they would hang him as well.

40.31 "short cord": Probably an allusion to "short shrift and a tight cord," in Walter Scott's *Quentin Durward* (1823).

44.25 "Hangman's day": Friday has been traditionally considered a day of bad luck; this expression dates from the 19th century.

45.27 "the Edisto": A river in central South Carolina formed by the confluence of the north and south forks of the Edisto south of Orangeburg. It empties into the Atlantic about thirty miles below Charleston.

46.2-3 "the camp of Marion, at the head of Cooper river": Marion had camped at Watboo Creek, a few miles southeast of Monck's Corner.

46.8 "Sumter, Maham": General Thomas Sumter (1734-1832) was a South Carolina partisan commander, nicknamed the "Game Cock" for his fighting spirit. Colonel Hezekiah Maham (1739-1789) was a South Carolina militia officer who frequently served with Marion, though he was not a member of Marion's Brigade.

46.9-13 "sleepless activity . . . by the enemy": After the British occupied Charleston in May 1780, and after the defeat of Gates at Camden the following August, partisans such as Marion and Sumter maintained the struggle against the British while there was not a single Continental soldier in the entire state who was not a prisoner of the British.

46.14-16 "The fact is . . . patriot army": It was Governor Mathews and his Council who decided that the militia should not be permitted to participate in the re-entry, because they feared retaliation by embittered partisans against the British and loyalists. This action upset Greene, who wrote Marion a letter on 22 November 1782 explaining that he had had nothing to do with the decision (James, *Life of Marion* [1821], p. 176).

47.9 "ducking gun": A fowling piece which carried a heavy charge in order to kill a large number of ducks in a flock with one shot.

47.10 "short fusee": Fusee is a corruption of "fusil"; a short fusil is a short-barrelled, lightweight musket.

47.10 "German yager": The German Jägers (literally "hunters") were Hessian light infantrymen.

47.11 "tower musket": A tower musket is a musket issued by the arsenal at the Tower of London, usually bearing the word "Tower" on the lock instead of the maker's name.

47.16-17 "Such equipment . . . brilliant showing": Actually, Greene's army was no better off than Marion's troops in terms of clothing. See note 17.18.

47.33-34 "disparaged, as they have been too frequently since": There has been a long debate over the relative merits and importance of the militia and the Continental Army in South Carolina during the Revolution. McCrady, like Simms, makes an impassioned defense of Marion and the militia (*The History of South Carolina in the Revolution* [1901-1902], II, 719-730); on the other hand, D. D. Wallace makes the same claims for the Continental Army (*South Carolina: A Short History* [1951], pp. 283n-285n).

48.3-7 "Nay, they had . . . to behold": For example, Greene summoned Marion to help keep order in his army when the Pennsylvania regulars mutinied in April 1782; see note 339.33-38.

49.14-15 "The cedars at Watboo": See note 46.2-3. According to James' *Life of Marion*, the camp was located "at Watboo, and on the side of the cedar trees" (p. 176).

49.22 "Orangeburg": A town eighty miles from Charleston on the north fork of the Edisto River. It was the site of a British post taken by Sumter on 11 May 1781.

49.22-23 "Waccamaw and Peedee": The areas watered by the Waccamaw and Pee Dee rivers in the low country of the northeastern part of the state.

49.24 "the two routes conducting to Charleston": One road led from Dorchester to Charleston; the other was formed by the conjunction of two roads from the Monck's Corner and St. James areas.

49.25-26 "the Ashley, the Edisto, the Ashepoo and the Savannah rivers": The rivers of the low country of the southernmost tip of the state, between Charleston and the South Carolina-Georgia border.

50.2 "a youth": Lance Frampton also appears in *The Partisan*, *Mellichampe*, *Katharine Walton* and *The Forayers*.

50.19-20 "of immense dimensions . . . son of Anak": The Anakim (Numbers 13:32-33; Deuteronomy 1:28, 2 *passim*, 9:1-2; Joshua 14:15, 15:13) were inhabitants of a part of the Promised Land and were reputed to be a race of giants and fierce fighters.

50.32-33 "At that time, there was not a surgeon in Marion's brigade": The lack of adequate medical attention for the wounded was a common problem during the Revolution. According to James, "Marion was often without a surgeon to dress his wounded, and if a wound reached an artery the patient bled to death" (p. 82n).

50.34 "Sergeant Millhouse": In addition to *Woodcraft*, Millhouse appears in *The Partisan*, *Katharine Walton* and *The Forayers*.

51.6 "Tom": Porgy's cook Tom is one of Simms' best slave characters, and also figures in *The Partisan*, *Mellichampe* and *The Forayers*. Tom is one of the slaves in the book (see also Jenny, 59.9; John, 69.39; Jupe, 119.18; and Charlotte, Betty, Sally and Bob, 313.13-37) who may be based on or named after Simms family slaves (*Letters*, I, clii; II, 590-591).

53.23-24 "Othello's occupation's gone": Shakespeare, *Othello*, III, iii.

54.39 "our colonel": Probably the fictional Robert Singleton who appears as a central character in *The Partisan* and *Katharine Walton*. Four historical Singletons, who were ancestors of Simms, fought with Marion.

57.32 "Parker's": A ferry on the Edisto River about thirty-five miles from Charleston.

58.5 "ancient Clubhouse": Robert· Mills' *Atlas* (1825) records a Pinkney Clubhouse near Quinby Creek in Charleston District.

58.6-7 "the parish country of South Carolina": In 1706 the low country was divided into parishes by the Church of England as divisions of ecclesiastical government. These divisions were maintained for civil government until after the Civil War.

58.20 "it was suddenly arrested": In his *History*, Simms notes that, after the war, "Lawless men traversed [the] forest-paths, for a time, with violence and impunity. Desperadoes, whom war and rapine had taught all their lessons, raged, torch in hand, around quiet and defence-less habitations" (p. 395).

61.2 "Fire Dick": A character called "Hell-fire Dick" appears in *The Forayers* and *Eutaw*, but is killed in the latter work. The use of *noms de guerre* is common throughout Simms' Revolutionary romances. This is especially true of his backwoods characters, yet Francis Marion, Thomas Sumter, Anthony Wayne, Henry Lee and other prominent officers were also known by such names.

62.26 "'life for life'": Exodus 21:23.

72.30-31 "In fear and trembling": Philippians 2:12.

81.25 "the prophet Daniel": The Hebrew prophet of the Babylonian captivity known for his ability to solve problems. His deeds, visions and prophecies are recorded in the canonical book of Daniel and apocryphal additions to it.

95.3 "'praised be rashness for it'": Shakespeare, *Hamlet*, V, ii.

95.6-7 "'Our indiscretion ... pall'": Shakespeare, *Hamlet*, V, ii.

101.25-26 "the furies that hunted the steps of Orestes": Orestes, the son of Agamemnon and Clytemnestra in classical mythology, is pursued by the Furies, the goddesses of vengeance for unpunished murder, after he kills his mother and her lover in revenge for their slaying of his father. The myth is the basis for the *Orestian Trilogy* by Aeschylus.

111.31 "'A fig for 'em all'": Robert Burns, "The Jolly Beggars," l. 292.

112.5 "ca. sa's, fi. fa's": *Capias ad satisfaciendum* is a writ which, after judgment, orders the imprisonment of the defendant until the plaintiff's claim is satisfied; *fieri-facias* is a writ which commands the sheriff to sell the defendant's goods and chattel and pay the plaintiff the sum for which judgment was given.

112.26-27 "old Humphries of Dorchester, father of our Bill": Bill Humphries is a fictional character and lieutenant in Porgy's company, and appears in *The Partisan, Mellichampe* and *Katharine Walton*. His father keeps the tavern called The Royal George in Dorchester, a small village a few miles inland from Charleston at the head of the navigable part of the Ashley River. Dorchester was an important post during the Revolution since it was a gateway to the back country, but was abandoned shortly afterward, and by Simms' time was little more than a ruin.

114.30 "Ellen Griffin": Lance Frampton's fiancée also appears in *The Partisan* and *Katharine Walton*.

116.29 "Cremona": A violin made in Cremona, Italy, where violin-making reached its greatest perfection in the 17th and early 18th centuries.

117.19 "'small deer'": Hunters' term for small animals as opposed to big game.

118.4-5 "Let the world slide!—Sessa": Shakespeare, *The Taming of the Shrew*, Induction, i.

120.18-19 "de leetle creek wha' run out of Turkey swamp": Turkey Creek, a tributary of the north fork of the Edisto River, drains Turkey Swamp.

127.17 "fatal sisters": The Valkyries in Scandinavian mythology chose the victors in battles and carried the brave dead to Valhalla.

128.26-27 "'grinned horribly a ghastly smile'": Milton, *Paradise Lost*, II, 846.

130.27 "'silver lining'": The money in the pockets, not the cloth from which the pockets were made.

131.3-4 "The memorial was of a nameless virtue": Shakespeare, *Two Gentlemen of Verona*, III, i. "Nameless" here is used in the sense of "bastard"; the implication is that the outlaw was not the true begetter of the feelings which the love token signifies.

141.22 "cambric needle": A very slender needle used to sew fine linen.

145.30-146.13 "The old idea of *regulation* . . . common weal": The lack of law and order in South Carolina in 1782 paralleled a similar problem in the back country fifteen years earlier. The Regulators were a group consisting mostly of respectable landholders who banded together in 1767 as a vigilante group to rid the back country of outlaws. They also took action against "lower people"—vagrants, petty thieves and other social undesirables. In 1768 Governor Montagu formed two companies of rangers composed of Regulators who purged the country of criminals within the year. The conflicts with the "lower people" were not so easily solved, however. The Regulators' attempts to enforce not only law, but also morals and industriousness, led to many abuses. In 1769 a Moderator movement arose among the "lower people," led by Joseph Coffell (also spelled Scovil or Scoffel), whose followers were frequently called Coffellites or Scovilites. Civil war between the two groups in March 1769 was averted only by the personal intervention of Richard Richardson, William Thompson and Daniel McGirt. The Regulators' excesses abated and a court and law enforcement system was established for the back country in 1769.

148.6 "mazzard": Nose.

148.28-29 "the Bow-street magistrate": Bow Street was the location of the principal metropolitan police court in London.

148.39 "we left swinging": Summary execution of criminals and deserters by hanging was a common practice.

148.39 "Four Holes": Four Holes Creek, a tributary of the Edisto River eleven miles from Dorchester; its banks are lined by a swamp of the same name.

149.2 "we dressed in tar and feathers": Tarring and feathering was one of the atrocities which the whigs occasionally practiced against loyalists; one of the earliest such victims was Thomas Browne, a vehement loyalist who was attacked by whigs in 1775.

149.2 "Monk's Corner": Also spelled Monck's Corner; a small village about thirty miles inland from Charleston at the headwaters of the navigable portion of the Cooper River. Like Dorchester it occupied a strategic position during the war because it was a gateway to the interior of the state.

152.4 "'Bear Castle'": In context, and in light of the place called "Muddicoat Castle" in *Eutaw*, this is probably a building or camp used by outlaws. It is also referred to in *The Forayers* (355.27). The location of Bear Castle may have been Bear Island, which appears on Mills' map of Colleton District between the Ashepoo River and Mosquito Creek.

152.29 "'The Question'": The application of torture as a part of a judicial examination.

156.27-29 "The bird . . . to *swing*": An allusion to and pun on the proverb, "The bird that won't sing must be made to sing," which dates from the early 17th century.

156.39 "Provost Marshal": The officer in charge of military police, whose responsibilities include the custody of prisoners.

159.25-26 "the culprit was drawn up slowly into the air": This method of obtaining information from a prisoner which also appears in *Mellichampe* (102.26) was fairly common. Johnson's *Traditions* records the hanging of a slave by the British who were trying to find where his master's horses were hidden (p. 104). B. F. Perry published a Revolutionary sketch in 1835 which also describes the use of hanging in this way (*Greenville Mountaineer*, 18 July 1835, p. 1). The victim, an old woman who was known to hide loyalist refugees from whig justice, was tortured by a Captain Mapp of the Spartanburg militia in his attempt to find where loyalist "out-lyers" were hiding.

169.19-20 "'The Philistines are upon thee, Samson!'": Judges 16:9.

172.4 "Marcus Tullius Cicero": Roman consul, rhetorician and philosopher (106-43 B.C.).

174.13 "Moultrie's memoirs": See note 35.18-19; the passage which follows (174.17-38) is excerpted from II, 354-356.

174.22 "Winyaw": Winyaw (also spelled Winyah) Bay is the body of water which connects Georgetown with the ocean.

175.26-27 "hailed his approach after a fashion such as Moultrie describes": The slaves' greeting of Porgy is drawn from Moultrie, II, 355-356.

178.33 "Sambo": In Simms' time, a generic name for a Negro; derived from the Spanish *zambo* (bandy-legged) or the African Foulah *sambo* (uncle).

183.3 "Saint Shadrach": One of the "Three Children" delivered unharmed from the fiery furnace (Daniel 3:26-27).

187.34 "the widow Griffin": The wife of Walter and mother of Ellen Griffin, this character appears in *The Partisan* and *Katharine Walton*.

188.25 "blue cat": Blue catfish.

189.6 "I sowed wheat only to reap tares": A possible allusion to Matthew 13:3-30, or to Chidiock Tichborne's "Elegy Written . . . in the Tower before His Execution" ("My crop of corn is but a field of tares . . .").

196.8 "pole-houses": Makeshift sleeping quarters for slaves, apparently fairly common in the 18th century, had given way to considerably more elaborate housing by Simms' time.

198.23 "chewing the bitter cud of thought and memory": Shakespeare, *As You Like It*, IV, iii.

199.30-31 "the famous allegory of Menenius Agrippa": The well-known set piece called the allegory of the belly in Shakespeare's *Coriolanus*, I, i.

200.2 "'the flower of all'": Shakespeare, *Coriolanus*, I, i.

201.21 "Deep thus continued for a season to call unto deep": Psalm 42:7.

204.37 "the seven sleepers": Seven youths of Ephesus were said to have hidden in a cave during the Decian persecution and to have slept there for several hundred years.

205.24-25 "like the old-fashioned pictures of winter, his big beard crested with icicles": The anthropomorphic representation of the seasons as well as abstract ideas was a common practice in book illustration, and was especially common in the emblem books of the Renaissance, in which the pictures were accompanied by a few lines of verse or prose describing them.

206.23-24 "our fathers lived too well, were too rapidly prosperous": Beginning in the 1730s, South Carolina experienced a period of economic expansion of unprecedented dimensions as a result of increased demand for rice, indigo and other staple products, and as a result of the new trade developing from the settling of the up country.

210.4 "by Acheron and Styx": The two rivers of the underworld in classical mythology by which the gods swore their most solemn oaths.

211.14 "the Scythian and Cumanche robber": The Scythians were ancient inhabitants of what is now southern European Russia; the Comanches were a Plains Indian tribe.

211.28-29 "the wayside cross . . . has perished": It was customary in Spain and other southern European countries to mark the site where travelers had been murdered by highwaymen.

222.23-223.20 "'A book!'. . . . 'turn agin him!'": This passage is strikingly similar to the incident in chapter V of Samuel Clemens' *Adventures of Huckleberry Finn* (1885), in which Huck reads to his father. This similarity, as well as the fact that Huck's father and Bostwick are essentially the same type of character—poor whites who drink too much, abandon their families and are criminally involved—suggests that Clemens may have drawn on this scene in *Woodcraft* in writing his own novel.

223.24-25 "the Acts of the Apostles, the first chapter": The subject of Acts 1 is the Ascension of Christ and the election of Matthias to replace Judas.

224.13 "men of Harden": Colonel William Harden, a native of Barnwell, joined Marion's brigade after the fall of Charleston, having served with distinction as an officer of militia since the early days of the war. In March 1781 he separated from Marion with a troop of seventy-six men to lead successful raids against the British in the southern part of the state.

224.33-34 "cooling board": An undertaker's slab.

225.10 "more sinned against than sinning": Shakespeare, *King Lear*, III, ii.

232.39-233.1 "Lord be marciful to them who ain't marciful to themselves": A variation on the proverb "God helps them that help themselves," from Benjamin Franklin's *Poor Richard's Almanac* (1757).

233.3 "Georgetown": A town at the confluence of the Black and Pee Dee rivers on Winyah Bay, sixty miles up the coast from Charleston.

233.3-4 "that blasted skrimmage at Quinby": The battle at Quinby Bridge on 17 July 1781 was a part of the general campaign by Sumter and Marion to shake royal authority in the low country during the summer of 1781. At Quinby Bridge, across an eastern branch of the Cooper River, Lee and Marion's cavalry surprised the British in their retreat towards Charleston, but failed to win a military victory due to Lee's indecisiveness. A full account of that battle and the ensuing engagement at Shubrick's plantation is provided in *Eutaw*, pp. 330-340, 354-366.

233.9 "when we were at camp 'pon the High Hills": The High Hills of Santee is a forty mile range of hills northwest of Charleston and Dorchester, extending twenty-two miles across to the Kershaw County line in the north and to within five miles of the east bank of the Wateree in the south. It was the site of Greene's camp during the summer of 1781.

233.13 "Lieutenant Withers": In his *Traditions* Johnson mentions that William Withers was one of Marion's most active and daring men (p. 285).

237.11-12 "Physic and physicians were not to be had in that sparsely-settled region": Mills' *Atlas* (1825) lists only one doctor by title in his map of Colleton District.

239.12 "mouths of the Edisto": The Edisto (see note 45.27) meets the ocean at two points, the mouths of the North and South Edisto rivers, about fifteen miles apart at either end of Edisto Island.

239.31-33 "Like those of the Druid Bards ... elegy of the same writer": In Thomas Gray's ode "The Bard," a single Welsh bard curses Edward I for ordering the execution of the bards after the conquest of Wales. Simms also alludes to Gray's "Elegy Written in a Country Church-yard."

239.39-240.1 "'castled crags of Drachenfell's'": In Germanic myth, Drachenfells is the site of a cave on the Rhine where the dragon which Siegfried killed had lived.

242.7 "brag and poker": Two similar card games which became popular in America around the middle of the 19th century. See note 242.13-14.

242.13-14 "old-sledge, seven-up, all-fours, &c.": Variant names for a card game, a forerunner of the modern game of poker, popular in England and America from the 18th to the mid-19th century.

251.38-252.3 "that German fancy . . . astonished master": Goethe, *Faust* (1808, 1832).

260.4 "French vessels-of-war": The French allies were patrolling the Southern coast to prevent British incursions on their holdings in the Caribbean after the evacuation of Charleston.

263.13 "Doctor Warley": The name Warley appears in several places on Mills' map of Colleton District.

267.23 "Virginia snake-root": The root of *Polygala Senega* or *Aristolochia serpentaria* from which a medicinal preparation can be made.

267.25 "grain of tartar": Probably tartar-emetic (potassio-antimonious tartrate), a poisonous substance used to induce vomiting.

273.11 *"nem. diss.":* *Nemine dissiente*, a legal phrase meaning "with no one dissenting."

279.35 "Oakenberg": Dr. Oakenberg, who also appears in *The Partisan* and *Mellichampe*, does not appear to be based on any historical person, although he does share a few of the traits described in Johnson's sketch of Dr. Skinner; see note 20.26.

280.9-10 "scrimmage . . . with Fraser at Parker's Ferry": On 31 August 1781 Marion and Harden led an ambush of Major Charles Fraser's troops. This well-conducted battle had an important result, for it effectively reduced the number of cavalry available to the British at the Battle of Eutaw Springs eight days later. See note 57.32.

281.12 "more kicks than coppers": More trouble than profit.

281.16 "Dennison": The poet George Dennison is an apparently fictional character who also appears in the revised version of *The Partisan*, and in *Mellichampe*, *Katharine Walton*, *The Forayers* and *Eutaw*.

282.10 "to stick like a pitch plaster, and to draw like a mustard": Pitch and mustard plasters were medical remedies commonly used in the 18th and 19th centuries.

285.12-13 "the forced march . . . Great Pedee": Major Micajah Gainey was a loyalist from the Pee Dee area; the incident referred to here is probably Marion's pursuit of Gainey in 1782 in order to negotiate a treaty which was signed on 8 June to end the civil strife in that area.

285.34 "It could neither sow nor spin": Matthew 6:28.

292.24 "'hew it down and cast it into the fire'": Matthew 3:10; Luke 3:9; John 15:6.

309.35-36 "the tender-hearted wanton who flung herself away for love of the phlegmatic Phaon": Sappho (c. 600 B.C.), poetess of Lesbos, fell in love with Phaon, a boatman, and threw herself into the sea when he rejected her.

311.18 "peaks of Teneriffe": The mountains of the largest of the Canary Islands.

318.19 "great cave of Kentucky": Mammoth Cave, limestone caverns in central Kentucky.

324. chapter title "SANS-CULOTTISM": Literally, going without trousers; also, the principles and practices of the republicanism of the poorer classes during the French Revolution.

331.2-3 "the knights of the English Harrys and Edwards": Probably an allusion to the Wars of the Roses, 1455-1485; Henry VI (r. 1422-1461, 1470-1471), Edward IV (r. 1461-1470, 1471-1483), Edward V (1483), and Henry VII (1485-1509).

331.37-38 "'valley de sham'": Alternate spelling of *valet de chambre*; man servant.

339.33-38 "'There was a Sergeant Mil*ler* . . . continentallers in order'": A reference to the mutiny of the Pennsylvania regulars against Greene in April 1782, supposedly caused by their lack of clothes and dislike of rice; the same regiment had mutinied the year before in New Jersey. The ringleader of the plot was a Sergeant Gornell who was executed for treason after the conspiracy was discovered. After Gornell was arrested, others involved in the plot escaped to the British.

340.24-27 "with Gineral Middleton . . . Ingin skrimmage": Colonel Thomas Middleton (1719-1766) led a provincial regiment in the campaign against the Cherokee in 1761. He fought an ineffectual duel with Colonel James Grant (1720-1806), the commander of the regular troops, over his accusation that Grant was indifferent to suggestions made by the provincial officers.

341.31 "great muster of the loyalists, near Coosawhatchie": On 3 May 1779, Colonel John Laurens imprudently brought on an engagement with a superior force under General Prévost at Coosahatchie in what is now Beaufort County. This passage may refer to that incident.

345.24-25 "Samson and Zebeedee, the Philistians": Samson was a Hebrew hero (Judges 13-16); Zebedee was the father of the apostles James and John (Matthew 4:21); neither was a Philistine.

350.13 "Charles Cotesworth Pinckney": Pinckney (1746-1825) was an eminent Carolina lawyer who had been a member of the Council of Safety and the provincial and state legislatures. As a colonel of militia, he helped defend Charleston against the British siege in 1780 and opposed surrendering the city. He was taken prisoner when the British occupied the city and was released in 1782. After the war he helped settle many disputes over debts, served as a delegate to the Constitutional Convention, and was a minister to the French government from America.

358.3-4 "Gineral Arnold": Benedict Arnold (1741-1801) betrayed West Point to the British on 21 September 1780 out of anger with Congress, his need for money and indignation over the French alliance.

369.25-31 "Porgy . . . less moral, period": The English poets William Shakespeare (1564-1616), John Milton (1608-1674), and John Dryden (1631-1700) have been recognized for centuries as the most important English writers of the 17th century. William Wycherley (dramatist, 1640?-1716), John Vanbrugh (dramatist, 1664-1726), William Congreve (dramatist, 1670-1729), Robert Wilmot (dramatist, fl. 1568-1608), George Etherege (dramatist, 1635?-1691) and John Wilmot, Lord Rochester (poet, 1648-1680) enjoyed considerable popularity in the 17th and 18th centuries.

370.20 "'fair, fat, and forty'": The subtitle of the book when first published (1852), this epithet appeared in Walter Scott's *St. Ronan's Well* (1823) and *Redgauntlet* (1824). See note 7.36-38.

435.38-436.1 "the ferocious Blue Beard in the opera . . . her brother":
No opera about Blue Beard written before *Woodcraft* has been
identified.

436.16-17 "forgive my merry men": Probably a reference to the
legend of Robin Hood who, with his band of "merry men," harassed
the sheriff of Nottingham in the twelfth century.

436.23-24 "strangling his wife . . . Othello": Shakespeare, *Othello*,
V, ii.

437.25 *"Sacre"*: A French oath which means literally "sacred" but
which is used elliptically to mean "by all that's holy."

437.26 *"Demonios"*: A Spanish oath meaning "what the devil?"

438.13-14 "stir up the bile and black blood": According to an ancient
system of physiology and psychology originating with the Greeks, a
person's health and personality were determined by the balance of four
humours within his body: blood, phlegm, choler (or yellow bile) and
black bile (or black blood). Depending on the humour which domi-
nated, the personality was said to be sanguine, phlegmatic, choleric
or melancholy.

442.30-31 "He had a red head . . . red waistcoat": It was thought that
a red-haired, red-faced person suffered from an excess of choler or bile.
See note 438.13-14.

443.24-452.39 "We must leave him . . . other documents": This anecdote is apparently based on an incident in the life of Colonel Hezekiah
Maham related in Johnson's *Traditions* (p. 291). Maham too forced the
deputy to swallow the writ, but was then arrested by the sheriff.

443.38 "Rhadamanthus": The son of Zeus and Europa in classical
mythology who was one of the judges of the underworld. The name is
often applied to an inflexible judge or severe master.

449.6 "the times of Elizabeth": Elizabeth I of England (b. 1533;
r. 1558-1603).

452.8 *"locus sigilli"*: The place of the seal.

456.18-21 "a virtuous puritan captain, of Rhode Island . . . senate of
the United States": Neither of these persons has been identified; however, it has been observed that most of the slaves purchased by South
Carolinians, when slave trade opened again after the Revolution, were
sold by Rhode Island or English merchants.

470.39-471.1 "Johnny Ketch, the born rope-stretcher": Jack Ketch
(d. 1686) was an official English executioner notorious for his excessive

barbarity, either through cruelty or incompetence. The name is used allusively for an official executioner.

486.10 "the broad tail of a fiery comet, at the advent of an earth-quake": Popular superstition since ancient times has regarded the appearance of a comet as an omen of earthquakes, floods, wars and other natural and political disasters.

488.20-23 "Charles Cotesworth Pinckney ... president of the United States": Pinckney was the Federalist Party nominee for president in 1804 and 1808.

500.11 "small-pox": This extremely infectious disease was common in the West Indies and in South Carolina during the period. The partisans, mostly backcountrymen who were far less familiar with the disease than city-dwellers, were so frightened of smallpox that they refused to enter Charleston in February 1780 to defend the city.

500.23 "all inoculated": Although inoculation for smallpox was not perfected until 1796, it was commonly practiced in a crude form in the mid-18th century.

507.4-5 "'Draw the curtain close ... meditation'": Shakespeare, 2 *Henry VI*, III, iii.

509.6-7 "that cluster of parishes which lie between the Ashley and the eastern margin of the Savannah": These parishes are St. Andrew's, St. George's, St. John's Colleton, St. Paul's, St. Bartholomew's, St. Helena's, Prince William's and St. Peter's.

509.14 "hush-money": It is almost certain that Simms has subtly used this expression to emphasize the fact that Porgy has still not made the necessary readjustment to civilian life by accepting civilian law.

511.39-512.1 "'come to the sticking point'": An allusion to Shakespeare, *Macbeth*, I, vii.